# SENTIME[...]

GUSTAVE FLAUBERT was b[...] [...]vas
chief surgeon at the hospital. [...]ris,
but gave up that career for w[...] [...]46
with his widowed mother and niece. Notwithstanding his attachment to
them (and to a number of other women), Flaubert's art was the centre of his
existence, and he devoted his life to it. His first published novel, *Madame
Bovary*, appeared in 1856 in serial form, and involved Flaubert in a trial
for irreligion and immorality. On his acquittal the book enjoyed a *succès de
scandale*, and its author's reputation was established.

Flaubert is often considered a pre-eminent representative of 'realism' in
literature. It is true that he took enormous trouble over the documentation
of his novels. Even his historical novel *Salammbô* (1862), set in Carthage at
the time of the Punic Wars, involved a trip to North Africa to gather local
colour. But Flaubert's true obsession was with style and form, in which he
continually sought perfection, recasting and reading aloud draft after draft.

While enjoying a brilliant social life as a literary celebrity, he completed
a second version of *L'Éducation sentimentale* in 1869. *La Tentation de
Saint Antoine* was published in 1874 and *Trois contes* in 1877. Flaubert
died in 1880, leaving his last (unfinished) work, *Bouvard et Pécuchet*, to be
published the following year.

HELEN CONSTANTINE has published three volumes of translated stories,
*Paris Tales*, *French Tales*, and *Paris Metro Tales*, with OUP. She has also
translated Gautier's *Mademoiselle de Maupin* and Laclos's *Dangerous
Liaisons* for Penguin and Balzac's *The Wild Ass's Skin* and Zola's *The
Conquest of Plassans* for Oxford World's Classics.

PATRICK COLEMAN is Professor of French at the University of Los
Angeles, California. He has edited Rousseau's *Confessions* and *Discourse on
Inequality*, and Balzac's *The Girl with the Golden Eyes and Other Stories* and
*The Wild Ass's Skin* for Oxford World's Classics. His most recent book is
*Anger, Gratitude, and the Enlightenment Writer* (OUP, 2011).

## OXFORD WORLD'S CLASSICS

*For over 100 years Oxford World's Classics have brought
readers closer to the world's great literature. Now with over 700
titles—from the 4,000-year-old myths of Mesopotamia to the
twentieth century's greatest novels—the series makes available
lesser-known as well as celebrated writing.*

*The pocket-sized hardbacks of the early years contained
introductions by Virginia Woolf, T. S. Eliot, Graham Greene,
and other literary figures which enriched the experience of reading.
Today the series is recognized for its fine scholarship and
reliability in texts that span world literature, drama and poetry,
religion, philosophy, and politics. Each edition includes perceptive
commentary and essential background information to meet
the changing needs of readers.*

OXFORD WORLD'S CLASSICS

GUSTAVE FLAUBERT

# Sentimental Education
## The Story of a Young Man

*Translated by*
HELEN CONSTANTINE

*With an Introduction and Notes by*
PATRICK COLEMAN

OXFORD
UNIVERSITY PRESS

# OXFORD
### UNIVERSITY PRESS

Great Clarendon Street, Oxford, ox2 6DP
United Kingdom

Oxford University Press is a department of the University of Oxford.
It furthers the University's objective of excellence in research, scholarship,
and education by publishing worldwide. Oxford is a registered trade mark of
Oxford University Press in the UK and in certain other countries

First published as an Oxford World's Classics paperback 2016

Impression: 10

Published in the United States of America by Oxford University Press
198 Madison Avenue, New York, NY 10016, United States of America

British Library Cataloguing in Publication Data

Data available

Library of Congress Control Number: 2015943762

ISBN 978-0-19-968663-6

Printed and bound in Great Britain by Clays Ltd, Elcograf S.p.A.

# CONTENTS

# INTRODUCTION

THE seductive appeal, but also the unsettling ambiguity, of Flaubert's 'story of a young man' begins with its title. In common parlance, an *éducation sentimentale* refers to a person's initial instruction in love. It includes the sensual discoveries of one's sexual awakening, the emotional knowledge that comes from experiencing the force and the fragility of intimate relationship, and the worldly wisdom achieved by gaining some perspective on all of it. One way we seek such perspective is by reading stories about the sentimental education of other people, and one of the important functions of the French novel, from Mme de Lafayette through Stendhal and Flaubert to Proust and beyond, has been to provide us with such stories. In the broadest sense, of course, the theme is a common one in the novels of many cultures. To take just one example, what is the theme of that other great 1860s 'story of a young man', *Great Expectations*, but the sentimental education of Dickens's hero Pip? Yet the widespread notion that the expression *éducation sentimentale*, like *savoir-faire*, has no exact English equivalent is based on its association with a particular attitude, at once open-minded and disenchanted, towards the lessons of desire that we find, or think we find, in the great French novelists.

There is, however, another reason for focusing on the translation of Flaubert's title: it brings to the fore an ambiguity not immediately apparent in the French, but which was pointed out by Marcel Proust a century ago. Proust had given his own great novel of education a title rich in ambiguity.[1] Based on his attentive reading of Flaubert's *L'Éducation sentimentale*, Proust sensed that his predecessor might be exploiting the conflicting possibilities of the one he chose. From a strict grammatical point of view, Proust says, *éducation sentimentale* can be read in two contradictory ways. It can mean 'education of the sentiments', with the latter term referring, not just to feelings as such, but to the opinions and judgements that emerge in and

---

[1] Briefly, is the 'lost time' of *In Search of Lost Time* (*A la recherche du temps perdu*) a past good time to be retrieved, time wasted and in need of redemption, or some combination of both?

from those feelings. This meaning of 'sentiment' can be found in eighteenth-century English as well. Adam Smith's *Theory of Moral Sentiments* (1758), for example, is an extended examination of this interaction of feeling, opinion, and judgement.[2] A sentimental education of this sort is not complete until the whole complex of impulses that together make up what we now call our emotional intelligence is tested and refined through intellectual reflection. Whether stories of sentimental education end happily or not, they should culminate in wisdom of a critical, self-aware kind. On the other hand, an education may be 'sentimental' in the more negative sense of one short-circuited by sentimentality. Shying away from the challenges of critical self-awareness, sentimentality collapses the distinction between thinking and feeling, making the one merely the intensification or intellectualization of the other. Stories of this second type offer only a parody of wisdom, complacently or cynically closing off further reflection—for cynicism may be a self-satisfied shadow of sentimentality.

In real life, of course, distinguishing between these two forms of sentimental education may not be an easy task. Our upbringing may prompt us to question what we might call the emotional regime of our culture; it also pressures us to bow to the way things are, in our personalities or in the world around us. Over the last three centuries, novels dramatizing critical and conformist sentimental educations have illustrated this tension in various ways. Some have tried to portray an authentic sentimental education through the struggles of exemplary protagonists. Others have dramatized in admonitory fashion the deadening effects of excessive compromise. In so doing, the best of these novels model a sentimental education of a higher, more sophisticated sort. That is to say, they illustrate an approach to the ongoing task of discerning the difference between the critical and conformist shaping of emotion and of negotiating the tension between them. What we value in writers such as Dickens and George Eliot, for example, contemporary with Flaubert, and in the great novelists who learned from him, including Henry James, Proust, Joyce, and Mann, are the ways they help us to understand what this process involves and, just as importantly, what it feels like.

---

[2] As is also, in its own way, Sterne's *Sentimental Journey* (1768), which, several times translated as *Voyage sentimental*, was instrumental in introducing the adjective into French. For Sterne's and Smith's use of the term, see Laurence Sterne, *A Sentimental Journey and Other Writings*, ed. Ian Jack and Tim Parnell (Oxford, 2003), pp. xxvii–xxviii.

By making 'sentimental education' his title, Flaubert suggests that what we will find in his novel is an enactment of this process of discernment. His use of the definite article underscores his ambition. The novel does not give us *a* sentimental education but *the* sentimental education.[3] The exemplariness of the case study might be found at various levels of the text. It might be illustrated in the story of a hero who struggles in representative fashion with the consciousness and social contradictions of his time. It might be found at the level of the narrative, in the evolution of the perspectives we are invited to consider as we follow the hero's story. In a writer as subtle as Flaubert, we expect that ultimately it will be the interplay between story and narrative, between theme and form, which will show us what constitutes 'the' sentimental education, so that at the end we will be better equipped to distinguish between sentiment and sentimentality at every level of experience and reflection. As readers of Flaubert's earlier novel *Madame Bovary*, we have been given a negative lesson about what happens when these levels are confused; we come now to *Sentimental Education* in the expectation of seeing what a properly differentiated structuring of feeling should look like. Indeed, the title promises so much that some early reviewers attacked Flaubert for the extravagance of his claim.

What no doubt provoked them even more, and continues to perplex readers today, is that the novel confounds the expectations it raises. The hero, Frédéric Moreau, is enticed by women sufficiently various and engaged by such widely differing political ideals as to provide ample opportunity to examine his feelings. As a law student, he meets other young men who challenge his provincial views, and as the beneficiary of a substantial inheritance that allows him to settle permanently in Paris he mingles with economic and artistic entrepreneurs who stir his ambitions. The Revolution of 1848 offers him the possibility of a political career, but also the chance to discover the underside of political manoeuvres. Although he thinks he has met the

---

[3] Flaubert could also have omitted the article altogether, letting the reader decide just how generalizable the pattern is supposed to be. English usage does not allow the translator to make this distinction in phrases like this one that involve an abstract noun. 'The Sentimental Education' would not be idiomatic (nor would 'The Great Expectations'; the French translation of Dickens as *Les Grandes Espérances* is also an interpretative choice). The presence or absence of optional articles in English titles can be significant, too. Compare *The Portrait of a Lady* (Henry James) and *Portrait of the Artist as a Young Man* (James Joyce).

love of his life when in 1840, as a newly minted *bachelier*, he is dazzled by the sight of Mme Arnoux, over the following decade he will become entangled with three other women, each endowed with a particular charm: the mistress of Mme Arnoux's husband, a *lorette* or courtesan whom other lovers pursue as well; a home-town girl whose early crush on him grows into womanly passion; and a society lady of refined taste and jealous demands. That all of these different women should find Frédéric attractive means they see some intriguing potential in him, yet Henry James spoke for many readers when he complained that Frédéric is so vague in thought and ineffectual in action that even his failures fail to instruct. Even more disconcerting is the impersonality of the narrative. Flaubert's refusal to have his narrator judge Madame Bovary's adultery was the chief reason he was prosecuted for publishing it, but sophisticated readers could see the logic in refraining from telling us *what* to think about a provincial woman like Emma, whose delusions and deviant passions were all too liable to be summarily condemned by narrow-minded moralists. But what could be the point of refusing to tell us at least *how* to think about the aspirations of a young man of middling talent and muddled motives as he and the friends around him negotiate their personal and political relationships in the capital of France? The novel seems to belie its title.

## *The Genesis of* Sentimental Education

We know from Flaubert's correspondence that he was in fact not very happy with the title, but not because he felt it was inappropriate. Inadequate it might be, but in the end it was the only one that fitted.[4] Though he does not say so, the real reason is that Flaubert had already written a novel with the title 'L'Éducation sentimentale' many years before, when he was in his twenties, which was never published. The story follows two childhood friends as they experience the thrills and disappointments of love: Henry with a married woman, Jules with a free-spirited actress. The former moves to Paris, with an interlude in America; the latter remains in the provinces but at the

---

[4] 'I don't say the title is good. But so far it's the one that best renders what I had in mind.' Letter to George Sand, 3 April 1869, in *The Letters of Gustave Flaubert 1857–1880*, edited and translated by Francis Steegmuller (Cambridge, Mass., 1982), 129.

end of the book departs for the 'Orient' (that is to say, the eastern Mediterranean). Henry settles for a conventional career, marrying the niece of a government minister, while Jules commits to the solitary life of the artist. The contrast between the two characters is schematically drawn and the comments of the narrator awkwardly intrusive, and so it is not surprising that Flaubert never published the book. A deeper problem is his handling of the main theme. The young author displays a striking ability to use the notion of sentimental education as a springboard for exploring the early stages of young men's imaginative experience. Yet, the range of both the experience and the exploration is pre-emptively circumscribed. Flaubert's one use of the title phrase in a story within the story does not, as one would hope, add an additional layer of meaning; instead it undercuts the point of writing the main novel. Any realistic story of sentimental education will be tinged to some degree with disenchantment, but the emblematic little anecdote Flaubert inserts into the middle of the 1845 'Sentimental Education' takes that tendency to an extreme. On his way to New York, Henry meets a black man named Itatoé, who works for the captain of the ship:

His father had sold him for a box of nails; he had come to France as a servant. He had stolen a scarf for a chambermaid he loved; they had sent him to the galleys for five years. He had returned on foot from Toulon to Le Havre to see his mistress again; he hadn't found her. He was going back now to the land of the Blacks.

Like any other man, he, too, had got his sentimental education.[5]

In putting Africans and Europeans on the same level, this passage supports the author's claim that sentimental education as he understands it is the same for everyone, but in its refusal to enter the character's subjectivity and in its throwaway conclusion, the text implies that the pattern is a common one only in its denial of difference. There is nothing new to discover in another instance of this education and nothing new to say about it.

The 1845 'Sentimental Education' reflected how Flaubert thought about his own life at the time he wrote it. A year earlier he had suffered

---

[5] Gustave Flaubert, *Œuvres de jeunesse* (*Œuvres complètes*, vol. i), ed. Claudine Gothot-Mersch and Guy Sagnes (Paris: Gallimard, 2001), 978. Except where indicated, translations from the French are my own.

a series of seizures generally thought to be epileptic in nature. They had forced (or, perhaps better, allowed, given the probability of some psychosomatic element in their genesis and the convenience of their timing) the 23-year-old young man to abandon the law studies he hated. From then on Flaubert would devote himself entirely to reading and writing, living at Croisset near Rouen with his mother. The link between them was reinforced when Flaubert's father and beloved sister Caroline died within a few months of each other in 1846. Starting that same year, when his health had recovered, Flaubert would again visit Paris for various periods of time, but not long after completing his novel, he wrote this in a letter to the closest companion of his youth:

By dint of being in a bad way, I'm in a good way . . . I have weaned myself from so many things that I feel rich in the midst of the most absolute destitution. I still have some way to go. My sentimental education isn't finished, but I may graduate soon. Have you sometimes thought, dear sweet friend, how many tears the horrible word 'happiness' is responsible for?[6]

The young Flaubert is eager to embrace disappointment and be done. He deliberately renounces what is in any case denied him, all in the name of art. What produces his disenchantment, however, is not any actual experience of the transience of happiness; it is scepticism about the promise contained in the word itself. Flaubert is renouncing what he has lived only in his mind, and so it is no wonder his conception of sentimental education should be so thin and abstract. Ironically, within a year of declaring his education almost complete, Flaubert found himself caught up in a tempestuous love affair, one very different from the one he attributes to his fictional Henry. His relationship with Louise Colet, a free-living poet struggling to make her way in the Paris literary world, brought him more pleasure and pain than he could ever have anticipated. Begun in 1846, the affair was broken off in 1848 and then resumed in less intense form in 1851, when Flaubert was setting to work on *Madame Bovary*. By the time their relationship ended for good in 1855, when that book was almost finished, it had also provided the catalyst for a decisive development of Flaubert's aesthetic ideas. In responding to Louise's

---

[6] Letter to Alfred Le Poittevin, 17 June 1845, in *The Letters of Gustave Flaubert 1830–1857*, edited and translated by Francis Steegmuller (Cambridge, Mass., 1980), 34.

sincerely humanitarian but often mawkish writings, Flaubert sharp-
ened his views about the necessary impersonality of art. In addition,
her feminist ideas and emotional assertiveness also challenged his
tendency to view women in simplistic terms as either idealized or
sexualized figures in the drama of a man's sentimental education. If
in the end he did not amend his views—he chose to remain single
rather than accede to Louise's demands for a more stable and ongoing
intimacy—he was certainly forced to acknowledge their partiality.

Another crucial moment in Flaubert's sentimental education
came when in 1849 he followed the footsteps of the fictional Jules
and travelled to the Orient. The inspiration he would find during his
eighteen-month trip exceeded anything he might have imagined for
his character. In the Egyptian dancer and prostitute Kuchuk Hanem,
Flaubert discovered a woman of enigmatic, archetypal sexual power.
His encounter with her (purely physical, since they did not have
a common language in which to communicate) became a source of
endless reverie. Kuchuk's enduring influence on Flaubert's emotional
imagination, and his art, can be detected in the second *Sentimental
Education* of 1869. Flaubert's use of the term 'apparition' to describe
the moment when on the boat to Nogent, Frédéric first sees Mme
Arnoux, 'etched out against the blue sky' in the novel's first scene,
would for the French reader of the time most likely connote the
widely discussed apparitions of the Virgin Mary at La Salette in 1846
and at Lourdes in 1858. No doubt Flaubert intended this allusion,
but for the author the image recalled a very different and private
event: his unforgettable first sight of Kuchuk Hanem, 'surrounded
by light and standing against the background of blue sky' at the top of
an Egyptian staircase, looking down at a man who was also travelling
in a boat up a river, not the Seine but the Nile.[7]

While these unexpected real-life experiences upset Flaubert's
desire to bring his sentimental education to an early close, he also
began to curb his tendency to pre-emptive closure in his aesthetic
conception of the theme. As he looked backwards, he gained a clearer
perception of how his views had been shaped by the world in which
he had grown up. It was understandable that he should view his early
identification with the Romanticism of the preceding generation,

[7] Gustave Flaubert, *Flaubert in Egypt: A Sensibility on Tour*, trans. and ed. Francis
Steegmuller (1979; repr. Harmondsworth: Penguin, 1996), 114.

that of Lamartine and Hugo, which had been made all the more attractive because it had been attacked as vulgar and subversive by his classical-minded schoolmasters, as immature and in the end all too conventional. But as Flaubert grew into adulthood he became aware of just how much even the ostensibly more radical stance of a Byron had turned into a cultural cliché. Not only did he realize his struggle for originality was not unique; what was more disturbing, he saw that his spiritual disenchantment, like the sowing of sexual wild oats, could be considered without shock as just a stage in a young man's development. He tried to maintain the edge of his internal rebellion by sharpening it with the nihilism of the Marquis de Sade and the corrosive laughter of Rabelais, but no writer of the past could help him articulate his most profound insight into the nature of the world around him or handle the challenge it presented to him as a writer. This was the sense that no matter how hard a man tried to maintain a creative tension between critique and conformity, and no matter what efforts an artist made to give creative artistic representation to that dialectic of idealistic feeling and ironic reflection that lies at the heart of a genuine sentimental education, modern culture would absorb that tension and neutralize that dialectic by the deadening power of what he called 'received ideas'.

Clichés and conventional opinions pervade every culture, of course. What distinguishes the *idées reçues* of a modernity that prides itself in already being enlightened and critically aware is that they are not recognized as such and revised when artists point them out. Flaubert's personal experience had led him to modify his initial, and defensively reductive, definition of sentimental education. But in attempting to expand and deepen his conception of that education, he had to wonder how he could imagine and then convey it authentically, given that the usual strategies of idealizing or ironic distancing would offer no sure protection against the transformation of a work of art into another *idée reçue*.

Flaubert's path out of this impasse was a long and tortuous one. One solution was to tap the resources of the distant past. In *The Temptation of Saint Anthony*, a book about a fourth-century Egyptian monk, the first version of which was completed in 1849, sentimental education is reframed as a spiritual asceticism straining against all worldly temptations. Unfortunately, when Flaubert read the manuscript to his friends Maxime du Camp and Louis Bouilhet, they found it incomprehensible. It was just too eccentric. Only in 1874, five years after the publication of *Sentimental Education* and in the anxious atmosphere of a France reeling from military defeat in the Franco-Prussian War and shaken by the brutal repression of the Paris Commune, would Flaubert be able to recast the *Temptation* into a readable, though still challenging book.

A second strategy, as mentioned above, was to focus on a contemporary but marginal figure. Flaubert reframed his theme in a revolutionary way when he decided to write about the sentimental education of a woman, in the book that became *Madame Bovary*. A girl's discovery of love is one of the novel's most conventional themes, and fictional female heroines may be led to scrutinize their heart or learn the painful lesson of abandonment, but an *éducation sentimentale* of the more explicitly sexual and more intensely intellectual kind, involving experiences deviating from social rules and reflections detached from conventional moral considerations, was the prerogative of male protagonists. Rare exceptions such as the monstrous Mme de Merteuil in Laclos's *Liaisons dangereuses*, and the even more disturbing title character of Sade's *Juliette*, only proved the rule.

Flaubert's unpublished 1845 novel had made at least a gesture towards the inclusion of men of another race, but it did not challenge gender norms. *Madame Bovary* does so to disturbing effect. Emma's 'virile' qualities never obscure the reality or pathos of her womanly predicament, and Flaubert's re-examination of the gendered polarities of sentimental education is apparent in the way he mixes dreaminess and down-to-earth fact in narrating her erotic experiences. The prosecution of *Madame Bovary* for immorality confirmed his low opinion of bourgeois France, but it also validated his achievement in publishing a story that could not immediately be absorbed into the cultural repertoire—though of course in time Emma and her illusions would become as iconic a figure as any in a later modernity more acutely, if still too comfortably, aware of itself as an image factory.

After a return to the ancient world with *Salammbô* (1862), the story of a mercenary revolt against the government of Carthage and a rebel's doomed love for a local priestess, Flaubert began to think about setting another novel in contemporary France. At first, the central figure was again to be a woman, this time named Mme Moreau. According to the preparatory notes Flaubert began to sketch in 1862, the story, as in *Madame Bovary*, was to centre on an adulterous relationship, although in formulating it as one involving 'the husband, the wife, the lover, all loving each other, all cowardly',[8] Flaubert deviates from the pattern of the earlier novel in two significant ways. First, while her lovers may be cowardly, Emma Bovary is bold in her pursuit of them. By putting the three leading characters of the new book all on the same level Flaubert would seem to negate the energizing potential of its Parisian setting. Second, the working-out of that premiss was to be just as anaemic. The characters all 'understand their relative position and don't dare say it to each other. The feeling (*sentiment*) ends on its own. They separate . . . then, they die.'

The scope of the project begins to expand, paradoxically, with another deflationary move: Flaubert's decision that the lovers should not consummate their affair. Although the young man will become 'hardened' by his experience in society, he will remain too timid to pursue the wife, focusing his desires instead on *lorettes*, women looking for ongoing sexual arrangements with men prepared to 'keep' them in style. The result is a recentring of the book on a different kind of love triangle. Initially the central figure was the wife, torn between virtue and desire but unable to take the initiative the young man fails to seize himself—an inversion, in other words, of the situation dramatized in *Madame Bovary*. Now, Flaubert focuses his attention on the hero and his experience with two women, the 'honest' and the 'impure'. The transfer of the name 'Moreau' from the wife to the lover underscores this shift of emphasis. Flaubert finds himself wondering: is the story to be 'a sort of sentimental education'? One understands Flaubert's hesitation. Will this dramatization of the theme be an improvement on the first?

Flaubert's first innovation is to imagine the *bourgeoise* and the *lorette* as parallel rather than opposing characters. As objects of desire, they

---

[8] The following quotations are taken from what is known as 'Notebook 19', the earliest of the many sketches and drafts that provide a fascinating record of the novel's genesis. The contents of Notebook 19 were first published in 1950, but much of the other (and very considerable) material relating to *Sentimental Education* only became available to scholars after it was acquired by the Bibliothèque nationale in 1975. The full significance of these manuscripts is still being explored, but what are known as the 'scenarios' of the novel, the more extended notes and outlines intermediate between the notebooks and the drafts, have been published in a helpfully readable form. See Flaubert, *'L'Éducation sentimentale': Les Scénarios*, ed. Tony Williams (Paris, 1992). This volume also reproduces (pp. 324–33) the text of Notebook 19 as transcribed by Pierre-Marc de Biasi in his edition of Flaubert's *Carnets de travail* (Paris, 1988).

are equivalent to the point of the hero's being able to switch from one to the other without difficulty. By abolishing the ethical hierarchy between the hero's erotic alternatives, Flaubert undermines any easy identification of sentimental education with the achievement of an 'enlightened' moral judgement, whether of an edifying or cynical cast. Even so, Flaubert is reluctant to follow where his imagination is leading him. Something else was required to prevent critically shaped sentiment from collapsing into complacent sentimentality. The solution appeared when Flaubert discovered in the historical and political configuration of the setting a structural analogue to the dynamic of the story's personal relationships. 'Show', he advised himself in his notebook, 'that sentimentalism (its development since 1830) follows politics and replicates its phases.'[9] As he researched and wrote the book, Flaubert would modify this rather simplistic conception of sentimentalism as a mirror of politics. What he learned as he explored the events and writings of the period leading up to and through the Revolution of 1848, was that while every aspect of life was subject to the same flattening of moral difference and dynamism, that flattening took multiple forms. Moreover, because the various individual and collective expressions of this process proceeded at different speeds, they clashed with each other in ways that generated new and sometimes incongruous forms. By arranging his material in a carefully controlled pattern of echoes and contrasts, Flaubert found he could generate artistic energy from a contrapuntal orchestration of inertias.

## Sentimentalism 1: Inaction

The sentimentalism Flaubert portrays in the novel has three related aspects, and a brief exploration of how he treats each of them may offer helpful points of entry into the book. The first aspect is an inclination to vacuous reverie that precludes decisive action. Frédéric is an ineffectual dreamer possessed by images of happiness and social success so vivid and immediate that he feels the reality of them will follow by itself. If they don't there is no point in striving to attain them, because what is pursued with effort cannot match what is, and derives its charm from being, given. Even then, to have social success and

---

[9] In the manuscript, Flaubert capitalizes the word *Sentimentalisme*, but editors do not attribute much significance to his unsystematic use of capital letters.

personal fulfilment available for potential acquisition is better than to
have to take responsibility for actual possession. In a letter of 1864,
Flaubert told one of his women correspondents that the novel he was
writing was 'about love, about passion; but passion such as can exist
nowadays—that is to say, inactive'.[10] We like to think of 'modernity'
in terms of strenuous activity, of boldly transgressive assertions of
artistic as well as sexual desire, but for many male writers of the later
nineteenth century, erotic diffidence was the real mark of the modern.
This view is perhaps most memorably reflected in a remark made
by one of Flaubert's female acquaintances. In 1862, he and his friends
the writers Jules and Edmond de Goncourt were visited by the actress
Suzanne Lagier, who was known for her licentious songs and libertine
lifestyle. In *Sentimental Education*, Flaubert drew on her experiences
in creating the character of the courtesan Rosanette. The story (told in
the first chapter of Part Three) of how Rosanette lost her virginity is
taken directly from Lagier's own real-life account. Over the course of
the evening, Lagier made only half-joking advances to the three men
in turn. Disappointed by their lack of response, she exclaimed, 'Ah,
go on! You are all *moderns*, the three of you!'[11]

Flaubert does not say why modern passion should be so inactive,
and his brief account of Frédéric's childhood or early education does
not explain why he should be so lacking in initiative. To find a clue, we
must look around rather than behind Frédéric, to his circle of friends
rather than to his family origins, which are only briefly sketched. The
first thing we notice is that Flaubert's portrayal of the other young (or
youngish) men in the novel seems to be at odds both with his declared
focus on love and with his blanket characterization of their passions
as inactive. Their relationships with women do not lack initiative,
and some are not interested in love at all. Frédéric's closest companion from school, Charles Deslauriers, easily finds a mistress, but his
real passion is for power, the opportunity to dominate other people.
Significantly, the only women he tries to seduce are those with whom
his friend is involved. He only succeeds with one, but he tries his luck
with them all. Frédéric's other *lycée* classmate, Martinon, embarks on

---

[10] Letter to Mlle Leroyer de Chantepie, 6 October 1864, in *Letters of Flaubert 1857–1880*, ed. and trans. Steegmuller, 80.
[11] Edmond and Jules de Goncourt, *Journal: Mémoires de la vie littéraire*, ed. Robert Ricatte (Paris, 1989), i. 790 (23 March 1862).

a strategic affair with the wife of the wealthy M. Dambreuse and succeeds admirably in pivoting at the right moment to woo his daughter. Even the timorous aristocrat M. de Cisy, whom Frédéric meets at law school, is able to steal Rosanette away from him for a night, thanks to his wealth. The dandy journalist Hussonnet is evidently popular with the actresses he promotes. It is true that the irascible Regimbart, known as the 'citizen' for his militant nationalism (the 'citizen' of Joyce's *Ulysses* is partly inspired by him), neglects the wife who admires him, but we are told (in what now seems a remarkably offhand way) that the reason is his predilection for young girls (p. 214). In contrast to him, the good-hearted Dussardier shocks his friends when he tells them the only woman he wants is one he can love for the rest of his life. If he doesn't do much to find one, his poverty, his injury, and then his vigorous commitment to the Republican cause don't leave him the time. The two remaining friends display little interest in women, but they, too, are passionate about other things: the ascetic Sénécal for ideological authority, the aesthetic Pellerin for art.

Yet, if we look closer, we see that they are all 'inactive' in a deeper sense. They suffer from what Flaubert in his early notebook calls a 'radical failure of imagination', in paradoxical contrast with the futile excesses of their tastes, their sensuality, and their reveries. Precisely because they are mesmerized by seductive images of themselves enjoying the success they crave, they are incapable of the kind of creative self-projection that would enable them to pursue their goals more effectively. To take a small example, Deslauriers tells Frédéric they can make their way in the world by imitating Balzac's Rastignac, who rose from provincial poverty to Parisian success through charm, boldness, and wit. Yet, when he is frustrated in his desire to meet the Dambreuses by his lack of appropriate clothing—a very Balzacian situation—instead of begging, borrowing, or even stealing the outfit he needs, as Rastignac would have done, Deslauriers simply gives up. Or rather, he falls back into his habitual resentment of Frédéric and his wealth. The latter is equally satisfied with looking down on his friend's shabbiness, finding as usual in his own costly elegance some compensation for the feeling of inadequacy Deslauriers never fails to provoke in him (p. 143). It never occurs to either man to take a step back from their feelings in order to broker a deal. They desire success mostly to indulge their impulses more freely; in the crunch, the indulgence matters more than material advantage.

Near the end of the novel, Deslauriers seems finally to have made it when we see him coming out of the church where he has just married an heiress. He is wearing 'a blue suit with silver embroidery, a prefect's uniform' (p. 385). We soon learn that his success was short-lived: he was unable to leverage the status that came with the costume. What is true of Deslauriers is true of all the young men in the novel: they cannot be other than who they are. This is not because they possess a stable core identity stronger than any role. On the contrary, it is because their identity consists in a static set of attitudes they have internalized too unthinkingly to be able to adopt them more provisionally and in a detached manner. What Flaubert means by 'inactive' passion, therefore, is not emotion devoid of intensity; it is feeling that fails to get a grip on the world.

When they make themselves ridiculous, characters who cannot help being what they are, especially when they want to be different, are the stuff of comedy, and there are many occasions when Flaubert gives the actions of his young men a comic ineptness. At the end of the book Frédéric and Deslauriers themselves look back in laughter at their youth; they acknowledge themselves to be figures of fun. Yet we may find their laughter a little too comfortable in the narrow focus on their own earliest youth. People who cannot deviate from a self-image that has become second nature can also be frighteningly inhuman. Regimbart and Martinon are disturbingly impervious to the concerns of other people. Sénécal in particular is sinister in his implacability, and it is only because he has disappeared from sight that Frédéric can glide over the bloody moment when he last saw him. Flaubert challenges us with the suggestion that these characters illustrate the pervasiveness of sentimentality just as much as Frédéric does in his idealization of Mme Arnoux. Conversely, one is led to reflect in an equally challenging way on the nature of Frédéric's passion. A love as ridiculous as it is poignant is the stuff of romantic comedy, and so it is not that combination that bothers us, although the depiction earlier in the book of the virtuous and impure objects of his desire as interchangeable is somewhat disquieting. More disturbing is the possibility, expressed only implicitly, that Frédéric's sentimental fidelity to his ideal, in its inactivity, might be just as deathly in its way as the political constancy of Regimbart or Sénécal. We are unlikely to sympathize with the latter, but what does it say about us if we have identified more than a little with Frédéric?

This is one example of how Flaubert prompts us to scrutinize our own sentiments through subtle juxtaposition of material rather than by explicit commentary on it. That despite the overall pessimism of his vision he believes in the possibility of genuine reflection is indicated by the tenor of one of the rare instances in which the narrator intervenes in the story with a comment that does more than confirm what we can infer from the narrative itself. It comes at a point late in the story when Frédéric finds that to make love to Mme Dambreuse he needs to think about either Mme Arnoux or Rosanette, both of whom he has forsaken in order to gain 'a high position in society' through an affair with a society lady. The narrator speaks of the 'sentimental atrophy' (*atrophie sentimentale*) that has 'left his head completely clear' in this situation (p. 345). If Frédéric's feelings have atrophied, they must have had some tensile strength before, a strength he might yet recover. Yet, what has atrophied is his passion for the two interchangeable figures of the matron and the *lorette*. A foolish disposition that seemed at first to illustrate the flattening of desire now appears in retrospect as a comparatively commendable capacity to seek something beyond what can be seen with a clear head.[12] This is an even more radically flattened reality, symbolized here by Mme Dambreuse's 'thin bosom', the sight of which dampens what ardour Frédéric can muster when she arrives at his house dressed for the ball. The education of feeling, the reader's no doubt more than Frédéric's, is shaped by unexpected ironies such as these.

## Sentimentalism 2: Replication

If the first form of sentimentalism involves the 'inactive' quality of the agent, the second relates to the inert, even disabling results those agents achieve. Political conflict, including revolution, is shaped by the same tendency to strike a pose or inhabit a role that drives personal self-promotion, and by the same lack of genuine imagination. Like Marx, Flaubert saw the Revolution of 1848 and its aftermath as a farcical reprise of the tragic events of the decade that began in 1789. Louis Napoleon ('Napoleon the Little', as Victor Hugo would

---

[12] D. A. Williams makes the point well: 'If this is what the atrophy of sentiment leads to, sentiment cannot be all that bad.' *'The Hidden Life at its Source': A Study of Flaubert's* L'Éducation sentimentale (Hull, 1987), 169.

call him) has none of the grandeur of his uncle. At the political club where Frédéric hopes to secure popular support for his election to the Constituent Assembly, 'each person regulated himself on a model, some copying Saint-Just, some Danton, others Marat', while Sénécal, as chairman of the meeting, is an imitator twice removed, since 'he himself tried to be like Blanqui, who copied Robespierre' (p. 281).[13] The goals the revolutionaries seek are as comically (and yet dangerously) mimetic as their self-images. According to Flaubert, the French socialists of his time sought to establish a form of collectivism that while ostensibly modern in fact mirrored the oppressive corporatism of the Catholic Church. 'They are all little men deep into the Middle Ages and caste consciousness (*esprit de caste*).'[14] Socialism's rhetoric of 'fraternity' masked its hatred of individual freedom and of independent thinking. Introducing universal suffrage before the educational groundwork had been laid, in the belief that the people would naturally choose rightly, was a mistake. It only led to the crushing electoral victories the populist Louis Napoleon used to justify the re-establishment of authoritarian rule.

In this judgement, Flaubert agreed with some of the more clearsighted left-wing leaders, who had pleaded for elections under the new rules to be delayed until they could get their message out to the provinces. But Flaubert was not optimistic even about the long-term education of the masses. 'Philosophy will always be the portion of aristocrats', he told his friend George Sand, who for years had worked with the humanitarian socialist Pierre Leroux.[15] Against a rising tide of what he called 'democratic stupidity' Flaubert held fast to the more elitist and rationalist liberalism of the eighteenth-century

---

[13] 'Hegel observes somewhere that all the great events and characters of world history occur twice, so to speak. He forgot to add: the first time as high tragedy, the second time as low farce. Caussidière after Danton, Louis Blanc after Robespierre . . . The eighteenth Brumaire of the fool after the eighteenth Brumaire of the genius!' Karl Marx, *The Eighteenth Brumaire of Louis Napoleon*, in *Later Political Writings*, ed. and trans. Terrell Carver (Cambridge, 1996), 31. Marx's book was first published in 1852; by an interesting coincidence (Flaubert did not know anything about Marx's German work) a second edition appeared in 1869, the same year as *Sentimental Education*.

[14] Letter to Amélie Bosquet, July 1864, in Flaubert, *Correspondance*, ed. Jean Bruneau (Paris, 1973–2007), iii. 400. Flaubert's use of the term *caste* may also reflect his study of other religions, equally guilty in his eyes of stifling individuality, as he had shown in *Salammbô*.

[15] Letter to George Sand, 29 September 1868, in *Letters of Flaubert 1857–1880*, ed. and trans. Steegmuller, 120.

Enlightenment. 'If we had continued on the highroad of M. Voltaire, instead of veering off via Jean-Jacques, neo-Catholicism, the Gothic, and Fraternity, we wouldn't be where we are', he wrote in 1867.[16] The 'Gothic' here refers again to popular fascination with the Middle Ages, but it also evokes a genre of Romantic fiction, one of those that fed Emma Bovary's sentimental dreams. The image of the 'high road' (*grande route*) finds an echo, first in another letter to George Sand,[17] and then in the final chapter of *Sentimental Education*. There, Frédéric and Deslauriers agree that the former's fate can be attributed to his failure to 'steer a straight course' (p. 392) in life. 'I was too logical', Deslauriers says, 'and you were too sentimental.' The first part of the statement would have the ring of truth were it not for the clearly dubious claim Deslauriers makes for himself in adding that his own failure stemmed from 'an excess of rectitude'. Once again, Flaubert prevents us from endorsing too comfortably any summary judgement.

Another sign that Flaubert wants us to resist the stupidity (*bêtise*) of rushing to a conclusion[18] may be found in another of the narrator's exceptional interventions in the text. The judgement he offers seems so reasonable to readers today that we may not realize how much it jars with its context. When we are told with what venom the conservatives denounced the Second Republic of 1848 as a reincarnation of the Terror of 1793 Flaubert seems to be highlighting just another one of those stock historical analogies that stifle any new thinking. He goes on to say, however, that the regime being attacked was responsible for 'the most humane legislation there had ever been' (p. 275). The narrator does not specify what that legislation was, but given what we know of Flaubert's convictions such measures would surely include the ending of slavery in the French colonies and the first serious, if short-lived effort to guarantee a job for all those who wanted to work. But how could such innovative legislation have emerged from the motley beliefs and mimetic behaviour of those we are shown making the 1848 Revolution? The novel does not say. It records an effect without tracing its cause.

[16] Letter to Jules Duplan, [15] December 1867, in *Letters of Flaubert 1857–1880*, ed. and trans. Steegmuller, 111.

[17] Flaubert, *Correspondance*, ed. Bruneau and Leclerc, iii. 711.

[18] 'Yes, stupidity consists in wanting to reach conclusions.' Letter to Louis Bouilhet, 4 September 1850, in *Letters of Flaubert 1830–1857*, ed. and trans. Steegmuller, 128.

To simply repeat that Flaubert leaves the task of interpretation up to the reader is here to offer an inadequate response. Not telling us why people do what they do is one thing; character has its mysteries. Withholding an explanation of how historical action achieved a rare unequivocal good result suggests a failure of generosity; perhaps more crucially, it indicates a lack of trust. Indeed, Flaubert is sceptical of his readers' ability to arrive at authentic historical understanding. His own investigations into the Revolution of 1848 had so convinced him of the destructive effects of belief in the inevitability of progress and the sure triumph of goodness for him not to fear that any explanation he might offer would be incorporated into yet another naively teleological system. Yet he was even more worried that in attempting to offer historical explanations, no matter how rigorous, his novel would sacrifice its potential value as art.

The thoroughness of Flaubert's research has so impressed historians that some have treated _Sentimental Education_ as if it were a source document in its own right. In one sense, of course, it is. Flaubert had witnessed some of the February events at first hand, and in preparation for the novel he did an extraordinary amount of primary research, perusing entire runs of newspapers and reading deeply in books and pamphlets of every ideological stripe. Flaubert had also been an attentive reader of histories ever since his schooldays, when he was inspired by a teacher who had studied with the great Jules Michelet. Flaubert read each of the works Michelet himself continued to produce, as well as those of many others, including Hippolyte Taine, who became one of his friends. But just because of this familiarity with histories written over several decades, he was acutely conscious of how accounts of the past, and most notably of the French Revolution of 1789, were constantly being rewritten as new facts were unearthed and new ideologies became fashionable. He did not want to see his novel consigned to obsolescence, or, even worse, have it dismissed by later generations as blinkered by bias. The first fate he could forestall by dramatizing only specific moments and details he could document with certainty. He also refrained from linking them in extended causal chains that at best could only be provisional constructs and which could easily descend into mere speculation. Of course the work of narrative inevitably involves making connections, if only the ones created simply by putting facts in sequence. Flaubert thus sought to avoid the second fate by constructing patterns of juxtaposition using only material that, instead of fostering presumptuous hopes by suggesting that order could be discerned in disorder, would provoke an indignant reaction at the persistence of senseless violence or an ironic response to stubborn delusion about the most basic truths. Such reactions, he was convinced, are more timeless in quality than admiration; as the novel says of Dussardier, they refine one's sensibility (p. 215) yet are less likely to be vitiated by the sentimentality that infuses identification or the satisfaction that comes from grasping a manageable meaning. This does not entail, however, that hatred of oppression need be rooted or must result in personal animosity. On the contrary, and as Dussardier's attitude towards Vatnaz's criminality shows, if 'dissection is revenge', Flaubert insists one can never have enough 'sympathy', that is, disinterested appreciation, for the reality of human weakness.[19]

## *Sentimentalism 3: Perception*

The third form of sentimentality concerns the manner in which agency and achievement, such as they are, and stories about them, as they are told, are apprehended. Flaubert had already formulated the issue in a famous statement about the heroine of *Madame Bovary*. Emma, he wrote, 'had to derive a kind of personal profit from things, and rejected as useless anything that did not contribute directly to her heart's gratification—for her temperament was sentimental rather than artistic, and she longed for emotion, not scenery'.[20] The contrast here is between greedy incorporation and detached contemplation, of looking at things—or people, or books—as objects of consumption when they should be viewed, initially and finally, for who or what they are independently of us and in relationship with other things. By 'scenery' (*paysages*), Flaubert is not referring to a backdrop for one's personal drama but something like a landscape painting. This is a type of art without a 'subject', in the sense of a human situation or idea to the communication of which everything else is subordinated in the work. Instead, a landscape invites attention to the patterns of arrangement it discerns in the world it depicts. Feeling is not concentrated in a human

---

[19] The quotations are taken from Flaubert's letters to George Sand of 18–19 December 1867 and 10 August 1868 respectively, in *Letters of Flaubert 1857–1880*, ed. and trans. Steegmuller, 113, 118.

[20] Flaubert, *Madame Bovary*, trans. Margaret Mauldon (Oxford, 2004), 34.

figure representing that feeling to and for the viewer but dispersed in the scene as a whole, and is presented for an apprehension which precedes or perhaps supersedes the pleasure or instruction the viewer may draw from it. Of course, not all landscapes offer a disinterested apprehension of this kind, and conversely fostering such an apprehension is surely one of the goals of all great art. It is certainly one of Flaubert's. Here, he is using the *paysage* as a metaphor to make a point about the relentlessly self-interested attitude of his heroine, in order to contrast it with that of the book that tells her story.

The notebook recording the initial ideas for *Sentimental Education* picks up the theme. Anticipating the end of his story, Flaubert notes that the hero's excessive indulgence in reverie, coupled with his lack of genuine imagination, will have prevented him from being an artist. But while Flaubert may have had some such purpose in mind at the start, as the cowardly love triangle developed into a story about a young man's sentimental education the contrast between art and sentimentality became less clear-cut. For one thing, although Frédéric is certainly a consumer obsessed with the accoutrements he sees as necessary for the satisfaction of his desires, his appetites do not have the same urgency as Emma's. Of course, this is in part because, unlike Emma, Frédéric soon has an inheritance at his disposal and ample opportunity as a single man in Paris to do what he likes. Yet for a long time he remains content with merely contemplating Mme Arnoux, whose initial 'apparition' is described more as a kind of landscape image than as a personal meeting. Their eyes, for example, never quite meet. Instead, the sunlike radiance of her eyes conditions the lover's ability to see the things that surround her. In other words, there seems to be something artistic, or at least aesthetic, in Frédéric's way of loving. It is notable, too, that Flaubert shows Frédéric to be sensitive to landscape. In the episode in which he and Rosanette visit Fontainebleau (during which we glimpse the figure of an actual landscape painter), he escapes from the agitation of the 1848 Revolution in Paris to a historical site where the absence of people fosters a more melancholy view of the past precisely as past, not as prelude to a future eagerly expected to emerge from it.[21]

---

[21] For the literary as well as the artistic significance of this particular place, see Kimberly Jones et al., *In the Forest of Fontainebleau: Painters and Photographers from Corot to Monet* (New Haven, 2008).

In other situations, too, Frédéric remains an oddly passive specta-
tor. He is closely attentive, sometimes even in a hallucinatory way
that indicates a dispossession of self, to the arrangement of objects in
a scene. At the same time, he does not make the sustained effort needed
to understand the other characters in ways that would advance his
interests. Unlike his more prosaic companions, he does not integrate
isolated moments into instrumental chains of cause and effect. He is
entranced with surfaces, and if this is a sign of 'inactive' passion, it is
also similar enough to disinterested contemplation that although the
narrative must go around and beyond Frédéric's perceptions it does
not have to negate them in order to communicate an artistic vision of
the world. Frédéric is 'a man of innumerable weaknesses' (p. 277), but
some expressions of those weaknesses might be read as moments in
which sensual gratification is sacrificed for the sake of an ideal image.
This is certainly how Mme Arnoux interprets his actions during their
final meeting, though readers less partial to Frédéric (and to her) may
well disagree. On another level, Pellerin's endless dissatisfaction with
his art is a form of sentimental inaction in that he is so dominated
by the stances of previous artists that he can do no more than pas-
tiche them. Yet his anxiety about falling short of the true standard of
beauty has something admirable about it, and, as Alison Fairlie has
shown, some of his reflections mirror Flaubert's own thoughts on
the matter.[22] In the text as in the interpretation of it, the line between
sentiment and the sentimental becomes a hard one to draw.

There are critics for whom this is precisely Flaubert's point. They
would view the double meaning of *L'Éducation sentimentale*'s title as
undecidable rather than as merely ambiguous. According to this view,
the sentimental education the novel models for us culminates neither
in rueful wisdom nor in comfortable rumination but in a critical suspension and suspicion of judgement. There is ample warrant for this
inference, both in the novel and in Flaubert's famous statement about
conclusions. But one may think this too intellectual, and, in its own
way, too final a judgement to be a wholly satisfactory response to the
story Flaubert tells. Other readers, perhaps chiefly those who at one
point or another found themselves responding to the rhetoric of

---

[22] Alison Fairlie, 'Pellerin et le thème de l'art dans *L'Éducation sentimentale*', in Fairlie,
*Imagination and Language: Collected Essays on Constant, Baudelaire, Nerval, and Flaubert*
(Cambridge, 1981), 408–21.

romance and now feel they know better, will be less hesitant about taking ambiguity as bitter irony instead. They will see the novel as the expression of an ongoing work of disenchantment always expecting further confirmation, seeking to provoke that disenchantment in the reader, and finding in the latter's incomprehension or imperviousness something more to be disenchanted about. From this point of view, there is no conclusion for the simple reason that the process of disillusionment is never complete. The Flaubert who realized he had claimed too prematurely that his sentimental education was almost finished and had to eat his words would surely agree. This interpretation, however, faces the objection that the novel is never quite as unrelenting as this. We might cite as evidence a fact often overlooked because it is too obvious or perhaps because it would sound too caddish to present in this way. This is that Flaubert twice (if not three times) allows Frédéric to avoid a marriage that would have proved even more disastrous for him and more disenchanting for the reader than his actual fate.[23]

There is, however, a third possibility. In discussing the problem of how Flaubert's characters could be thought of as inactive despite the energy they display in the pursuit of their passions, I suggested that 'inactivity' consisted of an inability to be other than what they were. A similar approach might be taken to interpreting those aspects of Frédéric's and others' behaviour whose contemplative, selfless, or aesthetic qualities approximate to the artistic yet do not finally qualify as such. What is genuine in the idealized love Frédéric places above appetite and what is admirable in his lack of self-regard are not vitiated in the end by his sensual indulgence or his narcissism. Important as these failings are, Flaubert is not a moralist, and he can imagine a life in which these tendencies can coexist with other, nobler ones. What undermines Frédéric's 'aesthetic' aspirations is that he does not give them genuine embodiment (as opposed to merely associating them fetishistically with material objects), and what makes his self-sacrifices a vain exercise is that they do not stem from a self that has accepted its embeddedness in the world as it is (as opposed to merely fretting over its distance from the ideal and frantically trying to abolish it by magical thinking). One might put it like this: in ways just as crucial as those in which he cannot be other than what he is,

---

[23] See Jean Borie, *Frédéric et les amis des hommes* (Paris, 1995), 40–1.

Frédéric is unable to be other than what he is not. He is unable to view transcendence as a task, and not simply as a state of transport. He cannot move from dispossession to determination. From this point of view, what Flaubert does is to shape a narrative in which 'the' genuine sentimental education is not about achieving a higher level of consciousness or arriving at a lower view of humanity but more modestly about seeing the human landscape as landscape, that is, as a pattern of various and contradictory forces and facts that call for patient and sympathetic attention to their finitude. One could call the expression of such attention 'description', did not that word, by an ironic twist, connote a merely 'inactive' process in inartistic modern sensibilities. On the contrary, it is in scrupulous attention that reflection and feeling find their best discipline.[24]

---

[24] I would like to express my appreciation to Helen Constantine. Her fine translation has helped me to a much better understanding of the subtleties of Flaubert's text, which she conveys so well. It has been a pleasure to work with her a second time. I especially wish to say how grateful I am to the editor of Oxford World's Classics, Judith Luna, for the confidence she has shown in entrusting me with this and other projects. I have been privileged to benefit from her unfailing encouragement, gentle prompting, and insightful advice, all of which have been crucial to my work over the last two decades. Thanks also to Rowena Anketell, who as copy editor of this volume caught a number of slips and made many useful suggestions.

# NOTE ON THE TEXT

*L'ÉDUCATION SENTIMENTALE* was first published by Michel Lévy in November 1869, though with a title-page date of 1870. It was reprinted twice without changes in the following years, but a new edition published by Charpentier in November 1879, with a date of 1880, incorporated a large number of minor changes made by Flaubert. This edition was the last one to appear in the author's lifetime and so has served as the basis for all recent editions. Many of the modifications involve small stylistic adjustments of interest only to specialists, but one series of changes is worthy of remark. Flaubert eliminated almost 200 connective conjunctions and adverbs, including 131 instances of the word 'but'. Numerous instances of 'then', 'and', 'however', 'finally', and other such words were also deleted. The effect is to make the relationship between various statements less explicit. In the absence of such connectives, readers must rely on the rhythm and tone of the sentences to draw a possible, but perhaps never quite definite, pattern of connections among them.

In addition to these changes, which are clearly attributable to the author, the Charpentier edition includes a number of typographical errors, which have been silently corrected by modern editors. In some cases, however, it is not clear whether the anomalous feature is an error, an oversight, or an authorial decision. Editors have differed in their willingness to emend the text based on another printed or manuscript version that seems to offer a more coherent reading or to reflect Flaubert's most considered intention. Most of these variations are too minor to matter to all but the most specialist reader, but in the very few instances where the difference may be of more general interest, the alternative reading is recorded in the Explanatory Notes.

# TRANSLATOR'S NOTE

I HOPE English readers will enjoy this translation of one of the most important novels of nineteenth-century French literature. Translating a long novel is always difficult and demanding. Flaubert's use of the many tones and varieties of the language of sentiment in a wide variety of characters from differing social classes, against a backdrop of important historical events, presented an exciting challenge. It will be for the reader to judge if I have managed to carry the spirit of the novel across into my own language and culture.

Some of the questions I have had continually in mind for the last two years are: is that 'le mot juste'? Flaubert had a notorious interest in the exact word, whether writing about furnishings, dress, manufacture, or medicine. What *precisely* does Flaubert mean? Is that turn of phrase appropriate to the social context? Have I hit the tone of that dialogue? Does the sentence sound harmonious and 'natural' in English? These are problems all literary translators will recognize, and it was these rather than the peculiarities of Flaubert's style—among them the famous *style indirect libre*, for which there is an acceptable English stylistic equivalent—that presented tricky, though enjoyable, problems.

I have used Albert Thibaudet's Folio edition of the text, which has notes by S. de Sacy. This is based on the last edition published, by Charpentier, during Flaubert's lifetime. Thibaudet made a very few minor corrections to this last edition, in accordance with those indicated by Flaubert in a manuscript of 1879 preserved in Croisset. I have consulted previous versions of the novel and in particular Robert Baldick's (Penguin, 1964) to check and compare my translation.

I have been enormously helped in this two-year endeavour by the generous suggestions and expertise of David Constantine and Patrick Coleman. My grateful thanks also are due to Judith Luna at OUP who has constantly spurred me on, and to the ever-welcoming team in the Translation Centre at the Espace Van Gogh in Arles, where I have several times been privileged to work on my translations.

*Helen Constantine*

# SELECT BIBLIOGRAPHY

*Works in French*

The standard critical edition of Flaubert's *Œuvres complètes*, under the general editorship of Claudine Gothot-Mersch (Paris, 2001– ), 3 vols. to date, will include *L'Éducation sentimentale* in its fourth and final volume. Earlier separate editions of great value include those of Alan Raitt (Paris, 1979), P. M. Wetherill (Paris, 1984), and Claudine Gothot-Mersch (Paris, 1985). These are all out of print, but there are readily available editions in the Folio, GF, and Livre de poche series, the last two having especially helpful annotations by Stéphanie Dord-Crouslé and Pierre-Marc De Biasi respectively.

Flaubert's letters are essential to a full understanding of his work. His complete *Correspondance* has been edited by Jean Bruneau and Yves Leclerc (Paris, 1973–2007), 5 vols. plus separate index volume. In English, Francis Steegmuller has edited and translated an excellent selected *Letters of Gustave Flaubert* (Cambridge, Mass., 1980–2), 2 vols. There are also separate editions in English of Flaubert's correspondence with George Sand and Ivan Turgenev.

*Biography*

The most recent in English are Frederick Brown, *Flaubert: A Biography* (New York, 2006), and Geoffrey Wall, *Flaubert: A Life* (London, 2001). Older but still useful is Benjamin F. Bart, *Flaubert* (Syracuse, NY, 1967).

*Reference*

The website of the Centre Flaubert at the Université de Rouen offers many useful resources, including photographs and other visual material of interest to readers without extensive knowledge of French: http://flaubert. univ-rouen.fr/

Porter, Laurence M. (ed.), *A Flaubert Encyclopedia* (Westport, Conn., 2001).

*Critical Studies*

A useful introductory guide:

Paulson, William R., *Sentimental Education: The Complexity of Disenchantment* (New York, 1992).

Two classic essays by distinguished novelists:

James, Henry, 'Gustave Flaubert', in *Literary Criticism: French Writers, European Writers, the Prefaces to the New York Edition* (New York, 1984).

Proust, Marcel, 'On Flaubert's Style', in *Against Sainte-Beuve and Other Essays*, trans. John Sturrock (Harmondsworth, 1988).

A selected list of modern studies in English:

Alter, Robert, *Imagined Cities: Urban Experience and the Language of the Novel* (New Haven, 2005).
Berg, William J., and Martin, Laurey K., *Gustave Flaubert* (New York, 1997).
Brooks, Peter, *Reading for the Plot* (New York, 1984).
Burton, Richard D. E., 'The Death of Politics: The Significance of Dambreuse's Funeral in *L'Éducation sentimentale*', *French Studies* 50 (1996), 157–69.
Cortland, Peter, *The Sentimental Adventure: An Examination of Flaubert's* Éducation sentimentale (The Hague, 1967).
Culler, Jonathan, *Flaubert: The Uses of Uncertainty* (2nd edn., Ithaca, NY, 1984).
Danius, Sara, *The Prose of the World: Flaubert and the Art of Making Things Visible* (Uppsala, 2006).
Duvall, William, 'Flaubert's *Sentimental Education* Between History and Literature', *Historical Reflections/Réflexions historiques* 32 (2006), 339–57.
Fairlie, Alison, *Imagination and Language: Collected Essays on Constant, Baudelaire, Nerval, and Flaubert* (Cambridge, 1981).
Gans, Eric, '*Éducation sentimentale*: The Hero as Storyteller', *MLN* 89 (1974), 614–25.
Ginsburg, Michal Peled, *Flaubert Writing: A Study in Narrative Strategies* (Stanford, Calif., 1986).
Kelly, Dorothy, *Reconstructing Woman: From Fiction to Reality in the Nineteenth-Century Novel* (University Park, Pa., 2007).
Knight, Diana, *Flaubert's Characters* (Cambridge, 1985).
—— 'Object Choices: Taste and Fetishism in Flaubert's *L'Éducation sentimentale*', in Brian Rigby (ed.), *French Literary Thought and Culture in the Nineteenth Century: A Material World. Essays in Honour of D. G. Charlton* (Basingstoke, 1993), 198–217.
Orr, Mary, 'Reading the Other: Flaubert's *L'Éducation sentimentale* Revisited', *French Studies* 46 (1992), 412–23.
—— *Flaubert: Writing the Masculine* (Oxford, 2000).
—— 'Still Life and Moving Death in Flaubert's *Éducation sentimentale*', *Dix-Neuf* 5 (Sept. 2005); <http://dx.doi.org/10.1179/147873105790723312>.
Prendergast, Christopher, *Paris and the Nineteenth Century* (Oxford, 1992).
Roe, David, *Gustave Flaubert* (Basingstoke, 1989).

Sayeau, Michael, *Against the Event: The Everyday and the Evolution of Modernist Narrative* (Oxford, 2013).

Sherrington, R. J., *Three Novels by Flaubert* (Oxford, 1970).

Thorlby, Anthony, *Flaubert: The Art of Realism* (London, 1956).

Tooke, Adrianne, *Flaubert and the Pictorial Arts: From Image to Text* (Oxford, 2000).

Unwin, Timothy (ed.), *The Cambridge Companion to Flaubert* (Cambridge, 2004).

———— 'Gustave Flaubert (1821–1880): Realism and Aestheticism', in Michael Bell (ed.), *The Cambridge Companion to European Novelists* (Cambridge, 2012), 244–58.

Ward, Graham, 'Reading to Live: Miracle and Language', *Religion and Literature* 44/1 (2012), 1–21.

Wetherill, P. M., 'Flaubert and Revolution', in David Bevan (ed.), *Literature and Revolution* (Amsterdam, 1989), 19–33.

Williams, D. A., 'G. Flaubert: *Sentimental Education* (1869)', in Williams (ed.), *The Monster in the Mirror: Studies in Nineteenth-Century Realism* (Oxford, 1979).

———— *The Hidden Life at Its Source: A Study of Flaubert's L'Éducation sentimentale* (Hull, 1987).

Williams, Tony, 'Dussardier on the Barricades: History and Fiction in *L'Éducation sentimentale*', *Nineteenth-Century French Studies* 28 (2000), 284–97.

———— and Orr, Mary (eds.), *New Approaches in Flaubert Studies* (Lewiston, NY, 1999).

Wilson, Edmund, 'The Politics of Flaubert', in *The Triple Thinkers* (rev. edn., New York, 1948), 72–87.

Yee, Jennifer, 'Like an Apparition: Oriental Ghosting in Flaubert's *Éducation sentimentale*', *French Studies* 67 (2013), 340–54.

### Further Reading in Oxford World's Classics

Balzac, Honoré de, *Père Goriot*, trans. and ed. A. J. Krailsheimer.

Dickens, Charles, *Great Expectations*, ed. Margaret Cardwell, introd. Robert Douglas-Fairhurst.

Flaubert, Gustave, *Madame Bovary*, trans. Margaret Mauldon, introd. Malcolm Bowie.

Maupassant, Guy de, *Bel-Ami*, trans. Margaret Mauldon, ed. Robert Lethbridge.

Zola, Émile, *Money*, trans. and ed. Valerie Minogue.

# A CHRONOLOGY OF GUSTAVE FLAUBERT

1802 Achille Flaubert, Gustave's father, comes to Paris to study medicine.

1810 Achille Flaubert moves to Rouen to work as deputy head of the hospital (the Hôtel-Dieu).

1812 Achille Flaubert marries the adopted daughter of the head of the Hôtel-Dieu.

1813 Gustave's brother Achille-Cléophas born.

1819 Achille Flaubert appointed head of Hôtel-Dieu on the death of his superior.

1821 (12 December) Gustave Flaubert born.

1824 (July) Gustave's sister Caroline born.

1836 While at school in Rouen, writes several stories. On holiday at Trouville, falls in love with Elisa Foucault, a woman of 26, who shortly afterwards marries Maurice Schlésinger. The image of Elisa Schlésinger recurs in a number of Flaubert's writings: in particular, she is said to be the model for Madame Arnoux in *L'Éducation sentimentale*.

1837 More stories. One of these, *Une leçon d'histoire naturelle, genre Commis*, is published in a local journal; another, *Passion et vertu*, anticipates the story of *Madame Bovary* in certain respects.

1838 *Mémoires d'un fou*, an autobiographical narrative; *Loys XI*, a five-act play.

1839 Completes *Smarh*, a semi-dramatic fantasy which may be considered an embryonic version of *La Tentation de Saint Antoine*.

1841 (November) Registers as law student in Paris, though continuing to live at home.

1842 *Novembre*, another autobiographical narrative. Passes his first law examination.

1843 Begins the first version of *L'Éducation sentimentale*. Fails his second law examination.

1844 Has a form of epileptic seizure. Gives up law. (April) Flaubert's father buys a house at Croisset, near Rouen. (June) The Flaubert family moves to Croisset.

1845 *L'Éducation sentimentale* (first version) completed.

1846 Flaubert's father and sister die. He sets up house at Croisset with his mother and niece. Meets Louise Colet in Paris; she becomes his mistress.

1847 *Par les champs et par les grèves*, impressions of his travels in Brittany with his literary friend Maxime Du Camp.

1848 Together with Louis Bouilhet (another literary friend) and Maxime Du Camp, witnesses the 1848 uprising in Paris; he will later draw on these memories for scenes in *L'Éducation sentimentale*. Begins *La Tentation de Saint Antoine* (first version).

1849 Reads *La Tentation* aloud to Bouilhet and Du Camp, who consider it a failure. Leaves for a tour of the Near East with Du Camp.

1850 (February) They journey up the Nile; (May) they cross the desert by camel. (August) Death of Balzac; Flaubert and Du Camp reach Jerusalem. (September) They abandon plans to travel to Persia and turn west; (October) Rhodes; (November) Constantinople; (December) Athens.

1851 (April) Flaubert in Rome; Du Camp returns to Paris. (May) Flaubert returns to Croisset; resumes relations with Louise Colet. (19 September) Begins writing *Madame Bovary*.

1852 While working on *Madame Bovary*, recalls his earlier project for a *Dictionnaire des idées reçues*.

1854 End of affair with Louise Colet.

1856 *Madame Bovary* completed and published in serial form in *La Revue de Paris* (from 1 October). Begins to revise *La Tentation*.

1856–7 Fragments of *La Tentation* published in *L'Artiste*.

1857 Flaubert and *La Revue de Paris* prosecuted for irreligion and immorality; acquitted. The trial attracts a great deal of attention and makes *Madame Bovary* (now published as a complete novel) a *succès de scandale*. Begins work on *Salammbô*.

1858 Visits North Africa to gather material for *Salammbô*.

1862 *Salammbô* completed and published: an enormous success. Flaubert by now a famous literary figure.

1863 January: first letter to George Sand. February: first meeting with Turgenev.

1864 Begins work on *L'Éducation sentimentale*. In the course of the next five years gathers material for his novel, and at the same time enjoys a brilliant social life.

1866 (August) Nominated Chevalier de la Légion d'honneur. November: George Sand's first visit to Croisset.

1869 *L'Éducation sentimentale* (definitive version) completed and published. Death of Louis Bouilhet.

1870 Works on yet another version of *La Tentation de Saint Antoine*. (August) Franco-Prussian War begins; (December) victorious German troops arrive in Rouen.

1871 (January) Armistice signed with Prussia; (May) insurrection in Paris; (July) German troops leave Rouen.

1872 Flaubert's mother dies. Third version of *La Tentation* completed.

1874 *La Tentation* published. Begins work on *Bouvard et Pécuchet*.

1875–7 Writes *La Légende de Saint Julien l'Hospitalier*, *Un Cœur simple*, and *Hérodias (Trois contes)*.

1877 *Trois contes* published. Returns to *Bouvard et Pécuchet*.

1877–80 Works on *Bouvard*, which will remain unfinished.

1880 (8 May) Dies.

1881 *Bouvard et Pécuchet* published. House at Croisset sold and later demolished to make way for a distillery.

1882 (January) Death of brother, Achille Flaubert.

# SENTIMENTAL EDUCATION

# PART ONE

## I

ON 15 September 1840, at around six o'clock in the morning, *La Ville-de-Montereau*, almost ready to leave, was puffing out thick clouds of smoke alongside the Quai Saint-Bernard.

Passengers were arriving, out of breath; barrels, ropes, baskets of washing got in their way; the sailors made answer to no one; people bumped into one another; packages were piling up between the paddle boxes; and the din on the quay was absorbed in the hissing of the steam escaping through the metal plates, enveloping everything in a whitish mist, while the bell in the ship's bows sounded its insistent clanging.

At last the ship left, and the two riverbanks, lined with shops, workers' yards, and factories, slipped away like two wide ribbons being unspooled.

A young man of eighteen with long hair, holding a notebook under his arm, stood near the helm, not moving. He gazed through the mist at the church towers, at the buildings he could not put a name to; then in one last glance he embraced the Île Saint-Louis, the Cité, Notre-Dame; and before long, as Paris disappeared, he heaved a deep sigh.

Monsieur Frédéric Moreau, having just passed his baccalaureate, was going back to Nogent-sur-Seine to idle away two months before going to read for the Bar. His mother had sent him, with the necessary sum of money, to Le Havre to visit an uncle who, she hoped, would leave him something in his will; he had returned only the night before; and he was making up for not being able to stay in the capital by taking the longest route back to his home in the provinces.

The noise subsided; they had all found seats; but some remained standing close to the engine, warming themselves, and the funnel spat out, with a slow, rhythmic rattle, its plume of black smoke; tiny drops of dew trickled down the brass; the deck shuddered with a dull internal vibration and the two paddle wheels, turning at speed, churned up the water.

The riverbank had little sandy shores on either side. Sometimes they came across timber rafts and set them rocking with their wash; in his rowing boat a man sat fishing; then the drifts of fog melted, the sun appeared, and the hill, which followed the course of the Seine on the right, gradually fell away, while another, closer, rose up on the opposite bank.

On it was a crown of trees, amongst low houses with Italianate roofs. They had sloping gardens separated by newly built walls, wrought-iron fences, lawns, hothouses, and large pots of geraniums spaced at regular intervals on terraces you could lean over. Many a man, at the sight of those peaceful, stylish residences, felt the desire to be the owner of one, to see out his days there with a nice billiard room, a rowing boat, a wife—or some other pipe dream. The rather novel pleasure of a boat trip encouraged passengers to exchange confidences. The more droll amongst them were already beginning to laugh and tell jokes. Many sang songs. They were jolly together. They offered one another a drop to drink.

Frédéric thought of his room at home, the kind of play he might write, the pictures he might paint, and of future passions. The happiness his noble soul deserved seemed a long time coming. He recited melancholy verses to himself; he paced rapidly up and down the deck; he went to the far end by the ship's bell, and saw a man, in a group of passengers and sailors, flirting with a country girl, while fondling the gold crucifix she was wearing on her breast. He was a curly-haired fellow of some forty years. His stocky frame filled his black velvet jacket, two emeralds gleamed on his cambric shirt, and from beneath his wide white trousers protruded a pair of strange red boots, made of Russian leather tooled with a blue design.

The presence of Frédéric did not bother him. Several times he turned round and winked at him; then he offered everyone a cigar. But no doubt bored with this company, he moved away. Frédéric followed him.

The ensuing conversation was first about different kinds of tobacco; then it moved on, quite naturally, to the subject of women. The man in the red boots gave the young man advice. He expounded theories, told anecdotes, citing himself as an example, and delivered all this in a fatherly tone of voice, with an engagingly frank disregard for morals.

He was a Republican. He had travelled widely; he knew the inside of theatres, restaurants, newspapers, and all the celebrated artists, whom he referred to in a familiar way by their first names. Before long Frédéric was telling him about his plans; he encouraged him.

But he broke off to observe the ship's funnel and muttered a lengthy, rapid calculation, to work out 'how often each piston, at so many strokes per minute, would have to etc.'—and, once he had arrived at the answer, he talked about the beauties of the landscape. He said he was glad to have escaped from his work.

Frédéric felt a certain respect for him and couldn't resist the temptation to ask his name. The stranger replied all in one breath:

'Jacques Arnoux, proprietor of *L'Art industriel,** Boulevard Montmartre.'

A servant with gold braid on his cap came to say:

'Would Monsieur care to go below? Mademoiselle is crying.'

He disappeared.

*L'Art industriel* was a hybrid establishment, consisting of a publication about painting and a shop selling pictures. Frédéric had seen that title on several occasions in the window of the bookshop in his home town, on large posters bearing the name of Jacques Arnoux in large capitals.

The sun was directly overhead, making the iron sheathing around the masts, the metal on the rail, and the surface of the water gleam and glint. Around the prow the water parted in two furrows, which spread out to the very edge of the fields. At each bend in the river the same curtain of pale poplars came into view. The countryside was quite empty. Small white clouds hung overhead, inert, and the vague feeling of ennui pervading everything seemed to make the boat move more slowly and the passengers appear even more insignificant than before.

Apart from a few well-to-do people in the First Class, they were working men and women, shopkeepers with their wives and children. As it was usual at that time not to dress smartly for a boat trip, almost all were wearing old skullcaps or faded hats, flimsy black suits, rubbed threadbare by the office, or frock coats with the buttonholes stretched from being worn too often in the shop. Here and there, inside the occasional woollen jacket you saw a calico shirt stained with coffee; pinchbeck tiepins were stuck into shredded ties; list slippers were held together by sewn-on straps. Two or three disreputable-looking individuals holding bamboo canes braided with leather glanced around shiftily, and fathers of families asked questions and looked amazed.

They talked standing up or squatting on their luggage; others slept in corners; several were eating. The deck was littered with walnut shells, cigar stubs, the peelings of pears, the detritus of sausage that had been brought wrapped in paper. Three besmocked cabinetmakers had stationed themselves outside the canteen; a ragged harp-player was resting, leaning on his instrument. Now and again you could hear the fires being stoked with coal, a raised voice, someone laughing.—And the captain on the bridge paced incessantly to and fro between the paddle boxes. To get back to his seat, Frédéric pushed open the gate to the First Class and two sportsmen with their dogs had to move out of his way.

It was like an apparition:

She was sitting in the middle of a bench all by herself, or at least, with no one else that he could see, so dazzling was the light from her eyes. She raised her head as he went past; in an involuntary gesture he inclined his shoulders slightly, and when he had walked on a little, along the same side of the boat, he looked at her.

She wore a wide straw hat with pink ribbons that fluttered out behind her in the breeze. Her black hair framed her large eyebrows, and reached down very low on her oval face, seeming to press against it lovingly. Her pale dress of spotted muslin billowed out in numerous folds. She was engaged in some embroidery; and her straight nose, her chin, and indeed her whole person, was etched out against the blue sky.

As she didn't change her position, he took several steps to right and left to conceal his manoeuvring; then he stationed himself next to her sunshade, which was propped against the seat, and pretended to be observing a rowing boat on the river.

Never had he seen such beautiful dark skin, such an attractive figure, such delicate, translucent fingers. He contemplated her work basket in wonder, as though it were an extraordinary object. What was her name? Where did she live? What did she do? What was her past? He wanted to know how her room was furnished, all the dresses she had ever worn, what people she knew; and even the desire to possess her physically evaporated beneath a deeper yearning, a painful and infinite curiosity.

A Negro woman with a scarf tied round her head, appeared, holding by the hand a little girl who was already quite tall. The child, who had tears in her eyes, had just woken up; she took her on her lap.

Mademoiselle hadn't been a good girl, even though she'd soon be seven. Her mother wouldn't love her any more, she was too spoiled. And Frédéric was delighted by hearing all this, as though he had made a discovery, an acquisition.

He supposed her to be of Andalusian extraction, possibly Creole;* had she brought this Negro woman back with her from the islands?

A long shawl with purple stripes had been placed behind her back, on the brass rail. How many times, in the middle of the ocean, in the course of the damp evenings, must she have wrapped it round her figure, covered her feet with it, slept in it! But it was being dragged down by its fringe, it was gradually slipping and was about to fall into the water. Frédéric, in one leap, caught it. She said:

'Thank you, Monsieur.'

Their eyes met.

'Are you ready, my dear?' cried Arnoux, appearing at the hatch to the companion way.

Mademoiselle Marthe ran to him, and clinging to his neck, pulled at his moustache. There came the sounds of a harp, she wanted to see who was playing; and soon the player, fetched by the Negro woman, entered the First Class. Arnoux recognized him as a former painters' model; he spoke familiarly to him, to the surprise of those present. At last the harpist tossed his long locks over his shoulders, stretched out his arms, and started to play.

It was an oriental romance, full of daggers, flowers, and stars. The man in rags gave a spirited rendering; the thrumming of the engine distorted the tempo; he plucked harder; the strings vibrated, and their metallic notes seemed to sob out the lament of a proud love vanquished. On both sides of the river woods bowed down to the water's edge; a breath of cooler air wafted across; Madame Arnoux looked vaguely into the distance. When the music stopped, her eyelids fluttered several times as if waking from a daydream.

Respectfully, the harpist came forward. While Arnoux was searching for his change, Frédéric stretched out his closed fist, and opening it unostentatiously, dropped a gold coin* into the hat. It wasn't vanity which drove him to give money in her presence, but a generous impulse in which she was associated, a religious urge, almost.

Arnoux, indicating the way, cordially invited him to go down. Frédéric said he had just lunched; in fact he was dying of hunger; and there was not one centime in the bottom of his purse.

Then it occurred to him that he had as much right as anyone else to go into the saloon.

The well-to-do were sitting eating at round tables, a waiter was circulating; Monsieur and Madame Arnoux were at the back on the right; he picked up a newspaper lying on the long velvet-covered bench, and sat down.

At Montereau they were to take the coach to Châlons. Their trip to Switzerland would last a month. Madame Arnoux scolded her husband for being indulgent with the child. He whispered something in her ear, no doubt a compliment, for she smiled. Then he got up to close the curtain at the window behind her.

A harsh light was reflected from the low, all-white ceiling. Frédéric seated opposite could make out the shadow under her eyelashes. She moistened her lips in her glass, crumbled a little bread between her fingers; the lapis lazuli locket attached by a gold chain to her wrist chinked occasionally against her plate. Yet the people sitting around her did not seem to notice.

Sometimes through the portholes you could see the side of a boat come alongside the steamer to fetch or drop off passengers. People at the tables leaned towards the openings and put names to the places they passed along the banks.

Arnoux was complaining about the food: he objected vociferously to the bill and got it reduced. Then he carried the young man off to the bows to have a grog. But before long Frédéric came back to the awning, under which Madame Arnoux had seated herself again. She was reading a slim volume with a grey cover. Her mouth curled at the corners from time to time and her face lit up in a flush of pleasure. He was jealous of whoever had invented those things she seemed so interested in. The more he observed her, the more he felt a gulf opening up between them. He was thinking that he would have to leave her soon, for ever, without having snatched a word with her, without leaving even a memory.

Flat fields stretched out on the right-hand side; on the left pastures rose gently to a hill, where vineyards, walnut trees, a windmill could be espied among the greenery, and the little paths beyond formed zigzags on the white rock, which touched the rim of the sky. How blissful it would be to climb up and up, his arm around her waist and her dress brushing against the yellow leaves, listening to her voice, under the radiance of her eyes! The ship could halt, all they had to do was get out; and yet such a simple action was more impossible than moving the sun's orb.

A little further along they saw a castle with a pointed roof, with little square turrets. There was a wide flower bed in front of it; black archways down tall avenues of lime trees disappeared into the distance. He imagined her walking beneath their branches. At that moment a young man and woman appeared on the steps, between the tubs planted with orange trees. Then everything vanished.

The little girl was playing around him. Frédéric wanted to give her a kiss. She hid behind her nurse; her mother scolded her for not being nice to the gentleman who had rescued her shawl. Was that an indirect approach?

'Is she going to talk to me at last?' he wondered.

Time was getting short. How could he get an invitation to the Arnouxes'? All he could think of was to make a remark about the autumn tints, adding:

'Soon it'll be winter, time for balls and dinners!'

But Arnoux was totally taken up with his luggage. The shore of Surville appeared, the two bridges came closer. They sailed past a rope-maker's, and then a line of low houses; below them there were cauldrons of tar, wood shavings; and children ran along the sand, doing cartwheels. Frédéric recognized a man in a long-sleeved jacket and shouted:

'Hurry up!'

They were docking. After a painstaking search for Arnoux in the throng of passengers, he shook hands, and the latter said:

'I hope we meet again, Monsieur!'

Once he was on the quay, Frédéric turned round. She was standing near the tiller. He sent her a look in which he tried to put his entire soul but she remained unmoved, as though he had done nothing. Then, taking no notice of his servant's greeting, he said:

'Why didn't you bring the carriage over here?'

The poor man apologized.

'What a fool! Give me some money!'

And he went off to eat in the inn.

A quarter of an hour later he had a sudden urge to go into the yard where the coaches were, as if by chance. Perhaps he would see her again?

'What's the use?' he told himself.

And the cab carried him off. His mother did not own the two horses. She had borrowed the one belonging to Monsieur Chambrion, the tax collector, to harness it next to hers. Isidore had set off the day before, had rested at Bray until evening and spent the night at Montereau, so that the animals, now refreshed, were trotting along with a spring in their step.

Harvested fields stretched around them, as far as they could see. There were two rows of trees along the roadside, one stone pile after another: and gradually, Villeneuve-Saint-Georges, Ablon, Châtillon, Corbeil, and the rest of his entire boat journey came back to him; he could now remember new and more intimate details: under the last fold of her dress her foot had vanished into a thin silk boot of a maroon colour; the canvas awning had formed a wide canopy above her head, and the little red acorns along its edge continually fluttered in the breeze.

She resembled the women in romantic novels. He wanted to take nothing from, nor add anything to, her person. The world had suddenly got larger. She was the luminous point at which all things converged. Rocked by the motion of the cab, with his eyes half-shut, staring at the clouds, he gave himself up to a dreamy, infinite delight.

At Bray he did not wait until the horses had been given their oats, he went ahead down the road by himself. Arnoux had called her Marie. He shouted 'Marie!' as loud as he could. His voice was lost on the breeze.

Crimson flamed wide across the western sky. Large stacks of corn rising from the midst of the stubble threw out gigantic shadows. A dog began to bark in a farm in the distance. He shivered, uneasy for no reason.

When Isidore caught up with him, he took the driver's seat. His weakness had passed. He was very determined to obtain an introduction into the Arnoux household and to get to know them. Their house must be interesting, and besides he liked Arnoux; then, who knew? At that point he blushed: his head whirled, he cracked the whip, shook the reins, and drove the horses so fast that the old coachman said more than once:

'Gently, gently! You'll tire them out!'

Gradually Frédéric calmed down and heeded what his servant was telling him.

They were all very excited about seeing Monsieur. Mademoiselle Louise had cried to be allowed to go in the carriage.

'Who's Mademoiselle Louise?'

'Monsieur Roque's little girl, you remember?'

'Oh yes, I forgot!' answered Frédéric, carelessly.

Meanwhile the two horses were exhausted. They were both limping; and nine o'clock was striking in Saint-Laurent when they arrived at the Place d'Armes outside his mother's house. This spacious dwelling with a garden that gave on to open countryside, added to the standing of Madame Moreau, the most respected lady in those parts.

She was from an old aristocratic family, now defunct. Her husband, a plebeian, whom her parents had forced her to marry, had died by the sword during her pregnancy, leaving her a fortune that was encumbered. She entertained three times a week and gave the occasional lavish dinner party, though the number of candles was calculated in advance, and she was always impatient for her rents. This financial hardship, concealed as though it were a vice, made her a somewhat sober person. However, her good character, with no sign of prudery or harshness, was evident. Her smallest charities seemed a largesse. People asked her advice about the choice of servants, the education of their daughters, jam-making, and Monseigneur paid her visits during his bishop's rounds.

Madame Moreau cherished lofty ambitions for her son. She did not like to hear people criticizing the Government; she was wary, since he would first and foremost need patronage; then he might become councillor of State,* ambassador, or minister according to his own abilities. His successes in the college at Sens justified this pride, for he had carried off the highest prize.

When he entered the salon, everyone got up with loud cries of delight and embraced him and they made a wide semicircle around the hearth with their upright and easy chairs. Monsieur Gamblin immediately asked his opinion of Madame Lafarge. This trial, then preoccupying everyone, inevitably caused a violent argument; Madame Moreau put a stop to it, much to Monsieur Gamblin's regret; he judged it to be useful for the young man in his future career in law and he left the salon, rather put out.

Nothing should have surprised them about a friend of old Roque! And talking about Roque, they mentioned Monsieur Dambreuse, who had just acquired the Domaine de La Fortelle. But the tax collector drew Frédéric to one side to know what he thought of the latest work of Monsieur Guizot. They all wanted to know what he had been doing; and Madame Benoît started to find out in a roundabout way by asking news of his uncle. How was this kind relative? One didn't hear anything about him any more. Did he not have a distant cousin in America?

The cook announced that Monsieur's soup was ready. People tactfully withdrew. Then, as soon as they were alone in the room, his mother said to him in a low voice:

'Well?'

The old man had received him very civilly but had not given him any indication of his intentions.

Madame Moreau sighed.

'Where is she now?' wondered Frédéric.

She would be driving along in the coach and, wrapped in her shawl, no doubt, she would be asleep, resting her beautiful head against the lining of the carriage.

They were about to retire to their rooms when a boy from the Cygne de la Croix* brought a message.

'What is it then?'

'It's Deslauriers, he needs me,' he said.

'Oh, your friend!' said Madame Moreau in a scornful voice. 'He chooses his moment, I must say!'

Frédéric hesitated. But friendship was the stronger. He picked up his hat.

'At least don't be too late!' his mother said.


## II


THE father of Charles Deslauriers, a former captain of the line who had resigned his commission in 1818, had come back to Nogent to get married and with the money from his bride's dowry had bought the office of bailiff, which was barely enough to make ends meet. Embittered by long injustices, suffering from his old wounds and continually regretting the days of the Empire, he vented the bad temper which was choking him on his family. Not many children were beaten more than his son. But in spite of the blows, the boy didn't weaken. When his mother tried to intervene, she came in for the same harsh treatment. Finally the captain took him into his own employment, and kept him bent over his desk all day long copying out legal documents, which made his right shoulder visibly stronger than the left.

In 1833, at the request of Monsieur le Président, the captain sold his post. His wife died of cancer. He went to live in Dijon; then he set up as recruiting officer in Troyes; and having obtained a half-bursary for Charles he sent him to school in Sens, where Frédéric recognized him. But he was twelve and Charles fifteen; and besides they were separated by a great many differences of character and background.

Frédéric kept all sorts of provisions in his chest of drawers, valuable things like a toilet bag, for instance. He liked to sleep late in the mornings, watch the swallows, read plays; he missed the comforts of home, and found school life harsh.

To the bailiff's son it seemed a good life. He worked so hard that at the end of the second year he went into the fourth form. But, because of his poverty or his quarrelsome nature, he provoked a veiled animosity in those around him. Once when a servant had called him the son of a beggar right in the middle-school yard, he jumped at his throat and would have killed him if three teachers had not intervened. Frédéric, filled with admiration, threw his arms around him. From that day on, their intimacy was sealed. The affection of an older boy no doubt flattered the vanity of the younger one and Deslauriers gratefully accepted the devotion offered to him.

His father left him at school during the holidays. A translation of Plato opened at random inspired him. So he became passionate about metaphysics. He made rapid progress, for he absorbed the subject with youthful enthusiasm and the pride of an intelligence which has suddenly been set free; he read Jouffroy, Cousin, Laromiguière, Malebranche, the Scots,* everything the library had to offer. He had even had to steal the key to get hold of books.

Frédéric's leisure pursuits were not so serious. He did a sketch of the genealogy of Christ in the Rue des Trois-Rois, sculpted on a doorpost, and then the front portal of the cathedral. After reading some medieval plays he started on memoirs: Froissart, Commines, Pierre de l'Estoile, Brantôme.*

The images these readings conjured up in his brain obsessed him so much that he felt the need to do likewise. His ambition was to be one day the Walter Scott of France. Deslauriers was meditating a vast system of philosophy whose future ramifications would surely be far-reaching.

They chatted about all of these things, during recreation in the schoolyard, under the hortatory motto painted on the clock; they whispered about them in chapel, under the nose of Saint Louis; they dreamed about them in the dormitory, which looked out on to a cemetery. On the days when they went for walks they kept to the rear, behind the others, and talked and talked.

They spoke about what they would do later, when they had left college. First they would go travelling with the money that would be advanced to Frédéric out of his inheritance when he came of age. Then they would go back to Paris, work together, stay together; and to rest from their labours, they would have love affairs with princesses in satin boudoirs, or dazzling orgies with illustrious courtesans. Passionate hopes were succeeded by doubts. After these spasms of excited talk, they relapsed into deep silence.

On summer evenings when they had been for a long walk over stony paths along the vines, or along the main road in the sunshine, the corn undulating in the sun, the scent of angelica wafting through the air, they lay down on their backs feeling a kind of suffocation, heads whirling, intoxicated. The others in their shirtsleeves were playing 'prisoners' base', or flying kites. The *surveillant* called to them. They returned home along the gardens crossed by little streams, then along boulevards shaded by ancient walls; the deserted roads echoed beneath their feet; the gate opened, they went up to their rooms again; and they were cast down, as after some wild debauchery.

Monsieur le Censeur* claimed that they overexcited one another. However, if Frédéric worked hard in the higher classes it was only owing to the exhortations of his friend; and in the 1837 holidays he brought him home to his mother's.

Madame Moreau did not like the young man. He ate huge quantities of food, refused to go to church on Sundays, held forth on Republican matters; and besides, she suspected that he had probably led her son into places of disrepute. She kept a close eye on their relationship. It only made them more fond of one another. And when Deslauriers left college the following year to read law in Paris, their farewells were painful.

Frédéric was very much hoping to join him there. They hadn't seen each other for two years; and, after fondly embracing, they went out on to the bridge to chat more freely.

The captain, who was now in charge of a billiard saloon in

Villenauxe, had been livid when his son had demanded what was due to him from his mother's estate, and had gone as far as to stop his allowance there and then. But since he wanted to apply later for a chair at the university and didn't have any money, Deslauriers got himself a position as chief clerk in the chambers of a lawyer in Troyes. By economizing, he would save himself four thousand francs; and even if he didn't get anything from his mother's legacy, he would still have enough to allow him to work on his own for three years while he waited to obtain a post. They therefore had to abandon their old plans of living together in the capital, at least for the time being.

Frédéric was downhearted. This was the first dream to crumble.

'Never mind,' said the captain's son. 'Life is before us and we are young! We shall get together again. Think no more about it.'

He grasped his hands, and to take his mind off the subject, questioned him about his journey.

Frédéric had nothing special to report. But, when he remembered Madame Arnoux, his sorrow vanished. He did not speak of her, it was too private a matter. But to make up for that he dwelled upon the subject of Arnoux, recounting what he had said, what sort of man he seemed to be, the people he knew; and Deslauriers strongly urged him to cultivate this acquaintance.

Frédéric had not done any writing for a while. His literary opinions had altered. It was passion most of all that he held in high esteem. Werther, René, Franck, Lara, Lélia,* and other, more mediocre, characters inspired him almost equally. Sometimes it seemed to be music alone that was able to express his inner feelings; then he dreamed of symphonies; or he became obsessed by the appearance of things, and he wanted to paint. He had written some verses; Deslauriers said they were very fine, but didn't ask him for more.

As for Deslauriers, he was no longer interested in metaphysics. Political economy and the French Revolution preoccupied him. He was now a tall young man of twenty-two, slim, with a generous mouth and confident manner. That evening he wore a dowdy old worsted coat; and his shoes were white with dust, for he'd walked from Villenauxe on purpose to see Frédéric.

Isidore approached. Madame begged Monsieur to come home, and had sent along his coat as she was afraid he might be cold...

'Don't go!' said Deslauriers.

And they continued their walk from one end to the other of the two bridges connecting the narrow island formed by the canal and the river.

When they walked in the direction of Nogent they were opposite a group of slightly sloping houses. On the right the church could be seen behind the wooden watermills with their sluice gates closed, on the left the bushy hedges along the bank bordered gardens which were only just visible. But in the direction of Paris the main road went downhill in a straight line, and the fields were lost in the distance, in the mists of the night, which was silent and palely luminous. Scents of damp leaves wafted up to them, the weir gurgled a hundred paces away, the waves of it soft and sweet in the darkness.

Deslauriers stopped, and said:

'How strange to think that these good people are fast asleep in their beds. Just you wait! There's a new '89 brewing. People are sick and tired of constitutions, charters, sophistry, lies. Oh, if only I had a newspaper or a platform, I'd shake things up a bit, I can tell you! But if you want to do anything, you have to have money. What a curse it is to be the son of a publican and waste your youth in pursuit of bread!'

He looked down, bit his lips, and shivered under his thin clothes.

Frédéric threw half of his coat over his shoulders. They wrapped it around them both; and with their arms round each other's waist. They walked along in this fashion, side by side.

'How do you think I can live there without you?' said Frédéric. His friend's bitterness had made his melancholy return. 'I might have achieved something with a woman to love me... Why are you laughing? Love is the food and the very air of genius. Extraordinary emotions produce sublime works. As for looking for the woman I need, I give up! Anyway, if I ever found her she would reject me. I am from the race of the disinherited, and I shall cease to be, not knowing whether the treasure within me is a true diamond or a fake!'

A shadow fell across the cobbles, and they heard someone say:

'Your servant, Messieurs!'

The person who spoke was a small man, dressed in an ample brown greatcoat, wearing a peaked cap which only half-concealed his pointed nose.

'Monsieur Roque?' Frédéric asked.

'Himself!' the voice replied.

The man from Nogent explained that he was returning from an inspection of the wolf-traps in his garden leading down to the waterside.

'And so you're back in our part of the world? Very good! My little daughter told me. You are still in good health, I hope? And not going away again yet?'

And off he went, no doubt discouraged by Frédéric's manner.

Madame Moreau, it was true, never called on him; old Roque cohabited with his maidservant, and was not held in high regard, although he was the agent for elections and the steward for Monsieur Dambreuse.

'The banker who lives in the Rue d'Anjou?' Deslauriers continued. 'Do you know what you ought to do, my friend?'

Isidore interrupted them again. He had orders to take Frédéric home and that was that. Madame was worried about him being gone.

'Yes, yes, he's coming,' said Deslauriers. 'He won't be out all night.'

And when the servant had gone:

'You ought to ask that old man to introduce you to the Dambreuses. Nothing is as useful as an entrée into a wealthy house! You've got a black suit and white gloves, make the most of it! You can take me along later. A millionaire, think of it! Get him, and his wife too, to like you. Become her lover!'

Frédéric protested.

'But I'm giving you the classic advice, am I not? Remember Rastignac in *La Comédie humaine*.* You will succeed, I'm sure!'

Frédéric had such faith in Deslauriers, he felt quite shaken by his words, and forgetting Madame Arnoux, or else thinking of her at the prediction about this other woman, he could not repress a smile.

The clerk added:

'One last piece of advice: pass your exams! You will do well to have a qualification. And put your Catholic and satanic poets behind you; they are about as philosophically advanced as people were in the twelfth century. It's stupid to be pessimistic. Some very great men had more difficult beginnings, Mirabeau for a start. Besides, our separation will not last long. I will make my wretched father eat his words. It's time I was off. Farewell! Have you got a hundred sous for me to pay for my supper?'

Frédéric gave him ten francs, the rest of the sum Isidore had given him that morning.

However, several yards from the bridges, on the left bank, a light was blazing in the little window of a cottage.

Deslauriers saw it. Then he said with emphasis, removing his hat:

'Venus, queen of heaven, your servant! But penury is the mother of wisdom. And my word, didn't we get into trouble for that!'

This allusion to an adventure they had shared delighted them. They laughed out loud in the street as they walked along.

Then, having settled his expenses in the inn, Deslauriers went back with Frédéric as far as the crossroads at the Hôtel-Dieu. And after a long embrace, the two friends parted.

## III

ARRIVING one morning two months later in the Rue Coq-Héron, Frédéric's first thought was of his important visit.

Chance had been on his side. Old Roque had come, bringing a wad of papers, with a request to take them personally to Monsieur Dambreuse. And in the packet he had placed an unsealed note of introduction for his young neighbour.

Madame Moreau seemed surprised by this move. Frédéric had concealed the pleasure it gave him.

Monsieur Dambreuse's real name was the Comte d'Ambreuse; but from 1825 on, gradually abandoning his title and his party, he had turned to industry. And, with his ear to the ground in every workplace, his hand in all the business organizations, and on the lookout for a good opportunity, wily as a Greek and hard-working as an Auvergnat, he had amassed a fortune which by all accounts was considerable. Moreover, he was an officer of the Legion of Honour, on the board of the General Council of the Aube, a deputy, likely to get a peerage one day. Very willing to oblige, he pestered the minister with his constant demands for aid, for decorations, for licences to sell tobacco; and in his fallings-out with authority, he inclined to the Centre Left. His wife, pretty Madame Dambreuse, cited often in the fashion magazines, presided over charity meetings. By flattering duchesses she made peace with the embittered aristocrats in the faubourg* and let it be understood that Monsieur Dambreuse might still repent of his ways and be useful to them.

The young man had some qualms about going to their house.

'I would have done better to wear my tailcoat. I shall no doubt be invited to the ball next week? What are they going to say?'

His self-confidence returned when he remembered that Monsieur

Dambreuse was only a bourgeois, and he leaped down gaily from his cab on to the Rue d'Anjou.

Pushing open one of the two porte cochères, he crossed the court-yard, climbed the steps, and entered a hall paved in coloured marble.

A double staircase, carpeted red with brass rods, led straight up between high walls of shining stucco. At the bottom of the stairs was a banana palm, its broad leaves falling on to the velvet of the banisters. Two bronze candelabras held porcelain globes suspended on small chains; the air was warm with the exhalations from the vents on the heaters; and the only sound was the ticking of a great clock, standing under a panoply at the far end of the hall.

A bell rang; a servant appeared, and took Frédéric into a small room in which he could see two safes with compartments full of files. In the middle of the room, Monsieur Dambreuse was writing at a roll-top desk.

He scanned the letter from Père Roque, opened the cloth the papers were wrapped in with a pocketknife, and scrutinized them.

From a distance, because of his slim build, he might have passed for a young man. But his sparse white hair, his shaky limbs, and espe-cially his extraordinarily pale complexion signalled decrepitude. But a relentless energy lay in his grey-green eyes, colder than glass. He had protruding cheeks and gnarled hands.

At last he rose and asked the young man one or two questions about people they both knew, about Nogent and about his studies; then he dismissed him, with a bow. Frédéric went out through another pas-sage and found himself at the back of the yard near the coach houses.

A blue brougham, with a black horse in the shafts, was standing in front of the steps. The door opened, a lady got in, and the coach moved off with a thud on the sandy path.

Frédéric arrived simultaneously from the other side, under the porte cochère. Since the space was not wide enough, he was obliged to wait. The young woman, leaning out of the little window, was talking in a low voice to the concierge. All he could see was her back covered in a purple cloak. However, his eyes searched the interior of the car-riage upholstered in blue rep, with silk trimmings and fringes. The lady's clothes filled the whole space; there came a scent of iris from that little box with its hood, and an indefinable air of perfumed fem-inine elegance. The coachman loosened the reins, the horse brushed abruptly against the gate stone, and they all vanished.

Frédéric returned on foot, along the boulevards.

He was sorry not to have seen what Madame Dambreuse looked like.

A bit further up from the Rue Montmartre, a traffic jam made him turn his head; and opposite him on the other side he read on a marble plaque:

JACQUES ARNOUX

How was it that she hadn't crossed his mind earlier? It was Deslauriers's fault, and he went over to the shop, but didn't go in; he waited for *her* to appear.

The high, plate-glass windows displayed a judicious arrangement of statuettes, drawings, engravings, catalogues, copies of *L'Art industriel*; and the subscription prices were repeated on the door, in the centre of which were the publisher's decorated initials. Against the walls could be seen large brilliantly varnished paintings and at the back two sideboards laden with porcelain, bronzes, tempting objets d'art; they were separated by a little staircase, closed at the top by a heavy curtain; and a chandelier of Dresden china, a green rug on the floor, and an inlaid table made this room look more like a drawing room than a shop.

Frédéric pretended to be examining the drawings. After endless hesitation, he went in.

An employee lifted the curtain and answered that Monsieur would not be 'in the shop' before five. But if he wished to leave a message...

'No, I'll come back,' Frédéric answered quietly.

The following days were spent looking for lodgings; and he decided on a second-floor room in a furnished house in the Rue Saint-Hyacinthe.

Carrying a brand new blotter under his arm, he went to the first lecture. Three hundred bareheaded young men filled an amphitheatre where an old man in a red gown was droning on, while pens squeaked on paper. In this room he felt the chalky atmosphere of the classroom again, the same sort of chair, the same boredom. He attended the lectures for a fortnight. But he abandoned the Civil Code before they reached Article 3, and the *Institutes* at the *Summa Divisio personarum*.*

The delights he had promised himself did not materialize; and when he had exhausted the lending library, visited the collections in the Louvre, and been to the theatre several nights in succession, he lapsed into a bottomless pit of lethargy.

A myriad new experiences contributed to his depression. He had to count his items of linen himself and put up with the concierge, a rough fellow with the demeanour of a male nurse who came in the mornings to make his bed, grumbling and reeking of alcohol. He disliked his apartment, decorated with an alabaster clock. The walls were thin; he could hear the students making punch, laughing, and singing.

Tired of this solitary existence, he went to find one of his former schoolfriends, Baptiste Martinon, and tracked him down in a boarding house in the Rue Saint-Jacques, swotting up legal procedure in front of a coal fire.

Opposite him a woman in a calico dress was darning socks.

Martinon was what people call a very handsome man, tall, round-faced, with regular features and rather prominent pale blue eyes. His father, a prosperous agriculturalist, intended him for the judiciary; and wanting to look serious already, he wore his beard clipped and thin.

As Frédéric's distress had no reasonable cause and he was unable to blame it on any misfortune, Martinon could not understand his complaints about his life. He himself went to classes every morning, then for a walk in the Luxembourg, drank his small cup of coffee every evening, and with fifteen hundred francs a year and the love of this working-class girl, was perfectly content.

'What luck!' Frédéric exclaimed inwardly.

At the School of Law he had made another acquaintance, Monsieur de Cisy, a son of the nobility, somewhat girlish in his gentleness of manner.

Monsieur de Cisy was interested in drawing, liked Gothic art. On several occasions they went to admire the Sainte-Chapelle or Notre-Dame together. But the young nobleman's distinction concealed one of the meanest intelligences. Everything was a surprise to him. He laughed a lot at the slightest joke, and displayed such complete naivety that Frédéric at first took him for a joker, but ended up thinking him a fool.

There was then no one he could confide in; and he was still waiting for the Dambreuses' invitation.

On New Year's Day he sent them a visiting card but received none from them.

He had returned once more to *L'Art industriel*.

He went a third time and finally saw Arnoux who was arguing, surrounded by five or six people, and scarcely acknowledged his greeting. Frédéric was hurt. Nonetheless he tried to find a way of reaching *her*.

First he had the idea of visiting the shop often to haggle over pictures. Then he thought he would slip a few 'very powerful' articles into the journal's postbox, and that would bring about closer relations. Or would it be preferable to rush straight in and declare his love? So he composed a twelve-page letter, full of passionate lyrical passages and apostrophizing. But he tore it up and did nothing, attempted nothing, paralysed by the fear of failure.

Above Arnoux's shop there were three windows on the first floor, lit up every evening. Shadows moved around behind them, especially one. It was hers; and he came a long way to look at those windows and contemplate that shadow.

A Negro woman he saw one day in the Tuileries holding a little girl by the hand reminded him of Madame Arnoux's Negress. She must come here, just like the others. Each time he crossed the Tuileries his heart started thumping in the expectation of meeting her. On sunny days he carried on walking to the end of the Champs-Élysées.

Women, sitting back nonchalantly in barouches, veils floating in the breeze, passed close by him. Their horses trotted along at a steady pace, swaying very slightly; the varnished leather cracked. More and more carriages appeared and, slowing down after the Rond-Point, they took up the entire road. Manes were next to manes, lamps next to lamps; steel stirrups, silver curb chains, brass buckles glinted here and there among the jodhpurs and the white gloves and the furs which spilled out over the coats of arms on the carriage doors. He felt as if he were lost in some other world. His eyes wandered over the heads of the women and vague likenesses brought Madame Arnoux to mind. He imagined her in the middle of them all, in one of those little coupés, just like the one belonging to Madame Dambreuse. But the sun was going down and the cold wind was whirling up clouds of dust. Coachmen stuck their chins into their neckcloths, the wheels began to turn more quickly, the macadam squeaked; and all the coaches moved down the long avenue at a trot, brushing against each other, passing, spacing out, then dispersing at the Place de la Concorde. Behind the Tuileries the sky took on the colour of slate. The trees in the gardens formed two huge shapes, tinged with violet at the top. The gaslights came on; and the entire greeny stretch of the Seine tore itself into silvery shards of silk against the pillars of the bridges.

He went to have dinner for forty-three sous in a restaurant in the Rue de la Harpe.

He looked with distaste at the old mahogany counter, the stained napkins, the dirty silver, and the hats hung on the wall. The people around him were students like him. They talked about their professors, their women. As if he cared about their professors! And since when did he have a mistress? To avoid their merriment he arrived as late as possible. The remains of food littered all the tables. The two tired waiters slept in corners and a smell of cooking, oil lamps, and tobacco filled the deserted room.

Then he slowly went back up through the streets. The street lamps swung to and fro, their long yellow reflections flickered on the mud. Shadows with umbrellas stole by on the kerb. The paving stones were slimy, the mist was coming down, and it seemed to him as if the damp darkness wrapping him round were coming to dwell in his heart for ever.

He felt a pang of remorse. He went back to his classes. But since he did not understand the first thing about the subjects being explained, he found even very simple things difficult to grasp.

He started to write a novel entitled *Silvio, the Fisherman's Son*. It was set in Venice. The hero was himself; the heroine, Madame Arnoux. She was called Antonia;—and to win her he assassinated several noblemen, burned down half the town, and sang beneath her balcony, where the red damask curtains of the Boulevard Montmartre fluttered in the breeze. But he noticed and was discouraged by the number of echoes of other novels; he went no further with it and felt more than ever at a loose end.

Then he begged Deslauriers to come and share his room. They would manage on his allowance of two thousand francs; anything was better than this unbearable existence. Deslauriers couldn't leave Troyes. He urged him to keep himself busy and to contact Sénécal.

Sénécal was a mathematics tutor, a very intelligent man and a convinced Republican, a future Saint-Just, according to the clerk. Frédéric climbed up five floors on three occasions without managing to see him. He didn't go back again.

He decided to enjoy life. He attended balls at the Opéra. The roar of gaiety made him go cold as soon as he reached the door. In any case he was held back by the fear of financial humiliation, imagining that supper with a masked dancer would lead him into considerable expense, a huge risk.

However, it seemed to him that he was lovable. Sometimes he woke with his heart full of hope, dressed carefully as if he were going to a rendezvous, and walked through the city for hours and hours. Whenever a woman crossed his path or came towards him, he said to himself: 'Here she is!' Each time it was another disappointment. The thought of Madame Arnoux strengthened his desire. Perhaps he would come across her on the street? He imagined complicated circumstances that might allow him to approach her, the extraordinary perils he would save her from.

And so the days went by, repeating the same worries and the daily habits he had acquired. He leafed through brochures under the arcades of the Odéon, went to read the *Revue des deux mondes** in a café, went into a room in the Collège de France, listened to a lecture on Chinese or political economy for an hour. Every week he wrote a long letter to Deslauriers, dined with Martinon from time to time, saw Monsieur de Cisy occasionally.

He hired a piano and composed German waltzes.

One evening at the theatre at the Palais-Royal, he saw Arnoux in a stage box with a woman sitting next to him. Was it her? The screen of green taffeta, pulled across the edge of the box, was hiding her face. Finally the curtain went up, the screen came down. It was someone tall, about thirty, rather faded, her large lips uncovering splendid teeth when she laughed. She was chatting familiarly with Arnoux and tapping him on the fingers with her fan. Then a blonde girl, her eyelids a little red as if she had just been weeping, sat down between them. From then on Arnoux talked to her, leaning against her shoulder, while she listened without responding. Frédéric racked his brains wondering who these women were, modestly attired in dark dresses with their collars turned down.

At the end of the play he hastened into the corridors. They were packed with people. Arnoux, in front of him, was going down the stairs, step by step, offering his arm to both women.

Suddenly a gas lamp illuminated him. Round his hat was a black band. Could she possibly be dead? This thought tormented Frédéric so much that he rushed along to *L'Art industriel* the next day, and, quickly paying for one of the engravings displayed at the front of the window, he asked the boy in the shop how Monsieur Arnoux was.

The boy replied:

'Very well!'

Pale, Frédéric added:

'And Madame?'

'Madame is very well too!'

Frédéric left, forgetting to take his engraving.

Winter ended. He was not so gloomy in the spring; he set himself to swotting for his exams, and having passed them without distinction, left for Nogent.

In order to avoid his mother's remarks, he didn't go to Troyes to see his friend. Then, when he went back to study, he left his accommodation and took a couple of rooms, which he furnished, on the Quai Napoléon. He had given up hope of an invitation to the Dambreuses'. His passion for Madame Arnoux began to fade.

## IV

ONE December morning, on his way to the lecture on judicial procedure, he thought he could detect more activity than usual in the Rue Saint-Jacques. The students were hurrying out from the cafés, or shouting to each other through open windows from one house to the next; the shopkeepers were looking on anxiously in the middle of the pavement; shutters were pulled down; and when he reached the Rue Soufflot, he saw a big gathering round the Panthéon.

Young men, in groups of half a dozen or a dozen or so, were walking along arm in arm and approaching the larger groups standing around. Men in smocks at the back of the square against the railings were delivering speeches, while the police, tricornes cocked and hands behind backs, patrolled along the walls, their sturdy boots striking the stones. All had a strange, perplexed expression on their faces; they were obviously waiting for something. Each had an unspoken question on his lips.

Frédéric found himself next to a fair-haired young man, with a pleasant face, sporting a moustache and a little beard like a dandy from the reign of Louis XIII. He asked him the reason for the disorder.

'I have no idea,' he replied, 'and nor do they. That's what people are like nowadays. What a joke!'

And he burst out laughing.

For the past six months in Paris, the petitions for Reform they were making people sign in the National Guard, along with the Humann census,* and other events as well, led to inexplicable demonstrations, and they were becoming so frequent that the newspapers no longer bothered to report them.

'There's neither shape nor colour in them,' he went on. 'Methinks, Messire, that we are going to the dogs! Bring back the good old days of Louis, the Eleventh of that name, even of Benjamin Constant, there was more mutiny amongst the scholars then. I think them meek as sheep, stupid as cucumbers and, God help me, fit only to be grocers! And that's what they call the Young Scholars!'

He made a sweeping gesture with his arm, like Frédéric Lemaître in *Robert Macaire.**

'Bless you, young scholars!'

Then, addressing a rag-and-bone man who was rummaging through oyster shells outside a wine seller's:

'You there, are you a young scholar?'

The old man lifted a hideous face in which were visible, in the midst of a grey beard, a red nose and two stupid wine-sodden eyes.

'No! You seem to me rather *one of those men of sinister aspect who are seen around in divers groups, scattering handfuls of gold coins...* Oh, scatter, old patriarch, scatter! Corrupt me with the treasures of Albion! *Are you English?* I do not reject the gifts of Artaxerxes. Let's talk a little about the Customs Union.'*

Frédéric felt someone touch his shoulder; he turned. It was Martinon, ghostly pale.

'So—another riot,' he said, with a deep sigh.

He was fearful of being dragged into it, and was unhappy. Men in smocks especially bothered him, they were sure to belong to some secret society.

'Do secret societies exist?' said the young moustachioed man. 'It's an old Government trick to scare the bourgeoisie!'

Martinon urged him to keep his voice down, for fear of the police.

'Do you still believe in the police? In fact, how do you know, Monsieur, that I'm not a spy myself?'

And he stared at him in such a way that Martinon was very upset and didn't realize at first that he was joking. The crowd was jostling them and they had all three been obliged to get on to the little row of steps leading through a passage to the new amphitheatre.

Soon the throng split up of its own accord; you could recognize several faces; they greeted the illustrious Professor Samuel Rondelot,

who, wrapped in his large topcoat, raising his silver-rimmed spectacles and puffing asthmatically, was unhurriedly going to deliver his
lecture. This man was a paragon among nineteenth-century jurists,
the rival of the Zachariaes and the Ruhrdorffs.* His recent elevation
to the peerage had not changed his behaviour at all. People knew he
was poor and he was treated with the greatest respect.

However, at the back of the square some were shouting:

'Down with Guizot!'

'Down with Pritchard!'

'Down with the traitors!'

'Down with Louis-Philippe!'

The crowd hesitated, and then, pushing at the door to the courtyard
which was closed, prevented the professor from going any further. He
stopped in front of the steps. Soon he was noticed on the topmost of
the three steps. He spoke; a hum of noise drowned out his words.
Although they had approved of him a little while before, they hated
him now because he represented Authority. Each time he tried to
make himself heard, the shouts began again. With a grand, sweeping
gesture he urged the students to follow him. He was answered with
a universal roar. He shrugged disdainfully and disappeared down the
passage. Martinon had taken advantage of his position to vanish at
the same time.

'What a coward!' said Frédéric.

'Just being cautious,' his companion responded.

The crowd broke into applause. They considered this professorial
retreat a victory. At all the windows, the curious were looking out. Some
struck up the Marseillaise.* Others suggested going to Béranger's.

'To Laffitte's!'

'To Chateaubriand's!'

'To Voltaire's!'* yelled the young man with the blond hair.

The sergeants were attempting to move among the crowd, saying
as calmly as they could:

'Move along, Gentlemen, move along now!'

Someone shouted:

'Down with the butchers!'

That was the insult commonly used since the September troubles.* They all echoed it; they jeered and whistled at the guardians of
public order, who began to turn pale. One could not restrain himself,
and, seizing hold of a boy who was getting too near and laughing at

him, he pushed him so roughly he fell on his back five feet away, outside the wine merchant's shop. They all retreated. But almost immediately the policeman went down himself, brought to the ground by a sort of Hercules whose hair, like a bundle of hemp, spilled out from under an oilcloth cap.

Having stopped for some minutes on the corner of the Rue Saint-Jacques, he had suddenly let go of a large box he was carrying, bounded towards the policeman, and, pinning him down beneath him, was punching him in the face as hard as he could. The other officers came running. The terrifying young man was so strong that it took four to hold him down. Two shook him by the collar, two others were pulling at his arms, a fifth was kneeing him in the back, and all were calling him a thug, an assassin, a rabble-rouser. Bare-chested and his clothes in rags, he protested his innocence. He had never been able to stand calmly by when he saw a child beaten.

'My name's Dussardier! I'm at Messieurs Valinçart *frères*, lace and fancy goods, Rue de Cléry. My box!'

But he calmed down and, with a stoical air, allowed himself to be led to the station in the Rue Descartes. A stream of people followed him. Frédéric and the moustachioed young man were walking immediately behind, full of admiration for the shop assistant and in revolt against the violence of the authorities.

As they advanced the crowd thinned out.

The police from time to time turned round and threatened them. And the troublemakers, who had nothing more to do, and the curious, who had nothing to see, all gradually drifted away. Passers-by took one look at Dussardier and passed outrageous comments. An old lady at her door even shouted that he had stolen some bread. This unjust accusation increased the two friends' annoyance. Finally they arrived outside the guardhouse. Only a score of people were left. The sight of the soldiers was enough to make them go away.

Frédéric and his friend boldly demanded to see the man they had just taken prisoner. The sentry threatened to clap them in gaol themselves if they carried on. They asked for the officer in charge and gave their names and status as law students, declaring that the prisoner was one of them.

They were made to enter a bare room where four benches had been placed along a plastered, smoke-blackened wall. At the back a hatch opened. Then the robust face of Dussardier appeared, who in the disorder of his hair, with his small honest eyes and his pug nose, reminded one vaguely of a trusty dog.

'Don't you recognize us?' said Hussonnet.

That was the name of the moustachioed young man.

'Er...' stammered Dussardier.

'Don't be a fool,' went on the other. 'We know you're a law student, like us.'

Despite their winks, Dussardier did not guess what they meant. He appeared to gather his wits and then suddenly said:

'Did anyone find my box?'

Frédéric raised his eyes in despair. Hussonnet replied:

'Oh, the box you put your lecture notes in? Yes, yes, don't worry!'

They went through the whole pantomime again. Finally Dussardier understood that they had come to help him; and he was silent, afraid of getting them into trouble. Moreover, he felt a sort of shame at seeing himself elevated to the social rank of student and the equal of these young men who had such white hands.

'Do you have a message to give to anybody?' Frédéric asked.

'No thanks, nobody!'

'What about your family?'

He hung his head without answering. The poor boy was illegitimate. The two friends were astonished at his silence.

'Have you got something to smoke?' asked Frédéric.

He felt deep in his pockets and took out the remains of a pipe— a fine meerschaum pipe, with a stem of black wood, a silver lid, and an amber mouthpiece.

For three years he had been labouring to make this pipe into a masterpiece. He had been careful to keep the bowl always safely protected in its chamois case, smoking it as slowly as possible, without ever putting it on a marble surface, and each evening, hanging it beside his bed. But now he shook the pieces in his hand, his nails bleeding; and, his chin on his chest, eyes fixed, mouth open, he contemplated the ruin of his pride and joy with an ineffable sadness.

'Suppose we gave him some cigars, what do you think?' Hussonnet whispered, making as if to get some out.

Frédéric had already put a full cigar case on the edge of the counter.

'Take these. Goodbye, don't despair!'

Dussardier seized the two hands that were held out to him. He shook them frantically, his voice jerky with sobs.

'What? Do you mean me?'

The two friends brushed away his expressions of gratitude, left the building and went to have lunch together in the Café Tabourey in front of the Luxembourg.

As he cut into his steak, Hussonnet told his companion he worked in fashion journals and wrote advertisements for *L'Art industriel.*

'Jacques Arnoux's place?' Frédéric asked.

'Do you know him?'

'Yes! No!... I mean I've seen him, I've met him.'

He asked Hussonnet casually if he ever saw his wife.

'Now and then,' the bohemian replied.

Frédéric did not dare to pursue this line of questioning. This man had just taken on an immeasurably important role in his life. He paid the bill for lunch without the least protest from his companion.

The friendship was mutual; they exchanged addresses and Hussonnet cordially invited him to accompany him to the Rue de Fleurus.

They were in the middle of the garden when Arnoux's employee took a deep breath, and with a horrendous grimace made a crowing noise like a cockerel. Immediately all the cocks in the neighbourhood answered him with a prolonged cock-a-doodle-doo!

'It's a signal,' said Hussonnet.

They stopped near the Théâtre Bobino,* outside a house which you approached through a narrow passage. A young woman appeared at an attic window, between pots of nasturtiums and sweet peas, bare-headed, in her underwear and leaning on the ledge of the gutter.

'Good morning, darling, good morning, my sweet,' Hussonnet said, blowing kisses.

He kicked open the gate and disappeared.

Frédéric waited for him the whole week. He dared not go to his lodgings, not wanting to appear anxious to be invited to dinner; but he looked for him everywhere in the Quartier Latin. One evening he found him and took him back to his room on the Quai Napoléon.

They talked for a long time. They exchanged confidences. Hussonnet hoped to achieve fame and fortune in the theatre. He was collaborating in unsuccessful vaudevilles, 'had thousands of plans', wrote lyrics, sang some of them. Then, seeing on Frédéric's shelves a volume by Hugo and another by Lamartine, he made copious sarcastic remarks about the Romantics. Those poets had no common sense or correctness, and above all, they weren't French! He prided himself on knowing his own language and dissected the finest phrases with the scathing seriousness, the pedantic judgement, typical of those of a playful nature when they come to serious works of art.

Frédéric was offended by his tastes; he felt like breaking off relations. Why not risk straight away uttering the word on which his happiness depended? He asked his literary friend if he could get him an introduction to Arnoux's house.

A simple matter! They arranged to meet the next day.

Hussonnet did not turn up. He did not turn up on three further occasions. He appeared one Saturday towards four. But, using Frédéric's carriage, he first stopped at the Théâtre Français to buy a ticket; he made another halt at a tailor's, and at a sempstress's; he wrote notes in concierges' lodges. Finally they reached the Boulevard Montmartre. Frédéric crossed the shop and climbed the stairs. Arnoux recognized him in the mirror placed in front of his desk; and without breaking off his writing, he held out one hand to him over his shoulder.

Five or six people stood around, filling the narrow apartment which was lit by a single window overlooking the courtyard. A sofa covered in brown woollen damask occupied the interior of the window recess at the back, between two curtains of similar material. On the mantelpiece littered in papers was a bronze Venus. Two candelabras decorated with pink candles were set one on each side. On the right, next to an adjoining room, a man still wearing his hat was reading the newspaper in an armchair; the walls had vanished under prints and pictures, rare engravings or sketches by contemporary masters, all adorned with dedications expressing the most sincere affection for Jacques Arnoux.

'How are you?' he said, turning towards Frédéric.

And without waiting for his reply he whispered to Hussonnet:

'What's your friend's name?'

Then, aloud:

'Please help yourself to a cigar from the box on the cabinet.'

*L'Art industriel*, situated in the heart of Paris, was a convenient meeting place, neutral territory where rivals could rub shoulders with one another. That day Anténor Braive, the painter of royal portraits, was there; Jules Burrieu, who was starting to popularize

the wars in Algeria through his drawings; Sombaz the caricaturist, Vourdat the sculptor, and more, not one of whom matched the
student's expectations. Their manners were unaffected and their
conversation uninhibited. The mystic, Lovarias, told a dirty story;
and the inventor of the oriental landscape, the famous Dittmer, wore
a woollen vest under his waistcoat and took the omnibus home.

First they were discussing a certain Apollonie,* a former model,
whom Burrieu claimed to have recognized on the boulevard, in
a coach and four. Hussonnet attributed this transformation to the
succession of men who kept her.

'This fellow certainly knows his Parisian women!' Arnoux remarked.

'After you, Sire—if there is anything left!' replied the bohemian
with a military salute in imitation of the grenadier offering his water
bottle to Napoleon.

Then some canvases were discussed, in which Apollonie's head
had figured. Absent colleagues were criticized. Astonishment was expressed at the price of their works; and they were all complaining of
not earning enough. Then in came a man of medium build, bright-
eyed, rather crazed in his expression, his coat held together by a single button.

'What a lot of bourgeois you are!' he said. 'What does it matter, for
pity's sake! The Old Masters never cared about the money. Correggio,
Murillo...'*

'And Pellerin,' Sombaz put in.

But, without heeding this *mot*, he carried on ranting so vehemently
that Arnoux was twice obliged to say:

'My wife wants you to come along on Thursday, don't forget.'

These words brought Frédéric's thoughts back to Madame Arnoux.
No doubt there was access to her rooms through the dressing room
near the divan? Arnoux had just opened the door to get a handkerchief; Frédéric spied a washbasin at the back. But a sort of grumbling
noise was coming from near the mantelpiece. It was the man reading
the newspaper in the armchair. He was five foot nine, grey-haired, his
eyelids a little droopy, and with an imposing demeanour. His name
was Regimbart.

'What's the matter then, Citizen?' Arnoux asked.

'Yet another low trick by the Government!'

It was about the dismissal of a schoolmaster; Pellerin reverted to
comparing Michelangelo and Shakespeare. Dittmer left. Arnoux

went after him and put two banknotes in his hand. Then Hussonnet, thinking it was an auspicious moment, said:

'You couldn't give me an advance, could you, my dear fellow?'

But Arnoux had sat down again and was berating a dirty-looking elderly man with blue glasses.

'You're a fine one, Isaac! Three works of art denounced, finished. Everyone laughing at me. What am I supposed to do with them? Now everyone knows which they are. I'll have to send them to California!... Or to the devil! Do shut up!'

This old fellow's speciality consisted in putting the signatures of the Old Masters at the bottom of these pictures. Arnoux refused to pay him. He was harshly dismissed. Then, changing his manner, he greeted a man with medals on, stiff and starchy with his side whiskers and white necktie.

Leaning on the window catch, he spoke to him at length in hon-eyed tones. Finally he burst out:

'Well, I don't have trouble finding brokers, Monsieur le Comte!'

The nobleman capitulated, Arnoux paid him twenty-five louis,* and as soon as he had gone:

'Such a bore, the nobility.'

'Wretched creatures, all of them,' muttered Regimbart.

As time passed, Arnoux became more and more busy. He filed art-icles, unsealed letters, drew up accounts. At the sound of hammering in the shop, he went out to keep an eye on the packing, then came back and resumed his work. And, even as his pen was racing over the paper, he was keeping up with the repartee. He had to dine with his lawyer that evening, and was leaving the next day for Belgium.

The others were chatting about the topics of the day: the portrait of Cherubini, the assembly of the Council for the Beaux Arts, the forth-coming exhibition. Pellerin was railing against the Institute.* Gossip and argument intermingled. The room with its low ceiling was so crowded you couldn't move, and the light from the pink candles pierced the cigar smoke like rays of sun through a mist.

The door near the sofa opened, and a tall slim woman came in, her staccato gestures setting all the watch-charms tinkling on her black taffeta dress.

It was the woman he had glimpsed last summer at the Palais-Royal. Some, calling her by name, shook hands with her. Hussonnet had finally managed to extract fifty francs. The clock struck seven. Everyone left.

Arnoux told Pellerin to stay behind and led Mademoiselle Vatnaz into the adjoining room.

Frédéric couldn't hear their words, they were whispering. But the female voice was then raised:

'The deal was done six months ago and I'm still waiting!'

There was a prolonged silence. Mademoiselle Vatnaz reappeared. Arnoux had made her another promise.

'Oh, later on, we'll see!'

'Farewell, lucky man!' she said as she left.

Arnoux quickly went back into the dressing room, smoothed some oil on his moustache, hoiked up his braces to tighten his trouser straps, and, as he washed his hands, said:

'I need two panels for above the door at two hundred and fifty francs each, in the style of Boucher.* Is that all right with you?'

'Agreed,' the artist said, reddening.

'Good, and don't forget my wife!'

Frédéric accompanied Pellerin to the end of the Faubourg Poissonnière, and asked permission to call on him now and then, a favour that was graciously granted.

Pellerin was reading every book on aesthetics he could lay his hands on to discover the true theory of Beauty, since he was convinced that by discovering it he would create masterpieces. He surrounded himself with all the things he could think of that might be helpful, drawings, plaster casts, models, engravings; and he searched, it gnawed at him; he blamed the weather, his nerves, his studio, he went out to seek inspiration in the street, thrilled when he thought he had found it, but then abandoned his work and dreamed about something else which was to be even more beautiful. Tormented in this way by a longing for fame, but wasting his time in discussion, a thousand ridiculous ideas, systems, criticism, and on the importance of rules or the reform of art, by the time he was fifty he had only managed to produce a few sketches. His resolute pride prevented him from being at all discouraged, but he was constantly irritable, in that hyperactive state at once factitious and natural that is characteristic of people in the acting profession.

As you entered his studio, your attention was caught by two large paintings, in which the first colours, placed here and there, made brown, red, and blue marks on the white canvas. A web of chalky lines stretched out over them, like stitches in a net mended many times.

It was impossible to make anything of them. Pellerin explained what these two compositions were all about by pointing with his thumb to the parts still missing. One was to represent 'The Madness of Nebuchadnezzar', the other 'Nero's Burning of Rome'. Frédéric admired them.

He admired the nudes with their hair streaming out, landscapes strewn with tree trunks twisted by the storm, and especially the pen-and-ink sketches inspired by Callot,* Rembrandt, or Goya, the originals of which he was unfamiliar with. Pellerin no longer cared for these youthful works; now he was all for *le grand style*; he discoursed eloquently on Phidias and Winckelmann.* The objects around him reinforced the power of his words: there was a skull on a prayer stool, yataghans,* and a monk's robe which Frédéric put on.

When he arrived early, he found Pellerin in his humble truckle bed, concealed by a tattered counterpane, for, being an assiduous theatre-goer, he retired to bed at a late hour. He had an old woman in rags for servant, dined in an eating house, and did not keep a mistress. His knowledge, accumulated here, there and everywhere, made his paradoxes amusing. His hatred for the ordinary and the bourgeois flowed over into superbly lyrical sarcasm, and he had such a religious devotion to the Masters that he was almost elevated into their number.

But why did he never mention Madame Arnoux? As for her husband, sometimes he spoke of him as a good fellow, at other times a charlatan. Frédéric waited for him to confide in him.

One day as he was leafing through one of his folders, Frédéric found a portrait of a gypsy that bore some resemblance to Mademoiselle Vatnaz, and as he was interested by this woman, he wanted to know all about her.

Pellerin thought she had been a schoolteacher in the provinces; now she gave lessons and tried to get published in minor journals.

If her behaviour towards Arnoux was anything to go by, Frédéric supposed, she might be his mistress.

'Oh, I don't know—he has plenty of others!'

Then the young man, averting his face, which was reddening in shame at the outrageous idea, added boldly:

'I suppose his wife gives as good as she gets?'

'Not at all! She's a virtuous woman!'

Frédéric was filled with remorse, and turned up at the newspaper offices more regularly.

The capital letters composing the name Arnoux on the marble plaque over the shop seemed unique and laden with significance to him, like holy script. The downward slope of the wide pavement quickened his steps, the door turned almost of its own accord; and the handle, smooth to his touch, was soft and sensitive like a hand in his own. Imperceptibly he became as punctual as Regimbart.

Each day Regimbart would sit down by the fire in his armchair, take the *National*,* and hang on to it, telling the world what he thought, with exclamations or simple shrugs. From time to time he wiped his brow with his pocket handkerchief rolled up into a sausage shape on his chest, tucked in-between two buttons on his green overcoat. He wore trousers with creases, short boots, and a long tie. And from a distance his hat with a turned-up rim made him an easily identifiable figure in a crowd.

At eight in the morning he walked down from the heights of Montmartre to have a glass of white wine in the Rue Notre-Dame-des-Victoires. His lunch, followed by several games of billiards, took him to three o'clock. Then he made his way to the Passage des Panoramas to have a glass of absinthe. After his visit to Arnoux's he went into the Bordelais *estaminet* to have a vermouth. Then, instead of going home to his wife, he often chose to eat alone in a little café on the Place Gaillon, where he wished to partake of 'home-made, wholesome food'! Finally he betook himself to another billiard room and stayed there till midnight, till one o'clock in the morning, till the moment when the gaslight had been extinguished, the blinds drawn, and the exhausted proprietor begged him to leave.

It wasn't a love of alcohol which drew Citizen Regimbart to these places, but his old habit of talking politics. With age his enthusiasm had waned. All that remained was a silent moroseness. Seeing his serious expression, you would have thought that the whole world was turning on its axis inside his head; but nothing came out of it, and nobody, not even his friends, knew what his job was, although he put it around that he ran a business agency.

Arnoux appeared to have the highest regard for him. One day he said to Frédéric:

'My word, he knows a thing or two, he does! What a clever chap!'

On another occasion Regimbart spread out some papers about the kaolin mines in Brittany on his desk; Arnoux relied greatly on his knowledge and experience.

Frédéric was careful to be polite to Regimbart—to the point of offering him an absinthe from time to time; and although he thought him stupid, he often stayed with him for a good hour solely on account of his being friends with Jacques Arnoux.

After helping contemporary painters to establish themselves, the art dealer, a man who believed in progress, while keeping up appearances of being an art lover, did his best to make a financial profit at the same time. He sought the emancipation of the arts, the sublime at cut-price. All the luxury trades of Paris came under his influence, which was good for the small ones but disastrous for those that were more important. With his overwhelming desire to pander to public opinion, he turned aside talented artists from their path, corrupted the strong, exhausted the weak, and elevated the mediocre; he used them, through the people he knew and through his journal. The ambition of young painters was to see their works in his window, and upholsterers and decorators modelled their furnishing on his patterns. Frédéric supposed him to be at one and the same time a millionaire, a dilettante, a man of action. But many things surprised him, for Monsieur Arnoux was cunning in his buying and selling of pictures.

He would have sent to him from a remote part of Germany or Italy a canvas he himself had bought in Paris for one thousand five hundred francs, displaying an invoice raising the price to four thousand, and sell it on for three thousand five hundred, as a favour. One of his usual tricks was to ask the painter for a small copy of the picture, as commission, on the pretext of publishing the engraving; he always sold the copy but the engraving never appeared. To those who complained of being exploited he responded by a dig in the ribs. Excellent in other respects, he was generous in dispensing cigars, was familiar with people he didn't know, enthused over a painting or a person, and stuck to his opinion, throwing himself into a round of visits, correspondence, advertisements, with no expense spared. He thought himself a very decent man, and because he needed to confide in others, he innocently told them all about his little tricks.

Once, to annoy a colleague who was having a big celebration to launch another art journal, he asked Frédéric to write notes to the guests, under his supervision, that it was cancelled, shortly before the event was to take place.

'There's no dishonour involved, you understand?'

And the young man did not dare refuse him this service.

The next day as he went into his office with Hussonnet, Frédéric caught sight of the vanishing hem of a dress through the door that opened on to the stairs.

'A thousand apologies!' said Hussonnet. 'If I'd supposed there were any ladies...'

'Oh, that was only my wife,' replied Arnoux. 'She came to pay me a little visit on the way home.'

'What?' said Frédéric.

'Yes, she's going back home.'

The objects around him suddenly lost their charm. The vague aura which pervaded the room had just dissipated, or rather had never existed. He felt immense surprise and sorrow, as though he had been betrayed.

Arnoux, rummaging in his drawer, was smiling. Was he having a joke at his expense? The assistant placed a bundle of damp papers on the table.

'Oh, the posters!' cried the art dealer. 'No dinner for me till late tonight!'

Regimbart took his cap.

'What, are you going?'

'Seven o'clock!' said Regimbart.

Frédéric followed him.

At the end of the Rue Montmartre, he turned. He looked at the first floor windows, and laughed inwardly, with self-pity, remembering the love he'd felt when he'd gazed at them on frequent occasions before. So where was she living? How could he meet her now? There opened up around his desire a desolation that was more immense than ever!

'Are you coming to have one?'

'Have... who?'

'An absinthe!'

Humouring Regimbart and his obsessions, Frédéric allowed himself to be conducted to the Bordeaux *estaminet*. While his companion, leaning on his elbow, was examining the carafe and glancing to right and left, he caught sight of Pellerin's profile outside on the pavement and tapped sharply on the window. The painter had not even sat down before Regimbart asked him why he didn't see him any more at *L'Art industriel*.

'I'll be damned if I'm going back there! He's a brute, a bourgeois, a wretch, you can't trust him!'

These insults gratified Frédéric. Yet he was hurt, for it seemed to him they reflected badly on Madame Arnoux too.

'Why, what's he done to you?' enquired Regimbart.

Pellerin tapped the floor with his foot and breathed hard instead of answering.

He was secretly engaged in doing chalk and charcoal portraits and pastiches of the Old Masters for lovers of art who didn't know very much about it. And as this work made him feel ashamed, he had rather keep quiet about them on the whole. But 'that swine Arnoux' was too much for him. And out it all came.

Complying with an order, which Frédéric had been party to, he had brought along a couple of pictures. The art dealer had seen fit to be critical of them! He had criticized the composition, the colour, drawing, especially the drawing, in short hadn't wanted them at any price. But forced into it by the non-payment of a bill, Pellerin had handed them over to Isaac, a Jew; and two weeks later Arnoux himself sold them to a Spaniard for two thousand francs.

'Two thousand no less! What a crook! And I'm not the only one, I can tell you! We'll see him in court one of these days.'

'You're exaggerating!' Frédéric said in a timid voice.

'So, you think I'm exaggerating?' cried the artist, bringing his fist down hard on the table.

This violent reaction restored the younger man's self-confidence. No doubt Arnoux might have been more considerate; but if he really thought those two canvases...

'Bad! Go on, say it! So have you seen them? Is that your profession? Well, my boy, get this straight. I don't hold with amateurs!'

'Oh, it's none of my business!' Frédéric said.

'So what's your interest in sticking up for him?' Pellerin asked coldly.

The young man faltered:

'Well... he's a friend of mine.'

'Then give him my love! Goodnight!'

And the painter left in a rage, and, of course, without a word about paying for his drink.

In defending Arnoux, Frédéric had also managed to convince himself. He warmed to his own eloquence and felt a sudden compassion for this kind, clever man whom his friends insulted and who, deserted by them, was now working on his own. He could not resist the strange impulse to go and see him again straight away. Ten minutes later he was pushing open the door of the shop.

Arnoux was working with his apprentice on some enormous posters for an exhibition of paintings.

'Well, what brings you back here?'

This all too simple question embarrassed Frédéric; and, not knowing what to say, he asked if anyone had by any chance found his notebook, a little blue leather one.

'The one where you keep your love letters?' said Arnoux.

Frédéric, blushing like a virgin, protested against this supposition.

'Your poems then?' pursued the dealer.

He was handling the proofs spread out on the table and was discussing the form, colour, borders; and Frédéric felt increasingly irritated by his preoccupied air, and especially by his hands as they moved over the posters—fat, rather flabby hands with flat fingernails. Arnoux got up finally, and saying, 'That's it!' he chucked Frédéric in a familiar fashion under the chin. This liberty displeased Frédéric who recoiled and then left the premises, for the very last time in his life, or so he believed. It was as though Madame Arnoux herself was diminished by her husband's coarse behaviour.

That same week he received a letter from Deslauriers announcing his arrival in Paris the following Thursday. So then he put all his energies back into cultivating this friendship, which was altogether more substantial and on a higher plane. Such a man was worth any woman. Now he didn't need Regimbart, Pellerin, Hussonnet, or anyone else! In order to make his friend more comfortable, he bought an iron bedstead, a second armchair, divided his bed linen in two, and on Thursday morning was just getting ready to go and meet Deslauriers when there was a loud ring on his doorbell. Arnoux came in.

'Just a quick word! Yesterday someone sent me a beautiful trout from Geneva. We expect you this evening at seven o'clock sharp... It's Rue de Choiseul, 24*bis*. Don't forget!'

Frédéric had to sit down. He felt weak at the knees. He said to himself over and over: 'At last! At last!' Then he wrote to his tailor, his hatmaker, his bootmaker; and he had these three notes carried by three different messengers. The key turned in the lock and the concierge appeared with a trunk on his shoulder.

Frédéric, seeing Deslauriers, started to tremble like an adulterous woman who has to face her husband.

'Whatever's the matter with you?' Deslauriers asked. 'You must have had my letter?'

Frédéric didn't have the courage to tell a lie.

He threw his arms around Deslauriers and hugged him.

Afterwards the clerk told him what had been happening to him. His father had refused to show him the accounts of his guardianship, on the supposed grounds that they were due only every ten years. But knowing about legal procedure, Deslauriers had in the end got possession of his mother's inheritance, seven thousand francs in total, and kept it on him in an old wallet.

'It's my reserve in case of an emergency. I must find out about where to invest it and get fixed up with a job myself tomorrow morning. But today it's a proper holiday and I am all yours, my old friend!'

'Oh, don't put yourself out!' said Frédéric. 'If you had anything important to do this evening...'

'Of course not! I'd be a selfish wretch...'

This phrase, casually flung out, cut Frédéric to the quick, as if it had been some deliberate and insulting allusion.

On the table by the fire the concierge had set out cutlets, galantine,* a lobster, a dessert, and two bottles of Bordeaux. Such a fine reception touched Deslauriers deeply.

'My word, you are treating me like royalty!'

They talked about the past, the future; and from time to time they grasped each other's hands across the table, looking at each other affectionately for a minute or two. Then a messenger brought in a new hat. Deslauriers remarked on its shiny new lining.

Then the tailor himself arrived with the suit he had pressed.

'You'd think you were going to get married,' Deslauriers said.

An hour later a third person appeared and took a pair of splendid patent-leather boots out of a big black bag. While Frédéric was trying them on, the bootmaker was sardonically observing the footware of the man from the provinces.

'Does Monsieur need anything?'

'No thank you,' replied the clerk, tucking his old lace-up shoes under his chair.

This humiliation embarrassed Frédéric. He shrank from making his confession.

'Oh, heavens above! I was forgetting!'

'What?'

'I'm dining out this evening!'

'At the Dambreuses'? Why do you never speak of them in your letters?'

'Not at the Dambreuses', but at the Arnouxes'.'

'You should have let me know!' Deslauriers said. 'I could have come a day later.'

'Impossible!' Frédéric answered curtly. 'I only got the invitation this morning, a short time ago.'

And in order to redeem his fault and distract his friend from the matter, he untied the knotted ropes on his trunk, put away all his things in the drawers, offered to give him his own bed and sleep in the box room. Then at four o'clock he began to get ready.

'You're in plenty of time!' said his friend.

Finally he was dressed, and he left.

'There's wealth for you!' Deslauriers thought.

And he went off to eat in the Rue Saint-Jacques at a little restaurant he knew.

Frédéric stopped several times on his way up the stairs, his heart was beating so fast. One of his gloves was too tight and tore, and while he was tucking the torn part under the cuff of his shirt, Arnoux, coming up behind him, took him by the arm and ushered him in.

The hall, decorated in the oriental style, had a painted lantern hanging from the ceiling and bamboos in each corner. Crossing the salon, Frédéric tripped over a tiger skin. The candelabra had not been lit, but two lamps were burning in the boudoir beyond.

Mademoiselle Marthe came to say her mother was dressing. Arnoux picked her up and lifted her to head height to kiss her. Then, wanting to go and choose certain bottles of wine in the cellar himself, he left Frédéric with the little girl.

She had grown a lot since the trip to Montereau. Her brown hair fell in long ringlets on to her bare arms. Under her dress, more bouffant than a ballet skirt, you could see her pink calves, and the whole of her lovely little person smelled as fresh as a bunch of flowers. She received the gentleman's compliments with a coquettish grace, stared at him intently, then slunk away like a little cat between the furniture.

His nervousness had gone. The globes of the lamps, covered in paper lace, gave out a creamy light which softened the colour of the walls, hung with mauve satin. Through the bars in the fireguard, which resembled a large fan, you could see the coal in the hearth. In front of the clock there was a box with silver clasps. Domestic items were scattered here and there: a doll in the middle of the sofa, a scarf on the back of a chair, and on the worktable some knitting with two ivory needles sticking out, their ends pointing down. The room was peaceful, civilized, and homely at one and the same time.

Arnoux came back; and through the other door Madame Arnoux appeared. As she was enveloped in shadow, at first he could see only her head. She wore a dress of black velvet and in her hair was a long Algerian headdress in red silk net, which was twisted around her comb and fell on to her left shoulder.

Arnoux introduced Frédéric.

'Oh, I remember Monsieur Frédéric very well,' she said.

Then, almost simultaneously, the guests arrived: Dittmer, Lovarias, Burrieu, Rosenwald the composer, Théophile Lorris, the poet, two art-critic colleagues of Hussonnet, a paper manufacturer, and finally the illustrious Pierre-Paul Meinsius, the last representative of classical painting, who bore his fame, his eighty years, and his embonpoint with a cheerful good humour

When they moved into the dining room, Madame Arnoux took his arm. A chair was left vacant for Pellerin. Arnoux liked him, even though he exploited him. In any case he was scared of his sharp tongue—so that, to appease him, he had published his portrait in *L'Art industriel* along with hyperbolic praise: and Pellerin, who cared more about fame than money, appeared at eight, quite out of breath. Frédéric supposed they had made up their differences long ago.

The company, the food, everything was to his liking. The room resembled a medieval parlour, with embossed leather on the walls; in front of a Dutch whatnot there was a rack of chibouks;* and around the table Bohemian glass in various colours lit up the surrounding fruit and flowers like a garden.

He had to choose from among ten kinds of mustard. He ate gazpacho, curry, ginger, blackbirds from Corsica, Roman lasagne; he drank extraordinary wines, lip-fraoli and Tokay.* Arnoux certainly prided himself on being a good host. He knew all the drivers of post-chaises, with a view to stocking his larder, and he was on friendly terms with chefs from the big houses, who passed their sauce recipes on to him.

But the most entertaining thing for Frédéric was the conversation.

His liking for travel was indulged by Dittmer, who talked about the East; he satisfied his curiosity about the theatre as he listened to Rosenwald's tales of the Opéra; and the horrors of bohemian life took on a fascination for him when Hussonnet gaily narrated in picturesque fashion how he had spent the whole of one winter with nothing but Dutch cheese to eat. Then, a discussion between Lovarias and Burrieu about the Florentine School revealed masterpieces to him, opened new horizons, and he could hardly contain his enthusiasm when Pellerin cried:

'Oh, your hideous reality be damned! What does reality mean, anyway? Some look on the black side, others through rose-tinted spectacles, most don't see anything at all. Nothing's more artificial than Michelangelo, but nothing's greater! This questing after external truth proves how low we have sunk nowadays; and if we go on like this, art will become something merely farcical, less poetic than religion and less interesting than politics. You will not get to its real goal—yes, its goal—which is to make us feel an impersonal exaltation, you won't get there with small works, however cleverly executed. Look at Bassolier's paintings for instance: they're pretty, attractive, clean, and extremely light! You can put them in your pocket or take them on holiday! Lawyers will pay twenty thousand francs for them, and the ideas in them are not worth a sou. But without ideas, no grandeur! And without grandeur, no beauty! Olympus is a mountain! The boldest monument will always be the Pyramids. Exuberance is worth more than taste, the desert worth more than a pavement, and a savage more than a barber!'

While he listened to these remarks, Frédéric was watching Madame Arnoux. They dropped into his mind like metals into a furnace, increasing his passion, engendering love.

He was sitting three places below her on the same side. From time to time she leaned over a little, turning her head to say a few words to her daughter; and as she smiled then, a dimple appeared in her cheek, making her face gentler and more delicate.

When the liqueurs were served, she disappeared. The conversation became very free; Monsieur Arnoux spoke brilliantly and Frédéric was astonished by the cynicism of these men. But their preoccupation with women established a sort of equality between them and himself which raised him in his own estimation.

Coming back into the salon, assuming a nonchalant air, he picked up one of the albums lying on the table. The great artists of the age had illustrated it with their drawings, and had written lines of prose or verse, or simply signed them; among the well-known names were many that were unknown, and the interesting remarks were lost under a surfeit of platitudes. All contained a direct or indirect homage to Madame Arnoux. Frédéric would have been afraid to write a single line next to theirs.

She went into her boudoir to fetch the box with the silver clasps that he had noticed on the mantelpiece. It was a present from her husband, a piece from the Renaissance. Arnoux's friends complimented him, his wife thanked him. He was overcome with tenderness and kissed her in front of everybody.

Then they all dispersed and chatted in groups; the worthy Meinsius sat by Madame Arnoux in an armchair by the fire; she was leaning forward to say something into his ear and their heads were touching;— and Frédéric would not have minded being deaf, infirm, or ugly had he had a famous name and white hair, in short, anything which would establish him in such intimacy as that. He was anguished, furious at being young.

But then she came over to the corner of the salon where he was, asked him if he knew any of the guests, whether he liked paintings, how long he had been studying in Paris. To Frédéric, every word she spoke was a revelation, one she alone could have occasioned. He studied the strands of hair which had escaped from her coiffure and were caressing her bare shoulder. He couldn't take his eyes off them, his soul was lost in this white female flesh. But he did not dare raise his eyes and look at her full in the face.

Rosenwald interrupted them by asking Madame Arnoux to sing. She waited while he played the introductory bars; then she parted her lips and a pure long-drawn-out sound rose into the air.

Frédéric couldn't understand a word of the Italian.

It began with a solemn rhythm like plainsong, then, gathering to a crescendo, a myriad notes burst forth in diapason before it suddenly quietened again; and then the melody returned, lovingly, languidly, in sweeping waves of sound.

She stood near the pianoforte, hands at her sides, with a rapt expression. Occasionally, to read the music, she bent her head and her eyes were half-shut for a moment. In the lower notes her contralto voice took on a mournful tone that made your blood run cold, and then her beautiful face with the large eyebrows leaned sideways on to her shoulder. Her breast swelled, her arms stretched out, and as the notes trilled forth in rapid succession from her throat, she gently tilted back her head, as though the air was kissing her. She sang three high notes, came down the scale again, reached even higher, and after a silence finished on a long-drawn-out final chord.

Rosenwald did not leave the pianoforte. He carried on playing for his own pleasure. Now and then one of the guests would vanish. At eleven as the last of them left, Arnoux went off with Pellerin, on the pretext of seeing him back to his house. He was one of those people who say they'll be ill if they 'don't take their after-dinner walk'.

Madame Arnoux had moved forward into the hall. Dittmer and Hussonnet were saying goodbye and she gave them her hand. She also gave her hand to Frédéric and the shock of it went right through him.

He left his friends; he needed to be alone. His heart was overflowing. Why had she given him her hand? Was it a casual gesture or to encourage him? 'Come now, I am off my head!' What did it matter anyway, since now he could go and see her whenever he wished, breathe the air she breathed.

The roads were deserted. The occasional heavy cart went by, juddering over the cobbles. House after house appeared with their grey facades, their closed windows. He thought pityingly of all the creatures asleep behind those walls who lived their lives without ever seeing her, not even one of them suspecting her existence! He wasn't aware of his surroundings, the space around him, anything at all; and striding along, tapping the shutters on the shops with his stick as he went, he marched straight ahead, vaguely, drawn along at random. Damp air enveloped him and he realized he was walking along the banks of the river.

The shining street lamps stretched away in two straight lines and long red flames flickered in the depths of the water. The river was the colour of slate, whereas the sky, which was lighter, seemed to be supported by the great masses of shadow which rose on either side of the river. Buildings not visible to the eye intensified the darkness. A luminous mist floated beyond them over the rooftops. All noises dissolved into a single murmur. A light breeze was blowing.

He had stopped halfway across the Pont Neuf and, bareheaded, his coat open, he breathed in the night air. And he felt something rising from within him, inexhaustibly, an increasing love which made him giddy, like the movement of the waves beneath his eyes. A church clock chimed the hour, slowly, like a voice calling to him.

Then he was seized by one of those tremors of the soul in which you feel you are being transported into a higher world. An extraordinary power—for what, he did not know—had come upon him. He seriously wondered whether to become a great painter or a great poet. And made up his mind to be a painter, for the demands of that profession would bring him closer to Madame Arnoux. He had found his vocation then! The aim of his life was now clear to him and his future was assured.

Closing his door, he heard someone snoring in the dark closet by the bedroom. It was his friend. He had forgotten he was there.

He caught sight of his face in the mirror. Good-looking, he thought; and for a minute or two he remained there in contemplation of himself.

## V

BEFORE noon the following day he had bought a paintbox, paint-brushes, an easel. Pellerin agreed to give him lessons, and Frédéric took him to his lodgings to see if he needed any more equipment.

Deslauriers had come back. A young man was sitting in the second armchair. The clerk said, by way of introduction:

'This is the man! Here he is, Sénécal!'

This fellow was not to Frédéric's liking. His swept-back hair accentuated his high forehead. There was a hard, cold look in his grey eyes, and his long black frock coat, his whole dress, reeked of pedagogy and the Church.

First they chatted about current events, about Rossini's Stabat* amongst other things. Sénécal, when asked, declared he never went to the theatre. Pellerin opened the paintbox.

'Is all that for you?' said the clerk.

'Of course!'

'How strange!'

And he leaned over the table where the maths tutor was leafing through a volume of Louis Blanc. He had brought it with him and was reading passages aloud in a low voice while Pellerin and Frédéric examined the palette, the palette knife, the bladders; then they got round to discussing the dinner at Arnoux's.

'The art dealer?' Sénécal asked. 'He's a rascal.'

'Why's that?' Pellerin asked.

Sénécal answered:

'A man who makes money by political corruption!'

And he started to tell them about a famous lithograph, representing all the royal family in edifying occupations: Louis-Philippe was holding a copy of the Code, the Queen a missal, the Princesses were embroidering, the Duc de Nemours was putting on his sword; Monsieur de Joinville was showing his young brothers a map; in the background you could see a bed with two compartments. This picture, entitled *A Worthy Family*, had delighted the bourgeoisie but made the patriots despair. Pellerin, crossly, as though he had painted it himself, replied that everybody was entitled to their own opinion. Sénécal disagreed. The only aim of Art was to improve the morals of the masses! One should depict only subjects which would encourage virtuous actions; anything else was harmful.

'But that depends on how they are done!' cried Pellerin. 'I might paint masterpieces!'

'Too bad for you then! You don't have any right...'

'What?'

'No, Monsieur, you haven't the right to try to interest me in things I disapprove of. What use have we for tedious nonsense, from which it's impossible to derive any benefit, from these Venuses, for example, with all your landscapes. I see no education of the masses there. Show me their misery instead! Inspire us with the sacrifices people make! There's no shortage of subjects, for heaven's sake: the farm, the workshop...'

Pellerin was spluttering with indignation and, believing he had hit on an argument, asked:

'Do you approve of Molière?'

'Indeed I do,' admitted Sénécal, 'I admire him as a precursor of the French Revolution.'

'Oh, the Revolution! What art! Was there any period in history more lamentable!'

'None greater, Monsieur!'

Pellerin crossed his arms and looking him straight in the eyes:

'You sound just like a member of the National Guard!'*

His antagonist, used to argument, answered:

'Well I'm not a member, and I hate them as much as you do. But with such principles one can corrupt multitudes. That's typical of the Government anyway. It wouldn't have any power without the complicity of rogues like ours.'

The painter came to the defence of the art dealer, for Sénécal's opinions exasperated him. He even dared maintain that Jacques Arnoux had a true heart of gold, was devoted to his friends and very fond of his wife.

'Huh! If he could get a good price he would let her pose for anybody.'

Frédéric went pale.

'Has he done you a great wrong then, Monsieur?'

'Me? No. I once saw him in a café with a friend, that's all.'

Sénécal was speaking the truth. But he was annoyed every day by the advertisements he saw for the *Art industriel*. For him Arnoux represented a world he judged to be fatal for democracy. He was an austere Republican and suspected all those who lived stylishly to be corrupt; he himself had no need of anything, and was of uncompromising probity.

It was difficult to carry on this conversation. Quite soon the painter remembered he had an appointment, the tutor remembered his students; and when they had gone, after a long silence, Deslauriers asked various questions about Arnoux.

'You'll introduce me later on, my friend, won't you?'

'Of course,' replied Frédéric.

Then they attended to the business of planning their life together. Deslauriers had obtained without difficulty a position as junior clerk to a solicitor, registered at the School of Law, and bought the necessary books. The life they had dreamed of for so long began.

It was delightful, thanks to the grace that comes with youth. Deslauriers not having mentioned any arrangement about money, Frédéric didn't either. He paid for everything they needed, stocked the larder, managed the housekeeping. But if it was necessary to give the concierge a talking-to, the clerk took responsibility for it, continuing, as at school, in his role of protector and elder brother.

They were apart in the day, but together every evening. Each took his place by the fireside and set to work. It wasn't long before work was interrupted. They confided in each other endlessly, laughed a great deal for no reason, and sometimes quarrelled about a lamp that was smoking or a book that was lost, momentary bursts of temper that were soon allayed by merriment.

The door of the box room remained open and they chatted at a distance, from one bed to the other.

In the mornings they walked on their balcony in their shirtsleeves. The sun rose, a thin mist drifted over the river, shrill voices could be heard from the nearby flower market; and the smoke from their pipes made rings in the clear air that awakened their eyes, still puffy from sleep; they could sense, as they breathed, boundless possibilities stretching out before them.

On Sundays, when it wasn't raining, they went out, and roamed the streets, arm-in-arm. They almost always had the same thoughts at the same time, or else they chatted, oblivious to their surroundings. Deslauriers's aim was to make money, as a means of exercising power over other men. He wanted to influence lots of people, make a name for himself, have three secretaries to order around, and give a big political dinner each week. Frédéric imagined himself living in a Moorish palace, lying on cashmere divans listening to the murmur of a fountain, attended by Negro attendants. And these things he dreamed of in the end became so clear to him that they made him miserable, as though he had lost them.

'What's the good of talking about all that,' he would say, 'since we shall never have it!'

'Who knows?' said Deslauriers.

In spite of his democratic opinions he urged him to get a foot in the Dambreuse household. Frédéric objected that he had already tried.

'Try again. They'll invite you!'

Towards the middle of March some steep bills arrived, one from the restaurateur who provided their dinner. Not having enough money, Frédéric borrowed a hundred écus from Deslauriers. He asked him for the sum again a fortnight later and the clerk grumbled at him for spending so much money in Arnoux's shop.

It was true he wasn't restrained in his purchases. A view of Venice, a view of Naples and another of Constantinople occupying the middle of the three walls, pictures of horses by Alfred de Dreux hanging here and there, a group portrait by Pradier* on the mantelpiece, back numbers of *L'Art industriel* on the piano, as well as the boxes on the floor in the corners, so filled the lodgings that there was scarcely any elbow room or space to put a book. Frédéric claimed he needed all that for his painting.

He was working at Pellerin's place. But often the latter was dashing about, being accustomed to attending all the burials and events that newspapers were likely to report; and Frédéric spent hours in the studio entirely on his own. The calm of this large room—where all you could hear was the scampering of mice—the light falling from the ceiling and even the soft roaring of the stove, all plunged him at first into a sort of intellectual well-being. Then his gaze, straying from his work, would range over the mouldings on the walls, between the ornaments on the shelves, along the unfinished pieces where the layers of dust looked like velvet rags; and, like a traveller lost in the middle of a wood who is constantly brought back to the same spot whichever road he takes, he found, underlying every idea, the memory of Madame Arnoux.

He decided on the days when he would go to her house. Having climbed the stairs, he paused at her door, uncertain whether to ring or not. Footsteps approached, the door opened, and at the words 'Madame is out' he would feel a sort of deliverance, as if a weight had been lifted off him.

Yet he did meet her on occasion. The first time she was with three ladies; another afternoon Mademoiselle's writing tutor arrived. But the men that Madame Arnoux received did not make regular visits and so, out of discretion, he did not return.

But he made sure of turning up at *L'Art industriel* regularly on a Wednesday in order to get an invitation to the Thursday dinner; and he stayed later than all the rest, longer than Regimbart, till the last minute, pretending he was looking at an engraving, or reading a newspaper. In the end Arnoux would say: 'Are you free tomorrow evening?' He said yes before the question had been asked. Arnoux seemed to have taken a shine to him. He showed him the art of differentiating between wines, of brewing punch, of making woodcock stew. Frédéric meekly followed his advice, loving everything that had to do with Madame Arnoux, her furniture, her servants, her house, her street.

He scarcely spoke during these dinners. He gazed at her. On her right temple she had a small beauty spot; her bandeaux were darker than the rest of her hair and always, as it seemed, a little moist round the edges. She stroked them from time to time with just two fingers. He knew the shape of each of her nails, it thrilled him to hear the swish of her silk dress when she passed near the doors. Secretly he smelled the scent of her handkerchief; her comb, her gloves, her rings were for him special, significant, like works of art, almost taking on a life of their own. They all had a hold on his heart and increased his passion.

He'd not had the strength to hide it from Deslauriers. When he came back from the Arnouxes', he woke his friend as if by accident, so that he could talk about her.

Deslauriers who slept in the box room next to the cistern gave a long yawn. Frédéric sat down at the foot of his bed. First he talked about the dinner, then he recounted a thousand insignificant details, in which he detected marks of scorn or affection. Once, for example, she had refused his arm, and taken Dittmer's instead, and Frédéric had been in despair.

'Oh, don't be so silly!'

Or else she had called him her 'friend'.

'Then make the most of it!'

'But I don't dare,' Frédéric said.

'Well then, forget it! Goodnight.'

Deslauriers turned to face the wall and fell asleep. He couldn't understand this passion, a weakness, in his opinion, left over from adolescence; and since he supposed that his own friendship was not enough for Frédéric, he had the idea of getting together a little group of their friends once a week.

They came on Saturday towards nine. The three Algerian curtains were carefully drawn across. The lamp and four candles were burning. In the middle of the table the tobacco jar, full of pipes, stood among bottles of beer, a teapot, a flask of rum, and some petits fours. They discussed the immortality of the soul, the relative qualities of their professors.

One evening Hussonnet brought along a tall young man dressed in a coat whose sleeves were too short, and who looked very embarrassed. It was the lad they had tried to get out of the police station the year before.

Unable to give back the box of lace lost in the fracas, he had been accused by his master of stealing it, and threatened with a court action. Now he was working as a haulier. Hussonnet had met him that morning on a street corner, and was bringing him along, for Dussardier, wishing to express his gratitude, wanted to see 'the other man'.

He gave Frédéric the cigar box, which was still full, and which he had hung on to religiously in the hope of being able to return it. The young men asked him to come again. He did.

Everybody got on very well. In the first place their hatred for the Government had reached the level of indisputable dogma. Martinon was the only one to stand up for Louis-Philippe. The others over-whelmed him with the platitudes being published in the papers: Paris was becoming like a Bastille, the Laws of September, Pritchard, 'Lord' Guizot*—so Martinon held his tongue, afraid he might offend someone. In his seven years at school he had never once got a detention, and at the School of Law he knew how to please the professors. Usually he wore a big putty-coloured frock coat with rubber overshoes. But one evening he turned up dressed like a bridegroom: a velvet shawl gilet, a white tie, a gold chain.

Their astonishment increased when it was known that he had come from the Dambreuse household. In fact, Dambreuse the banker had just purchased a substantial stretch of woodland from Martinon's father. The latter had introduced his son and Dambreuse had invited them both to dinner.

'Were there a lot of truffles?' Deslauriers asked. 'And have you had your arm round his wife's waist in some dark corner, *sicut decet*?'*

Then the conversation turned to women. Pellerin would not admit that there were any beautiful women (he preferred tigers); moreover, the female of the species was an inferior creature in the aesthetic hierarchy:

'What is attractive about them is precisely what is degrading to women as an idea. I'm talking about their breasts, their hair...'

'But', Frédéric objected, 'long black hair with big black eyes...'

'Oh, I know all about that!' cried Hussonnet. 'I've had enough of floozies from Andalusia. Women of antiquity? You can keep them! For, seriously, a *lorette*'s* more fun than the Venus de Milo! Let's be Gauls, my dear boy! And Regency rakes if possible!

> "Flow forth good wine! Ladies, show us your smiles!"

You have to progress from brunettes to blondes!—What do you think, Dussardier, my friend?'

Dussardier said nothing. They all urged him to tell them what he thought.

'Well,' he said, blushing, 'I should like to love one woman for ever!'

It was said in such a way that there was a moment's silence, some surprised at this candour, and the rest perhaps realizing it was what they secretly longed for in their hearts.

Sénécal put his beer mug down on the mantelpiece and dogmat-ically declared that since prostitution was a tyranny and marriage immoral, the best thing to do was abstain. For Deslauriers women were for entertainment and nothing more. Monsieur de Cisy was terrified of having anything to do with them.

Brought up under the watchful eye of a religious grandmother, he found the company of these young men as tempting as a den of vice and as enlightening as the Sorbonne. They were generous with their tuition and he was full of zeal, even wanting to smoke although it made him feel sick every time he did. Frédéric was extravagant in his praises. He admired the shade of his cravat, the fur on his overcoat, and especially his boots whose leather was as soft as his gloves and seemed almost offensively immaculate and genteel. His carriage used to wait for him below in the street.

One evening when he had just left and it was snowing outside, Sénécal said he felt sorry for his coachman. Then he railed against the yellow gloves of the Jockey Club.* He had more regard for workmen than for such gentlemen.

'I go to work at least! I need the money!'

'That's obvious!' Frédéric was in the end exasperated.

The tutor did not forgive him for these words.

But when Regimbart told him that he knew Sénécal a little, Frédéric, wishing to be polite to a friend of Arnoux, asked him to come along to the Saturday meetings. The patriotic pair enjoyed meeting each other.

Their opinions, however, differed.

Sénécal, with his pointed head,* was only concerned with theories. Regimbart on the other hand saw only the facts. His main concern was the borders of the Rhine.* He claimed to be an artillery expert, and had his clothes made by the tailor to the École Polytechnique.

The first day when he was offered cakes, he raised his shoulders in contempt, saying that cakes were for women. And he was scarcely more gracious on subsequent occasions. When conversation reached a certain level he would murmur: 'Oh please—no utopias, no visions!' In relation to art (although he frequented artists' studios, where, to be obliging, he would sometimes give fencing lessons) his opinions were not of the highest order. He compared M. Marrast to Voltaire, and Mademoiselle Vatnaz to Madame de Staël, because of an ode to Poland* which 'had feeling'. In brief, Regimbart exasperated everybody and Deslauriers in particular, for the Citizen was a friend of Arnoux. Now the clerk's ambition was to be a visitor at his house,

hoping to make useful acquaintances. 'When are you going to introduce me?' he would ask Frédéric. Arnoux was overwhelmed with
things to do, or was going away; or then again it wasn't worth it because soon they wouldn't be giving any more dinners.

If he had been required to risk his life for his friend, Frédéric
would have done so. But as he was concerned to appear to as much
advantage as possible and kept a careful watch on his language, manners, and on his dress—so much so that his gloves when he arrived at
the offices of *L'Art industriel* must always be immaculate, he was afraid
that Deslauriers with his old black suit, his attorney's demeanour, and
his extravagant remarks might be displeasing to Madame Arnoux,
and that could compromise him, and lower him in her opinion. He
was willing to admit the others, but this particular friend would have
embarrassed him infinitely more than anyone else. The clerk saw that
he did not want to keep his promise and Frédéric's silence seemed to
him to add insult to injury.

He would have liked to have absolute control over him, watch him
develop in accordance with their youthful ideals, and this inertia infuriated him; it felt like disobedience and betrayal. It was a fact that
Frédéric, obsessed with Madame Arnoux, talked frequently about her
husband; and Deslauriers began to poke fun at him, repeating his
name over and over at the end of each sentence, a hundred times
a day, like an idiot. When someone knocked at the door, he would say:
'Come in, Arnoux!' At the restaurant he would ask for a portion of
'Brie Arnoux' and at night, pretending to have had a bad dream,
he would wake his companion crying: 'Arnoux, Arnoux!' So that finally one day Frédéric, driven to distraction, expostulated:

'For heaven's sake leave me alone with your Arnoux!'
'Never!' the clerk replied.

> ' "Always him, him everywhere! In flames or in ice,
>    The image of Arnoux..." '*

'Just shut up!' cried Frédéric, raising his fist.
He went on more calmly:
'It's a sore point, as you very well know.'
'Oh, I'm so sorry, my friend,' Deslauriers replied, with a deep bow.
'Henceforth we shall respect Mademoiselle's nerves! Forgive me, for-
give me, a thousand apologies!'
And that was the end of the joke.

But one evening three weeks later he said:

'By the way, I saw Madame Arnoux just now.'

'Where?'

'At the Palais de Justice with the lawyer, Balandard. A brunette, medium height, is that right?'

Frédéric nodded. He waited for Deslauriers to say more. At the slightest word of praise he would have spoken volumes about her, being more than ready to be nice to him. The other remained silent. Finally, not able to hold back any longer, he asked casually what he thought of her.

Deslauriers thought she was 'not bad, but nothing out of the ordinary'.

'Oh,' said Frédéric, 'is that what you think?'

The month of August came, time for his second exam. According to most people, two weeks should be enough for revising the subjects. Frédéric, not doubting his ability, devoured the first four books of the Code of Procedure whole, the first three of the Penal Code, several sections of the Criminal Law, and a section of the Civil Code with notes by Monsieur Poncelet. The evening before, Deslauriers tested him on it, and it went on all night. And to make the most of the last fifteen minutes, he carried on testing him as they walked along the pavement.

As there were several exams on simultaneously, there were a lot of people in the courtyard, Hussonnet and Cisy amongst them. People with friends taking these exams always made sure to come along too. Frédéric put on the traditional black gown. Then he went in, followed by the crowd, three other students with him, into a large room, lit by curtainless windows and furnished with little benches along the walls. In the middle were leather chairs around a table covered with green baize. It divided the candidates from the red-robed examiners, who all wore ermine on their shoulders and had hats with gold stripes.

Frédéric was next to last in his group, a bad position. At the first question about the difference between an agreement and a contract, he confused one with the other; and the professor, a kindly man, said: 'Don't be nervous, Monsieur, compose yourself!' Then, having asked two easy questions, which were met with muddled answers, he passed on to the fourth candidate. Frédéric was demoralized by this poor start. Deslauriers, sitting opposite in the public seats, signalled to him that all was not yet lost, and at the second round of questions

about criminal rights, he did passably well. But after the third, about
the sealed will,* the examiner remaining impassive throughout, his
anxiety increased. Hussonnet put his hands together as though about
to clap, while Deslauriers repeatedly shrugged his shoulders. Finally
the time came for him to answer on Procedure. The subject was third-
party opposition.* The professor, shocked to have heard theories at
variance with his own, asked him in a brusque tone:

'And you, Monsieur, is that your opinion? How do you reconcile
the principle of Article 1351 of the Civil Code with this extraordinary
line of attack?'

Frédéric had a terrible headache, not having slept all night.
A ray of sunlight, entering through a slat in the blind, fell on his face.
Standing behind the chair he rocked back and forth on his heels and
pulled at his moustache.

'I'm waiting for your answer!' intoned the man in the gold cap.

And no doubt irritated by Frédéric's fidgeting:

'You won't find the answer in your beard!'

This sarcastic remark provoked merriment in the auditorium.
The professor, mollified, became more conciliatory. He asked him
two more questions about summons and summary procedure, then
nodded in approval; the public interrogation was over. Frédéric went
back into the vestibule.

While the beadle was divesting him of his gown, to pass it on to another student immediately, his friends surrounded him, managing to
confuse him utterly with their conflicting opinions about the result of
the exam. It was announced before long in a sonorous voice at the
entrance to the room: 'The third candidate was referred.'

'Messed up!' said Hussonnet. 'Let's go!'

Outside the concierge's lodge they found Martinon, red-faced,
excited, smiling, and with the aureole of triumph on his brow. He
had just passed his last exam successfully. Only his thesis remained.
Another two weeks and he would have his degree. His family knew
a minister—'a fine career' lay ahead.

'He's got the better of you, after all,' Deslauriers said.

Nothing is more humiliating than to see fools succeed in the enterprises where you yourself have failed. Frédéric was cross and replied that he didn't give a damn. His ambitions were higher. And as
Hussonnet looked as if he were about to leave he took him on one
side and said:

'Not a word to them about all this, of course!'

It was easy to keep it secret since Arnoux was leaving for a trip to Germany next day.

In the evening when he got home the clerk found his friend strangely different: he was executing pirouettes, whistling; and when Deslauriers expressed surprise at this mood, Frédéric declared he wouldn't go back to his mother's, he would be busy working in his holidays.

Learning of Arnoux's departure, he had been filled with delight. He could go and call over there as he pleased, without fear of his visits being interrupted. He would take courage from being reassured of absolute safety. In short, he would not have to be far away, separated from her! Something stronger than iron chains attached him to Paris, a voice inside was telling him to stay.

There were obstacles in his way. He got over them by writing to his mother. First he confessed his failure, which was because of changes to the course programme—a chance occurrence, an injustice—and anyway all the great lawyers (he mentioned their names) had failed their exams. But he was hoping to take them again in November. So not having any time to lose, he would not go home this year. And in addition to the money for this term, would she send two hundred and fifty francs for law tuition, that would be extremely useful. All this was padded out with expressions of regret, sympathy, endearments, and protestations of filial affection.

Madame Moreau, expecting him the next day, was doubly cast down. She concealed her son's misfortune and told him 'to come anyway'. Frédéric did not give in. A quarrel ensued. But at the end of the week he nevertheless received the term's money with the sum for tutorials, and used it to buy a pair of pearl-grey trousers, a white felt hat, and a gold-topped cane.

When he was in possession of all these things he thought:

'Supposing it's just a silly idea of mine?'

And he was thrown into a terrible state of indecision.

To make up his mind whether to go to Madame Arnoux's he tossed a coin up in the air three times. Each time the auspices were favourable. So fate had decreed it. He took a cab to the Rue de Choiseul.

He climbed the stairs rapidly, pulled the bell cord. It didn't ring; he felt he was about to faint.

Then he tugged furiously at the heavy red silk bell-cord. A peal rang out, gradually faded and then... nothing. Frédéric was afraid.

He put his ear to the door. Not a sound! He put his eye to the key-hole and could see nothing in the hall but the tips of two reeds on the wall amongst the flowers on the wallpaper. Finally he was just about to turn and go when he changed his mind. This time he gave a little light pull. The door opened and in the doorway Arnoux appeared, dishevelled, red-faced, and annoyed.

'Well, well! What the devil brings you here? Come in!'

He invited him, not into the boudoir or his sitting room, but into the dining room where a bottle of champagne and two glasses could be seen; and in a brusque voice, he said:

'Did you have something you wanted to ask me, my friend?'

'No, nothing, nothing,' stammered the young man, racking his brains for a pretext for his visit.

Finally he said that he had come to find out news of him since Hussonnet had said he was in Germany.

'Nonsense!' said Arnoux. 'What a scatterbrain that boy is, always getting it wrong!'

In order to conceal his discomfiture Frédéric walked up and down. As he bumped into a chair leg he knocked over a parasol that was placed on it. The ivory handle broke.

'Oh, heavens!' he exclaimed. 'I'm so sorry, I've broken Madame Arnoux's parasol!'

At these words the dealer raised his head and gave an odd smile. Frédéric, taking the opportunity to talk about her, added timidly:

'Shall I not be seeing her?'

She had gone back to her home, to be near her sick mother.

He dared not question him about how long this absence might last. He made do with asking where Madame Arnoux's home was.

'Chartres. Does that surprise you?'

'Me? No, not in the least.'

After that they had nothing at all to say to each other. Arnoux, who had rolled a cigarette, walked around the table, puffing away. Frédéric, standing with his back to the stove, gazed at the walls, the shelves, the floor, and delightful images went through his mind, or rather before his eyes. Finally he took his leave.

A piece of scrunched-up newspaper was lying on the floor in the hall. Arnoux picked it up. And standing on tiptoe he stuffed it into the bell, to continue, as he said, his interrupted siesta. Then, grasping him by the hand:

'Please tell the concierge I'm not at home!'

And he closed the door behind him, banging it shut.

Frédéric went downstairs one step at a time. This failure discouraged him from risking any further attempts. Then three tedious months began. As he had no work, idleness increased his melancholy.

From his balcony he spent hours looking down at the river flowing between the grey quays, blackened in places where water from the drains dribbled into it; or at a pontoon for washerwomen moored against the bank, and where sometimes children had fun in the mud giving a poodle a bath. His eyes were continually drawn from the stone bridge of Notre-Dame away to the right and the three suspension bridges, to a clump of old trees on the Quai des Ormes, which looked like the limes in the port at Montereau. The Tour Saint-Jacques, the Hôtel de Ville, Saint-Gervais, Saint-Louis, Saint-Paul rose opposite amongst the tangle of roofs;—and the Spirit of Liberty on the July Column glittered in the east like a great golden star, while on the other side of the city the round dome of the Tuileries made a solid blue shape against the skyline. It was behind the dome, over there, that Madame Arnoux's house must be.

He went back into his room; then, stretched out on his couch, he gave himself up to his confused thoughts: his artistic projects, plans of action, visions of his future. At last, to get away from himself, he went out.

He strolled idly around the Quartier Latin, which was normally so busy, but at that time of year was empty, for the students had gone home to their families. The high walls of the colleges, which seemed higher in the silence, looked even more dismal than usual. You could hear all sorts of peaceful sounds, the beating of wings in cages, the hum of a lathe turning, a cobbler hammering. And the clothes-sellers, in the middle of the streets, looked questioningly, but in vain, up at every window. At the back of the cafés the women behind the bars yawned, between their full decanters; the newspapers remained unopened on the reading-room tables; in the laundry shops sheets were shaking gently in the little draughts of warm air. From time to time he stopped outside a display of books. An omnibus came down the boulevard, close to the pavement and made him turn round. He got as far as the Luxembourg and didn't go any further.

Sometimes, hoping for some entertainment, he made his way to the boulevards. After the dark, dank little streets he reached large deserted squares, dazzling with lights, where monuments cast jagged shadows on to the edge of the pavement. But soon there were more barrows and shops, and the crowd made him dizzy—especially on Sundays when, from the Bastille to the Madeleine, there was a huge flood of humanity on the asphalt in the dust, in a continual hum of noise. He felt sick at the sight of their vulgar faces, the idiotic remarks, the foolish satisfaction on their sweaty foreheads! However, the knowledge that he was worth more than these people lessened the fatigue he felt contemplating them.

He went to *L'Art industriel* every day. And, to find out when Madame Arnoux would return, he made lengthy enquiries about her mother. Arnoux's reply was always the same: she was still doing well. His wife, with her little girl, would be home next week. The longer she stayed away, the more anxious Frédéric became—so much so that Arnoux, touched by this great concern, took him out to dine five or six times.

Frédéric, in these long heart-to-heart conversations, realized that the art dealer was not an especially witty man and that Arnoux might notice his flagging interest; but here was an opportunity to return his hospitality a little.

So, keen to do things properly, he sold all his new clothes for about eighty francs to a second-hand clothes dealer; and, adding the hundred francs he still had left, he arrived at Arnoux's to take him out to dinner. Regimbart was there. They all went to the Trois-Frères-Provençaux.

The Citizen began by removing his frock coat, and, confident that the others would defer to him, wrote out the items he wanted on the menu. But it was no use him going into the kitchen to have a word with the chef, or down to the wine cellar, where he was familiar with every nook and cranny, or getting the proprietor to come up, and give him a good ticking-off, neither food nor wine nor service met with his approval! With each new dish, each different bottle, as soon as he had tasted the first mouthful, he put down his fork or pushed his glass away. Then, resting his arms on the tablecloth, he declared that it was impossible to dine out in Paris any longer! Finally, undecided about what to eat, Regimbart ordered 'a simple dish' of beans in oil, which were more or less all right and mollified him somewhat. Then he had a conversation with the waiter about former waiters at the Provençaux. What had become of Antoine? And that fellow Eugène?

And little Théodore who always served downstairs? In those days you really did eat exceptionally well and there were burgundies the like of which you'd never see again.

Then the talk was of how much land would fetch in the suburbs, a speculation of Arnoux's that was bound to be absolutely safe. In the meantime he was losing on the interest since he wouldn't sell at any price. Regimbart was finding someone for him. And the two gentlemen, with the help of a pencil, did their sums, right until dessert was over.

They left to have a coffee in a tavern in the Passage du Saumon, downstairs. Frédéric stood and watched interminable games of billiards, washed down with innumerable beers;—and he stayed there until midnight, not quite knowing why, through cowardice, stupidity, in the vague hope of something happening that might advance his love affair.

When would he see her again then? Frédéric was desperate. But one evening towards the end of November Arnoux said to him:

'You know my wife came back yesterday?'

The following day he went to see her at five o'clock.

He began by congratulating her on the recovery of her mother who had been so ill.

'Why, no! Who told you that?'

'Arnoux!'

'Ah!' she said lightly, and then added that she had first been very concerned about her, but her worries had now subsided.

She was sitting near the fire, in the upholstered armchair. He was on the couch, his hat between his knees; the conversation was painful, she continually let it lapse. He couldn't find a way of making the transition to talking about his feelings. But as he was complaining about studying pettifogging legal matters, she replied: 'Yes... I can well imagine... business...' and bowed her head, suddenly absorbed in her own thoughts.

He was longing to know what they were and indeed could not think about anything else. Twilight was gathering its shadows around them.

She got up, having to go out on some errand, then reappeared in a velvet cap and a black cloak edged with squirrel-fur. He plucked up his courage and offered to accompany her.

Outside, they could scarcely see. It was cold and a heavy stench of fog hung in the air, blotting out the fronts of the houses. Frédéric breathed it in with delight; for he could feel the shape of her arm through the softness of her cloak. And her hand, tightly enclosed in a chamois glove with two buttons, her little hand that he so wanted to cover with kisses, was resting on his sleeve. They swayed around a little on the slippery pavement; he felt that the two of them were being rocked by the wind in the centre of a cloud.

The sparkling lights on the boulevard brought him back to reality. The opportunity was good, time was running out. He gave himself until they reached the Rue Richelieu to declare his love. But she stopped short, almost immediately, outside a china shop and said:

'Here we are, thank you very much! Shall we see you on Thursday as usual?'

The dinners began again. The more he saw of Madame Arnoux, the more lovelorn he became.

The contemplation of this woman enervated him, like a perfume that was too strong. It went down into the depths of his being, and was becoming almost a general mode of feeling, a new way of living.

The prostitutes that he saw in the gaslight, the singers trilling their arias, the galloping horsewomen, the housewives on foot, the grisettes* at their windows, all these women reminded him of her, by reason of their resemblance or their violent dissimilarities. In the shop windows he looked at the cashmeres, the lace, the jewels hanging from the earrings, imagining them draped around her waist, sewn to her corsage, lighting up her black hair. On the flower stalls, the blooms existed only for her to choose as she passed by; in the shoemakers' window the little satin slippers with the swansdown trim seemed to be waiting only for her foot. All streets led to her house: cabs parked on their squares were only there in order to reach it more rapidly. Paris existed only in relation to Madame Arnoux, and all the voices of the great city resounded like an immense orchestra around her.

When he visited the Jardin des Plantes, the sight of a palm tree made him dream of faraway places. They were travelling together on the backs of dromedaries, on an elephant, under the awning, in the cabin of a yacht among blue archipelagos, or side by side on two mules with little bells, stumbling over broken columns in the grass. Sometimes he stopped in the Louvre in front of old paintings. And his love reached out into vanished centuries to embrace her, replaced the people in the paintings with her. Wearing a wimple, she prayed on her knees behind a leaded window. A Lady of Castile or Flanders, she sat in a starched ruff and whalebone bodice and large puff sleeves. Or she was coming down some grand staircase of porphyry in a brocade gown, surrounded by senators, under a canopy of ostrich feathers. At other times he dreamed of her in yellow silk trousers on cushions in a harem; and everything that was beautiful, the twinkling stars, certain melodies, a harmonious sentence, a silhouette, brought her abruptly and unconsciously into his mind.

As for trying to make her his mistress, he was sure that all attempts would be in vain.

One evening Dittmer arrived and kissed her on her forehead; Lovarias did likewise, saying:

'May I? As a friend?'

Frédéric faltered:

'I suppose we are all friends?'

'Not all old friends!' she rejoined.

Indirectly, she was keeping him at bay.

Anyway, what should he do? Tell her he loved her? She would be sure to rebuff him. Or else take offence and banish him from her house! He preferred to suffer anything rather than the terrible fate of not seeing her again.

He was jealous of the talents of pianists, the battle scars of soldiers. He hoped he might catch some dangerous disease and gain her sympathy in that manner.

One thing that surprised him was that he wasn't jealous of Arnoux. And he couldn't imagine her without her clothes on—so natural did her modesty seem, her sex remote in some mysterious shadowland.

However, he dreamed of the happiness of living with her, of calling her 'Tu', of slowly caressing the bands tied in her hair, or of kneeling with his arms around her waist and drinking up her soul with his eyes. To do that, he would have had to subvert Fate; and, incapable of action, cursing God and blaming himself for being a coward, he turned in his desire like a prisoner in a cell. He was choked with anguish the whole time. He sat for hours without moving, sometimes giving way to tears. And one day when he had not been able to hold them back, Deslauriers said:

'For heaven's sake, what's the matter with you?'

Frédéric 'was suffering from his nerves'. Deslauriers didn't believe a word of it. In the face of such pain, he felt his fondness for his friend revive, and comforted him. A man like him letting himself be brought down in that way, how silly was that? It was all very well when you were young, but when you were older it was a waste of time.

'My Frédéric has been ruined for me! I demand the old one back again. Waiter, same again! I liked him how he was. Come on now, smoke your pipe, old chap. Pull yourself together! You make me feel terrible.'

'It's true,' said Frédéric. 'I'm crazy!'

The clerk went on:

'Oh, my old troubadour, I know what's tormenting you! Your little heart? Admit it! But you lose one, you gain four! You have to console yourself for the virtuous ones with the ones who are not. Do you want me to introduce you to a few women? You only have to go to the Alhambra.' (It was a dance hall recently opened at the top of the Champs-Élysées, and which went bankrupt in its second season by premature overspending on this kind of establishment.) 'It seems you can have a good time there. Let's go! You can bring your friends if you like; I'll even let you bring Regimbart!'

Frédéric did not invite the Citizen. Deslauriers did without Sénécal. They took only Hussonnet and Cisy with Dussardier. And the same cab put all five of them down at the door of the Alhambra.

Two parallel arcades in the Moorish style stretched out on the left and right. The house wall took up all the far end and the fourth side, which was the restaurant, looked like a Gothic cloister with stained glass windows. A kind of Chinese pagoda sheltered the stage where the musicians played. The ground around it was covered in asphalt, and from a distance Venetian lanterns on poles made a crown of multicoloured lights over the dancers. Here and there a pedestal supported a stone basin, from which there rose a thin jet of water. Plaster statues could be seen among the leaves, Hebes* or Cupids, all sticky with oil paint. And the numerous paths laid out with very yellow sand and carefully raked made the garden seem much bigger than it actually was.

Students were walking with their mistresses; assistants from the fancy-goods shops strutted around with their canes between their fingers. Schoolboys smoked cheroots; old bachelors combed their dyed beards; there were English, Russians, people from South America, three Oriental gentlemen in tarbooshes.* *Lorettes*, grisettes, prostitutes had come, hoping to find a protector, a lover, a gold coin, or simply for the pleasure of dancing. And their tunic dresses of aquamarine, blue, cerise, or purple fluttered by in-between the laburnum and the lilac. Almost all the men wore checks, some had white trousers in spite of the coolness of the evening. The gas lamps were lighted.

Through his contacts with the fashion magazines and the small theatres Hussonnet knew a lot of women. He blew them kisses and from time to time left his friends and went to chat to them.

Deslauriers was jealous of his charming manners. He cynically accosted a tall blonde, dressed in yellow nankeen. After looking him up and down in a disapproving fashion, she said:

'No, I don't trust you, young man!' And turned on her heels.

He began all over again with a large brunette, who must have been insane, for at his first words she jumped up, and threatened to call the police if he carried on. Deslauriers gave a forced laugh; then, discovering a young woman sitting on her own under a lamp, he suggested a dance.

The musicians, perched on stage and posturing like monkeys, were blowing and scraping with wild enthusiasm. The conductor stood and beat time mechanically. There were crowds on the dance floor, everyone was having a good time. Ribbons on hats hung loose and brushed against ties, boots disappeared under skirts, everything leapt in rhythm. Deslauriers pressed the girl against him and, possessed by the cancan, thrashed about in the middle of the dancers like a huge marionette. Cisy and Dussardier continued their walk. The young aristocrat peered at the girls with his lorgnette but did not dare address them despite the clerk's encouragement, imagining that with those sorts of women there was always 'a man hiding in the wardrobe with a pistol who comes out to make you sign away your money'.

They returned to join Frédéric. Deslauriers wasn't dancing any more. They were all wondering what to do for the rest of the evening when Hussonnet cried:

'Look! There's the Marquise d'Amaëgui!'*

This was a pale woman with a turned-up nose, gloves up to her elbows, and great black curls hanging down her cheeks like the ears of a spaniel. Hussonnet said to her:

'Should we organize a little party at your place? An oriental orgy? Try and dig up a few of your friends for these French cavaliers? Well, what's stopping you? Are you waiting for your hidalgo?'

The Andalusian bowed her head. Knowing the not-exactly-luxurious life her friend led, she was afraid she would have to pay for the refreshments. At last, when she uttered the word 'money', Cisy offered five gold pieces, all he had with him. And so it was resolved. But Frédéric was no longer there.

He had thought he recognized Arnoux's voice, had caught sight of a woman's hat, and had dived rapidly into the nearby arbour. Mademoiselle Vatnaz was alone with Arnoux.

'I'm sorry, am I intruding?'

'Not in the least!' protested the dealer.

Frédéric, catching the last words of their conversation, thought he must have hurried along to the Alhambra to speak to Mademoiselle Vatnaz about an urgent matter. And probably Arnoux wasn't entirely happy about something, because he was saying to her in a worried tone:

'Are you positive?'

'Absolutely! We all love you! Oh, what a man!'

And she pouted at him, pushing out her full lips, so red they looked almost as if they were bleeding. But she had wonderful eyes, fawn-coloured with dots of gold in the iris, full of intelligence, love, and sensuality. They lit up the slightly yellow tone of her thin face. Arnoux seemed to enjoy her rebuffs. For his part he leaned over to her, saying:

'How sweet you are. Give me a kiss!'

She took hold of his two ears and planted a kiss on his forehead. At that moment the dancing stopped; and in the place of the conductor a young man appeared, good-looking but rather plump and with a waxy countenance. He had long black hair arranged rather in the manner of Christ, a velvet waistcoat with large gold palms on, and looked as proud as a peacock and stupid as a turkey cock. When he had greeted the audience he began a song. It was about a peasant describing his trip to the capital. The artiste spoke in the accent of Lower Normandy, and pretended to be drunk.

> 'Oh, such a good time, hee hee hee
> With that old harlot, gay Paree!'

This refrain aroused much enthusiastic stamping. Delmas, a 'soulful singer', was too shrewd to let his audience go. Quickly somebody passed him a guitar and he groaned out a romance entitled 'The Albanian Girl's Brother'.

The words reminded Frédéric of those sung by the man in rags on the boat between the paddle boxes. His eyes were involuntarily fixed on the hem of the dress spread out in front of him. After each couplet there was a long pause; and the breath of the wind in the trees resembled the sound of the waves.

Mademoiselle Vatnaz, brushing aside the branches of a privet which was obscuring her view of the stage, was staring at the singer with her nostrils flared, her eyes half-closed, as if lost in a solemn joy.

'Aha,' Arnoux said. 'I understand now why you are at the Alhambra tonight! You *like* Delmas, my dear.'

She did not want to admit it.

'Oh, don't be shy!'

And pointing to Frédéric:

'Is it because of him? You needn't worry—there is no one more discreet than this young man!'

The others, who were searching for their friend, entered the arbour. Hussonnet introduced them. Arnoux distributed cigars and treated everyone to sorbets.

Mademoiselle Vatnaz had blushed at the sight of Dussardier.

After a minute or two she got up and, extending her hand, said: 'Don't you remember me, Monsieur Auguste?'

'How do you know her?' Frédéric asked.

'We used to work for the same firm,' he said.

Cisy was tugging his sleeve, and they left; but they had scarcely vanished before Mademoiselle Vatnaz began to sing his praises. She even added that he had 'a genius for the heart'.

Then they chatted about Delmas, who might have some success as a mime in the theatre; and a muddled conversation ensued about Shakespeare, Censorship, Style, the People, the takings at the Porte Saint-Martin, Alexandre Dumas, Victor Hugo, and Dumersan.* Arnoux had known a lot of famous actresses; the young men leaned forward to hear what he was saying. But his words were drowned out by the din from the band. And as soon as a quadrille or a polka was over they all made for the tables and gaily summoned the waiter. Bottles of beer and fizzy lemonade popped amongst the greenery, women screeched like hens; occasionally two men wanted to start a fight. A thief was arrested.

When the galop was played, the dancers crowded into the paths. Red in the face, puffing and panting, they went by in a rush that lifted the tailcoats and the skirts. The trombones roared louder. The beat quickened. From behind the medieval cloister came the crackle and bang of firecrackers. Catherine wheels began to turn. For a moment Bengal lights illuminated all the garden emerald green; at the final rocket the crowd gave a long sigh.

They drifted away. A cloud of gunpowder hung in the air. Frédéric and Deslauriers were edging along through the crowd when they were brought up short by a surprising sight. Martinon was getting change at the cloakroom, and he was with an unattractive woman of about fifty, marvellously attired and of unclear social standing.

'That fellow', Deslauriers remarked, 'is not as straightforward as you might think. But wherever is Cisy?'

Dussardier pointed to the eating house, where they saw that child of the nobility with a bowl of punch before him, in the company of a pink hat.

Hussonnet, who had been absent for five minutes, reappeared at the same moment.

A girl was hanging from his arm, loudly calling him '*mon petit chat*'.

'No!' he was saying. 'Not in public! Call me Vicomte instead! That gives me the air of a cavalier, Louis XIII and velvet boots, I like that! Yes, my friends, an old flame! Isn't she sweet?' He chucked her under the chin. 'Say hello to these gentlemen, they are all heirs to a peerage, every one of them! I keep in with them so that they'll propose me for ambassador.'

'You are quite mad!' sighed Mademoiselle Vatnaz.

She asked Dussardier to see her home.

Arnoux saw them go and then, turning to Frédéric:

'Is La Vatnaz to your liking? And by the way, you are not very candid in such matters. I believe you keep your love affairs secret.'

Frédéric went pale and swore he was keeping nothing secret.

'It's just that you are not known to have a mistress,' went on Arnoux.

Frédéric wanted to pluck a name out of the blue. But someone might tell *her*. He replied that that was correct, he didn't have a mistress.

The dealer scolded him.

'You missed your chance this evening! Why didn't you do like the others and go with a woman?'

'Well, and what about yourself?' said Frédéric, becoming impatient at his persistence.

'Oh, it's different for me, my boy. I am going back to my wife!'
He called a cab and disappeared.

The two friends walked off. An east wind was blowing. Neither said anything. Deslauriers was sorry he hadn't made an impression on the director of a journal, and Frédéric was plunged deeper into melancholy. He finally declared the dance hall stupid.

'Whose fault is that? If you hadn't left us for your Arnoux...'

'Bah! It wouldn't have made any difference!'

But the clerk had his own view. If you wanted something badly enough you could get it.

'But you yourself, just now...'

'As if I cared!' Deslauriers said, stopping his friend from alluding to it. 'I'm not going to get entangled with women.'

And he ranted on about their affectations and stupidity. In short, he didn't care for them.

'Don't pretend!' Frédéric said.

Deslauriers said no more. Then, suddenly:

'Do you want to bet a hundred francs that I can't get off with the first woman who comes along?'

'Yes, you're on!'

The first one who came along turned out to be a hideously ugly beggarwoman, and they were thinking luck was not on their side when in the middle of the Rue de Rivoli they caught sight of a tall girl carrying a small cardboard box.

Deslauriers drew level with her beneath the arcades. She turned abruptly in the direction of the Tuileries, and soon reached the Place du Carrousel; she glanced to right and left. She ran after a cab; Deslauriers caught her up. He walked beside her, talking animatedly. At last she took his arm and they continued along the banks of the Seine. Then, level with Châtelet, they walked up and down the pavement for a good twenty minutes like two sailors pacing the deck. But suddenly they crossed the Pont au Change, to the Marché aux Fleurs, the Quai Napoléon. Frédéric went into the entrance behind them. Deslauriers gave him to understand that he would be in the way, and that he should copy him.

'How much have you got left?'

'Two hundred-sou coins!'

'That's enough then. Goodnight!'

Frédéric was astonished at the success of the practical joke. 'He's having me on,' he thought. 'Supposing I went back?' Deslauriers would perhaps imagine he was jealous of his affair. 'As though I didn't have one myself, and one that's a hundred times rarer, nobler, stronger?' A kind of rage drove him on. He arrived at Madame Arnoux's door.

None of the windows outside belonged to her rooms. Despite that, he stayed staring at the facade as though he thought he might crack the walls with the force of his gaze. Now, he supposed, she must be resting, peaceful as a sleeping flower, with her beautiful black hair spread out on the lace on her pillows, her lips half-closed, her head on her arm.

Arnoux's head appeared. He drew back to escape this vision.

Deslauriers's advice came into his mind. It horrified him. He wandered aimlessly about the streets.

When a pedestrian approached he tried to make out his face. From time to time a ray of light passed between his legs, described a wide arc on the pavement; and a man would rise up out of the shadows with basket and lantern. In certain places the wind shook a metal chimney stack. Distant sounds rose and mingled with the buzzing in his head, and he thought he could hear the muffled ritornello of a quadrille. This feeling of intoxication was sustained by the motion of walking. He found himself on the Pont de la Concorde.

Then he remembered that evening of the previous winter before last—when, leaving her house for the first time, he had been obliged to stop, so quickly had his heart been beating in the grip of hope. All those hopes were dead now!

Dark clouds passed rapidly across the face of the moon. He gazed at it, dreaming of the grandeur of space, the misery of existence, the nothingness of life. Daylight came. His teeth were chattering; and, half asleep, wet with fog and full of tears, he wondered why he should not end it all. One move would be enough. The weight of his forehead dragged him forward, he saw his body floating in the water. Frédéric leaned over. The parapet was rather wide, and it was because of weariness that he did not try to climb over.

Terror seized hold of him. He got back to the boulevards and collapsed on a bench. He was wakened by the police, who supposed he'd been 'living it up'.

He started walking again. But as he was famished and all the restaurants were shut, he went to have supper in an eating place in Les

Halles. After that, judging it to be still too early, he wandered the streets around the Hôtel de Ville until a quarter past eight.

Deslauriers had packed his woman off a long time before, and was writing at his table in the middle of his room. Towards four, Monsieur de Cisy entered.

The previous evening, thanks to Dussardier, he had got himself a lady-friend. And he had even taken her back to her door in a cab with her husband, and she had arranged to meet him. He was coming away from that meeting now. And she wasn't a woman with a name for that sort of thing!

'What do you want me to do about it?' Frédéric asked.

At that the nobleman was deliberately evasive; he talked about Mademoiselle Vatnaz, the Andalusian girl, and all the rest. At last in a very roundabout way he gave the reason for his visit. Trusting his friend to be discreet, he had come for his help in doing something after which he would be able to consider himself, once and for all, a man. And Frédéric did not refuse. He related the story to Deslauriers, without telling the truth about his personal involvement.

The clerk thought 'he was doing all right now'. This deference to his advice increased his good mood.

It was because of this good humour that he had seduced, on the very first day, Mademoiselle Clémence Daviou, who embroidered gold braid on military uniforms, the sweetest person there ever was, slim as a reed, with blue eyes always wide with astonishment. The clerk abused her innocence, going so far as to make her believe he had the Legion of Honour; he put a red ribbon on his coat when they were together, but took it off in public, so as not to embarrass his employer, he said. He generally kept her at a distance, allowed himself to be caressed like a pasha, and called her a 'daughter of the people', as a joke. Each time she came she brought him little bunches of violets. Frédéric would not have wanted a woman like that.

However, when they walked out together arm in arm, to go to a private room at Pinson's or Barillot's, he felt a peculiar sadness. Frédéric did not realize how much he had made Deslauriers suffer each Thursday for the last twelve months when he brushed his nails before going to dine in the Rue de Choiseul!

One evening when, from the height of his balcony he had just watched them leave, he saw Hussonnet a little way off, on the Pont de l'Arcole. The bohemian began to signal to him and when Frédéric had come down his five flights of stairs, he said:

'Now here's a thing: Madame Arnoux's name day is next Saturday, the twenty-fourth.'

'How is that possible, since her name is Marie?'*

'Angèle as well... And what does it matter? They are celebrating in their country house in Saint-Cloud. I've been told to give you notice of it. You'll find transport at three o'clock at the Journal. So it's agreed then? Sorry to disturb you, I must dash!'

Frédéric had scarcely turned before his porter handed him a letter:

Monsieur and Madame Dambreuse request the pleasure of Monsieur F. Moreau's company at dinner next Saturday, the twenty-fourth. RSVP.

'Too late,' he thought.

Nevertheless he showed the letter to Deslauriers who cried:

'At last! But what's wrong? You don't look very pleased.'

Frédéric, after some hesitation, said he'd had another invitation for the same day.

'Do me the pleasure of giving the Rue de Choiseul a miss! And don't be so stupid! I'll write an answer for you if you don't want to.'

And the clerk wrote an acceptance in the third person.

Since he had never viewed society except through the fever of his ambition, he imagined it to be an artificial creature, functioning according to the laws of mathematics. A dinner in town, meeting a man in a good position, the smile of a pretty woman could, by a series of actions, each logically leading to the next, bring about amazing results. Some Parisian salons were like those machines which take matter in its most basic form and mould it into something a hundred times more precious. He believed in courtesans advising diplomats, in rich marriages obtained through intrigue, in the genius of criminals, in the malleability of fate in the hands of the strong. In short, his opinion was that going to see the Dambreuses would be extremely useful and he was so eloquent on the subject that Frédéric no longer knew what he should do.

It was nevertheless important to give Madame Arnoux a present, seeing it was her name day. He had the idea of giving her a parasol, naturally, in order to make amends for his clumsiness. He found one in grey silk with a little carved ivory handle which had just arrived from China. But it cost a hundred and seventy-five francs and he didn't have a centime. Indeed he was already living on credit from his allowance for the following term. However, he wanted it, he would have it, and in spite of his reluctance to do so, he asked Deslauriers.

Deslauriers replied that he had no money.

'I need it,' Frédéric said. 'I need it badly.'

And when his friend repeated his excuse, he lost his temper.

'You might occasionally...'

'What?'

'Oh, nothing!'

The clerk had understood. He got together the sum in question from the money he had put aside and when he had doled it out coin by coin:

'I'm not asking for a receipt since I am living off you.'

Frédéric threw his arms round him, with many protestations of affection. Deslauriers remained impassive. Then the next day when he saw the parasol on the piano:

'Oh, so that's what it was for!'

'Perhaps I'll send it to her,' Frédéric said weakly.

Fortune was on his side, for that evening he received a card with a black border: Madame Dambreuse, announcing the death of an uncle, apologized for postponing the pleasure of making his acquaintance.

He was already at the offices of the Journal by two o'clock. Instead of waiting to drive him there in his cab, Arnoux had left the previous day, giving in to an urgent need for fresh air.

Every year when the first leaves appeared, he rose early on several successive days and made lengthy treks across the fields, drank milk in the farms, flirted with the village girls, asked about the harvests, and brought back lettuce plants in his kerchief. In the end, realizing an old dream of his, he had bought a house in the country.

While Frédéric was talking to the assistant, Mademoiselle Vatnaz appeared and was disappointed not to see Arnoux. He would perhaps be away for some days yet. He advised her to go over; she could not. Write him a letter? She was afraid the letter would go astray. Frédéric offered to take it himself. She wrote a rapid note and made him swear to deliver it when nobody else was around.

Forty minutes later he arrived at Saint-Cloud.

The house, a hundred yards beyond the bridge, was halfway up a hill. The garden walls were concealed by two rows of lime trees, and a wide lawn stretched down to the river. The gate in the railings was open, Frédéric went in.

Arnoux was stretched out on the grass playing with a litter of kittens. This occupation seemed to amuse him greatly. The letter from Mademoiselle Vatnaz roused him from his torpor.

'Oh, damnation! How annoying! She's right—I'll have to go back.'

Then having stuffed the missive into his pocket he took pleasure in showing Frédéric round. He showed him everything, the stables, the outhouses, the kitchen. The sitting room on the right was on the Paris side, and looked out on a leafy arbour covered with clematis. Above their heads there was a sudden singing. It was Madame Arnoux, believing herself to be alone. She was practising scales, trills, arpeggios. There were long-drawn-out notes which seemed to be suspended in the air. Others cascaded down like drops from a fountain. And her voice coming through the shutters cut the great silence and rose into the blue sky.

She stopped abruptly when two neighbours, Monsieur and Madame Oudry, arrived.

Then she herself appeared at the top of the steps and as she was going down he saw her foot. She was wearing small open-toed shoes in gold leather, with three cross-straps that made a pattern of gold stripes on her stockings.

The guests arrived. Apart from Maître Lefaucheux, a lawyer, they were the same people as on Thursdays. Everyone had brought a present: Dittmer a Syrian scarf, Rosenwald a song album, Burrieu a watercolour, Sombaz a caricature of himself, and Pellerin a charcoal drawing, representing a kind of *danse macabre*, a hideous fantasy of mediocre quality. Hussonnet had absolved himself from giving a present.

Frédéric waited till last to give her his.

She thanked him warmly. Then he said:

'Well, it was practically a debt I owed you! I was so cross!'

'What about?' she replied. 'I don't understand!'

'Dinner's served!' said Arnoux, catching hold of his arm; then, whispering in his ear:

'Not very quick on the uptake, are you!'

Nothing was so delightful as the dining room, decorated in aquamarine. At one end a stone nymph dipped her toe in a basin in the shape of a shell. Through the open windows the whole garden could be seen, with its long lawn and an old Scots pine, three-quarters stripped of its needles, on one side. Here and there the lawn was broken up by a clump of flowers. And beyond the river, in a wide semicircle, stretched the Bois de Boulogne, Neuilly, Sèvres, Meudon. Immediately in front of the railings a little sailing boat was tacking to and fro.

First the conversation was of the view and then of landscape in general. And the discussions were just beginning when Arnoux ordered his servant to harness the cab for about nine-thirty. A letter from his cashier called him back to Paris.

'Would you like me to come with you?' asked Madame Arnoux.

'Of course!' And making her an elaborate bow: 'As you are aware, Madame, it is not possible to live without you!'

They all complimented her on having such a good husband.

'Oh, it's because I am not alone!' she replied sweetly, indicating her little daughter.

Then, the conversation having reverted to painting, they spoke about a Ruysdael,* which Arnoux expected to fetch a considerable price, and Pellerin asked him if it was true that the famous Saul Mathias of London had come last month to offer him twenty-three thousand francs for it.

'He did indeed!' And, turning to Frédéric: 'That is in fact the gentleman I was showing around the Alhambra the other day, very much against my will, I assure you, for these Englishmen are not much fun to be with!'

Frédéric, suspecting there was some female intrigue in the letter from Mademoiselle Vatnaz, admired Sieur Arnoux's ease in finding a plausible means to get away. But this new lie, absolutely uncalled-for, made him open his eyes wide.

The dealer added in a casual tone:

'What's his name then, that tall young friend of yours?'

'Deslauriers,' Frédéric said quickly.

And to repair the wrongs he felt he had done to him, he boasted about his superior intelligence.

'Oh really? But he doesn't seem such a good fellow as your haulier friend?'

Frédéric cursed Dussardier. She would think he kept company with common people.

Then they talked about the improvements to the capital, the new districts, and the worthy Oudry happened to mention Monsieur Dambreuse as being one of the most important speculators.

Frédéric, seizing the chance to shine, said he was an acquaintance of his. But Pellerin started ranting about tradesmen; he couldn't see any difference between selling candles or money. Then Rosenwald and Burrieu discussed porcelain. Arnoux chatted about gardening with Madame Oudry while Sombaz, a farceur of the old school, was busy teasing her husband. He called him Odry, like the actor, and declared he must be a descendant of the Oudry who painted dogs, for the animal bump* was visible on his forehead. He even tried to feel his skull, but Oudry wouldn't allow it on account of his wig. And dessert came to an end amid peals of laughter.

When they had finished their coffee and smoked under the limes, and strolled several times round the garden, they went for a walk along the river.

The company halted in front of a fisherman who was cleaning eels in a shed selling fish. Mademoiselle Marthe wanted to see them. He emptied his box on to the grass. And the little girl threw herself on to her knees to catch them, laughed in delight, and shouted in fright. They all slithered away. Arnoux paid for them.

Then he took it into his head to go for a boat trip.

One side of the horizon began to pale while on the other side the sky turned orange, spreading wide, more violet-coloured at the peaks of the hills, which had grown completely dark. Madame Arnoux was sitting on a rock, with the fiery colours blazing behind her. The others were wandering here and there. Hussonnet down below on the bank was skimming pebbles across the water.

Arnoux came back, with a large old rowing-boat. Against all good advice, he piled his guests in. It began to sink; they all had to climb out.

The candles were already lit in the drawing room decorated throughout in blue-green, with crystal candelabra along the walls. Old Madame Oudry was quietly falling asleep in an armchair and the others were listening to Monsieur Lefaucheux discoursing on the glories of the Bar. Madame Arnoux was by herself next to the window. Frédéric went over to her.

They chatted about the subjects under discussion. She admired people who could talk well. He preferred the achievement of those who could write. But, she went on, it must be a greater pleasure to appeal to crowds directly, to see one's own feelings influencing theirs. This kind of success did not tempt Frédéric at all as he had no ambition.

'Oh, why not?' she said. 'You have to have a little!'

They were standing close to each other in the window recess. The night stretched out before them like a vast black veil, studded with silver. It was the first time they had not talked about trivialities. He even got to know what she liked and disliked: certain perfumes made her feel nauseous, history books interested her, she believed in dreams.

He broached the subject of love. She bemoaned the disasters of passion, but was disgusted by hypocrisy and corruption. And this righteousness of spirit accorded so well with the perfect beauty of her face that the one seemed to derive from the other.

Sometimes she smiled, and her eyes dwelled for a moment on him. Then he felt her looks go deep into his soul like those bright rays from the sun that penetrate the depths of the water. He loved her unconditionally, absolutely, without hope of any return. And in this silent elation, which was like a leap of gratitude, he wanted to shower kisses on her brow. Meanwhile within he felt rapt away by something stronger than himself. It was a desire for self-sacrifice, the need to devote himself immediately to someone, all the stronger because he could not assuage it.

He did not leave with the others, nor did Hussonnet. They were supposed to go back in the cab. And the cab was waiting at the foot of the steps when Arnoux came down into the garden to pick some roses. Then the bunch was tied with string, as the stems were all different lengths. He rummaged in his pockets which were full of papers, took one out at random, and after wrapping the flowers, finished off his work with a large pin and presented it to his wife with a certain emotion.

'Here you are, darling, I am sorry I forgot you!'

But she gave a little cry; the pin, clumsily placed, had hurt her and she went up to her room again. They waited almost a quarter of an hour for her. She finally reappeared, and taking Marthe with her, jumped into the cab.

'What about your flowers?' asked Arnoux.

'No, no! Don't bother!'

Frédéric ran off to get them; she shouted after him: 'I don't want them!'

But he soon retrieved them, saying he had just put them back in the paper, for he had found the flowers on the ground. She shoved them down the leather pocket by the seat and they left.

Frédéric, seated next to her, noticed she was shaking all over. Then after crossing the bridge, as Arnoux turned left, she cried:

'No you've gone wrong! It's that way, to the right!'

She seemed irritated; everything annoyed her. Finally when Marthe had closed her eyes, she pulled the flowers out and flung them out of the window, then caught hold of Frédéric's arm, signalling to him with her other hand never to mention it.

After that she pressed her handkerchief to her mouth and did not move.

The other two on the front seat were talking about printing, and subscribers. Arnoux, who was driving and not paying attention, got lost in the middle of the Bois de Boulogne. They set off down side-tracks. The horse was going at walking pace. The branches of the trees brushed against the hood. All Frédéric could see of Madame Arnoux were her two eyes in the shadow. Marthe was sprawling across her and he was holding her head up.

'You'll get tired,' said her mother.

He replied:

'Oh no, not at all!'

Clouds of dust rose slowly. They were going through Auteuil. All the houses were shut up. Here and there a street lamp lit the corner of a wall, then they went back into the dark again. Once he noticed her weeping.

Was it remorse? Desire? What was it? This pain, which he had not known about, affected him as though he himself was suffering. Now between them there was a sort of complicity; and he said to her as tenderly as he could:

'Are you unwell?'

'Yes, a little,' she said.

The cab continued to roll along, and the honeysuckle and lilac spilled over garden walls, sending out wafts of delicious perfume. The numerous folds of her dress covered her feet. It seemed to him he was wholly in connection with her through the child's body stretched out between them. He bent over the little girl and pushing back her pretty chestnut hair, kissed her gently on her forehead.

'How kind you are!' Madame Arnoux exclaimed.

'Why?'

'Because you love children.'

'Not all of them!'

He didn't say any more but stretched out his left hand on his side and allowed it to remain open—imagining that she might do the same and that he would touch hers. Then he was ashamed of himself and withdrew it.

Soon they reached the cobbled streets. The cab picked up speed, there were more and more gas lamps, they had arrived in Paris. Hussonnet jumped down outside the Garde-Meuble.* Frédéric waited until they had arrived in the courtyard. Then he hid at the corner of the Rue de Choiseul and saw Arnoux slowly* going back up the boulevard.

The very next day he began to work as hard as he possibly could.

He could picture himself at the assizes, on a winter's evening, making his closing speech; the jury was pale, the audience breathless and almost bursting through the partitions of the courtroom. He had been speaking for the last four hours, summing up all his arguments, finding new ones and feeling at every sentence, every word and gesture, the blade of the guillotine, suspended behind him, lifting. Then he was at the tribune in the Chamber, an orator carrying the salvation of a whole people on his lips, overwhelming his adversaries with his prosopopeia, crushing them with one riposte, with thunder and music in his voice, ironic, pathetic, passionate, sublime. She would be somewhere there in the middle of the crowd, hiding tears of enthusiasm beneath her veil. They would meet afterwards; and no disappointments, calumny, or insults would touch him just so long as she said: 'Oh, that was beautiful!' and over his forehead lightly passed her hands.

These images shone bright as lighthouses on his horizon. His excited intellect became more agile and more robust. He shut himself away until August and passed his last exam.

Deslauriers, who had had such trouble drilling him through the second at the end of December and the third in February, was amazed at how hard he worked. Then the old hopes returned. In ten years, Frédéric had to be a deputy. In fifteen, a minister—well why not? With the inheritance that would come to him quite soon, he would be able to found a newspaper. That would be the start; then later, they would see. As for him, his ambition was to get a chair at the School of

Law. And he defended his thesis for the doctorate so expertly that it earned the compliments of the professors.

Three days after that, Frédéric defended his. Before going on holiday he hit on the idea of having a picnic to round off the Saturday get-togethers.

He was very cheerful. Madame Arnoux was now with her mother in Chartres. But he would see her soon and would end up becoming her lover.

Deslauriers, who had been admitted the very same day to the Orsay debating chamber,* had given a much-lauded speech. Though normally a sober man, he got drunk and said to Dussardier at dessert:

'You're an honest fellow! When I'm rich I'll make you my manager.'

They were all in a good mood. Cisy would not finish his law degree; Martinon was going to continue his probationary period in the provinces where he would be appointed assistant public prosecutor; Pellerin was preparing to paint a big picture called *The Spirit of the Revolution*. Next week Hussonnet was going to read the summary of a play to the director of the Délassements,* and was sure it would be accepted:

'Everyone knows I'm good at putting a play together. And as far as feelings are concerned, I've been knocking around long enough to know about them; and as for witticisms, well that's my job!'

He made a leap, landed on his hands, and walked for a little way around the table, his legs in the air.

This childish behaviour did not cheer up Sénécal. He had just been driven out of his boarding house for thrashing the son of an aristocrat. He was getting poorer, and started criticizing the social order, cursing the rich. And he poured it all out to Regimbart who was more and more disillusioned, melancholy, disgusted. The Citizen turned towards questions of finance now and accused the Camarilla of wasting millions in Algeria.*

As he couldn't sleep unless he had stopped by at Alexandre's eating house, he vanished at eleven o'clock. The others retired later. And Frédéric, saying farewell to Hussonnet, learned that Madame Arnoux was supposed to have returned the night before.

So he went to the Messageries to change his reservation for the next day, and towards six in the evening went to her house. Her return had been put off for a week, the concierge told him. Frédéric dined alone, then wandered along the boulevards.

Trails of pink clouds, like a long scarf, floated out beyond the roofs. Shopkeepers were beginning to wind up their awnings. The water-carts sprayed rain on the dust and an unexpected freshness mingled with the smells coming from the cafés, showing through their open doors, between silverware and gilt, sheaves of flowers reflected in the tall mirrors. The crowd moved along at a leisurely pace. In the middle of the pavement groups of men were chatting, and women went by with a softness in their eyes and that camellia-like complexion they have when exhausted by very hot weather. Vast possibilities opened up and enveloped the houses around him. Never had Paris seemed so beautiful. He could see his future as nothing but an unending series of years filled with love.

He came to a halt outside the theatre in the Porte Saint-Martin, and looked at the poster. And, for want of something to do, he bought a ticket.

They were putting on an old *féerie*.* There weren't many in the audience and up in the gods daylight came through the small windows in little blue squares, while the footlights—which were small oil lamps—formed one glowing yellow line. The stage was set to represent a Peking slave market, with little bells and drums, sultans' wives, pointed bonnets, and bad puns. When the curtain came down he wandered around the foyer on his own and admired a large green landau at the bottom of the steps harnessed with two white horses held by a coachman in knee-breeches.

He was going back to his seat when upstairs in the first box in the circle a lady and gentleman came in. The husband had a pale face, with a strip of grey beard on his chin, wore an officer's rosette, and had that icy demeanour that diplomats are said to have.

His wife, at least twenty years younger than him, neither tall nor short, ugly nor pretty, wore her blonde hair swept up in a bun in the English fashion; her dress had a flat bodice and she held a wide fan of black lace. For anyone of this standing in society to come to a play at this time of the year, one had to assume it was just by chance or because of the boredom of spending their evening alone together. The lady was chewing her fan, and the gentleman was yawning. Frédéric was trying to recall where he had seen that face before.

During the next interval he met them both as he was crossing a corridor. At his vague gesture of greeting, Monsieur Dambreuse recognized him, stopped him, and apologized straight away for his unforgiveable negligence. This was an allusion to the numerous visiting cards Frédéric had sent, in accordance with Deslauriers's advice. But he was confused as to which generation of students Frédéric belonged to, supposing him to be in the second year of his law degree. He was envious of his going to the country. Himself, he needed a rest, but business kept him in Paris.

Madame Dambreuse, leaning on his arm, inclined her head slightly, and her animated expression contrasted with her bored look a little while before.

'Yet there are very entertaining things to do here,' she said at her husband's last remark. 'How ridiculous this play is! Don't you think so, Monsieur?' And all three stood chatting about the theatre and the new plays.

Frédéric, used to the grimacings of women from the provinces, had never seen in any other woman such an easy manner or the refined simplicity which the naive take to be the expression of an instant sympathy.

He must call as soon as they got back; Monsieur Dambreuse asked to be remembered to Père Roque.

Frédéric made sure to tell Deslauriers about this meeting when he got home.

'Excellent!' replied the clerk. 'And don't let your maman get her way with you. Come back immediately.'

The day after his arrival, Madame Moreau took her son into the garden after they'd had lunch.

She said she was happy to see him in a good position since they were not as well-off as they had thought. The land was bringing in very little. The farmers were not paying up. She had even found it necessary to sell the carriage. In brief she told him what their situation was.

When she had been in financial difficulties in the early days of her widowhood, Monsieur Roque, a clever man, had lent her money; those debts had been renewed and prolonged against her wishes. He had come to demand repayment, suddenly. And she had accepted his conditions, letting him have the farm at Presles for a derisory sum. Ten years later, she lost her capital in the collapse of her bank in Melun. Having a horror of mortgages and wishing to keep up appearances that might influence her son's future career, when Père Roque turned up again, once more she listened to him. But now she was rid of him. The long and short of it was that they had about ten thousand francs a year left, of which two thousand three hundred were his, as his total inheritance.

'It can't be true!' cried Frédéric.

She shook her head, indicating that it was only too true.

But would his uncle not leave him something?

It was far from certain.

And they walked round the garden in silence. Finally she drew him to her and in a voice choked with tears said:

'Oh, my poor boy! I have had to abandon so many dreams.'

He sat down on a bench in the shade of the tall acacia tree.

Her advice was to take a position as clerk at Maître Prouharam's, the lawyer, who would leave him the practice; then, if he did well, he would be able to sell it later, and make a good marriage.

Frédéric was no longer listening. Absently he was looking over the hedge into the other garden, opposite.

A little girl of about twelve with red hair was there on her own. She had made herself earrings out of rowan berries. Her grey cotton blouse left her shoulders bare, rather bronzed by the sun. Her white skirt was spotted with jam stains; and there was a kind of grace, like a wild animal's, about her body, both nervous and slight. The presence of an unknown person must have astonished her, for she had stopped abruptly with her watering can in hand, flashing him a look with eyes that were a limpid turquoise.

'That's Monsieur Roque's daughter,' said Madame Moreau. 'He has just married his housekeeper and made his child legitimate.'

# VI

RUINED, robbed, done for!

He had stayed sitting on the bench, as though in shock. He cursed his fate, wished he could hit someone; and to make his despair even worse he felt a kind of insult, a disgrace weighing him down. For Frédéric had imagined that his patrimony would be as much as fifteen thousand francs one day and in a roundabout way he had given the Arnouxes to understand that this was the case. So he was going to look like a braggart, a laughing stock, a jumped-up little nobody who had wormed his way into their home in the hope of getting something out of it! And Madame Arnoux—how could he see her again now?

In any case that was quite impossible, since he had only three thousand francs' income! He could not remain as a lodger on the fourth floor, have the porter as his servant, and go visiting with shabby black gloves going blue at the fingertips, a greasy hat, and the same frock coat all year. No, no, never! And yet life was unbearable without her. Lots of people without a fortune managed to live well. Deslauriers for one. And he thought he was cowardly to attach such importance to trivialities. Poverty would perhaps increase his abilities a hundredfold. He felt inspired, thinking about the great men who worked in their attic rooms. A soul like Madame Arnoux's would surely be moved by that sight and she would take pity on him. So this catastrophe was a stroke of luck after all. Like the earthquakes in which treasures are uncovered, it had revealed to him the secret riches of his character. But there was only one place in the world where they could be shown for what they were worth: Paris! For in his mind art, science, and love (those three faces of God, as Pellerin would have said) belonged only to the capital.

That evening he told his mother he was going back. Madame Moreau was surprised and indignant. It was a madness, absurd. He would do better to follow her advice: stay at home near her and work in a legal practice. Frédéric shrugged:

'For heaven's sake!'—and felt insulted by this proposition.

So the worthy lady tried another tactic. In a pathetic voice and with a catch in her throat she began to tell him how lonely she was, that she was getting old, she had made so many sacrifices. Now she was more unhappy than ever, he was abandoning her. Then, alluding to her future demise:

'Be patient a while, for goodness' sake! You'll be a free man soon!'

These complaints were repeated twenty times a day, for three months. And at the same time the comforts of home were spoiling him. He was happy to sleep in a softer bed, have napkins without holes in. So, tired and enervated, finally overcome by the terrible seductions of a quiet life, Frédéric allowed himself to be taken to Mâitre Prouharam's.

He showed neither knowledge nor aptitude. He had been considered up to that point to be a young man of great ability who would bring glory to the department. Everyone was disappointed.

First he said to himself: 'I must tell Madame Arnoux about it.' And for a whole week in his head he wrote her dithyrambic letters and short notes in a sublime, lapidary style. The fear of revealing his situation held him back. Then he thought that it would be better to write to her husband. Arnoux was a man of the world and would understand.

Finally after hesitating for a fortnight:

'Too bad, I mustn't see them again. Let them forget all about me! At least I shan't have come down in her estimation! She'll think I'm dead and will miss me... perhaps.'

Since it cost him very little to make extravagant resolutions, he swore never to return to Paris and not even to enquire about Madame Arnoux.

However, he missed it all, even the smell of gas and the rattling of the buses. He thought constantly about all the words she had ever said to him, her tone of voice, the light in her eyes. And, considering himself a dead man, he did absolutely nothing at all.

He got up very late and from his window watched the wagoners go by. The first six months were especially dreadful.

On some days, however, he felt a sort of indignation with himself. Then he would go out. He went off into the fields that were half covered in winter by the Seine flooding. They were divided by lines of poplars. Here and there rose a little bridge. He would wander around till evening, kicking through the yellow leaves, breathing in the mist, jumping over ditches. As his blood beat faster, the longing for violent action swept over him. He wished he could be a trapper in America, serve a pasha in the East, sign up to be a sailor; and he poured out his melancholy in long letters to Deslauriers.

The latter was doing his utmost to make a name for himself. His friend's cowardly behaviour and his everlasting jeremiahs struck him as stupid. Soon their letters dwindled to almost nothing. Frédéric had given all the furniture to Deslauriers who was keeping his room. His mother spoke to him about it from time to time. Finally one day he admitted that he had given it all away and she was scolding him, when he received a letter.

'Whatever's the matter?' she said. 'You're trembling.'

'It's nothing,' Frédéric replied.

Deslauriers informed him that he had taken Sénécal in and for the last two weeks they had been living together. Sénécal was now comfortably at home among things that had come from Arnoux's shop!

He might sell them, make remarks, joke about them. Frédéric felt hurt to the depths of his being. He went up to his room. He wanted to die.

His mother called him. It was to consult him about planting something in the garden.

The garden, set out in the English style, was cut through the centre by a wooden fence and half of it belonged to Père Roque who owned another, for vegetables, down by the river. Since their quarrel the two neighbours avoided being there at the same time. But since Frédéric had come home, the old man had begun to appear more often and to be excessively polite to Madame Moreau's son. He pitied him for living in a small town. One day he told him that Monsieur Dambreuse had been asking after him. Another time he held forth about how it was customary in Champagne to inherit a title through the mother.

'In those days you would have been a lord, because your mother was called de Fouvens. And say what you like, it's quite something to have an aristocratic name! After all,' he added, with a sly look, 'it's up to the Keeper of the Seals.'*

This pretension to aristocracy was singularly at odds with his appearance. As he was small, his long brown frock coat made his upper body look longer. When he took off his cap he had an almost feminine face with an extremely pointed nose. His yellow hair resembled a wig. He made deep bows to everyone, brushing against the walls.

Until he was fifty, he had been happy with the services of Catherine, a woman from Lorraine, the same age as him and very scarred by smallpox. But around 1834 he brought back a fine blonde woman from Paris, dumb-looking, with a queenly bosom. She was seen shortly after that flaunting big earrings and all became clear when a daughter was born, registered in the name of Élisabeth-Olympe-Louise Roque.

Catherine, who was jealous, was expecting to detest this child. But in fact she adored her. She surrounded her with care, attention, and caresses, to supplant her mother and render her hateful, an easy thing to do, for Madame Éléonore totally neglected her little daughter, preferring to gossip with the shopkeepers. The very day after her wedding she went visiting at the sub-prefecture, no longer fraternized with the servants, and felt it a mark of respectability to be strict with the child. She was present at her lessons. The teacher, an old bureaucrat from the town hall, didn't know how to go about teaching her. The child rebelled, got slapped, and went to cry in Catherine's lap, and she always sided with her. Then the two women quarrelled. Monsieur Roque silenced them. He had married out of love for his daughter and did not want them to make her life a misery.

She often wore a white ragged dress with knickers edged with lace. And on feast days she went out dressed like a princess, to upset the bourgeois, who stopped their offspring from playing with her, because she was illegitimate.

Her life was spent on her own in her garden, swinging on her swing, running after butterflies, and then suddenly stopping to look at the beetles that settled on the rose bushes. It was no doubt these habits which gave her face an expression of both boldness and dreaminess. What's more, she was the same size as Marthe, so that the second time they met Frédéric said to her:

'May I give you a kiss, Mademoiselle?'

The child raised her head and replied:

'You may!'

But the wooden fence separated them.

'You'll have to climb up,' Frédéric said.

'No, lift me!'

He leaned over, reached out and, lifting her up, gave her a kiss on both cheeks. Then in the same way he put her back on her side of the fence. This was the procedure on subsequent occasions.

With no more reserve than a four-year-old, she would rush to meet her friend as soon as she heard him approaching, or else, hiding behind a tree, would bark like a dog, to scare him.

One day when Madame Moreau had gone out, he took her up to his room. She opened all the scent bottles and poured them on to her hair; then, not in the least abashed, she lay on the bed and remained there stretched out, eyes wide open.

'I'm pretending to be your wife,' she said.

The next day he saw her in floods of tears. She admitted she was 'weeping for her sins' and as he wanted to know what they were she replied, lowering her eyes:

'Don't ask any more questions!'

Her First Communion was approaching. She had been taken to confession that morning.

The sacrament did not make her behave any better. Sometimes she would get into a really terrible temper. They sought Monsieur Frédéric's help in calming her down.

He often took her for walks with him. He was lost in his own thoughts as he strolled along, while she picked poppies along the edge of the cornfields; and when she saw he was more downcast than usual she tried to comfort him with kind words. Deprived of love, he threw himself into friendship with this child. He drew funny faces for her, told her stories, and started to read books with her.

He began with *Annales romantiques*, an anthology of verse and prose that was famous at the time. Then, forgetting how young she was, so delighted was he by her prowess, he read *Atala*, *Cinq-Mars*, and *Les Feuilles d'automne*,* one after the other. But one night (that evening she had listened to *Macbeth* in the plain translation by Letourneur) she woke up screaming: 'The spot! The spot!' Her teeth were chattering, she was trembling, and fixing her terrified eyes on her right hand, she rubbed it, saying: 'There's still a spot!' Finally the doctor arrived and advised avoiding any more emotional upsets.

The neighbours saw in this nothing but a sign that she would go to the bad. They said that 'the Moreau boy' wanted to make her into an actress later.

There was soon another event, namely the arrival of Uncle Barthélemy. Madame Moreau hospitably gave him her bedroom and went so far as to serve meat on days of abstinence.

The old man was not all that amiable. He made constant comparisons between Le Havre and Nogent, where he found the air stuffy, the bread bad, the streets ill-paved, the food mediocre, and the inhabitants lazy. 'Business is in a parlous state here!' He criticized the extravagant life led by his late brother; he himself had got himself twenty-seven thousand francs a year income! He finally left at the end of the week, and stepping into the carriage, uttered these far from reassuring words:

'I'm very pleased to see you are comfortably off.'

'You won't get a thing!' said Madame Moreau, as she went back inside.

He had only come at her pressing invitation; and for a whole week she had tried, perhaps too obviously, to get him to broach the subject. She was sorry she had acted like that and sat in her armchair with her head down, tight-lipped. Frédéric, opposite, observed her; and neither said anything, as had been the case five years before when he returned from Montereau. This coincidence, suddenly striking him, reminded him of Madame Arnoux.

At that moment he heard the crack of a whip under the window and a voice called to him.

It was Père Roque, alone in his wagonette. He was going to spend the day at la Fortelle with Monsieur Dambreuse, and he suggested in a friendly fashion that Frédéric should come too.

'Don't worry, you don't need an invitation if you are with me.'

Frédéric was inclined to accept. But what explanation could he give for his decision to settle in Nogent? He didn't have a decent summer outfit; and besides, what would his mother say? He declined the invitation.

From that time on, his neighbour was less friendly. Louise was growing up. Madame Éléonore fell dangerously ill. And the connection ceased, much to the relief of Madame Moreau who feared that frequenting such people would harm her son's career.

Her ambition was to buy him the post of clerk of the court; Frédéric was not totally against this idea. Now he went to Mass with her, played cards in the evenings, became accustomed to life in the provinces, lived it fully; and even his love affair had taken on a sort of gloomy pleasure, a soporific charm. By dint of pouring out his sorrow in his letters, seeing connections with it in whatever he read, taking it on walks with him, and extending it to every part of his life, he had almost succeeded in exhausting it completely, so that Madame Arnoux was like a dead woman for him, and he was surprised not to know where her grave was, so calm and resigned had his love become.

One day, 12 December 1845,* towards nine in the morning, the cook brought a letter up to his room. The address in big letters was by an unknown hand; and Frédéric, half asleep, was in no hurry to break the seal. Finally he read:

From the Court of Conciliation at Le Havre, 3rd arrondissement.
Dear Monsieur,
Your uncle, Monsieur Moreau, having died intestate...

He had inherited!

As though fire had broken out on the other side of the wall he jumped out of bed, barefoot, in his nightshirt: he passed his hand over his face, unable to believe his eyes, thinking he must be still dreaming, and in order to get a firm hold on reality, he opened the window wide.

Snow had fallen; the roofs were white; and in the courtyard he could even see the washtub he had tripped over the previous evening.

He reread the letter three times in succession. It was absolutely true! The whole of his uncle's fortune! Twenty-seven thousand a year! And he was overcome by a frenzy of joy at the thought of seeing Madame Arnoux again. He had a fantasy of going to visit her, in her house, bringing her some present or other wrapped in silk paper, with his tilbury, no, his brougham, rather, waiting at the door. A black brougham with a servant in brown livery; he could hear the horse snorting and the sound of the curb chain mingling with the murmur of their kisses. That would happen day after day, indefinitely. He would entertain them himself in his house; the dining room would be in red leather, the boudoir in yellow silk, sofas everywhere! And such display cabinets! Such Chinese vases! Such carpets! These images were arriving so tumultuously he felt his head whirling. Then he remembered his mother and went downstairs still holding the letter in his hand.

Madame Moreau tried to contain her emotion and felt faint. Frédéric took her in his arms and kissed her on her forehead.

'Dear Mother, you can buy back your carriage now. Smile, don't cry, be happy!'

Ten minutes later the news had reached the outskirts of the town. Then, Maître Benoist, Monsieur Gamblin, Monsieur Chanbion, all their friends came hurrying over. Frédéric escaped briefly to write to Deslauriers. Other visitors appeared. The afternoon went by in receiving congratulations. 'Roque's wife', now 'very poorly', was forgotten in all this.

In the evening when they were on their own, Madame Moreau advised her son to set up as a lawyer in Troyes. Since he was better known in his own part of the country than anywhere else, he might more easily make a good match there.

'Oh, that's the limit!' he cried.

He scarcely held happiness in his hands before someone was trying to wrest it from him. He stated his firm resolve to go and live in Paris.

'What will you do there?'

'Nothing!'

Madame Moreau, surprised at his attitude, asked him what he was hoping to become.

'A Cabinet minister!' Frédéric replied.

And he assured her that he was deadly serious, that he was aiming at a diplomatic career, that his studies and his inclinations pushed him in that direction. First he would enter the Council of State under the protection of Monsieur Dambreuse.

'So you know him?'

'Yes, through Monsieur Roque.'

'That's odd,' Madame Moreau said.

He had reignited in her heart her old dreams of glory. Secretly she indulged them and spoke no more of the others.

If he had been able to accommodate his own impatience to be off, Frédéric would have left that very instant. But all the seats in the coaches were booked for the next day. He fretted until seven in the evening of the following day.

They were sitting down to dinner when they heard the church bell toll three times, slowly; and the maidservant entered and announced that Madame Éléonore had just passed away.

This death, all things considered, was no misfortune for anyone, not even her daughter. The young girl would be only the better for it later on.

As the two houses adjoined, they could hear a great to-do and much talking. And the thought of this dead body so close to them cast a sombre atmosphere over their imminent parting. Madame Moreau wiped her eyes two or three times. Frédéric's heart was heavy.

When the meal was over and he was leaving, Catherine stopped him. Mademoiselle insisted on seeing him. She was waiting for him in the garden. He went out, leaped over the hedge, and sometimes bumping into trees, made for Monsieur Roque's house. Lights were shining from a window on the second floor. Then a shape appeared in the shadows and a voice whispered:

'It's me.'

She seemed taller than normal, because of her black dress no doubt. Not knowing what to say to her at first, he made do with taking her hands and sighing:

'Oh, my poor Louise!'

She did not answer. She looked deep into his eyes for a long time. Frédéric was afraid he would miss the coach. He thought he could hear the wheels in the distance, and to put an end to the conversation he said:

'Catherine told me you had something...'

'Yes, that's right! I wanted to tell you...'

She addressed him as 'vous' which astonished him. And since she still did not speak, he said:

'Well, what is it?'

'I can't remember. I've forgotten! Is it true that you are going away?'

'Yes, now in a minute.'

She repeated:

'Now, in a minute?... For ever?... Shan't we see each other ever again?'

She was choking with tears.

'Farewell, farewell! Kiss me then!'

And she clasped him passionately in her arms.

# PART TWO

## I

WHEN he had taken his seat inside the coach, it gave a sudden jolt as the five horses simultaneously leapt forward, and he felt waves of joy sweep over him. Like an architect designing a palace, he planned out his life in advance. He filled it with luxuries and magnificence; it soared to heaven; things appeared in abundance. And he was so deep in this contemplation, the objects around him vanished.

At the bottom of the hill at Sourdun, he noticed where they were. They had only gone five kilometres at the very most! He was cross. He lowered the window to look at the road. He asked the driver several times exactly how long it would be before they arrived. But he regained his composure and remained in his corner with his eyes wide open.

The lantern, suspended from the postilion's seat, lit up the cruppers of the nearer horses. Beyond that he could see only the white undulating manes of the others; their breath made an opaque mist each side of the shafts. The iron chains rattled, the windows shook in their frames, and the heavy vehicle rolled on at a steady pace over the cobbles. Here and there you could see the wall of a barn or an isolated inn. Sometimes as they passed through the villages a baker's oven threw out a fiery blaze of sparks and the monstrous shadows of the horses ran along the house opposite. At the staging posts, once they had been unharnessed, there was a hush for a minute. Someone was stamping his feet on the roof, under the awning, while a woman standing in a doorway sheltered her candle with her hand. Then the driver jumped on to the step and the coach set off again.

At Mormans the clock could be heard striking a quarter past one. 'So it's today,' he mused. 'It's really today. Not long now!'

But little by little his hopes, his memories, the Rue de Choiseul, Nogent, Madame Arnoux, his mother, everything blurred together in his head.

The dull rattle of planks woke him; they were crossing the Pont de Charenton. It was Paris. Then his two companions, one taking off his cap and the other his scarf, put on their hats and began to chat. The first, a fat man with a red face in a velvet frock coat, was a business-man; the second had come to the capital to consult a doctor; and, afraid that he had disturbed him during the night, Frédéric offered him a spontaneous apology, he was so well disposed to everyone by reason of his own happiness.

The station road must have been flooded, as they went straight on and were in the countryside again. In the distance tall factory chim-neys were smoking. Then they turned into Ivry. They went up one street and suddenly he saw the dome of the Panthéon.

The plain was in a dreadful state; it looked completely ruined. The fortifications* bulged out in a long line; and on the unmade-up tracks which lined the road, small trees without branches were protected by wooden struts bristling with nails. Chemical works alternated with timber yards. High gateways, like those you see on farms, through their half-open doors showed sordid courtyards full of refuse and with pools of dirty water in the middle. Long taverns of a dark red colour dis-played two crossed billiard cues on a wreath of painted flowers between two windows on the first floor; here and there a half-built plastered shack had been abandoned. After that the double row of houses was continuous, and on the bare facades you occasionally saw a giant metal cigar poking out, that told you it was a tobacco shop. Midwives' prem-ises were indicated by a matron wearing a bonnet, dandling a baby in a lacy quilt. Posters covered gable ends and, three-quarters hanging off the walls, were flapping like rags in the wind. Workers in smocks went by and brewers' drays, laundry vans, butchers' carts. A light rain was falling, it was cold, the sky was pale, but two eyes which were brighter to him than the sun shone through the mist.

At the barrier* they stopped for some considerable time. Egg-sellers, hauliers, and a flock of sheep were holding things up. The guard on duty, his cap pulled down, strode back and forth in front of his booth to keep warm. The toll-clerk climbed on to the top of the coach and the fanfare of a cornet was heard. They trotted briskly down the boulevard, the swingletrees rattling, the traces streaming in their wake. The crack of the long whip sounded in the damp air. At the driver's shout of 'Make way! Make way!', roadsweepers stepped aside, pedestrians jumped back, mud splattered against the window; they met carts, carriages, omnibuses. Finally they were alongside the iron railings of the Jardin des Plantes.

The yellow waters of the Seine had risen nearly level with the tops of the bridges. They gave off a chilly breeze. Frédéric drank it in, in deep gulps, savouring the good Paris air that seemed to contain both the outpourings of love and the emanations of the intellect. Seeing the first cab he was moved almost to tears. He loved even the straw-filled doorways of the wine sellers, even the shoeblacks with their boxes, even the grocers' boys shaking their coffee-roasters. Women were tripping along under their umbrellas. He leaned out to see their faces—Madame Arnoux might chance to be out for a walk.

They passed several shops, the crowd got denser, the noise got louder. They drove over the Quai Saint-Bernard, the Quai de la Tournelle, and the Quai Montebello and took the Quai Napoléon. He strained to see her windows, but they were too far away. Then they crossed back over the Seine again, over the Pont Neuf, and on to the Louvre; and by way of the Rue Saint-Honoré, Croix-des-Petits-Champs, and Rue du Bouloi, they reached the Rue Coq-Héron and arrived in the hotel courtyard.

To prolong his pleasure, Frédéric got dressed as slowly as he could, and even went on foot to the Boulevard Montmartre. He smiled at the thought that soon he would again see that beloved name on the marble plaque. He raised his eyes. No shop window, no pictures, nothing!

He ran to the Rue de Choiseul. Monsieur and Madame Arnoux did not live there any more and a neighbour was looking after the porter's lodgings. Frédéric waited for him. Finally he appeared, it wasn't the same man. He didn't know their address.

Frédéric went to a café and whilst he was eating, consulted the *Almanach du commerce*. There were three hundred Arnouxes, but no Jacques Arnoux. So where were they staying? Pellerin must know.

He betook himself to the top of the Faubourg Poissonnière, to his studio. Since there was neither bell nor knocker he hammered on the door, shouted, called his name. He was met with silence.

Next he thought of Hussonnet. But where should he go to find a man like him? He had gone with him on one occasion to his mistress's house, Rue de Fleurus. Once he reached the Rue de Fleurus, Frédéric realized he did not know the girl's name.

He went to the Prefecture of Police for help. He wandered from staircase to staircase, office to office. The information desk was closing. They told him to come back tomorrow.

Then he went into all the art shops he could find, to see if anyone knew Arnoux. Monsieur Arnoux was no longer in business.

Finally, disheartened, fretted, feeling ill, he went back to his lodgings, to bed. Just as he was stretching out between the sheets, a thought made him sit up in delight.

'Regimbart! What an idiot I was not to think of him!'

The next day at seven sharp he reached the Rue Notre-Dame-des-Victoires and a bar where it was Regimbart's custom to drink white wine. It wasn't yet open. He went for a walk around and after half an hour returned. Regimbart had just left. Frédéric rushed into the street. He even thought he could see his hat. A hearse and some funeral carriages got in the way. By the time it had passed this vision had disappeared.

Luckily he remembered that the Citizen lunched at eleven o'clock sharp every day in a small restaurant on the Place Gaillon. He had to be patient. And after wandering interminably, as it seemed, from the Bourse* to the Madeleine, and from the Madeleine to the Gymnase,* Frédéric entered the restaurant in the Place Gaillon on the stroke of eleven, sure of finding Regimbart there.

'Never heard of him!' said the bar owner roughly.

Frédéric wouldn't take no for an answer. But he repeated:

'I still don't know him, Monsieur!' and raising his imperious eyebrows, he shook his head mysteriously.

But when they had last talked, the Citizen had mentioned the Alexandre eating house. Frédéric swallowed a brioche and, jumping into a cab, enquired of the driver if there were a certain café called Alexandre's somewhere on the heights on Sainte-Geneviève. The driver took him to Rue des Francs-Bourgeois-Saint-Michel to an establishment of that name and to his question: 'Monsieur Regimbart, please?' the café owner replied with an obsequious smile:

'He hasn't been in yet, Monsieur'—this, with a conspiratorial glance to his wife, who was sitting at the counter.

And forthwith, turning towards the clock:

'But he'll be here, I hope, within ten minutes, or a quarter of an hour at the latest. Célestin, quick, the newspapers—What would Monsieur like to drink?'

Although he did not want anything to drink, Frédéric downed a glass of rum, followed by a glass of kirsch, then a glass of curaçao, then various grogs, cold as well as hot. He read the whole of the day's *Le Siècle*, and read it again. He studied the cartoon in the *Charivari*,* right down to the grain of the paper. By the time he had finished, he knew the small advertisements by heart. Now and again there came the sound of boots on the pavement; it must be him! A silhouette could be seen against the window. But it always passed on.

To relieve the boredom, Frédéric moved to another table. He went to one at the back, then one on the right, then one on the left. And he sat there in the middle of the bench with both arms stretched out. But a cat, delicately scratching at the velvet on the back of the seat, scared him by jumping up suddenly to lick the drips of syrup on the tray. And the child of the house, an unbearable little brat, four years old, played with a rattle on the steps of the counter. His mother, a pale little woman with bad teeth, smiled a dumb smile. What on earth was Regimbart doing? Frédéric waited for him, sunk in his immeasurable gloom.

The rain came down like hail on the hood of the carriage. Pulling aside the muslin curtain he could see the poor horse in the road, more immobile than if he had been made of wood. The gutter had become a great river and was flowing between the spokes of the wheels, and the driver, sheltering under the covers, was half-asleep. But afraid his gentleman might give him the slip, he opened the café door now and again; the rain streamed off him. And if you could wear out an object by looking, Frédéric would have dissolved the clock with his gaze. But the hands kept moving forward. Monsieur Alexandre was walking up and down, repeating: 'He'll be along soon! He'll be here!' And to keep him amused he chatted to him, talked politics. In his desire to be obliging he went so far as to propose a game of dominos.

Finally at four-thirty Frédéric, who had been there since midday, jumped up and said he would wait no longer.

'I can't understand it myself,' replied the café owner with an air of total honesty. 'It's the first time Monsieur Ledoux has missed!'

'What do you mean, Monsieur Ledoux?'

'Yes, Monsieur Ledoux.'

'I said *Regimbart*!' cried Frédéric, at his wits' end.

'Oh, I'm so sorry! You've made a mistake!—Didn't Monsieur say Monsieur Ledoux, Madame Alexandre?'

And accosting the waiter:

'You heard him as well, didn't you?'

The waiter only smiled, no doubt to get his own back on his master.

Frédéric had himself conveyed to the boulevards, cross at the time he had wasted, angry with the Citizen, imploring his presence as though he were a god, and quite resolved to dig him out of the most distant cellar. His cab annoyed him, he dismissed it. His thoughts became confused. Then all the names of the cafés he had ever heard uttered by that imbecile sprang out of his memory all at once like thousands of fireworks exploding: Café Gascard, Café Grimbert, Café Halbout, Estaminet Bordelais, Havanais, Havrais, Bœuf-à-la-mode, Brasserie Allemande, Mère Morel. And he visited them all in turn. But in one, Regimbart had just left; in another, he might turn up; in the third, they hadn't seen him for six months; elsewhere, the previous day he had ordered a leg of mutton for Saturday. Finally at Vautier's tavern, Frédéric, opening the door, bumped into the waiter.

'Do you know Monsieur Regimbart?'

'Do I know Monsieur Regimbart? It is I who have the honour of serving him. He is upstairs, finishing his dinner!'

And with his napkin under his arm the manager of the establishment himself accosted him:

'Are you asking for Monsieur Regimbart, Monsieur? He was here a moment ago.'

Frédéric uttered an oath, but the proprietor declared that he would without any doubt find him in Bouttevilain's.

'I give you my word! He left a bit earlier than usual, because he has a business meeting with some gentlemen. But, as I said, you will find him at 92, Rue Saint-Martin, second flight of steps on the left at the back of the courtyard, first floor, right-hand door!'

And there he was, finally, in the fug of tobacco smoke, sitting alone, at the back of the café behind the pool table with a beer glass in front of him, his chin down, deep in thought.

'Aha! I've been looking for you for ages!'

Regimbart, unmoved, simply proffered him two fingers and, as if he had only seen him the day before, uttered a few trivial observations about the opening of the session of parliament.

Frédéric interrupted, saying as innocently as he could:

'How's Arnoux?'

The answer was a long time coming, Regimbart was gargling with his drink.

'He's all right!'

'So where does he live now?'

'In the Rue Paradis-Poissonnière of course,' the Citizen replied in surprise.

'What number?'

'Thirty-seven, for goodness' sake! How odd you are!'

Frédéric got up:

'What, are you leaving?'

'Yes, I've got something to do. I was forgetting. Goodbye!'

Frédéric left the *estaminet* and went to the Arnouxes', as though he was being wafted along by a warm wind with that supernatural ease you experience in dreams.

He soon found himself on the second floor outside a door whose bell was ringing. A maid appeared. A second door opened. Madame Arnoux was sitting by the fire. Arnoux jumped up and hugged him. On her lap was a little boy of about three;* her daughter, now as tall as her, was standing on the other side of the fireplace.

'Allow me to introduce this young man,' said Arnoux, picking his son up under the armpits.

And he amused himself for a few minutes throwing him up in the air, very high, and then catching him again in his arms.

'You'll kill him! Stop, stop, for heaven's sake!' Madame Arnoux cried.

But Arnoux, swearing there was no danger, continued, even addressing his son fondly in his native lisping dialect, the patois of Marseilles. 'Who's a little darling? Who's his Daddy's pet then?' Then he asked Frédéric why he had not written for so long, what on earth he had been doing down there, what brought him to Paris again.

'As for me, my dear friend, I am in the porcelain business now. But let's talk about you!'

Frédéric blamed a long court case, his mother's health. He went into it all in great detail, to make it sound more interesting. To conclude, now he was staying in Paris for good. And he said nothing of the inheritance, afraid they might look askance at his previous life.

The curtains, like the furniture, were in brown wool damask. Two pillows lay side by side against the bolster. A hot-water jar was heating up in the coals. And the lampshade placed on the edge of the sideboard dimmed the apartment. Madame Arnoux wore a deep blue merino dressing-gown. Her face turned to the fire and one hand on the little boy's shoulder, she was undoing the ties on his vest. The toddler, half-undressed, was crying and scratching his head, like Monsieur Alexandre *fils*.

Frédéric had expected to feel spasms of joy; but passions wilt when transplanted, and not finding Madame Arnoux in the place he had known her before, it seemed to him that she had lost something, had diminished in some indefinable way, in other words, that she was not the same woman. He was astonished by how calm he felt. He asked about the old friends, about Pellerin, among others.

'I don't see him very often,' Arnoux said.

She added:

'We don't entertain as we used to!'

Would he not receive any invitations in the future? But Arnoux, cordial as ever, chided him for not dropping in for dinner, on the off-chance, and he explained why he had changed his line of business.

'What do you expect in a time of decadence like ours? Great painting is no longer fashionable! But in any case one can have art in any sphere of life. I love beauty, as you know! One of these days I must take you along to my factory.'

And straight away he wanted to show him some of his products in his shop downstairs.

Dishes, soup tureens, plates, and bowls lay all over the floor. Wide flooring tiles for bathrooms and lavatories leaned against the walls, with mythological designs on them in the style of the Renaissance, while in the middle, a double shelf-stand which reached to the ceiling held jugs for ice, flower vases, candelabra, small jardinières, and large multicoloured statuettes representing Negroes or Pompadour shepherdesses. Frédéric, who was cold and hungry, was bored by Arnoux's displays.

He hurried off to the Café Anglais, supped royally, and as he ate, he said to himself:

'What an idiot I was to break my heart over her! She hardly recognized me. How bourgeois she is!'

And in a sudden rush of health and animal strength, he resolved to live exactly as he pleased. His heart felt as hard as the table his elbows leaned on. So now he could throw himself fearlessly into society. He thought of the Dambreuses; he could make use of them. Then he thought of Deslauriers. 'Oh well, too bad!' However, he sent him a note, by messenger, making a rendezvous with him to have lunch the following day at the Palais-Royal.

Fortune wasn't smiling so brightly on Deslauriers.

He had presented a thesis on 'the right to make a will' at the State examination for teaching posts, where he maintained that this right should be restricted as far as possible; and his adversary provoked him into saying silly things, and he had said many, without the examiners flinching. Then, as luck would have it, he had randomly drawn the subject 'Statute of Limitations'* for the subject of his lecture. At that point Deslauriers propounded deplorable theories. The old cases should be treated just like the new ones. Why should a proprietor be deprived of his wealth just because within the period of thirty-one years he had not been able to prove his legal right to it? It was tantamount to giving the security of an honest man to the son of a thief who had got rich. Every kind of injustice was sanctified by an extension of this right—which was tyranny, the abuse of power! He had even cried:

'Let's abolish it. And the Franks will no longer oppress the Gauls, the English the Irish, the Yankees the Redskins, the Turks the Arabs, the Whites the Blacks, Poland...'

The chairman had interrupted him:

'That will do, Monsieur! We don't want your political opinions. You can present yourself again at a later date.'

Deslauriers did not want to present himself again. But that wretched Article 20 of Book III of the Civil Code had become for him an enormous stumbling block. He was drafting out a vast tome on 'The Statute of Limitations Considered as the Basis of Civil Law and the Natural Right of Peoples', and he was deep into Dunod, Rogérius, Balbus, Merlin, Vazeile, Savigny, Troplong,* and other such worthies. In order to devote more time to this, he had resigned his position as master clerk. He lived by giving private lessons and helping write theses. And at the sessions of the debating chamber,* by his virulence he put the fear of God into the conservatives, all of those young doctrinaires of the Guizot school, so much so that in some quarters he enjoyed a kind of celebrity, rather mixed with mistrust of him as a person.

He arrived at the rendezvous wearing a bulky coat lined with red flannel like the one Sénécal used to wear in the old days.

Decency prevented them hugging each other too tightly in public, but they went along as far as Véfour's arm in arm, laughing with pleasure, tears in their eyes. Then, as soon as they were on their own, Deslauriers cried:

'Splendid! Now we can have it easy!'

Frédéric did not care for this manner of associating himself immediately with his good fortune. His friend was expressing too much delight for them both and not enough for Frédéric alone.

Then Deslauriers told him all about his failure and bit by bit recounted his works, his life, talking stoically about himself and with bitterness about everyone else. He hated everything. There was not a man in office who wasn't a cretin or a cad. He railed at the waiter for giving him a badly rinsed glass and, at Frédéric's mild protest, said:

'As if I am going to bother about fools like that who are earning six or eight thousand francs a year, who have the vote, and could probably even stand for election to the Chamber!* Oh no, no!'

Then gaily:

'But I was forgetting I am talking to a capitalist, to a Mondor*—for you are a Mondor now!'

And, returning to the subject of the inheritance, he expressed the opinion that collateral successions (in themselves unjust, although he was delighted about this one) would be abolished one of these days, come the next revolution.

'Do you believe so?' asked Frédéric.

'You may depend upon it!' he replied. 'It can't go on like this! We are suffering too much! When I see people like Sénécal living in poverty...'

'Sénécal again!' Frédéric thought.

'What's new, anyway? Are you still in love with Madame Arnoux? Past history, is it?'

Frédéric, not knowing what to say, closed his eyes and bowed his head.

On the subject of Arnoux, Deslauriers told him that his journal now belonged to Hussonnet, who had transformed it. It was called *Art*, 'a literary institution, a company with shares at a hundred francs each and an authorized capital of forty thousand francs'. Every shareholder was entitled to supply copy to the magazine. For 'the aim of the company is to publish the works of unknown writers, to spare talent, genius perhaps, the trials and torments by which it may be overwhelmed etc.... etc.... The usual stuff!' However, there was something that could be done, viz. to raise the tone of the said magazine, then all of a sudden, while keeping the same contributors and promising to continue with the serial, to provide subscribers with a political journal. The sum required would not be huge.

'Well, what do you think? Do you want to be in on it?'

Frédéric didn't rebuff this suggestion. But he had to wait for his affairs to be put in order.

'So, if you need anything...'

'No thanks, my friend!' Deslauriers said.

Then, leaning on the plush windowsill, they smoked cheroots. The sun was shining, the air was mild, swarms of birds flew down into the garden; statues of bronze and marble washed by the rain glistened. Aproned maids sat chatting on chairs. And you could hear children laughing, along with the continuous murmur of the fountain.

Frédéric had felt very troubled by Deslauriers's resentment. But under the influence of the wine circulating in his veins, half asleep, bemused and with the light full in his face, he felt nothing but an immense sense of well-being, a dull voluptuousness, like a plant saturated in warmth and wet. Deslauriers was looking vaguely into the distance from between half-closed eyelids. His chest swelled and he began:

'Oh, those were the days, when Camille Desmoulins, standing on a table over there, urged people to the Bastille. Then you were really alive, you could stand up for yourself, prove your strength! Simple lawyers ordered generals about, beggars vanquished kings, whereas nowadays...'

He stopped talking and then suddenly cried:

'No matter, the future is great!'

And drumming with his fingers on the windows he declaimed this verse of Barthélemy:*

> ' "The dread Assembly will appear again
>    Forty years on still troubling your thoughts,
>    Colossus on the march, fearless, with mighty tread." '

'I can't remember the rest! But it's late, should we be going?'

And in the street he carried on expounding his theories.

Frédéric, who was not listening, examined the objects and the furniture in the shop windows to see what would suit his rooms. And it was perhaps the thought of Madame Arnoux which made him stop outside the display of a second-hand dealer's, at the sight of three china plates. They were decorated with yellow arabesques with a metallic sheen and cost a hundred écus apiece. He had them put on one side.

'If it were me,' Deslauriers said, 'I should prefer to buy silver', by this love of opulence revealing his humble origins.

As soon as he was on his own, Frédéric went to the famous Pomadère's where he ordered three pairs of trousers, two suits, a fur coat, and five waistcoats; thence to a bootmaker's, a shirtmaker's, and a hatmaker's, urging them to be as quick as possible.

Three days later, in the evening, on his return from Le Havre, he found his complete wardrobe waiting for him and, impatient to make use of it, he resolved to go and visit the Dambreuses straight away. But it was too early, scarcely eight o'clock.

'Supposing I went to see the others?' he mused.

Arnoux was on his own, shaving in front of the mirror. He suggested taking him to a place where he would enjoy himself, and, at the mention of Monsieur Dambreuse:

'Oh yes! You will be able to meet some friends of his. Do come then, it will be fun!'

Frédéric was excusing himself, when Madame Arnoux recognized his voice and greeted him through the partition, for her daughter was unwell and she herself was poorly. And you could hear the tinkle of a spoon against a glass and things being gently moved around as invariably happens in the bedroom of a sick person. Then Arnoux disappeared to say goodbye to his wife. He gave one excuse after another for going out:

'It's important you know! I have to go, I need to, they are expecting me.'

'Go on, my dear. Enjoy yourself.'

Arnoux hailed a cab.

'Palais-Royal! Galerie Montpensier, No. 7.'

And, sinking down on to the cushions:

'Oh, how weary I am, my friend. It'll be the death of me. Well, I can tell *you* all about it at any rate.'

He leaned over to whisper mysteriously in his ear:

'I am trying to find the coppery red of the Chinese potters.'

And he explained the nature of a glaze and slow firing.

When they reached Chevet's he was handed a huge basket which he told them to take to his cab. Then he chose, for 'his poor wife', grapes, pineapples, as well as other exotic delicacies and ordered them to be delivered early the following morning.

Then they went to the costumier's; they needed clothes for a fancy-dress ball. Arnoux bought blue velvet trousers, a jacket of the same material, a red wig; Frédéric a domino; and they went down the Rue de Laval, to the front of a house lit up by coloured lanterns on the second floor.

As soon as they got to the bottom of the stairs, they could hear the sound of violins.

'Where on earth are you taking me?' Frédéric asked.

'To see a lovely girl! Don't be scared!'

A footman opened the door and they went into the hall, where waistcoats, coats, and shawls had been thrown in a pile on the chairs. A young woman in a Louis XV dragoon's costume was passing through at that moment. It was Mademoiselle Rose-Annette Bron, the mistress of the establishment.

'Well?' enquired Arnoux.

'It's done!' she replied.

'Oh, thank you, my angel!'

And he made to kiss her.

'Be careful, stupid! You'll spoil my make-up.'

Arnoux introduced Frédéric.

'Put it right here, Monsieur! You are very welcome!'

She parted a curtain behind her and began to shout:

'Master Arnoux, the kitchen-boy, and a noble friend of his.'

At first Frédéric was dazzled by the lights. All he could see was silk, velvet, bare shoulders, a mass of colour swaying to the strains of an orchestra camouflaged by the greenery, between walls covered in yellow silk, with pastel portraits here and there and crystal sconces in the style of Louis XVI. Tall lamps with frosted globes resembling snowballs towered over baskets of flowers placed on small tables in the corners. And opposite, beyond the second, smaller, room, you could see into a third in which there was a bed with twisted legs and, beside it, a Venetian mirror.

The dancing stopped and there was some delighted applause at the sight of Arnoux walking into the room with a basket heaped with things to eat on his head.

'Mind the chandelier!' Frédéric raised his eyes; it was the old blue Dresden chandelier which had hung in the shop in *L'Art industriel.* Memories of the old days flashed through his head; but a scantily clad foot-soldier with the sort of stupid expression on his face one normally associates with conscripts, planted himself in front of him with a sweep of his arms that betokened astonishment; and, in spite of the terrifying black, excessively pointed moustache, which disfigured him, he recognized his old friend Hussonnet. Speaking half-Alsatian half-pidgin, the bohemian showered him with congratulations, and addressed him as 'colonel'. Frédéric, abashed by all these people, was tongue-tied. A bow was tapped on a desk, and the dancers all took their places.

There were about sixty of them, the women were mostly dressed as village girls or marquises and the men, almost all of mature years, were dressed as wagoners, stevedores, or sailors.

Frédéric, drawn back against the wall, watched the quadrille in front of him.

An elderly man, handsome and dressed as a Doge of Venice in a long purple silk *simarra*, was dancing with Madame Rosanette who wore a green jacket, knitted breeches, and soft boots with gold spurs. The couple opposite consisted of an Albanian loaded with yataghans and a Swiss girl with blue eyes, milk-white, plump as a chicken, in shirtsleeves and red corselet. To show off her hair which reached down to her calves, a tall blonde girl, who had walk-on parts at the Opéra, had got dressed up as a wild woman; she wore only a leather loincloth over her brown leotard, with glass bracelets and a tinsel diadem from which there rose a tall plume of peacock's feathers. In front of her a Pritchard, decked out in a grotesquely wide black coat, was beating time with his elbow on his snuffbox. A little Watteau shepherd, blue and silver as moonlight, was tapping his crook against the thyrsus of a Bacchante,* crowned with grapes, a leopard skin on her left thigh and wearing buskins trimmed with gold ribbons. On the other side a Polish girl in a salmon-coloured velvet spencer swung her gauzy skirt over pearl-grey stockings encased in pink boots edged with white fur. She was smiling at a big-bellied man in his forties, disguised as a choirboy, who was leaping high in the air, lifting his surplice with one hand and holding on to his red skullcap with the other. But the queen of all, the star, was Mademoiselle Loulou, the famous dancer of the *bals publics*. Being at present well-off, she was wearing a wide lace collar over a plain velvet waistcoat. And her wide trousers of poppy red silk, hugging her hips, were tied round the waist by a cashmere sash and had real little white camellias all along the seams. Her pale, rather puffy complexion and turned-up nose were made even jauntier by her tousled wig topped by a man's grey felt hat, which she had dented with her fist and cocked over her right ear. And in her leaps her diamond buckled slippers almost touched the nose of her neighbour, a tall medieval baron, who was encumbered in a suit of armour. There was also an Angel, a gold sword in hand, two swansdown wings on her back, who, as she danced back and forth, kept losing her partner, a Louis XIV, and, not understanding the figures of the dance, got in everybody's way.

Looking at these people, Frédéric felt abandoned and ill at ease. He still had his mind on Madame Arnoux and it seemed to him he was taking part in some hostile activity that threatened her.

When the quadrille was over, Madame Rosanette accosted him. She was panting a little, and her gorget, gleaming like a mirror, rose and fell gently below her chin.

'What about you, Monsieur?' she asked. 'Are you not dancing?'

Frédéric apologized. He couldn't dance.

'Is that right? Not even with me? Are you sure?'

And, resting her weight on one foot, the other knee drawn back a little, stroking the mother-of-pearl pommel of her sword with her left hand, she contemplated him for a minute with a half-imploring, half-ironic expression. Finally she said 'Bonsoir!', executed a pirouette, and vanished.

Frédéric, dissatisfied with himself, and not knowing what to do, began to wander through the house.

He went into the boudoir. It was lined with blue silk, embroidered with bunches of wild flowers and, on the ceiling encircled by gilded wood, Cupids emerging from an azure sky frolicked on clouds of eiderdown. These elegant adornments, which would in our own day be considered of little consequence by the likes of Rosanette, dazzled him. He admired everything: the artificial convulvulus decorating the edges of the mirror, the curtains over the fireplace, the Turkish divan, and, in an alcove, a kind of tent with pink silk hangings, covered in white muslin. In the bedroom was black furniture inlaid with brass and on a dais covered in swanskin, stood the huge canopied bed with ostrich feathers. Pins bejewelled with precious stones were stuck into pincushions, rings lay around on trays, gold-framed lockets and silver caskets could be made out in the dim light shed by a Bohemian glass bowl suspended on three little chains. Through a small half-open door you could see a conservatory which took up the entire width of the terrace and was bounded at the far end by an aviary.

This was indeed a space meant to be pleasing. In a sudden upsurge of youthful feeling he swore he would make the most of it, and grew bolder. Coming back to the drawing room, where there were more people now (everything was moving around in a sort of luminous dusty haze), he stood contemplating the dancers, squinting to see more clearly—and breathing in the soft scents of the women floating by like one immense universal kiss.

But there next to him on the other side of the door was Pellerin—Pellerin in full evening dress, his left arm tucked into his coat and in his right hand, together with his hat, a torn white glove.

'Well! We haven't seen you for a long time! Where on earth have you been? Travelling? In Italy? A bit of a bore, don't you think? Not so marvellous as they all say? Never mind! Show me your sketches one of these days?'

And without waiting for an answer, the artist began talking about himself.

He had made considerable progress, having realized how ridiculous it was to emphasize the importance of Line. One ought not to strive for Beauty and Unity in a work of art so much as for character and variety.

'Everything exists in Nature, so everything is a legitimate subject for painting. All you have to do is strike the right note. I have discovered the secret!' And with a nudge of the elbow he repeated several times:

'I've discovered the secret! See that little woman with the sphinx coiffure dancing with a Russian postilion, it's crisp, exact, firm, all planes and strong colours. Indigo under the eyes, a scarlet dab on the cheek, shading at the temples. One! Two!'—and he made imaginary brush strokes in the air with his thumb. 'While the fat woman over there', he continued, pointing out a fishwife, in a dress of cerise, a gold cross round her neck and a lawn scarf knotted over her back, 'is nothing but curves. Her nostrils flare like the wings of her bonnet, the corners of her mouth turn up, her chin drops, all is rich, melting, lush, tranquil and sunny, a real Rubens! Yet they are both perfect! So where is the ideal type?' He was warming to his subject. 'What is a beautiful woman? What is beauty? Ah, beauty! You'll tell me...'

Frédéric interrupted him to ask about a Pierrot who looked like a goat in profile, who was in the process of blessing all the dancers in the middle of a pastorelle.

'He's nobody! A widower, father of three boys. He lets them go around half-naked, spends his time at the club, and sleeps with the maidservant.'

'And what about that one dressed as a judge who's talking to a Marquise de Pompadour* in the window?'

'The marquise is Madame Vandael, the former actress at the Gymnase, the mistress of the Doge, the Comte de Palazot. They've been together for twenty years, nobody knows why. She had such beautiful eyes once, that woman! As for the citizen next to her, they call him Captain Herbigny, one of the old guard, with nothing to his name except his Croix d'honneur and his pension. He is a kind of uncle to the girls on solemn occasions, he arranges duels and dines out.'

'A scoundrel?' said Frédéric.

'Not at all! He's a thoroughly decent member of society!'

'Oh!'

The artist gave him the names of yet others, and then, catching sight of a gentleman who was wearing a long gown of black serge like Molière's doctors, open from head to toe so as to show off all the trinkets on his chain:

'And that fellow is Doctor Des Rogis, furious that he is not famous. He's written a pornographic medical book, is happy to lick the boots of those in high places, and is discreet. Their ladyships adore him. He and his wife (that scraggy chatelaine in a grey dress) trail around together in all public places. Despite the lack of money in their household, they hold their "day"—arty tea parties where they read poetry together. Oh, watch out!'

And, sure enough, the doctor came over to talk to them, and before long the three of them had formed a group chatting at the entrance to the drawing room. Hussonnet joined them, then the lover of the Wild Woman, a young poet who, under a short cloak à la François I, revealed the puniest of anatomies. And finally, a witty lad dressed as a Turkish peddler. But his gold braided jacket had been around for such a long time on the back of travelling dentists, his wide turned-up trousers were of such a faded pink, his turban, rolled up like a fried eel, looked so shabby, and all his costume was so disgustingly true to life, that the ladies could not hide their revulsion. The doctor made it up to him by singing the praises of his mistress the Stevedore. This Turk was the son of a banker.

Between two quadrilles Rosanette made her way towards the fireplace where a fat little old man, in a brown suit with gold buttons, was sitting in an armchair. In spite of his withered cheeks which drooped on to his high white neckerchief, his hair, still fair and curling naturally like the fur of a poodle, gave him a rather playful air.

She listened to him, bending over towards him. Then she brought him a glass of fruit syrup. And nothing was as sweet as her hands in the lacy cuffs showing from the sleeves of her green tunic. When this worthy man had drunk, he kissed them.

'Why, it's Monsieur Oudry, Arnoux's neighbour!'

'Neighbour no more!' said Pellerin, laughing.

'What?'

A postilion from Longjumeau* seized her by the waist, a waltz was beginning. Then, all the women sitting on sofas around the salon suddenly sprang up in a line. And their skirts, their stoles, their coiffures began to whirl around.

They were spinning in such proximity to him that Frédéric could see the drops of perspiration on their foreheads. And this twirling and whirling, ever faster and more regular, produced a kind of intoxication in his giddy brain and filled it with other images as they passed him in a dazzling vision, each exciting him differently according to the kind of beauty she possessed. The Polish girl, who abandoned herself in a languorous way, made him want to clasp her to his heart, and go sledging along, the two of them, over snow-covered fields. The Swiss girl, waltzing with her body held straight and her eyebrows lowered, promised long days of voluptuous tranquillity in a chalet on the edge of a lake. Then suddenly the Bacchante, her dark head tilted back, made him dream of greedy kisses in groves of oleander, in stormy weather, to the muffled sound of tambourines. The Fishwife, out of breath with dancing so fast, was laughing out loud. And he would have liked to have a drink with her at Les Porcherons* and crumple her neckerchief in his hands, as in the days of old. But the Stevedore, whose little toes scarcely touched the floor, seemed to harbour in the suppleness of her limbs and the seriousness of her face all the refinements of modern love, which combines the precision of science with the mobility of a bird. Rosanette was twirling round, hand on her hip. Her wig in the shape of a knot bobbing up and down on her collar, sent orris powder out around her. And each time she came round, she almost caught Frédéric with the tips of her gold spurs.

At the last chord of the waltz Mademoiselle Vatnaz appeared. She had an Algerian kerchief on her head, a lot of piastres on her forehead, mascara around her eyes, and a kind of black cashmere coat falling over a light-coloured skirt of silver lamé, and she was holding a tambourine.

Behind her walked a tall young man, in the classic garb of Dante. He was, and she no longer tried to conceal the fact, the former singer from the Alhambra, whose name was Auguste Delamare. He had originally called himself Anténor Dellamarre, then Delmas then Belmar and finally Delmar, thus modifying and improving his name to match his growing fame; for he had left the music hall for the theatre, and had indeed just made his debut to great acclaim at the Ambigu in *Gaspardo le Pêcheur*.*

When Hussonnet saw him he scowled. Since the rejection of his play he hated actors. You would not believe how puffed-up those people are, especially that fellow! 'What a poseur! Just look at him!'

After briefly greeting Rosanette, Delmar had gone to stand with his back to the fireplace; and he remained there motionless, one hand on his heart, left foot in front of him, looking at the ceiling, with his crown of gold laurel leaves around his hood, trying his best to put a deal of poetry into his gaze, to fascinate the ladies. At a distance they formed a large circle around him.

But when La Vatnaz had embraced Rosanette at length, she came over to ask Hussonnet to revise, from a stylistic point of view, an educational work that she wished to publish: *The Young Person's Garland*, an anthology of literature and ethics. The man of letters promised to help. So then she asked him if, in one of the newspapers he had access to, he might write enthusiastically about her friend and perhaps even get him a part later. Hussonnet was so taken aback that he forgot to take a glass of punch.

It was Arnoux who had concocted the punch. And followed by the count's footman carrying an empty tray, he offered it around to the guests with a satisfied air.

When he came to Monsieur Oudry, Rosanette stopped him.

'Well, what about that business matter?'

He reddened a little; then, addressing himself to the old man, he said:

'Our friend here says you might be so kind as to...'

'Why of course, neighbour, I am at your service!'

And the name of Monsieur Dambreuse was mentioned. As they were talking together in hushed tones, Frédéric could not hear them very well. He went over to the other corner of the fireplace, where Rosanette and Delmar were chatting.

This poseur of an actor had a common face, intended, as if on the stage, to be viewed at a distance, thick hands, big feet, a heavy jaw. And he poured scorn on the most famous actors, looked down on poets, talked of 'my vocal organ, my physique, my method', embellishing his speech with words he didn't rightly understand, such as '*morbidezza*',* 'analogous', and 'homogeneity'.

Rosanette was listening to him, giving little approving nods. You could see the admiration spread over her cheeks beneath her make-up, and something moist passed like a veil over her bright eyes, which were an indefinable colour. How could such a man be attractive to her? Frédéric worked himself up to despise him even more, perhaps to banish a kind of envy he felt.

Mademoiselle Vatnaz was now with Arnoux. And laughing very loudly, she glanced now and then at her friend, whom Monsieur Oudry was still studying carefully.

Then Arnoux and La Vatnaz disappeared. The old man came to whisper to Rosanette.

'All right then, it's settled! Leave me alone.' And she asked Frédéric if he'd go and see if Monsieur Arnoux was in the kitchen.

The floor was covered with rows of half-empty glasses. And the saucepans, the cooking pots, the turbot kettle, the frying pan were vibrating on the stove. Arnoux was ordering the servants around familiarly, beating the remoulade, tasting the sauces, and joking with the maid.

'Right,' he said. 'Tell her we'll dish up.'

The dancing had stopped, the women had just sat down again, the men were walking round. In the middle of the drawing room one of the curtains hanging at the window was billowing out; and the Sphinx, in spite of everyone commenting on it, was stretching out her perspiring arms to the draught. But where was Rosanette? Frédéric looked for her all over the place, going as far as the boudoir and into the bedroom. Some people had escaped there, to be by themselves, or with partners. The darkness mingled with the whispers. There were little laughs stifled by handkerchiefs, and the fluttering of fans could be seen on necklines, slow and gentle like the beating wings of a wounded bird.

Entering the conservatory, he saw under the broad leaves of a caladium near the fountain, Delmar, lying on the sofa with his face turned towards Rosanette sitting by him. She was running her fingers through his hair and they were gazing into each other's eyes. At that moment Arnoux entered by the other door near the aviary. Delmar leaped up, then left quietly without looking round, and even stopped by the door to pick a hibiscus flower which he stuck in his buttonhole. Rosanette leaned over. Frédéric, seeing her in profile, saw that she was weeping.

'Why, what's the matter?' said Arnoux.

She shrugged without answering.

'Is it because of him?' he enquired.

She clasped her arms around his neck and, kissing him on the forehead, slowly said:

'You know quite well that I'll love you for ever, my darling. Let's think no more about it! Let's go and have supper!'

A brass chandelier with forty candles lit up the room, the walls disappearing beneath the ancient porcelain hanging there. And this harsh light, falling directly on to it, made an enormous turbot, surrounded by the hors d'oeuvres and the fruit, appear even whiter. It occupied the centre of the tablecloth, while dishes full of bisque soup had been placed around the edge. With a rustle, the women gathered up their skirts, their sleeves and stoles, and sat down next to each other. The men waited in the corners. Pellerin and Oudry were placed next to Rosanette; Arnoux was opposite. Palazot and his mistress had just left.

'Bon appétit!' she said. 'Let's start!'

The Choirboy, a man of wit, made a large sign of the cross and began to recite the *Benedicite*.

The ladies were scandalized, especially the Fishwife, who had a daughter she wished to make into a respectable woman. Arnoux 'did not care for that sort of thing' either, opining that one ought to be respectful towards religion.

A German clock, decorated with a cockerel, chiming two, gave rise to many jokes about cuckoos. All kinds of remarks followed: witticisms, anecdotes, boasts, wagers which passed for truths, improbable assertions, a tumult of words which soon fractured into individual conversations. The wines circulated, the dishes succeeded one another, the doctor carved. An orange was thrown, a cork; people left their places to chat with others. Rosanette kept turning round to Delmar, who stood motionless behind her; Pellerin was gossiping, Monsieur Oudry was smiling. Mademoiselle Vatnaz ate the dish of crayfish almost on her own, and the shells crunched between her long teeth. The Angel, perched on the piano stool (the only place her wings allowed her to sit), was chewing away placidly and determinedly.

'What an appetite!' the Choirboy kept saying in amazement. 'What an appetite!'

And the Sphinx was drinking brandy, shouting at the top of her voice, leaping around wildly like a demon. Suddenly her cheeks puffed up, and unable to hold back the blood which was choking her, she put her napkin to her lips and threw it under the table.

Frédéric had seen her.

'It's nothing!'

And when he urged her to go home and look after herself, she answered slowly:

'Oh, what's the use? It might as well be that as anything else. Life's not a bowl of cherries.'

Then he shuddered, seized by an icy melancholy, as though he had seen a vision of endless worlds of misery and despair, a charcoal stove near a truckle bed, the bodies in the Morgue in leather aprons and the cold water from a tap dripping on to their hair.

Meanwhile Hussonnet, crouching at the feet of the Wild Woman, was braying in a rasping voice in imitation of Grassot, the actor:

'Do not be cruel, O Celuta!* This little family celebration is charming! Fill my senses, my loves! Let us frolic, let us gambol!'

And he began kissing all the ladies on their shoulders. They shuddered, tickled by his moustache. Then he hit on the idea of breaking a plate over his head, giving it a gentle tap. Others copied him. The pieces of china flew up in the air like slates in a gale, and the Stevedore cried:

'Carry on! It doesn't cost anything! The man who makes them gives them to us!'

All eyes turned to Arnoux. He replied:

'Oh, I'll send the bill,' no doubt wishing to give the impression that he was not, or was no longer, Rosanette's lover.

But two furious voices were raised:

'Fool!'

'Swine!'

'At your service!'

'At yours!'

It was the medieval knight and the Russian postilion quarrelling. The latter had maintained that armour dispensed with the need for bravery, the other had taken that as an insult. He wanted to pick a fight, everyone intervened, and in all the uproar the captain tried to make himself heard.

'Messieurs, listen to me! One word! I know what I'm talking about!'

When Rosanette had tapped on a glass with her knife, she finally managed to get silence. And addressing the knight who kept his helmet on, then the postilion with a shaggy fur headdress:

'Take your saucepan off! It makes me hot just to look at you!—and you over there with your wolf's head.—Do as I tell you, damn you, do as you're told! Look at my epaulettes! I am your Maréchale!'

They took them off and all applauded, shouting:

'Vive la Maréchale! Vive la Maréchale!'

Then she took a bottle of champagne which was standing on the stove and poured it from a height into the glasses held out to her. Since the table was too wide, the guests, and especially the women, leaned over towards her, and stood on tiptoe or on the bars of chairs, for a moment forming a pyramid of coiffures, naked shoulders, leaning bodies. And long jets of wine spurted out all over, for Pierrot and Arnoux, in two corners of the room, had each opened a bottle and were splashing everyone's faces. The little birds in the aviary, whose door had been left open, invaded the room, flying round the chandelier in fright, hitting the windowpanes and the furniture. And some perched on heads, looking like great flowers in the midst of people's hair.

The musicians had left. The piano was dragged from the entrance hall into the drawing room. La Vatnaz sat down to play and, accompanied by the Choirboy who was beating a tambourine, she began a furious quadrille, striking the keys like an impatient horse, and swaying to and fro to keep time with the beat. The Maréchale seized Frédéric, Hussonnet did cartwheels, the Stevedore performed acrobatics like a clown. The Pierrot behaved like an orang-utan, the Wild Woman with her arms spread wide imitated the rocking of a barge on the river.

Finally they all stopped, exhausted. Someone opened a window.

Daylight entered, with the freshness of morning. There was an exclamation of astonishment and then silence. The yellow flames flickered, sometimes cracking their candle-rings; ribbons, flowers, and pearls were strewn across the floor. Marks from the punch and the juices stained the small tables; the chair-covers were soiled, the costumes crumpled and covered in powder; hair hung over shoulders; and greasepaint, mixed with sweat, ran down pale faces, with red, blinking eyelids.

The Maréchale, fresh as though she had just got out of the bath, had pink cheeks, shining eyes. She threw her wig away. And her hair fell around her like a fleece, covering her entire costume apart from her breeches, and producing an effect that was both comical and sweet.

The Sphinx, whose teeth were chattering with fever, needed a shawl.

Rosanette ran into her bedroom to get one, and as the other woman was following her, quickly shut the door in her face.

The Turk observed aloud that nobody had seen Monsieur Oudry leave. Nobody took any notice of this malicious remark, they were all so tired.

Then as they waited for the cabs, they got wrapped up in their cloaks and coats.

Seven o'clock chimed. The Angel was still in the room, sitting at the table with a purée of sardines and butter in front of her; and the Fishwife, next to her, was smoking cigarettes while at the same time dispensing advice about Life.

Finally the cabs arrived and the guests left. Hussonnet, who was employed as a correspondent for a provincial journal, had to read fifty-three newspapers before lunch; the Wild Woman had a rehearsal at her theatre, Pellerin had to see a model; the Choirboy had three assignations. But the Angel, who was struggling with the first symptoms of indigestion, could not get up. The medieval baron carried her to her cab.

'Mind her wings!' yelled the Stevedore through the window.

They were on the landing when Mademoiselle Vatnaz said to Rosanette:

'Farewell, darling! Your party was lovely!'

Then, whispering in her ear:

'Hang on to him!'

'Until better times,' answered the Maréchale, slowly turning her back.

Arnoux and Frédéric left together, just as they had come. The china dealer looked so downcast, his companion thought he must be unwell.

'Me? Not at all!'

He was chewing his moustache, his brow was furrowed. Frédéric asked him if it was perhaps his business affairs that were worrying him.

'Absolutely not!'

Then, suddenly:

'You used to know him, didn't you? Père Oudry?'

And in a bitter tone:

'The old scoundrel has a pile of money!'

Then Arnoux talked of an important firing that had to be finished today in the workshop. He wanted to see it. The train left in an hour. 'But I must go and kiss my wife.'

'Oh, his wife!' Frédéric thought.

Then he went to bed, with an unbearable headache. And he drank a flask of water to calm his thirst.

He had acquired another thirst, for women, for luxury, and for all that goes to make up life in Paris. He felt a little bewildered, like a man getting off a ship. And in the hallucination of the first sleep, he saw passing back and forth in front of him the Fishwife's shoulders, the Stevedore's back, the Pole's ankles, the Wild Woman's hair. Then two big black eyes which were not at the ball appeared. And light as butterflies, burning like torches, they darted here and there, quivered, flew up to the cornice and down again to his mouth. Frédéric was desperate to see whose eyes they were, but failed. Already the dream had taken over. He seemed to be harnessed next to Arnoux in the shafts of a cab and the Maréchale, astride him, was disembowelling him with her gold spurs.

## II

FRÉDÉRIC found a small mansion at the end of the Rue Rumfort and he bought, all at the same time, a brougham, a horse, some furniture, and two jardinières from Arnoux's to place each side of the door in his salon. Behind this room were a bedroom and a dressing room. He thought of putting Deslauriers in that room. But then how should he entertain *her*, his future mistress? The presence of a friend would be embarrassing. He knocked down the partition to enlarge the salon and made the dressing room into a smoking room.

He bought the works of poets he liked, travel books, atlases, dictionaries, for he had numerous work projects; he hurried up the workmen, scoured the shops, and in his impatience to enjoy his purchases, bought everything without bargaining.

When he received the tradesmen's bills, Frédéric saw that before long he would need to pay about forty thousand francs, not including the legacy dues, which would come to more than thirty-seven thousand. As his fortune lay in his land, he wrote to the lawyer in Le Havre that he should sell some of it, to free himself of his debts and have some money at his disposal. Then, wanting to get to know this vague entity, glittering and indefinable, that is called 'society', he wrote the Dambreuses a note asking if he could visit them. Madame responded that they would expect his visit the following day.

It was their day for entertaining. Cabs were parked along the courtyard. Two valets hurried out under the awning, and a third, standing at the top of the staircase, began to walk ahead of him.

He went through the hall, a second room, then a large drawing room with high windows where a monumental fireplace supported a spherical carriage clock and two monstrous porcelain vases from which two clusters of sconces sprang up like golden bushes. Pictures in the manner of Ribera* were affixed to the walls. The heavy tapestry curtains on the doors hung in majestic folds and the furnishings, side tables, all the furniture, which was in the Empire style, had something imposing and ambassadorial about it. Frédéric couldn't help smiling with pleasure.

Finally he reached an oval room, with rosewood panels, crammed full of pretty furniture and lit by one single window giving on to a garden. Madame Dambreuse was by the fire, a dozen people forming a circle around her. With a friendly word she invited him to sit down, but without showing surprise at not having seen him for so long.

When he went in they were praising the eloquence of the Abbé Cœur.* Then they were deploring the immoral behaviour of servants, after a theft committed by a valet. And one piece of tittle-tattle led to another. Old Lady Sommery had a cold. Mademoiselle de Turvisot was getting married, the Montcharrons were not coming back till the end of January, nor were the Bretancourts. People stayed later in the country nowadays. And the pettiness of the conversation was as though emphasized by the luxury surrounding them. But what was said was not so inane as the manner in which it was uttered, without any aim, continuity, or vigour. Yet men of some consequence were there: a former minister, the priest of a large parish, two or three gentlemen who occupied important positions in government. They confined themselves to the most hackneyed of commonplaces. Some resembled tired dowagers, others had manners like horse traders, and old men accompanied wives who might have been their grand-daughters.

Madame Dambreuse received them all graciously. As soon as they said someone was sick her brow furrowed in pain, and if the conversation was of balls and parties she brightened up. She would soon have to do without them, since she was taking her husband's niece—an orphan—out of school. Her dutifulness was praised. She was behaving like a proper mother.

Frédéric observed her. The dull skin on her face looked taut and pink, but without a sheen, rather like a preserved fruit. But her hair was in corkscrew curls in the English fashion, and was finer than silk, her eyes were a brilliant azure blue and all her gestures graceful. Sitting at the back, on the sofa, she was caressing the red tassels on a Japanese screen, no doubt to show off her hands—long, narrow, rather thin hands, with fingers which turned up at the ends. She wore a dress of grey shot silk with a high neckline, like a Puritan.

Frédéric asked if she would be going to La Fortelle this year. Madame Dambreuse had no idea. Well, he could understand that; she must find Nogent boring. More and more people arrived. There was a continual rustling of dresses on the carpet. The ladies perched on the edge of their chairs, uttered little giggles, made one or two re-marks, and after five minutes, left with their daughters. Soon the con-versation was impossible to follow and Frédéric was just leaving when Madame Dambreuse said:

'Every Wednesday then, Monsieur Moreau?', redeeming by that single phrase the indifference she had shown.

He was happy. Nevertheless, once in the street he breathed in a deep breath of air. And needing a less artificial environment, Frédéric remembered he owed the Maréchale a visit.

The front door was open. Two lapdogs came rushing out. A voice shouted:

'Delphine, Delphine! Is that you, Félix?'

He stood still. The two little dogs were still yapping. Finally Rosanette appeared, enveloped in a kind of bathrobe in white muslin enbroidered with lace, her bare feet in Turkish slippers.

'Oh, I beg your pardon, Monsieur! I took you for my hairdresser. One minute! I'm coming back!'

And he stood alone in the dining room.

The Venetian blinds were drawn down. Frédéric scanned the room, and was remembering the din of the other night, when he noticed on the table an old dented felt hat, greasy and dirty. Whose was this hat then? It seemed to be showing off its torn lining as much as to say: 'Anyway, what do I care? I'm master here!'

The Maréchale arrived. She picked it up, opened the conservatory and threw it inside, shutting the door on it. (Other doors at the same time opened and closed.) Ushering Frédéric through the kitchen, she took him into her dressing room.

You could immediately see that it was the most used room in the house, the real focal point. The walls, the furniture, and a huge sprung divan were covered in chintz in a bold leaf pattern. On a white marble table were laid two large blue china bowls. Crystal shelves above were laden with bottles, brushes, combs, cosmetic sticks, powder boxes. The fire was reflected in a high mirror, a sheet was hanging over the side of a bath and the scent of almond and benzoin filled the air.

'Please excuse the mess! I am dining out tonight.'

And as she turned on her heels, she almost stepped on one of the small dogs. Frédéric said they were delightful. She picked them both up and raising their black snouts to his face, said:

'Come on now, be a nice doggy and give the gentleman a kiss.'

A man dressed in a dirty frock coat with a fur collar came in suddenly.

'Félix, my dear,' she said, 'that little matter will be settled next Sunday, without fail.'

The man began dressing her hair. He gave her news of her friends: Madame de Rochegune, Madame de Saint-Florentin, Madame Lombard, all of them noble, like the people in the Dambreuse establishment. Then he talked about theatres; there was a special show on at the Ambigu that night.

'Will you go?'

'Oh no, I'll stay at home.'

Delphine appeared. Rosanette scolded her for going out without her permission. The latter said she was coming back from the market.

'Well, bring me your book!—Forgive me, won't you?'

And, muttering aloud while she read it, Rosanette made remarks about every item. Her maid had added it up wrong.

'Give me back four sous!'

Delphine gave them to her and when Rosanette had dismissed her:

'Oh, Mother of God! What one has to suffer with these people!'

Frédéric was shocked by this recrimination. It reminded him too much of the others and established a sort of uncomfortable similarity between the two households.

Delphine had come back and went over to whisper a word in her ear.

'Oh no, I won't!'

Delphine again appeared.

'Madame, she insists.'

'Oh, how annoying! Show her out!'

At that moment an old lady dressed in black pushed open the door. Frédéric heard nothing, saw nothing. Rosanette had hurried into the room to meet her.

When she reappeared, her cheeks were red and she sat down in one of the armchairs, without speaking. A tear fell on to her cheek. Then turning to the young man, she said gently:

'What do they call you?'

'Frédéric.'

'Oh, Federico! Do you mind if I call you that?'

And she gazed at him in a flirtatious fashion, almost lovingly.

Suddenly she uttered a cry of delight at seeing Mademoiselle Vatnaz.

The artiste had no time to waste, since she had to preside over her guest table at six o'clock precisely. And she was tired and out of breath. First she drew out of her bag a watch chain with a paper, then other objects, things she had acquired.

'Did you know there are some magnificent suede gloves for thirty-six sous in the Rue Joubert! They still need another week to clean the curtains. I've said we'll call back for the lace trim. Bugneaux has received the account. That's all I think? You owe me one hundred and eighty-five francs!'

Rosanette went over and took ten napoleons out of a drawer. Neither had any change. Frédéric offered.

'I'll pay you back,' said La Vatnaz, stuffing fifteen francs into her bag.* 'But you are a naughty boy. I don't like you any more, you didn't ask me for a single dance the other day.—Oh, my dear, I found a frame of stuffed humming-birds on the Quai Voltaire, simply divine! If I were you I'd buy them. Look! What do you think of this?'

And she got out an old piece of pink silk that she had bought at the Temple to make a medieval doublet for Delmar.

'He was here today, wasn't he?'

'No!'

'That's odd!'

And a minute later:

'Where are you going this evening?'

'To Alphonsine's,' Rosanette said. That was the third version of how she intended to spend the evening.

Mademoiselle Vatnaz went on:

'And what news of the Old Man of the Mountain?'*

But with a sudden wink the Maréchale ordered her to keep quiet. And she accompanied Frédéric back to the hall, to find out if he were going to see Arnoux soon.

'Ask him to come and see me. Not in front of his wife, obviously!'

At the top of the steps an umbrella was placed against the wall, near a pair of overshoes.

'La Vatnaz's galoshes. Look at the size! She's a big girl, my little friend is!'

And in a melodramatic voice, rolling the last letter, she said:

'Can't trust herrrr!'

Frédéric, feeling taken into her confidence and emboldened by it, tried to kiss her on the neck. She said coldly:

'You are welcome! It doesn't cost anything!'

His heart was light as he came out. He did not doubt that the Maréchale would become his mistress before long. This desire awoke another. And in spite of the kind of grudge he bore towards her, he felt the urge to see Madame Arnoux.

Anyway he needed to go there, for Rosanette's commission.

'But at the moment,' he thought, because six o'clock was striking, 'Arnoux will certainly be at home.'

He put off his visit till the following day.

She was in the same place as on the first day, sewing a child's shirt. The little boy at her feet was playing with wooden animals. Marthe was writing, a little way off.

He began by complimenting her on her children. She answered him without any silly maternal exaggeration.

The room had a peaceful look. Bright sunshine streamed through the window, the corners of the furniture gleamed, and as Madame Arnoux was sitting near the window, a large ray of light falling on the curls on her neck flooded her amber skin with gold. Then he spoke:

'This young lady has grown up in the last three years! Do you remember, Mademoiselle, when you fell asleep on my knees in the coach?' Marthe couldn't remember. 'One night when we were coming back from Saint-Cloud?'

Madame Arnoux looked extremely sad. Did that mean she forbade him to make any allusion to the shared memory?

Her beautiful black eyes, with their brilliance, moved slightly beneath their rather heavy lids, and in the depths of her pupils, there was an infinite tenderness. He was seized again by a love which was stronger and more intense than ever. This contemplation transfixed him, but he shook himself out of it. How could he impress her? What could he do? And, casting about, Frédéric could find no better subject than money. He began to talk about the weather, which was not so cold as in Le Havre.

'Is that where you have been?'

'Yes, on family business... an inheritance.'

'Oh, I'm so pleased,' she answered, with such obvious sincerity that he was touched, as if she had done him a great service.

Then she asked what he planned to do, a man needed to have some occupation. He remembered his lie and said he was hoping to become councillor of State, with the help of Monsieur Dambreuse, the deputy.

'Perhaps you know him?'

'Only by name.'

Then in a low voice:

'*He* took you to the ball the other day, didn't he?'

Frédéric was silent.

'That's what I wanted to know. Thank you.'

Then she asked him two or three discreet questions about his family and his home. It was very nice of him to have stayed over there so long and not forget them.

'But... how could I?' he went on: 'Did you ever think I would?'

Madame Arnoux rose.

'I think you are a good, loyal friend to us. Farewell... we shall see you again soon?'

And she held out her hand to him in a frank and forthright way. Did that signify an understanding, a promise? Frédéric felt elated. He had to stop himself from bursting into song, he felt a need to open out to the world, to do good, to give alms. He looked around him to see if there was anyone in need of his help. No beggar was passing. And the generous impulse passed, for he was not a man to go out of his way to look for such opportunities.

Then his mind returned to his friends. The first one he thought of was Hussonnet; the second, Pellerin. The lowly position of Dussardier naturally deserved thinking about. As for Cisy, he was delighted to be able to show off his fortune to him a little. He therefore wrote to all four to come to a house-warming the following Sunday at exactly eleven o'clock, and he enjoined Deslauriers to bring along Sénécal.

The tutor had been dismissed from his third school for arguing against the prize-giving ceremony, which he regarded as injurious to equality. He was now with a machine manufacturer, and had not been lodging with Deslauriers for the last six months.

Their separation had been on cordial terms. Lately Sénécal had been receiving visits from men in smocks, all patriots and all workmen, worthy fellows but whose company the lawyer found tiresome. Moreover, he disliked some of his friend's ideas, however excellent they might be as weapons of war. Deslauriers kept quiet, out of ambition, hoping to guide him through persuasion, for he was confidently expecting a huge upheaval in which he hoped to make a niche, carve out a place for himself.

Sénécal's convictions were more disinterested. Every evening after work he came back to his attic room and did some research in his books for the justification of his dreams. He had made notes on the *Social Contract*. He devoured the *Revue indépendante*.* He was acquainted with the work of Mably, Morelly, Fourier, Saint-Simon, Comte, Cabet, Louis Blanc, the whole load of socialist writers, those who require humanity to descend to the level of the barrack room, send it to a brothel for its pleasure, or force it to bend over a counter. And from a hotchpotch of all these ideas, he had constructed an ideal of virtuous democracy, a cross between a farm and a factory, a sort of American Sparta where the individual would exist only to serve Society, which would be more omnipotent, absolute, infallible, and divine than the Great Lamas or the Nebuchadnezzars. He had no doubts this idea would be realized before very long. And everything that he judged to be hostile to it, Sénécal fought against, with the logic of a mathematician and the faith of an inquisitor. Titles, decorations, plumes, and especially liveries and even over-lauded reputations scandalized him; every day his studies and his suffering revived his fundamental hatred of any mark of distinction or superiority.

'What has that man ever done for me that I should treat him courteously? If he wants to see me he can come here!'

Deslauriers dragged him along.

They found their friend in his bedroom. Blinds and thick lined curtains, Venetian mirror—nothing was lacking. Frédéric, in a velvet jacket, was lying back in an easy chair, smoking a Turkish cigarette.

Sénécal glowered, like a Puritan brought to a pleasure den. Deslauriers took in everything with one glance. Then, with a deep bow to Frédéric:

'Monseigneur! My most humble respects!'

Dussardier threw his arms around him.

'So are you rich now? Good for you, old chap, damn good for you!'

Cisy appeared with a crêpe ribbon round his hat. Since the death of his grandmother he possessed a considerable fortune, and wanted not so much to enjoy it as to distinguish himself from other people, so as not to be like everyone else; in short, 'to have some *cachet*'. That was the word he used.

Now it was noon and everyone was yawning. Frédéric was expecting someone. At Arnoux's name, Pellerin made a face. He considered him a traitor since he had abandoned the arts.

'Supposing we did without him? What do you think?'

Everybody agreed.

A servant in long leggings opened the door and the dining room with its high oak skirting-board embossed with gold and two dressers loaded with porcelain tableware could be seen. Bottles of wine were warming on the stove; the blades of new knives gleamed beside the oysters. The milky tone of the muslin glasses looked inviting, and the table vanished under the game, the fruit, and the extraordinary dishes. All this was lost on Sénécal.

He began by asking for some ordinary bread, as coarse as possible, and with this in mind talked of the murders of Buzançais and the food crisis.*

Nothing of all that would have come about if they had done more to protect agriculture, if everything were not given over to competition, to anarchy, to the lamentable maxim of 'Laissez-faire, laissez-passer'! That's how the feudalism of money, which was far worse than the other kind, came about! But they should watch out! The people would grow tired of it in the end and make the capitalists pay for it, either through bloody proscriptions or by pillaging their fine houses.

Frédéric saw, in a sudden flash, men with bare arms flooding into Madame Dambreuse's large drawing room, smashing the mirrors with their pikes.

Sénécal had not finished. In view of the inadequate wages, workers were worse off than helots, Negroes, or pariahs, especially if they had children.

'Must he rid himself of them by smothering them, as advised by that English doctor who followed Malthus?'

And turning to Cisy:

'Shall we be reduced to following the advice of that dreadful Malthus?'

Cisy, who knew nothing of the dreadful teaching or even the existence of Malthus, replied that in any case many poor folk were helped and that the upper classes...

'Oh, the upper classes!' jeered the socialist. 'In the first place there are no upper classes. Only the heart raises a person up. We don't want charity, do you understand? Only equality, and a just distribution of goods.'

What he wanted was that workers should become capitalists, just as a soldier could be a colonel. At least the old guilds, by restricting the number of apprentices, had prevented the workers becoming too numerous, and the sense of fraternity had been sustained by festivals and banners.

Being a poet, Hussonnet regretted the passing of the banners; so did Pellerin, a taste he had acquired at the Café Dagneaux, listening to the Phalansterians* talk. He declared that Fourier was a great man.

'Come now,' Deslauriers said. 'That old fool! He sees the effects of divine justice in the fall of empires. It's like old Saint-Simon and his church, with his hatred of the French Revolution. A band of jokers who would give us Catholicism again!'

Monsieur de Cisy, to enlighten himself, no doubt, or to have people think well of him, began to say timidly:

'Do those two fine minds not agree with Voltaire then?'

'As for *him*, you can keep him!' said Sénécal.

'What? But I thought...'

'Oh no, he didn't care for the people!'

Then the conversation descended to talking about contemporary events: the Spanish weddings, the corruption in Rochefort, the re-organization of the chapter in Saint-Denis,* which would entail an increase in taxes. In Sénécal's view, they were paying enough already.

'And why, for God's sake? To build palaces for the monkeys in the Museum, to hold parades for illustrious staff officers in our squares, or maintain an etiquette that is positively Gothic amongst the lackeys at court!'

'I read in *La Mode*,'* said Cisy, 'that on Saint Ferdinand's day at the Tuileries ball, everyone came in fancy dress.'

'Pathetic!' said the socialist, shrugging his shoulders in disgust.

'And look at the museum in Versailles!' cried Pellerin. 'What about that? Those fools have cut off a Delacroix and lengthened a Gros! In the Louvre they have restored, scratched, and retouched all the canvases so thoroughly that in ten years it's possible not one will remain. As for the mistakes in the catalogue, a German has written a whole book about it. Foreigners are having fun at our expense!'

'Yes, we are the laughing stock of Europe,' Sénécal said.

'That's because Art is in hock to the Crown.'

'Not until we have universal suffrage...!'

'No, thank you!' said the artist, who had not had an exhibition in a Salon for twenty years, and was furious with those in power. 'We want to be left alone. I ask for nothing! But the Chambers* should legislate in the interests of Art. A chair of aesthetics ought to be set up, and the professor, who should be both a practitioner and a theorist, might manage, I hope, to get together a general constituency.'

'You would do well, Hussonnet, to mention it in your paper?'

'Is the Press free? Are *we* free?' asked Deslauriers fiercely. 'When you think you have to fill in anything up to twenty-eight forms before you can even put a little boat on the river, I feel like going to live with the anthropophagi! The Government is devouring us! Everything belongs to them, philosophy, law, the arts, the very air we breathe. And France frets herself to death beneath the policeman's boot and the priest's soutane.'

Thus the future Mirabeau spewed out his bile. Finally he raised his glass, got up, and, his hand on his hip and his eyes flashing, said:

'I drink to the total destruction of the current order, that is to say, of everything whose name is Privilege, Monopoly, Control, Hierarchy, Authority, State...' And in a louder voice: '...I should like to smash it—like this!' And he threw down on the table the beautiful stemmed glass which smashed into a thousand pieces.

They all clapped, Dussardier loudest of all.

The sight of any injustice made his gorge rise. He worried about Barbès. He was the sort who would throw himself under a cab to help a fallen horse. His erudition was limited to two works, one called *Royal Crimes*, the other *Mysteries of the Vatican*.* He had listened to the lawyer open-mouthed with delight. Finally, no longer able to contain himself:

'What I blame Louis-Philippe for is abandoning the Poles!'

'Wait a moment!' said Hussonnet. 'First, Poland does not exist. It's something dreamed up by Lafayette. As a general rule, the Poles are all from the Faubourg Saint-Marceau, the real ones drowned with Poniatowski.' In short, 'he didn't believe in that any more'. He had 'done with all that'. It was like the sea serpent, the revocation of the Edict of Nantes, and 'the old lies' about Saint Bartholomew's Day.*

Without defending the Poles, Sénécal reiterated the poet's last words. They had been unfair to the Papacy, who, after all, was on the side of the people, and he called the League* 'the dawn of democracy, a great egalitarian movement against the individualism of the Protestants'.

Frédéric was rather surprised by these ideas. They probably bored Cisy, for he turned the conversation to the *tableaux vivants* at the Gymnase which were drawing in a lot of people lately.

Sénécal was upset about this. Such spectacles, with their insolent display of luxury, corrupted the daughters of the proletariat. So he approved of the Bavarian students who had insulted Lola Montès.* Like Rousseau, he set greater store by the wife of a charcoal-burner than the mistress of a king.

'You must be joking!' replied Hussonnet grandly, and he defended these ladies, citing Rosanette as an example. Then as he was speaking of her ball and of Arnoux's costume, Pellerin said:

'They say he's in trouble, don't they?'

The picture dealer had just been involved in a lawsuit over his land in Belleville and was at present in a company from Lower Brittany dealing in kaolin,* along with others of his sort.

Dussardier was better informed. His own employer, Monsieur Moussinot, had made enquiries about Arnoux from the banker Oscar Lefebvre, who, knowing of some of his renewed debts, had opined that he was not sound.

Dessert was over. They went through into the drawing room, which was hung, like the Maréchale's, with yellow damask, and furnished in the style of Louis XVI.

Pellerin chided Frédéric for not choosing a neoclassical style. Sénécal struck matches on the hangings; Deslauriers passed no comment then, but he did in the library, which he called a 'little girl's library'. Most contemporary writers were there on the shelves. It was impossible to discuss their books, for Hussonnet immediately started to tell personal anecdotes about them, passing remarks about their faces, habits, and dress, elevating fifteenth-rate intellects and denigrating first-rate ones, and of course deploring modern decadence. A folk song contained more poetry than all the lyrics of the nineteenth century. Balzac was overrated, Byron discredited, Hugo did not understand the first thing about the theatre etc. etc.

'Why haven't you got any volumes of our worker-poets?' enquired Sénécal.

And Monsieur de Cisy, who knew about literature, was surprised not to see on Frédéric's table 'some of those new physiologies, the Physiology of the Smoker, of the Fisherman, of the Toll-keeper'.*

They eventually succeeded in annoying him so much he wanted to kick them out of his house. 'But I'm being silly!' And taking Dussardier on one side he asked if there was anything he could do for him.

The honest fellow was touched. But with his position as cashier, he needed nothing.

Afterwards Frédéric took Deslauriers into his bedroom and taking two thousand francs out of his desk, said:

'Here, my friend, put this in your pocket! It's the rest of what I owe you.'

'But... what about the Journal?' the lawyer asked. 'I spoke to Hussonnet about it, as you know.'

And to Frédéric's reply that he was a little hard up at present, his friend gave an unpleasant smile.

After the liqueurs, they drank beer. After beer, punch. Pipes were smoked again and again. At last, at five, all departed. And they were walking all together, next to each other without talking, when Dussardier remarked that Frédéric had been a perfect host. All agreed.

Hussonnet said the lunch was a bit heavy. Sénécal criticized the frivolousness of the decor. Cisy was of the same opinion. It lacked '*cachet*', totally.

'In my opinion,' said Pellerin, 'he could have commissioned a picture from me.'

Deslauriers said nothing, clutching the banknotes in his trouser pocket.

Frédéric was left alone. Thinking about his friends, he felt as if there was a vast dark gulf between him and them. He had reached out to them, but they had not responded to his friendly overtures.

He was remembering what Pellerin and Dussardier had said about Arnoux. Perhaps that was an invention, a calumny? If so, why? And he imagined Madame Arnoux ruined, weeping, selling her furniture. He was tormented all night by this thought. The next day he went to visit her.

Not knowing how to broach the subject of what he knew, he asked, by way of conversation, if Arnoux still had his plot in Belleville.

'Yes, he still has it.'

'Now he's with a company for Breton kaolin, I think?'

'That's right.'

'His factory is going well, I suppose?'

'Well... I imagine so.'

And, seeing him hesitate:

'Why, what's the matter? You scare me!'

He told her about the renewal of the bills. She lowered her head and said:

'I feared as much!'

In fact, Arnoux had refused to sell his plots, hoping to make a killing. He had taken out a large loan, and, not finding any buyers, had thought he would make good the deficit by setting up a factory. The costs had exceeded the income. She didn't know any more than that; he avoided all her questions and constantly protested that it was all going well.

Frédéric tried to reassure her. It was perhaps a temporary difficulty. And anyway, if he heard anything he would let her know.

'Oh yes, you will, won't you?' she said, putting her two hands to-gether, beseeching him, in a way that was very becoming.

So, he could be useful to her. He was entering her life, her affections!

Arnoux appeared.

'Oh, how nice of you to come and take me out for dinner!'

Frédéric did not know what to say.

Arnoux made small talk, then told his wife that he would be back late, having an appointment with Monsieur Oudry.

'At his house?'

'Yes, of course.'

He admitted as they went downstairs that since the Maréchale was free they would spend the evening at the Moulin Rouge and since he always needed someone to confide in, he had Frédéric take him to her door.

Instead of going in, he walked up and down on the pavement, looking at the windows on the second floor. Suddenly the curtains were pulled back.

'Oh good, Père Oudry has left! Goodnight!'

So she was being kept by Père Oudry? Now Frédéric didn't know what to think.

From that day on Arnoux was even more friendly than before. He invited him to dinner at his mistress's house, and before long Frédéric was a regular at each of the two households.

He enjoyed going to Rosanette's house. They went there in the evenings when they left the club or the theatre. They had a cup of tea or a game of lotto. On Sundays they played charades. Rosanette, who was more boisterous than the others, distinguished herself by her funny inventions, like scampering around on all fours, or dressing up in a cotton nightcap. She put on a leather helmet to look at passers-by through the window. She smoked Turkish pipes, sang Tyrolean songs. In the afternoon, to pass the time, she cut out flowers from a piece of chintz, stuck them on her windows, painted her two little dogs with rouge, burned incense, or told her fortune. Incapable of resisting an impulse, she fell in love with a trinket she had seen, couldn't sleep for wanting it, and rushed out to buy it, exchanged it for another, wasted dress material, lost her jewels, squandered money, and would have sold her chemise for a box at the theatre. She often asked Frédéric the meaning of a word she had read, but didn't wait for his answer, skipping quickly on to another idea, asking more and more questions.

Spasms of gaiety were succeeded by childish rages. Or else she sat dreaming on the floor by the fire, head down and hugging her knees, more inert than a torpid snake. She got dressed in front of him, not paying attention to his presence, slowly pulling up her silk stockings, then splashed water all over her face, leaning back like a shivering water-nymph; and her laughing white teeth, sparkling eyes, her beauty, and her gaiety dazzled Frédéric and set him on edge.

Almost always he found Madame Arnoux teaching her toddler to read, or standing behind Marthe's chair as she practised scales on her piano. When she was working at her sewing it was a great pleasure for him to pick up her scissors occasionally. All her movements had a quiet dignity; her small hands seemed made to dispense alms, to wipe away tears. And her voice, naturally rather soft, was caressing and light as a breeze.

She had no great enthusiasm for literature but he found her simple and profound remarks charming. She liked travelling, the sound of the wind in the trees and walking bareheaded in the rain. Frédéric listened to these things with delight, believing that he could detect in them the beginnings of her surrender.

The company of these two women made a sort of twofold music in his life: one was playful, violent, entertaining; the other serious and almost religious. And the two melodies playing at the same time steadily swelled and became gradually intertwined. For if Madame Arnoux brushed him with her finger, the image of the other woman appeared before him as an object of desire, because he had more of a chance with her. And when in Rosanette's company his emotions happened to be stirred, he immediately remembered his one true love.

This confusion was created by the similarities between the two households. One of the chests that he had noticed in the apartment in the Boulevard Montmartre was at present gracing Rosanette's dining room, the other was in Madame Arnoux's drawing room. In the two houses the dinner services were identical, and even the same velvet skullcap could be seen lying on an armchair. Then there were any number of small gifts, screens, boxes, fans that travelled between the mistress's house and the wife's; for, without the least embarrassment, Arnoux took back what he had given to the one to give to the other.

The Maréchale and Frédéric laughed at his wicked ways together. One Sunday after dinner she took him behind the door and showed him a bag of cakes in his overcoat, just lifted from the table, no doubt in order to give his children a treat. Monsieur Arnoux behaved with a roguishness that bordered on the immoral. He thought it was one's duty to evade taxes. He never paid for tickets at the theatre, claimed he always got into a first-class compartment with a second-class ticket and said—with glee—that he always put a trouser button instead of a ten-sou coin in the assistant's collecting box at the swimming baths. Yet that didn't stop the Maréchale from liking him.

However, one day she said, speaking about him:

'Oh, I'm fed up with him! God knows I've had enough! Too bad, I'll find someone else!'

Frédéric thought the 'someone else' had already been found and was called Monsieur Oudry.

'So,' said Rosanette. 'What difference does that make?'

Then, in a trembling voice:

'Yet I ask him for so little! And the old fool won't, he won't! But when it comes to promises, oh, that's another story!'

He had even promised her a quarter of his profits in the notorious kaolin mines; but there were no profits, any more than there was cashmere, which he had been tempting her with for the last six months.

Frédéric immediately thought he would make a present of it to her. Arnoux might take that as a reprimand and get angry.

Yet Arnoux was generous, his wife herself said so. But mad! Instead of inviting everyone to dinner at his house, nowadays he treated his acquaintances to dinner in a restaurant. He bought things that were completely useless, such as gold chains, clocks, household items. Out in the passage Madame even showed Frédéric an enormous quantity of hot water jars, foot-warmers, and samovars. Finally one day she admitted she was worried: Arnoux had made her sign a bill made out to Monsieur Dambreuse.

In the meantime Frédéric kept on with his literary projects, because he had made this something of a point of honour. He had in mind to write a history of aesthetics, the result of his conversations with Pellerin, then dramatize various periods of the French Revolution and compose a great comedy, through the indirect influence of Deslauriers and Hussonnet. In the course of his work often the face of one woman or the other would float before his eyes. He struggled against the desire to see her, but soon gave in; and he was more depressed when he returned from seeing Madame Arnoux.

One morning when he was nursing his melancholy by the fireside,

Deslauriers came by. Sénécal's incendiary speeches had worried his employer and once again he found himself without any money.

'What do you want me to do about it?' Frédéric enquired.

'Nothing! You don't have any money, I know, but it wouldn't be too much trouble for you to find him a job, either through Dambreuse or Arnoux?'

The latter must need engineers in his business. Frédéric had an inspiration. Sénécal could let him know when her husband was absent, carry letters, help him out on a thousand possible occasions. Men always did things like that for one another. Moreover, he would find ways of using him without him being aware of it. Chance was offering him a helper, that was a good sign, one must seize the opportunity. And adopting a casual tone, he replied that it might be possible to arrange it, and that he'd see what he could do.

He saw to it without delay. Arnoux was taking great pains over his work in the factory. He was seeking to reproduce the copper red of the Chinese. But his colours were evaporating in the firing process. In order to avoid flaws in his china he mixed lime with his clay; but the pieces were mostly breaking, the enamel on the decorations bubbled before they were fired, his large plates buckled. And blaming these misfortunes on the bad tools in his factory he wanted to order new grinders and other drying equipment. Frédéric remembered some of these things, and went to him saying he had found a very clever man capable of achieving his famous red. Arnoux leaped up at this news, and then, having heard him out, replied that he didn't need anyone.

Frédéric extolled Sénécal's prodigious knowledge—he was engineer, chemist, and accountant all in one, being a first-class mathematician.

The porcelain maker agreed to see him.

They argued over the pay. Frédéric intervened and at the end of a week managed to bring them to an agreement.

But because the factory was situated at Creil, Sénécal couldn't be of any use. This very simple realization disheartened Frédéric, as though it were a great misfortune.

He thought that the more Arnoux was away from his wife, the more chance he would stand with her. So he began by taking Rosanette's side all the time. He cited the many wrongs he had done to her, told him about the vague threats she had made the other day, and even mentioned the shawl, saying she had accused him of being mean.

Arnoux, stung by these words, and in any case starting to get worried, took Rosanette the cashmere but chided her for having complained to Frédéric. She told him she had reminded him of his promise a hundred times, but he claimed he had forgotten, he'd had too many things to do.

The next day Frédéric went to see her. Although it was two o'clock, the Maréchale was still in bed. And at her bedside Delmar, sitting at a little table, was finishing a slice of foie gras. She shouted from afar 'I've got it, I've got it!' then taking hold of Frédéric by his ears, she kissed him on the forehead, thanked him profusely, addressed him as 'tu', and even urged him to sit on her bed. Her pretty soft eyes were sparkling, her moist lips were smiling, her two shapely arms protruded from her sleeveless chemise. And occasionally he could feel through the soft lawn the firm contours of her body. Delmar, during that time, was rolling his eyes.

'Really, my dear,' he said. 'My dear friend!'

It was the same on subsequent occasions. As soon as Frédéric arrived she stood on a pouffe so that he could kiss her properly, called him a sweet boy, a darling, stuck a flower in his buttonhole, straightened his cravat. These attentions were always exaggerated when Delmar was there.

Were they advances? Frédéric thought so. As for deceiving a friend, Arnoux wouldn't have any scruples about that if it were him! And he had every right not to be virtuous with his mistress, having been constantly virtuous with his wife; for he was persuaded that he had been, or rather he wanted to persuade himself of it to justify his remarkable cowardice. But he thought his conduct stupid and resolved to make a bold play for the Maréchale forthwith.

So one afternoon as she was bending down in front of a chest of drawers he drew nearer to her and made a movement so unambiguously suggestive that she stood up again, scarlet-faced. He repeated his attempt. At that she burst into tears saying she was very unhappy but that was no reason to treat her with contempt.

He tried again. She changed tactics, making fun of him every time. He thought it would be clever to respond in the same way but even more so. But he was too jolly for her to take him seriously. And their camaraderie proved an obstacle to their expressing any true emotion. Finally one day she said she wouldn't accept someone else's leftovers.

'Whose?'

'Madame Arnoux's of course—go back to her!'

For Frédéric talked about her often. Arnoux for his part had the same obsession. In the end she grew impatient hearing about this woman, and her remark was a kind of revenge.

Frédéric resented her for it.

In any case, he was starting to find her intensely irritating. Sometimes, posing as a woman of experience, she passed insults about love with a cynical laugh that made him itch to slap her. A quarter of an hour later love was the only thing in the world and, crossing her arms on her breasts, as though to squeeze a man to her, she would murmur 'Oh, it's so good, so good!', her eyelids half-closed and swooning as if half-drunk. It was impossible to know what she meant—to know, for example, if she loved Arnoux, for she made fun of him and seemed jealous of him too. It was the same with La Vatnaz, whom she called a bitch, but at other times her best friend. In short, there was something indefinable about her, even in the way she wore her chignon, that amounted to a challenge. And he desired her, especially for the pleasure of conquering and dominating her.

What could he do? For often she sent him unceremoniously away, opening the doors only a little and hurriedly whispering: 'I'm busy. See you this evening!' Or else he found her surrounded by a dozen people. And when they were on their own there were so many interruptions you would have sworn a wager had been laid against him. He invited her to dinner; she always refused. Once she accepted, but didn't turn up.

He hit on an idea, worthy of Machiavelli.

Aware of Pellerin's complaints about him from Dussardier, he thought of commissioning a life-size portrait of the Maréchale, which would require a lot of sittings. He would not miss a single one. The painter's habitual unpunctuality would mean they would often be alone together. He persuaded Rosanette to sit for her portrait, so that she could offer her likeness to her dear Arnoux. She accepted, for she saw herself in the place of honour in the middle of the Grand Salon* with a crowd of people in front of her, and the newspapers talking about her, which would launch her immediately in society.

As for Pellerin, he seized on the project with alacrity. This portrait would make his name as a great painter, it would be a masterpiece.

In his mind he went through all the Old Masters' portraits he was familiar with and decided finally on a Titian, with touches of

Veronese.* So he would execute his idea without artificial shadows, in a bright light illuminating the flesh in a single tone and making the accessories sparkle.

'Suppose I painted her in a pink silk dress with an oriental burnous?' he wondered. 'Oh no, not a wretched burnous! What if I dressed her instead in blue velvet on a grey background, very colourful? I could give her a little collar of white lace with a black fan and a scarlet curtain behind her.'

Casting around like this, he expanded his idea every day and marvelled at it as it developed.

His heart started beating hard when Rosanette accompanied by Frédéric arrived at his house for the first sitting. He posed her standing on a kind of dais in the centre of the apartment. And, complaining about the light and wishing he were back in his old studio, he got her first to lean against a pedestal, then sit in an armchair. Now he would step back, now go closer to adjust the folds of her dress with a flick of his fingers; he looked at her with his eyes half-closed and asked Frédéric for his opinion.

'Why no!' he cried. 'I'm going back to what I thought before! I'll do you as a Venetian lady!'

She would have a crimson velvet dress with a jewelled belt, and her wide sleeve trimmed with ermine would reveal her bare arm, which would be resting on the balustrade of a staircase rising behind her. On her left a high column would reach to the top of the canvas and join the curving architecture above. Below, you would just be able to make out some clumps of orange trees, almost black, against a blue sky streaked with white clouds. On the carpeted stairs there would be a bouquet of flowers on a silver platter, an amber rosary, a dagger, and an old yellowing-ivory box overflowing with gold sequins, some of which would even have spilled on to the floor and would form a series of bright splashes, thus leading the eye to the tip of her foot, for she would be posed on the last step but one in a natural attitude in full light.

He went to get a packing case, which he put on the dais to represent the step. Then he took a stool to serve as the balustrade and laid on it, as accessories, his jacket, a shield, a tin of sardines, a packet of pens and a knife, and when he had scattered a dozen copper coins in front of Rosanette he made her take up her pose.

'Imagine that those things are riches, splendid presents. Move your

head to the right a little. Perfect! Keep very still! That queenly attitude matches your type of beauty very well.'

She was wearing a tartan dress with a large muff and was trying to
stifle her giggles.

'As for the coiffure, we'll plait a string of pearls in it—that always
looks well in red hair.'

The Maréchale objected that she didn't have red hair.

'Nonsense! The painter's red isn't the same as ordinary red!'

He began sketching out the different areas of the subject. And he
was so preoccupied with the great Renaissance painters that he talked
about them for an hour; he envisaged their magnificent lives full of
genius, glory and luxury, their triumphal entries into cities and torchlight feasts between half-naked women beautiful as goddesses.

'You were born to live in that age. A creature of your calibre would
have deserved a prince!'

Rosanette found these compliments very charming. They fixed the
date of the next sitting. Frédéric took it upon himself to bring the
accessories.

As the heat of the stove had rather fuddled her, they walked home
via the Rue du Bac and stopped on the Pont Royal.

It was fine weather, sharp and bright. The sun was going down.
A few windows of houses in the Cité glittered in the distance like gold
plaques, while behind them on the right the towers of Notre-Dame
stood out blackly against the blue sky, which was bathed in a soft grey
mist on the horizon. It was windy; Rosanette declared she was hungry
and they entered the Pâtisserie anglaise.

Young women with children were standing eating at the marble-
topped counter, where plates of cakes were piled up under glass
covers. Rosanette devoured two cream cakes. The icing sugar made
a moustache at the corners of her mouth. From time to time she drew
a handkerchief from her muff to wipe it off. And her face under her
green hood looked like a full-blown rose among its leaves.

They resumed their walk. In the Rue de la Paix she stopped in front of
a jeweller's to look at a bracelet. Frédéric wanted to buy it for her.

'No,' she said. 'Keep your money.'

He was hurt by this.

'What's the matter with my sweet? Is he sad?'

When the conversation began again, he came round as usual to
declaring his love for her.

'You know it's impossible!'

'Why?'

'Oh, because...'

They walked side by side, she leaning on his arm, and the flounces of her dress flapped against his legs. Then he remembered how one winter twilight Madame Arnoux had walked like that beside him. And that memory so absorbed him that he no longer noticed or thought of Rosanette.

She was looking vaguely in front of her, dragging back a little like an indolent child. It was the time when people were returning from their outings and carriages were rolling briskly along the dry cobbles. Pellerin's flattering words must have occurred to her again for she uttered a sigh.

'Oh, some women are so lucky! I was made for a rich man, there's no doubt about it.'

He answered roughly:

'But you have one!' For Monsieur Oudry was said to be a multimillionaire.

She was doing her best to get rid of him.

'Who's stopping you?'

And he made acid comments about this old bewigged business-man, saying that a relationship like that was unworthy of her and that she ought to break it off.

'Yes,' the Maréchale replied. 'No doubt I shall in the end!'

This waning of interest delighted Frédéric. She was walking more slowly, he supposed she was tired. She insisted she did not want a cab and, blowing him a kiss with her fingertips, she sent him away at her door.

'What a shame! And to think that some fools think I am rich!'

He was in a sombre mood when he reached his house.

Hussonnet and Deslauriers were waiting for him.

His bohemian friend was sitting at the table drawing Turks' heads,* and the lawyer in muddy boots was dozing on the divan.

'Oh, at last!' he cried. 'But how cross you look! Can you listen to what I have to say?'

As a tutor, his star was waning, for he crammed his pupils' heads with theories that were unhelpful in their exams. He had defended cases once or twice and lost, and each new disappointment drove him further and further towards his former ambition: a newspaper where he could give voice to his ideas, take his revenge on society, spew forth his bile and his opinions. Fortune and renown in any case would follow. It was to this end that he had won over Hussonnet, for the bohemian owned a periodical.

At present he was printing on pink paper. He invented gossip, composed word games, tried to start controversies, and even (despite the unsuitable venue) attempted to put on concerts. A year's subscription 'gave one the right to a seat in the stalls in one of the principal theatres in Paris. What's more, the management took on the responsibility for providing foreign visitors with all the information they might require, artistic or otherwise.' But the printer was issuing threats, three terms' rent was owing, all sorts of difficulties were arising. And Hussonnet would have let *L'Art* perish had it not been for the exhortations of the lawyer who supported and encouraged him, day in, day out. He had brought him along in order to lend his proposition more weight.

'We've come about the newspaper,' he said.

'Oh, so you are still thinking about that?' Frédéric replied distractedly.

'Of course I'm thinking about it!'

And he expounded his plan again. Through articles on the Bourse, they would get to know financiers and obtain from them the necessary hundred thousand francs. But in order to transform the broadsheet into a political newspaper, they first had to have a wide circulation, and must therefore resolve to make some outlay to meet the cost of the paper, the printing, the administration, in short to spend the sum of fifteen thousand francs.

'I haven't got the funds,' Frédéric said.

'Nor have we!' said Deslauriers, folding his arms.

Hurt by this attitude, Frédéric replied:

'Is that my fault?'

'Oh, all right! A man may have fuel for his fire, truffles on the table, a comfortable bed, a library, a carriage, all the little luxuries! But if someone else shivers in a garret, pays twenty sous for a meal, works like a slave, or is mired in poverty, is that his fault?'

And he repeated: 'Is that his fault?' with a Ciceronian irony which had echoes of the law court. Frédéric tried to say something but Deslauriers interrupted him.

'Oh, I know, I understand, as an aristocrat, one has one's needs... no doubt for some woman...'

'Well, what of it? Am I not free to do as I please?...'

'Oh yes, very free!'

And after a moment's silence, Deslauriers remarked:

'Making promises is easy!'

'Damn you, I'm not going back on them!' Frédéric said.

The lawyer went on:

'At school we promise to form a phalanx, like Balzac's "Les Treize"!* Then, when we get together again it's, "Goodbye old chap, get lost!" For the one who could be of use to the others keeps all his wealth for himself.'

'What?'

'Yes, you haven't even introduced us to the Dambreuses!'

Frédéric contemplated him. With his shabby overcoat, his dirty spectacles, and his pale face, the lawyer cut such a wretched figure that he couldn't repress a scornful smile. Deslauriers noticed it and reddened.

He had already picked up his hat to leave. Hussonnet, worried stiff, attempted to calm him down with a beseeching look and as Frédéric turned his back he said:

'Come now, my friend! Be my Maecenas! Give your patronage to the arts!'

In an abrupt gesture of resignation Frédéric took a sheet of paper and scribbling a line or two on it, held it out to him. The bohemian's face lit up. Then, passing the letter over to Deslauriers, he said:

'Say you are sorry, Milord!'

Their friend had requested his solicitor to send him fifteen thousand francs as quickly as possible.

'Ah, that's the friend I used to know!' said Deslauriers.

'By God!' added the bohemian. 'You are a good fellow. We'll have to put you in the gallery of benefactors!'

The lawyer went on:

'You won't lose by it. It's an excellent investment!'

'It certainly is!' Hussonnet cried. 'I'd place my head on the block!'

And he said so many foolish things and promised so many miracles (in which he perhaps believed) that Frédéric no longer knew if he were making fun of other people or of himself.

That evening he received a letter from his mother.

She was surprised he hadn't been made a Cabinet minister already and teased him lightly about it. Then she talked about her health, and told him that Monsieur Roque was a frequent visitor these days. 'Since he has been made a widower I thought it was all right for him to visit. Louise is greatly improved.' And as a PS: 'You don't mention your fine acquaintance, Monsieur Dambreuse. In your shoes I would make use of him.'

Well, why shouldn't he? His intellectual pretensions had deserted him and his fortune (as he was well aware) was insufficient. For, once he had paid his debts and lent the agreed sum of money to the others, his income would be diminished by at least four thousand francs! Moreover, he felt the need to escape from this way of living, and to start getting involved in something. So next day as he was dining at Madame Arnoux's, he said his mother was nagging him to take up a profession.

'But I was under the impression', she answered, 'that Monsieur Dambreuse was to effect your entrée into the Council of State? That would suit you to perfection.'

So she was in favour of it. He did as he was told.

The banker was sitting at his desk as before, and with a wave indicated he should wait a few minutes, because a gentleman, who had his back turned to the door, was discussing important matters with him. It was about coal and the merger that was to take place between different companies.

The portraits of General Foy and Louis-Philippe could be seen hanging on either side of the mirror. Filing cabinets standing against the wall stretched to the ceiling, and there were six rush chairs, for Monsieur Dambreuse did not need a more luxurious office for his business affairs. The room resembled those dark kitchens where great feasts are prepared. Frédéric's attention was especially drawn to two enormous safes standing in the corners of the room. He wondered how many millions they might hold. The banker opened one and the iron plate turned, revealing nothing but blue notebooks.

Finally the man turned and passed in front of Frédéric. It was old Oudry. They reddened as they exchanged greetings, which seemed to surprise Monsieur Dambreuse. As for him, he was very charming. Nothing was easier than to recommend his young friend to the Keeper of the Seals. They would be very happy to have him. And he extended his courteousness so far as to invite him to a party he was giving a few days later.

Frédéric was just getting into his cab when a note came for him from the Maréchale. In the light of the carriage lamps he read:

My dear, I've followed your advice. I've just got rid of my Osage.* From tomorrow evening I am free! Am I not a brave woman?

That was all. But it was an invitation to fill the vacant place. He uttered an exclamation, folded the note tightly in his pocket, and set off.

Two mounted gendarmes were stationed in the road. A row of Chinese lanterns blazed over the two gates and servants in the yards were shouting, to get the cabs to move forward to the bottom of the steps under the awning. Then suddenly the noise in the vestibule ceased.

Tall trees filled the space below the stairs; the porcelain globes were shedding a light which cast ripples of white shot silk on the walls. Frédéric ascended the steps with a light heart. An usher shouted out his name: Monsieur Dambreuse stretched out his hand; almost immediately Madame Dambreuse appeared.

She was wearing a mauve dress with a lace trim, the slides on her hair more abundant than usual, and not a single jewel.

She chided him for not visiting often enough, made a few bland remarks. The guests arrived. By way of greeting they inclined sideways, bent double, or simply bowed their heads. Then came a married couple, a family, and all disappeared into the drawing room which was already crowded.

Beneath the chandelier in the middle, on an enormous pouffe, stood a jardinière whose flowers, bending like plumes of feathers, hung over the heads of the women sitting in a circle around it; others occupied the easy chairs, forming two straight lines symmetrically broken by the long curtains of rich red velvet and the high doors with their golden lintels.

The crowd of men standing around, hats in hands, seen from afar formed a dark mass, the ribbons* on their buttonholes creating red dots here and there against the black, which was made darker by the uniform white of the ties. Apart from some youths with incipient beards, they all looked bored. Some sullen-faced dandies were rocking back and forth on their heels. Grey heads, wigs were plentiful. Occasionally you saw the gleam of a bald pate. And the faces, either purple or very pale, showed in their creases and wrinkles the traces of an immense fatigue, the people present being involved either with politics or business. Monsieur Dambreuse had also invited several scientists, magistrates, two or three famous doctors; he modestly dismissed the compliments heaped on him about his party as well as the allusions to his wealth.

Numerous footmen with wide gold braid were circulating through the rooms. Great candelabras bloomed like fiery bunches of flowers above the drapes and were reflected in the mirrors. And at the back of the dining room which had a trellis of jasmine lining its walls, the buffet resembled the high altar of a cathedral or an exhibition of jewels, there were so many dishes, covers, place settings, silver and silver-gilt spoons, in the midst of the cut glass with its iridescent lights sparkling above the food. The other three drawing rooms were bursting with works of art: landscapes of the Old Masters on the walls, ivories and porcelain around the tables, chinoiseries on the consoles. There were folded lacquered screens in front of the windows, bouquets of camellias filled the fireplaces; and there was a soft hum of music in the background like the buzzing of bees.

Not many were dancing and those who were, to judge by the indifferent manner in which they dragged their feet, seemed only to be going through the motions. Frédéric heard snatches of conversation such as:

'Were you at the last Charity Ball at the Hôtel Lambert, Mademoiselle?'

'No, Monsieur!'

'It's going to be very hot here soon!'

'Yes, I can't breathe!'

'Who wrote this polka I wonder?'

'Heavens, Madame, I do not know!'

And behind him three ageing juveniles who had taken up their position in a recess were whispering obscene remarks to one another. Others were chatting about the railway, or free trade; a sportsman was telling a hunting story. A Legitimist and an Orléanist* were having an argument.

Wandering from group to group he reached the card room, where, in a circle of serious-looking men, he recognized Martinon, now attached to the Public Prosecutor's office in the capital.

His large waxen face comfortably filled his beard, which was a real marvel, the black hairs of it being so remarkably well trimmed. And, retaining a moderate balance* between the elegance demanded by his age and the dignity necessitated by his profession, he poked his thumb into his armpit in the manner of a dandy, then put his arm into his waistcoat like a doctrinaire. Although he had very shiny patent-leather boots, he shaved his temples to give himself the appearance of an intellectual.

After a few cool remarks to Frédéric, he turned back to continue his confabulation. A landowner was saying:

'It's a class that dreams of turning society upside down!'

'They are demanding the organization of labour!' said someone else. 'Can you believe that?'

'Well what do you expect', said a third, 'when you see Monsieur de Genoude giving his support to *Le Siècle*?'*

'And even conservatives calling themselves progressives! In order to bring about what? The Republic! As if that were possible in France!'

Everyone declared that a Republic was impossible in France.

'Still,' a gentleman remarked aloud, 'everyone's far too concerned with the Revolution. A very great deal is being published on that subject...'*

'Without mentioning the fact', Martinon said, 'that there must surely be far more serious subjects to write about!'

Someone from the Ministry got on to the scandals in the theatre:

'So, for example, this new play *La Reine Margot*\* is beyond the pale! Why was it necessary to tell us about the Valois? It all shows royalty in an unfavourable light! It's like your Press! The Laws of September,\* I don't need to tell you, are infinitely too lenient! There'd be court martials to gag the journalists if I had my way! At the least insolence, drag them in front of a war tribunal and see how they like that!'

'Oh careful, Monsieur, careful!' a professor cried. 'Don't attack our precious gains of 1830! Let's respect our liberties.'

They should decentralize, send the surplus from the towns into the country.

'The towns are diseased!' shouted a Catholic. 'They ought to strengthen Religion!'

Martinon was quick to add:

'It's a brake on them, that's true!'

All the problems lay in this modern craving for rising above one's station, wanting the good things in life.

'And yet', objected an industrialist, 'luxury is good for trade. So I approve of the Duc de Nemours insisting on knee breeches at his parties.'

'Monsieur Thiers went in trousers. Do you know what he said?'

'Yes, delightful! But he is turning into a demagogue and his speech on the question of the division of competences had quite an influence on the assassination attempt of 12 May.'*

'You don't say!'

'I do indeed!'

The group was forced to stand back to let a servant carrying a tray through; he was trying to get into the card room.

Beneath the green shades of the candelabra the table was covered with rows of cards and gold coins. Frédéric stopped in front of one, lost the fifteen napoleons he had in his pocket, swung right round, and found himself at the door of the boudoir where Madame Dambreuse happened to be.

It was full of women, packed tightly in and sitting on stools. Their long skirts, flounced out around them, looked like waves from which their waists rose, and their breasts could be seen emerging from their low-cut bodices. Nearly all of them carried a bouquet of violets. The matt tone of their gloves brought out the natural whiteness of their arms. Fringes and flowers hung down over their shoulders and one thought, when occasionally they shivered, that a gown might fall off. But their respectable faces tempered their titillating costumes. Several even had a sort of animal placidity and this gathering of half-naked women put you in mind of the inside of a harem. A cruder comparison came into the young man's mind. All sorts of beauties, in fact, were there: English girls with keepsake profiles, an Italian girl whose black eyes flared like Vesuvius, three sisters from Normandy, fresh as apple blossom, dressed in blue, a tall redhead with an amethyst necklace; and the glittering white diamonds which sparkled in their hair, the luminosity of stones displayed on their bosoms, and the soft gleam of pearls setting off their faces, mingled with the reflections of the gold rings, lace, powder, the small scarlet mouths, the mother-of-pearl teeth. The domed ceiling gave the boudoir the appearance of a basket of flowers; and the beating fans caused a current of scented air.

Frédéric, who had remained standing behind them with his monocle to his eye, did not consider all the shoulders faultless. He thought of the Maréchale and that kept temptation at bay, or at least afforded some consolation.

But he contemplated Madame Dambreuse and found her charming, for all that her mouth was a little too long and her nostrils too wide. But she was distinctly attractive. Her curly hair had a sort of passionate languor, and there seemed to be a lot going on behind that forehead, which was the colour of agate, and had an air of authority.

She had placed her husband's niece, a rather unattractive girl, next to her. Now and again she would get up and welcome the women just arriving; and the murmur of female voices growing steadily louder was like the chattering of birds.

They were discussing the Tunisian ambassadors and their costumes. One lady had attended the last reception given by the Académie française. Another was talking about Molière's *Don Juan* and the new production at the Théâtre Français. But with a glance towards her niece, Madame Dambreuse put a finger to her lips, though her smile, which she was unable to hide, belied this admonition.

Suddenly Martinon appeared, at the other door opposite. She rose. He offered her his arm. Frédéric threaded his way between the card tables so that he might observe his further gallantries, and rejoined the guests in the big drawing room. Madame Dambreuse promptly left her cavalier and struck up a friendly conversation with him.

She understood that he didn't play cards or dance.

'The young are so sad!' Then, taking in the dancing with one glance:

'But really, it's not much fun. For certain people, at any rate!'

And she halted in front of the line of armchairs, dispensing the odd kindly remark, while bespectacled old men came to pay court to her. She introduced Frédéric to a few. Monsieur Dambreuse touched him lightly on his sleeve and drew him outside on to the terrace.

He had seen the minister. It wasn't straightforward. Before being accepted as an official at the Council of State you had to take an exam. Frédéric, with an inexplicable burst of confidence, replied that he knew the required subjects.

The financier wasn't surprised, in view of how highly Monsieur Roque had spoken of him.

At the mention of this name Frédéric again saw little Louise, his home, his room; and he remembered nights like this when he had stood at his window listening to the wagons roll past. This memory of his melancholy brought back the thought of Madame Arnoux, and he was silent as he walked up and down the terrace. The windows made tall patches of red in the darkness; the noise of the ball was subsiding. The carriages were beginning to depart.

'But why', asked Monsieur Dambreuse, 'are you so keen on the Council of State?'

And he declared, as a man of the world, that public office did not lead to anything, he knew a thing or two about that. Business was more profitable. Frédéric objected that it was difficult to learn.

'Nonsense, I could teach you in a very short time!'

Was he wanting to involve him in his enterprises?

The young man saw, as in a lightning flash, the great fortune that would come to him.

'Let's go in,' said the banker. 'You are having supper with us, I hope?'

It was three o'clock, everyone was leaving. In the dining room a table was laid for close friends.

Monsieur Dambreuse saw Martinon and going over to his wife, said in a low voice:

'Was it you who invited him?'

She replied curtly: 'Yes!'

Their niece was not there. They drank well, they laughed aloud. And no one found the risqué jokes shocking, since they were all enjoying the relief which follows a rather long period of constraint. Only Martinon was serious. He considered it good form to refuse the champagne, but was otherwise extremely unctuous and polite, for Monsieur Dambreuse, who was narrow-chested, complained of breathlessness, and he enquired several times after his health. Then he turned his blue-eyed gaze on Madame Dambreuse.

She questioned Frédéric about which young ladies at the party he liked. He had not noticed anyone in particular, and in any case preferred women in their thirties.*

'Not such a bad idea perhaps!' she replied.

Then, as they were putting on cloaks and overcoats, Monsieur Dambreuse said to him:

'Come and see me for a chat one morning!'

At the bottom of the stairs Martinon lit a cigar. As he sucked at it, his face grew so grave, his companion couldn't help remarking:

'You look like a bear with a sore head!'

'This bear has turned a few heads in its time,' the young magistrate replied, in tones at once firm but irritated.

On his way to bed Frédéric went over the evening in his mind. First, his appearance (he had looked at himself in the mirror on more than one occasion) from the cut of his dress coat to the bow on his shoes, was irreproachable. He had talked to men of standing, had seen rich women at close quarters, Monsieur Dambreuse had proved extremely friendly and Madame Dambreuse almost engaging. He weighed her every word, her looks, a thousand details that could not be analysed and yet spoke reams. It would be a fine thing to have a mistress like her! And why not, after all? He was as good as the next man! Perhaps she wasn't so inaccessible? Martinon flashed into his mind again; and as he drifted off to sleep he smiled with pity for the poor fellow.

The thought of the Maréchale woke him; those words in her note: 'From tomorrow evening' implied a definite rendezvous for that very day. He waited till nine and then hurried over to her house.

Someone before him climbed the stairs and closed the door. He tugged at the bell. Delphine answered it and declared that Madame was not there.

Frédéric insisted, pleaded with her. He had something very important to tell her, just a word or two. Finally a hundred-sou coin did the trick and the maid left him alone in the hallway.

Rosanette appeared. She was wearing her nightdress, her hair hung down. And, shaking her head from a distance, she made a large gesture with both arms that she was not able to see him.

Frédéric went slowly downstairs. This caprice was worse than all the others. He failed to understand her.

In front of the porter's lodge, Mademoiselle Vatnaz stopped him.

'Did she agree to see you?'

'No!'

'Were you shown the door?'

'How did you know?'

'It's obvious! But come on, let's go out. I can't breathe!'

She took him into the street. She was panting. He felt her thin arm trembling against his own. All at once she burst out:

'Oh, the wretch!'

'Who?'

'Him, of course! Delmar!'

This revelation humiliated Frédéric. He went on:

'Are you absolutely sure?'

'I tell you I followed him!' La Vatnaz cried. 'I saw him going in! Now do you understand? I ought to have expected it anyway. I was fool enough to introduce him to her. And if you only knew what I did! I took him in, fed him, bought him clothes. And all the contacts I made with the newspapers! I loved him like a mother.' Then, with a scornful laugh: 'Oh, Monsieur has to have his velvet gowns! An investment on his part, if you can believe it. And her! When you think that I knew her when she was making underclothes! Without me she would have sunk into the mire more than a score of times. But I'll shove her down in it yet. Oh yes, I hope she dies in the workhouse, then everyone will know the whole story!'

And like a torrent of dishwater flushing away the garbage, her anger flooded Frédéric with the shameful doings of her rival.

'She's slept with Jumillac, Flacourt, young Allard, Bertinaux, Saint-Valéry, the one with the pockmarks—no, the other one! They are brothers, no matter! And when she was in trouble I managed everything for her. What did I gain from it? She is so mean! And besides you will agree it was good of me to be kind to her, for we don't belong to the same class! Am I a loose woman? Do I sell myself? And besides she's as thick as they come! She even writes "category" with a "k". Well, they go well together. They make a good pair, even though he calls himself an artist and believes himself to be a genius! But for heaven's sake! If he had any sense at all he would not have played such a dirty trick! You don't leave an intelligent woman for a whore! Well I don't care anyway. He's getting ugly, I hate him! If I met him now, you know what I'd do? I'd spit in his face.'—She spat.—'Yes, that's what I think of him now! And Arnoux, eh? Isn't it disgusting? He has forgiven her so many times! You can't imagine what sacrifices he's made. She ought to kiss his feet! He's so generous, so good.'

Frédéric was pleased to hear Delmar being dragged through the mud. He had resigned himself as far as Arnoux was concerned. Rosanette's perfidiousness seemed to him abnormal, unfair behaviour. And, persuaded by the indignation of La Vatnaz, he even started to feel affection for him. Suddenly he was there outside his door. Mademoiselle Vatnaz, without him noticing, had taken him down the Faubourg Poissonnière.

'Here we are,' she said. 'I can't go up. But you can.'

'What for?'

'To tell him everything, of course!'

Frédéric, as though waking up with a start, realized what sordid action he was being pushed into.

'Well?' she continued.

He raised his eyes to the second floor. Madame Arnoux's lamp was burning. It was true, nothing was stopping him from going up.

'I'll wait for you down here. Go on then!'

This order put him off completely, and he said:

'I shall be up there for some time. You'd do better to go home. I'll come to your house tomorrow.'

'No, no,' replied La Vatnaz, stamping her foot. 'Get hold of him! Take him along! Make him catch them red-handed!'

'But Delmar won't be there now!'

She bowed her head.

'Yes, perhaps that's true?'

And she stood there not speaking in the middle of the street between the cabs; then, fixing her wildcat eyes on him:

'I can trust you, can't I? Between us, it's a solemn promise! Go on then. Till tomorrow!'

Frédéric could hear two people speaking to each other as he went along the corridor. Madame Arnoux was saying:

'Don't tell lies! So don't tell lies!'

He went in. They were silent.

Arnoux was pacing up and down. Madame sat on the little chair by the fire, extremely pale and staring into the distance. Frédéric made to leave. Arnoux grasped him by the hand, happy that he had come to his aid.

'But I'm afraid...' Frédéric said.

'Please stay!' Arnoux whispered in his ear.

Madame went on:

'You must forgive us, Monsieur Moreau! One sometimes encounters things of this kind in a marriage.'

'That's because they are put there by women,' Arnoux said gaily. 'Women always have something against you. My wife isn't a bad sort, on the contrary! But she's been amusing herself for the last hour making up all sorts of stories to annoy me.'

'True stories!' Madame Arnoux replied impatiently. 'For in any case you bought it.'

'Me?'

'Yes, you! At the Persian shop.'

'The cashmere shawl!' Frédéric thought.

He felt he was to blame, and was afraid.

She added immediately:

'It was one Saturday last month, the fourteenth.'

'Oh, that day I was definitely at Creil! So you see...'

'That's not right. We dined with the Bertins on the fourteenth.'

'The fourteenth...?' Arnoux said, raising his eyes as if to search in his mind for a date.

'And the assistant who sold it to you was fair-haired!'

'Am I supposed to remember who sold it to me?'

'But he wrote the address at your dictation: 18, Rue de Laval.'

'How do you know that?' Arnoux asked, amazed.

She shrugged.

'Oh, it's quite simple: I went to get my shawl mended and a manager told me that another similar one had just been sent to Madame Arnoux's house.'

'So am I to blame if there is another Madame Arnoux in the same street?'

'No, but not Jacques Arnoux,' she replied.

Then he began to digress, protesting his innocence. It was a misunderstanding, a coincidence, one of those inexplicable things that sometimes happen. One ought not to condemn people on simple suspicion, vague evidence. He cited the example of the unfortunate Lesurques.*

'Well, anyway you're wrong! Do you want me to swear to it?'

'Don't bother!'

'Why?'

She looked him straight in the eyes without speaking. Then she stretched her hand out and took the silver box from the mantelpiece and held out an open bill.

Arnoux reddened to his ears and his discomposed face swelled.

'Well?'

'But,' he said slowly, 'What does that prove?'

'Ah,' she said, with a strange tone in her voice, and in which there was some pain and some irony. 'Ah!'

Arnoux kept hold of the bill, turning it over, his eyes glued to it as though he had expected to find there the solution to a huge problem.

'Oh yes, I remember,' he said finally. 'It was an errand. You must know about that, eh, Frédéric?' Frédéric said nothing. 'An errand I had to run for old Oudry.'

'And for whom?'

'For his mistress!'

'For yours!' cried Madame Arnoux, standing up.

'I swear to you...'

'Don't start that again! I know everything!'

'Oh, do you? So you're spying on me, are you?'

She replied coldly:

'Does that hurt your finer feelings?'

'When you get angry,' Arnoux went on, looking for his hat, 'and you can't be reasoned with...!'

Then with a deep sigh:

'Don't ever marry, my friend, take my advice!'

And he left, needing some fresh air.

Complete silence ensued. And everything in the room seemed more still than before. A luminous circle above the oil lamp whitened the ceiling, while from the corners the darkness extended like lengths of black gauze. You could hear the ticking of the clock and the crackling of the fire.

Madame Arnoux had just sat down in the armchair on the other side of the fireside. She was trembling and biting her lips. Her two hands were raised to her face, she could not prevent a sob, she was weeping.

He went to sit on the small chair. And in a gentle voice, as if talking to a sick person:

'You know I share...?'

She did not answer. But speaking her thoughts aloud:

'I give him his freedom! He had no need to lie to me!'

'Of course not!' Frédéric said.

It was no doubt the consequence of habits, he hadn't given it a thought, and perhaps in more important matters...

'What do you call more important matters?'

'Oh, nothing!'

Frédéric bowed his head with an obedient smile. Arnoux nonetheless had certain qualities: he loved his children.

'Oh, he is ruining them!'

It was because of his easy-going attitude. For it must be said he was a good sort.

'What does that mean, a good sort?' she cried.

He defended him like that as vaguely as he could, and while he sympathized with her, in his secret being he exulted. To have her revenge or in the need for affection she would take refuge in him. His hope increased immeasurably and strengthened his love.

She had never appeared so captivating to him, so thoroughly beautiful. From time to time her bosom heaved, her two eyes gazing fixedly seemed dilated by an internal vision, and her mouth remained half-open as if to send forth her soul. Sometimes she pressed her handkerchief hard against her lips. He would have liked to possess that little tear-sodden lawn handkerchief. In spite of himself he looked at the bed in the depths of the alcove, imagining her head on the pillow. And so vivid was his imagination, he had to stop himself taking her in his arms straight away. She closed her eyes, calm again, motionless. Then he went nearer, and leaning over her, he studied her face avidly. A noise of boots echoed in the corridor, it was Arnoux. They heard him closing the door of his room. Frédéric made a sign to Madame Arnoux to ask if he should go to him.

She mouthed back 'yes', and this mute exchange of thoughts was like a consent, like the beginnings of an adulterous liaison.

Arnoux, about to go to bed, was undoing his overcoat.

'Well, how is she?'

'Oh, not so bad!' said Frédéric. 'She'll get over it!'

But Arnoux was anxious.

'You don't know what she's like! Her nerves are so bad nowadays! Stupid shop assistant! That's what you get for being so generous. If I hadn't given Rosanette that damned shawl.'

'Don't be sorry about that. She is eternally grateful for it!'

'Do you think so?'

Frédéric was sure of it. The proof being that she had just got rid of old Oudry.

'Oh, the poor darling!'

And in an excess of emotion Arnoux wanted to rush round there forthwith.

'It's not worth it! I've just left her. She's poorly.'

'All the more reason to go!'

He put on his overcoat again and picked up his candlestick. Frédéric cursed himself for his foolish remark and pointed out to him that in all decency he ought to stay by his wife tonight. He couldn't desert her, that would be too bad of him.

'Frankly, you would be wrong to do that! There's no hurry to go over there! You can go tomorrow! Come now! Do that for me.'

Arnoux replaced his candlestick and, embracing him, said, 'You are a good fellow!'

## III

THEN a wretched existence began for Frédéric. He was the parasite of the house.

If anyone was sick, he went to enquire after their health three times a day; he went to see the piano tuner; he dreamed up a thousand ways to be helpful. And he smilingly put up with Mademoiselle Marthe's sulks and the kisses of young Eugène, who was forever putting his dirty hands all over his face. He was present at dinners where Monsieur and Madame, at opposite ends of the table, exchanged not a word, or else Arnoux would annoy his wife by making jocular remarks. Once the meal was over he played in the room with his son, hiding behind the furniture, or carrying him on his back, going down on all fours, like Henri IV.* Eventually he would take himself off, and she immediately started on her everlasting subject of complaint: Arnoux.

It wasn't his conduct that upset her. It was her pride that appeared to be hurt, and she let her disgust show for this man who was so devoid of finer feelings, dignity or honour.

'Or rather, he's mad,' she said.

Skilfully Frédéric elicited her confidences. Soon he knew the story of her life.

Her parents were petits bourgeois from Chartres. One day Arnoux, who had been sketching on the riverbank (he fancied himself as a painter back then) saw her coming out of church and asked for her hand in marriage. Because of his wealth, the family did not hesitate. Besides he was mad about her. She added:

'And he still loves me, after his fashion, for heaven's sake!'

During the first few months they had travelled in Italy.

In spite of Arnoux's enthusiasm for landscapes and the works of the Old Masters he had done nothing but complain the whole time about the wine, and, to amuse himself, had fixed up picnics with some English people. A few pictures that sold at a profit had encouraged him to make a career of buying and selling art. Then he had become obsessed with the manufacture of porcelain. Other speculations tempted him nowadays. And becoming more and more vulgar, he was falling into coarse and extravagant habits. It was not so much his vices she held against him, more his whole way of life. He would not change and nothing could be done about her own misfortune.

Frédéric affirmed that his life similarly was passing him by.

But he was very young. Why despair? And she gave him good advice: 'Work! Get married!' He replied with a bitter smile; for instead of expressing the true reason for his sadness he affected another, more elevated one: he was a bit like Antony,* there was a curse on him. Nor was such language totally at variance with what he believed.

For certain men the stronger their desire, the less likely they are to act. Lack of self-confidence holds them back, they are terrified of giving offence. Moreover, deep affections are like respectable women; they are afraid of being found out and go through life with their eyes cast down.

Though he had got to know Madame Arnoux better (and perhaps for that very reason) his cowardice was even greater than before. Each morning he swore he would be bold. An insuperable bashfulness prevented him, and he had no example from elsewhere to follow because she was not like other women. By the force of his dreams he had removed her to a place beyond the human condition. When he was by her side he felt less important on the earth than the scraps of silk which fell from her scissors.

Then he had monstrous thoughts, quite absurd: he would break in at night with skeleton keys, drug her—anything rather than having to face her scorn.

In any case the children, the two maids, the layout of the rooms created insuperable obstacles. So he resolved he would have her all to himself, go and live with her somewhere far away, in complete solitude. He looked for a lake blue enough, on the shores of a beach peaceful enough, either in Spain, Switzerland, or the Orient. And, deliberately choosing the days when she seemed most annoyed, he told her that she had to get out of this situation, think how to do it—and the only solution he could see was a separation. But because of her love for her children she could never go to such lengths. So much virtue increased his respect for her.

His afternoons were spent remembering the visit of the previous day, longing for the evening visit. When he did not dine with them, towards nine o'clock he went and stood on the corner of the street. And as soon as Arnoux had closed the front door, Frédéric would hurry up the stairs to the second floor and, with an innocent air, ask the maid:

'Is Monsieur at home?'

Then he would pretend to be surprised to find he wasn't there.

Often Arnoux came back unexpectedly and then he had to go with him to a little café in the Rue Sainte-Anne frequented nowadays by Regimbart.

The Citizen would begin by voicing some new complaint against the Crown; then they chatted, exchanging friendly insults. For the manufacturer held Regimbart to be a thinker of the highest order and, distressed to see such a waste of talent, he teased him about his laziness. The Citizen thought Arnoux full of soul and imagination but most certainly too immoral. So he treated him without the least indulgence and even refused to dine at his house because 'he couldn't bear ceremony'.

Sometimes as he was taking his leave, Arnoux was seized with hunger. He 'had to have' an omelette or baked apples; and since such things were never there on the premises, he sent out for them. They waited. Regimbart did not leave, and in the end grumpily said he would eat something.

Nevertheless he was filled with gloom* and would sit for hours with the same glass half empty in front of him. Since Providence was not ordering the world in accordance with his ideas he was becoming a hypochondriac, not even wanting to read the newspapers, and he would bellow with rage at the very mention of England. Once, when a waiter had not given good service:

'Have we not already had our fill of insults from foreigners!'

Apart from these crises he said very little, doubtless because he was planning 'something that would blow up the whole shebang'.

Whilst Regimbart was lost in thoughts like these, Arnoux, in a monotonous voice and with a rather drunken look in his eyes, recounted unbelievable exploits in which, thanks to his cool daring, he had always come out on top; and Frédéric (no doubt because deep down they resembled one another) felt rather drawn to him. He blamed himself for that weakness, thinking that on the contrary he should be hating him.

Arnoux complained about his wife's moodiness, her obstinacy, her unfair prejudices. She wasn't like that before.

'If I were you,' Frédéric said, 'I'd make her an allowance and live on my own.'

Arnoux did not reply. And a moment later he began praising her. She was good, devoted, intelligent, and virtuous. And going on to her physical qualities, he revealed one thing after another, in the careless manner of travellers who spread out their treasure in inns.

A catastrophe upset his equilibrium.

He had joined a kaolin company as a trustee; but believing everything he was told, he had signed reports that were inaccurate, and he had approved, without checking, annual inventories fraudulently drawn up by the manager. The business had folded and Arnoux, who was legally responsible, had just been condemned with the other trustees to pay damages amounting to about thirty thousand francs, a loss aggravated by the grounds on which judgement had been delivered.

Frédéric learned of this in the newspapers and hurried over to the Rue Paradis.

He was received in Madame Arnoux's room. It was breakfast time. Bowls of coffee lay around on a little table near the fire. Slippers littered the carpet, clothes the armchairs. Arnoux in his underpants and a knitted jacket was red-eyed and tousled. Little Eugène, on account of his mumps, snivelled as he nibbled at his bread and butter. His sister was eating quietly. Madame Arnoux, slightly paler than usual, was attending to all three.

'Well now,' said Arnoux, with a deep sigh, 'there we are!' And when Frédéric made a sympathetic gesture: 'You see! I've been a victim of my own good faith!'

Then he was silent. And he was so cast down, he pushed his breakfast away. Madame Arnoux raised her eyes, shrugging her shoulders. He passed his hand across his brow.

'After all, I'm not to blame. I've nothing to blame myself for. It's a bit of bad luck! We'll survive! It can't be helped!'

And he bit into a brioche, in obedience to his wife's entreaties.

That evening he wanted to have dinner alone with her in a private room at the Maison d'Or. Madame Arnoux did not understand this impulse, and even took offence at being treated like a *lorette*; but coming from Arnoux, it was a proof of his love for her. Then, as he was bored, he went off to amuse himself with the Maréchale.

Until then, he had been excused a lot of things thanks to his generous character. His court appearance tainted him. His household began to be cold-shouldered.

Frédéric made it a point of honour to go and see them more often. He rented a box at the Théâtre des Italiens and took them there each week. However, they were going through that period when, between an ill-matched couple, the concessions that have been made in the past produce an insuperable weariness and make life intolerable. Madame Arnoux struggled to suppress her feelings, Arnoux got more and more depressed. And the sight of these two unhappy creatures saddened Frédéric.

Since he was in Arnoux's confidence, she charged him with finding out about his affairs. But he was ashamed, and felt guilty when he ate dinner with them, since at the same time he had designs on his wife. Nonetheless he continued, giving as his excuse that he needed to protect her, and that he might sometime have an opportunity to be useful to her.

A week after the ball, he had visited Monsieur Dambreuse. The financier had offered him twenty shares in his coal company; Frédéric had not gone back again. Deslauriers had written him letters, they went unanswered. Pellerin urged him to come and see the portrait, he always prevaricated. Yet he gave in to Cisy who was pestering him for an introduction to Rosanette.

She received him very kindly but without flinging her arms round his neck as she had done before. His companion was delighted to be introduced to a woman of dubious morals and especially to talk to an actor. Delmar was there.

A historical drama in which he had played the part of a peasant who preaches at Louis XIV and prophesies 1789 had brought him such fame that similar roles were continually being created for him; and his function nowadays was to ridicule the monarchs of the whole wide world. As an English brewer he laid into Charles I; as a student from Salamanca he cursed Philip II; and as a concerned father he denounced La Pompadour—that was the best of all! Youngsters waited at the stage door to catch a glimpse of him. And his biography, which they sold in the interval, portrayed him as looking after his old mother, reading the Bible, helping the poor, in short, as having the qualities of a Saint Vincent de Paul* mixed with a Brutus and a Mirabeau. They called him 'Our Delmar'. He had a mission, he was becoming Christ.

All this had fascinated Rosanette and she got rid of old Oudry without a qualm, not being a grasping sort of person.

Arnoux, knowing her character well, had taken advantage of it for a long time, keeping her without too much expense to himself. The old man had arrived on the scene and all three of them had been careful to avoid too many explanations. Then, imagining that she was getting rid of Oudry for his sole benefit, Arnoux had increased her allowance. But her demands were renewed with a frequency that was perplexing—for she was not spending as freely as she had before. She had even sold her cashmere shawl, wishing to clear her long-standing debts, she said. And he paid up each time, she bewitched him, she abused him mercilessly. So the house was inundated with bills and writs. Frédéric felt a crisis impending.

One day he arrived to see Madame Arnoux. She had gone out. Monsieur was working down below in the shop.

Arnoux was in fact surrounded by his pots and trying to close with a young middle-class couple from the provinces. He spoke of turning and throwing, crackling and glazing; the others, unwilling to show their ignorance, made approving noises, and bought.

When his customers were outside he told Frédéric that he'd had a small altercation that morning with his wife. To prevent observations about his spending, he had declared that the Maréchale was no longer his mistress.

'And I even told her she was yours.'

Frédéric was furious. But if he blamed him he might give himself away. He stammered:

'Oh, you shouldn't have done that, you really shouldn't!'

'What difference does it make?' Arnoux asked. 'Where's the dishonour in being taken for her lover? I am! Would you not be flattered to be her lover?'

Had she talked? Was this an allusion? Frédéric hastened to reply:

'No, no dishonour at all! Quite the contrary.'

'Well then...'

'Yes, it's true, it doesn't make any difference.'

Arnoux went on:

'Why don't you go over there any more?'

Frédéric promised he'd go.

'Oh, I was forgetting! Could you... When you mention Rosanette to my wife... let something drop... I don't know, you'll think of something... to make her believe she's your mistress. I'm asking you to do this for me, you understand?'

For all reply the young man made a doubtful face. This calumny would spoil everything. He went that very evening to her house and swore Arnoux's allegation was false.

'Is that the truth?'

He appeared to be sincere. And when she had taken a deep breath, she said: 'I believe you', and gave him a lovely smile. Then she bowed her head and without looking at him said:

'In any case, nobody has any rights over you.'

So she did not guess, and she despised him, since she did not think he could love her enough to be faithful to her! Frédéric, forgetting his previous attempts with Rosanette, found her indulgence outrageous.

Then she begged him to go 'to that woman's house' from time to time to see what the situation was.

Arnoux arrived and five minutes later wanted to take him to Rosanette's.

The situation was becoming intolerable.

He was distracted by a letter from his solicitor who was going to send him fifteen thousand pounds next day; and, to make amends for his negligence towards Deslauriers, he went to share this good news with him straight away.

The lawyer was lodging in the Rue des Trois Maries, on the fifth floor, overlooking a courtyard. His study was a small square room, cold and papered with greyish wallpaper, in which the main decoration was a gold medal, the prize for his doctorate, inserted into an ebony frame over the mirror. A mahogany bookcase held about a hundred books behind glass. The desk, covered with sheepskin, stood in the centre of the room. Four old green velvet armchairs were in the corners; and sticks were burning in the hearth, where there was always a log waiting to be lit when the bell rang. It was his consultation time. The lawyer wore a white cravat.

The news of the fifteen thousand francs (he had probably given up expecting them by now) caused him to chuckle with pleasure.

'That's good, old fellow, that's good, that's very good!'

He threw some wood on the fire, sat down again, and immediately began to talk about the journal. The first thing to do was get rid of Hussonnet.

'That idiot is so tiresome! As for having a political standpoint, the fairest and the cleverest, in my view, is not to have any at all.'

Frédéric showed his surprise.

'But of course! It's time to treat politics scientifically. The old eighteenth-century philosophers were just beginning when Rousseau and the men of letters brought in philanthropy, poetry, and other things like that, to the great delight of the Catholics. This was a natural alliance, because modern reformers (as I can prove) all believe in Revelation. But if you celebrate Masses for Poland; if you replace the God of the Dominicans, who was an executioner, with the God of the Romantics, who is an upholsterer; if in short you don't have a broader concept of the Absolute than your ancestors, the monarchy will pierce through your Republican structures and your red bonnet* will only ever be a priest's calotte!* Except that solitary confinement will replace torture, offences against religion will replace sacrilege, a Concert of Europe will replace the Holy Alliance.* And in this fine order of things, this admirable society created out of the debris of Louis Quatorze and the ruins of Voltaire, with a little imperial whitewash and fragments of the English constitution, we will see the municipal councils trying to annoy the mayor, the general councillors their prefect, the chambers their king, the press whoever has power, and the administration annoying everybody! But there are good people who go into ecstasies about the Civil Code, a work which was constructed, whatever people say, in a mean-spirited, tyrannical spirit. For the legislator, instead of doing his job, which was to regularize tradition, thought he would shape society, as if he were Lycurgus!* Why does the law interfere with a father's rights when he wants to make a will? Why does it prevent the compulsory sale of buildings? Why punish vagrancy as a crime when it shouldn't even be a misdemeanour? And so on and so forth! I know them! So I am going to write a short novel called *A History of the Idea of Justice*, it'll be most entertaining! But I'm absolutely parched, are you?'

He leaned out of the window, and shouted to the porter to go and get some grog from the tavern.

'To sum up, I see three parties—no, three groups, none of which interests me. Those who have, those who used to have, and those who are trying their best to have. But they are all united in their foolish idolatry of Authority! Examples: Mably recommends that philosophers should be stopped from publishing their doctrines. The geometrician Monsieur Wronski calls the censure of the Press the "critical repression of speculative spontaneity";* old Enfantin blesses the Habsburgs for "reaching out a firm hand over the Alps to restrain Italy"; Pierre Leroux wants to force us to listen to an orator;

and Louis Blanc is inclined to a State religion, so mad is this race of vassals for government. However, not one of them is legitimate, despite their everlasting principles. "Principle" means "origin" so one has to go back all the time to a revolution, to an act of violence, to a transitory event. So our principle is national sovereignty, expressed in its parliamentary form, although the parliament doesn't agree! But why should the sovereignty of the people be more sacred than divine right?* One and the other are pure fictions. Enough of metaphysics, no more phantoms! There's no need for dogmas to keep the streets clean! I shall be accused of trying to overthrow society! Well what of it? What would be wrong with that? Your society is a pretty sight, I must say!'

Frédéric could have found a good many arguments in reply, but seeing that Deslauriers was very far removed from the ideas of Sénécal, he was full of indulgence. He made do with objecting that a system like that would make everyone hate them.

'On the contrary—as we shall have given each party a reason to hate its neighbour, they will all rely on us. You must get involved too and write us a Kantian critique now and then!'

They must attack accepted ideas, the Academie Française, the École Normale, the Conservatoire, the Comédie-Française, everything which could be thought of as an institution. That was the way to give a unified doctrine to their review. Then, when it was properly established, the journal would suddenly turn into a daily paper and they could start attacking individuals.

'And we shall be held in respect, you can be certain of that!'

Deslauriers was nearing his old ambition of being chief editor, which is to say the inexpressible pleasure of being in charge of other people, of making huge cuts in their articles, commissioning them, refusing them. His eyes sparkled behind his spectacles, he got very excited and drank small glasses of grog mechanically one after the other.

'You ought to give a dinner once a week. It's absolutely vital, even if half of your income goes into it. People will want to come, it will be a centre for other people, a lever up for yourself. And if we use the two handles of literature and politics to influence public opinion, you'll see that Paris society will be at our feet before six months is out.'

Listening to him, Frédéric felt rejuvenated, like a man who, after a long confinement in a bedroom, is transported into the fresh air. This enthusiasm won him over.

'Yes, you are quite right, I've been a lazy fool!'

'Excellent!' cried Deslauriers. 'That's my old Frédéric!'

And putting his fist under Frédéric's chin:

'Oh, how you've made me suffer! Never mind! I love you just the same.'

They stood there looking at each other fondly, close to hugging.

A woman's bonnet appeared in the door of the hallway.

'What brings you here?' asked Deslauriers.

It was Mademoiselle Clémence, his mistress.

She answered that, as she happened to be passing his house she couldn't resist calling on him. And she had brought some cakes, which she put on the table for them to have a little snack together.

'Be careful of my papers!' the lawyer said crossly. 'Anyway this is the third time I've forbidden you to come here while I'm consulting.'

She wanted to kiss him.

'Go away! Scram!'

He pushed her away. She let out a great sob.

'Oh, you are getting on my nerves!'

'But I love you!'

'I don't want to be loved, I want you to do as I ask!'

These harsh words stopped Clémence's tears. She stood in front of the window, and pressed her forehead against the glass, without moving.

Her attitude and her silence annoyed Deslauriers.

'When you've done you'll order your carriage, won't you?'

She swung round suddenly.

'Are you sending me away?'

'Precisely!'

She stared at him with her big blue eyes, in a last plea, no doubt, then crossed the two ends of her plaid, waited one more minute and then left.

'You should call her back,' Frédéric said.

'For heaven's sake!'

And as he needed to go out, Deslauriers went through into his kitchen which was also his dressing room. On the stone flags, next to a pair of boots, were the remains of a meagre lunch, and a mattress with a blanket rolled up in a corner on the floor.

'This shows you', he said 'that I don't entertain marquises very often. We can easily do without them. And the others as well!

Those who don't cost you anything waste your time. It's money by any other name. Now I am not a rich man. And anyway they are all so stupid! So stupid! Can *you* talk to a woman?'

They separated at the end of the Pont Neuf.

'So it's agreed then! You'll bring it tomorrow as soon as you have it?'

'Agreed,' said Frédéric.

The next day when he woke up the post brought him a bank draft for fifteen thousand francs.

This scrap of paper represented for him fifteen fat sacks of money. And he told himself that with this sum he could: first, keep his carriage for three years, instead of selling it as he would shortly have to do, or buy two beautifully damascened suits of armour that he had seen on the Quai Voltaire, and a heap of other things, paintings, books, and endless bouquets of flowers, presents for Madame Arnoux. In short, anything would have been better than risking, and losing, so much money in this journal! Deslauriers seemed to him presumptuous, his heartless behaviour of the previous day rather cooled Frédéric's feelings towards him, and he was giving himself up to these regrets when, to his great surprise, Arnoux arrived. He sat down heavily on the edge of his bed like a man defeated.

'Whatever's the matter?'

'I'm ruined.'

He had to repay that same day at the office of Maître Beauminet, a lawyer in the Rue Sainte-Anne, eighteen thousand francs lent to him by a man called Vanneroy.

'It's an inexplicable disaster! I gave him a mortgage which ought to have placated him. But he is threatening me with a court order if he's not paid this very afternoon!'

'So?'

'So it's very simple! He will expropriate my house. The first notice that goes up will ruin me, that's what! Oh, if I found someone to advance me that wretched sum, he could take Vanneroy's place and I should be saved. You wouldn't have it by any chance?'

The cheque was still on the bedside table, by a book. Frédéric lifted up the book and placed it on top, answering:

'Good heavens, no, my friend!'

But he felt bad refusing Arnoux.

'Can you really not find anyone who will...?'

'No one! And to think that in a week I shall have the money coming in. I am owed... perhaps fifty thousand by the end of the month.'

'Could you not ask the people who owe you money to advance you...?'

'That's not very likely!'

'But you have some securities, some bills?'

'No, nothing!'

'What can you do?'

'That's what I am wondering,' Arnoux replied.

He was silent, pacing up and down the room.

'It's not on my account, heaven knows! It's for my children and my poor wife!'

Then, articulating every word:

'Well, I shall be strong... I'll sell up... and go and seek my fortune... elsewhere!'

'Impossible!' cried Frédéric.

Arnoux replied calmly:

'How do you expect me to live in Paris now?'

There was a lengthy silence.

Frédéric ventured:

'When would you be able to pay?'

Not that he had it, not at all. But there was nothing to stop him asking friends and seeing what could be done. And he rang for his servant to get dressed. Arnoux was thanking him.

'You need eighteen thousand francs, is that right?'

'Oh, I could easily make do with sixteen. Because I could raise two thousand five hundred, perhaps three thousand with my silverware, as long as Vanneroy can give me till tomorrow. And I tell you again you can assure the lender, swear to him that in a week or even perhaps in five or six days, the money will be paid back. In any case the mortgage is there as guarantee. So there's no danger, you understand?'

Frédéric assured him that he understood and that he would go and see about it without delay.

He stayed in the house cursing Deslauriers, for he wanted to keep his word while still obliging Arnoux.

'Supposing I asked Monsieur Dambreuse? But on what pretext could I ask him for money? Quite the reverse, I'm the one who should be paying him for shares in the coal. Oh, to hell with the shares! I don't owe him anything.'

And Frédéric congratulated himself for being independent, as though he had refused to be of service to Monsieur Dambreuse.

'Well,' he thought next, 'since I am making a loss there—for I could make a hundred thousand with fifteen, that sometimes happens at the Bourse—but seeing I'm breaking my promise to Dambreuse, doesn't that mean I'm free? Anyway, even if Deslauriers had to wait... No, no, that's not a good idea. Oh, let's go and do it!'

He looked at his clock.

'Oh, there's no hurry! The Bank doesn't shut till five.'

And at four-thirty when he had withdrawn his money:

'No point now, I won't be able to find him. I'll go this evening!' thus giving himself a means to go back on his decision, for there always remains in one's conscience something of the sophisms one has poured into them. They leave an aftertaste like a bad liqueur.

He walked along the boulevards and dined on his own in a restaurant. Then, to entertain himself, he went to one act of a vaudeville. But his banknotes troubled him, as though he had stolen them. He would not have been sorry to lose them.

When he went back, he found a letter containing these words:

Any news?
My wife and I are hoping, dear friend, etc.

And a signature.

'His wife! She is begging me for help!'

At that same moment Arnoux appeared, to find out if he had got the sum he so urgently needed.

'Here it is,' said Frédéric.

And twenty-four hours later he sent a reply to Deslauriers:

'It hasn't arrived.'

The lawyer came back on three successive days. He pressed him to write to the solicitor. He even offered to make the journey to Le Havre.

'No, it's pointless. I am going to go!'

At the end of the week Frédéric timidly asked Monsieur Arnoux for his fifteen thousand francs.

Arnoux put him off till the next day, then the day after. Frédéric, afraid of being accosted by Deslauriers, ventured out only after dark.

One evening someone bumped into him at the corner of the Madeleine. It was Deslauriers.

'I'm on my way to get it,' he said.

And Deslauriers went with him to the door of a house in the Faubourg Poissonnière.

'Wait here!'

He waited. At last after forty-three minutes Frédéric came out with Arnoux, and indicated that he should wait a little longer. The porcelain dealer and his companion walked arm in arm to the Rue Hauteville and then went down the Rue de Chabrol.

The night was dark with warm gusts of wind. Arnoux walked slowly along, talking about the Galeries du Commerce, a succession of arcades which were planned to join up the Boulevard Saint-Denis and Châtelet, a marvellous enterprise which he was sorely tempted to take part in. And from time to time he stopped to look at the faces of the girls through the shop windows before resuming his conversation.

Frédéric could hear Deslauriers's footsteps behind him like so many reproaches, like blows at his conscience. But he didn't dare ask for the money, through false shame but also fearing it would be useless. The other was getting nearer. He made up his mind.

Arnoux, in a most casual tone, said that since the money he was owed had not been paid yet, he couldn't for the moment give back the fifteen thousand francs.

'I suppose you don't need it?'

At that moment Deslauriers caught Frédéric up and taking him swiftly on one side:

'Tell me straight, do you have the money, or don't you?'

'Well no,' said Frédéric. 'I've lost it!'

'Oh, and how?'

'Gambling!'

Deslauriers said not one word in reply, made a deep bow, and left. Arnoux had taken advantage of the situation to light up a cigar in a tobacconist's. He came back, and asked who the young man was.

'Nobody. A friend.'

And then three minutes later outside Rosanette's door:

'Go on up,' Arnoux said. 'She'll like to see you. How unsociable you are nowadays!'

A street lamp opposite lit him up. And with a cigar between his white teeth and his satisfied expression he looked quite insufferable to Frédéric.

'Oh, by the way, my solicitor went to see yours this morning about registering that mortgage. It was my wife who reminded me.'

'An intelligent woman!' Frédéric remarked mechanically.

'Indeed!'

And Arnoux began praising her again. There was no one like her for intellect, feeling, thrift; and he added under his breath and rolling his eyes:

'And for her body!'

'Adieu!' said Frédéric.

Arnoux was surprised.

'Why, what's the matter?'

And with his hand half-stretched out, he studied his face, quite disconcerted by the anger it expressed.

Frédéric replied coldly:

'Goodbye!'

He sped along the Rue de Bréda, furious with Arnoux, upset and abandoned, vowing never to set eyes on him again, nor on her either. Instead of the rupture he was expecting, here was her husband, on the contrary, starting to cherish and love her properly, from the hair on her head to the depths of her soul. The vulgarity of the man exasperated Frédéric. So he had it all, this fellow! He saw him again at Rosanette's door; and the mortification of a quarrel added to his impotent rage. Moreover, Arnoux's honesty in offering him security for his money humiliated him. He would have liked to strangle him. And underneath his chagrin the feeling of having acted in a cowardly way towards his friend floated around in his conscience like a fog. Tears choked him.

Deslauriers hurtled down the Rue des Martyrs, cursing aloud in his indignation. For his plans, like an obelisk which has been toppled, seemed to him of an extraordinary magnitude. He felt robbed, as if he had suffered a great injury. His friendship for Frédéric had died, and that made him feel a little better. That was some small compensation! A hatred of the wealthy pervaded him. He leaned towards the opinions of Sénécal and promised himself he would promote them.

During that time Arnoux, comfortably seated in an armchair by the fireside, was inhaling the warmth from his cup of tea, holding the Maréchale on his knee.

Frédéric did not go back to the Arnouxes'; and to distract himself from his disastrous passion, he took the first subject which came along, and decided to write a *History of the Renaissance*. On his table he piled up humanists, philosophers, and poets. He went to the print room to look at the engravings of Marcantonio.* He tried to understand Machiavelli. Gradually the soothing nature of the work calmed him. And delving into the personalities of others he forgot his own, which is perhaps the only way to avoid suffering from it.

One day as he was quietly taking notes, the door opened and the servant announced Madame Arnoux.

It really was her! Alone? No, for she was holding little Eugène by the hand followed by his nurse in a white apron. She sat down. And said, with a cough:

'It's a long time since you came to our house.'

And since Frédéric couldn't find any excuse, she added:

'It's very tactful of you.'

He answered:

'Why do you say that?'

'Because of what you did for Arnoux,' she said.

Frédéric made a gesture which meant: 'I don't give a damn about that. It was for you!'

She sent her little boy off to play with the nurse in the drawing room. They exchanged a word or two about their health and then the conversation faltered.

She was wearing a dress of brown silk, the colour of Spanish wine, and a jacket of black velvet, with a sable trim. This fur made him want to run his fingers over it, and his lips were drawn to her long, smooth hairbands. But something was bothering her, and, turning her eyes to the door:

'It's a little warm in here!'

Frédéric guessed the cautious intent which lay behind her look.

'Oh, I'm sorry. The door is not quite shut.'

'Oh yes, of course!'

And she smiled as much as to say: 'I'm not a bit afraid.'

He asked her immediately what brought her.

'My husband', she said, with an effort, 'asked me to come over, he did not dare come himself.'

'Why?'

'You know Monsieur Dambreuse, don't you?'

'Yes, a little!'

'Oh, only a little.'

She said nothing.

'No matter. Carry on.'

Then she told him that the day before yesterday Arnoux had not been able to pay the banker four bills of a thousand francs, which he had made her sign. She was remorseful about compromising the fortune of her children. But anything was better than dishonour; and if Monsieur Dambreuse could stop taking legal proceedings, it would certainly be paid. For she was about to sell a little house that she had in Chartres.

'You poor woman!' murmured Frédéric.—'I'll go and see him. Count on me.'

'Thank you!'

She got up to leave.

'Oh, there's no hurry!'

She stood there examining the trophy of Mongolian arrows hanging from the ceiling, the bookcase, the bindings, all his writing tools. She picked up the bronze bowl which contained his pens; her heels touched different places on the carpet. She had been to Frédéric's several times, but always with Arnoux. They were alone now, alone in his own house. It was an extraordinary event, almost a good omen.

She wanted to see his little garden. He offered her his arm to show her his thirty-foot-square domain, surrounded by houses, with shrubs in each corner and a flower bed in the middle.

It was the first few days of April. The leaves on the lilac bush were already green, a pure breath wafted through the air, and little birds were twittering, their song alternating with the far-off noise of the coachbuilder's forge.

Frédéric went to get a small shovel. And while they walked side by side the little boy made little piles of sand on the path.

Madame Arnoux did not think he would have much of an imagination later on, but he was an affectionate child. His sister, on the other hand, had a colder nature, which she sometimes found hurtful.

'She'll change,' Frédéric said. 'One must never give up hope.'

'One must never give up hope!' she repeated. This mechanical echoing of his words seemed rather encouraging. He picked a rose, the only one in the garden.

'Do you remember a certain bouquet of roses one evening in the cab?'

She blushed a little; then with an air of compassionate mockery:

'Ah, I was so young then!'

'And what about this one?' Frédéric asked. 'Will it suffer the same fate?'

Twirling the stem between her fingers, like the thread of a spindle, she replied:

'No! I shall keep it!'

She summoned the nurse, who took the child in her arms. Then in the doorway on to the street Madame Arnoux inhaled the scent of the flower, inclining her head on her shoulder, and with a look that was as sweet as a kiss.

Back in his study, he gazed at the armchair in which she had sat and all the objects she had touched. Something of her still moved in the air around him. The caress of her presence still lingered.

'So she was here!' he said to himself.

And the waves of an infinite love engulfed him.

The next day at eleven he went to see Monsieur Dambreuse. He was received in the dining room. The banker was lunching opposite his wife. Her niece was next to her and on the other side was the governess, an English woman whose face was badly pockmarked.

Monsieur Dambreuse invited his young friend to join them, and when he refused, asked:

'So what can I do for you? I'm listening.'

Frédéric, pretending indifference, confessed that he had come to make a request for a certain Arnoux.

'Oh yes, the former art dealer,' said the banker, with a silent laugh that exposed his gums. 'Oudry stood guarantor for him in the old days. They fell out.'

And he began to trawl through the letters and journals placed beside his plate.

Two servants were waiting on them, moving noiselessly over the wooden floor. And the high-ceilinged room, with its three tapestry door-hangings and two white marble fountains, the polished dish-warmers, the way the hors d'oeuvres were laid out, and even the crisp folded napkins, all this wealthy living reminded Frédéric, by contrast, of another dinner he'd had at Arnoux's. He did not dare interrupt Monsieur Dambreuse.

Madame noticed his embarrassment.

'Do you see our friend Martinon sometimes?'

'He'll be here this evening,' her niece intervened swiftly.

'Oh, you know that, do you?' her aunt replied, with a cold glance at her.

Then, one of the servants having leaned towards her ear:

'Your dressmaker, my child!... Miss Johnson!'

And the obedient governess disappeared with her pupil.

Monsieur Dambreuse, disturbed by the scraping of chairs, asked what was going on.

'It's Madame Regimbart.'

'Well I never! Regimbart! I know that name. I've come across his signature.'

Frédéric finally broached the subject. Arnoux deserved consideration. He was even about to sell a house belonging to his wife, with the sole aim of fulfilling his obligations.

'People say she's very pretty,' said Madame Dambreuse. The banker added jovially:

'Are you... an intimate friend?'

Without giving a precise answer, Frédéric said he would be extremely grateful if he would consider...'

'Well, if it makes you happy, let's do it! I'll wait! I have some time still. Shall we go down to my office?'

Lunch was over; Madame Dambreuse bowed slightly, smiling with a strange smile, at once full of politeness and irony. Frédéric did not have time to think about this, for as soon as they were alone, Monsieur Dambreuse said:

'You didn't come for your shares.'

And without allowing him to apologize:

'Never mind! It's a good idea for you to get to know the business better.'

He offered him a cigarette and began:

The *General Union of French Coal* was established; all they were waiting for now was the official go-ahead. The sole fact of the merger would lessen the costs of administration and labour and would increase the profits. What's more, the company had a novel idea, namely to involve the workers in the business. It would build houses, healthy accommodation for them. In short, it would constitute itself supplier to its employees, and would deliver everything they needed at cost price.

'And they will gain from it, Monsieur. That is true progress. That will answer the moans and groans of certain Republicans! We have on our board' (he displayed the prospectus) 'a peer of France, an academic from the Institute, a retired senior engineer, all well-known names! Such members will reassure timid investors and appeal to intelligent ones.—The Company will obtain orders from the State and also from the railways, steamships, iron and steel, gas, as well as households.—So we give people warmth and light, we reach deep into the humblest homes. But, you will ask, how can we be certain of sales? Thanks to import duties, my dear monsieur. And we shall make it our business to obtain those. Myself, by the way, I am a thorough protectionist! The country comes first!'

He had been appointed director. But he didn't have time to bother with some of the details, such as the writing of reports. 'I am a little hazy about my classical authors, I've forgotten my Greek! I need someone... who could translate my ideas on to paper.' And suddenly he said: 'Would you care to be that man, with the title of secretary general?'

Frédéric did not know what to say.

'Well, what's stopping you?'

His functions would be restricted to writing an annual report for the shareholders. He would be in contact on a daily basis with the most influential men in Paris. Representing the Company among the workers he would naturally win their affection and that would allow him later to progress to the General Council* and to becoming a deputy.

Frédéric's ears were buzzing. Where did all this goodwill come from? He thanked him, covered in confusion.

But the banker said he must not be dependent upon anyone. The best way was to buy some shares, 'a superb investment in any case, for your capital guarantees your position and your position your capital'.

'About how much do I need as capital?' enquired Frédéric.

'Good gracious, whatever you like; from forty to sixty thousand francs I suppose.'

This sum was so minimal for Monsieur Dambreuse and his authority was so great that the young man promptly decided to sell a farm. He accepted. Monsieur Dambreuse would fix a meeting one of these days to finalize their arrangements.

'So I can tell Jacques Arnoux...?'

'Anything you like! The poor fellow! Anything you like!'

Frédéric wrote a note saying that Arnoux could put his mind at rest, and sent the letter by his servant who was told:

'Very good!'

His efforts, however, deserved better than this. He was expecting a visit or at the very least a letter. He did not receive a visit. No letter arrived.

Had they forgotten, or was it intentional? Since Madame Arnoux had come once, what was stopping her from coming again? The kind of hint, confession she had made to him—was it only a manoeuvre executed out of self-interest? 'Are they making a fool of me? Is she in league with him?' Though he longed to return to their house, a sort of embarrassment prevented him.

One morning three weeks after their interview, Monsieur Dambreuse wrote that he wished to see him that same day, in an hour's time.

On the way the thought of Arnoux beset him once more. And, not finding a reason for their behaviour he was seized with a pang of dread, with an ominous presentiment. To rid himself of it he called a cab and drove to the Rue de Paradis.

Arnoux was away, on a journey.

'And Madame?'

'In the country, at the factory!'

'When will Monsieur be back?'

'Tomorrow, without fail!'

He would find her on her own. It was the right moment. An imperious voice cried out to him: 'Go on then!'

But what of Monsieur Dambreuse? 'Well, it's too bad! I'll say I was ill.' He ran to the station; then, in the railway carriage, thought: 'Perhaps I was wrong? Oh well, what's the odds?'

Green fields stretched to left and right; the train rolled along; the little station houses slipped past like stage sets; the engine emitted, always on to the same side, great white puffs of smoke which danced along the grass for a while and then dispersed.

Frédéric, alone on his seat, looked at all this out of boredom, immersed in the indolence caused by very excess of impatience. Cranes, shops appeared. It was Creil.

The town, built on the slopes of two low hills (the first bare and the second with a wood on top) with its church tower, its higgledy-piggledy houses and its stone bridge, seemed to him to have something cheerful, understated and wholesome about it. A big flat-bottomed boat was sailing downstream on the choppy water whipped by the wind. Hens pecked around in the straw at the base of the calvary. A woman passed by, carrying damp washing on her head.

Beyond the bridge he found himself on an island from which you could see the ruins of an abbey to the right. A mill wheel was turning, blocking across its width the second arm of the Oise, overlooked by the factory. The size of this building astonished Frédéric. His respect for Arnoux increased. Another three paces and he came to a small road ending in an iron gate.

He went in. The concierge called him back, shouting:

'Have you got a pass?'

'For what?'

'To visit the premises!'

Curtly Frédéric told her he had come to see Monsieur Arnoux.

'Who's Monsieur Arnoux?'

'The boss, the chief, the owner of course!'

'No, Monsieur, this is Messieurs Lebœuf and Milliet's factory.'

The woman was surely joking. Workers were arriving; he spoke to two or three; their reply was the same.

Frédéric went out of the yard, reeling like a drunk. And he had such a flabbergasted expression on his face that a local man smoking his pipe on the Pont de la Boucherie asked if he was looking for somebody. The man knew Arnoux's establishment. It was in Montataire.

Frédéric enquired about a cab. Only at the station. He went back there. A broken-down trap drawn by an old nag whose ragged harness trailed down between the shafts was stationed on its own in front of the luggage office.

A boy offered to go and find 'old Pilon'. He came back ten minutes later. Old Pilon was having his lunch. Frédéric left, unable to wait any longer. The gates of the level crossing were shut. He had to wait for two trains to go by. Finally he hurried into the countryside.

The monotonous green space looked like a huge billiard table. Heaps of iron waste lined both sides of the road like piles of pebbles. A bit further along, a row of factory chimneys was puffing out smoke. Opposite him on a rounded hill rose a small chateau with turrets and the four-square tower of a church. Long walls below formed irregular lines amongst the trees, and right at the bottom stretched the houses in the village.

They were single storey, with stairways built of three steps of blocks not held together by cement. At intervals the tinkling of a grocer's bell could be heard. Heavy shoes sank into black mud and a fine drizzle slashed the pale sky with a thousand little strokes.

Frédéric kept to the middle of the paved road. Then at the entrance to a lane he saw a large wooden arch on his left which bore the word POTTERY in gold letters.

It was not without good reason that Jacques Arnoux had chosen this location in Creil. By placing his factory here, as near as possible to the other one (which had enjoyed a good reputation for some time) he created in the public's mind a confusion which was favourable to his interests.

The main building stood on the very edge of a river which crossed the meadow. The master's house, surrounded by a garden, was distinguished by its flight of steps, adorned with four urns in which grew spiky cactus plants. Piles of white clay were drying under the hangars; others were outside in the air. And in the middle of the yard stood Sénécal in his eternal blue jacket with the red lining.

The former tutor held out his cold hand.

'Have you come to see the boss? He's not here.'

Frédéric, off his guard, answered stupidly:

'I know.' Then collecting his wits straight away: 'It's about a matter concerning Madame Arnoux. Is she at home?'

'Oh, I haven't seen her for three days,' Sénécal said.

And he started on a litany of grievances. When he'd accepted the manufacturer's conditions, he'd understood he would be living in Paris and not holed up in the country, a long way from his friends, without any newspapers. No matter! He had got over all that. But Arnoux seemed not to appreciate his qualities. Moreover, he was narrow-minded and backward-looking and ignorant as could be. Instead of putting his efforts into artistic improvements, it would have been better for him to install coal and gas heating. The boss was 'going under'. Sénécal emphasized these words. In short, his occupations displeased him and he was almost ordering Frédéric to put in a word for him so that his pay might be increased.

'Don't worry!' said Frédéric.

He met no one on the stairs. On the first floor he peered into an empty room; it was the drawing room. He called out very loudly. There was no reply. Probably the cook was out and the maid as well. At last reaching the second floor he pushed open a door. Madame Arnoux was on her own in front of a wardrobe mirror. The belt on her half-open dressing gown hung down over her hips. The whole of her hair on one side fell in dark waves over her shoulder. And both arms were lifted, one hand holding her chignon while the other was pushing a pin into it. She uttered a cry and disappeared.

Then she came back properly dressed. Her figure, her eyes, the rustle of her dress, everything delighted him. Frédéric scarcely restrained himself from covering her with kisses.

'I'm sorry,' she said, 'but I couldn't...'

He dared to interrupt:

'But... you looked very well... just as you were.'

She must have found the compliment a little vulgar, for her cheeks coloured. He was afraid he had offended her. She went on:

'What happy chance brings you here?'

He did not know what to answer. And after a little chuckle which gave him time to think:

'If I told you, would you believe me?'

'Why not?'

Frédéric explained that the other night he'd had a dreadful nightmare:

'I dreamed you were seriously ill, nearly dying.'

'Oh, my husband and I are never ill!'

'I only dreamed about you,' he said.

She looked at him quietly.

'Dreams don't always come true.'

Frédéric stammered, searched for words, and finally launched into a long discourse about kindred spirits. A force existed which could put two people in contact across space, inform them about each other's feelings, and cause them to be reunited.

She listened with head bowed, smiling her beautiful smile. He observed her with delight out of the corner of his eye and poured out his love more freely by way of commonplaces. She suggested showing him the workshops, and as she insisted, he accepted.

She began with something entertaining, showing him a sort of museum that decorated the staircase. The specimens hanging on the walls or placed on little shelves attested to the successive efforts and enthusiasms of Arnoux. After seeking the copper red of the Chinese he had tried his hand at majolica, faienza, Etruscan and oriental pots, these being first attempts which he had later refined. So the series included large vases covered with mandarins, bowls of an iridescent bronze, pots decorated with Arabic script, flagons in the style of the Renaissance; and large plates with two figures on, which were drawn in red chalk in a vapid and rather precious fashion. Nowadays he was making signboards and wine labels, but he was not gifted enough to create a work of Art, nor such a bourgeois that he would aim exclusively at profit, and so, pleasing nobody, he was ruining himself. Both of them were contemplating these things when Mademoiselle Marthe appeared.

'Don't you recognize this gentleman?' her mother asked.

'Of course!' she answered, as she greeted him, while her clear, suspicious look, her virgin gaze seemed to say: 'What are you doing here?' and she went up the steps with her head slightly turned on her shoulder.

Madame Arnoux took Frédéric out into the yard, then solemnly explained how the clay was crushed, cleaned, and sifted.

'It's important to prepare the pastes properly.'

And she took him into a room filled with vats, where a vertical axis with horizontal arms was turning. Frédéric was kicking himself that he had not declined her offer more definitely before.

'These are the blungers,'* she said.

He found the word grotesque and rather out of place in her mouth.

Wide belts ran from one side of the ceiling to the other, then wound around drums and everything moved in a continuous, mathematical, maddening rhythm.

They came out of there and passed by a derelict hut, which had once been used for putting garden tools in.

'It's no use any more,' said Madame Arnoux.

He replied, trembling:

'Room inside for happiness!'

The din of the fire pump drowned out his words and they went into the design room.

Men, sitting at a narrow table, were putting piles of clay on to a wheel in front of them. Their left hands were raking the inside, their right hands were smoothing the surface, and you could see pots rising like flowers opening.

Madame Arnoux showed him the moulds for the more difficult products.

In another room they were working on the fillets, grooves, projecting lines. On the floor above they were smoothing over the joins, and filling in with plaster the small holes left by the preceding operations.

Pots were lined up everywhere, on the grids, in the corners, in the middle of the corridors.

Frédéric began to be bored.

'Do you find this tiring, I wonder?' she said.

Fearing this might cut short his visit, he pretended that, on the contrary, he found it fascinating. He even regretted that he had not devoted himself to such work.

She seemed surprised.

'But of course! I could have been living near you!'

And, as he sought her eyes, Madame Arnoux in order to avoid his, took some little balls of clay from a console, some that had come off unsuccessful repairs, squashed them into a pancake shape, and printed her hand on it.

'Can I take that with me?' said Frédéric.

'Goodness, what a baby you are!'

He was going to say something when Sénécal came in.

At once the assistant manager noticed an infraction of the rules. The workshops had to be swept every week. It was Saturday and, as the workers had done nothing about it, Sénécal informed them they would have to stay an extra hour.

'It's your own fault!'

They leaned over their work, not saying a word; you could tell they were angry from the hoarse breathing in their chests. Moreover, they were rather unruly, all of them having been sacked from the big factory. The Republican was a hard taskmaster. A man of theory, he only took account of the masses and was pitiless towards individuals.

Hampered by his presence, Frédéric asked Madame Arnoux in an undertone if there were any possibility of seeing the kilns. They went down to the ground floor. And she was in the process of explaining the use of the saggers when Sénécal, who had followed them, intervened.

He continued the demonstration himself, expounding on the different kinds of combustible materials, on the loading of the kilns, pyroscopes, hearths, slip, glazes and metals, cramming his explanations full of chemistry terms—chloride, sulphur, borax, carbonate. Frédéric didn't understand a word, and kept turning towards Madame Arnoux.

'You are not listening,' she said. 'Yet Monsieur Sénécal is very clear. He knows all these things much better than I do.'

The mathematician, flattered by this praise, suggested showing him how the colours were applied. Frédéric looked questioningly and rather anxiously at Madame Arnoux. She remained impassive, no doubt wanting not to be left alone with him, nor to leave him. He offered her his arm.

'No—thank you, all the same. The stairs are too narrow.'

And when they were upstairs, Sénécal opened the door of a room full of women.

They were using paintbrushes, phials, shells, glass slides. Along the cornice against the wall engraved blocks stood in a row; scraps of paper were fluttering around; and an iron stove gave off a sickening heat mixed with the smell of turpentine.

Almost all the women had dirty overalls. One was remarkable, however, for having a madras kerchief and dangling earrings. Slim and yet well covered, she had the large black eyes and fleshy lips of a Negro woman. Her full breasts showed beneath her blouse, which was fastened around her waist by the tie on her skirt; and one elbow on the workbench, the other arm hanging loose, she was gazing vaguely into the distant countryside. Beside her was a bottle of wine and some sausage.

It was forbidden to eat in the workshops, to keep the products clean and for the workers' own health.

Sénécal, out of a sense of duty or the need to throw his weight about, shouted across the room, pointing to a framed notice:

'Hey, you over there, the girl from Bordeaux! Read me aloud Article 9.'

'What about it?'

'What about it, Mademoiselle? You'll pay a three-franc fine.'

She looked him straight in the face, impudently.

'What difference does that make? When the boss comes back he'll cancel the fine! I don't give a damn about you, you silly man!'

Sénécal, who was walking around with his hands behind his back, like a prefect in the classroom, made do with a smile.

'Article 13, insubordination, ten francs!'

The girl from Bordeaux went back to her work. Madame Arnoux, through a sense of propriety, said nothing but she frowned. Frédéric muttered:

'For a democrat, you are very harsh!'

Sénécal replied magisterially:

'Democracy doesn't mean an individual can do what he pleases. It means everyone's the same before the law, the division of labour, good order!'

'You are forgetting humanity,' Frédéric said.

Madame Arnoux took his arm; Sénécal, perhaps offended by this silent approbation, left.

Frédéric was extremely relieved. Ever since the morning he had sought the opportunity to declare his love. Now the time had come. Madame Arnoux's spontaneous gesture seemed to contain a promise. And he asked if he could come up and warm his feet in her room. When he was seated next to her, he was embarrassed to know what to say. Luckily Sénécal came to mind.

'How stupid that punishment was!' he said.

Madame Arnoux replied:

'Sometimes strictness is necessary.'

'What? You who are so kind! Oh, I was forgetting, you do enjoy making people suffer at times.'

'I don't understand riddles, my friend.'

And her severe look, even more than her words, stopped him in his tracks. Frédéric was determined not to be put off. A volume of Musset* lay by chance on the chest. He turned over a few pages then started to talk about love, of its despair and joy.

All that, according to Madame Arnoux, was criminal or artificial.

The young man felt wounded by this rebuttal. And to challenge her he cited as proof the suicides you read about in newspapers, praised the famous figures in literature, Phèdre, Dido, Romeo, Des Grieux.* His words got tangled up in his passion.

The fire in the grate had gone out. The rain beat against the window panes. Madame Arnoux rested both hands on the arms of her chair, without moving. The ribbons on her bonnet hung down like the hairbands of a sphinx. Her pure profile stood out palely among the shadows.

He wanted to throw himself on his knees. A board creaked in the corridor. He did not dare.

In any case he was held back by a kind of religious fear. Her dress merging into the shadows seemed to him immeasurable, infinite, impossible to lift. And precisely for that reason his desire for her increased. But in the fear of going too far, and of not going far enough, he lost all power of judgement.

'If she doesn't like me,' he thought, 'let her send me away. If she wants me, then let her encourage me.'

He said with a sigh:

'So you do not admit that a man may love... a woman?'

Madame Arnoux replied:

'When she is available, a man may marry her. When she belongs to someone else, he must keep his distance.'

'So is happiness impossible?'

'No! But it is never to be found in lying, worry, or remorse.'

'What does that matter if it is redeemed by sublime happiness?'

'The experience costs too dear.'

He wanted to attack her through irony.

'So virtue is nothing but cowardice?'

'Call it foresight, rather. Even for those who forget their duty or their faith, simple good sense may suffice. Selfishness is a solid basis for wisdom.'

'Oh, what bourgeois precepts you have!'

'But I do not claim to be a great lady.'

At that moment her little boy came running up.

'Maman, are you coming to supper?'

'Yes, in a minute!'

Frédéric rose. At the same time Marthe appeared.

He could not make up his mind to leave.

And with a beseeching look:

'These women you speak of are very unfeeling then?'

'No, but they are hard of hearing when it's necessary.'

And she stood there in the doorway of her room, with her two children at her side. He bowed, without a word. She acknowledged his bow in silence.

His initial reaction was one of extreme stupefaction. This manner of making him realize the hollowness of his hopes crushed him completely. He felt lost, like a man fallen into the bottom of a pit, who knows that no one will come to his aid and that he is bound to die.

He went on walking, blindly, at random. He tripped over stones. He took the wrong way. A noise of clogs echoed near his ear. It was the workers coming out of the foundry. Then he realized where he was.

On the horizon the lights from the railway traced a line of fire. He arrived just as a train was leaving, allowed himself to be shoved into a carriage, and fell asleep.

An hour later on the boulevards the gaiety of Paris at night put his journey back into a past that was already distant. He tried to be strong, and alleviated his suffering by denigrating Madame Arnoux with insults.

'She's a fool, a goose, a beast, let's not think about her any more!'

Back home, he found in his study an eight-page letter on glossy blue paper, signed R.A.

It began with friendly reproaches:

'What has become of you, my dear? I'm bored.'

The writing was so dreadful that Frédéric was going to throw away all the sheets when he saw the postscript:

'I am relying on you to take me to the races tomorrow.'

What did this invitation mean? Was it another of the Maréchale's tricks? But one doesn't make fun of the same man twice about nothing at all. And seized with curiosity, he reread the letter attentively.

Frédéric made out the words: 'Misunderstanding... went the wrong way... disappointments... We are poor creatures... Just like two rivers which run together!' And so on.

This style contrasted with the courtesan's normal style. What change had taken place then?

He held the pages in his hands for some time. They smelled of iris. And in the formation of the letters and the irregular spacing of the lines there was an aspect he found troubling, like a dress in disarray.

'Why not go?' he said finally. 'But what if Madame Arnoux knew? Oh, let her find out! So much the better. And let her be jealous. That shall be my revenge!'

## IV

THE Maréchale was ready and waiting.

'That's nice of you!' she said, gazing at him with her pretty eyes both tender and gay.

When she had tied the strings of her bonnet, she sat on the divan and remained silent.

'Are we going?' Frédéric said.

She looked at the clock.

'Oh no, not before half past one,' as though she had imposed this limit on her indecision.

Finally when it had struck the half-hour:

'Well, *caro mio, andiamo!*'*

She fixed her hair once more and gave Delphine her instructions.
'Will Madame be back for dinner?'
'Why should we? We shall be dining somewhere together in the Café Anglais, or wherever you like.'
'Fine!'
Her little dogs were yapping around her.
'We can take them with us, can't we?'
Frédéric carried them to the cab himself. It was a hired berlin* with two post horses and a postilion. He had placed his servant on the back seat. The Maréchale appeared to be satisfied with these preparations. Then as soon as he sat down she asked if he had been to see the Arnouxes recently.
'Not for a month,' Frédéric said.
'I saw him the day before yesterday. In fact, he was going to come today, but he's got all sorts of problems—another trial and I don't know what else. What a strange man!'
'Yes, very strange!'
Frédéric added indifferently:
'By the way, do you still see... What's his name?... That man who used to sing... Delmar?'
She replied curtly:
'No, it's over.'
So their rupture was final. Frédéric took heart.
They drove at walking pace down the Bréda district; since it was Sunday the roads were deserted, and the faces of the inhabitants appeared at their windows. The cab went faster. The sound of the wheels made passers-by turn their heads, the folded leather hood of the cab shone, the servant threw back his shoulders, and the two lap-dogs looked like fur muffs on the cushions. Frédéric let himself be rocked gently by the springs. The Maréchale turned her head to left and right and smiled.
Her pearly straw bonnet was trimmed with black lace. The hood of her burnous floated in the wind and she shaded herself from the sun under a parasol of lilac satin pointed at the top like a pagoda.
'What sweet little fingers!' said Frédéric, taking her other hand, the left one, tenderly in his; it was decorated with a gold curb-chain bracelet. 'Oh, it's really pretty; where did you get it?'
'Oh, I've had that a long time,' the Maréchale said.
The young man made no comment on this hypocritical reply. He

preferred to 'make the most of his opportunity', and still holding her wrist, he pressed his lips on it in the space between her glove and the end of her sleeve.

'Stop it, we shall be seen!'

'What's that matter?'

After the Place de la Concorde, they went along the Quai de la Conférence and the Quai de Billy, where there was a cedar tree in a garden. Rosanette thought that Lebanon was in China; she laughed at her own ignorance and asked Frédéric to give her geography lessons. Then, leaving the Trocadéro on the right, they crossed the Pont d'Iéna and halted finally in the middle of the Champ-de-Mars, near the other cabs already lined up in the Hippodrome.

The grassy slopes were crowded with the lower classes. You could see onlookers on the balcony of the École Militaire. And the two pavilions outside the paddock, the two stands inside, and a third below the royal enclosure were filled by a smartly dressed crowd who showed by their behaviour their reverence for this still quite novel entertainment. The racegoing public were more exclusive at that time, not so vulgar. It was the era of trouser straps, fur collars, and white gloves. The women wore brightly coloured dresses with dropped waists and, as they sat on the tiered rows, they looked like huge flower beds, flecked here and there by the dark costumes of the men. But all eyes were turned on the famous Algerian Bou-Maza,* who was sitting impassively between two staff officers in one of the private stands. In that of the Jockey Club there were only solemn-looking men.

The most enthusiastic spectators had gone down to the bottom, right next to the track, which was roped off by two rows of posts. In the huge oval formed by this track, vendors of liquorice water shook their rattles, others sold the race programme, cigar-sellers cried their wares, there was a great buzz and the municipal guards walked to and fro; then a bell hanging on a post covered in numbers, was rung. Five horses appeared and everyone went back to the stands.

However, large clouds were rolling over the tops of the elms opposite. Rosanette was afraid it might rain.

'I've got umbrellas,' said Frédéric. 'And everything we need to keep us happy,' he added, opening the boot, which contained provisions in a hamper.

'Bravo! We understand one another.'

'And we are going to understand one another even better, are we not?'

'Possibly!' she said, blushing.

The jockeys in their silk jackets were trying to keep their horses in line, reining them in with both hands. A red flag was lowered. All five started, the riders leaning low over the horses' manes. At first they stayed bunched together in a large mass but soon they spaced out and broke away; the jockey in yellow almost fell halfway round the first lap; for a long time Filly and Tibi were neck and neck; then Tom Thumb was in the lead; but Clubstick,* from behind since the start, caught up with them and won, beating Sir Charles by two lengths; it was a surprise; the crowd shouted; the wooden stands shook with their stamping.

'We are having such fun!' the Maréchale said. 'What a darling you are!'

Frédéric no longer doubted his good fortune. These last words of Rosanette confirmed it.

A hundred feet away in a victoria,* a lady appeared. She leaned out of the window, then quickly withdrew again. That was repeated several times. Frédéric could not see her face. A suspicion took hold of him, it looked like Madame Arnoux. But that was impossible! Why would she be here? He got out of the cab, on the pretext of having a walk round the enclosure.

'That's not very gallant of you!' said Rosanette.

He took no notice, but walked on. The victoria turned and started off at a trot.

At the same moment Frédéric was caught by Cisy.

'Hello, my friend! How are you? Hussonnet is over there. Listen!'

Frédéric tried to disengage himself and catch up with the victoria. The Maréchale was beckoning him to come back. Cisy caught sight of her and insisted on going to greet her.

Ever since he had come out of mourning for his grandmother he was achieving his ambition, managing to acquire some *cachet*. A tartan waistcoat, short coat, large tassels on his shoes, and the entry ticket tucked into his hatband, in fact nothing was missing in what he himself called his 'chic', a chic that was passionately Anglophile and *mousquetaire*.* He started by complaining about the Champ-de-Mars, an execrable turf, then talked about the races at Chantilly and the tricks they got up to there, swore he could drink twelve glasses of champagne while midnight was chiming, suggested to the Maréchale that she place a bet, gently caressed her two lapdogs; and leaning on one elbow against the carriage door, he carried on making fatuous remarks, sucking the top of his cane, his legs apart, his bottom poking out. Frédéric stood beside him, smoking, and trying to find out what had become of the victoria.

The bell rang and Cisy departed, to the great relief of Rosanette, who said she found him extremely annoying.

The second race was not very entertaining, nor the third, apart from a man being carried off on a stretcher. The fourth, in which eight horses battled it out for the Prix de la Ville, was more engaging.

The spectators in the stands had climbed on to the benches. The others, eyeglasses in hands, were standing in their carriages following the jockeys as they went round the course. They looked like red, yellow, white, and blue spots moving past the crowd lining the whole circuit of the Hippodrome. From a distance their speed did not seem very great. At the far end of the Champ-de-Mars they even seemed to slow down and only to be gliding along, the bellies of the horses touching the ground without bending their outstretched legs. But, coming back round rapidly, they got bigger. As they went past they cut the air, the ground shook, pebbles flew up. The wind billowing out the jockeys' jackets made them vibrate like sails. With great cracks of the whips they lashed their steeds to the finishing post. The numbers were removed and another was put up. And to the sound of applause, the victorious horse slowly walked towards the paddock, covered in sweat, its knees rigid, its head down, while its rider held his sides, as though in agonies on his saddle.

A dispute held up the last race. The crowd, bored, broke up. Groups of men were chatting below the stands. The talk was rather loose. Some society ladies left, shocked by the proximity of the kept women.

There were also celebrities from dance halls, boulevard actresses, and it wasn't the most beautiful who received the greatest homage. Old Georgine Aubert, whom some vaudevillist had once called the Louis XI of prostitution,* horribly made-up and occasionally giving a grunting sort of laugh, remained lying in her long barouche, wrapped in a sable tippet as if it were the depths of winter. Madame de Remoussot, whose trial had propelled her into the limelight, was queening it on the seat of a break in the company of Americans; and Thérèse Bachelu, looking as usual like a Gothic virgin, filled with her dozen flounces the entire interior of a carriage, its apron being replaced by a jardinière full of roses. The Maréchale was jealous of these celebrities. She began making extravagant gestures to get herself noticed and talked very loudly.

Some gentlemen recognized her and waved. She reciprocated, telling Frédéric their names. They were all viscounts, dukes, and marquises; and he swelled with pride, for all their eyes expressed a certain respect for his good fortune.

Cisy looked just as pleased with himself in the circle of older men who surrounded him. They smiled above their cravats as if they were making fun of him. Before long he shook the oldest man's hand and came over to the Maréchale.

She was eating a slice of foie gras with an affected greediness. Frédéric, balancing a bottle of wine on his knees, obediently did the same.

The victoria reappeared. It was Madame Arnoux. She went very pale.

'Give me some champagne!' Rosanette said.

And raising her filled glass as high as possible she cried:

'Good health there to respectable women—and to the wife of my protector!'

Laughter broke out all round. The victoria vanished. Frédéric, about to lose his temper, was tugging at her dress. But Cisy was there in the same attitude as before and, with a surfeit of confidence, he invited Rosanette to dinner that very evening.

'Impossible!' she replied. 'We are going to the Café Anglais together.'

Frédéric remained silent, as if he had not heard anything, and Cisy took leave of the Maréchale with a disappointed air.

While he was talking to her and leaning against the right-hand door, Hussonnet had come up on the left, and catching the reference to the Café Anglais, he said:

'That's a fine restaurant! Supposing we go there for a bite to eat?'

'As you please,' said Frédéric, slumped in a corner of the berlin, looking at the victoria disappearing on the horizon, feeling that something irreparable had just occurred and that he had just lost the love of his life. And with the other woman there next to him, the love that was both joyous and unproblematic! Weary, full of contradictory desires and not even knowing any more what he really wanted, he felt an infinite sadness, a wish to die.

Loud footsteps and voices made him look up. Children jumping over the ropes on the track had come to look at the stands. People were leaving. A few drops of rain were falling. The crush of traffic got worse. Hussonnet had disappeared.

'That's good!' Frédéric said.

'We'd rather be on our own, wouldn't we?' said the Maréchale, putting her hand in his.

Then a splendid landau with its brass and steel gleaming, passed in front of them. It was harnessed with four horses, driven by two jockeys in gold-trimmed velvet jackets. Madame Dambreuse was sitting next to her husband. Martinon was on the opposite seat. All three looked astonished.

'They recognized me!' Frédéric said.

Rosanette wanted to stop and get a better view of the procession. But Madame Arnoux might reappear. He shouted to the postilion:

'Go on! Go on! Get a move on!'

And the berlin shot off in the direction of the Champs-Élysées in the midst of the other carriages, barouches, britchkas, wurches, tandems, tilburys, dog carts, wagonettes with leather curtains full of workmen singing on their day out, go-carts driven carefully by fathers of families. In victorias crammed full of people, boys sat on other people's laps with their two legs dangling over the side. Large coupés with cloth-covered seats were taking dozing dowagers for a ride; a magnificent stepper went by, drawing a post-chaise, simple and smart like a dandy's black suit. But the downpour was heavier now. People got out their umbrellas, parasols, mackintoshes. They shouted to each other: 'Hello! You all right? Yes! No! See you later!' and faces went by with the speed of a shadow-show. Frédéric and Rosanette did not talk to each other, feeling slightly dazed at seeing all these wheels incessantly turning around them.

From time to time the rows of carriages were too close together and would all draw up at the same time in several lines. Then, everybody was side by side and they would all stare at one another. From the emblazoned panels indifferent looks were cast on the crowd; envious eyes gleamed from the back of cabs; disdainful smiles encountered the proud tossing of heads. Some gazed in foolish open-mouthed admiration. And the occasional *flâneur* in the middle of the road would jump back to avoid a rider who was galloping between the cabs, before managing to get through. Then everything started to move again.

The coachmen slackened the reins, lowered their whips; the spirited horses, shaking their bits, spattered foam around them, and the damp cruppers and harnesses steamed in the droplets catching the light of the setting sun. Passing under the Arc de Triomphe it created reddish rays, at a man's height, which made the hubs, the door knobs, the shaft ends, and the rings of the saddles gleam and sparkle. And on the two sides of the great avenue—like an undulating river of manes, clothes, human heads—the trees all gleaming with rain rose up like two green walls. The blue sky overhead reappearing here and there had the softness of satin.

Then Frédéric recalled the already far-off time when he had envied the inexpressible good fortune of being in one of those cabs next to one of those women. He was now the possessor of that good fortune, but it didn't make him any happier.

It had stopped raining. The passers-by, sheltering between the columns of the Garde-Meuble,* went on their way. Walkers in the Rue Royale were going back up the boulevard. In front of the Ministry for Foreign Affairs some idlers were standing on the steps.

Up by the Chinese Baths the berlin slowed down as there were some holes in the road. A man in a greenish overcoat was walking along the edge of the pavement. A splash of mud from under the springs went all over his back. The man turned round, furious. Frédéric went white. He had recognized Deslauriers.

At the door of the Café Anglais, he sent the cab away. Rosanette had gone in ahead of him while he was paying the postilion.

He found her on the stairs, chatting to a man. Frédéric took her arm. But in the middle of the corridor a second young lord stopped her.

'You go on!' she said. 'I'll be with you in a minute!'

And he went into the private room on his own. Through the two open windows you could see people at the casements of other houses opposite. Large puddles quivered like silk on the drying asphalt, and a magnolia placed on the sill of the balcony was scenting the room. The perfume and the cool air soothed his nerves. He sank on to the red divan beneath the mirror.

The Maréchale came in; and, kissing him on his forehead, said:

'Are we a bit sad, my pet?'

'Possibly,' he replied.

'You're not the only one!' That meant: 'Let's forget our own troubles and enjoy ourselves!'

Then she placed a flower petal between her lips, and held it out to him to nibble. This gesture which had a grace and an almost lascivious tenderness mollified Frédéric.

'Why do you make me sad?' he said, thinking of Madame Arnoux.

'Me? Make you sad?'

And standing facing him, she looked at him with her lids almost closed and her two hands on his shoulders.

All his morals, all his bitterness vanished in a boundless cowardice. He went on:

'Because you won't love me!'—drawing her on to his knee.

She let him do what he wanted. He put both arms round her waist. The rustle of her silk dress excited him.

'Where are they?' came the voice of Hussonnet from the corridor.

The Maréchale got up abruptly and went and stood at the other side of the room, turning her back to the door.

She asked for oysters; and they sat down to eat.

Hussonnet was not good company. Through writing daily on all sorts of subjects, reading many newspapers, hearing a lot of arguments and dealing in dazzling paradoxes, he had lost all exact sense of things and was blinded by his own damp squibs. The difficulties of what had once been an easy life, kept him in a state of perpetual agitation. And his ineffectuality, which he was unwilling to admit to himself, made him peevish and sarcastic. On the subject of *Ozaï*, a new ballet,* he came out strongly against dance; then, on the subject of dance, came out against operas; and on the subject of operas, against the Théâtre des Italiens, replaced now by a troupe of Spanish actors, 'as though we weren't sick to death of Castile'. Frédéric, romantically attached to Spain, was shocked, and in order to change the subject he asked him about the Collège de France, from which they had just excluded Edgar Quinet and Mickiewicz. But Hussonnet, an admirer of Monsieur de Maistre, declared himself in favour of Authority and Spiritualism. He had doubts, however, about the most well-proven facts, denied history, and disputed the most obvious truths, going as far as to cry out at the word geometry, 'What a joke geometry is!' All this was interspersed with imitations of actors, Sainville* being his chief model.

Frédéric was bored stiff by these imbecilities. In an impatient movement he caught one of the lapdogs under the table with his boot.

They both began to bark in an odious fashion.

'You ought to send them back!' he said brusquely.

Rosanette didn't trust anybody.

Then he turned to the bohemian.

'Come on Hussonnet, sacrifice yourself!'

'Oh yes, my sweet. That would be so nice of you!' Hussonnet left, without having to be asked twice.

How would he be rewarded for this complaisance? Frédéric put the thought from his mind. He was even beginning to enjoy his tête-à-tête when a boy entered.

'Madame, someone is asking for you.'

'What! Again?'

'Nevertheless I must see who it is.' Rosanette said.

He thirsted for her, needed her. Her disappearance seemed to him a treachery, a vulgarity almost. What did she want then? Was it not enough to have insulted Madame Arnoux? So much the worse for her, anyway! He hated all women now. He was choked with tears for his love was misunderstood and his desire thwarted.

The Maréchale came back again, and Cisy with her. 'I've invited this gentleman. That's all right, isn't it?'

'What! But of course!'

Frédéric, with a tortured smile, motioned to Cisy to sit down.

The Maréchale began to scan the menu, stopping when she reached the strange names.

'What if we had, for example, a turban of rabbit à la Richelieu and a pudding à la d'Orléans?'

'Oh no, not d'Orléans!' cried Cisy who was a Legitimist and thought he was being witty.

'Would you prefer a turbot à la Chambord?' she asked.

These courtesies annoyed Frédéric.

The Maréchale decided on a simple steak, crayfish, truffles, a pine-apple salad, and vanilla sorbets.

'Then we'll see. Meanwhile, let's get on with it. Oh, I was forgetting! Bring me some sausage, not with garlic!'

And she called the waiter 'young man', tapped her glass with her knife, threw pellets of bread at the ceiling. She wanted to drink a glass of burgundy straight away.

'You don't drink that at the beginning of a meal,' Frédéric said.

According to the viscount, it was sometimes done.

'Oh no, never!'

'I assure you it is!'

'Aha, you see!'

Her accompanying look said: 'He's a rich man, listen to what he says!'

But every minute the door opened, the waiters bawled orders, and someone thumped out a waltz on an infernal piano in the room next door. Then the races brought them round to talking about horses and the two rival systems. Cisy was defending Baucher, Frédéric the Comte d'Aure,* when Rosanette shrugged.

'That's enough, for goodness' sake! He knows more than you about it!'

She bit into a pomegranate, her elbows on the table; the candles on the candelabra in front of her flickered in the draught; the white light infused her skin with pearly tones, put a rose colour on her eyelids, and made the globes of her eyes shine. The red of the fruit blended with the crimson of her lips, her thin nostrils palpitated; and there was something insolent, drunk, and abandoned about her, which Frédéric found exasperating, and yet it filled him with an insane desire.

Then she asked calmly who the huge landau with the maroon livery belonged to.

'The Comtesse Dambreuse,' replied Cisy.

'They are very rich, aren't they?'

'Oh, immensely rich! Although Madame Dambreuse, who was plain Mademoiselle Boutron, daughter of a prefect, has just a modest fortune.'

Her husband on the other hand had certainly inherited several fortunes. Cisy enumerated them. Since he frequented the Dambreuses he knew all about the family.

To be disagreeable Frédéric obstinately contradicted him. He maintained that Madame Dambreuse was a *de* Boutron, he assured them she was of noble birth.

'I don't care!' the Maréchale said, leaning back on her armchair. 'But I wouldn't mind having her horses!'

And the sleeve of her dress, riding up a fraction, uncovered a bracelet set with three opals on her left wrist.

Frédéric saw it.

'Ah, isn't that...?'

All three looked at each other and blushed.

The door was discreetly opened a fraction, the brim of a hat appeared and then the figure of Hussonnet.

'Forgive me if I'm intruding, you lovebirds!'

But he stopped, surprised to see Cisy sitting there at table.

Another place was set. And as he was extremely hungry, he took random handfuls of whatever was left of the dinner, meat from one plate, a piece of fruit from a basket, one hand holding a drink, and with the other helping himself to the food, while at the same time reporting on his mission. The two little doggies had been taken back. There was nothing new at home. He had found the cook with a soldier—a fiction, made up simply to impress.

The Maréchale took her hat off the hook. Frédéric made haste to ring the bell, shouting to the waiter from across the room:

'A carriage!'

'Mine's here,' said the viscount.

'But Monsieur!'

'But really, Monsieur!'

And they stared at each other, pale and trembling. Finally the Maréchale took Cisy's arm and, pointing out the bohemian still sitting at the table:

'Take care of him, for goodness' sake! He's stuffing himself. I wouldn't want him to die through devotion to my dogs!'

The door banged shut.

'Well?' asked Hussonnet.

'Well what?'

'I thought...'

'What did you think?'

'Don't you...?'

He finished his sentence with a gesture.

'Oh no, not on your life!'

Hussonnet said no more.

He had an ulterior motive in inviting himself to dinner. His newspaper, which wasn't called *L'Art* any more but *Le Flambard** (with the epigraph: 'Gunners, to arms!'), was not doing very well at all, and he wanted to turn it into a weekly magazine—on his own, without the help of Deslauriers. He spoke of the former project and explained his new plan.

Frédéric, who did not precisely understand what he meant, gave a vague reply. Hussonnet took several cigars from the table, said: 'Goodbye my friend', and vanished.

Frédéric asked for the bill. It was steep. And the waiter, with his napkin under his arm, was waiting for his money when another person, a pasty individual who looked like Martinon, came to say:

'Excuse me, but we forgot to charge for the cab.'

'What cab?'

'The one that Monsieur ordered just now for the little dogs.'

And the waiter looked mournful, as though he felt sorry for the poor young man. Frédéric wanted to box his ears. He gave him the twenty-franc change as a tip.

'Thank you, Monseigneur!' said the man with the napkin, bowing deeply.

Frédéric spent the following day nursing his anger and humiliation. He blamed himself for not slapping Cisy's face. As for the Maréchale, he swore not to see her again. There were plenty of women as beautiful as her. And since you had to have money to possess those women, he would gamble what he got for his farm on the Bourse, he would be rich, he would crush the Maréchale and everyone else with his opulence. By the evening he was surprised that he hadn't given Madame Arnoux one thought.

'And just as well! What's the use?'

Two days later, at eight, Pellerin came to visit. He began by admiring the furniture, flattering Frédéric. Then, abruptly:

'You were at the races on Sunday?'

'Yes, more's the pity!'

Then the painter criticized the anatomy of English horses, praised Géricault's horses, the horses on the Parthenon.* 'Rosanette was with you?' And he began discreetly to sing her praises.

He was discouraged by Frédéric's cold manner. He could not think how to get round to the subject of the portrait.

His first intention had been to produce a Titian. But gradually the variety of colour in his model had seduced him. And he had worked boldly, stroke upon stroke, making layers of light. At first Rosanette was delighted. Her meetings with Delmar had interrupted the sittings and had left Pellerin plenty of time to marvel at his painting. Then, his admiration waning a little, he wondered if his painting lacked grandeur. He had been back to look at the Titians, had understood the difference, realized where he was going wrong, and begun simplifying the contours. Then he had tried to 'lose' them by blending the tones of the head with the background. And the face had become more substantial, the shadow more pronounced; it seemed to have become more solid. At last the Maréchale came back. She even permitted herself to make some criticisms; the artist naturally persevered. After raging about her stupidity, he admitted she might be right. So pangs of doubt began to set in, worries which caused him stomach cramps, sleeplessness, fever, self-loathing. He had found the courage to make some alterations, but his heart was not in it and he felt his work was poor.

He merely complained about being refused by the Salon, then blamed Frédéric for not coming to see the portrait of the Maréchale.

'I don't care a jot about the Maréchale!'

This declaration encouraged Pellerin to be bold.

'That wretched woman doesn't want it any more now, would you believe?'

What he didn't say was that he had asked her one thousand écus for it. Now the Maréchale did not worry overmuch about who would pay, preferring to get money from Arnoux for more urgent things.

'Well, what about Arnoux?' Frédéric said.

She had referred Pellerin to him. The former art dealer wanted nothing to do with the portrait.

'He maintains that it belongs to Rosanette.'

'That's right, it's hers.'

'What! She sent me to see you!' Pellerin replied.

If he had believed in the excellence of his work, he perhaps would not have thought of making use of it like that. But a sum of money (and a considerable sum at that) would be a slap in the eye for the critics, and a boost to his own self-confidence. In order to get rid of him Frédéric enquired politely what he wanted for it.

The exorbitant price shocked him. He replied:

'No, oh no!'

'But you are her lover, you commissioned it.'

'I'm sorry, but I was only the intermediary!'

'But I can't be left with that on my hands!'

The painter was getting angry.

'I did not believe you were so mean!'

'Nor you so avaricious! Good day!'

He had just left when Sénécal arrived.

Frédéric was worried and it showed.

'What is it?'

Sénécal told his story.

'At nine on Saturday Madame Arnoux received a letter recalling her to Paris. As chance would have it, nobody was there to go to Creil and get a cab. She wanted to send me, but I refused because it's not part of my job. She left and came back on Sunday evening. Yesterday morning Arnoux turned up at the factory. The girl from Bordeaux had made a complaint. I don't know what's going on between them but he revoked the fine in front of everyone. We had words. In short, he sent me packing and here I am!'

Then, articulating his words one by one:

'Anyway I'm not sorry. I did my duty. Too bad! It's all because of you.'

'What?' exclaimed Frédéric, afraid that Sénécal knew his secret.

Sénécal knew nothing of it, for he went on:

'I mean that but for you I would have perhaps found something better.'

Frédéric was seized with a kind of remorse.

'How can I help you now?'

Sénécal was wanting a job of some sorts, a position.

'It's easy for you. You know so many people, Monsieur Dambreuse, for one—from what Deslauriers told me.'

This reminder of Deslauriers was unpleasant for his friend. He wasn't at all anxious to return to the Dambreuses since the encounter on the Champ-de-Mars.

'I'm not sufficiently intimate with the family that I could ask a favour for anyone.'

The democrat took this refusal on the chin and after a minute's silence:

'All of that, I'm sure, is because of the girl from Bordeaux and your Madame Arnoux.'

This 'your' took away from Frédéric what bit of goodwill he still felt. However, as a courtesy he reached for the key of his desk.

Sénécal forestalled him:

'No, thank you!'

Then, forgetting his own problems, he started talking about national affairs, the Croix d'honneur given out so liberally at the King's birthday, a change in the Cabinet, the scandals of the time like the Drouillard and Benier* affairs; he railed against the bourgeois and predicted a revolution.

A Japanese kris* hanging on the wall caught his eye. He took hold of it, tried the handle, and then threw it down on the sofa with an air of disgust.

'Well goodbye! I have to go to Notre-Dame-de-Lorette.'

'Oh, why?'

'Today it's the memorial service for Godefroy Cavaignac. He died in harness! But all's not lost... Who knows?'

And Sénécal staunchly* held out his hand.

'We may never see each other again! Farewell!'

This farewell twice repeated, his frown as he studied the dagger, and above all his resigned attitude, made Frédéric wonder, but soon he thought no more about it.

In the same week his lawyer in Le Havre sent him the money for his farm, a hundred and seventy-four thousand francs. He divided it in two, placed the first in government securities, and took the second to a stockbroker to risk it on the Bourse.

He ate in fashionable restaurants, went to theatres, and made an effort to amuse himself. Then Hussonnet wrote him a letter in which he gaily announced that the Maréchale had sent Cisy packing the day after the races. Frédéric was pleased, and did not ask himself why the bohemian was telling him about this affair.

As chance had it, he ran into Cisy three days later. The nobleman put a brave face on it and even invited him to dinner for the following Wednesday.

That same morning Frédéric received an official notification in which Monsieur Charles-Jean-Baptiste Oudry informed him that through the judgement of the tribunal he had acquired a property situated in Belleville which belonged to Monsieur Jacques Arnoux, and that he was prepared to pay the two hundred and twenty thousand francs, the price of the sale. But in the same document he informed him that the sum of the mortgages exceeded the purchase price, so Frédéric's claim was null and void.

The whole problem derived from the mortgage not having been renewed in time. Arnoux had taken responsibility for this procedure and forgotten all about it afterwards. Frédéric flew into a rage with him, but when his anger had passed:

'Well what of it?... If it gets him out of a hole, so be it! It won't kill me! I'll put it behind me!'

But as he was riffling through his pile of papers on his table, he came across Hussonnet's letter and caught sight of the postscript which he hadn't noticed the first time round. The bohemian was asking for exactly five thousand francs to set up the newspaper.

'Oh, he's getting on my nerves!'

And he sent a curt refusal in a laconic note. After that he got dressed to go to the Maison d'Or.

Cisy introduced his guests, starting with the most respectable, a stout gentleman with white hair:

'Marquis Gilbert des Aulnays, my godfather. And Monsieur Anselme de Forchanbeaux,' he added. This was a slim fair-haired young man already going bald. Then, indicating an unassuming-looking man in his forties: 'Joseph Boffreu, my cousin; and this is my old teacher, Monsieur Vezou', a cross between a carter and a monk, with bushy whiskers and a long frock coat fastened with a single button at the bottom, so it stretched across his chest like a shawl.

Cisy was still expecting somebody, the Baron de Comaing 'who might be coming, he wasn't sure'. He kept going out of the room and seemed anxious. At last, at eight, they went through into a magnificently lit room that was too large for the number of guests. Cisy had chosen it on purpose to show off.

A silver gilt epergne laden with flowers and fruits occupied the centre of the table covered with silver dishes in the old French tradition; this was surrounded by plates of spices and seasonings for the hors d'oeuvres. Jugs of iced rosé wine were placed at intervals down the length of the table. Five glasses of different heights were lined up before each plate with countless ingenious eating devices whose use was a mystery. And there was, just for the first course: sturgeon's head drizzled with champagne, a York ham boiled in Tokay, thrushes au gratin, roast quail, a béchamel vol-au-vent, a sauté of red partridge, and to accompany all this, finely sliced potatoes combined with truffles. A chandelier and some candelabra lit up the room, which was hung with red damask. Four servants in black tailcoats stood behind the leather armchairs. At the sight of this the guests cried out in admiration, especially the tutor.

'My word, our host has quite let himself go! It's magnificent!'

'That?' the Vicomte de Cisy said. 'Oh, come now!'

And as soon as he had taken the first spoonful:

'Well, my friend des Aulnays, have you been to the Palais-Royal to see *Père et Portier*?'*

'You know very well I haven't the time!' replied the marquis.

His mornings were taken up in a course of forestry, his evenings by the Agricultural Club, and all his afternoons by visits to factories that made agricultural tools. Living in Saintonge for three-quarters of the year, he made the most of his journeys to the capital to educate himself. And his wide-brimmed hat set by on a side table was full of brochures.

But Cisy, noticing that Monsieur de Forchambeaux was refusing wine:

'For heaven's sake, drink up! You must make the most of your last meal as an unmarried man!'

When he said that, everyone bowed and congratulated him.

'And no doubt the young lady is charming?' said the tutor.

'Of course she is!' Cisy cried. 'But what does it matter? He's making a mistake, marriage is stupid!'

'You don't really mean it, my friend,' replied Monsieur des Aulnays, a tear rolling down his cheek at the memory of his dead wife.

And Forchambeaux said several times, with a laugh:

'You'll come round to it yourself, you'll come round to it!'

Cisy denied it. He would rather have a good time, 'be a Regency man'. He wanted to learn French boxing in order to visit the low haunts of the Cité, like Prince Rodolphe in the *Mystères de Paris*;* he drew a clay pipe out of his pocket, was harsh with the servants, drank copiously; and in order to impress everyone he criticized all the dishes. He even sent back the truffles; and the tutor, who was very much enjoying them, said obsequiously:

'They are not up to the "œufs à la neige" your grandmother used to make!'

Then he began to chat again with his neighbour, the agronomist, who considered there were many advantages to living in the country, not least being able to raise one's daughters to have simple tastes. The tutor congratulated him on his ideas and flattered him, supposing he had some influence on his pupil whose financial adviser he secretly wished to become.

Frédéric had come to Cisy's house full of bile, but his foolish behaviour was disarming. Nevertheless his gestures, his face, and all his person reminded him of the Café Anglais, and annoyed him more and more. And he was lending an ear to the rude remarks made sotto voce by Cousin Joseph, a worthy fellow without much money, who played the stock exchange and liked hunting. Cisy, for a laugh, called him 'swindler' several times; then, suddenly:

'Oh, here's the baron!'

At that moment there arrived a fellow of some thirty years, with rather rough features and a strong build, with his hat pulled over one ear and a flower in his buttonhole. This was the viscount's ideal man. He was delighted to have him. And because his presence excited him, he even risked a joke, for he said as they were passing round a *coq de bruyère*:

'This is the best of La Bruyère's* characters!'

He asked Monsieur de Comaing a host of questions about people nobody there knew; then, as if an idea had just occurred to him:

'By the way, did you remember me?'

Comaing shrugged.

'You are not old enough, my boy. It's impossible!'

Cisy had asked to be admitted to his club. But the baron, no doubt taking pity on his wounded pride, added:

'Oh, I nearly forgot! Many congratulations on your bet, dear boy!'

'What bet?'

'The one you made at the racecourse, that you'd go to that lady's house the same night.'

Frédéric felt he'd been struck by a whiplash. But he was immediately comforted by Cisy's abashed countenance.

In fact, the Maréchale the very next morning was feeling sorry for herself when her first lover, her man, Arnoux, had called to see her. Both of them had given the viscount to understand that he was de trop, and they had kicked him out unceremoniously.

He pretended not to have heard. The baron added:

'What's the news with our Rose?... Has she still got such nice legs?'—thus proving that he had been intimate with her.

Frédéric was put out by this revelation.

'You don't need to blush,' the baron added. 'She's a very fine woman!'

Cisy clucked:

'Huh, not so fine as all that.'

'Oh?'

'No, by Jove! In the first place I don't think she's anything out of the ordinary; and besides, you can pick up any number of women of her sort because... she's for sale.'

'Not to everybody!' Frédéric remarked acidly.

'He thinks he's different from the others,' Cisy replied. 'How very amusing!'

And a laugh went around the table.

Frédéric felt his heart beating as though it might burst. He swallowed two glasses of water one after the other.

But the baron had pleasant memories of Rosanette.

'Is she still with that fellow Arnoux?'

'No idea,' said Cisy. 'I don't know the man.'

Nevertheless, he suggested that he was something of a swindler.

'Hold on a moment!' cried Frédéric.

'But it's absolutely certain! He was even up in court.'

'That's a lie!'

Frédéric began to defend Arnoux. He guaranteed his probity, ended up believing it was true, invented statistics, proofs. The viscount, full of resentment, and also drunk, clung to his assertions so obstinately that Frédéric, in a serious tone, said:

'Are you trying to offend me, Monsieur?'

And he stared at him with eyes that gleamed as brightly as his cigar.

'Oh, not in the least! I even grant you that he has one good thing: his wife.'

'Do you know her?'

'Good heavens! Everyone knows Sophie Arnoux!'*

'What do you mean?'

Cisy had risen to his feet, and, slurring his words, said again:

'Everyone knows *her*!'

'Be quiet! You don't frequent women like her!'

'I hope not! I can do better than that!'

Frédéric threw a plate at his face.

It flew across the table like a streak of lightning, knocked over two bottles, destroyed a fruit dish, and smashed into three pieces against the surtout, hitting the viscount in the stomach.

Everyone got up to restrain him. He struggled, shouted, was seized with a kind of frenzy. Monsieur des Aulnays repeated:

'Calm down, dear boy, come now, calm down!'

'This is terrible!' exclaimed the tutor.

Forchambeaux, yellow as the plums, was trembling. Joseph was laughing out loud. The servants were mopping up the wine, picking up the mess from off the floor. And the baron went to shut the window, for the din, in spite of the noise of the traffic, could have been heard from the boulevard.

As everybody had been talking at once when the plate was thrown, it was impossible to discover the reason for the attack, whether it was because of Arnoux, Madame Arnoux, Rosanette, or someone else. What was certain was Frédéric's unqualified savagery, for which he positively refused to show any sign of regret.

Monsieur des Aulnays attempted to pacify him; so did Cousin Joseph, the tutor, and even Forchambeaux. During this time the baron was comforting Cisy, who, yielding to an attack of nerves, was shedding tears. Frédéric, on the other hand, was getting more and more annoyed, and they would have been there till daybreak if the baron had not said, to bring the business to a conclusion:

'The viscount will send his seconds to you tomorrow, Monsieur.'

'What time?'

'At midday, if you please.'

'With pleasure, Monsieur.'

Once outside, Frédéric took a deep breath. He had kept his feelings bottled up for too long, and had just relieved them. He felt something like a virile pride, a superabundance of inner strength which was intoxicating. He needed two seconds. The first one he thought of was Regimbart, and he went immediately to a tavern in the Rue Saint-Denis. The shutters were down, but there was a light shining from a pane of glass above the door. It opened and he went in, bending low under the entrance.

A candle on the edge of the counter lit up the deserted room. All the stools, with their legs in the air, had been placed on the tables. The proprietor and his wife were having supper with the waiter in the corner by the kitchen. And Regimbart, hat on head, was sharing their meal, and was even getting in the way of the waiter, who had to turn his head a little each time he took a mouthful. Having given him a brief account of what had happened, Frédéric asked him to help. The Citizen did not reply straight away. He rolled his eyes and seemed to be thinking it over, walked around the room a few times and finally said:

'Yes, gladly!'

And his face broke into a murderous smile when he learned that the adversary was noble.

'Never fear, we'll see him off! For a start, with a sword...'

'But perhaps I haven't the right...' Frédéric objected.

'I'm telling you it has to be swords!' the Citizen answered roughly. 'Can you use one?'

'A little.'

'Oh, a little! That's what they all say! And they are crazy about fencing! What use is a fencing school, I ask you? Listen to me! Make sure you keep your distance, enclose yourself in circles and give ground, give ground! It's perfectly permissible. Tire him out, then lunge at him full on! And whatever you do, don't try any clever stuff. Nothing out of La Fougère.* No, straightforward one-two and disengage. Here, you see? Turn your wrist as if you are unlocking a door.— Père Vauthier, give me your stick! No, this'll do!'

He caught hold of the pole which was used to light the gas, made an arch with his left arm, bent his left, and began to execute thrusts at the partition. He stamped about, getting more and more excited, and even pretended to encounter a problem, shouting 'Are you with me? Are you with me?' the whole time, and his huge shadow projected itself on to the wall, with his hat which appeared to touch the ceiling. The proprietor said from time to time: 'Bravo! Very good!' His wife also admired him, although she was nervous. And Théodore, a former soldier and a big fan of Monsieur Regimbart, was transfixed with admiration.

The next day Frédéric hurried to Dussardier's shop. After going through rooms one after the other that were all full of materials, on the shelves or spread out on the tables, with shawls draped over wooden mushroom stands, he spied Dussardier standing at a desk, writing, in a sort of cage, surrounded by ledgers. The good fellow immediately dropped what he was doing.

The seconds arrived just before noon. Frédéric thought it would be tactful not to be present at the discussion.

The baron and Monsieur Joseph said they would be satisfied with a simple apology. But Regimbart who, on principle, never gave way and who wanted to defend Arnoux's honour (Frédéric hadn't mentioned anything else) demanded that the viscount apologize. Monsieur de Comaing was disgusted by this arrogance. The Citizen refused to back down. All conciliation becoming impossible, they would fight.

Other difficulties arose. For the choice of arms legally belonged to Cisy, the offended party. But Regimbart maintained that by sending the challenge he constituted himself as the aggressor. Cisy's seconds, however, protested that a slap in the face was the most cruel of insults. The Citizen quibbled about the term, being hit by a plate was not the same as a slap. Finally it was decided that they would ask the military; and the four seconds left to go and consult officers in some barracks or other.

They stopped at the one on the Quai d'Orsay. Monsieur de Comaing, having accosted two captains, explained what the dispute was about.

The captains couldn't make head or tail of his story, muddled as it was by incidental comments from the Citizen. In short, they advised these gentlemen to set out the facts of the matter in writing. After that they would come to a decision. Then the seconds went to a café. And for the sake of greater discretion, they even designated Cisy as H and Frédéric as K.

Then they went back to the barracks. The officers had gone out. They reappeared and declared that clearly the choice of weapons belonged to Monsieur H. They all went back to Cisy's house. Regimbart and Dussardier stayed outside in the street.

When the viscount learnt of the outcome, he was so worried that he made them repeat it several times. And when Monsieur de Comaing came to Regimbart's demands, he muttered 'All the same', almost ready to comply with them. Then he sank into an armchair and declared he wasn't going to fight.

'Eh? What?' asked the baron.

Then Cisy let out a flood of incoherent words. He wanted to fight with blunderbusses, at point-blank range, or with a single pistol.

'Or else we can put arsenic in one of two glasses and it will be chosen at random. People do that sometimes, I've read about it!'

The baron, who was naturally impatient, said roughly:

'These gentlemen are waiting for your reply. This is disgraceful. What's your weapon for heaven's sake? The sword?'

The viscount nodded in reply. And the meeting was fixed for the next day at the Porte Maillot at seven o'clock precisely.

Dussardier was obliged to go back to his shop, so Regimbart went to let Frédéric know.

He had been left the whole day without any news. His impatience had become unbearable.

'Good!' he cried.

The Citizen was satisfied with this determined attitude.

'They were asking for an apology from us, would you believe? Just a single word, nothing more! But I well and truly sent them packing! As I had to, didn't I?'

'Of course,' Frédéric said, thinking that he would have done better to choose a different second.

Then, when he was alone, he said over and over to himself several times:

'I'm going to fight! Well, I'm going to fight! How odd!'

And as he was walking back and forth in his room in front of his mirror, he noticed he was pale.

'Does that mean I'm frightened?'

A terrible anguish overcame him at the idea he might be afraid when on the duelling ground.

'But supposing I were killed? My father died the same way. Yes, I shall be killed!'

And suddenly he saw his mother in a black dress; disjointed images flashed one after another through his brain. His own cowardice exasperated him. He was seized by a paroxysm of bravado, a thirst for blood. A whole battalion would not have made him back down. Once this fever had abated he was delighted to find he felt unshakeable. To take his mind off it he went to the Opéra where they were performing a ballet. He listened to the music, feasted his eyes on the dancers through opera glasses, and drank a glass of punch during the interval. But when he went home the sight of his study, his furniture, which he was perhaps seeing for the last time, made him feel weak.

He went down into his garden. The stars were shining; he looked at them. The idea of fighting for a woman raised him a little higher in his own estimation, made him more noble. Then he went calmly to bed.

For Cisy, it was different. After the baron had gone, Joseph had tried to lift his spirits but as this had not had any effect on the viscount:

'My dear chap, if you'd anyway rather leave it there, I'll go and say so.'

Cisy did not dare to answer 'Please do', but he bore his cousin a grudge for not doing so without telling him.

He hoped that Frédéric would die of a stroke in the night, or that a riot would happen and that the next day there would be enough barricades to close all the approaches to the Bois de Boulogne, or that something would happen to prevent one of the seconds getting there; for without the seconds, a duel could not take place. He wished he could escape to somewhere—anywhere—on an express train. He was sorry he had not studied medicine, so that he might take something which would make people think he was dead, without endangering his life. He reached the point of wishing he was seriously ill.

In order to get some advice, some help, he sent for Monsieur des Aulnays. This excellent man had gone back to Saintonge when a telegram had arrived informing him that one of his daughters was ill. That seemed to Cisy to be a bad sign. Fortunately Monsieur Vezou, his old tutor, came to visit him. Then he poured forth his feelings.

'What am I going to do? My God, what am I going to do?'

'In your position, Monsieur le Comte, I should pay a strapping fellow from the market to give him a thrashing.'

'He would still know where that came from!' Cisy replied.

And from time to time he uttered a groan; then:

'But is it legal to fight duels?'

'It's a relic from barbarous times! What can you do?'

To be companionable, the tutor invited himself to dinner. His pupil ate nothing and after the meal felt the need to go out for a while.

He said as they passed a church:

'Should we go in for a while... and look around?'

Monsieur Vezou was more than happy to do so and even offered him some holy water.

It was May, the month of Mary, flowers were covering the altar, voices were singing, the organ was thundering. But he found it impossible to pray, the pomp of religion put him in mind of funerals. He imagined he could hear something like the droning of the *De Profundis*.

'Let's go! I don't feel well!'

They spent the night playing cards. The viscount tried to lose, by way of dispelling bad luck, which Monsieur Vezou took advantage of. Finally at daybreak Cisy, at the end of his strength, collapsed on to the card table and had a sleep which was full of unpleasant dreams.

Yet if courage consists in wanting to control one's weakness, the viscount was courageous, for when he saw his seconds coming to look for him, he was vain enough to see that retreat would be the ruin of him. He stiffened his sinews. Monsieur de Comaing complimented him on how well he looked.

But on the way the swaying of the cab and the heat of the morning sun got the better of him. He collapsed once more. He couldn't even recognize where they were.

The baron enjoyed increasing Cisy's terror by speaking about the 'corpse' and how it had to be got secretly back to the town. Joseph played along with him. Both of them judged the affair ridiculous and were persuaded that a peaceful solution would be found.

Cisy kept his head down on his chest. He raised it slightly and observed that they had not got a doctor.

'There's no point,' said the baron.

'So there's no danger then?'

Joseph replied in a grave voice:

'Let's hope not.'

And nobody in the carriage said another word.

At ten past seven they reached the Porte Maillot. Frédéric and his seconds were there, all in black. Instead of a cravat, Regimbart had a horsehair collar like a soldier. And he was carrying a sort of long violin case specially adapted for this kind of adventure. They exchanged a frosty greeting. Then they all plunged into the Bois de Boulogne by the Route de Madrid, to look for a suitable place.

Regimbart said to Frédéric who was walking between him and Dussardier:

'Now what if you are in a funk? So what? If you need anything just ask! I know how it feels! Fear is a natural emotion.'

Then he added in an undertone:

'Don't smoke, that'll make you feel weak!'

Frédéric threw away his cigar, which was bothering him, and moved forward with confidence. The viscount was coming along behind, leaning on the arms of his two seconds.

Occasionally they met someone out walking. The sky was blue, now and then you could hear rabbits scuttling about. Around a corner of the path a woman in a madras kerchief was chatting to a man in a smock, and in the main avenue under the chestnuts servants in linen coats were exercising their horses. Cisy was remembering the happy days when he used to ride along beside carriage doors on his sorrel mare with his monocle to his eye. These memories increased his anguish. An unbearable thirst was burning his mouth; the buzzing of the flies mingled with the beating of his arteries. His feet sank into the sand. It seemed to him that he had been walking for ever.

The seconds were scanning both sides of the road as they walked. They were trying to decide whether to go to the Croix Catelan or under the walls of Bagatelle. Finally they turned right. And they stopped in a sort of clearing between some pine trees.

The spot was chosen so as to divide up the level of the ground evenly. The two places where the adversaries were to stand were marked out. Then Regimbart opened his box. On a lining of red leather it contained four exquisite swords, with grooved blades and filigree hilts. A ray of sunlight filtering through the leaves fell upon them. And to Cisy they looked like shining silver vipers on a pool of blood.

The Citizen showed everyone that they were of equal length. He took the third himself, so that he could separate the combatants if necessary. Monsieur de Comaing was holding a cane. There was silence. They all looked at one another. There was something of fear or cruelty in every face.

Frédéric had taken off his coat and waistcoat. Joseph helped Cisy to do the same. When his tie was removed you could see a sacred medallion round his neck. That made Regimbart smile pityingly.

Then Monsieur de Comaing (to allow Frédéric a minute's reflection) tried to put some obstacles in their path. He claimed the right to wear a glove, and to seize hold of the adversary's sword with the left hand. Regimbart, who was in a hurry, raised no objection. Finally the baron, addressing himself to Frédéric, said:

'It all depends on you, Monsieur. There is never any dishonour in admitting one's mistakes.'

Dussardier nodded approval. The Citizen got annoyed.

'Do you suppose we've come here to pluck chickens, dammit? En garde!'

The combatants were facing one another, their seconds one each side of them. He shouted the signal.

'Go!'

Cisy went pale as death. The point of his sword was trembling like a riding crop. His head was thrown back, his arms flew out, he fell on his back, in a faint. Joseph picked him up, and pushing some smelling salts under his nostrils, shook him hard. The viscount opened his eyes and then threw himself like a madman on his sword. Frédéric had held on to his. And he waited with his eyes fixed on him and his hand raised.

'Stop, stop!' called a voice from the road, to the sound of galloping hooves. And the hood of a cab broke through the branches. A man leaned out, waving a handkerchief and shouting repeatedly: 'Stop, stop!'

Monsieur de Comaing, thinking the police had arrived to intervene, raised his walking stick.

'Let's stop! The viscount is bleeding.'

'Am I?' said Cisy.

In his fall he had indeed grazed the thumb on his left hand.

'But that was when he fell,' the Citizen said.

The baron pretended he hadn't heard.

Arnoux leaped out of the cab.

'Am I too late? No! God be praised!'

He hugged Frédéric, felt him all over, covered his face with kisses.

'I know the reason. You wanted to defend your old friend! That's good, very good! I'll never forget it! How good you are! Oh, my dear boy!'

He contemplated him and shed tears, simultaneously laughing with delight. The baron turned to Joseph.

'I think we are de trop in this little family reunion. It's over, Messieurs, is it not?—Viscount, put your arm in a sling. Here, take my scarf.' Then, with an imperious gesture: 'Come now! No hard feelings! That's only right!'

The two combatants shook hands limply. The viscount, Monsieur de Comaing, and Joseph vanished in one direction and Frédéric went off in the other with his friends.

As the Madrid restaurant was not far off, Arnoux suggested going there for a glass of beer.

'We might even have something to eat,' Regimbart suggested.

But since Dussardier did not have time, they made do with a drink in the garden.

They were all in that state of well-being which results from a happy outcome. However, the Citizen was cross that the duel had been interrupted at the crucial moment.

Arnoux had got to hear about it from a certain Compain, a friend of Regimbart. And on a sudden impulse he had rushed to prevent it, believing, moreover, that he was the cause of it. He begged Frédéric to fill him in on a few details. Frédéric, moved by this proof of his friendship, was careful to foster his illusions.

'Oh please, let's not talk about it any more.'

Arnoux thought Frédéric's reserve extremely tactful. Then with his usual volatility, he turned to another subject:

'What news, Citizen?'

And they began to discuss bills and dates of maturation. In order to be more comfortable they even went off to talk quietly on their own at another table.

Frédéric caught the words: 'You'll put me down for... Yes, but you for your part... I did a deal for three hundred. That was a good commission, I'd say.' In short, it was clear that Arnoux was doing a great deal of shady business with the Citizen.

Frédéric thought he would remind him about his fifteen thousand francs. But the recent events forbade any such reproaches, even the mildest. Anyway he felt tired and it wasn't the right place. He put it off for another day.

Arnoux, sitting in the shade of a privet, was smoking contentedly. He raised his eyes to the doors of the private rooms giving on to the garden, and said that he used to come there often in the old days.

'Not alone, I'm sure?' replied the Citizen.

'Indeed!'

'What a rogue you are! And you a married man!'

'Well, what about you?' replied Arnoux. And with an indulgent smile: 'I'm pretty sure this fellow has a room somewhere where he entertains little girls.'

With a simple lifting of the eyebrows the Citizen admitted the truth of this assertion. Then these two gentlemen brought their tastes out into the open: Arnoux nowadays preferred young ones, working girls; Regimbart hated 'stuck-up' women and liked the down-to-earth sort. The conclusion, advocated by the porcelain seller, was that one should not take women too seriously.

'And yet he loves his wife!' thought Frédéric, as he went home. And he decided he was a dishonest man. He bore a grudge against him for the duel, as though it had been for him he had just risked his life.

But he was grateful to Dussardier for his loyalty; the clerk, at Frédéric's insistence, took to calling on him every day.

Frédéric lent him books: Thiers, Dulaure, Barante, Lamartine's *Les Girondins*.* His good friend listened quietly to him and accepted his opinions as from a master.

He arrived one evening in a panic.

That morning on the boulevard a man running as fast as he could had collided with him. And when he had realized it was a friend of Sénécal, he said:

'They've arrested him, and I'm running for it!'

It was absolutely true. Dussardier had spent the day finding out what had happened. Sénécal was locked up, suspected of a political conspiracy.

Born in Lyons, the son of a foreman, and having been taught by a former disciple of Chalier, he had joined the Société des Familles* on arriving in Paris. His habits were well known and the police kept him under surveillance. He had fought in the battle of May 1839 and since that time had lain low but had become more and more fanatical, worshipped Alibaud,* associated his complaints against society with those of the people against the monarchy, and woke every morning in the hope of a revolution which in a couple of weeks or a month would change the world. Finally, sickened by the weakness of his colleagues, furious with the obstacles that were placed in the way of his ambitions and in despair over his country, he had, in his capacity as chemist, become involved in the incendiary bomb conspiracy. And he had been caught carrying gunpowder which he was going to try out in Montmartre in a supreme attempt to establish the Republic.

Dussardier was just as keen on the Republic, for in his opinion it meant freedom and universal happiness. One day—when he was fifteen—outside a grocer's shop in the Rue Transnonain, he had seen soldiers with bloody bayonets and with hair stuck to the butts of their rifles,* and ever since that moment he had hated the Government as the very incarnation of Injustice. Murderers and gendarmes were much alike to him; an informer in his eyes was as bad as a parricide. He naively attributed all the evil in the world to Power. And he hated it with an undying hatred that came from the depths of his being, which filled his soul and refined his sensibility. Sénécal's rhetoric had dazzled him. Whether he was guilty or no and his plotting horrifying, what did it matter! Once he had fallen victim to Authority, they must come to his aid.

'The Peers will condemn him, for certain! Then he'll be carted off like a convict and locked up in Mont Saint-Michel, where the Government gets rid of people! Austen went mad! Steuben committed suicide.* When they transferred Barbès to a cell they pulled him by the legs and hair. They stamped on his body and his head bounced on each step all the way down the stairs. What an abomination! Oh, the swine!'

He was choked with angry sobs and he walked round and round the room in great anguish.

'We must do something anyway. Look, I don't know! Supposing we tried to set him free, what do you think? While they are taking him to the Luxembourg we can throw ourselves on the escort in the corridor. With a dozen determined men you can do anything.'

There was so much passion in his eyes that Frédéric shivered.

Now Sénécal seemed to him greater than he had imagined. He recalled his sufferings, his austere life. Without sharing Dussardier's enthusiasm for him he did nevertheless feel the admiration inspired by every man who sacrifices himself for a cause. He told himself that if he had come to his aid, Sénécal wouldn't be in this situation. And the two friends sought laboriously for some way of saving him.

It was impossible for them to get to him.

Frédéric tried to find out from the newspapers what had become of him and for three weeks he made frequent visits to the reading rooms.

One day he came across several numbers of *Le Flambard*. The leading article was devoted to the demolishing of a famous figure. After that came the society news, the gossip. Then they made fun of the Odéon, Carpentras,* fish-farming, and, when there were any, of prisoners condemned to death. The disappearance of a packet boat provided material for a whole year's humour. In the third column a chronicle of the arts contained, in the form of an anecdote or a piece of advice, advertisements for tailors, with accounts of parties, announcements of sales, book reviews; it treated a volume of verse and a pair of boots in exactly the same way. The only serious part was the critique of the smaller theatres and there two or three directors were pilloried. And the interests of Art were invoked in connection with the decor at the Funambules or an actress at the Délassements.*

Frédéric was about to toss all this aside when his eye fell upon an article entitled 'The Pullet and the Three Cocks'. It was the story of his duel, narrated in sparkling and bawdy style. He could easily recognize himself, for he was designated in this jokey way as 'a young man from the college of Sens, and who hasn't any'. He was even portrayed as a poor fellow from the provinces, an obscure fool, attempting to cross swords with the nobility. As for the viscount, he had the hero's role, first at the supper, which he gatecrashed, and then in the bet, where he carried off the girl, and finally on the duelling ground where he behaved like a gentleman. Frédéric's bravery wasn't exactly denied but it was implied that an intermediary, the *protector* himself, had arrived in the nick of time. The article ended with this maliciously suggestive question:

'Where does their affection spring from? Who knows! And as Don Basilio* says, who on earth is deceiving whom here?'

It was, without the least doubt, Hussonnet's revenge on Frédéric because of his refusal to give him five thousand francs.

What was to be done? If he called him to account the bohemian would protest his innocence and he would be no better off. The best thing would be to put up with it and say nothing. Nodody read *Le Flambard* anyway.

Leaving the library he saw a crowd outside a picture-seller's shop. They were looking at a portrait of a woman with these words underneath in black: 'Mademoiselle Rose-Annette Bron, property of Monsieur Frédéric Moreau of Nogent.'

It was definitely her—or a passable likeness of her—seen full on, breasts bare, hair hanging loose, and in her hand a red velvet purse, while behind her a peacock was poking his beak over her shoulder, covering the wall with his great fan-like plumes.

Pellerin had created this display to force Frédéric to pay him, since he was persuaded he was famous and that the whole of Paris would bestir itself on his behalf and do something about his wretched circumstances.

Was this a conspiracy? Had the painter and the journalist planned the attack together?

His duel had not helped in any way. He was becoming a laughing stock. Everybody was making fun of him.

Three days later at the end of June, the Northern Line shares having risen by fifteen francs, he was in a position to make thirty thousand francs, as he had bought two thousand the previous month. This stroke of luck gave him back his confidence. He told himself he didn't need anyone, that all his difficulties stemmed from his shyness and indecisiveness. He should have started by dealing harshly with the Maréchale, refused Hussonnet from the outset, not compromised himself with Pellerin. And to show that he was not embarrassed he went to visit Madame Dambreuse at one of her regular parties.

In the middle of the hall Martinon, arriving at the same time, turned.

'What are you doing here?' He looked surprised and even put out to see him there.

'Why should I not be here?'

And still wondering why he should be greeted thus, Frédéric went on into the salon.

The light was dim, in spite of the lamps that were placed in the corners, for the three windows that were wide open formed three large black squares of shadow. Between them, in the spaces under the pictures, jardinières rose to head height. A silver teapot with a samovar was reflected in a mirror in the background. There was a discreet murmur of voices. You could hear the squeak of a patent leather shoe on the carpet.

He could make out black suits and a round table lit by a large shaded lamp, seven or eight women in summer clothes, and a little further away Madame Dambreuse in a rocking chair. Her silk dress of lilac taffeta had slit sleeves with muslin puffs, the soft tone of the material matching the colour of her hair. And she was leaning back slightly with her heel just resting on a cushion, as tranquil as an exquisite work of art or a rare bloom.

Monsieur Dambreuse and an old man with white hair were walking up and down the long salon. A few people were chatting, sitting forward on the small divans, here and there. Others, standing, formed a circle in the middle of the room.

They were talking about votes, amendments, counter-amendments, about Monsieur Grandin's speech, what Monsieur Benoist had said in reply. The Third Party* was definitely going too far! The Centre Left should have remembered where its origins lay! The minister had been dealt some serious blows! But it was reassuring that he had no obvious successor. In short, the situation was completely analogous to that of 1834.

As these matters bored Frédéric he went over to the women. Martinon was near them, standing up with his hat under his arm, three-quarters turned away from him and looking so correct that he resembled a piece of Sèvres porcelain. He picked up a *Revue des deux mondes* lying on the table between an *Imitation* and an *Almanach de Gotha* and loftily criticized a famous poet, said he was going to the Saint-François lectures,* complained about his throat, swallowed a lozenge now and then; and in-between times spoke of music and made small talk. Mademoiselle Cécile, Monsieur Dambreuse's niece, who was embroidering a pair of cuffs for herself, watched him covertly with her pale blue eyes. And Miss Johnson, the governess with the snub nose, had put down her tapestry because of him. Both of them seemed to be exclaiming inwardly, 'Oh, how handsome he is!'

Madame Dambreuse turned her attention to him.

'Give me my fan, then, it's over there on that table. No, not that one, the other one!'

She got up; and as he was coming back they met in the middle of the salon, face to face. She addressed a few words to him, no doubt telling him off, to judge by the haughty expression on her face. Martinon smiled weakly, then went to join the group of men having a serious conversation. Madame Dambreuse took her seat again and, leaning on the arm of her chair, said to Frédéric:

'I saw someone the day before yesterday who was speaking of you—Monsieur de Cisy. You know him, don't you?'

'Yes, a little.'

Suddenly Madame Dambreuse cried:

'Oh, Duchess! What a delight!'

And she went over to the door to greet a little old woman wearing a dress of brown taffeta and a lace bonnet with long ribbons. The daughter of an exiled companion of the Comte d'Artois* and the widow of a marshal of the Empire who had been created a peer in 1830, she was connected with the old Court as well as the new one and wielded a good deal of influence. Those who were standing around chatting made way for them before resuming their discussion.

They were now talking about pauperism,* the depictions of which, according to these gentlemen, were exaggerated.

'All the same,' Martinon objected, 'poverty exists, let's admit it! But the remedy does not depend on either Science or those in power. It is entirely a matter for the individual. When the lower classes make an effort to rid themselves of their vices they will be free of their needs. When the common people are more moral they will not be so poor!'

According to Monsieur Dambreuse, nobody would make any real progress without a substantial amount of capital. So the only possible way was to entrust 'as moreover the Saint-Simonians suggested (there was some good in them for heaven's sake, give the devil his due), to entrust, as I was saying, the cause of Progress to those who can increase the public purse'. Gradually they got round to discussing the big industrial enterprises, the railways, the coal industry. And Monsieur Dambreuse, addressing himself to Frédéric, whispered:

'You didn't come about that little business of ours?'

Frédéric said he had been ill. But sensing the excuse was too silly:

'Anyway, I needed my funds.'

'To buy a carriage?' asked Madame Dambreuse, who was passing with a cup of tea in her hand. And she looked at him for a moment, her head a little to one side.

She supposed him to be Rosanette's lover. The allusion was obvious. Frédéric even felt that all the ladies were looking at him and whispering. In order to find out what they thought of him he again approached their group.

From the other side of the table, Martinon, sitting beside Mademoiselle Cécile, was leafing through an album. They were lithographs illustrating Spanish costumes. He was reading the captions aloud: 'Woman from Seville,—Gardener from Valentia,—Andalusian Picador'; and going down to the bottom of the page he continued in one breath:

'Jacques Arnoux, publisher.—Friend of yours, isn't he?'

'Yes he is,' said Frédéric, annoyed by his attitude.

Madame Dambreuse went on:

'Oh yes, you came here one morning... about... a house, I believe? Yes, a house belonging to his wife.' (That meant, 'She's your mistress.')

He blushed to his ears and Monsieur Dambreuse who arrived at the same moment added:

'In fact, you seemed to be extremely interested in them.'

These last words completed Frédéric's discomposure. His embarrassment, which he thought must be obvious, would confirm their suspicions; then Monsieur Dambreuse came closer and said in a serious voice:

'I suppose you don't do business together?'

He denied it, shaking his head many times over, without understanding the intentions of the capitalist who wanted to give him some advice.

He wanted to leave. The fear of seeming cowardly held him back. A servant came and took away the teacups. Madame Dambreuse was chatting to a diplomat in blue. Two young girls, heads together, were showing each other a ring. The others sitting in a semicircle on arm-chairs slowly turned their pale faces, framed with black or blonde hair, this way and that. In short, nobody was paying him any atten-tion. Frédéric turned on his heel. And by a succession of lengthy zigzags, he had almost reached the door when, passing by a side table, he noticed a newspaper folded in two between a Chinese vase and the wooden panelling. He pulled it out a little and read the words: *Le Flambard*.

Who had brought it? Cisy! Nobody else, obviously. Well anyway, what did it matter? They would all believe, perhaps already did be-lieve, the article. Why was he being persecuted? An ironic silence enveloped him. He felt as if he were lost in a desert. But Martinon raised his voice.

'Speaking of Arnoux, I read the name of one of his employees, Sénécal, among the names of those arrested for the incendiary bombs. Is that our Sénécal?'

'The same,' Frédéric said.

Martinon repeated, shouting very loudly:

'What? Our Sénécal, our Sénécal!'

Then he was questioned about the plot. His position at the Public Prosecutor's office should mean he had information.

He admitted he had none. And he scarcely knew the man, having met him only two or three times. He felt sure he must be a rogue. Frédéric cried indignantly:

'Not at all! He's a very respectable fellow!'

'But, Monsieur,' said a landowner, 'being a conspirator is not repectable.'

Most of the men there had served in at least four governments. And they would have sold France or the whole human race to safe-guard their fortune, to spare themselves an awkward or difficult situation, or even out of mere servility and an instinctive worship of power. Every one of them declared political crimes to be inexcusable. Far better to forgive crimes that were committed through need! And they invariably held up the example of the father of a family stealing the eternal crust of bread from the eternal baker.

One official even cried:

'Well, as for me, Monsieur, if I found out that my brother was a conspirator, I would denounce him!'

Frédéric invoked the right of resistance; and, remembering a few phrases that Deslauriers had uttered in conversation, he cited Desolmes, Blackstone, the Bill of Rights in England, and Article 2 of the '91 Constitution.* It was as a result of this right that the deposition of Napoleon had been brought about. It had been recognized in 1830 and inscribed at the head of the Charter.

'Moreover, when the sovereign does not fulfil his contract justice requires that he be overthrown.'

'But that's dreadful!' exclaimed a prefect's wife.

All the other women kept quiet, vaguely shocked as if they had heard the noise of gunfire. Madame Dambreuse rocked back and forth in her chair and listened to him talk, a smile on her lips.

A captain of industry, an old *carbonaro*,* tried to prove to him that the Orléans were a fine family. Of course there was some bad behaviour...

'Well, then?'

'One mustn't mention it, my dear sir. If only you knew how all these complaints from the Opposition harm business!'

'I don't give a damn about business!' declared Frédéric.

He was exasperated by the corruption of these old men. And carried away by the bravura that sometimes overcomes even the shyest, he attacked the financiers, the deputies, the Government, the King, stood up for the Arabs, said many foolish things. A few encouraged him ironically: 'Yes, go on! Keep going!' while others muttered: 'Good God, what passion!' In the end he deemed it better to withdraw, and as he went, Monsieur Dambreuse said to him, alluding to the position of secretary:

'Nothing is settled yet. But hurry!'

And Madame Dambreuse said:

'We'll see you soon, won't we?'

Frédéric thought their farewell a final mockery. He was determined not to come back to their house or mix with people like that ever again. He supposed he had offended them, not knowing what a large fund of indifference society possesses! Those women especially made him cross. There was not one who would have stood up for him, even with a glance. He bore them a grudge for not having been able to move them by his words. As for Madame Dambreuse, she struck him as being at once languid and hard, which prevented him from labelling her according to a formula. Had she a lover? Who was it?

Was it the diplomat or someone else? Martinon perhaps? Impossible! However, he felt a kind of jealousy towards him, and an inexplicable resentment towards her.

Dussardier, who had come round that evening as usual, was waiting for him. Frédéric's heart was full, and his problems, although vague and difficult to understand, saddened the kindly shop-assistant. He even complained of feeling lonely. Dussardier hesitantly suggested going to Deslauriers's house.

At the lawyer's name, Frédéric was filled with the urgent need to see him again. His intellectual solitude was deep and Dussardier's company did not suffice. He answered that he could arrange whatever he liked.

Deslauriers too had felt that his life was lacking something since their quarrel. He promptly responded to his friendly overtures.

The two embraced, then began to chat about indifferent matters.

Frédéric was touched by Deslauriers's reserve. And to make reparation, as it were, he confided to him the next day his loss of fifteen thousand francs, without telling him that those fifteen thousand francs were originally meant for him. Nonetheless the lawyer was in no doubt this was so. This misadventure, which justified his prejudices against Arnoux, completely dispelled his resentment and he did not mention the former promise.

Frédéric, deceived by his silence, thought he had forgotten about it. A few days later he asked if there were any way of recovering his funds.

They could dispute the preceding mortgages, accuse Arnoux of fraudulent misrepresentation, or lay a claim to the house by proceeding against his wife.

'No, no, not against her,' cried Frédéric; and surrendering to the questions of the former clerk, he admitted the truth.

Deslauriers was convinced he was not telling him everything, no doubt through discretion. This lack of trust hurt him.

However, they were as close as they had been in the old days and they so much enjoyed each other's company that they felt Dussardier to be in the way. On the pretext of appointments they managed to gradually shake him off. There are men whose only mission it is to serve as intermediaries between others. One crosses over them like bridges and leaves them behind.

Frédéric hid nothing from his old friend. He told him about the coal business and Monsieur Dambreuse's proposition. The lawyer became thoughtful.

'That's strange! For that position they need someone who's very good at legal matters!'

'But you could help me,' Frédéric suggested.

'By God yes... of course I could!'

The same week he showed him a letter from his mother.

Madame Moreau blamed herself for misjudging Monsieur Roque, who had given a satisfactory explanation for his conduct. Then she spoke about his fortune and of the possibility of a marriage with Louise later on.

'That might not be such a bad idea,' said Deslauriers.

Frédéric dismissed it out of hand. Anyway, Père Roque was an old rogue. That didn't matter, according to the lawyer.

At the end of July, there was an inexplicable fall in the Northern Line shares. Frédéric hadn't sold his. He lost sixty thousand francs all at once. His income was greatly diminished. He had to either tighten his purse strings, or take up a profession, or make a rich marriage.

Then Deslauriers talked to him about Mademoiselle Roque. Nothing was preventing him from going to see the lie of the land for himself. Frédéric was a little tired. The country and his mother's house would restore him. He set off.

Driving through the streets of Nogent by moonlight revived old memories. And he felt a kind of anguish, like somebody who returns home after a long journey.

At his mother's house there were all the usual visitors: the Gamblins, Heudras and Chambrion, the Lebruns, the Auger girls; then Père Roque and, sitting opposite Madame Moreau at a card table, Mademoiselle Louise. She was a woman now. She rose with a cry. There was a general commotion. She stood motionless. The light of four candles in their silver holders on the table increased her pallor. When she went back to playing cards her hand was trembling. This emotion flattered Frédéric, whose self-esteem was ailing, out of all proportion. He said to himself: '*You* could love me!' and in revenge for the slights he had had to put up with in Paris, he acted the Parisian, the celebrity, talked about the latest plays, told anecdotes about famous people he had gathered from the gossip columns, and succeeded in dazzling that home-town company.

Next day Madame Moreau spoke at length about Louise's qualities. Then she listed the woods, the farms she would inherit. Monsieur Roque's fortune was considerable.

He had acquired his money by making investments for Monsieur Dambreuse, for he lent to people with reliable mortgage securities, which meant he could demand supplements or commissions. The capital, thanks to his watchfulness, did not incur any risk. Moreover, Père Roque never hesitated to foreclose. Then he bought back the property that was mortgaged, at a low price, and Monsieur Dambreuse, seeing his funds repaid, thought his business affairs were being conducted very successfully.

But this illicit manoeuvring compromised him with his agent. He could not refuse him anything. It was in response to Roque's urging that he had given Frédéric such a warm welcome.

Père Roque was in fact nursing a secret ambition in his heart. He wanted his daughter to be a countess; and to achieve this, without putting his daughter's happiness in jeopardy, he knew no other young man than Frédéric.

Through the protection of Monsieur Dambreuse he could be given the title of his ancestor, Madame Moreau being the daughter of the Comte de Fouvens, and related moreover to the oldest families in Champagne, the Lavenades, the d'Étrignys. As for the Moreaus, a Gothic inscription near the mills of Villeneuve l'Archevêque mentioned a Jacob Moreau who had rebuilt them in 1596; and the tomb of his son Pierre Moreau, first groom to the king in the reign of Louis XIV, could be seen in the Saint-Nicholas chapel.

So much nobility fascinated Monsieur Roque, the son of a former footman. But if the coronet of count was not to be, he would make do with something else. For Frédéric might attain the post of deputy when Monsieur Dambreuse was elected to the peerage and then help him with his business affairs, obtain orders and concessions for him. He liked the young man as a person. In short, he wanted him for his son-in-law, because for a long time he had cherished this idea and it appealed to him more and more.

Now he had taken to going to church; and he had won over Madame Moreau with the hope of a title more than anything else. She had been careful, however, not to give him a decisive answer.

So a week later, though no definite engagement had been made, Frédéric was considered Mademoiselle Louise's 'intended'. And

Père Roque, who was not overscrupulous, left them alone together sometimes.

## V

DESLAURIERS had taken the deed of subrogation* away from Frédéric's house, along with the power of attorney conferring on him full authority; but when he had climbed up the five storeys and was on his own in the middle of his gloomy study in his leather armchair, the sight of the stamped documents made him feel sick.

He was tired of these things, of cheap restaurants, trips in the bus, of his poverty, of all his efforts. He took up the wad of paper again. There was more besides. There were the prospectuses of the coal company with the list of mines and the details of what they contained. Frédéric had left all that for him to form his own opinion.

An idea occurred to him. He would introduce himself to Monsieur Dambreuse and ask him for a position as secretary. This position, naturally, would not come without the buying of a certain number of shares. He realized the folly of his plan and said to himself:

'Oh no, it would be wrong.'

Then he tried to think what to do to recover the fifteen thousand francs. A sum like that was nothing to Frédéric! But if he himself had such an amount, what a help that would be! And the former clerk was angry that Frédéric's fortune was so immense.

'What he spends it on is pitiful. He is selfish. Oh, I don't care about his fifteen thousand francs!'

Why had he lent the money? To please Madame Arnoux. She was his mistress! Deslauriers was sure of that. 'There's another thing that money can buy!' Hateful thoughts filled his head.

Then he thought about Frédéric as a person. He had always exercised an almost feminine charm over him. And he soon came round to admiring him for a success of which he acknowledged himself incapable.

But wasn't willpower the most important constituent of enterprise? And since one can conquer all things with that...

'Oh, that would be droll!'

He was ashamed of this disloyalty, but a minute later exclaimed:

'Bah! Why should I be afraid?'

Madame Arnoux, being so much talked about, had become an extraordinarily vivid presence in Deslauriers's imagination. The persistence of this love irritated him, as if it were a problem. His rather theatrical asceticism irritated him nowadays. Moreover, the lawyer was dazzled by this society lady (which he supposed her to be)—the symbol and epitome of countless pleasures that he'd never known. A poor man himself, he coveted luxury in its most blatant form.

'After all, if he gets angry, what does it matter! He's behaved so badly towards me, I've no need to hold back! I've no certainty that she is his mistress! He denied it. So I am a free man!'

The desire to go ahead with this plan would not leave him. It was a test of his own powers that he wanted; so much so that one day, all of a sudden, he polished his boots himself, bought white gloves, and started out, putting himself in Frédéric's place and almost thinking he *was* Frédéric, by a strange mental transformation in which there was both revenge and sympathy, imitation and daring.

He had himself announced as 'Doctor Deslauriers'.

Madame Arnoux was taken aback, not having summoned a doctor.

'Oh, many apologies! I am a doctor of law. I have come on a matter relating to Monsieur Moreau.'

This name seemed to disconcert her.

'Good!' thought the former clerk. 'Since she was willing to have him, she will have me!'—taking heart from the old adage that it is easier to supplant a lover than a husband.

He had had the pleasure of meeting her once at the Palais. He even gave the date. Such a memory astonished Madame Arnoux. He went on in a winning tone:

'You have already had... some problems... with your business affairs!'

She did not answer. So it was true.

He began to chat about this and that, about his lodgings, the factory. Then, catching sight of miniatures around the mirror:

'Ah, some family portraits I imagine?'

He noticed the picture of an elderly woman, Madame Arnoux's mother.

'She looks an excellent person, very much a woman from the South of France.'

And being told that she was in fact from Chartres:

'Chartres! Lovely town!'

He praised the cathedral and the pies; then returning to the portrait, found some resemblance to Madame Arnoux and paid her indirect compliments. She did not take offence. His confidence grew and he said he had known Arnoux for a long time.

'He's a fine fellow. But he gets into some compromising situations. With this mortgage, for example, you can't imagine a more foolish... '

'Yes, I know,' she said, with a shrug.

This involuntary show of contempt encouraged Deslauriers to go on.

'Perhaps you don't know that the kaolin affair almost went very badly wrong and even his reputation...'

He was brought up short by a frown.

Then falling back on generalities, he sympathized with poor women whose husbands squandered their fortune...

'But the fortune belongs to him, Monsieur. I have no money of my own!'

It was of no consequence. One never knew... An experienced person could be of help. He offered to devote himself to her, vaunted his own merits; and he looked at her straight in the eyes through his glinting spectacles.

She was overcome by a vague apathy. But suddenly said:

'To business, if you please!'

He took out the dossier and showed her.

'Here is Frédéric's power of attorney. With a document like this in the hands of an officer who makes a court order, nothing could be simpler... Within twenty-four hours...' (She remained impassive, he changed tactics.) 'But in any case I don't understand what's making him demand this sum of money, for he doesn't need it at all!'

'What! Monsieur Moreau has been kind enough...'

'Oh, I agree!'

And Deslauriers began to sing his praises, then moved to denigrating him, very gently, giving him out to be forgetful, egotistical, and mean.

'I thought he was your friend, Monsieur?'

'That does not prevent me from seeing his faults. For example, he does not always—how shall I put it—understand one's feelings...'

Madame Arnoux was turning the leaves of the thick notebook. She interrupted him, to ask him to explain a word.

He leaned over her shoulder and so near to her that he was touching her cheek. She blushed. This blush aroused Deslauriers. He kissed her hand hungrily.

'What are you doing, Monsieur?'

And standing with her back to the wall, she kept him transfixed by the angry look in her big black eyes.

'Listen to me! I love you!'

She burst out laughing, a shrill laugh, desperate, dreadful. Deslauriers felt so angry he could have strangled her. He contained himself. And with the expression of a victim begging for mercy, said:

'Oh, you are wrong! I wouldn't go like him and...'

'Who are you talking about?'

'About Frédéric!'

'Ah well, Monsieur Moreau is not a worry to me, I've already told you!'

'Oh, I do beg your pardon!'

Then in a cutting, drawling voice:

'All the same, I thought you'd be interested in him enough to be pleased to know...'

She went very pale. The former clerk added:

'He is to be married!'

'Married!'

'In a month's time, at the latest, to Mademoiselle Roque, the daughter of Monsieur Dambreuse's agent. He has even left for Nogent specifically for that purpose.'

She placed her hand on her heart, as though she had been dealt a physical blow. But she immediately rang the bell. Deslauriers did not wait to be thrown out of the house. When she turned round, he had gone.

Madame Arnoux found it rather hard to breathe. She went to the window to get some air.

On the pavement on the other side of the road a packer in shirt-sleeves was nailing up a crate. Cabs went by. She shut the window and sat down. The tall houses opposite blocked out the sun, cold light fell on the apartment. Her children had gone out, nothing moved round her. It was like a huge abandonment.

'He is to be married! Is that possible!'

And she started to tremble all over.

'Why am I like this? Do I love him?'

Then, all of a sudden:

'Yes, yes, I love him... I love him!'

It seemed to her she was falling into an infinite abyss. The clock chimed three. She listened to the vibrations die away. And she sat on the edge of her armchair, gazing at nothing, still smiling.

That same afternoon, at the same time, Frédéric and Mademoiselle Louise were walking in the garden that Monsieur Roque owned at the end of the island. Old Catherine was keeping watch on them, from a distance. They were walking side by side and Frédéric was saying:

'Do you remember when I used to take you into the country?'

'How nice you were to me!' she replied. 'You helped me make sandcastles, filled up my watering can, and pushed me on the swing!'

'What has happened to all your dolls that were called after queens or marquises?'

'Goodness, I've no idea!'

'And your little dog Moricaud?'

'He drowned, poor little thing.'

'And the Don Quixote with the engravings we coloured in together?'

'I've still got that!'

He reminded her of the day of her First Communion, and how sweet she had looked at Vespers with her white veil and her large candle, when they all processed around the choir and the bell was tolling.

These memories no doubt held little charm for Mademoiselle Roque; she couldn't think what to say. And a minute later:

'You are a bad boy, not sending me news of you even once!'

Frédéric defended himself on the grounds of having a great deal of work.

'What do you do?'

He was embarrassed by the question, then said he was studying politics.

'Oh!'

And without further questioning:

'You are busy with that, but as for me...'

And then she told him about her dreary existence, not having anybody to see, not the least pleasure, the slightest entertainment! She wanted to go riding.

'The curate says it's not respectable for a young lady. How stupid respectability is! In the old days I was allowed to do whatever I liked. Nowadays, nothing!'

'But your father loves you!'

'Yes, but...'

She gave a sigh as much as to say: 'That's not enough to make me happy.'

Then there was a silence. All they could hear was the crunching of the sand beneath their feet and the gurgling of the weir. For the Seine above Nogent branched into two. The arm which made the watermills turn disgorged its overflow here and rejoined the natural course of the river further down. And when you approached it from the bridges, you saw to your right, on the other bank, a grassy hill with a white house at the top. On the left, poplars stretched back through the fields and the horizon opposite was bounded by a bend in the river. It was smooth as a mirror; large insects scooted across the unruffled surface. Tufts of reeds and rushes grew at intervals along the edges; all sorts of plants which had taken root there opened in golden buds, yellow hanging blossoms, spikes of purple flowers, random green shoots. In a little inlet in the bank water lilies covered the water. And on this side of the islet a line of old willow trees, concealing spring-traps, were the only defence the garden possessed.

Beyond that, inside, four walls with a slate coping enclosed the kitchen garden in which newly dug plots formed brown patches of earth. The cloches on the melons gleamed, lined up on their narrow bed. The artichokes, the beans, the spinach, the carrots and tomatoes alternated as far as a bed of asparagus, which looked like a little feathery forest.

Under the Directory* all this land had been what was called a 'folly'. Since then the trees had grown out of all measure. Clematis choked the arbours, the paths were covered with moss, everywhere brambles abounded. Plaster flaked off ruined statues in the undergrowth. Your feet got caught in bits of old wire ornament. In the pavilion only two rooms on the ground floor remained, with shreds of blue wallpaper. Along the front was a pergola where, on brick pillars, a wooden trellis supported a vine.

The pair reached this point and as the light filtered through the greenery here and there, Frédéric, while talking to Louise at his side, was observing the shadow of the leaves on her face.

In the chignon at the back of her red hair, was a pin with a glass bead on the end resembling an emerald. And despite the fact that she was in mourning, her bad taste was so naive she wore straw slippers with a trim of pink satin, a vulgar new acquisition no doubt from some country fair.

He noticed this and complimented her ironically.

'Don't make fun of me!' she said.

Then, looking him up and down, from his grey felt hat to his silk socks:

'How elegant you are!'

Then she asked him to suggest some books she might read. He named several, and she said:

'How learned you are!'

When very young she had been overwhelmed with one of those childish passions which have both the purity of a religion and the violence of a need. He had been her comrade, her brother, her master, had kept her mind active, made her heart beat faster and unintentionally filled the depths of her being with a suppressed but constant intoxication. Then he had left her in the middle of a tragic crisis, her mother scarcely in her grave; these two sad events became confused in her mind. Absence had idealized him in her memory. He came back with a kind of halo round his head and she naively indulged her happiness at seeing him again.

For the first time in his life Frédéric felt loved. And this new pleasure, which did not amount to more than any other agreeable feeling, caused him a sort of secret pride, so that he spread his arms wide and threw back his head.

A large cloud passed overhead.

'It's moving in the direction of Paris,' said Louise. 'You'd like to follow it, wouldn't you?'

'Me? Why?'

'Who knows?'

And looking at him with her piercing eyes:

'Perhaps you have someone you'—she searched for the word—'are fond of?'

'Ha! I have no one!'

'Are you sure?'

'Yes, Mademoiselle, of course I'm sure!'

In less than a year an extraordinary transformation had taken place in the girl, which Frédéric found astonishing. After a minute's silence he added:

'We ought to say "tu" to each other, as we used to, don't you think?'

'No.'

'Why not?'

'Because!'

He insisted. She lowered her head and said:

'I don't dare!'

They had reached the end of the garden on the Livon beach. Frédéric boyishly began to play ducks and drakes with pebbles. She ordered him to sit down. He obeyed, then, looking at the weir, he said:

'It's like Niagara!'

He got to talking about far-off lands and long journeys. The idea of them appealed to her greatly. She wouldn't be afraid of anything, of raging tempests or lions.

Sitting side by side they scooped up handfuls of sand, then, as they talked, let them trickle through their fingers. And the warm breeze coming off the fields wafted over the scents of lavender and tar from a boat behind the lock. The sun was striking the water cascading down. The greenish stones of the little wall over which the water flowed appeared to be covered by a sheet of silver gauze unrolling for ever. A long line of foam at the bottom resurfaced at regular intervals. It boiled and bubbled into whirlpools, into a thousand cross-currents finally uniting in one single limpid sheet of water.

Louise murmured that she envied the life of fish.

'It must be so nice to roll around in it as you like and feel it caress you all over.'

And she shivered with little shocks of sensual delight.

A voice cried:

'Where are you?'

'Your maidservant is shouting for you,' said Frédéric.

'All right! All right!'

Louise did not move.

'She'll get cross,' he went on.

'I don't care. And anyway...' Mademoiselle Roque gave him to understand by a gesture that she could do as she pleased with her.

But she got up, then complained of a headache. And as they were passing a vast shed stacked with faggots:

'Supposing we went in, into the *égaud*?'*

He pretended not to understand that dialect word and he even teased her about her accent. Gradually the corners of her mouth came together, she bit her lips. She went a little way off, sulking.

Frédéric walked over to her again, swore he had never meant to hurt her and that he loved her a lot.

'Is that true?' she cried, smiling at him with a smile that lit up the whole of her somewhat freckled face.

He could not resist this openness, this youthful freshness, and said:

'Why would I lie to you?... You don't believe me, do you?' And he put his left arm around her waist.

A cry, soft as the cooing of a dove, sprang from her throat. Her head went back, she almost fainted, he held her up. And his moral scruples were useless; faced with this young girl who was offering herself to him, he panicked. He helped her to take a few steps, gently. His tender words had ceased and, since now he wished to say nothing of any significance, he talked about people in Nogent.

Suddenly she pushed him away and said bitterly:

'You wouldn't have the courage to take me away.'

He remained motionless, looking completely bewildered. She burst out sobbing and buried her head in his chest:

'How can I live without you!'

He tried to calm her. She put her two hands on his shoulders to look straight at him and fixed her green eyes on his almost fiercely, through her tears:

'Will you be my husband?'

'Well...' Frédéric replied, searching for words. 'Of course... I couldn't wish for anything better...'

At that moment Monsieur Roque's cap poked up from behind a lilac bush.

He took his 'young friend' off for two days on a little tour of his properties in the neighbourhood; and when Frédéric came back he found three letters at his mother's.

The first was a note from Monsieur Dambreuse inviting him to dinner on the Tuesday before. What did this courtesy mean? Had he been forgiven for his uncivil behaviour?

The second was from Rosanette. She thanked him for having risked his life on her behalf. Frédéric did not understand at first what she meant. Finally after much shilly-shallying she wrote that, seeing he was her friend, trusting in his finer feelings, in view of her urgent need, she asked him on her knees, as though she were begging for bread, if he would help her with a little loan of five hundred francs. He decided immediately that he would.

The third letter, coming from Deslauriers, spoke of subrogation and was long and obscure. The lawyer had not yet taken a decision. He enjoined him to stay where he was: 'It's pointless you coming back!' And he insisted, curiously, on this.

Frédéric sank into all sorts of conjectures and wanted to go back to Paris. This attempt to influence his comings and goings annoyed him.

In any case, a nostalgia for the boulevards was beginning to take hold. Besides, his mother was nagging him, Monsieur Roque was being so attentive, and Mademoiselle Louise was so much in love with him that he could not stay any longer without declaring himself. He needed time to think, he would be a better judge of things at a distance.

As a pretext for his journey, Frédéric made something up and left, telling everyone, and believing himself, that he would be back soon.

## VI

HIS return to Paris gave him no pleasure. It was an evening towards the end of August and the boulevards were deserted. People went by, one after another, looking glum; here and there a cauldron of asphalt was smoking, many houses had their shutters completely closed. He reached his house. Dust covered the hangings; and, dining alone, Frédéric felt strangely abandoned. Then he started thinking about Mademoiselle Roque.

The idea of getting married no longer seemed extravagant to him. They would travel, go to Italy, to the Orient! And he could imagine her standing on a little hill looking at the landscape, or leaning on his arm in a Florentine gallery stopping in front of the pictures. What a delight it would be to see this lovely young thing blossoming before the splendours of Art and Nature. Once removed from her present surroundings she would make a charming companion in no time. Moreover, he was tempted by Monsieur Roque's fortune. Yet such a plan was repugnant to him as though it were a weakness, a corruption.

But he was quite determined to change his life (whatever that involved)—that is to say, not to waste his feelings on fruitless passions, and he even hesitated to fulfil the commission Louise had charged him with. This was to buy for her at Jacques Arnoux's two big polychrome statues of Negroes, like those which were in the prefecture in Troyes. She knew the trademark and wouldn't have any other. Frédéric was afraid, if he returned to visit *them*, that he would slip back into his old love for Madame Arnoux.

These thoughts occupied him the entire evening. And he was just about to go to bed when a woman arrived.

'It's me,' smiled Mademoiselle Vatnaz. 'I've come on behalf of Rosanette.'

So had they made friends again?

'Goodness gracious yes! I'm not vindictive, you know very well. What's more, the poor girl... It would take too long to tell you.'

In short, the Maréchale wanted to see him, was expecting a reply, her letter having been forwarded from Paris to Nogent. Mademoiselle Vatnaz did not know what it contained. Then Frédéric asked about the Maréchale.

She was now 'with' a very rich man, a Russian, Prince Tzernoukoff, who had seen her at the races on the Champ-de-Mars last summer.

'We have three carriages, a saddle horse, livery and groom in the best English fashion, a country house, a box at the Théâtre des Italiens, and a lot more besides. So there you are, my dear.'

And La Vatnaz, as though she had profited from this change in Rosanette's fortunes, seemed jollier, very cheerful. She took off her gloves and examined the furniture and trinkets in the bedroom. She estimated the exact price of them, like a second-hand dealer. He ought to have consulted her to get them cheaper. And she congratulated him on his good taste:

'Oh, how sweet! Superlative! You have such good ideas!'

Then, catching sight of a door by the bed in the alcove:

'So that's the door the women leave by?'

And she chucked him under the chin in a friendly way. He shuddered at the contact of her long hands, that were at one and the same time thin and soft. Around her wrists she had lace cuffs and on the front of her green dress gold braiding like a hussar. Her hat, of black tulle with a dropped brim, half hid her forehead. Her eyes sparkled beneath it. A scent of patchouli escaped from her hair. The oil lamp placed on a stool lit her from below like footlights in a theatre, giving prominence to her jaw; and suddenly in front of this ugly woman who undulated like a panther, Frédéric felt an enormous lust, a bestial desire for pleasure.

In an unctuous voice, pulling three squares of paper from her pocket, she said:

'You're going to take these!'

It was three tickets for a benefit show for Delmar.

'What? For him?'

'Of course!'

Mademoiselle Vatnaz, without further explanation, added that she adored him more than ever. The actor, if one could believe her, was definitely to be classed among the 'leading figures' of his time. And it wasn't such-and-such a character he portrayed but the spirit of France, of the People! He had a 'humanitarian soul'; he understood the 'holy vocation of art'! Frédéric, to spare himself this eulogy, gave her the money for the three tickets.

'No point you talking about it to her! Goodness me, look at the time! Oh, I was forgetting to give you the address: It's 14, Rue Grange-Batelière.'

And on the way out:

'Farewell, O breaker of hearts!'

'Whose heart?' Frédéric wondered. 'What a peculiar woman!'

And he again recalled that Dussardier had said to him one day about her: 'Oh, she's not much good!' as though alluding to tales that did not show her in a good light.

The next day he went to the Maréchale's. She lived in a new house, with awnings jutting out over the street. On each landing there was a mirror on the wall, a rustic flower-stand in front of the windows, and canvas covering on the stairs. To anyone arriving from outside, the coolness of the staircase was refreshing.

It was a manservant who came to open the door, a footman in a red waistcoat. On the bench in the hall a woman and two men, tradespeople no doubt, were waiting as though in a minister's antechamber. On the left through the half-open door of the dining room, empty bottles were visible on the sideboards, napkins on the backs of the chairs. And running parallel was a gallery, where gold sticks were supporting a rose espalier. Down below in the courtyard two boys, with arms bare, were polishing a landau. Their voices rose up to the landing, along with the intermittent sound of a curry comb being beaten on a stone.

The servant came back. 'Madame would receive Monsieur.' And he took him through a second antechamber, then a large salon hung with yellow brocade, with cable-mouldings in the corners, which met in the middle of the ceiling and seemed to be continued by the cable-shaped branches of the chandelier. No doubt there had been a party the night before. Ash from cigars had been left on the side tables.

At length he entered a kind of boudoir lit unevenly by stained glass. Above the doors were decorations of trefoils carved into the wood; behind a balustrade three crimson mattresses formed a divan, and the pipe of a platinum hookah was lying on it. Instead of a mirror the mantelpiece had shelves in the form of a pyramid, displaying a whole collection of curios on different levels: old silver watches, Bohemian vases, jewelled clasps, jade buttons, enamels, Chinese porcelain figures, and a little Byzantine virgin in a silver cope; and all that merged in a golden twilight, with the bluish colour of the rug, the mother-of-pearl gleam of the stools, the fawn tint of the walls covered in maroon leather. In the corners on pedestals were bronze vases containing bunches of flowers, their scent heavy in the air.

Rosanette appeared, dressed in a pink satin jacket with a pair of white cashmere trousers, a necklace of piastres, and a red cap with a spray of jasmine twined round it.

Frédéric gave a start. Then, saying that he had brought the 'thing in question', presented her with a banknote.

She looked at it flabbergasted; but as he was still holding the banknote and didn't know where to put it:

'Well, take it then!'

She snatched at it; then, throwing it on to the divan:

'That's very kind of you.'

It was to go towards buying a piece of land at Bellevue that she was paying for through annual instalments. Such casual manners offended Frédéric. Apart from that, so much the better. It avenged him for the past.

'Sit down,' she said. 'There, a bit nearer.' And in a serious tone of voice: 'First, I have to thank you, my dear, for risking your life for me.'

'Oh, it was nothing!'

'What do you mean? It was magnificent!'

The Maréchale's gratitude embarrassed him, for she must have thought that he had fought exclusively because of Arnoux; the latter, supposing that to be the case, must have given in to the temptation to say something to her.

'She's perhaps making fun of me,' Frédéric thought.

There was nothing more to say, so, saying he had an appointment, he rose.

'Oh, no! Stay!'

He sat down again and complimented her on her attire.

She replied, with an air of weariness:

'Yes, it's the prince, he likes me like this! And we have to smoke those contraptions,' Rosanette added, showing him the hookah. 'Shall we try one? Would you like to?'

A light was brought. The tombac* took a long time to light and she began to walk up and down in her impatience. Then she was overcome with lethargy. And she stayed motionless on the divan, a cushion under her armpit, her body a little twisted, one knee bent, the other leg straight. The long snake of red leather formed rings on the floor, and coiled round her arm. She pressed the amber mouthpiece to her lips and was looking at Frédéric through eyes half-closed across the smoke rings which were enveloping her. Her breathing made the water gurgle, and from time to time she murmured:

'The poor sweetheart! The poor darling!'

He tried to find an agreeable subject of conversation. He lit on La Vatnaz.

He said he thought her extremely elegant.

'Yes, I'll say!' said the Maréchale, 'She's very lucky to have me.' That was all she said, conversation between them being difficult.

Both of them felt constrained, as though there was something between them. In fact, the duel, of which Rosanette imagined she was the cause, had flattered her vanity. She had been astonished that he didn't hurry along and take advantage of his action. And in order to make him come back she had dreamed up this need for five hundred francs. How was it that Frédéric did not ask for a little loving in return! It was a refinement that amazed her, and on an impulse she said:

'Would you like to come to the seaside with us?'

'Who is "us"?'

'Me and my friend. I'll pass you off as my cousin, like in the old comedies.'

'Spare me!'

'Well then, you can take lodgings near ours.'

The idea of hiding from a rich man was humiliating.

'No, that's out of the question!'

'As you please!'

Rosanette turned aside with a tear on her eyelid. Frédéric saw it, and to show his concern for her, he said he was glad to see her so well off at last.

She shrugged. What was the trouble then? Was it that nobody loved her?

'Oh, they always love me!'

She added:

'The only thing is *how* they love me.'

Saying that she found the heat stifling, the Maréchale undid her jacket. And with no other item of clothing but a silk chemise around her bottom, she inclined her head on his shoulder in the attitude of a slave-girl, full of provocation.

The idea that the viscount, Monsieur de Comaing, or someone else might suddenly arrive would not have occurred to a man less obsessed with himself; but Frédéric had too often been duped by those same looks to compromise himself in fresh humiliation.

She wanted to know whom he was seeing, what he did for entertainment. She even managed to find out about his business affairs and offered to lend him money if necessary. Unable to stand it any more, Frédéric picked up his hat.

'Well then, my dear, have a lovely time at the seaside. Au revoir!'

She opened her eyes wide; then said curtly:

'Au revoir!'

He went back through the yellow drawing room and the second hall. On the table between a bowl full of visiting cards and a writing case was a little box, of chased silver. It was Madame Arnoux's! He was suddenly emotional and, at the same time, felt that a terrible sacrilege had taken place. He wanted to touch it with his hands, to open it, but he was afraid of being seen, and left.

Frédéric was virtuous. He did not go back to Arnoux's house.

He sent his servant off to buy the two Negroes, having told him exactly what to look for; and the box went off to Nogent that same evening. The next day, as he was going to Deslauriers's, at the corner of the Rue Vivienne and the boulevard, he came face to face with Madame Arnoux.

Their first instinct was to draw back. Then the same smile came to the lips of both, and they went towards each other. For a whole minute neither spoke.

She was swathed in sunshine. And her oval face, her long lashes, her black lace shawl, tracing the shape of her shoulders, her dove-grey silk dress, the bouquet of violets on the corner of her bonnet—everything struck him as extraordinarily beautiful. An infinite softness issued from her lovely eyes. And saying the first thing that came into his head, Frédéric stuttered:

'How is Arnoux keeping?'

'Fine, thank you.'

'And the children?'

'Very well.'

'Ah, er...! What lovely weather we are having, aren't we?'

'Magnificent, really!'

'Are you shopping?'

'Yes.'

And with a slight inclination of her head:

'Goodbye!'

She had not shaken his hand, or uttered one affectionate word, had not even invited him to come to see her, but no matter! He would not have exchanged this encounter for the most marvellous adventure in the world, and he savoured its sweetness as he continued on his way.

Deslauriers, surprised to see him, hid his disappointment—for he still obstinately retained some hope with regard to Madame Arnoux. And he had written to Frédéric to stay in Nogent so as to be freer in his own manoeuvres.

However, he said that he had been to see her, in order to find out if their marriage contract stipulated a common estate, in which case one could have taken proceedings against the wife. 'And she had a strange expression on her face when I told her about your wedding!'

'Good heavens! Why invent a story like that!'

'I had to, to show her that you needed your capital. A person who was indifferent would not have gone into a sort of swoon, like she did.'

'Did she really?' cried Frédéric.

'Aha, you old rogue, you're giving yourself away! For goodness' sake, tell the truth!'

An immense cowardice took possession of this man who was in love with Madame Arnoux.

'No, I assure you! On my word of honour!'

These feeble denials managed to convince Deslauriers he was right. He complimented him. He asked him for 'some details'. Frédéric offered none, and even resisted the urge to make some up.

As for the mortgage, he told him not to do anything, but wait. Deslauriers thought him wrong and was actually quite violent in his remonstrances.

Altogether he was more gloomy, malevolent, and irascible than ever. Within the year if his fortunes did not improve, he would embark for America or blow his brains out. In short, he appeared to be so furious with everything and was so absolute in his radicalism that Frédéric couldn't help saying:

'You are just like Sénécal.'

Talking of whom, Deslauriers told him that he had been released from Sainte-Pélagie,* doubtless because at the preliminary hearing there hadn't been enough evidence to bring him to trial.

To celebrate this freedom, Dussardier wanted 'to throw a punch party' for him and asked Frédéric along as well, but warning him at the same time that Hussonnet would be there, and that the latter had been very supportive of Sénécal.

In fact, *Le Flambard* had just become an agency as well, describing itself in its prospectus: 'Wine bureau—Publicity Office—Debt Collecting, Information, etc.' But the bohemian feared these commercial activities might harm his literary reputation and so he had taken the mathematician on to keep the accounts. Although the position was not well paid, Sénécal would have died of hunger without it. Not wishing to upset the kindly clerk, Frédéric accepted his invitation.

Three days in advance, Dussardier had waxed the red tiles in his attic himself, beaten the armchair, and dusted the mantelpiece, on which you could see an alabaster clock in a glass globe between a stalactite and a coconut. As his two candelabras and the small bedside candle did not throw out enough light he had borrowed two sconces from the concierge and these five lights were shining on the chest of drawers which was covered with three napkins in order to provide a more respectable setting for the macaroons, biscuits, a brioche, and twelve bottles of beer. Against the facing wall, covered in yellow wallpaper, a small mahogany bookcase contained the *Fables* of Lachambeaudie, *Les Mystères de Paris*, Norvin's *Napoléon*—and in the middle of the alcove the face of Béranger smiling out from its ebony frame.

The guests (apart from Deslauriers and Sénécal) were: a newly qualified pharmacist, who did not have enough money to set up in business; a young man from Dussardier's firm; a traveller in wines; an architect; and a gentleman who worked in insurance. Regimbart had not been able to come. They were sorry about that.

They welcomed Frédéric very cordially, since everyone knew from Dussardier what he had said at the Dambreuses'. Sénécal made do with shaking hands with him in a dignified manner.

He remained standing next to the mantelpiece. The others, sitting and smoking their pipes, listened to him talk about universal suffrage, which would result in the triumph of democracy and the realization of the principles of the Gospel. Moreover, the time was drawing near; in the provinces reformist banquets* were proliferating; Piedmont, Naples, Tuscany...

'It's true,' Deslauriers said, cutting him short, 'it can't go on much longer!'

And he began to map out the situation.

We sacrificed Holland to obtain recognition of Louis-Philippe from England; and that famous English alliance was lost thanks to the Spanish marriages! In Switzerland Monsieur Guizot, towed along by the Austrian, was upholding the treaties of 1815. Prussia, with its Zollverein, was going to make difficulties for us. The Eastern question* remained unresolved.

'Just because the Grand Duke Constantine* sends presents to Monsieur Aumale is no reason to trust Russia. As for Home Affairs, you never saw such blindness, such stupidity! Even their majority does not hold together any more! In short, as has been said, there is nothing, nothing, nothing! And in the face of this disgraceful state of affairs,' the lawyer went on, putting his hands on his hips, 'they declare they are satisfied!'*

This allusion to a famous vote drew a round of applause. Dussardier uncorked a bottle of beer; the froth splashed the curtains, he took no notice. He filled the pipes, cut the brioche, offered it round, went down several times to see if the punch was on its way. And very soon all were in a state of excitement, since everyone was exasperated by and hated those in power. It was a violent hatred, the one reason being their detestation of injustice. And with their legitimate grievances were mixed the silliest of recriminations.

The pharmacist grumbled about the lamentable state of the navy. The insurance broker could not bear Marshal Soult's two sentries.

Deslauriers denounced the Jesuits who had recently settled publicly in Lille.* Sénécal detested Monsieur Cousin a great deal more; for eclecticism, which taught one to use reason to arrive at the truth, encouraged egotism, destroyed solidarity. The traveller in wine, who did not understand very much about such matters, remarked aloud that Sénécal was forgetting a lot more scandals.

'The royal carriage on the Northern Line is supposed to be costing eighty thousand francs. Who's going to pay for it?'

'Yes, who's going to pay for it?' echoed the clerk, as furious as if they had milked the money from his own purse.

Recriminations followed against the sharks in the Bourse and the corruption of civil servants. According to Sénécal you needed to go higher up and first lay the blame at the door of the princes who were reviving the customs of the Regency.

'Did you hear that the friends of the Duc de Montpensier coming back from Vincennes recently, no doubt drunk, disturbed the workers in the Faubourg Saint-Antoine with their singing?'

'People were even shouting: "Down with the robbers!",' said the pharmacist. 'I was there, I was shouting!'

'Good for you! The People are waking up at last, after the trial of Teste-Cubières!'*

'That trial made me feel bad', said Dussardier, 'because it dishonoured an old soldier.'

'Do you know', Sénécal went on, 'that they discovered at the Duchesse de Praslin's...?'*

At that moment someone kicked open the door. Hussonnet came in.

'Greetings, my lords!' he said, sitting down on the bed.

Nobody alluded to his article, for which he was sorry in any case, the Maréchale having given him a good scolding about it.

He had just seen *Le Chevalier de Maison-Rouge** at the Dumas theatre and found it 'excessively boring'.

Such criticism astonished the democrats—this drama by its political slant, or rather its setting, flattered their beliefs. They protested. Sénécal, to settle the matter, asked if the play served the cause of Democracy.

'Yes... perhaps. But the style is...'

'Well then, it's a good play. What is style anyway? It's the idea that counts!'

And not allowing Frédéric to speak:

'I was putting forward the view that in the Praslin affair...' Hussonnet interrupted.

'Oh, that's another old story. It makes me sick!'

'And you're not the only one!' Deslauriers replied. 'It's caused five newspapers to be shut down, that's all! Listen to this piece.'

And taking out his notebook, he read:

'Since the establishment of the "best of all Republics", we've had twelve hundred and twenty-nine press trials, from which have resulted, for writers: three thousand one hundred and forty-one years of prison, together with a paltry fine of seven million one hundred and ten thousand five hundred francs.—Wonderful, isn't it?'

They all gave a cynical laugh. Frédéric, fired up like the rest of them, said:

'The *Démocratie pacifique*\* is being prosecuted for its serial, a novel entitled: *A Woman's Share.*'

'Come now!' Hussonnet said. 'I hope they won't forbid our share of women!'

'But what's not forbidden?' cried Deslauriers. 'It's forbidden to smoke in the Luxembourg, forbidden to sing the hymn to Pius IX!'\*

'And they are forbidding the printers' banquet,' a muffled voice said.

This was the architect, hidden in the shadow in the alcove and silent until now. He added that last week a certain Mullet had been convicted for lese-majesty.

'Mullet is fried,' said Hussonnet.

This joke seemed so indecent to Sénécal that he accused him of sticking up for 'the juggler at the Hôtel de Ville, the friend of the traitor Dumouriez'.

'Me? Quite the opposite!'

He thought Louis-Philippe a common plod—a grocer in a cotton nightcap! And putting his hand on his heart, the bohemian recited the sacramental phrases: 'It is always with renewed pleasure... the Polish nation will not perish... Our great works will be carried through... Give me money for my little family...' Everyone laughed a lot and pronounced him a great wit. Their delight increased at the sight of a bowl of punch brought by a bar owner.

The flames of the alcohol and those of the candles quickly warmed the apartment, and the light from the attic window crossing the courtyard lit up the edge of a roof opposite, along with a chimney pot which stood out black against the night. They were talking at the tops of their voices, all at once. They had taken off their coats; they were banging into the furniture, clinking glasses.

Hussonnet cried:

'Let the high-class ladies come up, let's be more Tour de Nesle,* local colour, and Rembrandt into the bargain!'

And the pharmacist, who was stirring the punch over and over, gave a full-throated rendering of

'I've two large oxen in my stable
Two large white oxen...'*

Sénécal put a hand over his mouth, he did not care for rowdy behaviour. And the tenants appeared at their windows, surprised by the unusual noise that was coming from Dussardier's apartment.

This good fellow was enjoying himself, saying that it reminded him of the little sessions they used to have on the Quai Napoléon; though several were missing, Pellerin among them...

'We can do without him,' Frédéric said.

Deslauriers enquired about Martinon.

'What's become of that fascinating gentleman?'

Immediately, giving full rein to his malevolence towards him, Frédéric attacked his mind, his character, his false elegance, the whole man. He was the perfect specimen of a jumped-up peasant! The new aristocracy, the bourgeoisie, could not hold a candle to the old, the nobility. He expressed this opinion and the democrats agreed—as though he belonged to one sort of aristocracy and that they had mixed with the other. They were delighted with him. The pharmacist even compared him to Monsieur d'Alton-Shée, who, though a peer of the realm, supported the People's cause.

It was time to go. They all took leave of each other with much shaking of hands; companionably, Dussardier accompanied Frédéric and Deslauriers home. As soon as they were out in the street, the lawyer appeared to be lost in thought, and after a moment's silence:

'Do you really bear a grudge against Pellerin then?'

Frédéric did not hide his resentment.

However, the painter had withdrawn the notorious painting from the window. One ought not to pick a quarrel over nothing! What was the point of making enemies?

'He gave way to an outburst of temper, excusable in a man who is on his beam ends. *You* can't comprehend that!'

And once Deslauriers had gone home, the clerk did not leave off, even urging him to buy the portrait. In fact, Pellerin had given up hope of intimidating him and had asked the two of them to persuade him to take it.

Deslauriers brought up the subject again after that, and pressed the point. The claims of the artist were reasonable.

'I'm sure that for, say, five hundred francs...'

'Oh, give it to him! Here it is,' said Frédéric.

The picture was delivered that very evening. He thought it even more abhorrent than when he first saw it. The half-tones and the shadows had become muddied under too many reworkings, and they seemed too dark in relation to the highlights which, remaining brilliant here and there, contrasted sharply in the overall effect.

Frédéric avenged himself for having had to buy it, denigrating it bitterly. Deslauriers believed him and approved of his behaviour, for his ambition was still to constitute a phalange of which he would be leader. Certain men delight in making their friends do what they don't want to do themselves.

In the meantime, Frédéric had not returned to the Dambreuses'. He lacked the necessary capital. There would be no end of explanations; he hesitated. Perhaps he was right? Nothing was safe nowadays, the coal business no more than anything else. He must get out of this high society. Finally Deslauriers managed to turn him against the enterprise. His hatred was making him virtuous; and anyway he liked Frédéric better in mediocrity. In that way he remained his equal and enjoyed a more intimate relationship with him.

The commission for Mademoiselle Roque had been carried out very badly. Her father wrote to tell him so, providing him with precise details and ending his letter with the joke: 'At the risk of making you work like a Negro.'

Frédéric had no choice but to return to the Arnoux's. He went up into the shop and saw nobody. The business was failing and the employees were following the example of their boss, and neglecting it.

He walked the length of the room, past the long shelf loaded with china, which occupied the middle. Then, at the end, by the counter, he stamped his feet to attract attention.

The portière was raised and Madame Arnoux appeared.

'What, are you here? You!'

'Yes,' she stammered, rather troubled. 'I was looking for...'

He noticed her handkerchief near the desk and guessed she had gone down to her husband's shop to see how things were and clear up something that was bothering her.

'But... do you need something?' she enquired.

'Nothing, Madame.'

'These clerks are intolerable! They are always away!'

One shouldn't blame them. On the contrary, he was very glad they were not there.

She looked ironically at him.

'Well, what about your wedding?'

'What wedding?'

'Yours!'

'Me? Never!'

She brushed aside his denial.

'What if it were true? One takes refuge in the ordinary, in despair of the ideal one has dreamed of.'

'However, all your dreams were not so... innocent.'

'What do you mean?'

'When you go to the races with... certain people.'

He cursed the Maréchale; then remembered something.

'But it was you who asked me to go and see her before, on Arnoux's behalf!'

She shook her head:

'And you took advantage of it for your own amusement.'

'For goodness' sake, let's forget all those stupidities!'

'We must, because you are going to get married.'

And she bit her lips, to prevent a sigh.

Then he cried:

'I tell you once more it isn't true! Can you really believe that I, with my need for intellectual company, my habits, I should go and bury myself in the provinces to play cards, supervise builders, and walk around in clogs! Whatever for? They have told you that she's rich, haven't they? Oh, as though I care about money! Do you think that after wanting all that is the best in life, the loveliest, the most enchanting, a sort of paradise in human form, and finally finding this ideal, when that vision overshadows all the rest...'

And taking her head in his hands, he began to kiss her eyelids, saying over and over:

'No, no, no, I shall never marry! Never never!'

She received his kisses, transfixed by surprise and delight.

The shop door on to the stairs closed. She started. And she stayed with her arm outstretched as if to order him to be quiet. Footsteps approached. Then someone outside said:

'Is Madame there?'

'Come in!'

Madame Arnoux was leaning on the counter and calmly twirling a pen in her fingers as the bookkeeper opened the door.

Frédéric rose.

'Madame, my respects. The dinner service will be ready, won't it? I can count on it?'

She made no reply. But this silent complicity made her face flame with all the blushes of adulterous love.

The next day he went back to see her and she let him in. And straight away without preamble, in order to follow up his advantage, Frédéric began by justifying the encounter on the Champ-de-Mars. It was mere chance that had found him in the company of that woman. Even admitting that she was pretty (which wasn't true), how could she occupy his thoughts for a single minute, since he loved someone else?

'You know that quite well. I told you so.'

Madame Arnoux bowed her head.

'I'm sorry you said that to me.'

'Why?'

'The most elementary proprieties demand now that I never see you again.'

He protested that his love was innocent. The past should answer for the future. He had promised himself not to trouble her, nor importune her with his grievances.

'But yesterday my heart was brimming over.'

'We must not think of that moment any longer, my friend!'

Yet what would be wrong with two poor creatures sharing their sadness?

'For you are not happy either! Oh, I know you, you have nobody to answer your need for love, devotion. I'll do anything, anything you ask! I won't offend you any more, I swear.'

And he fell on his knees in spite of himself, collapsing under the unbearable weight of his feelings.

'Get up!' she said. 'I order you!'

And she imperiously declared that if he did not obey he should never see her again.

'Oh, I defy you to stop me!' Frédéric rejoined. 'What should I do in this world? Others strive for riches, celebrity, power! I have no profession. You are my exclusive occupation, my total fortune, the aim, the centre of my life, my thoughts. I cannot live without you, any more than the air I breathe. Do you not feel the aspiration of my soul towards yours and that they must mingle and that I am dying because of it?'

Madame Arnoux began to tremble all over.

'Oh, go, go, I beg you!'

The distraught expression on her face stopped him in his tracks. Then he moved towards her. But she drew back, joining her two hands together.

'Leave me! In heaven's name, please!'

And Frédéric loved her so much that he left.

Soon he was filled with anger against himself, declared he was a fool, and came back twenty-four hours later.

Madame was not in. He remained on the landing, in a turmoil of rage and indignation. Arnoux appeared and told him that his wife had left that very morning to move into a little house in the country, that they were renting in Auteuil, since they no longer had the one in Saint-Cloud.

'Yet another of her caprices! Never mind, if it makes her happy! And I am happy anyway. So much the better! Shall we dine together this evening?'

Frédéric made the excuse of having urgent business, then hurried straight to Auteuil.

Madame Arnoux let out a cry of delight. Immediately all his resentment vanished.

He did not speak of his love. To make her trust him more he became even more reserved. And when he asked if he could come back she replied: 'Of course', giving him her hand which she withdrew again almost immediately.

From then on Frédéric visited her often. He promised the coachman large tips. But often the sluggish horse made him impatient, and he got out. Then, breathless, he would climb into an omnibus. And with what disdain he studied the faces of the passengers sitting in front of him; they weren't going to see *her*!

He recognized her house from a long way off by the enormous honeysuckle covering one side of the planks on the roof. It was a sort of Swiss chalet, painted red, with a balcony outside. In the garden were three old chestnut trees and in the middle, on a mound, a thatched sunshade supported by a tree trunk. Beneath the slate coping of the walls a large vine had come down and was hanging in places like a rotten rope. On the iron gate the bell, somewhat hard to pull, rang on and on and it was always a long time before anyone came. Each time he felt an anguish, a vague fear.

Then he would hear the maid's slippers pattering along the sandy path; or Madame Arnoux herself would appear. He arrived one day behind her when she was crouching down by the lawn looking for violets.

Her daughter's temperament had obliged her to put her in a convent. Her little boy spent the afternoon at school. Arnoux had long lunches at the Palais-Royal with Regimbart and their friend Compain. Nobody could come and disturb them.

It was perfectly understood they could not belong to one another. This agreement, which guaranteed they would not be in danger, made their confidences easier.

She told him about her former life in Chartres at her mother's house; her devoutness at around twelve years old; then her passion for music when she sang until nightfall in her little bedroom, from which you could see the ramparts. He told her about his fits of melancholy at school and how in his poetic heaven the face of a woman shone out, so clearly that when he saw her for the very first time he had recognized her.

These conversations usually only related to the years they had known each other. He reminded her of small details, the colour of her dress at such-and-such a time, who had visited her on a particular day, what she had said on such-and-such an occasion. And she replied, marvelling:

'Yes, I remember!'

Their tastes, their opinions were the same. Often the one who was listening to the other would cry:

'So do I!'

And in turn the other would cry:

'So do I!'

There followed interminable railings against Fate:

'Why did heaven not ordain it? If only we had met...'

'Oh, if I'd been younger!' she sighed.

'No, if I'd been a little older.'

And they imagined a life of love alone, fertile enough to fill the vast solitude, exceeding all delights, defying all misery, where the hours would have slipped by in a continual effusion of their souls and which would have created something resplendent and noble like the pulsing of the stars.

Almost always they stood in the open air at the top of the steps. The treetops, yellowed by the autumn, arched unevenly before them, meeting the edge of the pale blue sky. Or they went to the end of the avenue into a summer house where the only item of furniture was a grey linen sofa. There were black marks on the mirror; the walls exuded a smell of damp;—and they stayed there talking about themselves, other people, anything at all, in raptures. Sometimes the rays of the sun filtering through the shutters stretched from the ceiling on to the tiles like the strings of a lyre, specks of dust whirled round in these luminous bars. She liked to break them with her hand. Frédéric would take her hand, and gently examine the little pathways of veins, the tiny marks in her skin, the shape of her fingers. Each finger was, for him, more than a thing, almost a person.

She gave him her gloves, a week later her handkerchief. She called him 'Frédéric', he called her 'Marie', adoring that name, just made, so he said, to be breathed in ecstasy, and seeming to contain clouds of incense, trails of roses.

They eventually took to fixing the days he would visit in advance. And going out, as if by chance, she would come to meet him on the road.

She did nothing to excite his love, for she was in the carefree state that is typical of great happiness. The whole season she wore a wrap in brown silk with matching velvet trim, a loose garment which suited her softness and her serious expression. Besides she was reaching the month of August in a woman's life, a period of both reflexion and tenderness, when the start of maturity kindles a warmer look of passion, when the strength of the heart mingles with the experience of life, and the whole woman finally blossoms and overflows with a wealth of beauty. She had never been so gentle, so indulgent. Sure of not falling, she abandoned herself to a feeling that seemed to her a right she had won through her sorrows. It was so lovely, in any case, and so novel!

What a gulf there was between the coarseness of Arnoux and the adoration of Frédéric!

He was terrified of losing, by a misplaced word, all he thought he had won, telling himself one can retrieve an opportunity but never make up for a foolish remark. He wanted her to surrender herself, and not take her by force. The assurance of her love for him delighted him like a foretaste of possession, and her physical charms troubled his heart more than his senses. It was an indefinable bliss, such an intoxication, that he forgot even the possibility of absolute joy. When away from her a rage of desire devoured him.

Quite soon there were long intervals of silence in their conversation. Sometimes a sort of sexual modesty made them blush when they were together. All precautions to hide their love only made it more transparent. The stronger it grew, the more reserved they were in their manner. Living this lie, their sensibility grew more acute. They took delicious pleasure in the scent of wet leaves, they suffered from the east wind, they were irritable or had gloomy presentiments for no good reason. The noise of footsteps, the creak of a floorboard caused them terror, as though they had done something wrong. They felt as if they were being pushed towards a precipice. They lived as though under storm clouds. And when Frédéric uttered a complaint, she blamed herself.

'Yes, it's my fault! I'm like a coquette! So don't come any more!'

Then he would repeat the same promises, and she would listen to him each time with pleasure.

His return to Paris and the busyness of New Year* put a stop to their conversations for a while. When he came back there was something bolder about his manner. She kept going out of the room to give her orders and, in spite of his entreaties, received all the neighbours who came to visit. Then they got involved in conversations about Léotade, Monsieur Guizot, the Pope, the insurrection in Palermo,* and the banquet in the 12th arrondissement,* which was giving rise to some anxiety. Frédéric consoled himself by ranting against those in power, for, like Deslauriers, he desired a universal upheaval, he was so embittered nowadays. Madame Arnoux for her part was downcast.

Her husband, indulging in one extravagance after another, was keeping a working girl from the factory, the one they called 'the girl from Bordeaux'. Madame Arnoux told Frédéric about it herself. He wanted to use this as an argument, 'since she was being betrayed'.

'Oh, that doesn't trouble me at all!' she said.

This declaration seemed to him to consolidate their intimacy. Did Arnoux suspect anything?'

'No, not now.'

She told him that one evening he had left them deep in conversation, then had returned and listened behind the door, but as they were both speaking of indifferent matters, since then he had not been at all anxious.

'With good reason,' Frédéric acidly remarked.

'Yes, of course.'

She would have done well not to risk saying such things.

One day she wasn't at home at the time when he usually came. To him, that was a betrayal.

Then he was cross at seeing the flowers he brought always stuck in a glass of water.

'Well, where do you expect me to put them?'

'Oh, not there! But at least they are not so cold there as against your heart.'

Some time after that he scolded her for going to the Théâtre des Italiens the night before without telling him. Other people had seen her, admired her, perhaps fallen in love with her. Frédéric insisted on these suspicions solely to pick a quarrel with her, to torment her, for he was starting to hate her and it was only right that she shared his suffering!

One afternoon (towards the middle of February) he found her very upset. Eugène was complaining of a sore throat. Yet the doctor had said it was nothing, a bad cold, a fever. Frédéric was surprised to see the boy looking so poorly. Nonetheless he reassured his mother, cited as examples several children of his age who had just had similar infections and had got over them quickly.

'Really?'

'Yes, of course!'

'Oh, how kind you are!'

And she took his hand. He squeezed it in his own.

'Oh! Let go!'

'What difference does it make, since you offered it to the man comforting you?... You believe I am good for that sort of thing but you... do not believe me when I speak of my love.'

'I do believe you, my poor friend.'

'Why this lack of trust, as though I were a wretch capable of abusing you.'

'Oh, no!'

'If I only had proof...'

'What sort of proof?'

'What you would give to anyone at all, what you once granted me too.'

And he reminded her about the time when they had gone out together one winter's evening at twilight, when it was foggy. What a long time ago it all was now! So what was preventing her being seen on his arm in front of everyone, without her being afraid, without any ulterior motive on his part, with no one around to get in their way?

'All right!' she said, with such decisiveness that Frédéric was at first astounded.

But he answered her quickly:

'Shall I wait for you at the corner of the Rue Tronchet and the Rue de la Ferme?'

'Goodness! But...' faltered Madame Arnoux.

He added, without giving her time to think about it:

'Next Tuesday, then?'

'Tuesday?'

'Yes, between two and three.'

'I'll be there!'

And she averted her face in shame. Frédéric put his lips to the nape of her neck.

'Oh, don't,' she protested. 'You will make me regret it.'

He moved away, fearing she might change her mind, as women have a tendency to do. Then at the door, said softly, as though it was fully agreed:

'Till Tuesday!'

She lowered her beautiful eyes in a modest and resigned gesture.

Frédéric had a plan.

He hoped that he would be able to make her stop in a doorway to shelter from the rain or the sun and that once in the doorway she would enter the house. The difficulty was finding a suitable one.

He set himself to search and towards the middle of the Rue Tronchet, he read on a distant sign: *Furnished rooms.*

The porter immediately understood what he wanted and showed

him upstairs to a room with one adjoining that had two exits. Frédéric booked it for a month and paid in advance.

Then he went to three shops to buy the rarest perfume. He bought a piece of imitation lace to replace the ugly red cotton counterpane, and selected a pair of blue satin slippers. It was only the fear of seeming vulgar that made him rein in his purchases. He returned with them. And with even more devotion than those who create an altar of repose, he changed the furniture around, hung the curtains himself, put heather on the mantelpiece and violets on the chest of drawers. He would have liked to pave the room with gold. 'It's tomorrow, really tomorrow! I'm not dreaming!' he said to himself. And he felt his heart beating fast in the delirium of his hope. Then, when all was ready, he put the key in his pocket as if the happiness sleeping there might have flown away.

At home a letter from his mother was waiting for him.

Why have you been away so long? Your behaviour begins to appear ridiculous. I understand that to a certain extent you have hesitated about this marriage, but think about it!

And she gave relevant details: forty-five thousand francs' income. And besides 'people were talking' and Monsieur Roque was expecting a definite answer. As for the young lady, her situation was embarrassing. 'She is very much in love with you.'

Frédéric threw the letter aside without finishing it, and opened another one, a note from Deslauriers.

My dear friend,
'The pear is ripe.'* We are counting on you, as you promised. We are meeting tomorrow at dawn in the Place du Panthéon. Go into the Café Soufflot, I have to talk to you before the demonstration.

'Oh, I know all about their demonstrations. Spare me! I have a more pleasant rendezvous.'

And the next day by eleven Frédéric was out and about. He wanted to check his preparations one last time. Then, who knew, she might by some chance be early? Coming out from the Rue Tronchet, he heard a great noise behind the Madeleine. He went on and at the other end of the square on the left he saw people in smocks and others in street clothes.

And in fact a manifesto published in the newspapers had summoned all the subscribers to the Reform banquet to that spot. Almost immediately the Ministry sent out a proclamation forbidding it. The evening before, the parliamentary opposition had given up the plan, but the patriots, unaware of their leaders' resolution, had arrived at the meeting point followed by a large number of curious onlookers. A deputation from the schools had just been to Odilon Barrot's house. It was now at the Ministry of Foreign Affairs; and nobody knew if the banquet would take place, if the Government would follow up its threat, or if the National Guard would appear. There was as much ill will to the deputies as there was to those in power. The crowd was getting steadily larger when suddenly the strains of the Marseillaise reverberated through the air.

The column of students was arriving. They were marching steadily in two lines in good order; they were not armed but looked angry, and were all shouting at intervals:

'Long live the Reform! Down with Guizot!'

Frédéric's friends were bound to be there. They would see him and take him along with them. He escaped quickly to the Rue de l'Arcade.

When the students had made their way twice round the Madeleine, they went down to the Place de la Concorde. It was packed; and the crowd from a distance resembled a field of black corn waving in the breeze.

At the same moment the soldiers organized themselves into a battle line to the left of the church.

The groups meanwhile held their positions. To bring the demonstration to a halt plain-clothes policemen seized the most unruly and brutally carted them off to the police station. Despite his indignation, Frédéric remained silent. They might have arrested him along with the rest and he would have missed Madame Arnoux.

A short time after that the helmets of the municipal guard appeared. They struck out around them with the flat of their swords. A horse went down. People rushed to help it. And as soon as the rider was in the saddle they all left.

Then there was a deep silence. The drizzle which had wetted the asphalt was no longer falling. Clouds were drifting over, swept along by the west wind.

Frédéric began to walk up and down the Rue Tronchet, looking in front and behind him.

At last two o'clock chimed.

'Ah, it's now!' he thought. 'She's leaving her house, she's getting closer.' A minute later: 'She should be here by now.' He tried to remain calm until three o'clock. 'No, she's not late. I must be patient.'

And he looked idly into the few shops in the street: a bookseller's, a saddler's, an undertaker's. Soon he was familiar with all the titles of the books, the kinds of harness, the funeral materials. The shopkeepers, seeing him constantly walking back and forth past their shops, were at first surprised and then alarmed, and pulled down their shutters.

She must have been held up and she would be suffering too. But soon, what delight! For she would come, for certain. 'She promised me faithfully!' Yet an unbearable anguish was taking hold of him.

On an absurd impulse he went back into the house, as though she might have been there. At that same moment she was perhaps coming down the street. He rushed out. Nobody! And again he began his pacing up and down.

He contemplated the cracks in the pavement, the holes of the drainpipes, the street lamps, the numbers over the doors. The most trivial things became companions for him, or rather ironic spectators. And the regular fronts of the houses seemed to him heartless. His toes were cold. He felt he was dissolving in desperation. The sound of his own footsteps made his head throb.

When he saw by his watch that it was four o'clock, he felt a sort of vertigo, a panic. He tried to repeat some lines of poetry, to work out a mathematical problem, to invent a story. Impossible! The image of Madame Arnoux obsessed him. He wanted to run and meet her, but which way should he go so as not to miss her?

He stopped an errand boy, gave him five francs, and told him to go to the Rue Paradis, to Jacques Arnoux's house, to find out from the porter if 'Madame was at home'. Then he took up a position on the corner of the Rue de la Ferme and the Rue Tronchet, so that he could look simultaneously down both streets. At the end of his line of vision vague crowds passed by on the boulevard. He could see the occasional plume of a dragoon, or a woman's hat. And he strained his eyes to pick her out. A smiling child in rags who had a marmot in a cage asked him for money.

The man in the velvet coat came back. 'The porter had not seen her go out.' What was keeping her? If she'd been ill, they would have said! Was someone visiting? Nothing was easier than saying you were not at home. He struck his forehead.

'Oh, how stupid I am! It's the riot!' This obvious explanation comforted him. Then, suddenly: 'But it's quiet where she lives.' And he was assailed by an unspeakable thought. 'Supposing she wasn't coming? Supposing her promise was only a trick to get rid of me? No, No!' What was preventing her surely was an extraordinary chance event, one of those things that cannot be foreseen. In that case she would have written. And he sent the errand boy to his own house in the Rue Rumfort to find out if there was a letter there.

No letter had been brought. He found this absence of news reassuring.

He looked for omens in the number of coins he took at random in his hand, in the faces of the passers-by, in the colour of horses; and when the auguries were not good, he tried not to believe them. In his rage at Madame Arnoux, he insulted her under his breath. It made him first almost weak enough to faint, and then hope would leap into his heart again. She was about to appear. She was there behind him. He turned. Nobody! Once he caught sight of a woman of the same height with the same dress. He went up to her; it was not her!

Five o'clock came, five-thirty, six! The gas lamps were lit. Madame Arnoux did not arrive.

The night before she had dreamed that she had been on the pavement of the Rue Tronchet for ages. She was waiting for something indeterminate but nevertheless significant and, without knowing why, she was afraid of being seen. But a cursed little dog attacking her was biting the hem of her dress. It kept coming back and barking ever more loudly. Madame Arnoux woke up. The barking of the dog went on. She listened. It came from her son's bedroom. She hurried in, in bare feet. It was indeed the boy, who was coughing. His hands were burning, his face was red and his voice peculiarly hoarse. His breathing grew steadily more laboured every minute. She stayed there till daylight came, leaning over his coverlet, watching him.

At eight o'clock the drumming of the National Guard warned Monsieur Arnoux that his friends were waiting for him. He got dressed rapidly and left, promising he would call straight away on their doctor, Monsieur Colot. At ten o'clock, since Monsieur Colot had not come, Madame Arnoux sent her maidservant. The doctor was away, in the country, and the young man who was replacing him was on his rounds.

Eugène was holding his head on one side on the bolster, frowning, with his nostrils dilated. His poor little face was becoming whiter than the sheets. And from his larynx every breath he took caused a whistling sound that got increasingly shorter and drier, and rather metallic. His cough was like the bark of those crude devices inside toy dogs.

Madame Arnoux was gripped with panic. She threw herself at the bell pulls, calling for help, shouting:

'A doctor! A doctor!'

Ten minutes later an old gentleman in a white tie and with grey well-trimmed whiskers arrived. He asked lots of questions about the habits, age and temperament of the sick boy, then examined his throat, applied his ear to his back, and wrote a prescription. The unruffled nature of this man was odious. He reminded one of the embalming room. She felt like hitting him. He said he'd come back in the course of the evening.

Before long the horrible coughing started again. From time to time the child suddenly sat up. Convulsive movements shook the muscles in his chest and when he drew breath his stomach hollowed out as if he was gasping for breath after a race. Then he sank down on the bed again with his head back and his mouth wide open. With infinite care Madame Arnoux tried to make him swallow the contents of the medicine bottles, some syrup of ipecacuanha, a potion of antimony. But he pushed the spoon away, with a little moan. His words seemed to come puffing out of his mouth.

From time to time she read the prescription again. The formula frightened her. Perhaps the pharmacist had made a mistake! Her impotence made her despair. Monsieur Colet's student arrived.

He was a young man of modest appearance, new to the job, and did not conceal his impression of the invalid. He was at first undecided, fearful of compromising himself, and finally he prescribed the application of an ice pack. They could not find any ice for some time. The bladder holding the pieces burst. The nightshirt had to be changed. All this upset provoked a new attack that was even worse.

The boy began to tear the linen bandage from his neck as though he were trying to pull away the thing that was choking him, and he scratched at the wall, clutching at the curtains round his bed, looking for something to hold on to, to help him breathe. His face was bluish now, and his whole body, soaked in a cold sweat, seemed to be thinner. His haggard eyes fastened on his mother in terror. He threw his arms around her neck, and clung to her in desperation. She stammered out loving words as she held back her tears:

'Yes, my love, my angel, my treasure!'

Then moments of calm ensued.

She went to find some toys, a puppet, a collection of pictures, to distract him and spread them on his bed. She even tried to sing.

She began a song she used to sing in the old days when she rocked him and swaddled him on the same small tapestry chair. But a shudder ran through the whole of his body, like a wave in a gust of wind. His eyeballs protruded. She thought he was going to die and turned aside so as not to see him.

A moment later she had enough strength to look at him. He was still alive. Hours went by, heavy, bleak, interminable, desperate; and she only counted the minutes by the progress of his agony. The spasms in his chest threw him forward, as though they would break him. Finally he vomited up something strange that resembled a tube of parchment.* What could it be? She imagined he had spat out a piece of his insides. But he was breathing freely, regularly. This apparent improvement frightened her more than anything. She remained as if turned to stone, hands to her sides, eyes staring, when Monsieur Colot arrived. The boy was out of danger, in his opinion.

At first she didn't understand and asked him to repeat what he had said. Was it not one of those consoling phrases that doctors were wont to use? The doctor left, looking satisfied. Then it was just as if the strings of her heart had been severed.

'Out of danger! Can it be true?'

Suddenly the thought of Frédéric came to her in a clear and inexorable fashion. It was a warning from Providence. But the Lord in his mercy had not wished to punish her completely! What an expiation would be necessary later if she persevered in that love! No doubt her son would be insulted because of her. And Madame Arnoux saw him as a young man, wounded in some duel, brought back dying on a stretcher. She jumped up and flung herself on to the little chair, and with all her strength sending her soul up to heaven, she offered up to God as a sacrifice her first passion, her only weakness.

Frédéric had gone home. He sat in his armchair without even having enough strength to curse her. He sank into a kind of sleep. And through his nightmare he could hear the rain falling, still believing that he was down there on the pavement.

The next day, in a final cowardice, he sent another messenger boy to Madame Arnoux.

Either the man failed to deliver the message, or she had too much to explain in a brief note, but the same reply came back. This rudeness was outrageous. He was filled with angry pride. He swore to himself he would never again feel the least desire for her. And like leaves carried away in a hurricane, his love vanished. He felt relief, a stoical joy, then a need for violent action; and he went off walking at random through the streets.

Men from the faubourgs were going past, armed with guns and old swords; some were wearing red bonnets and all were singing the Marseillaise or the Girondins.* Here and there a soldier of the National Guard hurried to get to his local town hall. Drums were beating in the distance. They were fighting at the Porte Saint-Martin. There was a jolly, warlike feeling in the air. Frédéric went on walking. He found the excitement of the capital exhilarating.

Up by Frascati's* he could see the windows of the Maréchale. He had a crazy idea, a young man's reaction. He crossed the boulevard.

The main gate was being closed. And Delphine, the maid, who was in the process of writing over it with a piece of charcoal: 'Arms surrendered', said to him quickly:

'Oh, Madame is in such a state! She dismissed her groom who was rude to her this morning. She thinks they are going to pillage everything. She's petrified! All the more because Monsieur has left.'

'Which Monsieur?'

'The prince!'

Frédéric entered the boudoir. The Maréchale appeared in her petticoat, hair down her back, very upset.

'Oh, thank you, you've come to save me! That's the second time. *You* never ask for payment!'

'Forgive me,' said Frédéric, seizing her round the waist with both hands.

'What? What are you doing?' stammered the Maréchale, taken by surprise but pleased by his behaviour.

He replied:

'I'm in fashion. I've reformed.'

She allowed herself to be pushed back on to the sofa, and carried on laughing at him through his kisses.

They spent the afternoon watching the mob in the street. Then he took her off to have dinner at the Trois-Frères-Provençaux. The meal was long and the food delicious. They came back on foot, as there were no cabs.

At the news of a change of regime Paris was transformed. Everyone was in high spirits. People were out on the streets, and strings of lights on every floor meant that it was bright as day. The soldiers went slowly back to their barracks, harassed and gloomy. People greeted them, shouting 'Long live the infantry!' Making no reply, they continued on their way. In the National Guard, on the other hand, the officers, red-faced with enthusiasm, were brandishing their swords, shouting: 'Long live Reform!' and that word each time made the two lovers giggle. Frédéric joked and was very gay.

They reached the boulevards by way of the Rue Duphot. Chinese lanterns, hung from the houses, formed fiery garlands. Below was a seething throng; here and there in the midst of this dark mass gleamed white bayonets. A great din arose. The crowd was too packed, it was impossible to go straight back. And they were turning into the Rue Caumartin when suddenly behind them there was a noise like the tearing of a huge piece of silk. It was the fusillade on the Boulevard des Capucines.*

'Oh, they are killing off a few bourgeois,' Frédéric said unconcernedly, for there are occasions when the least violent of men is so detached from others that he would see the whole human race perish without batting an eyelid.

The Maréchale, hanging on to his arm, her teeth chattering, declared she could not go another twenty yards. So in a further refinement of his hatred, as a further mental insult to Madame Arnoux, he took Rosanette to the Rue Tronchet, to the lodgings he had prepared for the other woman.

The flowers were still fresh. The lace was spread out across the bed. He took the little slippers out of the wardrobe. Rosanette thought these preparations extremely delicate.

Towards one o'clock, she was roused by the distant sound of wheels; and she saw him sobbing, his head buried in the pillow.

'What's the matter, dearest?'

'A surfeit of happiness,' Frédéric said. 'I've been wanting you for too long!'

# PART THREE

## I

THE noise of gunfire suddenly woke him; and despite Rosanette's pleading, Frédéric wanted at all costs to go and see what was going on. He went down* the Champs-Élysées, from where the shots had come. At the corner of the Rue Saint-Honoré, men in smocks met him, shouting:

'No, not that way! To the Palais-Royal!'

Frédéric followed them. The railings of the church of the Assumption had been torn down. Further on he observed three paving stones in the middle of the road, the beginnings of a barricade, no doubt, then broken bottles and bundles of wire intended to obstruct the cavalry. Suddenly a tall, pale young man rushed out of an alley, his black hair streaming over his shoulders, wearing a kind of vest with coloured spots. He was holding a long musket and was running along on tiptoe, as supple as a tiger and with the air of a man sleepwalking. At intervals you could hear an explosion.

The previous evening the spectacle of the cart carrying five corpses collected from among those on the Boulevard des Capucines had changed the attitude of the common people. And while one aide-de-camp succeeded another at the Tuileries, and Monsieur Molé, in the process of creating a new cabinet, did not return, and Monsieur Thiers was trying to assemble another, and the King, undecided, was shilly-shallying, now giving total command to Bugeaud and at the same time preventing him from exercising it, the insurrection, as though organized by one mind, grew to formidable strength. Men were haranguing the crowd with frenzied eloquence on street corners. Others were ringing church bells for all they were worth. Lead was melted, cartridges were rolled. The trees on the boulevards, the public urinals, the benches, the railings, the gas lamps were all pulled out or turned upside down. By morning Paris was covered with barricades. Resistance did not last long. The National Guard intervened everywhere; so much so that by eight o'clock, the people, by consent or force, had taken five barracks, almost all the local town halls, and the strongest strategic positions. The monarchy was dissolving quietly and rapidly all by itself. And the mob was attacking the Château d'Eau guardhouse to set free fifty prisoners who were not there.

Frédéric was stopped from entering the square, which was full of armed men. Infantry companies were occupying the Rue Saint-Thomas and the Rue Fromanteau. An enormous barricade sealed off the Rue de Valois. The smoke hanging over it dispersed a little, men ran at it gesturing wildly and disappeared. Then the firing began again. There was an answering volley from the station, though no one could be seen inside. Its windows, defended by oak shutters, were pierced with loopholes and the building with its two storeys, two wings, its fountain on the first level and its small door in the middle began to show white pockmarks where the bullets hit. Its flight of three steps was deserted.

Next to Frédéric a man in a Phrygian cap* and carrying a cartridge pouch slung over his wool jacket was arguing with a woman wearing a kerchief in her hair. She was urging him:

'Come back! Come back!'

'Leave me alone!' her husband replied. 'You can easily look after the lodge yourself. Citizens, I ask you, is it fair? I have always done my duty, in 1830, '32, '34, and '39! Today we are fighting! I have to fight!—Go away!'

And the porter's wife in the end gave in to his protests and to those of a nearby member of the National Guard, a man in his forties whose kindly face was trimmed with a fair beard. He loaded his firearm and fired, still conversing with Frédéric, as unconcerned in the middle of the riot as a gardener on his plot of land. A young boy in a tradesman's apron was cajoling him to give him some caps so that he could fire his weapon, a fine hunting gun that a 'gentleman' had given him.

'Grab the ones behind me,' said the man, 'and make yourself scarce! You'll get yourself killed.'

The drums were beating the charge. Shrill cries, triumphant cheers rose. The crowd surged in a continual motion. Trapped between two dense masses, Frédéric could not move, fascinated in any case and enjoying himself enormously. The wounded who were falling and the dead who were laid out on the ground did not look as though they were really wounded, really dead. It seemed to him he was watching a play.

In the middle of the throng, over their heads, you could see an old man in a black suit on a white horse with a velvet saddle. In one hand he was holding a green branch, in the other a piece of paper, and he was shaking them insistently. Finally, despairing of making himself heard, he withdrew.

The infantry had disappeared and the municipal guards remained defending the station on their own. A wave of fearless men surged up the flight of steps. They fell and others took their place; the door echoed with the sound of iron bars battering at it. The guards did not give way. But a carriage filled with hay and burning like a giant torch was dragged up against the walls. Wood was quickly brought, together with straw and a keg of alcohol. The flames crept up the walls and the building began to send up smoke everywhere like a sulphur spring. Large flames at the top leapt out with a great hiss from between the balustrades on the terrace. The first floor of the Palais-Royal was crowded with the National Guard. There was firing from all the windows on the square. The bullets whistled. The water from the broken fountain was mixed with blood and made puddles on the ground. In the mud you slipped around on clothes, on shakos, on weapons. Frédéric felt something soft underfoot. It was the hand of a sergeant in a grey overcoat, lying face down in the gutter. New groups of people kept arriving, pushing the combatants into the station. The firing became more intense. The wine shops were open. From time to time people went to smoke a pipe, drink a glass, then came back to fight. A lost dog was howling. It made people laugh.

Frédéric was suddenly shaken by a man falling heavily on to his shoulder, groaning, with a bullet in his back. At this shot, which might have been directed against him, he felt enraged. And he was rushing into the fray when a member of the National Guard stopped him.

'It's pointless! The King has just gone. Oh, if you don't believe me, go and look!'

This assertion calmed Frédéric. The Place du Carrousel looked quiet. The Hôtel de Nantes was still there alone. And the houses behind, the dome of the Louvre in front, the long wooden gallery on the right and the undistinguished wasteland which stretched as far as the shopkeepers' stands, seemed to melt into the grey air, and distant murmurs to merge into the mist. But at the other end of the square a harsh light falling through a gap in the clouds on the facade of the Tuileries* picked out all its windows in white. Near the

Arc de Triomphe a dead horse lay on the ground. Behind the railings groups of five or six were chatting. The doors of the palace were open; the servants at the entrance let people in.

Down below in a small room, people were serving bowls of milky coffee. Some of the curious went and sat at the table, for a joke. The others remained standing, and amongst them, a coachman. He grabbed a jar full of caster sugar, threw an anxious look right and left, then began to eat greedily, his nose plunging into the neck of the jar. At the bottom of the great staircase a man was writing his name in a register. Frédéric recognized him from behind.

'Well I'm damned—Hussonnet!'

'Yes,' replied the bohemian. 'I am presenting myself at Court. What a farce, isn't it?'

'Shall we go on up?'

And they reached the Hall of the Marshals. The portraits of these illustrious gentlemen, apart from Bugeaud's which had been pierced through the stomach, were all intact. They were leaning on their swords, gun carriages behind them, and in terrifying poses which ill befitted the circumstances. A big clock told the time: twenty past one.

Suddenly the Marseillaise rang out. Hussonnet and Frédéric leaned over the ramp. It was the People. They rushed up the stairs, in a dizzying flood of bare heads, caps, red bonnets, bayonets and shoulders, so violently that people disappeared in this swarming mass which kept on rising with a great roar, like a spring tide pushing back a river under an irresistible force. Once up, they dispersed and the hymn died away.

All you could hear was the tread of shoes and the babble of voices. The inoffensive crowd looked on curiously. But from time to time a cramped elbow would break a windowpane, or a vase, a statuette would roll off a table on to the ground. The pressure on the woodwork made it crack. All the faces were red, sweat ran off them in large drops. Hussonnet remarked:

'Heroes don't smell very nice!'

'Oh, don't be so irritating!' rejoined Frédéric.

And being pushed forward in spite of themselves, they entered a room where a canopy of red velvet stretched across the ceiling. On the throne, at the bottom, was seated a proletarian with a black beard in an open-necked shirt, grinning stupidly like an ape. Others were climbing on to the platform to sit where he was.

'What a myth,' said Hussonnet. 'Behold the sovereign people!'

The throne was swung up into their arms and made its unsteady way across the floor.

'Good heavens, look how it's pitching! The ship of State is tossed on a stormy sea! Look at it, it's doing the cancan!'

They had brought it as far as the window and amidst boos and hisses, they threw it out.

'Poor old thing!' Hussonnet exclaimed, as he watched it fall into the garden, where it was rapidly seized and carried aloft to the Bastille and burnt.

At that point a frenzy of joy erupted, as if, in place of the throne, a future of unlimited happiness had appeared. And the people, less for vengeance than through wanting to assert control, smashed and ripped out curtains, lamps, sconces, tables, chairs, stools, all the furniture, even albums full of drawings, even needlework baskets. Since they were victorious, why should they not enjoy themselves! The rabble draped themselves ironically in lace and cashmere. Gold fringes were entwined round the sleeves of smocks, hats with ostrich feathers decorated the heads of blacksmiths, ribbons of the Legion of Honour made sashes for prostitutes. They all satisfied their whims. Some danced, some drank. In the Queen's bedroom a woman made her hair shine with pomade. Behind a screen two gamblers were playing cards. Hussonnet pointed out an individual to Frédéric leaning on the balcony and smoking a clay pipe. And the noise of revelry was increased by the continuous din of china being broken and pieces of crystal tinkling as they smashed like the keys of a harmonica.

Then the frenzy became more threatening. Obscene curiosity made them pillage all the cabinets, all the corners, open all the drawers. Jailbirds thrust their arms into the beds of the princesses, and rolled around on them to make up for not being able to rape them. Others with more sinister faces wandered about silently, spying out what they might steal. But the crowd was too numerous. Through the doorways, you saw through the endless line of rooms nothing but a dark throng of folk in a cloud of dust between the gilded furnishings. Everyone's chest was heaving; the heat became more and more stifling; the two friends, fearing they might suffocate, went out.

In the entrance hall, standing on a pile of clothes, was a prostitute posing as the Statue of Liberty—motionless, with her eyes open wide in a terrifying fashion.

They had only taken a couple of steps outside the door when a squad of municipal guards in topcoats advanced on them. Taking off their police hats and at the same time uncovering their somewhat bald heads, they bowed low to the people. At this display of respect the ragged conquerors swelled with pride. Hussonnet and Frédéric also took a certain pleasure from it.

They went back to the Palais-Royal in enthusiastic high spirits. Bodies of soldiers were piled up on straw in front of the Rue Fromanteau. They walked past them, unconcerned, and even took pride in not showing any emotion.

The palace was thronged with people. Seven bonfires burned in the inner courtyard. They were throwing pianos, wardrobes, clocks out of the windows. Fire pumps squirted water on to the roofs. Some hooligans were trying to cut through the hoses with their swords. Frédéric tried to get a military cadet to intervene. The cadet did not understand him and in any case seemed a halfwit. All around the two galleries the mob, who had got into the wine cellars, were indulging in a horrifying orgy. Wine was flowing in rivers, wetting people's feet, ruffians were drinking out of the bottoms of broken bottles and reeling around, shouting.

'Let's get out of here,' said Hussonnet. 'These people disgust me.'

All along the Orléans gallery the wounded were lying on mattresses, with crimson curtains for covering. And womenfolk from the area were bringing them soup, clean linen.

'Nevertheless,' Frédéric said. 'In my view the people are sublime!'

The great hall was filled by a swirling and furious crowd. Men were trying to climb up to the higher floors to complete the work of destruction. On the steps the National Guard were struggling to hold them back. The most intrepid of them was a bareheaded rifleman, his hair standing on end, and his outfit in tatters. His shirt was hanging out between his trousers and his coat, and he was struggling desperately in the midst of the others. Hussonnet, with his sharp eyes, recognized Arnoux from a distance.

Then they reached the Tuileries gardens, where they could breathe more easily. They sat down on a bench, and stayed there for a few minutes with eyes closed, so exhausted, they didn't have the strength to speak. Passers-by addressed one another. The Duchesse d'Orléans was appointed regent, it was all over; and everyone felt that sort of well-being that follows rapid solutions to a crisis, when, at each of the attic windows of the castle, servants appeared, tearing up their livery. They threw it into the garden as a sign they were renouncing it. The crowd booed them. They withdrew.

The attention of Frédéric and Hussonnet was diverted to a tall man walking swiftly between the trees with a rifle over his shoulder. A cartridge belt held his red tunic tight to his waist, a kerchief was twined around his forehead under his cap. He turned his head. It was Dussardier; and throwing himself into their arms he cried:

'Oh, I'm so happy, my old friends!' That was all he could say, he was so out of breath with joy and fatigue.

He had been up for two days. He had worked at the barricades in the Quartier Latin, had fought in the Rue Rambuteau, had saved three dragoons, had entered the Tuileries with the Dunoyer column, had gone after that to the Chamber and then to the Hôtel de Ville.

'I've just come from there. All's well! The people have triumphed! The workers and the bourgeoisie are embracing. Oh, if you only knew what things I've seen! What wonderful people, how good it all is!'

And, not noticing that they weren't armed:

'I was sure you'd be here. It was bad for a while, but it doesn't matter now!'

A drop of blood was running down his cheeks and to the questions put by the other two:

'Oh, it was nothing, a scratch from a bayonet.'

'But you ought to get it seen to.'

'Pah, I'm all right! What's the odds? The Republic is declared! We shall be happy now! Some journalists who were chatting near me just now were saying that we shall liberate Poland and Italy! No more kings, do you understand? The whole world free! The whole world free!'

And, sweeping the horizon with a glance, he flung out his arms in a triumphant attitude. But a long line of men was running along the terrace by the edge of the water.

'Oh damn, I was forgetting! The forts are still occupied. I must get over there! Adieu, Adieu!'

He turned round to brandish his gun and shout:

'Vive la République!'

From the chimneys on the chateau enormous whirls of black smoke were escaping, carrying sparks with them. The ringing of the bells made a sort of frightened bleating noise. From right and left, everywhere the victors discharged their firearms. Although Frédéric was no warrior, he felt his Gallic blood leap. The zeal of the enthusiastic crowds mesmerized him. Sensuously, he breathed in the stormy air, full of the smell of gunpowder. And at the same time he trembled in the throes of a vast love, a love that was supreme and universal, like the heart of the whole of humanity beating in his breast.

Hussonnet said with a yawn:

'Perhaps it's time to go and educate the masses.'

Frédéric followed him to his office in the Place de la Bourse and sat down to compose an account of the events in lyrical style for the Troyes gazette—a good piece of work, which he signed. Then they dined together in a tavern. Hussonnet was in a thoughtful mood. The eccentricities of the Revolution were even more pronounced than his own.

After coffee when they got to the Hôtel de Ville in search of news, his boyish nature resurfaced. He climbed the barricades like a goat and cracked patriotic jokes in reply to the sentry's challenges.

They heard the proclamation of the Provisional Government,* by torchlight. At last, at midnight, Frédéric, utterly exhausted, got back to his house.

'Well,' he said to his servant, who was helping him undress, 'are you happy now?'

'Yes of course, Monsieur! But what I dislike is seeing the mob marching!'

The next day when he woke, Frédéric thought of Deslauriers. He hurried round to his house. The lawyer had just left, having been appointed commissioner in the provinces. The evening before he had got to speak to Ledru-Rollin and, by pestering him in the name of the law schools, had managed to extract from him a post, a project. In any case, said the porter, he was going to write next week to send his address.

After that Frédéric went to see the Maréchale. She received him sourly, she bore him a grudge for abandoning her. Her resentment vanished when he assured her that peace had returned. Everything was calm now, no reason for alarm. He kissed her, and she declared her allegiance to the Republic—as the Archbishop of Paris had done, and as would do, with a zealous speed that was nothing if not miraculous, the Judiciary, the Council of State, the Institute, the Marshals of France, Changarnier, Monsieur Falloux, all the Bonapartists, all the Legitimists, and a considerable number of Orléanists.

The fall of the Monarchy had been so prompt that, after the first shock was over, there was astonishment among the bourgeoisie that they were still alive. The summary execution of a few thieves, shot without being brought before a judge, seemed entirely fair. People repeated the words of Lamartine about the red flag, 'which had merely been carried round the Champ-de-Mars, whereas the *tri-colore...*'* and so on. And they all lined up under the shadow of the flag, each side only perceiving its own colour among all the others and promising itself, as soon as it was stronger, to tear down the other two.

As business was suspended, anxiety and curiosity brought every-one out on the streets. The casual nature of dress made the differ-ence between the classes less marked, hatred was concealed, hope was everywhere, and the mob was in a gentle mood. Pride in having attained their rights shone on every face. There was a carnival atmos-phere, like camping out. Nothing was as enjoyable as Paris during those early days.

Frédéric took the Maréchale on his arm and they walked around the streets together. She liked to see the rosettes decorating all the button-holes, the flags hanging from every window, placards of every colour on the walls, and here and there she threw some coins into the box for the wounded, placed on a chair in the middle of the road. Then she stopped to look at the caricatures which depicted Louis-Philippe as a pastry-cook, as an acrobat, as a dog, as a leech. But the men around Caussidière, with their swords and scarves, frightened her a little. At other times it was a liberty tree that was being planted. The clergy were rushing to the ceremony, blessing the Republic, escorted by servants with gold stripes; and the crowd thought that was wonderful. The most frequent spec-tacle was that of all manner of deputations going to petition for some-thing at the Hôtel de Ville. For each trade, each industry, was expecting from the Government the definitive end to its wretchedness. Some, it was true, went to offer advice or to congratulate or quite simply to pay a call on the Government and see the machinery at work.

One day towards the middle of the month of March when he was crossing the Pont d'Arcole, having to run an errand for Rosanette in the Quartier Latin, Frédéric saw a column of men with strange hats and long beards advancing. A Negro was at the head, beating a drum; he was a former studio model and the man carrying the ban-ner, floating in the breeze, bearing the inscription 'Pictorial Artists', was none other than Pellerin.

He waved to Frédéric to wait for him, then, having some time to spare, because the Government was receiving the stonemasons at that moment, reappeared five minutes later. He and his colleagues were going to ask for the creation of a Forum of Art, a kind of stock exchange where they would thrash out aesthetic matters. This would result in sublime works of art, since those working on them would pool their genius. Soon Paris would be covered with gigantic monuments. He would decorate them. He had even already begun a painting of the Republic. One of his comrades came to collect him, for a deputation from the poulterers was hard on their heels.

'What nonsense!' grumbled a voice in the crowd. 'What a lot of jokers. No substance to them!'

It was Regimbart. He did not greet Frédéric but took advantage of the opportunity to pour forth his bile.

The Citizen spent his days wandering the streets, pulling at his moustache, rolling his eyes, receiving and spreading gloomy news. And he had only two phrases: 'Take care, we shall be outflanked!' or 'For God's sake, they're filching the Republic!' He was dissatisfied with everything, and especially the fact that we had not taken back our natural frontiers. The very name of Lamartine made him shrug his shoulders. He considered Ledru-Rollin was not 'man enough for the job' and treated Dupont (from the Eure) as an old duffer, Albert as a madman, Louis Blanc as a Utopian, Blanqui as an extremely dangerous individual, and when Frédéric asked what one should have done, he answered, seizing his arm in a grip that hurt:

'Taken the Rhine, dammit, taken the Rhine!'

Then he blamed the forces of reaction.

They were beginning to show their hand. The sack of the chateaux of Neuilly and Suresnes, the fire at Batignolles, the troubles in Lyons, all the excesses, all the grievances were starting to be exaggerated, like Ledru-Rollin's circular, the forced issue of banknotes, the fall in Government bonds down to sixty francs, in short, as the ultimate wickedness, the last straw, as the worst horror, the forty-five centimes' tax!*—And on top of all that there was still socialism! Although these theories, about as new as the game of Mother Goose, for the last forty years had been thrashed out enough to fill whole libraries, they still scared the bourgeois, like a hail of meteorites. People were angry, with that hatred that any idea provokes, just because it is an idea, a detestation in which it will one day glory and by which its enemies will always be humbled, however mediocre an idea in itself it might be.

Then Property was elevated in people's minds to the level of Religion and got muddled up with God. Attacks made against it appeared sacrilegious, almost cannibalistic. In spite of the most humane legislation there had ever been, the spectre of '93 reappeared, and the sound of the guillotine echoed through all the syllables of the word 'Republic'—which did not stop them pouring scorn on it for its weakness. France, feeling she no longer had a master, began to shout with fear like a blind man without a stick, or like a small child who has lost its nurse.

Of all the French, the one who was the most in fear of the future was Monsieur Dambreuse. This new state of affairs threatened his fortune, but, more than that, undermined his experience of life. Such a good system, such a wise king! Was it possible? The world was collapsing around him. The very next day he dismissed three of his servants, sold his horses, bought a soft hat to wear outside, even wondered whether to let his beard grow; and he stayed at home, resentfully perusing the newspapers that were the most hostile to his ideas, and growing so gloomy that even the jokes about Flocon's pipe could not make him smile.

As a supporter of the late monarchy, he feared the people would take revenge on his properties in Champagne; then Frédéric's effusions in the journal came to his notice and he concluded that his young friend was a very influential person, and if he could not be useful to him, at least he might defend him. So one morning Monsieur Dambreuse came to pay him a visit, accompanied by Martinon.

The only reason for this visit, he said, was to have a little chat with Frédéric. All things considered, he was delighted about what had happened and he adopted wholeheartedly 'our sublime motto: Liberté, Égalité, Fraternité', having been always a Republican at heart. If he had voted with the Ministry under the other regime, it was simply to hasten its inevitable downfall. He even inveighed against Monsieur Guizot 'who has got us into a pretty mess, you can't deny it!' On the other hand he greatly admired Lamartine who had shown himself to be 'magnificent, my word, when he had said that the red flag...'

'Yes, I know,' said Frédéric.

After that he declared himself in sympathy with the workers.

'For when all's said and done, we are all more or less working class!'

And he pushed his impartiality so far as to admit that there was some logic in Proudhon. 'Oh, a great deal of logic, by God!' Then with the detachment of a superior intelligence he chatted about the exhibition in which he had seen the painting by Pellerin. He thought it was original, well executed.

Martinon encouraged him with approving remarks. He too thought one had to 'throw in one's lot wholeheartedly with the Republic', and, acting the peasant, the man of the people, he talked of his father, who ploughed the fields. Soon the conversation turned to the elections for the National Assembly and the candidates for the Fortelle district.* The Opposition candidate had no chance.

'You ought to take his place!' Monsieur Dambreuse said. Frédéric demurred.

'But why not?' He would obtain the votes of the Left, because of his personal opinions, and the conservative vote, given his background. 'And perhaps also', added the banker with a smile, 'my influence might help a little.'

Frédéric objected that he would not know how to go about it. There was nothing easier, by getting himself recommended to the patriots of the Aube* through a Paris club. He would have to make, not a profession of faith of the sort you heard every day, but a serious statement of principle.

'Bring the speech to me! I know what goes down well in these parts! And, I repeat, you could give invaluable service to the country, to all of us, to myself.'

In such times they had to help each other out, and if Frédéric needed anything, he or his friends...

'Oh, how generous of you, Monsieur!'

'You'll do the same for me one day!'

The banker was a splendid fellow, decidedly.

Frédéric could not stop thinking about his advice, and soon he was dazzled by the dizzying prospect.

The great figures of the Convention* passed before his eyes. It seemed to him that a wonderful dawn was about to break. Rome, Vienna, Berlin were in a state of revolt, the Austrians driven out of Venice, the whole of Europe in ferment. It was the moment to rush into the movement and perhaps give it added impetus. And he was attracted by the costume that, so they were saying, the deputies would wear. He could already see himself in a waistcoat with lapels and a *tricolore* sash. And this longing, this hallucination, grew so powerful that he confided in Dussardier.

The enthusiasm of his worthy friend had not waned.

'Yes, yes, go on! Put your name forward!'

Nonetheless Frédéric consulted Deslauriers. The stupid opposition that was holding back the commissioner in his provincial post had increased his liberalism. He immediately sent him violent exhortations.

In the meantime Frédéric needed to get approval from more people, and he told Rosanette about it one day when Mademoiselle Vatnaz was there.

She was one of those Parisian unmarried ladies who each evening, when they have finished giving lessons, or tried to sell little drawings or place pitiful manuscripts, go back to their apartment with mud on their skirts, make dinner, eat it alone, then, feet on a warming jar by the light of a dirty lamp, dream of love, a family, a home, money, everything they don't have. So in common with many others she greeted the Revolution as the harbinger of revenge. And she gave herself up to a frenzy of socialist propaganda.

The emancipation of the proletariat, according to La Vatnaz, was only possible through the emancipation of women. She wanted women to have access to all positions, an investigation into the paternity of illegitimate children, a new legal code, the abolition of marriage, or at least 'a more intelligent regulation of the institution'. Every Frenchwoman would have to marry a Frenchman or adopt an old person.* Nurses and midwives must become paid civil servants. There should be a jury to examine women's books, special editors for women, a women's polytechnic, a National Guard for women, everything for women! And since the Government wasn't aware of their rights, they must defeat force with force. Ten thousand women citizens well armed could make the Hôtel de Ville tremble!

Frédéric's candidature seemed to her to favour these ideas. She encouraged him, showing him the glory on the distant horizon. Rosanette was delighted to have a man who would speak in the Chamber.

'And they will perhaps give you a good post.'

Frédéric, a man of innumerable weaknesses, was persuaded by the general folly. He wrote a speech and went along to show it to Monsieur Dambreuse.

At the sound of the front gate closing, a curtain opened slightly behind a window and a woman appeared. He did not have time to see who it was, but in the hall a picture made him halt—Pellerin's picture, placed on a chair, temporarily no doubt.

It depicted the Republic, or Progress, or Civilization, in the figure of Jesus Christ driving a locomotive, crossing virgin forest. After a minute's studying it, Frédéric exclaimed:

'How contemptible!'

'Indeed!' said Monsieur Dambreuse arriving as Frédéric said that and imagining it referred not to the painting but to the doctrine glorified by the picture. Martinon arrived simultaneously. They went through to the study, and Frédéric was just pulling a piece of paper out of his pocket when Mademoiselle Cécile, coming in suddenly, said, with an innocent expression:

'Is my aunt here?'

'You know very well she isn't,' replied the banker. 'But it doesn't matter. Make yourself at home, Mademoiselle.'

'Oh, no thank you, I'll go.'

She had only just gone when Martinon acted as if he were searching for a handkerchief.

'I've left it in my coat, please excuse me!'

'Of course,' Monsieur Dambreuse said.

He was obviously not taken in by this manoeuvre and even seemed to be conniving in it. Why? But soon Martinon reappeared and Frédéric began his speech. On the second page, which drew attention to the shameful dominance of monetary interests, the banker made a face. Then, getting on to the subject of reforms, Frédéric called for the end of all restrictions on trade.

'What...? But if you'll allow me...!'

Frédéric was not listening and carried on. He demanded a tax on income, a progressive tax, a European federation, and the education of the masses, and the most generous encouragement for the fine arts.

'If the country gave men like Delacroix and Hugo a hundred thousand, what would be wrong with that?'

The speech ended with advice to the upper classes.

'Do not be sparing, you have means! Give, give!'

He stopped and remained standing there. His two listeners, who were sitting, said nothing. Martinon was wide-eyed and Monsieur

Dambreuse went rather pale. Finally, hiding his emotion beneath a sour smile:

'Your speech is perfect!' And he praised the form, so that he had no need to comment on the substance.

This passion on the part of an inoffensive young man terrified him, especially as a symptom. Martinon tried to reassure him. Before long the conservatives would surely take their revenge. In several towns the commissioners of the Provisional Government had been driven out. The elections were not until 23 April. There was ample time. In short, it was incumbent upon Monsieur Dambreuse himself to stand for the Aube; and from then on Martinon did not leave him, became his secretary, and surrounded him with filial attentions.

Frédéric arrived at Rosanette's very pleased with himself. Delmar was there and informed him that he was 'definitely' going to stand in the elections of the Seine. In a poster addressed to 'the People' and in which he spoke to them familiarly, the actor boasted that he understood them, and for their sake, he had been 'crucified by Art', so that he was their incarnation, their ideal; indeed, he believed that he had had an enormous influence on the masses, and later, in a ministerial office he even offered to quell a revolt all by himself; and asked what means he would employ, he replied:

'Never fear, I'll show them my face!'

In order to annoy him Frédéric told him of his own candidature. As soon as his future colleague said he had the provinces in mind, the actor declared he was at his service and offered to take him round the clubs.

They visited all of them, or almost all, the red and the blue, the furious and the peaceful, the puritanical and the bohemian, the mystical and the drinking clubs, the clubs where they promised death to kings, the ones where they denounced swindling in grocers' shops; and everywhere tenants cursed owners, the smock attacked the suit, and the rich conspired against the poor. Several wanted to press charges for compensation for what they had once suffered at the hands of the police, others begged for money to develop inventions. There were plans for phalansteries,* projects for village bazaars, schemes to please the public. Then, here and there, a light of intelligence would appear in these clouds of foolishness, impassioned speeches, sudden as a splash of water, a point of law established by an oath, flowers of eloquence on the lips of a worker wearing a sword belt on his bare chest. Sometimes too there was a gentleman, an aristocrat of humble bearing, making plebeian remarks, who hadn't washed his hands so as to make them appear callused. A patriot would recognize him, the most virtuous would jeer, and he would go away with anger in his heart. To be thought a person of common sense one had to constantly denigrate lawyers, and to pepper one's speech with phrases like: 'adding one's stone to the edifice—social problems—workshop'.

Delmar never missed an occasion to take the floor. And when he couldn't think of anything else to say, he resorted to striking a pose, hand on hip, the other arm in his waistcoat, turning to the side, sharply, so that his head could be clearly seen. Then there would be applause, from Mademoiselle Vatnaz, at the back of the hall.

In spite of the mediocrity of the speakers, Frédéric did not dare try his hand. All these people seemed to him too ill-educated or too hostile.

But Dussardier made enquiries and announced that there was a club called the Club de l'Intelligence in the Rue Saint-Jacques. Such a name inspired hope. And what was more, he would bring friends.

He brought the people he had invited to his punch party: the bookkeeper, the traveller in wines, the architect; Pellerin himself was there, perhaps Hussonnet would come. And on the pavement outside the door Regimbart stood with two men, the first his faithful friend Compain, a rather stocky man, pockmarked and red-eyed. And the second, an ape-like creature, black and extremely hairy, and whom he knew simply as 'a patriot from Barcelona'.

They went down an alleyway, then were ushered into a large room, apparently used as a carpenter's workshop, whose new walls smelled of plaster. Four oil lamps hanging in a row threw out an unpleasant light. On the platform at the far end there was a desk with a bell on it, below it a table which was the rostrum, and on either side two lower tables for the secretaries. The audience occupying the benches was composed of old painters, school ushers, and unpublished writers. Among these lines of overcoats with greasy collars could be seen the occasional woman's bonnet or workman's overall. The back of the hall was in fact full of workers who had come there, no doubt because they had nothing better to do or who had been brought along by the speakers to applaud them.

Frédéric was careful to place himself between Dussardier and Regimbart, who, having scarcely sat down, put both hands on his walking stick, rested his chin on his hands and closed his eyes, while at the other end of the hall, Delmar was on his feet, a domineering presence in the assembled company.

Sénécal appeared at the chairman's desk.

Dussardier thought this surprise would please Frédéric. It made him cross.

The crowd showed great deference to its chairman. He was one of those who, on 25 February, had called for the immediate organization of labour. The next day at the Prado* he had said he was in favour of attacking the Hôtel de Ville; and as each person regulated himself on a model, some copying Saint-Just, some Danton, others Marat, he himself tried to be like Blanqui, who copied Robespierre. His black gloves and his short-cropped hair gave him a severe look, which was extremely appropriate.

He opened the sitting with the Declaration of the Rights of Man and the Citizen, the usual act of faith. Then a loud voice started to sing the 'Souvenirs du Peuple' by Béranger.

Other voices were raised:

'No, no, not that one!'

The patriots at the back began to roar out 'La Casquette'.*

And they all sang the popular song, in unison:

> 'Take your hat off to my cap,
> On your knees to the working man!'

At a word from the chairman the auditorium fell silent. One of the secretaries proceeded to the opening of the letters. 'Some young men announce that every evening outside the Panthéon they are burning an issue of the *Assemblée nationale*,* and they urge all patriots to follow their example.'

'Bravo! Carried!' the crowd responded.

'Citizen Jean-Jacques Langreneux, a typographer in the Rue Dauphine, would like us to put up a monument to the Thermidor martyrs.'*

'Michel-Évariste-Népomucène Vincent, ex-teacher, hopes that European democracy will adopt a universal language. A dead language, such as reformed Latin, for instance, could be used.'

'No, not Latin!' cried the architect.

'Why not?' a schoolmaster asked.

And these two gentlemen started a debate in which others joined, each one trying to impress with his wit, and which soon became so tedious that many started to leave.

But a little old man, wearing green spectacles low on his remarkably high forehead, asked permission to take the floor for an urgent communication.

It was a memorandum on the allocation of taxes. The numbers came pouring forth, it was never-ending! First, people's impatience became evident in their mutterings and chatter; but nothing put him off. Then they started to whistle, they called out 'Azor';* Sénécal chided them; the speaker continued like a machine. The only way to stop him was to take hold of his elbow. The fellow looked as if he was waking from a dream, and, calmly raising his spectacles, said:

'Forgive me, Citizens, forgive me! I have done! A thousand apologies!'

The failure of this reading disconcerted Frédéric. He had his speech in his pocket, but something improvised would have been better.

At last the chairman announced they would move on to the main business of the evening, the question of the elections. They would not discuss the long Republican lists. However, the Club de l'Intelligence had the complete right, like any other, 'with all due respect to the pashas in the Hôtel de Ville', to draw up its own, and the citizens who were seeking a mandate from the people could state their qualifications.

'Go on!' Dussardier urged Frédéric.

A man in a soutane, curly-haired and with a petulant expression, had already raised his hand. He mumbled that his name was Ducretot, and he was a priest and an agronomist, the author of a work called *Manure*. He was packed off to join a horticultural club.

Then a patriot in a smock climbed up on to the platform. He was a plebeian, broad-shouldered, with a large, very gentle face and long black hair. He scanned the assembly with an almost voluptuous look, threw his head back and finally, spreading out his arms:

'Brothers, you have rejected Ducretot! And you were right to do so. But you did not reject him out of impiety, for we are all of us pious.'

Several listened with open mouths, with a look of children in a catechism class, in ecstatic attitudes.

'It is not because he is a priest either, for we are all of us priests! The worker is a priest, as was the founder of socialism, the Master of us all, Jesus Christ!'

The time had come to inaugurate the kingdom of God! The Bible led us straight to '89! After the abolition of slavery would come the abolition of the proletariat. The era of hatred had passed, the age of love was about to begin.

'Christianity is the keystone and the foundation of the new edifice...'

'Are you making fun of us?' cried the wine salesman. 'Who has let this wretched priest in?'

This interruption caused a great to-do. Almost all got up on the benches and showed their fists, shouting: 'Atheist! Aristocrat! Scum!' Whereat the chairman's bell rang and rang and the cries of 'Order, Order!' redoubled. But the intrepid traveller, sustained by three 'coffees' which he had drunk before he arrived, defended himself in the midst of the crowd.

'What? Me? An aristocrat? Come now!'

Finally allowed to explain himself, he declared that we should never be happy as long as there were priests around, and since they had spoken just now about saving money, it would be a wonderful saving if churches, holy vessels, and indeed all kinds of worship were to be suppressed.

Someone objected that he was going a bit far.

'Yes, I am! But when a ship is suddenly caught in a storm...'

Without waiting for the end of the comparison, someone else replied:

'I agree! But that is destroying the whole edifice in one go, like a stonemason without any sense.'

'You are insulting masons!' cried a citizen, covered in plaster. And insisting on believing that he had been provoked, he spat out curses, tried to pick a fight, clung to his bench. It took three men to get rid of him.

Meanwhile the worker was still standing on the platform. The two secretaries warned him to get down. He protested at the injustice being done to him.

'You won't stop me swearing everlasting love to our beloved France! Everlasting love to the Republic too!'

'Citizens!' said Compain. 'Citizens!'

And by dint of repeating 'Citizens', he obtained a degree of silence, and, placing his two red stumpy hands on the table, leaned forward with half-closed eyes:

'I think we must widen the scope for the calf's head!'

Everybody was quiet, thinking they must have misheard.

'Yes! The calf's head!'*

Three hundred laughs broke out all at once. The ceiling shook. In front of all these faces convulsed with laughter, Compain drew back. He went on in a furious voice:

'What! Don't you know about the calf's head?'

Delirious guffaws of laughter ensued. They were holding on to their sides. A few even fell to the floor under the benches. Compain, unable to bear it, took refuge beside Regimbart and tried to make him leave.

'No, I'm waiting till it finishes!' the Citizen said.

This reply decided Frédéric. And as he sought his friends' support from right and left, he caught sight of Pellerin on the platform. The artist took a superior tone with the crowd.

'I'd like to know where the candidate for Art is in all this? I have painted a picture...'

'We don't give a fig for pictures!' a thin man, with red patches on his cheeks, answered harshly.

Pellerin protested that he was being interrupted.

But the other man in a tragic tone of voice said:

'Should the Government not have already abolished prostitution and poverty by decree?'

And this speech having immediately gained the approval of the mob, he raged about the corruption in the large towns.

'Shame and infamy! We should catch the bourgeois as they come out of the Maison d'Or and spit in their faces! The Government ought not to encourage debauchery anyway! But the city revenue officers behave shamefully with our daughters and our sisters...'

A voice from the back shouted:

'That's funny!'

'Throw him out!'

'They demand taxes to fund their debauchery! All that money going to actors...'

'I can't let that pass!' cried Delmar.

He bounded on to the stage, shoving everyone out of the way, and struck an attitude. Declaring that he condemned such inane accusations, he expatiated upon the civilizing mission of the actor. Since the theatre was the home of national education, he was voting for the reform of the theatre. And for a start, no more managers, no more privileges!

'Yes, not of any kind!'

The actor's speech whipped up feeling in the crowd and subversive motions went back and forth.

'No more academies! No more institutes!'

'No more missions!'

'No more Baccalaureate!'

'Down with university degrees!'

'Let's keep them,' said Sénécal, 'but confer them by a universal vote, by the People—the only real judge.'

Besides, that wasn't the most useful thing to do straight away; you first had to level down the rich. And he painted a picture of them wallowing in crime under their gilded ceilings while the poor, writhing in hunger in their attics, cultivated all the virtues. The applause grew so loud that he stopped. For a few minutes he remained with his eyes closed and his head thrown back, as though he were being rocked to and fro by the rage he was fomenting.

Then he started speaking again—dogmatically, in phrases, in words as authoritative as laws. The State should take over the banks and the insurance companies. Inheritances would be abolished. A social fund for workers would be set up. Many other measures would be good in future, but those would be sufficient for the moment. And reverting to the subject of the elections:

'We need honest citizens, men who are totally new to politics! Is there anyone who will come forward?'

Frédéric rose. There was a buzz of approval from his friends. But Sénécal, making a face like Fouquier-Tanville's, began to question him about his name, first names, antecedents, life, and habits.

Frédéric answered him briefly, biting his lips. Sénécal asked if anyone could see a just impediment to this candidature.

'No! No!'

Sénécal, however, could. Everyone leaned forward and pricked up their ears. The citizen who had put his name forward had not delivered over a certain sum which had been promised for a democratic foundation, a magazine. What was more, on 22 February, although he had been given due warning, he had failed to be there as arranged in the Place du Panthéon.

'I swear he was at the Tuileries!' Dussardier cried.

'Can you swear that you saw him at the Panthéon?'

Dussardier bowed his head. Frédéric said nothing. His friends, in consternation, looked anxiously at him.

'At the very least,' Sénécal continued, 'do you know a patriot who will answer for your principles?'

'I will!' said Dussardier.

'Oh, that won't do. Someone else!'

Frédéric turned to Pellerin. The artist answered with a variety of gestures, which meant:

'Oh, my dear! They have rejected me. Dammit, what do you expect!'

Then Frédéric elbowed Regimbart forward.

'Yes, it's true. It's time, here I go!'

And Regimbart strode on to the platform. Then, indicating the Spaniard who had followed him:

'Citizens, let me introduce a citizen from Barcelona!'

The patriot made a deep bow, rolled his silvery eyes like an automaton, and with his hand on his heart, said:

'*Ciudadanos! Mucho aprecio el honor que me dispensáis, y si grande es vuestra bondad mayor es vuestra atención.*'

'I demand a hearing!' cried Frédéric.

'*Desdeque se proclamó la constitución de Cadiz, ese pacto fundamental de las libertades españolas, hasta la última revolución, nuestra patria cuenta numerosos y heroicos martires.*'

Frédéric again tried to make himself heard:

'But citizens!...'

The Spaniard continued:

'*El martes próximo tendrá lugar en la iglesia de la Magdalena un servicio funebre.*'

'For heaven's sake, nobody understands!'

This remark annoyed the crowd.

'Out with him!'

'Who, me?' asked Frédéric.

'Yes, you!' said Sénécal imperiously. 'Out!'

He rose to leave, and the Spaniard's voice followed in his wake.

'*Y todos los Españoles desearian ver alli reunida las deputaciones de los clubs y de la milicia nacional. Une oración funebre en honor de la libertad española y del mundo entero, será pronunciada por un miembro del clero*'

*de Paris en la sala Bonne-Nouvelle. Honor al pueblo francés, que llama-*
*ria yo el primero pueblo des mundo, si no fuese ciudadano de otra nación!'\**

'Aristo!' barked a lout, shaking his fist at Frédéric, who rushed out
into the courtyard in high dudgeon.

He cursed his passion for the Republic, without stopping to reflect
that the accusations against him were fair, after all. What a fool he had
been to put forward his candidature! But what donkeys! What dolts!
He compared himself to these men, and comforted his hurt pride
with the thought of their stupidity.

Then he felt the need to go and see Rosanette. After so much ugli-
ness and intensity her gentle person would be a relief. She knew that
he had been due to present himself at a club that evening. However,
when he came in she did not ask him a single question.

She was by the fire, unpicking the lining of a dress. Such an occupation was a surprise to him.

'Goodness, what are you doing?'

She said drily:

'As you see, I am mending my clothes. It's for your Republic.'

'Why *my* Republic?'

'Is it mine, then?'

And she began to chide him for everything that had been going on
in France for the last two months, accusing him of having caused the
Revolution; it was his fault if people were ruined, if rich people were
deserting Paris, and if she died an early death in the workhouse.

'All right for you to talk, with your private income! But if things
carry on the way they are, you won't have that for very long.'

'That's quite likely,' said Frédéric. 'The most loyal are always the
most misunderstood. And if you didn't have your conscience to
hang on to, the animals you are forced to compromise yourself with
would make you sick of self-sacrifice.'

Rosanette looked at him, between half-closed eyelids.

'Eh? What? What self-sacrifice? Hasn't Monsieur had any success
then? Well, good! That'll teach you to make patriotic donations! Oh,
don't tell lies! I know you gave them three hundred francs, for that
Republic of yours needs supporting! Well, enjoy yourself with her,
my dear!'

Beneath this avalanche of silly remarks Frédéric moved from one
disappointment to one he found even harder to bear.

He had withdrawn to the back of the room. She came over.

'Look! Be sensible! In a country, as in a house, you have to have a master, or everyone's got his finger in the pie. We all know Ledru-Rollin is up to his ears in debt! As for Lamartine, how do you expect a poet to understand politics? Oh, it's no use shaking your head and thinking yourself more intelligent than other people. What I'm saying is true! But you are always quibbling. No one else can get a word in edgeways. Look at Fournier-Fontaine's shops in Saint-Roch. Do you know how much they lost? Eight hundred thousand francs. And Gomer the carter across the road, he's another Republican, he broke the tongs on his wife's head and drank so much absinthe they're going to put him in the madhouse. That's what they're all like, these Republicans. A Republic on the cheap. Oh yes, you can be proud of it!'

Frédéric left. The girl's stupidity, revealing itself suddenly in her vulgar talk, disgusted him. He even felt he was becoming rather patriotic again.

Rosanette's bad temper only grew worse. She was irritated by Mademoiselle Vatnaz's zeal. The latter felt she had a mission and made furious speeches, lecturing and catechizing her friend and overwhelming her with arguments, as she was cleverer than her in these matters.

One day she arrived very indignant with Hussonnet, who had just allowed himself to make ribald jokes at the Women's Club. Rosanette approved of his behaviour, declaring that she herself would 'dress up as a man to go and tell it to them straight, and whip them'. Frédéric arrived at that moment.

'You'll come with me, won't you?' she asked him.

And in spite of him being there, the women squabbled, one taking the housewife's part, the other the intellectual's.

According to Rosanette women were born exclusively for love or to raise children and keep house.

According to Mademoiselle Vatnaz women should take their place in society. In olden times Gaulish women passed laws, Anglo-Saxon women did too, and the Huron wives formed part of the Council. The work of civilization was common to both sexes. Everyone had to contribute and substitute fraternity for selfishness, community for individualism, collectives for smallholdings.

'So you know all about agriculture now, do you?'

'Well, why not? It's all about the future of humanity!'

'Take care of your own!'

'That's up to me!'

They grew crosser with each other. Frédéric intervened. La Vatnaz was getting hot under the collar, and even spoke in favour of communism.

'How stupid!' Rosanette said. 'As if that could ever come about.'

Her friend cited the Essenes as proof, the Moravian Brothers, the Jesuits of Paraguay, and the Pingons* near Thiers in the Auvergne. And as she was throwing her arms about, her watch chain caught on a little gold sheep hanging on her charm bracelet.

All of a sudden Rosanette went visibly pale.

Mademoiselle Vatnaz went on disentangling her charm.

'Don't give yourself so much trouble,' Rosanette said. 'Now I know your political opinions.'

'What?' answered La Vatnaz, who was blushing like a virgin.

'Aha! You know what I mean!'

Frédéric did not know what she meant. Between the two of them it was obvious something had arisen that was more important and more personal than socialism.

'What of it?' La Vatnaz replied, drawing herself up brazenly. 'I've borrowed it my dear, a debt for a debt!'

'I don't deny my debts for heaven's sake! For a few thousand francs, are you serious? At least I borrow, I don't steal from people!'

Mademoiselle Vatnaz made an effort to laugh.

'Oh, it's the truth—I'll put my hand in the fire!'

'Be warned. It's dry enough to burn!'

The old maid held out her right hand in front of Rosanette's face:

'But some of your friends find it attractive!'

'People from Andalusia I suppose! They play it like castanets!'

'Slut!'

The Maréchale made a deep bow.

'How very charming!'

Mademiselle Vatnaz said nothing. Drops of perspiration appeared on her forehead. Her eyes were fixed on the carpet. She was breathing hard. At last she reached the door and, banging it loudly:

'Goodnight. You haven't heard the last of this!'

'My pleasure!' said Rosanette.

She had bottled up her rage, but now collapsed. She fell on to the sofa, shaking all over, stammering out insults, shedding tears. Was it the threat from La Vatnaz that was torturing her? Oh no, see if she cared! Could it be that the other woman owed her money? No, it was the gold sheep, a present. And in the midst of her tears, she let slip the name of Delmar. So she loved the actor!

'Then why did she take me?' Frédéric wondered. 'How is it that he's come back? Who's forcing her to stay with me? What does it all mean?'

Rosanette's little sobs continued. She was still lying on her side on the edge of the sofa, her right cheek on her hands—and seemed such a delicate, helpless, unhappy creature, that he drew closer to her and kissed her gently on her forehead.

Then she assured him of her love. The prince had just left her, they would be free. But for the moment she had some... problems. 'You saw that for yourself the other day when I was using up my old linings.' No more carriages now! And that wasn't all; the upholsterers were threatening to take back the furniture from the bedroom and the big drawing room. She did not know what to do.

Frédéric wanted to reply: 'Don't worry! I'll pay!' But the lady could be lying. Experience had taught him that. He made do with consoling her.

Rosanette's fears were not in vain; she had to give back the furniture and leave the pretty apartment in the Rue Drouot. She took another on the Boulevard Poissonnière on the fourth floor. The knick-knacks from her former boudoir were enough to make the small flat cosy. She had Chinese blinds, a terrace with an awning, in the sitting room a second-hand rug that was still new, and tuffets of pink silk. Frédéric had contributed generously to these acquisitions; he was enjoying the pleasures of a newly-wed who finally had a house of his own, a wife of his own; and as he felt very much at home in it, he came to spend most nights there.

One morning as he was coming out on to the landing on the third floor he caught sight of the shako of a national guard climbing the stairs. Where on earth was he going? The man kept on going up, his head lowered. He looked up. It was Arnoux. The situation was obvious. They blushed at the same time, for the same reason.

Arnoux was the first to resolve the problem.

'She's getting better, isn't she?' as if, Rosanette being ill, he had come to find out how she was.

Frédéric took advantage of that gambit.

'Yes, she certainly is. At least, her maid told me so,' wanting to give him to understand that he had not seen her.

Then they remained there face to face, both hesitant, eyeing one another. It was a toss-up who would leave first. Arnoux once more bit the bullet.

'Oh well, I'll come back later. Where were you going? I'll keep you company!'

And when they were outside he chatted as naturally as ever. Without doubt he wasn't a jealous man, or else he was too good-natured to get cross.

In any case his country preoccupied him. Nowadays he wore his uniform all the time. On 29 March he had protected the offices of *La Presse*.\* When the Chamber had been taken over, his bravery had stood out, and he was at the banquet given by the National Guard in Amiens.

Hussonnet, always on duty with him, took advantage more than anyone else of his brandy and his cigars; but being by nature irreverent, he liked to contradict him; he poked fun at the poor grammar in the decrees, the lectures in the Luxembourg, the Vesuvians, the Tyroleans,\* everything, down to the farm tractor drawn by horses instead of oxen and escorted by ugly young women. Arnoux on the contrary defended those in power and dreamed of unity among the parties. Meanwhile his business affairs were going from bad to worse. He was mildly worried.

The relations between Frédéric and the Maréchale had not depressed him. For this discovery licensed his conscience to cancel the allowance he had been making her again ever since the prince had left. He pleaded difficult circumstances. He bewailed his fate and Rosanette was generous. Then Monsieur Arnoux considered himself her 'true lover'—which raised his self-esteem and made him feel younger. Never doubting that Frédéric was giving the Maréchale money, he thought he was 'playing a capital trick on him'; he managed to keep it secret, and left Frédéric the freedom to do as he wished when they met.

Frédéric found having to share painful, and he thought his rival's politeness a joke that was wearing rather thin. But had they quarrelled he would have had to renounce any chance of going back to Madame Arnoux's, and in any case it was his only opportunity to find out any news of her. The porcelain manufacturer, out of habit or perhaps to make mischief, readily mentioned her in the course of conversation, and even asked him why he didn't come and visit her any more.

Having exhausted all pretexts, Frédéric assured him he had been to see Madame Arnoux on several occasions, but she had not been at home. Arnoux was convinced, for he frequently exclaimed to her about the absence of their friend, and she always said she had been out when he called. So these two lies, instead of contradicting, corroborated one another.

The gentleness of the young man and the delight of pulling the wool over his eyes increased Arnoux's affection for him. He pushed familiarity to the absolute extreme, not out of contempt but because he trusted him. One day he wrote that urgent business required him to spend the day away from Paris. He asked him to take his place on duty. Frédéric dared not refuse and went to the guard-post at the Carrousel.

He had to put up with the company of the National Guardsmen! And except for a refiner, a fussy man who drank like a fish, they all seemed more dumb than the haversacks they wore. The main topic was the replacement of their leather belts by inferior ones. Others were angry with the National Workshops.* One said: 'Where will it end?' The person who had been addressed would open his eyes and answer, as though on the edge of an abyss, 'Yes, where will it end?' Then another, bolder, would cry: 'It can't go on like this. It's got to stop!' And at the same words being repeated over and over again till nightfall, Frédéric was bored to death.

To his great surprise, at eleven o'clock, Arnoux appeared. He said straight away that he was coming to relieve him since his business was over.

There had been no business. He had invented it to spend a day alone with Rosanette. But the good fellow had overtaxed his strength, and in his lassitude had been overcome with remorse. He had come to thank Frédéric and to invite him to supper.

'Thank you, but no. I'm not hungry. I only want my bed.'

'That's an even better reason to eat together later. How feeble you are! But you can't go home yet. It's too late. It would be dangerous.'

Again Frédéric gave in. Arnoux, whom they had not expected to see, was spoiled by his comrades-in-arms, and chiefly by the refiner. Everyone loved him. And he was such a good-natured man that he was even sorry Hussonnet wasn't there. But he had to have just forty winks.

'Come over by me,' he said to Frédéric, stretching out on a camp bed, without taking off his equipment.

Fearing an alert and in spite of the regulations, he kept his rifle by him, then muttering a few words: 'My darling... my little angel', he quickly fell asleep.

Those who were talking, stopped, and gradually a deep silence fell on the station. Frédéric, tormented by fleas, looked around him. Halfway up the yellow wall there was a long shelf upon which the knapsacks formed a series of little bumps, while below them, the lead-coloured muskets were stacked next to each other; and snores could be heard, from the National Guards, whose bellies stuck out indistinctly in the darkness. An empty bottle and plates littered the stove. There were three straw-bottomed chairs around the table, where a card game was spread out. A strap hung down from a drum in the middle of the shelf. The warm wind coming through the door made the oil lamp smoke. Arnoux slept, with arms outstretched. And as the shaft of his gun was placed at a slightly oblique angle, the muzzle reached into his armpit. Frédéric noticed and was alarmed.

'No, I'm being silly. There's nothing to be afraid of. But supposing he were to die!'

And right away endless images passed before his eyes. He saw himself with her in a post-chaise at night; then by the river one summer evening, and in the lamplight at home in their house. He even dwelt on household accounts, domestic arrangements, seeing and already sensing his future happiness—and in order to realize his desires all it would take would be to cock the musket! A little poke with the end of his toe! The shot would be fired, it would be an accident, nothing more than that.

Frédéric pondered this thought like a dramatist composing a play. Suddenly it occurred to him that it wasn't far off being put into practice, and that he was going to play his part, that he wanted to do it. Then he was filled with terror. In the midst of this anguish he felt a kind of pleasure and sank ever deeper into the terrifying feeling that his scruples were vanishing. In his mad reverie the rest of the world was blanked out. And he was conscious of himself only because of an unbearable tightening in his chest.

'Shall we have some white wine?' said the refiner, waking up.

Arnoux jumped up. And once they had drunk some white wine, he insisted on taking over Frédéric's guard duty.

Then he carried him off to lunch at Parly's in the Rue de Chartres. And as he needed to restore his strength, he ordered for himself two plates of meat, a lobster, a rum omelette, a salad and so on, all washed down with an 1819 Sauternes, a '42 Romanée, as well as champagne at dessert and then liqueurs.

Frédéric said nothing to discourage him. He was embarrassed, as if Arnoux had been able to guess what he had been thinking from the expression on his face.

Arnoux, his two elbows on the edge of the table, and leaning over very low, fixed his steadfast gaze on him and told him of his plans.

He wanted to lease all the embankments on the Northern Line and plant them out with potatoes, or else organize a gigantic cavalcade on the boulevards, in which the 'celebrities of the day' would figure. He would rent out all the windows, which at the rate of three francs on average would bring in a goodly sum. In short, he dreamed of seizing some monopoly and thereby becoming very rich. But he had his principles, condemned excess and bad behaviour, talked about his 'poor father', and said that every evening he examined his conscience before offering his soul to God.

'A drop of curaçao perhaps?'

'By all means!'

As to the Republic, things would get sorted out. Anyway he was, in his view, the happiest man in the world. And forgetting himself, he boasted about Rosanette's qualities, even comparing her with his wife. She was something quite different! You wouldn't believe what beautiful thighs she had.

'Your good health!'

Frédéric clinked his glass. To be polite, he had drunk a little too much. Besides, the bright sun was dazzling him. And when they went up the Rue Vivienne together their epaulettes brushed against each other in a fraternal fashion.

Once back home, Frédéric slept till seven o'clock. Then he went off to the Maréchale's. She had gone out with somebody. Perhaps Arnoux? Not knowing what to do, he carried on walking along the boulevard, but couldn't get any further than the Porte Saint-Martin, there were so many people.

Poverty had left a considerable number of workers to their own devices. And they came here every evening, as though on parade and waiting for a signal. In spite of the law prohibiting assemblies, these 'clubs of the desperate' were increasing in a frightening way, and many of the better-off went along every day to watch, through bravado or because it was the thing to do.

Suddenly Frédéric saw Monsieur Dambreuse with Martinon a few yards away. He turned aside, for since Monsieur Dambreuse had been elected to the Assembly, he bore him a grudge. But the capitalist stopped him.

'A word, Monsieur! I owe you some explanation.'

'I don't want any.'

'Please! Listen.'

It wasn't in any way his fault. He had been begged, forced, in a way, to stand. Martinon immediately corroborated his account. A deputation from Nogent had come to his home.

'In any case, I assumed I was free from the moment when...'

A crowd pushing past on the pavement obliged Monsieur Dambreuse to move out of the way, A minute later he reappeared, saying to Martinon:

'That was a good turn you did me! You won't regret it...'

All three leaned against a shopfront, to chat more freely.

From time to time there was a cry of: 'Vive Napoléon! Vive Barbès! Down with Marie!' The huge crowds were chattering at the tops of their voices, and the echo sent back by the houses was like the continual slapping of waves in a harbour. At certain moments they were quiet and then the Marseillaise struck up. In the carriage gateways mysterious-looking men were selling swordsticks. From time to time two individuals passing one in front of the other would wink and then go speedily on their way. Groups of idlers blocked the pavements. A dense crowd swarmed on the cobbled street. Entire bands of police, emerging from the side streets, vanished at once into the multitude. Here and there small red flags flickered like flames. From their elevated positions, coachmen waved their arms about and drove off. So much movement, so much to see and enjoy!

'How Mademoiselle Cécile would have loved all this!' Martinon said.

'As you know, my wife wouldn't have liked my niece to be here with you,' Monsieur Dambreuse replied, with a laugh.

You wouldn't have known it was the same man. For the last three months he had been shouting: 'Vive la République!' and had even voted for the banishment of the Orléans family. But no more concessions! He was so furious that he carried a cosh in his pocket.

Martinon had one as well. Since judicial posts were no longer for life, he had retired from the Public Prosecutor's office and was now even more violent in his views than Monsieur Dambreuse.

The banker hated Lamartine in particular (because he had supported Ledru-Rollin) and with him Pierre Leroux, Proudhon, Considerant, Lamennais, all the hotheads, all the socialists.

'Anyway, what do they want? The tax on meat has been abolished and so has imprisonment for debt. Now they are working out plans for a mortgage bank. The other day it was a national bank! And there's five million on the budget for the workers! But luckily that's finished with, thanks to Monsieur Falloux. Good riddance! Let them go!'

In fact, at a loss to know how to feed the hundred and thirty thousand men from the national workshops, the Minister for Public Works had that very day* signed an order which asked all citizens between the ages of eighteen and twenty to serve as soldiers, or else go as farm labourers in the countryside.

This alternative made them angry, they were convinced they were trying to destroy the Republic. Life away from the capital seemed to them as bad as exile. They saw themselves dying of fever out in the wilds. Moreover, for many who were used to more skilled work, agricultural labour seemed a debasement. It was a trap, a mockery, a formal denial of all they had been promised. If they resisted, force would be used against them. They did not doubt this and got ready to forestall it.

Towards nine, the gatherings that had formed at the Bastille and Châtelet spilled out on to the boulevard. From the Porte Saint-Denis to the Porte Saint-Martin all you could see was a huge swarm, a single dark blue, almost black, mass of people. The men you saw had fire in their eyes, pale complexions, faces that were thin from hunger, passionate with the injustice of it. Meanwhile clouds were gathering. The thunder in the sky generated electricity in the crowd, which whirled uncertainly around, surging back and forth. And you felt an immeasurable force in its depths, an elemental energy. Then they all started to chant: 'Lights! Lights!' Several windows did not light up; stones were thrown at their panes. Monsieur Dambreuse thought it prudent to leave. The two young men accompanied him home.

He foresaw great disasters. The people might invade the Chamber again; and saying this, he recounted how he would have died on 15 May without the loyalty of one of the National Guard.

'But it was your friend, I was forgetting! Your friend the porcelain manufacturer, Jacques Arnoux!'—The rioters were on top of him. This good citizen had put his arms round him and got him out of harm's way. So since then a kind of bond had developed.—'One of these days we should all have dinner together, and since you see him often, assure him that I like him very much. He is an excellent man, unfairly criticized in my view. And he has his wits about him, the rogue! My compliments once more! Have a very good evening...'

After leaving Monsieur Dambreuse, Frédéric went back to the Maréchale's house, and with a very serious expression, said she had to choose between him and Arnoux. She replied sweetly that she could not understand 'such rubbish', that she didn't love Arnoux, and was not in the least attached to him. Frédéric was desperate to leave Paris. She did not try to dissuade him from this whim and they left for Fontainebleau the very next day.

The hotel where they stayed was different from the others in that it had a fountain splashing in the middle of the courtyard. The bedroom doors opened on to a corridor, like the ones in monasteries. The room they were given was spacious, well appointed, hung with chintz, and was quiet because of the few visitors. Well-to-do citizens with time on their hands wandered by on the street. At dusk beneath their windows children were playing prisoners' base; and after the tumult of Paris this peace and quiet was a surprise and a relief to them.

Early in the morning they went to visit the castle. Entering through the main gate, they saw the whole of the facade with its five towers, their pointed roofs and the horseshoe staircase at the back of the courtyard, with two lower buildings to the right and left of it. The lichen on the cobbles blended with the fawn of the bricks in the distance. And the entire chateau, the colour of rust like an old suit of armour, had an air of impassive royalty, a sort of melancholy, military grandeur.

At last a servant appeared, carrying a bunch of keys. He first showed them the Queen's apartments, the Pope's oratory, the gallery of François I, the small mahogany table where the Emperor signed his abdication, and, in one of the rooms which divided the former Galerie des Cerfs, the place where Christina had Monaldeschi murdered.* Rosanette listened carefully to that story, then turned to Frédéric and said:

'It must have been because he was jealous. You be careful!'

Next they crossed the Council Chamber, the guards' room, the throne room, Louis XIII's drawing room. A bright light poured from the high, uncurtained windows. There was a light layer of dust on the handles of the catches, the brass legs of the tables. Everywhere there were thick linen cloths covering the armchairs. Above the doors could be seen hunting parties of Louis XV, and here and there tapestries representing the gods of Olympus, Psyche, or the battles of Alexander.

When she passed in front of the mirrors, Rosanette stopped for a moment to smooth her hair.

After the keep and the Saint-Saturnin chapel, they reached the banqueting room.

They were dazzled by the splendour of the ceiling, divided into octagonal sections, enhanced with gold and silver, more finely carved than a jewel, and by the multitude of paintings covering the walls, stretching from the gigantic fireplace, where crescents and quivers surrounded the arms of France, as far as the musicians' gallery built right at the other end of the enormous room. The ten arched windows were wide open. The sun cast a lustre on the paintings, the azure sky continued the ultramarine of the curving arches into infinity, and from the depths of the wood, with its hazy treetops lining the horizon, you could almost hear the echo of the mort blown by the ivory hunting horns and see the mythological ballets of princesses and lords disguised as wood nymphs and satyrs gather beneath their branches—a time when science was young, passions were violent and art was sumptuous, when people dreamed of voyaging to the Hesperides, and the mistresses of kings might be set among the stars. The most beautiful of these famous women had herself painted— on the right—as Diana the Huntress, and even as Diana of the Underworld, no doubt to denote her powers stretching to beyond the grave. All these symbols strengthened her glory. And there remained in that place something of her, a muffled voice, a continuing radiance.

Frédéric was seized by an inexplicable craving for these dead women. In an effort to distract himself from this desire, he began to contemplate Rosanette tenderly, asking her whether she would have liked to be that woman.

'Which woman?'

'Diane de Poitiers!'

He repeated:

'Diane de Poitiers, the mistress of Henri II.'*

She uttered nothing but a little 'Oh!'

Her silence clearly showed she knew nothing, understood nothing, so that, wanting to be kind to her, he asked:

'Perhap you are bored?'

'Oh no, not at all!'

And raising her chin and looking around her with the vaguest of expressions, Rosanette murmured:

'It brings back memories!'

However, you could see on her face she was trying hard to be respectful. And as this serious expression made her all the prettier, Frédéric forgave her.

She was more amused by the carp pond. For a quarter of an hour she threw crumbs of bread into the water to see the fish jump.

Frédéric had sat down next to her under the lime trees. He thought about all the people who had walked beneath these walls, Charles V, the Valois, Henri IV, Peter the Great, Jean-Jacques Rousseau, and the 'lovely ladies who wept in the stage boxes'.* He thought about Voltaire, Napoleon, Pius VII, Louis-Philippe. He felt surrounded, jostled by this throng of the dead. He was dazed, but at the same time fascinated by such a plethora of images.

At last they came out into the garden.

It was a vast rectangle, allowing you to take in at a glance its wide ochre paths, its square lawns, its ribbons of box, its yew trees in the form of pyramids, its shrubs and its narrow beds, in which clumps of flowers scattered here and there bloomed on the grey soil. At the end of the garden was a park, bisected by a long canal.

Royal residences possess a special melancholy. No doubt this has something to do with their dimensions which are too big for the small number of people who live there, with their silence which comes as a surprise after so many fanfares, and with their unchanging luxury which proves by its antiquity the fleeting nature of dynasties, the misery at the heart of all things. And the exhalation of the centuries, deadening and funereal like the scent of a mummy, is felt even by the simplest among us. Rosanette could not stop yawning. They went back to the hotel.

After lunch an open carriage came for them. They left Fontainebleau by a wide crossroads, then trotted up a a sandy road in a wood of small pine trees. The trees were taller here, and the coachman from time to time said: 'Those are the Siamese Twins, the Pharamond, the Bouquet-du-Roi', omitting none of the famous sites, and sometimes even stopping so that they might admire them.

They entered the Forest of Franchard. The carriage glided over the grass like a sledge. Invisible pigeons cooed. Suddenly a waiter from a café appeared, and they alighted near a garden fence where there were round tables. Then, leaving the walls of a ruined abbey on their left, they climbed down over some big rocks and before long reached the bottom of the gorge.

On one side it was covered by a mixture of sandstone rocks and juniper, while on the other, the earth, which was almost bare, sloped down to the valley floor where a path made a pale streak through the coloured heather. And far in the distance you could see a flat-topped hill with a telegraph tower* behind.

Half an hour later they got down from the coach again to climb the heights of Aspremont.

The path zigzagged up between the dwarf pines, beneath jagged rocks. All this part of the forest had a hush about it, and felt rather wild and secret. You could imagine hermits, the companions of great stags wearing a fiery cross between their antlers, who welcomed with a fatherly smile the good kings of France kneeling before their caves. A scent of resin filled the warm air, vein-like roots entwined on the ground. Rosanette tripped over them, was in despair, nearly in tears.

But at the top her spirits revived when she discovered under a canopy of branches a sort of tavern where they sold wood carvings. She drank a bottle of lemonade, bought a stick made out of holly; and, without glancing at the view from the top of the hill, she visited the Cave of the Brigands preceded by a boy carrying a torch.

Their carriage was waiting in Bas-Bréau.

A painter* in a blue smock was working at the foot of an oak tree, with his box of paints on his knees. He looked up and watched them go by.

In the middle of the hill at Chailly there was a cloudburst which made them put the hood up. Almost immediately the rain stopped, and when they returned to the town the cobbles in the streets were shining in the sun.

Some travellers who had just arrived told them that there was terrible bloodshed in Paris. Rosanette and her lover were not surprised. Then everyone left, peace reigned again in the hotel, the gaslight went out, and they fell asleep to the murmur of the fountain in the courtyard.

The next day they went to visit the Gorge-au-Loup, the Mare-aux-Fées, the Long-Rocher, La Marlotte. The day after, they set off again at random, wherever their coachman took them, not asking where they were and often even missing the famous sites.

They felt so comfortable in their old landau, low as a sofa and upholstered with a faded stripy material! Ditches choked with growth passed in a continuous, gentle rhythm. White rays of sun darted through the tall ferns. At times a disused path appeared before them in a straight line, with weeds growing on it languidly here and there. At the centre of every crossroads a signpost extended its four limbs. Elsewhere stakes leaned over like dead trees and little curving paths losing themselves under the leaves made you yearn to follow them. And precisely at such moments the horse would turn, they went in and sank into the mud. A little further on, moss was growing along the edges of the deep ruts.

They thought they were far away from the world, all on their own. But then suddenly a gamekeeper came by with his gun, and a group of women in rags dragging large bundles of faggots on their backs.

When the carriage stopped, a universal silence descended. All you could hear was the panting of the horse in its shafts, and the very faint, insistent cry of a bird.

Light falling on the edge of the wood in certain spots left the depths in shadow; in the foreground it was more a kind of twilight, while in the distance it made purplish streaks and a white light. In the middle of the day the sun, shining straight down on to the large expanses of greenery, showered them with light, suspended silvery drops on the ends of branches, streaked the grass with trails of emerald, cast golden dots over the beds of dry leaves. If you threw back your head you could see the sky between the treetops. Certain enormous trees looked like patriarchs and emperors or, linking their branches, they formed triumphal arches with their long trunks; others, growing up at an angle from the ground looked like columns about to fall.

This host of great vertical lines opened out to reveal huge waves of green unfurling unevenly down to the bottom of the valleys; then the crest of other hills moved into view, overlooking yellow plains which vanished in a hazy pale colour.

Standing next to the other on a rise in the landscape they felt as if they breathed in the wind, and a sort of pride in a freer life entered their souls, with an abundance of strength, an inexplicable joy.

The diversity of the trees made a changing spectacle. The beeches, with their smooth white bark, entwined their crowns; the ash bowed down its grey-green branches; holly, burnished like bronze, bristled in the hornbeam coppices; then came a line of slender birches bent in elegiac attitudes; and the pine trees, symmetrical as organ pipes, swaying to and fro, seemed to be singing. There were enormous gnarled oaks, heaving themselves in convulsions out of the earth, twisting round one another; firm on their trunks like torsos, they raised their naked arms in a clamour of furious menace and despair, like a group of Titans immobilized in their rage. Something heavier, a feverish languor, hovered over the ponds whose surface was bordered by hawthorns; the lichens on the bank where the wolves came to drink were the colour of sulphur, burnt as though by witches' footprints, and the ceaseless croaking of frogs answered the cries of the crows wheeling overhead. They crossed some unremarkable clearings planted with a few odd saplings. The sound of iron, numerous heavy blows, echoed all around. On the slopes of a hill a gang of quarrymen were striking at the rock. These rocks became more widespread, increasing gradually until they filled the whole terrain; they were cube-shaped like houses, flat like paving stones, propping each other up, overhanging one another, merging like the unrecognizable and monstrous ruins of some vanished city. But the turbulence of their chaos put you in mind of volcanoes, of floods, of great unknown cataclysms. Frédéric said they had been there since the beginning of the world and would be there till the end; Rosanette looked away, declaring it 'would drive her mad', and went off to pick heather. Their small purplish flowers were bunched up close together and the crumbling soil beneath made a sort of black fringe along the sand that was spangled with mica.

One day they climbed halfway up a hill that was all sand. Its untrodden surface was striped with symmetrical waves; here and there rocks like promontories on a dry ocean bed rose in the shape of animals, tortoises poking out their necks, slithering seals, hippopotami and bears. Nobody. Not a sound. The sand sparkled in the sun, and suddenly in this vibration of light the animals seemed to move. Frédéric and Rosanette hurried back down, dizzy, in flight, almost.

The solemnity of the forest entered into them. And there were hours of silence when, letting themselves be rocked by the springs of the cab, they remained motionless, in a state of quiet intoxication. His arm around her waist, he listened to her chatter while the birds twittered, and took in with almost the same glance the black grapes on her bonnet and the berries on the junipers, the way her veil hung, the curling clouds. And when he bent over her, the freshness of her skin mingled with the strong scent of the forest. They enjoyed it all; they showed one another the spiders' webs hanging on the bushes, hollows full of water in the centre of stones, a squirrel on a branch, two butterflies flying after them. Twenty paces away a doe walked quietly under the trees, noble and gentle with her fawn at her side. Rosanette wanted to run after her and kiss her.

She was very scared once when a man suddenly appeared and showed her three vipers in a box. She threw herself into Frédéric's arms; he was glad of this weakness and that he felt strong enough to look after her.

That evening they dined at an inn by the Seine. The table was by the window, Rosanette was facing him, and he gazed at her nose which was small, delicate and white, her pouting lips, her limpid eyes, her loose chestnut hair, her pretty oval face. Her cream-coloured dress of soft cotton clung to her slightly rounded shoulders; her two hands, emerging from the plain cuffs, moved across the tablecloth to cut the bread and pour the wine. They were served a spread chicken, an eel stew in a pipe-clay dish, rough wine, bread that was too hard, knives that were chipped. All that increased their pleasure, the illusion. They could almost believe themselves to be on a journey, in Italy, on their honeymoon.

Before they left they went for a stroll along the bank.

The soft blue dome of the sky reached down to the horizon, to the jagged outline of the woods. At the end of the meadow opposite there was a bell tower in a village, and further along on the left, the red roof of a house was reflected in the river, which did not appear to move at all throughout its bends; but reeds were leaning over and the water was gently rocking the sticks placed along the edge to hold the nets. A wicker eel-pot was there and two or three old rowing boats. Near the inn a girl in a straw bonnet was drawing a bucket from a well. Each time it came up Frédéric heard, with inexpressible delight, the squeaking of the chain.

He was sure he was going to be happy enough to last him the rest of his life, so natural did his happiness seem to him, so integral to his life and the presence of this woman. He felt he must whisper amorous things to her. She replied tenderly, with little pats on his shoulder, a surprising gentleness which he found charming. He discovered in her a completely new beauty which was perhaps nothing more than the reflection of the lovely things around them, unless their secret virtues had made it blossom.

When they were resting in the middle of the countryside, he laid his head on her lap in the shade of her parasol. Or else they would lie flat on the grass gazing into each other's eyes, thirsting and slaking that thirst constantly, and then, with half-closed lids, saying nothing.

Sometimes they heard drum rolls in the distance. It was the call to arms they were beating in the villages, to go and defend Paris.

'Well, well, it's the rioting!' said Frédéric with scorn, all of this excitement striking him as trivial in comparison with their love and with eternal nature.

And they chatted about this and that, about things they already knew, about people who did not interest them, about a thousand foolish things. She talked to him about her maidservant and her hairdresser. One day she forgot herself so far as to tell him her age: twenty-nine. She was getting old.

And several times without meaning to she told him little things about herself. She had been 'a shop girl', had made a trip to England, begun studying to be an actress. All of that was told incoherently, and he couldn't reconstruct any whole narrative from it. She told him more one day when they were sitting under a plane tree on the edge of a meadow. Below on the side of the road a little girl, barefoot in the dust, was leading a cow to graze. As soon as she saw them she came to ask for money. And holding her ragged skirt in one hand, with the other she scratched her shock of black hair, like a Louis XIV wig, which framed her brown face that was lit by a pair of splendid eyes.

'She will be very pretty later,' Frédéric remarked.

'As long as she doesn't have a mother!' replied Rosanette.

'What's that you say?'

'Yes. If I hadn't had mine...'

She sighed and began to talk about her childhood. Her parents had been silk weavers at La Croix-Rousse.* She was apprenticed to her father. The poor man wore himself out with work but his wife nagged him and sold all their possessions to buy drink. Rosanette could see their bedroom now with the looms ranged along between the windows, the stockpot on the stove, the bed painted to look like mahogany, a cupboard opposite, and the dark closet she had slept in till she was fifteen. Then a gentleman had arrived, a fat man with a face the colour of boxwood, sanctimonious, dressed in black. Her mother and he had talked and the result, three days later... Rosanette stopped and with a look that was full of brazenness and bitterness said:

'And that was that!'

Then, replying to Frédéric's gesture:

'As he was married (he would have been afraid of being found out in his own house) he took me to a room in a tavern and I was told I'd be happy and get a lovely present.

'The first thing that struck me as I walked through the door was a silver chandelier on a table laid for two. It was reflected in a mirror on the ceiling and the blue silk drapes on the walls made the whole apartment resemble the alcove of a bedroom. I was astonished. You realize that I was a poor creature who had seen nothing of the world! In spite of being dazzled I was afraid. I wanted to leave. But I stayed.

'The only seat there was a divan by the table. It was soft to sit on. The heating vent in the carpet sent warm air up at me and I stayed there, not touching anything. The waiter stood by and urged me to eat. Immediately he poured me a large glass of wine. My head was spinning. I tried to open a window, he said: "No, Mademoiselle, that's forbidden." And then he left me. On the table were heaps of things I didn't recognize. Nothing tempted me. I made do with a pot of jam and still waited. I don't know what kept him. It was very late, at least midnight, I was exhausted. I pushed back one of the pillows to stretch out more comfortably and my hand grasped a kind of album, a notebook. In it were obscene pictures... I was sleeping on top of it when he came back.'

She bowed her head and remained thoughtful.

The leaves around them rustled. In a clump of weeds a tall foxglove swayed, the light streamed like a wave on to the grass. And the silence was broken at frequent intervals by the grazing of the cow that had disappeared from view.

Rosanette stared at a point on the ground three paces away, fixedly, her nostrils quivering, absorbed in her own thoughts. Frédéric took her hand.

'My poor darling, how you have suffered!'

'Yes,' she said, 'more than you think! So that I wanted to end it all. They fished me out of the river.'

'What?'

'Oh, don't let's think about that any more!... I love you, I am happy!

Kiss me!' And she removed one by one the prickles from the thistles that had caught in the hem of her dress.

Frédéric was thinking mostly of what she hadn't told him. By what steps had she managed to escape from her poverty? To what lover did she owe her education? What had happened in her life up to the day he had arrived at her house for the first time? Her last admission forbade any more questions. He only asked her how she had got to know Arnoux.

'Through La Vatnaz.'

'Didn't I see you with them both once at the Palais-Royal?'

He gave her the exact date. Rosanette made an effort.

'Yes, you are right!... I wasn't so very gay back then!'

But Arnoux had been kind to her. Frédéric did not doubt it. However, their friend was a queer fish and full of faults. He was at pains to enumerate them. She agreed.

'Never mind! He's a lovable old rascal!'

'Still?' asked Frédéric.

A blush crept over her face, half laughing, half cross.

'Oh no, it's ancient history. I'm not hiding anything from you. And even if I were, he's different! Anyway, I don't think you are being very nice to your victim.'

'My victim?'

Rosanette chucked him under the chin.

'Of course!'

And in baby talk, like a nursemaid:

'We've not always been a good boy! We've been to beddy-byes with his wife!'

'Me! Never!'

Rosanette smiled. He was hurt by her smile, a proof of indifference, he thought. But she went on gently and with the look of a woman begging to be lied to:

'Are you sure?'

'I am positive!'

Frédéric swore on his honour that he had never thought of Madame Arnoux, since he was too much in love with someone else.

'Who, then?'

'You, of course, my love!'

'Oh, don't tease me! You make me cross!'

He judged it prudent to invent a story, a passion. He invented circumstantial details. This woman moreover had made him very miserable.

'Decidedly, you've not had much luck,' said Rosanette.

'Oh, I don't know about that...'—wanting to suggest by this remark several examples of good fortune in order to make her think better of him, in much the same way as Rosanette did not admit to all her lovers so that he would have a higher opinion of her. For, even in the midst of the most intimate of confidences, false shame, delicacy or pity invariably cause a certain reticence. You discover in the other person, or in yourself, precipices or quagmires which prevent you from going further. In any case, you feel you will not be understood. It's difficult to express anything precisely, whatever it may be, so perfect unions are a rare thing.

The poor Maréchale had never known anything better. Often when she looked at Frédéric tears came to her eyes, then she would raise her head or gaze at the horizon as if she had caught sight of a great dawn, vistas of limitless happiness. Finally, one day, she admitted that she would like to have a Mass said 'to bring good luck to our love'.

So how was it that she had resisted him for so long? She didn't know herself. He asked her the question several times, and she replied, enfolding him in her arms:

'It was because I was afraid of loving you too much, darling.'

That Sunday morning Frédéric read in a newspaper the name of Dussardier among the list of wounded. He gave an exclamation, and, showing Rosanette the paper, declared he had to leave immediately.

'Why?'

'To go and see him and look after him.'

'You are not going to leave me on my own, I suppose?'

'Come with me.'

'Oh, I'm not going to get mixed up in a brawl! No thank you!'

'But I can't...'

'Rubbish! There's no shortage of nurses in the hospitals. Anyway what business was it of his? Everyone for himself, say I!'

He was shocked at her egotism and he blamed himself for not being in Paris with the others. So much indifference to the misfortune of France had something mean-spirited and bourgeois about it. His love suddenly seemed to weigh on him, as if he had committed a crime. They sulked for an hour with one another.

Then she begged him to wait and not to expose himself to danger.

'Supposing you got killed!'

'Then I should only have done my duty!'

Rosanette jumped up. His first duty was to love her. It must be because he didn't want her any more! It didn't make any sense! What a silly idea!

Frédéric rang for the bill. But going back to Paris wasn't easy. The Leloir mail coach had just left, the Lecomte berlins were not running, and the stagecoach from the Bourbonnais would only pass through late at night and might be full. Nobody could tell. When he had wasted a great deal of time trying to find out, he thought he would hire a post-chaise. The postmaster refused to provide horses, since Frédéric did not have a passport.* Finally he hired a landau (the same one they had used on their outings) and they pulled up outside the Hôtel du Commerce in Melun towards five o'clock.

Arms were stacked all over the Place du Marché. The prefect had forbidden the National Guard to go to Paris. Those who were not in his department wanted to carry on marching. There was shouting. There was uproar in the inn.

Rosanette in a panic declared she would go no further, and again begged him to stay. The innkeeper and his wife added their voices to hers. A man who was having his dinner got involved, declaring that the battle would be over very soon. Anyway, you had to do your duty. Then the Maréchale's sobs got louder. Frédéric was exasperated. He gave her his purse, kissed her swiftly, and disappeared.

At the station in Corbeil they told him that the insurgents had cut through the rails in places and the coachman refused to drive him any further. His horses, he said, were 'dead-beat'.

Through his influence, however, Frédéric got hold of a driver who, in a shabby cabriolet, for the sum of sixty francs without counting the tip, would take him as far as the Porte d'Italie. But a hundred feet from the barrier this driver made him get out, and turned back. Frédéric was walking along the road when suddenly a sentinel barred his way with a bayonet. Four men seized hold of him yelling:

'This is one of them! Watch out! Search him! Brigand! Scum!'

And he was so totally flabbergasted that he allowed himself to be dragged to the guard post at the barrier, at the very crossing point where the Boulevard des Gobelins, the Boulevard de l'Hôpital, and the Rues Godefroy and Mouffetard meet.

Four barricades at the end of these four streets were formed by enormous ramparts of paving stones. Torches sputtered here and there. In spite of the clouds of dust rising he could make out some infantrymen and National Guards, all with black faces, dishevelled and haggard.

They had just taken the square and shot several men; they were still angry. Frédéric said he was coming from Fontainebleau to help a wounded comrade lodging in the Rue Bellefond. No one would believe him at first. They examined his hands and even sniffed his ears to ascertain whether he smelt of gunpowder.

However, by dint of repeating the same thing, he ended up persuading a captain who ordered two riflemen to conduct him to the guard post in the Jardin des Plantes.

They went down the Boulevard de l'Hôpital. A strong wind was blowing. It revived him.

Then they turned into the Rue du Marché-aux-Chevaux. The Jardin des Plantes was a big black mass on the right, while on the left the entire facade of La Pitié, with all its windows lit up, blazed as if on fire, and shadows passed rapidly behind the panes.

The two men with Frédéric left. Another accompanied him to the École Polytechnique.

The Rue Saint-Victor was in total darkness, with no gaslight, nor lights in any of the houses. Every ten minutes you heard:

'Sentries! Attention!'

And this shout cast into the silence went echoing forth like the sound of a stone falling into an abyss.

Sometimes the tramp of heavy feet could be heard approaching. It was a patrol of a hundred men at least. Whisperings, the muffled clicking sound of metal came from that confused mass. And moving rhythmically away it melted into the darkness.

In the centre of the crossroads a dragoon sat motionless on horseback. From time to time a despatch rider went by at a gallop and then silence descended again. Guns moving over the cobbles in the distance made a dull, frightening rumble; your heart tightened at these noises which were so different from all the sounds of everyday. They seemed even to increase the silence which was deep, absolute— a black silence. Men in white smocks would come up and speak to the soldiers, and then vanish like ghosts.

The guard post at the École Polytechnique overflowed with people. Women blocked the entrance demanding to see their sons or husbands.

They were sent to the Panthéon which had been made over into a repository for corpses. And they didn't listen to Frédéric. He persisted, swearing that his friend Dussardier was expecting him, that he was dying. Finally they detailed a corporal to take him to the top of the Rue Saint-Jacques, to the town hall in the 12th arrondissement.

The Place du Panthéon was full of soldiers lying on straw. Dawn was breaking. The campfires were going out.

The uprising had left terrible traces in that area of the city. The surface of the roads was pockmarked along its whole length. On the ruined barricades there were omnibuses, gas pipes, cartwheels; small black puddles in certain parts were obviously blood. The houses had been holed by projectiles and their timbered structure could be seen through the crumbling plaster. Blinds, held only by a nail, hung like rags. The staircases having collapsed, doors opened on to a void. You could see inside the rooms, their wallpaper in shreds. Occasionally a few fragile items had been preserved. Frédéric noted a clock, a parrot's perch, some engravings.

When he went into the town hall, the National Guards were talking incessantly about the deaths of Bréa and Négrier, the deputy Charbonnel, and the Archbishop of Paris. They were saying that the Duc d'Aumale had landed in Boulogne, that Barbès had escaped from Vincennes, that the artillery was coming from Bourges, and that help was flooding in from the provinces. Towards three o'clock somebody brought good news. Spokesmen from the uprising were talking to the President of the Assembly.

At this, everyone was delighted. And as he still had twelve francs, Frédéric sent out for twelve bottles of wine, hoping by that means to hasten his freedom. Suddenly they thought they could hear firing. The drinking stopped. They looked at the stranger suspiciously. Perhaps he was Henri V.

To absolve themselves of all responsibility for him they took him to the town hall in the 11th arrondissement,* which he was not allowed to leave until nine o'clock next morning.

He ran to the Quai Voltaire. At an open window an old man in shirtsleeves was weeping, his eyes lifted to the heavens. The Seine flowed calmly along. The sky was completely blue; birds sang in the trees in the Tuileries.

Frédéric was just crossing the Carrousel when a bier came by. The guard at once presented arms, and the officer, touching his shako, said: 'All honour to our fallen hero.' This phrase had become almost obligatory; the man uttering it always appeared deeply moved. A group of angry people were escorting the stretcher, shouting:

'We will avenge you! We will avenge you!'

The carriages circulated on the boulevard and women at their doors were shredding linen. However, the riot had been suppressed, or as good as; a proclamation from Cavaignac, put up just a short time ago, announced this fact. At the top of the Rue Vivienne a squad of Mobile Guards* appeared. Then the well-to-do, the respectable citizens uttered enthusiastic cries, raising their hats, clapping, dancing, wanting to kiss them, giving them drinks; flowers thrown by the ladies fell from balconies.

Finally at ten o'clock when the cannons were roaring and preparing to attack the Faubourg Saint-Antoine, Frédéric reached Dussardier's place. He found him in his attic, lying on his back asleep. From the neighbouring room a woman tiptoed out. Mademoiselle Vatnaz.

She took Frédéric on one side and told him how Dussardier had been wounded.

On Saturday, from the top of the barricade in the Rue Lafayette, a boy, wrapped in a *tricolore*, was shouting to the National Guard: 'Will you fire on your brothers?' As they advanced, Dussardier had thrown his gun on the ground, got the others out of the way, jumped on to the barricade, and with one kick had brought down the insurgent, tearing the flag off him. He had been discovered under the debris, pierced in the thigh by a length of copper. They had to cut round the wound and remove the projectile. Mademoiselle Vatnaz had arrived that same evening and since then had not left his side.

She skilfully prepared all that he needed in the way of bandages, helped him drink, anticipated his slightest wish, came and went, light as a fairy, casting loving glances in his direction.

For two weeks Frédéric came back to see him every morning. One day when he mentioned La Vatnaz's devotion, Dussardier shrugged:

'Oh no, it's self-interest!'

'D'you think so?'

'I'm sure of it,' he replied, offering no further explanation.

She showered him with attentions, even bringing him the newspapers in which his brave conduct was commended. This praise seemed to embarrass him. He even admitted to Frédéric that his conscience was not clear.

Perhaps he ought to have gone over to the other side and joined the working people; for it must be said they had been promised a whole lot of things which had not been delivered. Their conquerors hated the Republic, and had been extremely hard on them. They were wrong, no doubt, but not entirely. And the young man was tormented by the idea that he might have been fighting against justice.

Sénécal, imprisoned in the Tuileries beneath the terrace on the riverbank, had none of these worries.

They were there, nine hundred men piled up pell-mell in filth, blackened by gunpowder and congealed blood, shivering with fever and shouting in anger. And the ones who had died were not removed from the rest. Sometimes there was the sudden report of a rifle and they thought they were all going to be shot. Then they rushed to the wall, and fell back again, so numbed with pain, they seemed to be living in some nightmare, in a dreadful hallucination. The lamp hanging from the ceiling looked like a bloodstain. And small green and yellow flames darted around, produced by the vapours from the cellar. Fearing an epidemic, a commission of enquiry was appointed. At the very first steps the chairman jumped back, appalled at the stench of excrement and corpses. When the prisoners approached the grating, the National Guards who were on duty there to stop them shaking the bars, shoved their bayonets at random into the mass.

They were mostly without mercy. Those who had not been fighting now wanted to make their mark. It was an explosion of panic. They were taking revenge all at the same time on the newspapers, clubs, assemblies, doctrines, on everything which had enraged them for the last three months. And despite having won, equality (as if to punish its defenders and deride its enemies) manifested itself triumphantly as an equality of brute beasts, a common level of bloody crimes; for the fanaticism of the rich balanced out the frenzy of the needy, the aristocracy was as furious as the rabble, and the cotton nightcap was just as hideous as the red bonnet. Public reason was as shaken as after a huge natural catastrophe. Intelligent people lost their sanity for the rest of their lives.

Père Roque had grown very daring, almost foolhardy. He had arrived in Paris on the twenty-sixth with the company from Nogent but instead of going home with them he had joined the National Guard, which was encamped in the Tuileries. And he was very happy to be placed on sentry duty outside on the river terrace. At least there he had the rogues under his watchful eye! He rejoiced in their defeat, their abjection, and could not stop himself insulting them.

One of them, an adolescent with long blond hair, put his face up to the bars to ask for bread. Monsieur Roque commanded him to be quiet. But the young man repeated in a pitiful voice:

'Bread!'

'Why should I have any!'

Other prisoners appeared at the grating, with their bristling beards and their eyes blazing, all pushing and screaming:

'Bread!'

Père Roque was angry at seeing his authority flouted. To frighten them he aimed his musket at them and the young man, carried up to the ceiling by the throng of people suffocating him, threw back his head and shouted one more time:

'Bread!'

'Here's some bread for you!' said Père Roque, firing his gun.

There was a terrible wail, then silence. Something white was left on the edge of the grating.*

After that Monsieur Roque went home, for he owned a house in the Rue Saint-Martin and had kept a room there. The damage caused by the rioting to the frontage of his building had played no small part in making him angry. It seemed to him when he saw it again that he had made too much of this damage. His action just now soothed him, as though he had been compensated.

It was his own daughter who opened the door. She said immediately that she had been worried by his long absence. She'd feared something had happened, that he'd been wounded.

This proof of filial affection won his heart. Her father was surprised she had travelled there without Catherine.

'I sent her off to do something for me,' said Louise.

And she asked after his health, and this and that. Then in an indifferent tone of voice she asked if he had happened to see Frédéric.

'No. Not at all.'

It was for him and only him that she had made the trip.

There were footsteps in the corridor.

'Oh, excuse me!'

And she disappeared.

Catherine had not found Frédéric. He had been away for some days and his close friend Monsieur Deslauriers now lived in the provinces.

Louise appeared again, trembling, unable to speak. She leaned against the furniture.

'What's wrong? What's the matter?' her father exclaimed.

She gestured that it was nothing, and recovered herself with a great effort of will.

The caterer opposite brought the soup. But Père Roque had suffered a violent upset. 'It wouldn't go down.' And at dessert he had a sort of fainting fit. A doctor was hurriedly sent for and he prescribed some medicine. Then when he was in bed, Monsieur Roque demanded as many blankets as possible to bring out the fever. He sighed, he groaned.

'Thank you, dear Catherine! Give your old father a kiss, my pet! Oh, these revolutions!'

And as his daughter was scolding him for having made himself ill on her account he replied:

'Yes, you are right. But it's stronger than me. I am too sensitive!'


## II


MADAME DAMBREUSE was sitting in her boudoir between her niece and Miss Johnson, listening to Monsieur Roque recounting his hardships in the military.

She bit her lips, and seemed to be in pain.

'Oh, it's nothing. It will pass.'

And graciously:

'We shall be having one of your acquaintances to dinner— Monsieur Moreau.'

Louise shuddered.

'And then only a few close friends, Alfred de Cisy, amongst others.'

And she praised his manners, his looks, and especially his behaviour.

Madame Dambreuse was not being as hypocritical as she supposed. The viscount was very anxious to get married. He had said as much to Martinon, adding that he was sure Mademoiselle Cécile would find him attractive and that her parents would accept him.

To dare to confide in him like that, Cisy must have some inside information about the dowry. Now Martinon suspected Cécile of being the illegitimate daughter of Monsieur Dambreuse and it would probably have been a clever move to take a chance and ask for her hand himself. But such boldness was not without its dangers; so Martinon until now had been careful not to compromise himself. Besides, he didn't know how to get rid of her aunt. Cisy's words decided him. And he had put his request to the banker, who, not seeing any obstacle to the marriage, had just informed Madame Dambreuse.

Cisy appeared. She got up, saying:

'I thought you'd forgotten us... Cécile, *shake hands*.'

At that moment Frédéric arrived.

'Oh, at last! There you are!' Père Roque cried. 'I've called on you three times this week with Louise!'

Frédéric had taken care to avoid them. He said he had spent every day with a wounded comrade. For a long time, moreover, he had been greatly taken up. He endeavoured to invent excuses. Luckily the guests arrived. First, Monsieur Paul de Gremonville, the diplomat he had seen at the ball. Then Fumichon, the industrialist whose loyalty to the conservative cause had scandalized him one evening. The old Duchesse de Montreuil–Nantua followed them.

But two voices were raised in the hall.

'I'm certain of it,' said one.

'My dear lady! My dear lady!' replied the other. 'Calm down, I beg you!'

It was Monsieur de Nonancourt, an old dandy, looking like a mummy in cold cream, and Madame de Larsillois, the wife of a prefect of Louis-Philippe. She was trembling all over, for she had just heard a polka played on a barrel organ, a signal between the insurgents. Many among the bourgeoisie imagined such things. It was thought that men in the catacombs were going to blow up the Faubourg Saint-Germain; strange noises had been heard from the cellars and suspicious goings-on at the windows had been observed.

However, everyone did their best to calm Madame de Larsillois. Order was restored. There was nothing to fear any more. 'Cavaignac has saved us!' As though the horrors of the revolt had not been enough, they were being exaggerated. There had been no fewer than twenty-three thousand convicts on the side of the socialists!

They were positive that the food was being poisoned, that Mobile Guards had been sawn in half between two pieces of wood, that flags had borne incitement to arson and pillage.

'And that's not all,' hinted the former prefect's wife.

'Oh, my dear!' Madame Dambreuse exclaimed with a discreet glance at the three young ladies.

Monsieur Dambreuse emerged with Martinon from the adjoining room. She turned her head and responded to Pellerin's greeting as he came over. The artist was studying the walls uneasily. The banker took him on one side and gave him to understand that he had found it necessary to hide his revolutionary canvas for the time being.

'Of course!' Pellerin replied, his failure at the Club de l'Intelligence having somewhat modified his opinions.

Monsieur Dambreuse added politely that he would of course commission more paintings from him.

'Oh, excuse me!... My dear friend, how lovely to see you.'

Arnoux and Madame Arnoux came face to face with Frédéric.

He felt dizzy. Rosanette had got on his nerves the whole afternoon with her admiration for the soldiers. His old love awoke in him.

The butler came to announce to Madame Dambreuse that dinner was served. With one look she commanded the viscount to take Cécile's arm, saying in an undertone to Martinon: 'Scoundrel!' and they went through into the dining room.

Under the green leaves of a pineapple in the centre of the table was a sea bream, with its mouth pointing to a haunch of venison and its tail touching a pile of crayfish. Figs and enormous cherries, pears, and grapes (the early produce from the hothouses of Paris) were piled up in pyramids in baskets of old Dresden china. Sprays of flowers at intervals alternated with bright silverware. The blinds of white silk drawn down in front of the windows filled the apartment with a soft light. The air was cooled by two fountains in which there were cubes of ice. And tall servants in knee breeches were serving the guests. All of this seemed even better after the turmoil of the preceding days. The enjoyment of the things that they had worried about losing was restored to them. Nonancourt expressed the feeling of the whole party when he said:

'Ah, let us hope that our Republican friends will allow us to have dinner!'

'In spite of their fraternity!' Père Roque quipped.

These two worthy men were on the right and left of Madame Dambreuse. Opposite her sat her husband, between Madame de Larsillois—she had the diplomat next to her—and the old duchess, who rubbed shoulders with Fumichon.

Then came the painter, the porcelain manufacturer, and Mademoiselle Louise. And thanks to Martinon, who had exchanged places with him in order to sit next to Cécile, Frédéric found himself beside Madame Arnoux.

She was wearing a black silk dress, a gold bracelet round her wrist and, like the first time he had dined at her house, something red in her hair, a sprig of fuchsia entwined in her chignon. He could not help saying to her:

'We haven't seen each other for a long time.'

'No!' she replied coldly.

He went on, with a gentleness in his voice which softened the impertinence of his question:

'Have you thought of me sometimes?'

'Why should I think of you?'

Frédéric was hurt by these words.

'Perhaps you are right after all.'

But quickly repenting of it, he swore he had not spent one single day without being ravaged by the memory of her.

'I don't believe a word of it, Monsieur.'

'And yet you know I love you.'

Madame Arnoux was silent.

'You know I love you.'

She was still silent.

'Well, go to the devil,' he thought.

And, looking up he saw Mademoiselle Roque at the other end of the table.

She had thought she would look nice dressed all in green, a colour that clashed crudely with her red hair. The buckle on her belt was too high, her little collar was too tight; this lack of elegance had no doubt contributed to Frédéric's cool greeting. She was observing him curiously from a distance. And Arnoux sitting next to her was being very gallant, but in vain, for he could not get a word out of her, so he gave up trying to be charming and listened to the conversation. The subject now was the pineapple purées at the Luxembourg.*

According to Fumichon, Louis Blanc owned a mansion in the Rue Saint-Dominique and refused to rent it out to workers.

'What I find bizarre,' said Nonancourt, 'is Ledru-Rollin hunting in the Royal estates!'

'He owes twenty thousand francs to a goldsmith!' Cisy added. 'And they are even saying . . .'

Madame Dambreuse interrupted him.

'Oh, how boring it is to get worked up about politics! A young man like you, for goodness' sake! Why not look after your neighbour and talk to her instead!'

After that the serious conversation turned to newspapers.

Arnoux defended them. Frédéric got involved, calling them commercial enterprises like any other. Their journalists in general were fools or jokers. He pretended he knew them and attacked Arnoux's generous sentiments with sarcastic remarks. Madame Arnoux did not notice that he was taking his revenge on her.

Meanwhile the viscount was racking his brains how to win Mademoiselle Cécile. First he displayed his artistic taste by criticizing the shape of the carafes and the chasing on the knives. Then he talked about his stables, his tailor, and his shirtmaker. Finally he got on to the subject of religion and found a way of giving her to understand that he fulfilled all his pious duties.

Martinon was doing better. Keeping up a steady flow of talk and, with his eyes constantly on her, he praised her bird-like profile, her faded blonde hair, her stubby hands. The unattractive girl revelled in the shower of compliments.

Nothing of this could be heard, since everyone was talking loudly. Monsieur Roque wanted France to be ruled 'by an iron hand'. Nonancourt was even sorry that the scaffold had been abolished for political crimes. They should have killed all those rogues en masse!

'In fact, they are cowards,' said Fumichon. 'I can't see anything brave about sheltering behind a barricade.'

'Apropos, let's talk about Dussardier,' Monsieur Dambreuse said, turning to Frédéric.

The brave shop assistant was now a hero, like Sallesse, the brothers Jeanson, the Péquillet woman,* and the rest.

Frédéric was glad to recount what had happened to his friend. He basked in his reflected glory.

They began to relate, quite naturally, different manifestations of bravery. It was not difficult to face death, according to the diplomat; witness men who fought duels.

'We can ask the viscount,' said Martinon.

The viscount blushed red.

The guests looked at him. And Louise, more surprised than the others, murmured:

'What is that about?'

'He funked a duel with Frédéric,' whispered Arnoux.

'Do you know about this, Mademoiselle?' Nonancourt asked instantly. He passed on her answer to Madame Dambreuse, who, leaning forward a little, began to stare at Frédéric.

Martinon did not wait for Cécile to question him. He told her that this affair concerned someone of unspeakable morals. The girl drew back slightly on her chair as if to escape contact with this immoral person.

The conversation had begun again. The fine Bordeaux wines were circulating, people were becoming more animated. Pellerin bore a grudge against the Revolution because of the total destruction of the Spanish museum. Since he was a painter, that was what distressed him most... When he said this, Monsieur Roque questioned him.

'Would you be the creator of a very remarkable painting?'

'Possibly! Which?'

'It depicts a lady... rather scantily clad... with a purse and a peacock behind her.'

It was Frédéric's turn to go red. Pellerin pretended not to have heard.

'Nevertheless it's by you! For it has your name at the bottom and a line on the frame says it's the property of Monsieur Moreau.'

One day when Père Roque and his daughter were waiting for Frédéric at his house, they had noticed the portrait of the Maréchale. Monsieur Roque had even supposed it to be 'a Gothic work'.

'No!' replied Pellerin, cruelly. 'It's the portrait of a woman.'

Martinon added:

'Of a woman who is very much alive, isn't that the case, Cisy?'

'Ah? I don't know anything about it!'

'I thought you knew her. But if I have spoken out of turn, please forgive me!'

Cisy lowered his eyes, proving by his embarrassment that he must have played a sorry part in the affair of the portrait. As for Frédéric, the model could only be his mistress. That was one of the conclusions that everyone jumped to straight away, and the faces of the gathering clearly showed this.

'How he lied to me!' Madame Arnoux said to herself.

'So that's the reason he went off and left me!' Louise thought.

Frédéric imagined that these two stories could compromise him and when they were in the garden he expressed his anger to Martinon.

Mademoiselle's Cécile's lover laughed in his face.

'Oh no, you are quite wrong. It will stand you in good stead! Onward!'

What did he mean? Anyway, why this unaccustomed benevolence? Without any explanation Martinon went to the end of the garden where the ladies were sitting. The men were standing and Pellerin in their midst was throwing out one idea after another. The best thing for the arts was a monarchy of course. Modern times disgusted him, 'the National Guard itself being reason enough'. He looked back with regret to the Middle Ages, Louis XIV. Monsieur Roque congratulated him on his opinions, even admitting that they dispelled all his prejudices about artists. But almost immediately he went away, attracted by Fumichon's voice. Arnoux tried to say that there were two socialisms, a good one and a bad. The industrialist couldn't see any diffference, his head spinning with rage at the word 'property'.

'It's a right consecrated by nature! Toys are important to children. All peoples share my opinion and all animals too! Even the lion, if he could talk, would declare himself to be a landowner.* Thus, Messieurs, I began with fifteen thousand francs' capital! For thirty years, you know, I got up regularly at four in the morning. I had the devil of a job making my fortune! And now they come and maintain I am not the master of it, that my money is not my money. In other words, property is theft!'

'But Proudhon...'

'Don't give me Proudhon! If he were here I think I'd strangle him.'

And he would have, too. After the liqueurs especially, Fumichon did not know what he was doing. And his apoplectic face was near to exploding like a shell.

'Hello, Arnoux,' said Hussonnet, walking briskly across the grass.

He was bringing the front page of a brochure called *The Hydra* for Monsieur Dambreuse to see, for the bohemian was now the mouthpiece of a reactionary club, and the banker introduced him as such to his hosts.

Hussonnet entertained them, maintaining first that the candlemakers were paying three hundred and ninety-two urchins to shout 'Light up!' every evening, then making a joke about the principles of '89, the emancipation of the Negroes, the orators of the Left. He even went so far as to act out *Prudhomme on the Barricade*,* perhaps out of a naive jealousy of these bourgeois who had just enjoyed a very good dinner. The joke did not go down very well. Their faces grew longer.

In any case it was no time for joking. Nonancourt said as much, reminding them of the death of Monseigneur Affre and that of General Bréa. They were always cited in arguments. Monsieur Roque called the death of the archbishop 'sublime beyond words'. Fumichon gave the military man the greater honour, and instead of simply deploring these two murders, they argued over which should arouse the stronger indignation. A second parallel followed, Lamoricière and de Cavaignac, Monsieur Dambreuse extolling Cavaignac and Nonancourt Lamoricière. Nobody in the gathering, apart from Arnoux, had been able to see these two at work. Nevertheless they all delivered final judgements on their actions. Frédéric declined to discuss it, admitting that he had not taken part in the fighting. The diplomat and Monsieur Dambreuse gave him an approving nod. For those who had fought against the mob had in fact defended the Republic. The result, though favourable, made it stronger and now they were rid of the conquered, they wished to be rid of the conquerors as well.

Hardly had she reached the garden when Madame Dambreuse, taking Cisy aside, upbraided him for his ineptness. At the sight of Martinon, she dismissed him, then tried to discover from her future nephew the reason for his jokes about the viscount.

'No reason.'

'And all that as if it were for the glory of Monsieur Moreau! What was your aim?'

'No aim. Frédéric is a charming boy. I'm very fond of him.'

'So am I. I'd like a word with him. Go and get him!'

After two or three banal remarks, she began denigrating her guests slightly, which placed him in a superior position. He made sure of running down the other women a little, which was a clever way of complimenting her. But now and then she left him, it was her soirée and ladies were arriving. Then she returned to where she had been sitting and the way the chairs happened to be set out allowed their conversation not to be overheard.

She was by turns gay, serious, melancholic, and thoughtful. Current affairs did not greatly interest her. There was a whole order of feelings that were less ephemeral. She complained about poets who distort the truth, then raised her eyes to the sky, asking him the name of a star.

Two or three Chinese lanterns had been hung in the trees. The wind blew them, coloured stripes flickered over her white dress. As usual she was sitting a little back in her chair, with a stool in front of her; you could see the toe of a black satin slipper. And Madame Dambreuse at intervals raised her voice and even sometimes laughed out loud.

These coquettish ways did not impress Martinon, who was busy with Cécile. But they were observed by Louise Roque, who was chatting to Madame Arnoux. She was the only one of the women who did not seem to her snobbish. She had come to sit next to her; then, giving in to a need for confidences:

'Monsieur Moreau talks very well, don't you think?'

'Do you know him?'

'Yes, very well. We are neighbours, he used to play with me when I was little.'

Madame Arnoux gave her a meaningful look which said: 'I suppose you are not in love with him?'

The girl's untroubled look was plain: 'Oh yes, I am!'

'Then do you see him frequently?'

'Oh no, only when he comes to see his mother. He hasn't been for ten months. But he did promise to come before.'

'One mustn't put too much faith in men's promises, my dear.'

'But he hasn't deceived me!'

'He's deceived others.'

Louise shivered: 'Had he by any chance made a promise to her as well?' Her face was taut with mistrust and hatred.

Madame Arnoux was almost afraid of her. She would have liked to take back her words. They both fell silent.

As Frédéric was sitting opposite on a folding chair, they looked at him, one modestly from the corner of her eye, the other frankly open-mouthed, so that Madame Dambreuse was minded to say to him:

'Turn round so that she can see you!'

'Who?'

'Monsieur Roque's daughter of course!'

And she teased him about the love of this girl from the provinces. He protested, forcing a laugh.

'You are joking! I ask you, a plain little thing like that!'

But he was enjoying a huge boost to his vanity. He was remembering his humiliation of that other evening, when he had left, and gave a profound sigh of relief. He felt quite at home in this society as though all of it, including the Dambreuse household, belonged to him. The ladies clustered round to listen to him. And in order to shine he pronounced himself in favour of the re-establishment of divorce,* which ought to be made so easy that couples could leave each other and take each other back again whenever they liked. They exclaimed in astonishment; others whispered; faint voices could be heard in the shadow, at the bottom of a wall covered with creeper. It was like the clucking of happy hens. And he developed his theory, with the confidence that springs from the knowledge of success. A servant brought a tray loaded with ices into the arbour. The gentlemen came across. They were discussing the arrests.

At that point Frédéric took his revenge on the viscount by giving him to understand that perhaps they would arrest him as a Legitimist. Cisy objected that he had not moved from his rooms; his adversary piled up the bad things that might befall him. Messieurs Dambreuse and de Gremonville were enjoying themselves. Then they congratulated Frédéric, at the same time regretting that he was not using his gifts for the defence of law and order. But their handshakes were cordial; henceforth he could count on them. In the end, as everyone was leaving, the viscount made a deep bow to Cécile.

'Mademoiselle, I have the great honour of wishing you good evening.'

She replied curtly:

'Good evening,' and threw Martinon a smile.

Père Roque, with the idea of continuing his discussion with Arnoux, suggested accompanying him 'and Madame' to their home, since they were going the same way. Louise and Frédéric were walking in front. She had taken hold of his arm and when she was a little way away from the others:

'Oh, finally! I've suffered enough all evening. How spiteful those women are! What snobs!'

He tried to defend them.

'In the first place, you could have come to talk to me when you arrived, you haven't been home for twelve months.'

'It hasn't been twelve,' Frédéric said, happy to pick her up on this point in order to avoid the rest.

'Well, all right. But it seemed a long time to me. And throughout that dreadful dinner anyone would have thought you were ashamed of me. Oh, I understand, I don't have what it takes to please a man, as they do.'

'You are wrong,' said Frédéric.

'Truly? Swear to me you don't love any of them.'

He swore.

'And it's only me you love?'

'Of course!'

This reassurance made her merry. She would have liked them to lose their way in the streets and walk the whole night long.

'It was a torture for me at home. They talked about barricades the entire time. I saw you falling to the ground, covered in blood. Your mother was in bed with her rheumatism. She didn't know anything about it, I had to keep quiet! I couldn't bear it any longer. So then I took Catherine and left.'

And she recounted her departure, her journey, and how she had lied to her father.

'He's taking me back in two days' time. Come tomorrow evening, just drop in casually and use the occasion to ask him for my hand in marriage.'

The idea of marriage had never been further from Frédéric's mind. In any case Mademoiselle Roque seemed to him a rather silly little girl. What a difference there was between her and a woman like Madame Dambreuse! He had a very different future ahead of him! He was sure of it now; so it was not the moment to engage himself, on a sentimental impulse, in a decision of such importance. He had to be realistic now, and anyway he had seen Madame Arnoux again. Yet Louise's frankness embarrassed him. He replied:

'Have you really thought about what this would involve?'

'What!' she cried, frozen with surprise and indignation.

He said that it would be folly to get married now.

'So you don't want me?'

'But you are not understanding what I'm saying!'

And he embarked on an extremely complicated string of explanations to persuade her that he was held up by important business, that he was overloaded with work, that even his fortune was in jeopardy (here Louise cut him short with a word) and, finally, that political circumstances were against it. So the most sensible thing would be to wait awhile. Things would no doubt work out; at least he hoped so. And as he searched in vain for more reasons, he pretended to remember suddenly that he should have been with Dussardier two hours ago.

Then, saying goodbye to the others, he disappeared down the Rue Hauteville, went round the Gymnase,* came back on the boulevard, and ran up the four flights of stairs to Rosanette.

Monsieur and Madame Arnoux left Père Roque and his daughter at the entrance to the Rue Saint-Denis. They went home silently; he, exhausted from his talking, and she, feeling a terrible weariness; she even leaned her head on his shoulder. He was the only man who had given proof of any honest feelings the whole evening. She felt very indulgent towards him. However, he was rather resentful towards Frédéric.

'Did you see his expression when they were talking about his portrait? When I told you he was her lover, you wouldn't believe me!'

'Oh yes, I was wrong!'

Arnoux, satisfied with his victory, carried on.

'I bet he left us just now to go and meet her! He's with her now, you bet! He's spending the night with her.'

Madame Arnoux pulled her hood down very low over her face.

'You are trembling!'

'That's because I'm cold,' she answered.

As soon as her father was asleep, Louise went in to Catherine's room and shook her by the shoulder:

'Get up... Quick! And go and get me a cab.'

Catherine told her there were none at that hour.

'Then you can take me there yourself!'

'Where?'

'To Frédéric's house.'

'I can't do such a thing. Why?'

It was to speak to him. She couldn't wait. She wanted to see him immediately.

'How can you think of it! To go and see someone like that in the middle of the night! In any case he'll be asleep now.'

'I'll wake him up!'

'It's not respectable for a young lady.'

'I'm not a young lady, I'm his wife! I love him! Come, put on your shawl.'

Catherine, standing by her bed, was thinking. At last she said:

'No, I won't!'

'Stay here then. I'm going!'

Louise slid downstairs like a snake. Catherine rushed after her, caught up with her on the pavement. Her objections were in vain; and she followed her, finishing knotting her camisole as she went. It seemed a very long way. She complained of her old legs.

'And I don't have anything to make me go, like you do!'

Then she softened.

'Poor little thing! You only have your Cathy, you see.'

She was beset by scruples from time to time.

'Oh, this is a fine thing you are making me do! Supposing your father woke up? My Lord, let's hope nothing dreadful happens!'

Outside the Théâtre des Variétés a patrol of the National Guard stopped them. Louise told them quick as a flash that she was going to the Rue Rumfort with her nurse to find a doctor. They let them through.

At the corner of the Madeleine they came across a second patrol, and Louise having given the same explanation, one of the citizens replied:

'Is it for a nine months' sickness, darling?'

'Gougibaud!' the captain exclaimed. 'No smutty remarks in the ranks! Pass, ladies!'

In spite of the reproof, the banter continued:

'Have a good time!'

'My compliments to the doctor!'

'Beware of the big bad wolf!'

'They like a joke,' Catherine remarked aloud. 'They are young.'

At last they arrived at Frédéric's house. Louise pulled hard at the bell, several times. The door opened halfway and the concierge replied to her enquiry:

'No!'

'But he must be in bed?'

'No I tell you! He's not slept at home for three months!'

And the little window on the lodge came down with a slam like a guillotine. They remained in the darkness under the arch. A furious voice shouted:

'Go away!'

The door opened again; they left.

Louise had to sit down on a milestone, and she wept copiously, her head in her hands, crying her heart out. Day dawned, carts passed.

Catherine took her home, supporting her, kissing her, giving her all sorts of good advice from her own experience. She mustn't get so fretted up about these young men. If this one let her down, she would find plenty of others.

# III

WHEN Rosanette's enthusiasm for the Mobile Guards had abated, she became more charming than ever and Frédéric gradually got used to living at her house.

The best part of the day was in the morning on the terrace. In a soft cotton gown and slippers on her bare feet she pottered to and fro around him, cleaned her canary cage, topped up the goldfish bowl, or did some gardening with a coal-shovel in the tub filled with earth, from which nasturtiums climbed up the trellis on the wall. Then, leaning on their balcony, together they watched the cabs and the passers-by, and they warmed themselves in the sun and made plans for the evening. He was never away for more than two hours. Then they took a box in the theatre. And Rosanette, with a big bunch of flowers in her hand, listened to the music, while Frédéric whispered funny remarks or sweet nothings in her ear. At other times they took a landau to the Bois de Boulogne. They stayed out a long time, until late into the night. Finally they came back via the Arc de Triomphe and the Grande Avenue, drinking in the air, with the stars up above and all the gaslights lined up as far as the eye could see, like a double row of shining pearls.

Frédéric always had to wait for her when they were going out. She would take her time placing the two ribbons of her hood around her chin and smile at her reflection in the mirror on the wardrobe. Then she would put her arm on his and, forcing him to look in the mirror next to her:

'We make a pretty pair like that, side by side! Oh, my poor darling, I could eat you!'

He was now her property, her possession. Because of that she had a constant radiance in her face, at the same time seeming more languorous in her manners, rounder in her curves. And without being able to say why, he thought she was somehow different.

One day she told him importantly that Monsieur Arnoux had just opened a drapery shop for a former employee in his factory. He went there every evening and 'spent a great deal on her—only the week before last he had given her a set of rosewood furniture'.

'How do you know that?' said Frédéric.

'Oh, I just know!'

Delphine, carrying out her wishes, had made some enquiries. She must like Arnoux a lot then to be so preoccupied with his doings! He made do with replying:

'What's that to you?'

Rosanette seemed surprised by this question.

'That scoundrel owes me money! It's disgusting to see him spending it on trollops!'

Then, with a triumphant expression of hatred:

'Anyway, she makes a fool of him. She's got three other men. Good for her. Let her drain him to the very last penny!'

It was true that Arnoux was letting himself be exploited by the girl from Bordeaux, whom he indulged, in the way of old men in love.

His factory had ceased all production. Altogether, his businesses were in a lamentable state, so much so that in order to make them viable again he first had the idea of establishing a café with singers who would only sing patriotic songs. If the minister gave him a grant, this establishment would become at one and the same time a centre of propaganda and a source of profit. The balance of power having shifted, he had to abandon this plan. Now he was thinking of a large military hatshop but lacked the funds to set it up.

He was no happier in his domestic situation. Madame Arnoux was not so nice to him as before, and was sometimes even frankly unsympathetic. Marthe always took her father's side. That increased the bad feeling and the house became intolerable. Often he left very early in the morning, spent the day doing one thing or another in order to tire himself out, then dined, alone with his thoughts, at night in a country tavern.

Frédéric's prolonged absence upset his usual routine. So Arnoux appeared one afternoon and begged him to come and visit as he used to, and Frédéric promised to do so.

He was afraid of going back to Madame Arnoux's. He felt he had betrayed her. But that was to behave like a coward. He had no excuse for staying away. One evening he decided to have done with it, and he set off.

As it was raining, he had just entered the Passage Jouffroy when, in the light of the shop windows, a fat little man in a cap stopped him. Frédéric immediately recognized Compain, the man who had made speeches and caused so much merriment with his motion at the club. He was leaning on the arm of an individual in a red zouave cap,* with a very long upper lip, a complexion yellow as an orange, and a short beard, who was contemplating him with wide eyes which glistened with admiration.

No doubt Compain was proud of him, for he said:

'May I introduce this chap! He's a bootmaker friend of mine, a patriot! Shall we have a drink?'

When Frédéric declined, he immediately started to sound off about the Rateau proposal,* a manoeuvre by the aristocracy. To put a stop to all that, you needed '93 all over again! Then he asked after Regimbart and a few others just as famous, like Masselin, Sanson, Lecornu, Maréchal, and that Deslauriers who had been compromised in the business with the carbines they had intercepted recently in Troyes.

This was all news to Frédéric. Compain knew no more than that. He left, saying:

'See you soon, because you are one of them, aren't you?'

'One of what?'

'The calf's head!'

'What calf's head?'

'Ha ha!' replied Compain, giving him a dig in the ribs.

And the two terrorists dived into a café.

Ten minutes later Frédéric had forgotten all about Deslauriers. He was on the pavement outside a house in the Rue Paradis, looking up at the glow of a lamp behind the curtains on the second floor.

At last he climbed the stairs.

'Is Arnoux there?'

The maidservant answered:

'No, but come in anyway.'

And opening the door abruptly:

'Madame, it's Monsieur Moreau!'

She rose, paler than her lace collar. She was trembling.

'To what do I owe the honour... of such an... unexpected visit?'

'Nothing! Just the pleasure of seeing old friends again.'

And, sitting down:

'How's my friend Arnoux?'

'He's very well. He's out.'

'Oh, I see. He still has his old habits in the evenings, then. A little relaxation.'

'Why not? After a day of working at figures, a man's brain needs a rest!'

She even praised her husband for his industry. This praise annoyed Frédéric. Then pointing to a piece of black fabric with blue braid which she had on her lap:

'What are you doing?'

'Altering a jacket for my daughter.'

'Speaking of whom, I don't see her around. Where is she?'

'In a boarding school.'

Her eyes filled with tears. She kept them back, pushing her needle to and fro rapidly. Affecting not to notice, he had taken up a copy of *L'Illustration* that was beside her on the table.

'These Cham* caricatures are very funny, don't you think?'

'Yes.'

Then they were silent again.

A sudden gust of wind shook the window pane.

'What awful weather!' said Frédéric.

'Yes, it's very good of you to come out in this dreadful rain.'

'Oh, rain doesn't bother me. I wouldn't let it put me off a rendezvous—though some would.'

'Who?' she asked innocently. 'What rendezvous?'

'Don't you remember?'

She shuddered and bowed her head.

He put his hand gently on her arm.

'You made me suffer a lot, I can tell you.'

There was a plaintive note in her voice:

'But I was afraid for my child!'

She told him about little Eugène's illness and all her anguish that day.

'Thank you, thank you, I believe you! I love you as much as ever!'

'Oh no, that's not true.'

'Why?'

She looked coldly at him.

'You are forgetting that other woman. The one you take to the races. The woman whose portrait you have, your mistress.'

'Well yes,' exclaimed Frédéric. 'I don't deny it. I am a poor wretch. Listen to me!'

If he had made her his mistress, it was through despair, like when you commit suicide. Anyway, he had made her very unhappy, to avenge himself for his own shame.

'What torture! Do you understand or not?'

Madame Arnoux turned her beautiful face to him and stretched out her hand. They closed their eyes, lulled in a mutual rapture that was delicious and complete. Then they remained in contemplation of one another, face to face, very close.

'How could you believe that I didn't love you any more?'

She replied in a low, very tender voice:

'No, in spite of everything, I felt in my heart of hearts that it was impossible and that one day the obstacles to our love would disappear.'

'So did I! And I nearly died of longing for you.'

'Once', she said, 'in the Palais-Royal I passed right by you!'

'Really?'

And he told her about his joy at finding her at the Dambreuses.

'But how I hated you that evening, when we left.'

'Poor boy!'

'My life is so miserable.'

'Mine too!... If it were only my sadness, worries, humiliations, all that I put up with as a wife and mother, I shouldn't complain, since we all have to die one day. But what is so dreadful is my loneliness, with nobody...'

'But now I am here!'

'Oh yes!'

A passionate sob had made her rise to her feet. Her arms were open. And, standing, they kissed, in a long embrace.

There was a creak on the wooden floor. A woman stood there—Rosanette. Madame Arnoux recognized her. Her eyes, open as wide as possible, looked at her, full of surprise and indignation. At last Rosanette said:

'I've come to speak to Monsieur Arnoux about some business.'

'He's not here, as you can see.'

'Ah, that's true,' said the Maréchale. 'Your servant was right! Many apologies!'

And turning to Frédéric:

'So you are here, darling?'

This intimacy in front of her was like a slap across the face. Madame Arnoux reddened.

'He's not here, I told you!'

Then the Maréchale, looking around, said calmly:

'Shall we go home? I've got a cab waiting.'

He pretended not to have heard.

'Come on!'

'Oh yes, it's a good opportunity, go, go!' said Madame Arnoux.

They went. She leaned over the banisters to take a last look at them. And a shrill, heart-rending laugh assailed them from the top of the stairs. Frédéric pushed Rosanette into the cab, sat opposite her but said not a word the entire journey.

He himself was the cause of the disgrace whose repercussions so angered him. He felt at one and the same time a crushing humiliation and regret for his lost happiness. Just when it was within his grasp at last it had gone for ever! And through the fault of this woman, this girl, this whore! He wanted to strangle her. He was choking with rage. When they got home he threw his hat on to a chair and tore off his tie.

'Oh, that was a fine thing you did there!'

She stood her ground, facing him.

'What of it? What's wrong with that?'

'What, are you spying on me?'

'Is that my fault? Why should you go and enjoy yourself with respectable women?'

'That's not the point. I won't have you insulting them!'

'How have I insulted her?'

He did not have an answer; but in a tone of increased hatred:

'The other day at the Champ-de-Mars...'

'Oh, don't go on about your old flames!'

'Bitch!'

He raised his fist.

'Don't kill me! I'm pregnant!'

Frédéric recoiled.

'You're lying!'

'Look at me!'

She took a torch, and lighting up her face:

'Do you know what this is?'

There were little yellow spots on her skin which was unusually bloated. Frédéric did not deny the obvious. He went and opened the window, paced up and down a little, then collapsed into a chair.

This was a calamity. First it meant he could not break off their relationship immediately—and beyond that, it ruined all his plans. Besides, the idea of becoming a father seemed grotesque, unthinkable. But why? If, instead of the Maréchale...? And he became so lost in his reverie that he had a kind of hallucination. On the rug in front of the fireplace he saw a little girl. She looked like Madame Arnoux, and a little like him; dark, with a pale face, black eyes, dark eyebrows, a red ribbon in her curly hair. (Oh, how he would have loved her!) And he thought he heard her voice: 'Papa! Papa!'

Rosanette, who had just undressed, drew near to him, saw a tear in his eye, and kissed him gravely on his forehead. He got up saying:

'Well, we shan't get rid of it!'

Then she started chattering. Of course it would be a boy! They would call him Frédéric. They had to begin getting together some clothes for him. And when he saw that she was so happy he took pity on her. As he felt no more anger now, he wanted to know the reason for what she had done earlier.

It was because Mademoiselle Vatnaz had sent her that very day a bill that was overdue and she had hurried to Arnoux's house to ask him for money.

'I would have given you some,' said Frédéric.

'It was easier to get from him what belonged to me, and to pay her the thousand francs.'

'Is that really all that you owe her?'

She answered:

'Certainly!'

The next day at nine in the evening (the time the porter suggested) Frédéric went to see Mademoiselle Vatnaz.

In the hall he stumbled against all the furniture lying around but he was guided by the sound of voices and music. He opened a door and found himself in the middle of a party. Standing in front of the piano played by a girl wearing spectacles, Delmar, solemn as a pope, was reciting humanitarian verses about prostitution. And his deep voice reverberated round the room, accompanied by emphatic chords. A row of women sat against the wall, dressed for the most part in dark colours without collars or cuffs. Five or six men, all intellectuals, were sitting around on chairs. In one armchair sat a former fabulist, a wreck of a man. The acrid smell of two lamps mingled with the aroma of chocolate in bowls that were crowding the card table.

Mademoiselle Vatnaz, an oriental sash around her hips, was standing in the corner by the mantelpiece. Dussardier was on the other side opposite her. He looked a little uncomfortable about where he was. In any case this artistic milieu overawed him.

Had La Vatnaz broken with Delmar? Perhaps not. Yet she seemed possessive of the worthy shop assistant. And when Frédéric had asked to have a word with her, she indicated that Dussardier should go into her room with them. When the thousand francs were counted out, she demanded interest as well.

'Don't bother about that,' said Dussardier.

'You be quiet!'

Frédéric found this cowardice pleasing in such a brave man, a justification for his own. He took the receipt home and never spoke of the debacle at Madame Arnoux's again. But from then on he noticed all the Maréchale's little faults.

She had bad taste, about which nothing could be done; a laziness he found incomprehensible; a crass ignorance, which even extended to thinking Doctor Des Rogis was very famous. And she was very proud to entertain him and his wife because they were 'a married couple'. She ruled like a tyrant over the life of Mademoiselle Irma, a poor creature endowed with a little voice, who had a 'very nice gentleman' as her protector, an ex-employee in customs and very good at card tricks. Rosanette called him 'mon gros loulou'. Frédéric couldn't bear her repeating stupid expressions either, like 'Never in a month of Sundays!', 'I'll be glad to see the back of him!', 'Who'd have thought?', and so on. And she insisted on dusting her trinkets every morning with a pair of old white gloves. He was disgusted by her behaviour towards the maid, whose wages were constantly in arrears and who even lent her money. The days when they did their accounts they squabbled like two fishwives, then made it up with a kiss. Being on his own with Rosanette became rather depressing. It was a relief to him when Madame Dambreuse's parties began again.

At least she was entertaining! She knew all the scandal, the changes among the ambassadors, the personnel in the fashion houses. And if she made a few commonplace remarks, they were said in such a way that it was hard to tell if her banalities were respectful or ironic. She was at her best with a score of people talking all around her;

she left nobody out, elicited the answers she wanted, forestalled the dangerous ones. In her mouth the simplest anecdotes seemed like confidences. Her slightest smile was enchanting. Her charm, like the exquisite scent she normally wore, was subtle and indefinable. In her company Frédéric experienced the pleasure of discovery every time, whilst finding in her always the same serenity, like the reflections in a pool of clear water. But why was she so cold towards her niece? At times she threw her some very odd glances.

As soon as the question of marriage came up she had raised the issue of the 'dear girl's health' with Monsieur Dambreuse and had carried her off at once to the baths in Balaruc. When she came back she invented other excuses. The young man did not have a good position, this love did not seem very serious, it would be better to wait. Martinon replied that he would wait. His conduct was irreproachable. He sang Frédéric's praises. He did more: he told him how to please Madame Dambreuse, even suggesting that he knew the feelings of the aunt thanks to her niece.

As for Monsieur Dambreuse, far from being jealous, he showered his young friend with attentions, consulted him about various matters, worried about his future, so much so that one day when they were talking about Père Roque, he whispered meaningfully in his ear:

'You did the right thing there.'

And among Cécile, Miss Johnson, the servants, the porter, there was not one who was not charming to him in this house. He went there every night, abandoning Rosanette. Her future maternity made her more serious, even a little gloomy, as though she were tormented by worries. She replied to all his questions:

'You're wrong. I am doing very well!'

It was five bills, not one, that she had signed before, and, not daring to confess it to Frédéric after the first had been paid, she had gone back to Arnoux who had promised her in writing a third of his profits from lighting up the towns of Languedoc with gaslight—a magnificent enterprise!—but he advised her not to make use of the letter until the shareholders met. This meeting was postponed from one week to the next.

In the meantime the Maréchale needed money. She would have died rather than ask Frédéric for it. She didn't want any of his. It would have spoiled their love. He contributed generously to the household costs, but a small carriage rented by the month, and other indispensable sacrifices since he had become a regular visitor at the Dambreuses, meant he could not give his mistress any more. Two or three times when he came back at an unaccustomed hour he fancied he saw men's backs vanishing through doorways. And often she went out without saying where she was going. Frédéric did not dig any deeper. One of these days he would take a stand. He dreamed of another life which would be more noble, more amusing. This ideal made him indulgent towards the Dambreuse household.

It was a sort of annexe of the Rue de Poitiers.* There he met the great M. A., the illustrious B., the profound P., the eloquent Z., the wonderful Y., the old stagers of the Centre Left, the paladins of the Right, the veterans of the *juste milieu*, the eternal jokers of the political scene. He was taken aback by their terrible language, their small-mindedness, their spitefulness, their bad faith; all those people who had voted for the Constitution were now doing their best to ruin it. And they busied themselves a great deal with launching manifestos, pamphlets, biographies; Hussonnet's *Fumichon* was a masterpiece. Nonancourt busied himself with propaganda in the countryside, Monsieur de Gremonville worked for the clergy, Martinon rallied the young men of the bourgeoisie. Each contributed, according to his means, even Cisy himself. His mind nowadays was on serious matters the whole day long and he ran errands for the party in a cabriolet.

Monsieur Dambreuse, like a barometer, constantly recorded the party's latest variation. Nobody spoke of Lamartine without quoting what had been said by a man of the people: 'Enough poetry!' Cavaignac, in his view, was nothing but a traitor. The President,* whom he had admired for three months, began to fall in his estimation (he thought he did not possess 'the necessary energy'); and as he was always in need of a saviour, his gratitude since the business in the Conservatoire* belonged to Changarnier: 'Thank the Lord for Changarnier... Let's hope that Changarnier... Oh, there's nothing to fear as long as Changarnier...'

Monsieur Thiers was especially commended for his book against socialism in which he had proved himself to be as much philosopher as writer. They made enormous fun of Pierre Leroux who quoted passages from the Philosophes in the Chamber. They made jokes about the Phalansterian tail.* They went to applaud *La Foire aux idées** and they compared the authors to Aristophanes. Frédéric, like everyone else, went to see the play.

The political verbiage and the good food dulled his sense of moral-
ity. Although he thought these people mediocre, he was proud to
know them and inwardly hoped for their bourgeois approval. If he
had a mistress like Madame Dambreuse he would be well placed.

He set about doing what was necessary.

He put himself in her path when she took a walk, always made
sure of going to greet her in her box at the theatre; and knowing
what time she went to church, he stationed himself in melancholy
pose behind a pillar. There was a constant exchange of little mes-
sages about curios, about concerts, and much borrowing of books or
magazines. Apart from his evening visit he sometimes went to pay her
another at the end of the day; and his pleasure gradually increased as
he passed through first the front door, then the courtyard, the hall,
the two sitting rooms, and finally arrived in her boudoir, discreet as
the tomb, warm as a bedchamber, where visitors bumped into the
padded sides of furniture amongst all sorts of objects ranged around:
chests of drawers, screens, bowls and trays in lacquer, tortoiseshell,
ivory and malachite, costly trifles which she frequently replaced.
There were also simple things: three pebbles from Étretat which
she used as a paperweight, a Frisian bonnet hanging from a Chinese
sunshade. But all these articles looked well together, and the overall
impression was one of grandeur, perhaps because of the height of the
ceiling, the richness of the door hangings, and the long silk fringes
draped over the gilded legs on the stools.

She was almost always reclining on a small sofa, near the flower
stand which decorated the window recess. Sitting on the edge of
a large tuffet on castors, he paid her finely calculated compliments.
And she smiled at him, her head a little to one side.

He read her pages of poetry, putting all his soul into it, to move
her and to win her admiration. She would stop him with a critical
remark or a practical observation; and their conversation reverted
constantly to the eternal question of Love. They wondered what occasioned it, whether women felt it more than men, what were the differences between them on that subject. Frédéric tried to express
his opinion, avoiding both vulgarity and banality. It became a kind of
battle, pleasant at times and tedious at others.

He did not experience with her that rapture which transported him
to Madame Arnoux, nor the happy excitement he had felt at first with
Rosanette. But he coveted her as something unusual and challenging,

because she had class, because she was rich, because she was religious, imagining she had fine feelings as rare as her lace, with pious medals next to her skin and modest blushes in her lasciviousness.

He made use of his old love. He told her all he had felt for Madame Arnoux, his desires, his fears, his dreams—as though Madame Dambreuse inspired them. She listened, like someone who was used to hearing these things, not rebuffing him exactly but not yielding anything either. And he did not manage to seduce her any more than Martinon managed to marry her niece. To get rid of her niece's lover she accused him of wanting her money and even begged her husband to put him to the test. So Monsieur Dambreuse informed the young man that Cécile, being the orphan child of poor parents, had no hopes of inheritance and no dowry.

Martinon, thinking this couldn't be true, or too advanced in his courtship to pull out, answered wildly, in one of those stubborn and crazy impulses that turn out to be a master stroke, that his inheritance, fifteen thousand livres' income, would be enough for them both. This unforeseen disinterestedness moved the banker. He promised to obtain a post for him as tax inspector and to put up the caution money. And in May 1850, Martinon married Mademoiselle Cécile. There was no ball; the young couple left that very evening for Italy.

The next day Frédéric came to pay a visit to Madame Dambreuse. To him she looked paler than usual. She contradicted him about two or three unimportant matters. In any case, all men were selfish.

Yet there were some who were loyal—himself for instance.

'Oh yes, just like all the rest!'

Her eyelids were red. She was crying. Then, attempting a smile:

'Forgive me. It's wrong of me. I suddenly thought of something sad.'

He didn't understand her.

'It doesn't matter! She's not as strong as I supposed,' he thought.

She rang for a glass of water, drank a mouthful, sent it back again, and complained about the dreadful service. To amuse her, he offered to be her servant, claiming he could give out the plates, dust the furniture, announce guests, in fact be a valet or rather a footman, although they had gone out of fashion. He would have enjoyed riding behind on her carriage wearing a hat with a cockerel feather.

'And I would follow you proudly on foot, holding a lapdog in my arms.'

'You are very gay,' observed Madame Dambreuse.

'It's silly to be serious about everything in life, don't you think?'
said Frédéric. There was so much misery in the world, without adding to it. Nothing was worth breaking your heart over. Madame
Dambreuse raised her eyebrows, in vague approval.

This mutual feeling emboldened Frédéric. His earlier disappointments enabled him to see more clearly now.

'Our grandfathers knew how to live. Why not obey our impulses?'
Love, after all, was not as important as all that.

'But what you are saying is immoral!'

She had sat down on the sofa again. He sat on the edge, against
her feet.

'Can't you see I'm telling lies? To please women you have to display
the indifference of a clown or the ragings of a tragedian! They make
fun of us when we tell them quite simply that we love them. I think
those hyperbolic declarations they enjoy are a profanation of true
love. So one no longer knows how to say it, especially to those women
who are very intelligent.'

She gazed at him, with half-closed lids. He lowered his voice, leaning towards her face.

'Yes, you frighten me! Have I offended you?... I'm sorry!... I didn't
mean to say all that. It's not my fault. You are so beautiful!'

Madame Dambreuse closed her eyes and he was astonished at the
ease of his victory. The tall trees in the garden, which were rustling
softly, stood still. Motionless clouds streaked the sky with long red
trails, and it was as though the world had stopped. Then confused
memories of evenings like this one, with silences like this one, passed
through his mind. Wherever was it...?

He went down on his knees, took her hand, and vowed eternal love
to her. Then, as he was leaving, she beckoned him to come back and
whispered:

'Come back and have dinner. We shall be alone.'

It seemed to Frédéric as he went downstairs that he had become
another man, that the scented temperature of hothouses was surrounding him, that he was entering now for certain a higher world of
adulterous nobility and high intrigue. To reach the top, all he needed
was a woman like her. No doubt eager for power and action and
married to a mediocre man whom she had served magnificently,
she wanted someone strong to guide her? Nothing was impossible
now! He felt able to ride two hundred leagues on horseback, to work

several nights in a row without getting tired; his heart overflowed with pride.

On the pavement in front of him a man wearing an old overcoat was walking with such a look of exhaustion that Frédéric turned round to look at him. The man looked up. It was Deslauriers. He hesitated. Frédéric flung his arms round him.

'Oh, my dear friend! What, is it you?'

And he carried him off to his house, asking lots of questions all at once.

Ledru-Rollin's former commissioner told him first about the torments he had suffered. Since he preached brotherhood to the conservatives and respect for the law to the socialists the former had shot at him and the latter had brought a rope to hang him with. After the events of June he had been cruelly dismissed. He had thrown himself into a plot, the one connected with the weapons seized in Troyes. He had been released, for lack of evidence. Then the action committee had sent him to London, where he had come to blows with his colleagues in the middle of a banquet. Back in Paris...

'Why didn't you come and see me?'

'You were never there. Your concierge was very mysterious, I didn't know what to think. And I didn't want to come back in such a bad way.'

He had knocked at the doors of Democracy, offering himself to serve as its scribe, its speaker, its actions. Everywhere he had been repulsed. They were suspicious of him. And he had sold his watch, his books, his linen.

'It would be better to die with Sénécal on the prison-ships of Belle-Isle.'*

Frédéric was fixing his tie and did not seem very disturbed by the news.

'Oh, has our friend Sénécal been deported?'

Deslauriers replied, looking round the room enviously:

'Not everyone is as fortunate as you!'

'Forgive me,' said Frédéric, not noticing the allusion, 'but I am dining in town. They'll get you something to eat; order whatever you like and make use of my bed as well.'

In the face of this cordial generosity, Deslauriers's resentment disappeared.

'Your bed? But... I'll be in your way!'

'Oh no, I have others.'

'Aha! That's good,' the lawyer said with a laugh. 'Where are you having dinner then?'

'At Madame Dambreuse's house.'

'Would that be... by any chance...?'

'You are too curious,' Frédéric said with a smile that confirmed his suspicions.

Then having looked at the clock, he sat down again.

'That's how it is. And you mustn't despair, you, loyal defender of the people.'

'To hell with the people! Let others defend them for a change!'

The lawyer hated workers since he had suffered from them in his province, a coal-mining area. Each pit had appointed a provisional management of its own to give him orders.

'Their behaviour was charming everywhere, in Lyons, Lille, Le Havre, Paris. For like the manufacturers who want to exclude foreign goods, these gentlemen want the English, German, Belgian, and Savoyard workers expelled! As for their intelligence, what use were their famous guilds under the Restoration? In 1830 they joined the National Guard, without even having the good sense to control it! And the trade unions reappeared with their own flags the day after '48 was over! They even wanted their own representatives in the Chamber, who would have spoken only on their behalf, just like the deputies of beetroot who only care about beetroot!—Oh, I've had enough of those jokers, prostrating themselves in turn in front of Robespierre's scaffold, the Emperor's boots, Louis-Philippe's umbrella, the eternal scum, loyal to whoever stuffs their mouths with bread. People always shout about the venality of Talleyrand and Mirabeau, but the messenger down below would sell his country for fifty centimes if you promised to pay him three francs for every errand. Oh, what have we done? We ought to have set fire to the four corners of Europe!'

Frédéric answered:

'The spark was missing. You were only a lot of petits bourgeois and the best of you were pedants. As for the workers, they have a reason to complain; for, apart from a million subtracted from the Civil List, which you granted them with the most vile flattery, you have given them nothing but fine phrases. The wages book* remains in the hands of the employer, and the wage earner, even before the law, remains inferior to his master, since nobody believes a word he says. Anyway the Republic seems out of date to me. Who knows? Perhaps Progress is only able to be brought about by an aristocracy or by an individual? The initiative always comes from those on high. The people have not come of age yet, whatever you say.'

'You may be right,' said Deslauriers.

According to Frédéric most citizens only wanted peace and quiet (he had learnt this in the Dambreuse household) and it was the conservatives who had all the best chances. However, their party needed new faces.

'If you were to stand, I'm sure...'

He did not finish his sentence. Deslauriers understood, passed his hands over his forehead; then said abruptly:

'But what about you? Nothing's stopping you. Why shouldn't you be a deputy?'—Because of a double election, there was a vacancy in the Aube. Monsieur Dambreuse, re-elected to the Legislative Assembly, belonged to another district.* 'Would you like me to see what I can do?' He knew a lot of innkeepers, teachers, doctors, lawyers' clerks, and their employers. 'Anyway, you can make peasants believe whatever you like!'

Frédéric felt his ambitions revive.

Deslauriers added:

'You should find me a situation in Paris.'

'Oh, that won't be difficult, through Monsieur Dambreuse.'

'On the subject of coal,' the lawyer went on, 'what's become of his large company? That's the kind of work I need—and I would be useful to them, and still keep my independence.'

Frédéric promised they would go and see the banker within the next three days.

His meal alone with Madame Dambreuse was exquisite. She smiled at him across the table, over a basket of flowers, by the light of the hanging lamp. And as the window was open you could see the stars. They did not say very much, being undoubtedly a little mistrustful of themselves. But behind the servants' backs, they blew each other a kiss. He spoke of his idea of standing for election. She approved, and even promised to get Monsieur Dambreuse to work on it.

In the evening a few friends came to congratulate her and sympathize. She must be so sorry not to have her niece there any more!

But it was very good that the young couple had gone travelling. Later, things would be more difficult, children would come along. But Italy was not at all like the image one had of it. Still, they were in the age of illusions. And then the honeymoon put a shine on everything! The last two people to leave were Monsieur de Gremonville and Frédéric. The diplomat was reluctant to go. Finally at midnight he rose to leave. Madame Dambreuse made a sign to Frédéric that he should leave too and thanked him for his obedience with a squeeze of the hand, which was more delightful than all the rest.

The Maréchale gave a cry of joy when she saw him again. She had been waiting for him since five o'clock. He gave as his excuse some necessary business for Deslauriers. He wore a look of triumph, like a halo, which dazzled Rosanette.

'Perhaps it's because of your black tailcoat which suits you so well, but I think you have never looked so handsome! How handsome you are!'

In her transports of love she swore inwardly not to go with anyone else, whatever happened, even if she died in poverty!

Her pretty eyes glistened with such passion that Frédéric pulled her on to his lap, thinking: 'What a swine I am!', glorying in his own perversity.

## IV

WHEN Deslauriers came to see Monsieur Dambreuse, the latter was thinking of reviving his big coal business. But people were very critical of this merging of all the companies into one; they said it was a monopoly, as if, given such huge enterprises, a large capital were not essential!

Deslauriers, who had just read Gobet's book on purpose, as well as the articles by Monsieur Chappe* in the *Journal des mines*, was thoroughly familiar with the subject. He proved that the law of 1810 established that a licence holder had an inalienable right to the profits. Anyway, one could impart a democratic tone to the enterprise, by asserting that to forbid the coal mergers was an attack on the very principle of association.

Monsieur Dambreuse gave him some notes to draw up a memorandum. As to the manner in which his work would be paid, he made him some promises that were all the more generous for being vague.

Deslauriers came back to Frédéric's and told him about the discussion. And he had seen Madame Dambreuse at the bottom of the stairs when he was leaving.

'My congratulations there, old chap!'

Then they talked about the election. They had to devise a plan.

Three days later Deslauriers reappeared with a piece intended for the newspapers, a friendly letter in which Monsieur Dambreuse approved their friend's candidature. Proposed by a conservative and supported by a socialist, it ought to be successful. But how could a capitalist have signed such a document? The lawyer, without the slightest embarrassment, had shown it to Madame Dambreuse, who gave it her warm approval and had done whatever else was necessary.

This action took Frédéric by surprise. Yet he was glad of it; then, as Deslauriers was in touch with Monsieur Roque, he told him how he was placed vis-à-vis Louise.

'Tell them anything you like, that I've financial problems, that I'll sort them out. She can wait for me, she's young!'

Deslauriers left; and Frédéric thought he'd been very astute and decisive. At all events, he felt relief, a profound satisfaction. His joy at possessing a rich woman was unspoiled by any contrast. The feeling was in harmony with the milieu. Life now was universally sweet.

The most delightful thing perhaps was to observe Madame Dambreuse amongst a group of people in her salon. The propriety of her manners reminded him of other postures. While she was conversing in cool tones he recalled the words she had uttered in the throes of passion. All the respect for her virtue shown by others delighted him as if it were a homage to himself; and occasionally he wanted to shout: 'But I know her better than you! She belongs to me!'

Before long their liaison was something that was recognized and accepted. Madame Dambreuse drew Frédéric with her into society for the whole of that winter.

He almost invariably arrived before she did; and he saw her come in, arms bare, fan in hand, pearls in her hair. She stopped on the threshold—the door lintel framed her like a picture—and she hesitated a fraction, closing her eyes to see if he were there. She took him back in her carriage; the rain beat down on the windows. Passers-by flitted past through the mud like ghosts. And sitting close together they dimly noticed them, with a tranquil disdain. On various pretexts he remained another good hour in her room.

Madame Dambreuse had surrendered herself mainly out of boredom. But this last bid for love should not be wasted. She wanted a *grande passion*. She began showering him with flattery and caresses.

She sent him flowers; she made him a tapestry chair; she gave him a cigar case, a writing desk, a multitude of little items he could use everyday, so that, whenever he did anything, he would think of her. He found these gestures charming at first but soon began to take them for granted.

She would take a cab, send it back when she reached the entrance to a passage, and come out at the other end; then, stealing along the walls with a thick veil over her face, she would get to the road where Frédéric was waiting. He would take her arm briskly and conduct her into his house. His two servants would be out, the porter was away on an errand. She would glance around her. Nothing to fear! And she uttered a sigh like an exile who sees her native land again. Good luck made them bolder. Their meetings increased. And one night she even arrived suddenly in a ballgown. This sort of surprise could have been very risky; he scolded her for not being careful enough. In any case he didn't like the way she looked. Her décolletée showed her thin bosom too much.

He realized then what he had hidden from himself, the disillusionment of his senses. He nevertheless pretended to passionate feelings. But in order to feel them he had to conjure up images of Rosanette or Madame Arnoux.

This sentimental atrophy left his head completely clear, and it became more than ever his ambition to occupy a high position in society. Since he had a step up like this one, the least he could do was make use of it.

One morning towards the middle of January Sénécal came into Frédéric's study and, at his exclamation of surprise, replied that he was Deslauriers's secretary. He had brought a letter for him. It contained good news but scolded him for his negligence. He must go over and see him.

The future deputy said he would go the day after next.

Sénécal did not comment on his candidature. He talked about himself and the affairs of state.

Though they were in some ways lamentable, he was pleased about them, for things were going in the direction of communism. First, the Administration itself was tending that way, since every day there were more and more things under the control of the Government.

As to Property, the Constitution of '48, in spite of its weakness, had not favoured it. In the name of the public good, from now on the State could appropriate whatever it saw fit. Sénécal declared himself in favour of Authority; and Frédéric recognized in what he said the exaggeration of his very own words to Deslauriers. The Republican was even sounding forth about the inadequacy of the masses.

'Robespierre, by defending the right of the small number, brought Louis XVI in front of the National Convention and saved the people. The end justifies the means. Dictators are sometimes necessary. Long live tyranny, as long as the tyrant does good!'

Their discussion lasted a long time, and as he was leaving, Sénécal remarked (and that was perhaps the real reason for his visit) that Deslauriers was getting very impatient with Monsieur Dambreuse's silence.

But Monsieur Dambreuse was ill. Frédéric saw him every day, since, as a personal friend, he was a frequent visitor.

The dismissal of General Changarnier* had been extremely upsetting for the capitalist. That same evening he had a sharp burning sensation in his chest and a heaviness which meant he could not lie down. Leeches brought immediate relief. The dry cough disappeared, his breathing became more regular, and a week later he said, as he was swallowing some soup:

'Oh, that feels better! But I nearly made the ultimate journey!'

'Not without me!' cried Madame Dambreuse, implying in these words that she couldn't have survived him.

Instead of answering, he gave her and her lover a strange smile in which were resignation, indulgence, irony, and even a touch or hint of amusement.

Frédéric wanted to leave for Nogent, Madame Dambreuse did not want him to. And he unpacked and repacked his luggage, according to the vagaries of the illness.

Suddenly Monsieur Dambreuse was spitting a lot of blood. The 'princes of science' were consulted but did not have anything different to advise. His legs swelled, and he grew weaker. He had spoken several times of his wish to see Cécile who was at the other end of France, with her husband, who a month previously had been appointed tax collector. He expressly sent for her. Madame Dambreuse wrote three letters and showed him.

Not trusting even the nun who was nursing him, she did not leave him for a second, did not go to bed. The people who left their name at the concierge's lodge asked after her admiringly. And passers-by were in awe of the quantity of straw spread in the street under the windows.*

On 12 February at five o'clock he had a terrifying haemoptysis. The doctor looking after him said it was dangerous. They rushed to get a priest.

During Monsieur Dambreuse's confession, his wife watched him curiously from a distance. Then the doctor applied a blister and waited.

The light from the lamps, obscured by furniture, cast an uneven glow in the room. Frédéric and Madame Dambreuse, at the foot of the bed, watched the dying man. In the alcove the priest and the doctor were talking in low voices. The nun, on her knees, was mumbling prayers.

At last came the death rattle. His hands grew cold, his face began to turn pale. At times he drew a long-drawn-out breath. They became more and more rare. He uttered two or three confused words. He breathed a little breath as he turned up his eyes and his head fell back on one side on to the pillow.

Everyone, for a minute, was still.

Madame Dambreuse drew nearer. And, quite naturally, with the simplicity of a duty to fulfil, she closed his eyes.

Then she threw out her arms, twisting her body as though in the spasms of restrained despair, and left the apartment leaning on the doctor and the nun. A quarter of an hour later Frédéric went up to her room.

An indefinable scent was given off by the exquisite things with which it was filled. A black dress was laid across the bed, contrasting sharply with the pink counterpane.

Madame Dambreuse was standing by the fireside. Though he didn't imagine her to be in the depths of despair, he thought she was a little sombre; and in a sympathetic voice:

'Are you sad?'

'Me? No, not in the least.'

As she turned round, she caught sight of the dress and examined it; then she told him not to stand on ceremony.

'Smoke if you want to! You are in my home now.'

And sighing deeply:

'Oh, heavens, what a relief!'

Frédéric was astonished at this exclamation. He answered, kissing her hand:

'Yet we were free already.'

This allusion to the ease with which they had conducted their affair seemed to offend Madame Dambreuse.

'Oh, you don't realize all the things I did for him, and what worries I had!'

'What?'

'Oh yes! Was it safe to have his bastard always around, a child introduced into the house after five years together and who, without me of course, would have made him do something stupid?'

Then she explained her financial situation. They had got married under the system of separate assets. Her inheritance was three hundred thousand francs. In their marriage contract Monsieur Dambreuse had assured her that, in the event of her surviving him, she would have an income of fifteen thousand livres and the ownership of the mansion. But a short time later he had made a will, making over all his money to her. And she estimated it now, as far as it was possible to do so, at more than three million.

Frédéric opened his eyes wide.

'So it was worth it, wasn't it? I did my bit in any case. It was my property I was defending; Cécile would have stripped me of what was due to me.'

'Why has she not come to see her father?' Frédéric said.

At this question, Madame Dambreuse looked hard at him:

'I've no idea. Perhaps she didn't want to. Oh, I know her! She won't get a penny from me.'

She was scarcely any trouble, at least since her marriage.

'Oh, her marriage!' Madame Dambreuse exclaimed jeeringly.

And she bore a grudge at having treated that little minx too kindly; she was jealous, self-seeking, hypocritical. 'She has all her father's faults.' She heaped more and more insults on him. There was no one as deeply hypocritical, pitiless, hard as flint, 'a bad man, a bad man'.

Even the wisest of us can sometimes make mistakes. Madame Dambreuse had just made one by this outpouring of hatred. Frédéric was scandalized and, sitting in an armchair facing her, was deep in thought.

She got up and sat lightly on his knee.

'You are the only one who has a good heart! You are the only one I love!'

As she looked at him, her heart softened, a nervous reaction brought tears to her eyes and she whispered:

'Will you marry me?'

At first he thought he had not understood. This fortune made his head whirl. She repeated a little louder:

'Will you marry me?'

Finally he said with a smile:

'Can you doubt it?'

Then he was rather ashamed and in order to make it up to the dead man in some way he offered to watch over him himself. But as he was ashamed of this pious sentiment he added, casually:

'Perhaps that would show more respect.'

'Yes, perhaps,' she said, 'because of the servants!'

The bed had been pulled completely out from the alcove. The nun was at the foot of the bed. And at the bedside was a priest, another one, a tall, thin man, who looked rather Spanish and fanatical. On the bedside table covered with a white napkin three candles were burning.

Frédéric drew up a chair and looked at the dead man.

His face was yellow as straw. A little pink foam was visible at the corners of his mouth. He had a scarf round his head, a woollen waistcoat, and a silver crucifix on his chest between his folded arms.

That busy life, so full of anxieties, was over. How many times had he frequented ministers' offices, calculated figures, struck deals, listened to reports? How many flattering smiles, obsequious words had he uttered! For he had welcomed Napoleon, the Cossacks, Louis XVIII, 1830, the workers, all regimes, cherishing Power with such devotion that he would have paid to sell himself.

But he left behind him the domain of La Fortelle, three factories in Picardy, the Forest of Crancé in the Yonne, a farm near Orléans, and a considerable amount in stocks and shares.

So Frédéric totted up his fortune; it was going to belong to him! He thought first about 'what people would say', of a present for his mother, of his future coaches and pair, of an old family coachman he would make his concierge. The livery would have to be changed, of course. He would have the main salon as his study. And there was nothing against having a picture gallery on the second floor if they knocked down three walls. Perhaps there was a way they could install a Turkish bath in the basement. As for Monsieur Dambreuse's study it was not an attractive room, what could it be used for?

His dreams were rudely interrupted by the priest blowing his nose or the nun poking the fire. But reality confirmed them; the corpse was still there. His eyes had opened again; and the pupils, although they were sunk in viscous shadow, had an enigmatic expression Frédéric found hard to bear. He believed it was a kind of judgement on him, and he almost felt remorseful, for he had never had to complain about this man, who, quite the opposite, had... Oh, come on now, he was an old rascal! and he looked more closely at him, to regain his nerve, mentally crying out:

'Well then, what of it? I didn't kill you, did I?'

In the meantime the priest read his breviary. The nun dozed, not moving. The wicks on the three candles grew longer.

For two hours you could hear the muffled sound of carts rolling along to Les Halles. The windows misted over, a cab went past, then the noise of a troop of donkeys trotting along the road and hammer blows, cries of street vendors, trumpet blasts; everything now mingled in the great voice of Paris greeting the day.

Frédéric set to work. First he went to the town hall to declare the death. Then when the doctor in charge had issued a death certificate he went back to the town hall to tell them which cemetery the family had chosen and to make the arrangements with the funeral parlour.

The clerk showed him a drawing and a prospectus, one outlining the different classes of burial, the other the complete package of provision in detail. Did they want a hearse with a roof or one with feathers, plaits on the horses' manes, aigrettes for the bearers, initials or a coat of arms, funeral lamps, a man to bear the decorations of the deceased, and how many carriages? Frédéric did not stint on the arrangements. Madame Dambreuse was adamant no expense should be spared.

Then he went to the church.

The curate in charge of funerals began by criticizing the funeral directors' extravagance. It was really superfluous to have an officer bear the decorations. It was much better to spend the money on candles! They agreed on a low Mass with music. Frédéric signed the agreement with a binding obligation to pay all expenses.

After that he went to the Hôtel de Ville to buy the plot; one that was two metres long by one metre wide cost five hundred francs. Was it to be for a half-century or in perpetuity?

'Oh, in perpetuity!' Frédéric said.

He took it all seriously, took great pains over it. In the courtyard of the Dambreuse mansion a monumental mason was waiting to show him estimates and designs for Greek, Egyptian, and Moorish tombstones. But the family's architect had already spoken to Madame; and on the table in the vestibule were all kinds of brochures having to do with the cleaning of mattresses, the disinfecting of rooms, and various embalming procedures.

After dinner he went back to the tailor's to order the servants' mourning clothes. And he had one more thing to do, for he'd ordered beaver fur gloves whereas the done thing was to wear floss silk.

When he arrived the next day at ten the large drawing room was filling up with people, and almost all greeted one another with mournful faces, saying:

'I only saw him a month ago! Oh well, it's our common fate!'

'Yes, but let's try to put it off as long as possible!'

Then they gave a little satisfied laugh and even started conversations totally divorced from the circumstances. Finally the master of ceremonies, black-suited in the French manner, in knee-breeches, with a cloak, weepers, sword at his side and three-cornered hat under his arm, saluted and uttered the usual words: 'Gentlemen, if you please.' They left.

It was flower-market day on the Place de la Madeleine, mild and bright, and the breeze gently shaking the canvas on the stalls caused the huge black sheet fixed over the portal to lift at the edges. The crest of Monsieur Dambreuse in a velvet square was repeated three times. It was 'sable sinister arm Or, closed fist clenched and gauntleted Argent' with a count's coronet and the motto: 'By every path.'

The bearers carried the heavy coffin to the top of the staircase and the company went in.

The six chapels, the apse, and the chairs were draped with black. The catafalque at the far end of the choirstalls formed with its great candles one single blaze of yellow light. At the two corners the flames of ethanol burned on candelabras.

The most important people took their seats in the sanctuary, the rest in the nave, and the service began.

Apart from one or two, their ignorance on religious matters was so profound that the master of ceremonies had to indicate from time to time when they should stand, kneel, or sit down. Voices alternated with the organ and two double basses. In the intervals of quiet you could hear the muttering of the priest at the altar; then the music and singing began again.

A dim light came from the three cupolas. But through the open door a horizontal flood of white light struck all the bare heads; and in the air, halfway up to the roof, there was a shadow, pierced by the reflection of gold decorating the ribs of the pendentives and the foliage of the capitals.

To pass the time, Frédéric listened to the *Dies Irae*. He observed the people present, tried to see the paintings which were too high up and represented the life of Mary Magdalene. Luckily Pellerin came and sat by him and at once began a long lecture on the subject of frescoes. The bell tolled. They came out of the church.

The hearse, decorated with its hanging drapes and high plumes, made its way to Père-Lachaise, drawn by four black horses with plaited manes, and plumes on their heads, and enveloped down to their hooves in wide caparisons embroidered with silver. Their coachman, in groom's livery, wore a three-cornered hat with a long black crêpe. The ropes were held by four persons: a treasurer from the Chamber of Deputies, a member of the General Council of the Aube, a delegate from the mines, and Fumichon, as a friend. The dead man's barouche and twelve funeral carriages followed. Behind them, filling the middle of the boulevard, came the mourners.

Passers-by stopped to look. Women with babies in their arms stood on chairs, and people having a drink in the cafés appeared in the windows with billiard cues in their hands.

It was a long way; and as in ceremonial meals where one is rather reserved to begin with and then more talkative, before long people began to relax. The only subject was the Chamber's refusal to grant the President extra funds. Monsieur Piscatory had been too harsh, Montalembert 'magnificent' as usual, and Monsieur Chambolle, Monsieur Pidoux, Monsieur Creton, and indeed all the commission perhaps should have followed the advice of Monsieur Quantin-Bauchard and Monsieur Dufour.*

These conversations continued in the Rue de la Roquette, with its shops on either side displaying nothing but coloured glass chains and black medallions covered with patterns and gold lettering, which gave them the appearance of china shops or caves full of stalactites. But at the cemetery gates everyone instantly stopped talking.

The tombstones rose up between the trees, broken columns,

pyramids, temples, dolmens, obelisks, Etruscan vaults with bronze entrances. In one or two you could see a sort of funereal boudoir, with rustic chairs and folding stools. Spiders' webs hung like rags from the little chains on the urns; and dust covered the crucifixes and the bouquets tied with satin ribbons. Everywhere between the pillars of the balustrades on the tombstones were wreaths of dried immortelles and candlesticks, vases, flowers, black medallions with gold letters, plaster statuettes of little boys or girls, or little angels held in the air with brass wire; several even had a zinc roof over their heads. Huge ropes of spun glass, like boa constrictors, black, white and blue, snaked their way from the top of the steles to the base of the stones. The sun striking them made them sparkle among the black wooden crosses; and the hearse made its way down the wide avenues paved like the streets in a town. From time to time the axles creaked. Women on their knees with their dresses trailing in the grass talked softly to the dead. Little puffs of white smoke rose from the green yew trees—abandoned wreaths, rubbish that was being burned.

Monsieur Dambreuse's grave was in the same area as those of Manuel and Benjamin Constant. The ground fell away here in a steep slope. The tops of green trees were below the level of your feet. Further off, the funnels of the steam pumps and then the great city.

Frédéric was able to admire the landscape while the speeches were being made.

The first was on behalf of the Chamber of Deputies; the second on behalf of the General Council of the Aube, the third on behalf of the Mining Company of the Saône-et-Loire, the fourth on behalf of the Agricultural Society of the Yonne; and there was another representing a philanthropic society. Finally they were about to leave when a stranger began to read a sixth speech on behalf of the Amiens Society of Antiquaries.

And everyone took advantage of the occasion to attack socialism, of which Monsieur Dambreuse had died a victim. It was the spectacle of anarchy and his devotion to order which had shortened his life. They praised his intelligence, his probity, his generosity, and even his saying nothing in his capacity as deputy, for although not an orator, he possessed instead those solid qualities, a thousand times preferable etc. etc.... with all the obligatory phrases: 'premature death—everlasting sorrow—the other country—farewell, or rather no, till we meet again!'

The soil mixed with gravel, fell. The world was done with him.

They were still discussing him a little as they made their way down through the cemetery. And all manner of compliments were paid. Hussonnet, who had to write an account of the funeral for the papers, made fun of the speeches—for after all our friend Dambreuse had been one of the most famous 'palm-greasers' of the last reign. Then the funeral carriages took these good people back to their own busy lives; the ceremony had not lasted too long, they were pleased about that.

Wearily Frédéric went home.

When he arrived next day at the Dambreuse mansion, he was told that Madame was working downstairs in the office. Cardboard boxes, drawers were open all over the place, books of accounts thrown right and left. A roll of paper labelled 'Bad debts' was lying on the floor; he nearly tripped over it and picked it up. Madame Dambreuse was almost invisible, buried in the big armchair.

'Well, where are you? What's the matter?'

She leaped up.

'What's the matter? I am ruined, ruined! Do you hear?'

Monsieur Adolphe Langlois, the solicitor, had called her into his office and read a will her husband had made before his marriage. He was leaving everything to Cécile. And the other will was lost. Frédéric went white. Perhaps she had not searched properly?

'Well, look around you!' said Madame Dambreuse, indicating the room.

The two strongboxes were open, broken into with an axe, and she had turned the desk upside down, gone through the cupboards, shaken the doormats. Then suddenly she uttered a little scream and hastened to open a small box with a brass lock she had just noticed in a corner. She opened it: nothing!

'Oh, the swine! And I looked after him with such devotion!'

And she burst into tears.

'Could it be somewhere else?' Frédéric said.

'No, it was there in the strongbox. I saw it not very long ago. It's been burnt! I'm certain of it.'

One day at the start of his illness Monsieur Dambreuse had gone down to sign some papers.

'That's when he must have done it!'

And she collapsed into a chair again, defeated. Madame Dambreuse in front of the gaping strongboxes was more pathetic than a mother mourning her empty cradle. In short, her pain, in spite of its ignoble cause, seemed so profound that he tried to comfort her by saying that after all she would not be poor.

'I shall be poor,' she answered, 'because I cannot offer you a huge fortune!'

She only had thirty thousand francs' income, if you didn't count the house, which was worth perhaps eighteen to twenty.

Although this was luxury as far as Frédéric was concerned, he nevertheless felt disappointed. It was goodbye to all those dreams and the high life! Honour obliged him to marry Madame Dambreuse. He thought for a moment and then said, tenderly:

'I shall always have you!'

She threw herself into his arms. He squeezed her to his breast with a display of tenderness in which there was a little self-congratulation. Madame Dambreuse, whose tears had stopped, looked up, radiant with happiness and, taking his hand:

'Oh, I've never doubted you! I was counting on you!'

This confident anticipation of what he regarded as a noble action displeased the young man.

Then she took him into her room and they made plans. Frédéric must think about furthering his ambitions now. She even gave him admirable advice about his candidature.

The first thing was to learn a few phrases having to do with political economics. He must specialize in something, like horse-breeding, for instance, and write several memorandums on a question of local interest, have constantly at his disposal post offices or tobacco licences, perform a great many little services for people. Monsieur Dambreuse had been exemplary in that regard. For instance, once, in the countryside, he had stopped his charabanc full of friends in front of a shoemaker's and bought twelve pairs of shoes for his guests and some terrible boots for himself—which he had heroically worn for two weeks. This anecdote made them laugh. She recounted others, with a renewal of grace, youth and wit.

She approved his idea of going to Nogent immediately. They said fond farewells. Then as he left, she whispered again:

'You do love me, don't you?'

'For ever!' he replied.

A messenger was waiting at home with a pencilled note saying that

Rosanette was going into labour.* He had been so busy for the last few days that he had forgotten all about it. She had reserved a place in a special nursing home in Chaillot.

Frédéric took a cab and set off.

At the end of the Rue de Marbeuf he read in large letters on a wooden sign:

NURSING AND MATERNITY HOME UNDER THE MANAGEMENT OF MADAME ALESSANDRI, FIRST-CLASS MIDWIFE, FORMER STUDENT OF THE MATERNITY HOSPITAL, AUTHOR OF DIVERSE BOOKS, ETC.

Then on a smallish door further down the street, another sign repeated (omitting the word maternity): 'MADAME ALESSANDRI'S NURSING HOME', with all her qualifications.

Frédéric knocked hard.

A maidservant who looked like a soubrette took him into the sitting room furnished with a mahogany table, armchairs in plum-coloured velvet, and a clock in a glass case.

Madame appeared almost at once. She was a tall dark-haired woman of forty, slim, with beautiful eyes and used to dealing with people. She informed Frédéric of the safe delivery of the mother and took him up to her room.

Rosanette smiled in ineffable delight; and as if she were sinking, drowning in a tide of love, she whispered:

'It's a boy, look, look!' And pointed to a cot by the bedside.

He pulled back the curtain and saw something swaddled, yellowish-red and extremely wrinkled, that smelled bad and was wailing.

'Give him a kiss!'

He answered, in order to conceal his revulsion:

'But I'm afraid I'll hurt him.'

'No! No!'

So he gave his son a fleeting kiss.

'He's just like you!'

And she put her two frail arms round his neck with a passion such as he had never seen in her before.

He thought of Madame Dambreuse again. He blamed himself for his heinous behaviour in betraying this poor, simple creature who loved and suffered truly in all her being. For several days he kept her company till evening.

She was happy in this quiet house. The shutters at the front always remained closed. Her room, with bright chintz furnishings, looked out on to a large garden. Madame Alessandri, whose only fault was to talk about famous doctors as close friends, lavished attentions on her. Her companions, who were almost all girls from the provinces, were very bored, not having anyone to visit them. Rosanette realized they envied her and proudly said as much to Frédéric. However, they had to speak quietly, as the walls were thin and everyone was listening despite the constant tinkling of the piano.

He was finally about to leave for Nogent when a letter from Deslauriers arrived.

Two new candidates had applied, one conservative, the other a radical. A third, whoever he was, would have no chance. It was Frédéric's fault; he had let the right moment pass, he should have come earlier, bestirred himself. 'We didn't even see you at the agricultural show!' The lawyer reproached him for not having any connections in the newspapers. 'Oh, if only you had followed my advice! If only we had a news sheet of our own!' He went on at length about this. And besides, many who would have voted for him, out of consideration for Monsieur Dambreuse, would abandon him now. Deslauriers was one of them. Not having any more to expect from the capitalist he was letting his protégé go.

Frédéric took his letter to Madame Dambreuse.

'So you didn't go to Nogent?' she asked.

'Why do you say that?'

'I saw Deslauriers three days ago.'

Knowing about the death of her husband, the lawyer had come to bring back some reports from the mines and offer his professional services. That seemed strange to Frédéric. What was his friend doing there?

Madame Dambreuse wanted to know how he had spent his time away from her.

'I was ill,' he said.

'At least you might have told me.'

'Oh, it wasn't worth it.' In any case he'd had a lot of things to deal with, meetings, visits.

From then on he led a double life, scrupulously spending every night at the Maréchale's and the afternoon at Madame Dambreuse's, so that he scarcely had an hour free in the middle of the day.

The baby was in the country at Andilly. They went to see him every week.

The wet nurse's house was at the top of the village at the back of a small yard as black as a well, straw on the ground, hens here and there, a cart for vegetables in the shed. Rosanette would start by kissing her little baby frantically. And in a sort of delirium she went back and forth, tried to milk the goat, ate some farmhouse bread, breathed in the smell of the dung heap, and tried to put a little into her handkerchief.

Then they went for long walks. She would go into nursery gardens, pick branches of lilac hanging over the walls, cry 'Gee up there, Neddy!' when she saw a donkey pulling a cart, stop to look through the railings at beautiful gardens. Or the nurse would take the baby and put him in the shade of a walnut tree; and the two women would talk inane nonsense for hours on end.

Close by them, Frédéric was looking at the square vineyards on the slopes with their occasional bushes, the dusty paths like grey ribbons, the splashes of red and white houses amongst the greenery. And sometimes the smoke of a railway engine would leave a trail along the leafy valleys like a gigantic ostrich plume with its tail feathers disappearing into the air.

Then his eyes fell once more on his son. He imagined him as a young man, he would be his friend; but perhaps he would be a fool, certainly a failure. His illegitimacy would be a continual burden to him. It would have been better for him never to have been born, and Frédéric muttered: 'Poor baby!', his heart full of an incomprehensible sadness.

They often missed the last train home. Then Madame Dambreuse would scold him for being late. He made up stories.

He also had to make up stories for Rosanette. She didn't know what he did all evening. And when she sent someone to his house he was never there! One day when he was there they both turned up almost at the same time. He got the Maréchale out of the house and hid Madame Dambreuse, saying that his mother was coming.

Soon he took pleasure in this duplicity. He repeated to one the promises he made to the other, sent them two similar bouquets, wrote to them at the same time, then made comparisons between the two of them. There was a third woman always in his thoughts. The impossibility of possessing her was justification for his deceit. His pleasure was heightened by alternating between the two women, and the more unfaithful he was to one, the more she loved him, as if their loves increased reciprocally and in a sort of rivalry each wanted to make him forget the other.

'See how I trust you!' Madame Dambreuse said to him one day, unfolding a note informing her that Monsieur Moreau lived conjugally with a certain Rose Bron.

'Is that the young lady you took to the races, I wonder?'

'How ridiculous!' he said. 'Let me see.'

The letter, written in capitals, wasn't signed. At first Madame Dambreuse had put up with this mistress, as it concealed their own adultery. But as her love had grown, she had demanded he break off the relationship, which Frédéric claimed he had done long ago. And when he had finished protesting, she replied, narrowing her eyes, with a look like the veiled point of a dagger:

'Well, what about the other one?'

'What other one?'

'The wife of the porcelain dealer.'

He shrugged in a scornful manner. She didn't insist.

But a month later when they were talking about honour and loyalty and he was boasting about his own (in a casual way, for safety's sake) she said:

'It's true, you keep your promises, you don't go there any more.'

'Where?'

'To Madame Arnoux's.'

He begged her to tell him from whom she had this information. It was from her second seamstress, Madame Regimbart.

So she knew all about his life, while he knew nothing of hers!

However, he had found in her dressing room the portrait of a man with a long moustache. Was this the man about whom he had once been told a vague tale of suicide? But there was no way of finding out any more. What was the use, anyway? Women's hearts are like those secret little sets of drawers one inside the other. You struggle with them, you break your nails, and find at the bottom a dried flower, or dust or nothing at all! And besides he was afraid of getting to know too much.

She made him refuse invitations where she could not be with him, kept him by her side, was afraid of losing him. And in spite of this union which grew stronger every day, all of a sudden great abysses opened up between them about unimportant things, the appreciation of somebody's character, or a work of art.

She had a formal, stilted way of playing the piano. Her spiritualism (Madame Dambreuse believed in the transmigration of souls into the stars) did not prevent her from keeping an admirably clear eye on her finances. She was haughty to her servants, dry-eyed at the sight of the poor in rags. An instinctive selfishness shone out from her usual turns of phrase: 'What do I care about that? I'd be a fool to do that! Why should I?', and a thousand odious little actions that defied analysis. She would have listened behind doors; she must tell lies to her confessor. Asserting her dominance over him, she asked Frédéric to go to church with her on Sundays. He obeyed and carried her missal.

The loss of her inheritance had changed her considerably. These marks of grief, which people attributed to the death of Monseur Dambreuse, made her more interesting. And she entertained a lot, as before. Since Frédéric's electoral failure, her ambition was to obtain a legation in Germany for them both. So the first thing to do was to conform to the ideas prevailing at the time.

Some wanted the Empire, others the Orléans, others the Comte de Chambord; but everyone was agreed on the urgent need for decentralization, and several ideas for achieving this were put forward. For example: to divide Paris into numerous high streets and re-establish villages, transfer the seat of government to Versailles, put the university in Bourges, do away with libraries, entrust everything to the general staff. And they extolled country life, the uneducated man naturally having more sense than anyone else! Hatred was rife: hatred against primary-school teachers and wine merchants, against philosophy classes, history lessons, novels, red waistcoats,* long beards, all independence, any display of individuality. For it was necessary to 'restore the principle of authority', no matter where it came from, no matter in whose name it was exercised, just so long as it was Force, Authority! Conservatives now spoke like Sénécal. Frédéric was nonplussed; and he heard the same remarks, uttered by the same men, at Rosanette's!

The courtesans' salons (their importance dates from that time) were neutral territory, where reactionaries of different parties could meet. Hussonnet, who constantly disparaged well-known contemporary figures (which was a good thing for the restoration of Order), inspired Rosanette with the longing to give parties, like everyone else. He said he would write accounts of them. And he began by bringing along a serious man, Fumichon. Then Nonancourt appeared, Monsieur de Grémonville, Monsieur de Larsillois, the ex-prefect and Cisy who was now an agronomist in lower Brittany and more Christian than ever.

The Maréchale's old lovers also came, such as the Baron de Comaing, the Comte de Jumillac, and a few others; their easy manners offended Frédéric.

In order to assert his authority he raised the tone of the household. So they took on a groom, changed lodgings, and acquired new furniture. This expense served to make his forthcoming marriage seem less disproportionate to his fortune. So this diminished quite a lot—and Rosanette could make neither head nor tail of it all!

A bourgeoise déclassée, she loved domesticity, a quiet home life. However, she was happy to have her 'day'; she called women like herself: 'those women!'; she wanted to be a 'society lady' and believed she was one. She asked him not to smoke in the drawing room, and tried to make him observe fast days as it was more respectable.

She failed to play her role properly though, for she was becoming serious, and even before she went to bed was always rather melancholic; it was like when you see cypress trees outside a tavern.

He discovered the cause: she dreamed of marriage. She too! Frédéric was exasperated. And besides he was remembering how she had appeared at Madame Arnoux's house, and it still rankled that she had resisted him for such a long time.

But he nonetheless tried to discover who her previous lovers were. She denied them all. A kind of jealousy took hold of him. He was annoyed about the presents she had received and was receiving. And as her real character gradually irritated him more and more, a rough, animal attraction drew him to her, the illusions of a moment that began to turn into hatred.

Her words, her voice, her smile, everything about her started to annoy him, especially that look of hers, so limpid, feminine, and vacant. On occasion she infuriated him to such a degree that he would have not been sorry to see her dead. But how could he get cross with her? She was impossibly sweet.

Deslauriers turned up again and explained his stay in Nogent, saying he was trying to buy a lawyer's practice. Frédéric was glad to see him once more; here was somebody he could talk to! He made him the third person in their trio.

The lawyer dined with them from time to time and when there were any disagreements he always took Rosanette's side, so much so that once Frédéric said to him:

'Oh, go to bed with her if you like!' Such was his longing for an excuse to get rid of her.

Towards the middle of the month of June she received a writ from Maître Athanase Gautherot, bailiff, who ordered her to pay four thousand francs she owed to one Clémence Vatnaz. Failing that payment, he would come the next day to seize her belongings.

The fact was that only one of the four bills she had signed before had been paid. Any money she had managed to obtain since had been spent on other things.

She rushed to Arnoux's house. He lived in the Faubourg Saint-Germain but the porter didn't know which street. She went round to several friends, found nobody in, and came back in despair. She did not want to tell Frédéric, fearful that this new occurrence would put her marriage in jeopardy.

The next day Maître Athanase Gautherot arrived, flanked by two acolytes, one was pale, with a face like a weasel, and looked eaten up by envy. The other wore a collar, tight trouser straps, and a black taffeta stall on his index finger; they were both disgustingly dirty with greasy collars, and coat sleeves that were too short.

Their master, on the other hand, who was a fine-looking man, began by asking them to forgive his painful visit, looking round the apartment as he did so, 'full of pretty things, my goodness!' He added: 'apart from the ones that cannot be seized'. At a sign from him his two assistants disappeared.

Then his compliments redoubled. Was it possible that such a charming person did not have a friend to protect her? A forced sale was a catastrophe! You never get over it! He tried to frighten her. Then, seeing she was upset, suddenly adopted a fatherly tone. He had some experience of life, he'd had dealings with innumerable ladies. And as he named them, he was examining the framed pictures on the walls. They were old pictures belonging to Arnoux, drawings by Sombaz, watercolours by Burieu, three landscapes by Dittmer. It was obvious that Rosanette did not know how much they were worth. Maître Gautherot turned to her:

'Listen! To prove I am a decent fellow, let's make a deal. Give me those Dittmers and I'll settle the debt. What about it?'

At that moment Frédéric, who had been told about it by Delphine in the hall and had just seen the two assistants, stormed into the room, with his hat on his head. Maître Gautherot resumed his dignified air; and as the door remained open:

'Come, Messieurs, write this down! In the second room we'll say: an oak table, with two leaves. Two sideboards...'

Frédéric interrupted him, asking if there was any way of stopping the goods being seized.

'Oh, of course! Who paid for the furniture?'

'I did.'

'Well, put in a claim. You will gain time.'

Maître Gautherot finished his report quickly, citing Mademoiselle Bron, and withdrew.

Frédéric did not blame her. He looked at the muddy footprints left by the bailiff's assistants; and, talking to himself, said:

'I shall have to go and get some money.'

'Oh, how stupid I am,' said the Maréchale. She searched around in a drawer, took out a letter, and went quickly off to the Languedoc Lighting Company to get a transfer of her shares.

She came back an hour later. The shares had been sold to someone else. The clerk had replied, after studying the paper she brought with the promise written by Arnoux: 'This document doesn't make you a shareholder. The company does not recognize them.' In short, he had dismissed her; she was choking with rage. Frédéric must go to see Arnoux straight away to sort out the problem.

But Arnoux might suppose he had come indirectly to recover the fifteen thousand francs from his lost mortgage; and this claim from a man who had been his mistress's lover seemed to him a despicable action. Taking the middle way, he went to obtain the address of Madame Regimbart from the Dambreuse house, sent an errand boy, and thus discovered the café that the Citizen nowadays frequented.

It was a small café in the Place de la Bastille and he spent the whole day there in the right-hand corner at the back, as motionless as if he had been part of the furniture.

After passing in turn from coffee to grog, punch, mulled wine, and even wine with water, he had gone back to drinking beer. And every half-hour or so he would utter the word: 'Bock!' having cut his words down to the bare minimum. Frédéric asked if he ever saw Arnoux.

'No!'

'Oh, why?'

'He's a fool!'

Perhaps it was politics that divided them. Frédéric thought it might be a good idea to find out about Compain.

'He's an idiot!' Regimbart said.

'Why?'

'His calf's head!'

'Ah. Now do tell me what this calf's head business is.'

Regimbart smiled at him pityingly.

'Stupidities!'

Frédéric, after a long silence, went on:

'Has he moved then?'

'Who?'

'Arnoux!'

'Yes, Rue de Fleurus.'

'Which number?'

'Do you think I mix with Jesuits?'

'What do you mean, Jesuits?'

The Citizen replied angrily:

'That swine has set himself up as a rosary seller with the money from a patriot I introduced him to!'

'I don't believe it!'

'Go and see for yourself!'

It was absolutely true. Arnoux, who had been debilitated by a mild stroke, had turned to religion. Moreover, 'he had always been basically religious', and—with that combination of sincerity and commercial savvy which came naturally to him—he had established a business in religious artefacts, to bring about both his fortune and his salvation.

Frédéric found his shop easily, with the sign: '*The Gothic Arts*— Church Restoration—Ecclesiastical Decorations—Polychrome Sculpture—Incense of the Magi' etc. etc.

Two wooden statues stood in the two corners of the shop window, painted in gold, vermilion, and blue. Saint John the Baptist with his sheepskin and a Saint Geneviève, with roses in her skirt and a distaff under her arm. Then there were groups of plaster figures: a nun instructing a little girl, a mother on her knees by a cot, three schoolboys in front of the holy altar. The prettiest was a kind of chalet depicting the inside of the stable with the donkey, the ox, and baby Jesus laid on the straw, on real straw. You could see dozens of medallions lining the shelves, all kinds of rosaries, stoups in the shape of a shell, and the portraits of ecclesiastical worthies among whom shone out the smiling faces of Monseigneur Affre and the Holy Father.

Arnoux was dozing behind the counter, his head on the desk. He had aged enormously and even had around the temples a crown of rosy pimples* illuminated by the sun's rays, reflecting off the golden crosses.

Seeing this decline, Frédéric was overwhelmed with sadness. However, he resigned himself, out of loyalty to the Maréchale, and went in to see him. At the back of the shop Madame Arnoux appeared. He turned on his heels.

'I couldn't find him,' he said when he got home.

And it was no good him saying he would write straight away to his lawyer in Le Havre to get some money; Rosanette flew into a rage. Never had there been a man so weak, so feeble; while she endured a thousand deprivations, other people were living in luxury.

Frédéric was thinking of poor Madame Arnoux, imagining the desolating mediocrity of her house. He had sat down at the writing desk; and as Rosanette's shrill voice still nagged him:

'Oh, for God's sake, shut up!'

'You aren't going to defend them, are you?'

'Yes I am,' he cried. 'Why are you so determined to hate them?'

'And you, why don't you want them to pay? It's because you are afraid of hurting your old flame, admit it!'

He felt like hitting her with the clock; words failed him. He was silent. Rosanette, walking up and down the room, added:

'I'll take him to court, your precious Arnoux. Oh, I don't need you!' And, pinching her lips: 'I'll take advice.'

Three days later Delphine came in suddenly.

'Madame, Madame, there's a man here with a pot of glue and I'm scared!'

Rosanette went into the kitchen and saw a pockmarked ruffian with a withered arm, almost completely drunk and mumbling something.

It was Mâitre Gautherot's bill-paster. The objection to the seizing of goods had been overruled and naturally the sale was going ahead.

First he asked for a glass of wine for his trouble in climbing the stairs; then he asked another favour: theatre tickets, because he supposed Madame to be an actress. Then he spent several minutes winking incomprehensibly. Finally he declared that for forty sous he would tear off the corners of the poster he'd already put up downstairs on the door. Rosanette was named on it, which was an exceptionally severe measure and an indication of the strength of La Vatnaz's hatred.

In her young days she had a soft heart and once, having fallen unhappily in love, had written to Béranger for advice. But she had grown bitter under the blows life had dealt her; she had, in turn, given piano lessons, managed a boarding house, written for fashion magazines, let rooms, trafficked in lace among loose women, her contacts in that world then enabling her to be of service to a lot of people, including Arnoux. Before that, she had worked in a business.

She had been in charge of paying the female employees. And for each of them there were two account books, of which she kept one. Dussardier, who out of kindness kept one for a woman called Hortense Baslin, arrived one day at the cashdesk just as Mademoiselle Vatnaz was presenting this girl's account, 1,682 francs which the cashier paid her. Now the day before, Dussardier had only written 1,082 against Baslin's total in the account book. He asked for the book again, making some excuse, then, wanting to cover up this theft, told her he had lost it. The woman naively repeated his lie to Mademoiselle Vatnaz; the latter, to clear things up, and in a casual way, came to have a word with our kindly clerk. He said, 'I burned it.' And nothing more. She left the firm shortly afterwards without believing the story of the destruction of the book and imagining that Dussardier was still keeping it.

Hearing he had been wounded, she had hurried round to his house with the intention of getting it back. Then, not having found anything in spite of intensive searching, she had been filled with respect, and soon love, for this boy who was so loyal, gentle, heroic, and strong. Such good fortune at her age was unhoped for. She threw herself upon him with the appetite of an ogress, and abandoned literature and socialism's 'consoling doctrines and generous utopias', the lectures she gave on the De-subordination of Women, everything—even Delmar; to cut a long story short, she proposed marriage to Dussardier.

Although she was his mistress, he wasn't in the least in love with her. Moreover, he had not forgotten her theft. And she was too rich. He turned her down. Then she told him, weeping, of the dreams she had cherished: that they should run a dress shop together. She had the necessary capital, which would increase by four thousand francs the following week. And she told him about her action against the Maréchale.

This pained Dussardier on account of his friend. He remembered the cigar case he had given him at the guard-post, the evenings on the Quai Napoléon, so many good chats, books borrowed, Frédéric's thousand kindnesses. He begged La Vatnaz not to go ahead.

She laughed at his good nature, revealing an incomprehensible loathing for Rosanette. She only wanted money in order to crush her under the wheels of her carriage one day.

These depths of wickedness frightened Dussardier; and when he was sure of the day of the sale he went out. He called on Frédéric, looking very embarrassed.

'I owe you an apology.'

'Whatever for?'

'You must think me an ungrateful wretch, since...'

He faltered: 'Oh! I shan't see her any more. I won't be her accomplice!' And when Frédéric looked at him, astonished, he added: 'Are they not going to sell your mistress's furniture in three days' time?'

'Who told you that?'

'She did—La Vatnaz! But I am afraid of offending you...'

'That's impossible, my friend!'

'Oh, that's true, you are such a good friend to me!'

And he shyly held out a little leather purse to him.

It contained four thousand francs, his entire savings.

'What! Oh no, no!'

'I knew I would offend you,' replied Dussardier, tears in his eyes.

Frédéric wrung his hand and the good fellow went on despondently:

'Take it! Do me a favour! I am so desperate! Isn't it the end of everything anyway?—I thought when the Revolution came we should be happy. Do you remember how good it was? How we breathed again? But now we are worse off than before.'

And, fixing his eyes on the ground:

'Now they are killing our Republic, just as they killed the other one, the Roman Republic! And poor Venice, Poland, Hungary, what an abomination! First they cut down the liberty tree, then they restricted the right to vote, closed the clubs, reinstated censorship and handed education to the priests.* Next thing they'll do is bring in the Inquisition.

Well, why not? The conservatives would like to see the Cossacks back! People condemn newspapers when they speak out against the death penalty, Paris is packed with bayonets, sixteen departments are in a state of siege; and an amnesty has been put off yet again!'

He took his head in his hands, then, flinging his arms up as if in great distress:

'If only people tried! If they had good faith, they could get along. But no! You see, the workers are no better than the bourgeoisie. Recently in Elbeuf they refused to help put out a fire. Some wretches call Barbès an aristocrat. To make fun of the working class they want to appoint Nadaud, a builder, to be president! I ask you! There's nothing to be done about it. No remedy. Everyone is against us. Myself, I've done no wrong, and yet it's as though I've a weight on my stomach. I shall go mad if it continues. I want to kill myself. I tell you, I don't need my money. You can give it me back, for heaven's sake! Call it a loan.'

Frédéric, in financial difficulties, ended up accepting his four thousand francs. So, as far as La Vatnaz was concerned, they had nothing to worry about any more.

But Rosanette soon lost her case against Arnoux. Stubbornly, she said she would appeal.

Deslauriers did his level best to make her understand that Arnoux's promise constituted neither a gift nor a regular transfer. She wouldn't even listen to him, saying the law was unfair. It was because she was a woman, the men looked after one another. In the end, however, she took his advice.

He was so much at home in the house that he brought along Sénécal to dinner several times. This casual behaviour annoyed Frédéric who lent him money, even had him dressed by his own tailor. And there was the lawyer giving his old frock coats to the socialist whose means of subsistence were unknown.

He would have liked to be of use to Rosanette, however. One day when she was showing him a dozen shares she had in the kaolin company (the cause of Arnoux's being fined thirty thousand francs) he told her:

'But that's a very shady deal! That's wonderful!'

She had the right to sue him for the reimbursement of her shares. First she would prove that he was obliged to pay all the Company's debts, then that he had declared personal debts to be collective debts, and finally that he had misappropriated substantial funds from the Company.

'All of which makes him guilty of fraudulent bankruptcy, Articles 586 and 587 of the Code of Commerce; and we'll sort him out once and for all, my love, you may be sure!'

Rosanette put her arms around him. He recommended her the next day to his former boss, not being able to take care of the case himself, for he had to go to Nogent. Sénécal would write to him if there was any urgent need.

His negotiations for the buying of a practice were a pretext. He spent his time at Monsieur Roque's, where he had started not only to sing their friend's praises, but to imitate his manner and way of talking as nearly as possible. This had won Louise's confidence, and he was winning the trust of her father by railing against Ledru-Rollin.

If Frédéric didn't come back, it was because he was moving in high society; and bit by bit Deslauriers told them that he was in love, that he had a child, that he was keeping a mistress.

Louise's despair was immense, Madame Moreau's indignation just as great. She could see her son spinning towards the bottom of an unknown abyss, she was hurt in her—almost religious—sense of the proprieties and felt a personal shame. But then her face changed. When people asked her about Frédéric she replied with a knowing look:

'He's well, very well.'

She had found out about his marriage to Madame Dambreuse.

The date was decided, and he was even pondering how to make it acceptable to Rosanette.

Towards the middle of autumn she won her case concerning the shares in kaolin. Frédéric learned of it when he met Sénécal on his doorstep, who had just come from the hearing.

Monsieur Arnoux had been found complicit in all the fraudulent acts; and the former tutor had such a look of triumph that Frédéric forbade him to go any further, assuring him he would pass on the message himself. He went in to her, looking annoyed.

'Well, now I suppose you are happy!'

But without noticing his words:

'Come and look.'

And she showed him the baby lying in a cot by the fire. She had found him so poorly that morning at his nurse's she had brought him back to Paris.

All his limbs had become extraordinarily thin and his lips were covered in little white spots which looked like curdled milk inside his mouth.

'What did the doctor say?'

'Oh, the doctor claims that the journey worsened his... I don't know what, a word ending in "itis". He's got thrush.* Have you heard of that?'

'Of course,' said Frédéric quickly, and added that it was nothing.

But in the course of the evening he was frightened by the sickly look of the child and the spread of the white spots, like mildew, as though life, already deserting that small body, had left behind only a material on which vegetation could grow. His hands were cold; now, he couldn't drink any more; and the nurse, another nurse whom the porter had fetched at random from an agency, kept saying:

'He seems very low to me, very low!'

Rosanette was up all night.

In the morning she went to find Frédéric.

'Come and see. He's not moving.'

The child was dead. She took him up, shook him, hugged him, calling him the sweetest names, covered him in kisses and sobs, walked round and round, distraught, tore out her hair, uttered little cries; and collapsed on to the couch where she remained open-mouthed, with floods of tears issuing from her staring eyes. Then she was overcome with lethargy and all became calm in the apartment. The furniture was turned upside down. Two or three napkins lay around. Six o'clock struck. The night light went out.

When Frédéric saw this he felt rather as though he were dreaming. His heart tightened in anguish. It seemed to him that this death was but a beginning, and that an even greater misfortune was about to befall him.

Suddenly Rosanette said tenderly:

'We'll keep him, won't we?'

She wanted him to be embalmed. There were many reasons against it, the most cogent of which was that it was not feasible in the case of such a young child. A portrait would be better. She accepted this idea. He wrote a note to Pellerin and Delphine hurried to deliver it.

Pellerin arrived promptly, wishing to wipe out all memory of his conduct by this act. He said straight away:

'Oh, the poor little angel! Oh dear, how dreadful!'

But little by little (the artist in him taking over) he declared that he could do nothing with those dark eyes, that livid face, that it really was a still life, that you would need a lot of skill; and he muttered:

'Oh, not easy, not easy!'

'As long as it looks like him,' Rosanette said.

'Oh, I don't care about that! Down with Realism! It's the spirit you are painting. Let me get on with it. I must work out what it should be like.'

He thought hard, forehead in his left hand, holding his elbow with his right hand. Then abruptly:

'Ah, I've an idea! A pastel! With coloured half-tones, laid on almost flat, we could bring up just the outline in relief.'

He sent the maid to get his box of colours, then, with a chair beneath his feet and another by his side, he began making large lines, as calmly as if he had been working from a plaster cast. He extolled Correggio's infant Saint Johns, the Velázquez Infanta in a Pink Dress, the milky flesh-tints of Reynolds, the distinctive technique of Lawrence, and especially the child with the long hair on Lady Gower's lap.*

'Anyway, is there anything more charming than those little brats? The very model of the Sublime—Raphael proved it with his madonnas—is perhaps a mother with her child.'

Rosanette, choking with sobs, left the room. And Pellerin said immediately:

'Well, what about Arnoux!... You know what's happened?'

'No, what?'

'It was bound to end like that in any case.'

'Like what?'

'He may well be... Excuse me.'

The artist got up to raise the head of the small corpse.

'You were saying...?' Frédéric asked.

And Pellerin, half-closing his eyes to get the measurements right:

'I was saying our friend Arnoux may well be in clink by now.'

Then, satisfied:

'Take a look! Have I got it right?'

'Yes, it's very good! But what about Arnoux?'

Pellerin put down his crayon.

'According to what I've heard, he's being taken to court by someone called Mignot, a close friend of Regimbart, that idiot, you know? What a fool! Just imagine that one day...'

'We're not talking about Regimbart!'

'That's true. Well, Arnoux last night had to find twelve thousand francs or he was done for.'

'Oh, it's surely not as bad as all that?' said Frédéric.

'Indeed it is! It looked serious to me, very serious!'

At that moment Rosanette reappeared with red blotches under her eyes, as red as daubs of rouge. She drew close to the pastel and looked. Pellerin indicated that he had fallen silent out of respect for her but Frédéric took no notice:

'But I can't believe...'

'I tell you I met him last night in the Rue Jacob. He even had his passport on him just in case. And he was talking about getting a boat from Le Havre, him and all his tribe.'

'What! His wife too?'

'Of course! He's too much of a family man to live on his own.'

'Are you certain of it?'

'Yes, for heaven's sake! Where do you think he would have got twelve thousand francs from?'

Frédéric paced around the room two or three times. He was breathing hard and biting his lips. He seized hold of his hat.

'Where are you going?' said Rosanette.

He did not answer her, but disappeared.

## V

HE had to find twelve thousand francs or he'd never see Madame Arnoux again; and until that moment he had still entertained a hope in his heart that he could not extinguish. Was she not the very essence of his life, the very fount of his existence? For several minutes he stumbled around on the pavement, gnawed by anxiety, but happy nevertheless not to be with the other one.

Where could he get hold of some money? Frédéric knew from his own experience how hard it was to get it straight away, at whatever cost. There was one person alone who could help, Madame Dambreuse. She kept several banknotes in her desk. He went to see her; and in a bold voice:

'Can you lend me twelve thousand francs?'

'What for?'

It was someone else's secret. She wanted to know whose. He wouldn't tell her. They both stood their ground. In the end she declared she wouldn't give him anything unless he told her why. Frédéric blushed deeply. One of his friends had committed a theft. The sum had to be paid back that very day.

'What's he called? His name? Let's hear what his name is!'

'Dussardier!'

And he threw himself at her feet, begging her not to say anything.

'What sort of a woman do you think I am? One would think you were the thief. Stop acting so tragically! Here, here it is and much good may it do him!'

He rushed to Arnoux's house. The dealer was not in his shop. But he was still living in the Rue Paradis, for he had two houses.

In the Rue Paradis the porter swore that Monsieur Arnoux had not been there since yesterday. As for Madame, he wasn't sure where she was. And Frédéric, having leaped up the stairs, put his ear to the lock. Finally it was opened. Madame had left with Monsieur. The maid did not know when they would be back. Her wages had been paid. She was leaving too.

Suddenly a door slammed.

'Is somebody there?'

'Oh no, Monsieur, it's the wind!'

Then he withdrew. Nonetheless such a prompt disappearance had something strange about it.

Regimbart, being Mignot's friend, would perhaps be able to clear up the mystery? And Frédéric took a cab to his house in Montmartre, Rue de l'Empereur.

His house had a small garden along one side, enclosed by railings with sheets of metal behind. Three steps set off the white facade, and from the pavement you could see the two ground-floor rooms, the first being a drawing room with dresses lying around everywhere on the furniture, and the second a workshop where Madame Regimbart's seamstresses worked.

They were all persuaded that Monsieur had important work, important contacts, that he was a completely exceptional man. When he went along the corridor with his turned-up hat, his long serious face and his green frock coat, they stopped what they were doing. Besides he always spoke some encouraging words to them, some sententious courtesy; and later on when they got back to their own husbands they were dissatisfied, because he was their ideal.

None of them loved him as much as Madame Regimbart, however, an intelligent little woman who kept him on her earnings.

As soon as Monsieur Moreau had announced himself, she quickly came to greet him, knowing through the servants of his liaison with Madame Dambreuse. Her husband 'would be back any minute' and Frédéric, following her, admired the way the house was kept and the vast quantity of oilcloths everywhere. Then he waited a few minutes in a kind of study room to which the Citizen was in the habit of retiring, in order to think.

His welcome was less surly than usual.

He explained the Arnoux affair. The former porcelain manufacturer had persuaded Mignot, a patriot, and the owner of a hundred shares in *Le Siècle*, that he should, for the good of democracy, change the management and editorship of the magazine. And on the pretext of imposing this opinion on the next shareholders' meeting, he had asked for fifty shares, saying that he would pass them on to reliable friends, who would support his vote. Mignot would not have any responsibility, would not have any quarrel with anybody. Then, once assured of success, he would obtain a good position for him, earning at least five or six thousand francs. The shares had been made over to him. But Arnoux had promptly sold them, and with the money had gone into partnership with a dealer in religious objects; upon which Mignot had complained, and Arnoux had evaded the issue. Finally the patriot had threatened him with prosecution for fraud if he did not return the shares or the equivalent sum: fifty thousand francs.

Frédéric looked desperate.

'That's not all,' said the Citizen. 'Mignot, who's a good fellow, came down by twenty-five per cent. New promises from Arnoux, new play-acting of course. In short, the day before yesterday, in the morning, Mignot insisted that he give him back twelve thousand francs within twenty-four hours and without prejudice to the rest of the debt.'

'Here it is!' said Frédéric.

The Citizen slowly turned round:

'You are joking!'

'No, I'm not, the money's in my pocket. I was just bringing it.'

'Heavens, old chap, you haven't wasted any time! But anyway it's too late. The charge has been brought and Arnoux has gone.'

'Alone?'

'No, with his wife. Someone saw them at Le Havre station.'*

Frédéric went very pale. Madame Regimbart thought he was going to faint. But he recovered his self-possession and was even able to ask two or three questions about the whole affair. Regimbart was upset, since all of this harmed democratic principles. Arnoux had always been lacking in principles and stability.

'A real feather-brain! He burned the candle at both ends. Women have been the ruin of him. It's not him I pity, but his poor wife.' For the Citizen admired virtuous women and held Madame Arnoux in high esteem.

'She must have gone through a lot.'

Frédéric was grateful to him for this sympathy, and shook his hand warmly, as if he had done him a service.

'Have you done all that's necessary?' Rosanette asked when she saw him again.

He had not felt up to it, he replied, and had wandered around the streets to distract himself.

At eight they went into the dining room; but they sat in silence opposite each other, sighed deeply at intervals and pushed away their plates. Frédéric drank some brandy. He felt wrecked, crushed, annihilated, no longer feeling anything but extreme exhaustion.

She went to fetch the portrait. The red, yellow, green, and indigo clashed violently, and the picture was hideous, if not ridiculous.

In any case the dead baby was now unrecognizable. The purple of his lips made the whiteness of his skin stand out. His nostrils were even thinner, his eyes more hollow. And his head rested on a blue taffeta pillow between petals of camellias, late roses, and violets. That had been the maidservant's idea. Together, devotedly, they had arranged him. On the mantelpiece, covered with a lace cloth, were silver-gilt candlesticks interspersed with holy boxwood. In a vase at either end aromatic pastilles were burning. All this with the cradle as well created a kind of altar; and Frédéric remembered his vigil by the body of Monsieur Dambreuse.

Every quarter of an hour or so, Rosanette opened the curtains to look at her baby. She could imagine him beginning to walk in a few months' time, then at school, in the middle of the schoolyard playing prisoners' base, then as a young man of twenty; and all these images she conjured up seemed to her like all the sons she had lost—the extremes of grief multiplying her motherhood.

Frédéric, motionless in the other armchair, was thinking of Madame Arnoux.

She was probably on a train, her face pressed to the window in the compartment, and looking at the country rushing past her back to Paris; or else on the deck of a steamer, like the first time he had met her. But that ship was travelling on and on towards lands from which she would never return. Then he imagined her in the bedroom of an inn, with travelling trunks on the floor, wallpaper peeling off the walls, the door shaking in the wind. And what then? What would become of her? A teacher, a live-in companion, a chambermaid perhaps? She was at the mercy of all the vagaries of poverty. Not knowing what was happening to her tormented him. He should have opposed this flight, or gone after her. Was he not her true husband? And, thinking he would never meet her again, that it was well and truly over, he felt his whole being torn apart. His tears that had welled up since the morning overflowed.

Rosanette noticed.

'Oh, you are weeping, like me! Are you sad?'

'Yes, yes, very sad!'

He clasped her to him and they sobbed together, their arms around each other.

Madame Dambreuse was also weeping, lying on her bed, face down, her head in her hands.

Olympe Regimbart, having arrived that evening so that she could try on her first coloured dress,* had recounted Frédéric's visit, and even that he had twelve thousand francs ready to give to Monsieur Arnoux. So that money, her own money, was to prevent that woman leaving, to keep his mistress in Paris!

She flew into a rage at first. And she made up her mind to get rid of him, as she would a lackey. Her floods of tears calmed her down. It was better to bottle up her feelings and say nothing.

Next day Frédéric brought back the twelve thousand francs.

She begged him to keep them, in case he needed them for his friend, and she enquired in detail about this gentleman. Who was it who had pushed him towards this abuse of confidence? It was some woman, she was certain of it! Women drag you into all sorts of crime.

This teasing tone disconcerted Frédéric. He felt great remorse for his calumny. But it was reassuring that Madame Dambreuse could not know the truth.

She persisted, however, for the next day she asked again about his young friend and then about another, Deslauriers.

'Is he a reliable, intelligent friend?'

Frédéric praised him.

'Ask him if he'll come and see me one morning. I should like to consult him about something.'

She had found a roll of papers containing some of Arnoux's bills, correctly protested and signed by Madame Arnoux. It was for those that Frédéric had come once to Monsieur Dambreuse's house one lunchtime. And although the capitalist did not wish to sue for the money, he had obtained a judgement by the commercial tribunal not only against Arnoux, but his wife as well. She did not know about this; her husband had not seen fit to tell her.

This was a weapon! Madame Dambreuse had no doubt about it. But her own lawyer would perhaps advise her not to proceed; she would have preferred somebody obscure, and she remembered that fellow with the impudent expression who had once offered his services to her.

Frédéric innocently did what she asked. The lawyer was delighted to have dealings with such a fine lady.

He hurried over.

She informed him that the inheritance belonged to her niece, a further reason to get these debts settled. She would hand the money over to the Martinons, thus heaping coals of fire on their heads.

Deslauriers realized there was some mystery behind all this. He examined the bills thoughtfully. The sight of Madame Arnoux's signature conjured up her person before him, and how affronted by her he had been. Here now was an opportunity for revenge, why not take it?

He advised Madame Dambreuse to sell off at auction the bad shares that were left from the estate. An agent would buy them back secretly and would bring an action. He would be responsible for providing the agent.

Towards the end of November, Frédéric, passing down Madame Arnoux's street, raised his eyes to the windows and saw pasted to the door a notice in large capitals which read:

SALE OF FINE FURNITURE AND HOUSEHOLD EFFECTS, CONSISTING OF
KITCHEN UTENSILS, PERSONAL AND TABLE LINEN, CHEMISES, LACES,
UNDERSKIRTS, DRAWERS, FRENCH AND INDIAN CASHMERES, AN
ERARD PIANO, TWO RENAISSANCE OAK CHESTS, VENETIAN MIRRORS,
CHINESE AND JAPANESE PORCELAIN.

'It's their furniture!' Frédéric told himself, and the porter confirmed his suspicions.

As to the person who was making the sale, he didn't know his name, but the auctioneer, Maître Berthelmot, would perhaps be able to give him more information.

The official did not want at first to say which creditor had instigated the sale. Frédéric insisted on knowing. It was a certain Monsieur Sénécal, a business agent. And Maître Berthelmot was even gracious enough to lend him his *Petites Affiches*.*

When Frédéric arrived at Rosanette's he threw it down on the table, open at that page.

'Read that!'

'Well, what?' she said, with such an unconcerned expression that he was revolted.

'Oh, don't pretend you don't know!'

'I don't know what you are talking about!'

'You are the one making Madame Arnoux auction everything.'

She read the advertisement again.

'Where's her name?'

'Oh, it's her furniture! You know it as well as I do!'

'What's it to do with me?' Rosanette said, with a shrug.

'With you? You are taking revenge on her, that's all! It's the result of you persecuting her! Didn't you once insult her in her own home? A whore like you! And the saintliest, loveliest, best woman in the world! Why are you bent on ruining her?'

'You are mistaken, I assure you.'

'Come now! As though you didn't put Sénécal up to it!'

'Don't be so silly!'

Then he flew into a rage.

'You are lying, you wretch, you are lying! You're jealous of her! You've got a court order against her husband! Sénécal is already mixed up in your affairs! He hates Arnoux, and you hate his wife. I saw how delighted he was when you won your case over the kaolin. Don't tell me you're not in cahoots with him?'

'I give you my word...'

'Oh, I know all about your word!'

And Frédéric recited the names of all her lovers, with circumstantial details. Rosanette, turning paler and paler, was backing away from him.

'You are surprised? You thought I was blind because I closed my eyes. Now I've had enough! A man doesn't grieve to death when a woman like you betrays him. When a woman of your sort goes too far, he leaves her. He would demean himself by punishing her.'

She was wringing her hands.

'Dear heaven, what has altered you like this?'

'Only yourself!'

'And all that for Madame Arnoux!...' sobbed Rosanette.

He went on icily:

'She's the only one I've ever loved.'

At this insult, the tears stopped.

'That just goes to prove your good taste! A dumpy middle-aged creature with a complexion the colour of liquorice and eyes like holes in the wall and just as empty! Since you like that sort of thing, go and join her!'

'That's what I was waiting for! Thank you!'

Rosanette remained motionless, stupefied by this extraordinary behaviour. She even allowed the door to shut behind him; then with one swift movement she caught up with him in the hall and flung her arms around him:

'Don't be so crazy! It's absurd. I love you! In the name of our baby, for heaven's sake!' she begged.

'Admit you are the one who did it!' said Frédéric. She still protested her innocence.

'Won't you admit it?'

'No!'

'Well then, farewell—for ever.'

'Listen to me!'

Frédéric turned.

'If you knew me better you'd know I shan't go back on my word.'

'Oh, you'll be back!'

'Never!'

And he slammed the door.

Rosanette wrote to Deslauriers that she needed to see him urgently.

He arrived one evening five days later. And when she told him that Frédéric had left her, said:

'Is that all it was? Nothing serious then.'

At first she had thought he might be able to bring Frédéric back. But now all was lost. She had learned from her porter of his forthcoming marriage to Madame Dambreuse.

Deslauriers gave her a talking-to, was even especially cheerful and cracked jokes; and as it was very late, asked her permission to spend the night in an armchair. Then next day he left for Nogent, telling her he didn't know when they would see each other again. Probably there would soon be a great change in his life.

Two hours after his return, Nogent was in an uproar. They were saying Monsieur Frédéric was going to marry Madame Dambreuse. Finally the three Auger girls, no longer able to contain themselves, went to see Madame Moreau who proudly confirmed the news. Père Roque took it badly. Louise shut herself away. It was even rumoured that she had gone mad.

Frédéric, however, could not hide his depression. Madame Dambreuse redoubled her attentions, no doubt to distract him. Every afternoon she took him out in her carriage; and one day, as they went through the Place de la Bourse, she took it into her head to go into the auctioneers', just for amusement.

It was 1 December, the day of Madame Arnoux's sale. He remembered the date and made his distaste for the idea obvious, declaring the place unbearable because of the crowds and the noise. She only wanted to have a look. The carriage stopped. He had to go in after her.

In the yard you could see washstands without basins, bits of wood from armchairs, old baskets, broken china, empty bottles, mattresses. And men in smocks or in dirty frock coats covered in grey dust, with coarse faces, some carrying cloth bags on their shoulders, were chatting in separate groups or were bawling at each other.

Frédéric made objections to going any further.

'Oh, nonsense!'

They went upstairs.

In the first room on the right men with catalogues in their hands were examining some pictures; in another, they were selling a collection of Chinese weapons. Madame Dambreuse wanted to go downstairs. She looked at the numbers over the doors and took him to the end of the passage into a room that was packed with people.

He immediately recognized the two sets of shelves from *L'Art industriel*, her worktable, all her furniture! Piles of them at the back sloped upwards in order of height, from floor to ceiling. And on the other side of the room the rugs and curtains were hanging along the walls in a row. Below them were rows of seats on which old men were dozing. On the left was a kind of counter where the auctioneer in a white cravat was waving a small hammer around. Next to him was a young man, writing. And lower down stood a strong-looking fellow, a cross between a travelling salesman and a tout, shouting out the lots. Three lads brought them and put them on a table in front of which sat second-hand dealers and buyers. The crowd milled around.

When Frédéric came in, the skirts, scarves, handkerchiefs, even the chemises were passed from hand to hand and examined. Sometimes they were thrown across the room and suddenly the air was white with them. Then they sold her dresses, then a hat of hers, its feather broken and bent, then her furs, then three pairs of little boots. And the dividing-up of these relics, in which confusedly he could see the shape of her limbs, seemed to him an atrocity, as though he were watching carrion crows tearing at her corpse. The atmosphere in the room, with all these people's breath, made him feel sick. Madame Dambreuse offered him her smelling salts; she was enjoying herself hugely, she said.

They exhibited the bedroom furniture.

Maître Berthelmot named a price. The crier immediately repeated it, raising his voice. And the three commissioners waited calmly for the hammer to come down, then took the object into an adjoining room. And so one after the other there disappeared the large blue rug with camellias touched by her lovely feet as she came towards him; the little tapestry sofa where he always sat, opposite her, when they were on their own; the two firescreens whose ivory was softened by contact with her hands; a velvet pincushion with pins still sticking in it. It was as though pieces of his heart were vanishing along with these things. And the monotony of the same voices, the same gestures, paralysed him with fatigue, and caused him to sink into a morbid stupor, a dissolution.

There was a rustle of silk in his ear. Rosanette was touching him.

She knew of the sale from Frédéric himself. When she had got over her mortification, it struck her that she could take advantage of it. She had come to watch, wearing a white satin waistcoat with pearl buttons, a dress with flounces, tight gloves, and a triumphant look on her face.

He paled with anger. She looked at the woman with him.

Madame Dambreuse had recognized her. And for a whole minute they looked each other up and down, scrutinizing each other, in order to find fault, to criticize. The one perhaps envied the other's youth, and the younger one was discomfited by the high-class aristocratic simplicity of her rival.

Finally Madame Dambreuse looked away, with a smile of inexpressible insolence.

The crier had opened a piano—*her* piano! Remaining standing, he played a scale with his right hand and asked twelve thousand francs for the instrument, coming down to one thousand, eight hundred, seven hundred.

Madame Dambreuse gaily made fun of the old tin can.

Then they placed in front of the second-hand dealers a small jewellery box with silver medallions, corners and clasps, the very same one he had seen at the first dinner in the Rue de Choiseul; later it had been at Rosanette's, and had then come back again to Madame Arnoux's. Often in their conversations, his eyes encountered it. It was bound up with his dearest memories and his soul was melting with love, when Madame Dambreuse suddenly said:

'I shall buy it!'

'But it's of no interest,' he countered.

On the contrary, she considered it very pretty. And the crier was extolling the fine workmanship. 'A Renaissance jewel! Eight hundred francs, Gentlemen! And almost solid silver. With a little whiting, it will shine up a treat!'

And as she pushed her way through the crowd:

'What a peculiar idea!' said Frédéric.

'Does it annoy you?'

'No, but what use is this trinket?'

'Who knows? To put some love letters in, perhaps?' And she looked at him in a way that made the allusion perfectly obvious.

'All the more reason not to strip the dead of their secrets.'

'I didn't know she was as dead as all that.'

And she added in a clear voice: 'Eight hundred and eighty francs!'

'What you are doing isn't very kind,' muttered Frédéric. She laughed.

'But, my dear, it's the first favour I've asked of you. You won't be a very nice husband, you know!' Someone had just made a better offer. She raised her hand:

'Nine hundred francs!'

'Nine hundred francs!' repeated Monsieur Berthelmot.

'Nine hundred and ten... fifteen... twenty... thirty!' barked the crier, glancing round the audience with little jerks of the head.

'Prove to me I'm marrying a reasonable woman,' said Frédéric.

He propelled her gently towards the door.

The auctioneer continued.

'Come now, come now, Gentlemen, nine hundred and thirty! Any advance on nine hundred and thirty?'

Madame Dambreuse, who had reached the exit, halted; and said, in a ringing voice:

'A thousand!'

A shudder went through the crowd, then silence.

'One thousand francs, Gentlemen! A thousand! All done at a thousand? All done? Going, going, gone!'

The ivory hammer came down.

She passed her card, the jewel box was sent to her.

She pushed it into her muff.

Frédéric felt a grip of ice on his heart.

Madame Dambreuse was still holding tight to his arm. And she did not dare look at him until they reached the street, where her carriage was waiting.

She jumped in, like a thief escaping, and when she had sat down, turned to Frédéric. He had his hat in his hand.

'Will you not get in?'

'No, Madame.'

And, with a cold wave, he closed the door and signalled to the coachman to leave.

He felt joyful, as if he had recovered his independence. He was proud of having avenged Madame Arnoux by sacrificing a fortune. Then he was astonished by his action, and he was overcome by a feeling of infinite weariness.

The next morning* his servant told him the news. A state of siege was declared, the Assembly was dissolved, and some of the deputies were in Mazas prison. Public affairs left him indifferent, he was so preoccupied with his own private ones.

He wrote to some shops to cancel orders for several items to do with his wedding, which seemed to him now a rather ignoble specula- tion. And he was filled with disgust for Madame Dambreuse because she had almost made him do something dishonourable. For that rea- son he forgot the Maréchale, wasn't even worried about Madame Arnoux—thinking only of himself, and himself alone—lost in the ruins of his dreams, sick, fraught with grief and depression, and loathing the artificiality of this society in which he had suffered so greatly. He longed for the freshness of grass, the relaxation of the provinces, a sleepy life spent in the shade of the house where he was born, with simple people. On the Wednesday evening he finally went out.

Numerous groups were standing around on the boulevard. From time to time a patrol came to split them up; they re-formed after it had gone by. People spoke out freely, shouting jokes and insults after them, nothing more.

'What?' Frédéric asked a worker. 'Are you not going to fight?'

The man in the smock answered:

'We're not such fools as to get ourselves killed for a gang of bour- geois! Let them settle their own affairs!'

And a man grumbled, as he looked askance at the worker:

'Filthy socialists! If only we could get rid of them once and for all!'

Frédéric could not understand so much bitterness and foolishness. His disgust for Paris increased. And two days later* he left for Nogent by the first train.

The houses soon vanished, the countryside extended before him. Alone in his coach, his feet on the bench, he pondered the events of the last few days, and all his past. The memory of Louise returned.

'She loved me, that girl! I was wrong not to seize that chance of happiness... Oh well, don't let's think about it any more.'

But five minutes later:

'Yet... who knows? Later... why not?'

His thoughts, like his eyes, plunged into distant horizons.

'She was naive, a country girl, almost wild, but with a heart of gold!'

As he got nearer to Nogent, she became more real to him. When he crossed the plain of Sourdun, he could see her under the poplar trees as in the old days, cutting reeds by the pools. They arrived and he got out.

Then he leaned on the bridge, to look at the island and the

garden once more, where they had walked one sunny day; and dazed by the journey and the fresh air, and still weak from his recent upsets, he was filled with a sort of exaltation and said to himself:

'Perhaps she's out. Supposing I went to meet her!'

The bell of Saint-Laurent was tolling, and in front of the church in the square there was a gathering of poor people, and a barouche, the only one in the village (the one they used for weddings). Then suddenly at the church door there appeared a newly married couple in a large group of the well-to-do in white cravats.

He thought he was seeing things. No, it was definitely her, Louise, draped from her red hair to her heels in a white veil; and it was definitely him, Deslauriers! Wearing a blue suit with silver embroidery, a prefect's uniform.* What was the meaning of it all?

Frédéric hid in the recess of a house to let the procession pass.

Ashamed, defeated, crushed, he returned to the railway and went back to Paris.

The driver told him that the barricades were up between Château d'Eau and the Gymnase, and he went via the Faubourg Saint-Martin. At the end of the Rue de Provence Frédéric got out of the cab to reach the boulevards on foot.

It was five o'clock, a fine rain was falling. A crowd of bourgeois were occupying the pavement beside the Opéra. The houses opposite were all shut up. No one at the windows. Across the whole width of the boulevard, dragoons galloped by at full tilt, bent low over their horses, sabres drawn, and the plumes of their helmets and their vast white cloaks billowing out behind them passed beneath the gaslights which swung to and fro in the wind and the mist. The crowd watched, in terrified silence.

Between the charges of the cavalry, squads of police arrived to move everyone back into the side streets.

But on the steps of Tortoni's a man, remarkable from afar because of his tall figure, stood as immobile as a caryatid:* Dussardier.

One of the officers at the head, his tricorne over his eyes, threatened him with his sword.

Dussardier, taking a step forward, began to shout:

'Long live the Republic!'

He fell to the ground, his arms outstretched.

A howl of horror rose from the crowd. The officer looked around him, and Frédéric, open-mouthed, saw that it was Sénécal.

## VI

HE went travelling.

He knew the melancholy of the steamboat, cold mornings waking under canvas, the tedium of landscapes and ruins, the bitterness of interrupted friendships.

He came home again.

He moved in society, and he had more love affairs. But the constant memory of the first made them all seem insipid to him. And the violence of his desire, the very flower of the feeling, had gone. His intellectual ambitions had likewise diminished. Years passed; and he endured the inertia of his intelligence and the dulling of his heart.

Towards the end of March 1867, at dusk, when he was alone in his study, a woman came in.

'Madame Arnoux!'

'Frédéric!'

She grasped him by the hand, drew him over to the window, and looked at him, saying over and over:

'It's him! Yes, it's really him!'

In the half-light of dusk he could see only her eyes beneath the little black lace veil which hid her face.

Placing a small purse of wine-coloured velvet on the mantelpiece, she sat down. Both remained there smiling at one another, unable to speak.

Finally he asked her a host of questions about herself and her husband.

They lived in deepest Brittany in order to make ends meet and pay off their debts. Arnoux, who was almost always ill, now looked like an old man. Her daughter was married and living in Bordeaux and her son was garrisoned in Mostaganem.* She raised her head.

'But I have seen you again! I am so happy!'

Then he told her that on hearing the news of their disaster he had hurried to their house.

'I knew that!'

'How?'

She had caught sight of him in the courtyard and had hidden.

'Why?'

So with trembling voice and long intervals between her words:

'I was afraid. Yes... afraid of you... and of myself.'

This revelation sent a thrill through him. His heart beat fast. She continued:

'Please forgive me for not coming sooner.' Then, pointing to the little wine-coloured purse covered with golden palms:

'I embroidered it on purpose for you. It contains the money for which the land at Belleville was to stand security.'

Frédéric thanked her for the present, chiding her at the same time for going out of her way to give it him.

'No, I didn't come for that! This visit was important for me, now I shall go back... there.'

She talked to him about where she lived.

It was a low-built house with just one upper floor, a garden full of tall box trees and a double avenue of chestnuts sloping upwards to the top of the hill from which you could see the sea.

'I go and sit there on a bench, which I've named "Frédéric's bench".'

Then she began to look eagerly at the furniture, the trinkets, the framed pictures, as though to carry them home in her memory. The portrait of the Maréchale was half-covered by a curtain, but the golds and whites which showed up in the darkness attracted her attention.

'Do I know that woman?'

'Impossible!' Frédéric said. 'It's an old Italian painting.'

She confessed that she would like to take his arm and walk along the streets.

They went out.

The lamps from the shops lit up her pale face at intervals. Then the darkness enveloped it again. And in the midst of the cabs, the crowd and the noise, they carried on talking about themselves, hearing nothing, as if they were walking together in the country on dead leaves.

They talked of the old days, the dinners in the days of *L'Art industriel*, Arnoux's obsessions, his way of tugging at the ends of his collar, of greasing his moustache with pomade, and other things deeper and more intimate. How thrilled he had been when he had heard her singing for the first time! How beautiful she was on her feast day at Saint-Cloud! He reminded her of the small garden at Auteuil, the evenings in the theatre, the time they met on the boulevard, old servants, her Negro woman.

She was amazed at his memory. But she said:

'Sometimes your words come back to me like a distant echo, like the sound of a bell wafted by the wind. And when I read passages about love in books, then I believe you are there with me.'

'Everything that books are said to exaggerate, you have made me feel,' Frédéric said. 'I understand why young men like Werther are not put off by Charlotte and her slices of black bread.'*

'My poor dear friend!'

She sighed; and after a long silence:

'No matter, we shall have truly loved one another.'

'But not given ourselves to one another.'

'Perhaps it's better that way,' she said.

'No, no! What happiness we should have had!'

'Oh, I do believe it, with a love like yours.'

And it must have been very strong to last so long while they were apart.

Frédéric asked how she had realized he loved her.

'It was one evening when you kissed my wrist* between my glove and my sleeve. I told myself: "But he loves me, he loves me!" But I was afraid of being so certain of it. Your discretion was so charming that I took pleasure in that as if it were a continual and involuntary homage.'

He had no regrets. His old suffering was redeemed.

When they went back, Madame Arnoux took off her hat. The lamp, placed on a console, lit up her white hair. It was like a blow in the stomach.

To hide this disappointment he went down on his knees to her, and taking her hands began to speak words of love.

'Your person, your slightest movements, seemed to me to have a more than human importance in the world. My heart, like dust, rose up when I walked behind you. You had the effect on me of moonlight on a summer's night, when all is perfume, soft shadow, whiteness, infinity; and the delights of the flesh and the soul were encompassed in your name which I said over and over to myself, attempting to kiss it as it left my lips. I imagined nothing beyond that. It was Madame Arnoux, just as you were, with her two children, loving, serious, dazzlingly beautiful, and so kind! That image erased all the others. I did not even give them a thought, since I always had in the depths of my being the music of your voice and the splendour of your eyes.'

She delighted in this adoration for the woman she no longer was.

Frédéric, drunk with his own eloquence, began to believe what he was saying. Madame Arnoux, her back to the light, leaned towards him. He felt on his brow the sweetness of her breath, the hesitant touch of her body through her clothes. Their hands clasped. The tip of her little boot poked out a fraction from under her dress, and he said, almost fainting:

'I am troubled by the sight of your foot.'

She rose, out of modesty. Then, not moving, and with the tone of someone sleepwalking:

'At my age! Him! Frédéric!... No woman has ever been loved as I have been. No, no! What's the good of being young? I don't care, I despise them, all the women who come here!'

'Oh, not many do,' he replied, to please her.

Her face lit up and she wanted to know if he would marry.

He swore he never would.

'Are you certain? Why not?'

'Because of you,' said Frédéric, holding her tight in his arms.

She stayed there, leaning back, her lips open, her eyes raised. Suddenly she pushed him away in despair; and as he begged her to speak, she bowed her head and said:

'I should have liked to make you happy.'

Frédéric suspected Madame Arnoux of coming to give herself to him; and he was seized again by a desire that was stronger than ever, furious, raging. However, he felt something inexpressible, a revulsion, a terror as though of committing incest. Another fear stopped him, that of being disgusted afterwards. And how awkward it would be as well. Partly through prudence and partly so as not to degrade his ideal he swung round on his heels and began to roll a cigarette.

She looked at him in wonder.

'How fine you are! Only you! Only you!'

Eleven o'clock struck.

'Already!' she exclaimed. 'At a quarter past, I must go.'

She sat down again. But she watched the clock, and he walked to and fro, smoking. Neither could think of anything else to say. There is a moment in separation when the person we love is already no longer with us.

Finally, the hand having passed twenty-five, she slowly picked up her bonnet by the ribbons.

'Farewell, my friend, my dear friend! I shall not see you again. It was my last act as a woman. My soul will not leave yours. May all the blessings of heaven be upon you!'

And she kissed him on his forehead, like a mother.

But she seemed to be looking around for something, and asked him for some scissors.

She took out her comb and all her white hair tumbled down.

Roughly she cut off a long strand at the roots.

'Keep it. Farewell!'

When she had gone, Frédéric opened the window. On the pavement below Madame Arnoux hailed a passing cab. She got in. The cab vanished.

And that was all.

## VII

TOWARDS the beginning of this winter Frédéric and Deslauriers were chatting by the fire, reconciled by something irresistible in their nature which always brought them together in friendship. Frédéric explained his quarrel with Madame Dambreuse, who had got married again, to an Englishman.

Deslauriers, without saying how he had come to marry Mademoiselle Roque, told him that one fine day his wife had run off with a singer. Trying to lessen the ridicule this brought, he had compromised his position as prefect by an excess of zeal for the Government. He had been dismissed. After that, he had been director of colonization in Algeria, secretary to a pasha, administrator of a journal, advertising agent, and had ended up as a solicitor for an industrial company.

As for Frédéric, having got through two-thirds of his fortune, he was living the life of a modest member of the petits bourgeois.

Then they exchanged information about their friends.

Martinon was a senator now.

Hussonnet was highly placed, having in his remit all the theatres and all the press.

Cisy, deep into religion and father of eight children, was living in the chateau of his forebears.

Pellerin had dabbled in Fourierism, homoeopathy, table-turning, Gothic art and humanitarian painting, had become a photographer and could be seen on every wall in Paris, in a black suit with a small body and large head.

'And your friend Sénécal?' Frédéric asked.

'Gone! I don't know where! And what of your *grande passion*, Madame Arnoux?'

'She must be in Rome with her son, a cavalry lieutenant.'

'What about her husband?'

'Dead, last year.'

'You don't say!' said the lawyer.

Then, tapping himself on the forehead:

'By the way, the other day in a shop I met the Maréchale with a little boy she has adopted. She's the widow of a certain Monsieur Oudry and is very fat nowadays, she's enormous. How she has gone downhill! In the old days she was so slim.'

Deslauriers did not hide the fact that he had taken advantage of her despair to ascertain this himself.

'After all, you had given me permission.'

Confessing this, he thought to make up for saying nothing about his attempt to seduce Madame Arnoux. Frédéric would have forgiven him, since it had not been successful.

Although rather annoyed by Deslauriers's revelation, he pretended to find it amusing. And the thought of the Maréchale reminded him of La Vatnaz.

Deslauriers had not seen her at all, nor anyone else who came to the Arnouxes' house. But he remembered Regimbart perfectly.

'Is he still alive?'

'Only just! Every evening at the same time he hangs out in one café or another in the Rue de Grammont and the Rue Montmartre, on his last legs, bent double, finished, a ghost.'

'And what about Compain?'

Frédéric uttered a delighted cry and begged the former delegate of the Provisional Government to tell him about the mysterious affair of the calf's head.

'It's imported from England. To parody the ceremony which the Royalists celebrated on 30 January, some Independents founded an annual dinner at which calves' heads were eaten and red wine was drunk out of calves' skulls, while they toasted the extermination of the Stuarts. After Thermidor, terrorists organized a very similar club, which just goes to prove that stupidity engenders more stupidity.'

'You seem to have cooled down about political matters?'

'Advancing age,' the lawyer said.

And they looked back over their lives.

They had both failed, the one who had dreamed of love and the other who had dreamed of power. What was the reason?

'Perhaps it's because we didn't steer a straight course?' said Frédéric.

'That might be true in your case. But my sin was an excess of rectitude. I took no account of a thousand minor matters which were actually more important than everything else. I was too logical and you were too sentimental.'

Then they blamed fate, circumstances, the times into which they were born.

Frédéric went on:

'That's not how we thought we'd turn out in the old days, at Sens, when you wanted to write a critical history of philosophy and I a great medieval novel about Nogent, whose subject I had found in Froissart:* how Messire Brokars de Fénestranges and the Bishop of Troyes attacked Messire Eustache d'Ambrecicourt. Do you remember?'

And digging up their youth, at each sentence they said:

'Do you remember?'

They could see the school yard again, the chapel, the sitting room, the fencing hall at the foot of the stairs, the faces of the monitors and the pupils, a certain Angelmarre, from Versailles, who used to cut himself trouser-straps out of old boots, Monsieur Mirbal and his red whiskers, the two teachers of line drawing and design, Varaud and Suriret, who always disagreed, and the Pole, Copernicus's fellow countryman with his cardboard planetary system, a travelling astronomer whose talk had been paid for with a meal in the refectory. Then they remembered a terrific binge they had had when they were out once, their first pipes, the prizegivings, the joy of the holidays.

It was during the holidays of 1837 that they had been to the Turkish woman's house.

This was their name for a woman whose real name was Zoraïde Turc. And many thought she was a Muslim, a Turk, which added to the romantic appeal of her establishment, situated on the riverbank, behind the ramparts. Even in the height of summer there was shade around her house, which could be identified by a bowl of goldfish near a pot of mignonette on the windowsill. Girls wearing white shifts, with rouge on their cheeks and long earrings, tapped on the window when you went by, and in the evening in the doorway sang softly in husky voices.

This place of perdition dazzled the neighbourhood. It was referred to in an indirect way: 'you know that street I mean—a certain street—below the Bridges'. The farmers' wives in those parts trembled for their husbands, the bourgeoises were afraid for their maidservants, because the Sub-prefect's cook had been caught there, and it was, of course, the secret obsession of all the adolescents.

So one Sunday when people were at Vespers, Frédéric and Deslauriers, having previously had their hair curled, picked some flowers from Madame Moreau's garden, then went out of the field gate; and after making a long detour round the vineyard, came back via the Pêcherie and slipped into the Turkish woman's house, still clutching their huge bouquets.

Frédéric presented his, like a lover to his betrothed. But the heat, the fear of the unknown, a kind of remorse, and even the pleasure of seeing at a glance so many women at his disposal, affected him so powerfully that he went deathly pale and stood still, tongue-tied. They all laughed, delighted at his embarrassment. Thinking they were making fun of him, he fled. And as it was Frédéric who had the money, Deslauriers was obliged to follow him.

They were seen leaving. It was a local story, still remembered three years later.

They told it to each other at some length, each filling in what the other forgot. And when they had finished:

'Those were the best days of our lives!' said Frédéric.

'Yes, perhaps you are right,' Deslauriers said. 'The best days of our lives!'

# APPENDIX 1

## HISTORICAL SKETCH

WITH the exception of its last two chapters, which form a double epilogue, the action of Flaubert's novel is framed by two dates, clearly indicated in the text: the morning of 15 September 1840, the day Frédéric meets Mme Arnoux, and the evening of 4 December 1851, when he witnesses the death of his friend Dussardier. Such chronological precision is unusual even for the most realistic novels of the time, many of which, including Flaubert's own *Madame Bovary*, were content to indicate in a somewhat looser way the span of time within which they were set. In *Sentimental Education*, on the other hand, Flaubert invites us to consider the echoes, parallels, and ironic contrasts between the sequence of moments in the personal 'story of a young man' and that of the historical events occurring around him. Flaubert worried that the drama of the historical context, with its cast of famous political figures, might overwhelm the textual space occupied by his less-than-heroic fictional characters; yet to construct his novelistic world in terms of clearly gradated foreground and background features would be to betray his ambition to produce a flatter but more seamless pattern of relations. Historical realities therefore tend to appear in the narrative either as references without illustration or as tableaux without captions. Since in 1869 the events of 1848 were only twenty years old, Flaubert could rely on his readers' personal memories to fill in the gaps, and so the challenge today is much greater than it was then, and certainly greater than Flaubert intended it to be. This historical sketch is intended to contextualize the information provided in the Explanatory Notes and Appendix 2: Glossary of Historical Figures.

### Part One

The autumn of 1840, when the story begins, marks a turning point in the history of the July Monarchy, also called the Bourgeois Monarchy, of Louis Philippe. Ten years after the 1830 Revolution, the regime appeared to be well established, having survived a series of assassination attempts and insurrections, the latest and most dramatic of the latter occurring in 1839, when Blanqui and Barbès were arrested. The appointment of Guizot as Minister of Foreign Affairs and de facto Government leader also signalled the triumph of the 'Centre Right' faction of the King's supporters, those who believed 'the throne is not an empty chair', over the Centre

Left, who claimed the King should 'reign but not rule'. The latter had briefly formed a government under Thiers in the spring and summer of 1840 but had fallen because of Thiers's bellicose foreign policy. Guizot also enjoyed a close relationship with the British government of Robert Peel and especially with the Foreign Secretary Lord Aberdeen, whose Presbyterian faith he shared. While an important factor in establishing the *entente cordiale* between France and its former enemy, this relationship was criticized by many French nationalists such as Flaubert's Regimbart. Despite their differences, the Centre Right and the Centre Left were Orléanist in the sense of supporting the regime of Louis Philippe, the former Duc d'Orléans. To their right stood the Legitimists, or partisans of the elder Bourbon dynasty, overthrown in 1830. In the 1840s, they believed the surviving member of that dynasty, the Comte de Chambord, or 'Henri V', to be the rightful king of France. Some Legitimists, unwilling to take the oath required to serve as peers and deputies, withdrew from parliamentary politics while others worked within the system. On the Left were Republicans of various stripes, some of liberal, more of socialist tendencies, some of them moderates willing to work within the existing regime for its reform, others, with more radical views, engaging in underground organizations such as the Société des Saisons (Society of the Seasons). In 1840, the radicals seemed to have been neutralized, and Legitimist hopes for another Restoration appeared increasingly quixotic. If there continued to be demonstrations, like the one in 1841 during which Frédéric meets Dussardier, one of the two things Frédéric's ideologically diverse group of friends agree on is that nothing seems likely to change. The complacent attitude of Dambreuse reflects this perception, just as his wealth symbolizes the close ties between the regime and bourgeois financiers. The other attitude they share is national pride, or perhaps better, sensitivity to any political humiliation which resonates with their personal frustrations. If they do not follow Regimbart in his aggressive nationalism, even the cautious and conformist Martinon does not dissent from his indignation at Guizot's handling of the Pritchard affair, which came to a head in 1844 but which Flaubert quietly antedates to 1841, perhaps just to make the group friendship more plausible. It is worth remarking that when Frédéric returns to Nogent in 1843 for a period of two years (or more, see below), he takes no interest in political affairs, and the only reference to what one might call broader historical trends involves Roque's negotiations on behalf of Dambreuse.

On the other hand, no one in Frédéric's group makes much of another important feature of the early 1840s: the conquest of Algeria, begun in 1830 in the last days of the Bourbon regime and vigorously continued under Louis Philippe. France annexed the Algerian areas it occupied in 1834, and Louis Philippe's younger sons all served there in the army. Bugeaud, Cavaignac, and Changarnier, the three most prominent generals involved in fighting the workers in 1848 and the remaining years of the Second Republic, had previously fought campaigns in Algeria. At this period, however, Algerian conquest and colonization was not a major popular cause. Aside from a brief mention of Guizot's dealings with the sultan of Morocco, and a reference in the final chapter to Mme Arnoux's son being posted there, Algeria appears in the novel only indirectly, in the form of clothing and textiles inspired by Algerian designs. Also only alluded to late in the novel is another event of considerable symbolic impact that occurred in late 1840: the return of Napoleon's remains from St Helena to Paris and their December reburial at the Invalides before a huge crowd. Although hesitant to accept Thiers's proposal for the repatriation because he feared it would stir political unrest, Louis Philippe wanted to benefit from a gesture that appealed to widespread popular sentiment. Louis Napoleon may have misjudged the extent of this sentiment when in August 1840 he entered France illegally for the second time and failed again to provoke a Bonapartist rebellion, but nostalgia for the Napoleonic era was kept alive by the popular songs of poets such as Béranger. Neither here nor anywhere else, however, does Flaubert introduce Louis Napoleon as an actor in the story, and the few references to him in Part Three are indirect.

## Part Two

According to the date given in the text, this part begins on the evening of 14 December 1845, when Frédéric leaves for Paris two days after receiving news of his inheritance. For reasons detailed in the Explanatory Notes, this date seems to be inconsistent with other facts in the story, as well as with the references to historical events in the first chapters of this part, the earliest of which, the Spanish weddings, took place in October 1846. In any case, we are soon in 1847, and it is clear that the political atmosphere has changed. The marriage of Louis Philippe's son the Duc de Montpensier to the sister (and presumed heir) of the Spanish queen, a move Guizot opposed, has frayed France's ties with Britain, a problem aggravated by the appointment of Lord Palmerston, known for vigorously opposing French interests in Egypt, as British Foreign Secretary. A potato blight (like the one that precipitated the Irish famine) in 1845 and a bad grain harvest in 1846 caused food prices to spike, while the severe winter cold of 1846–7 halted construction projects and aggravated unemployment. The Government's reluctance to intervene, based on its laissez-faire principles, plus a series of scandals involving ministerial and military corruption, were undermining faith in the regime. Perhaps most serious in its consequences for the survival of the regime, Guizot and his allies (including Louis Philippe) opposed expanding the right to vote beyond those who possessed a substantial level of taxable property, a number that had in fact diminished because of the recession. Authors as different as Lamartine and Dumas were producing histories, novels, and plays that recalled the glory days of the French Revolution and stoked anti-monarchical feeling.

The year 1847 also saw the organization of a series of banquets (to avoid restrictions on political assembly, subscription meals with 'after-dinner' speakers). The extension of voting rights to smaller property owners and to educated elites who didn't meet the tax requirement was their main cause, but other grievances were aired as well. The banning of a Paris banquet scheduled for 22 February 1848 led to demonstrations that some participants saw as an opportunity to topple the regime. Despite the Government's contingency plans to prevent a repeat of the disorders of 1830 that had overthrown the previous regime, Louis Philippe's delay in dismissing the unpopular Guizot allowed the situation to spin out of the King's control. The new military commander, Bugeaud, was widely disliked by other officers and by the National Guard, many of whose middle-class members were disenchanted with the regime and changed sides. When on 23 February some regular soldiers fired on a crowd in the Boulevard des Capucines, riot turned to revolution.

Critics have often remarked on the ironic counterpoint at the end of Part Two between the political struggles in the streets and Frédéric's distracted awareness of them, preoccupied as he is with a planned rendezvous with Mme Arnoux, and on his use of the word 'reform' to designate a redirection of his erotic desire from one woman to another. Less obvious, perhaps, is that during the last months of 1847, the hero is often away from Paris visiting her in her country retreat. Yet, historical events affect his life in other ways. In Part One, Frédéric had travelled only by boat or coach. When he goes to see Mme Arnoux in Creil, he takes a train on a railway opened in 1844. While Arnoux's porcelain factory is a ramshackle operation, the more impressive plant nearby is another sign of a modernizing economy. Dambreuse's offer to employ Frédéric in the Coal Association he is leading reflects the savvy businessman's awareness of the discovery in 1847 of significant new coal deposits in northern France.

## Part Three

On 24 February, Louis Philippe's plan to abdicate in favour of his grandson, the Comte de Paris, with the widowed Duchesse d'Orléans as regent, was foiled when a crowd invaded the legislature before it could vote.

Instead, Lamartine and others went to the Hôtel de Ville and there proclaimed the institution of a Republic, with a Provisional Government to exercise power until elections could be called. The Tuileries Palace was sacked, but the proclamation of the 'right to work' on 25 February, the creation of the National Workshops on the 27th, and the establishment on the 28th of the Luxembourg Commission to study further employment measures helped calm the situation. Elections for a Constituent Assembly were held in April on the basis of the newly-proclaimed universal male suffrage, and in Paris political clubs were formed to vet candidates (such as Frédéric) and debate idealistic proposals, but the moderate to conservative majority resulting from the election disappointed the Republican and the socialist Left. Blanqui and others had argued that not enough time had been allowed to educate the rural masses, but even in Paris the Left did not do as well as expected, one reason being displeasure with the new taxation imposed in order to shore up State finances.

Conservatives such as Dambreuse, who had felt obliged to go along with the new Republic, were emboldened to push back against its progressive measures, which in any case the Government was unable to maintain. A popular demonstration on 15 May, in which the legislature was overrun by a crowd demanding its dissolution and proclaiming a revolutionary government, and which was quashed by a National Guard that saw itself as defending the Republic, helped discredit the Left. It is Arnoux's assistance to Dambreuse that day that earns him his invitation to the businessman's dinner in early June, and we also see his zeal during his watch with Frédéric. On 4 June, a set of by-elections brought more conservatives into the Assembly. The less easily classified Louis Napoleon was also elected, and though he soon after resigned under pressure from the Republicans, his popularity was increasing over this period, as reflected in the demonstration attended by Dambreuse and Martinon. The Luxembourg Commission was abolished, and then, on 21 June, the National Workshops. The next day, barricades were set up in Paris, but the workers' revolt was violently repressed on 24–6 June by troops led by Cavaignac, as well as by the Mobile Guards, units of fairly well-paid young men some insurgents thought would side with them because of a similar humble background but who did not in fact identify with the older and unemployed workers of the revolt. Dussardier's ambivalence about whether to help suppress the revolt (as Victor Hugo also did, and more wholeheartedly) reflects the dilemma of other liberal and left-wing Republicans at the time, but we learn about this after the fact, just as Frédéric, away in Fontainebleau with Rosanette, avoids having to taking a stand on the revolt itself and is shown reacting only to its vindictive aftermath.

Events after June 1848 are represented in less detail as Frédéric shuttles between Rosanette and the Dambreuses. For both parties, though in different ways, the Republic and its conflicts are bad for business. Dambreuse is unimpressed with the 'President' (i.e. Louis Napoleon) elected on 10 December 1848 under the new constitution proclaimed a month earlier. His defeat of Cavaignac was helped by many (including Hugo) who disliked the authoritarian general more than they liked the new Bonaparte. Dambreuse himself trusts the new military commander, Changarnier, to keep order more than he does the President, with his continued support for universal male suffrage and his populist views. Elections for a Legislative Assembly also established under the new constitution were held on 13 May 1849, with the so-called Party of Order, a coalition of monarchists and conservative Republicans, winning a clear majority.

In 1850, after Left Republicans regained some ground in the by-elections of April–May, the legislature restricted the right to vote by imposing a residency requirement that many workers could not meet because they often had to move to find work, made the Catholic Church once again an important force in education by ending the State monopoly on secondary schools and giving parish priests oversight on primary ones, and supported the restoration of the political power of the Pope in Italy. However, the legislature, mistrusting Louis Napoleon, refused to increase the President's budget (a topic of conversation at Dambreuse's funeral in Chapter 4 (February 1851)) or to change the constitution, which limited presidents to a single term, thus preventing Louis Napoleon from standing in the elections scheduled for 1852. Louis Napoleon, who was popular with the military and who had dismissed Changarnier in January 1851, executed a carefully planned *coup d'état* on 2 December of that year, easily suppressing the abortive revolt of 4 December evoked at the end of Chapter 5. That same day, Frédéric is able to make a longer journey by rail to Nogent in the morning and arrive back in Paris the same afternoon.

Chapter 6, set in March 1867, says nothing about the politics of the Second Empire of Napoleon III, inaugurated December 1852 after being approved by popular referendum. We are given a glimpse of the later careers of some characters, though again not of the state of public affairs, in the conversation between Frédéric and Deslauriers in Chapter 7, which is said to take place 'this winter'. *Sentimental Education* appeared in November 1869 (with a publication date of 1870). The reference would thus be to the winter of 1868–9, but, as with Balzac's *Wild Ass's Skin*, which begins with a reference to 'last October', the key point is that the time of the story is brought into close proximity with the moment the story is written and presumed to be read.

# APPENDIX 2
## GLOSSARY OF HISTORICAL FIGURES

AFFRE, AUGUSTE (1793–1848). Archbishop of Paris from 1840, killed (not clear by whom) during the June insurrection while trying to intervene in the conflict.

ALBERT (Alexandre-Albert Martin, 1815–95). Known as 'Albert the Worker', Martin was a machinist by trade. He was a socialist, a member of the Société des Saisons (Society of the Seasons), and the editor of the newspaper *L'Atelier* (*The Workshop*). A friend of Louis Blanc, he was made a member of the 1848 Provisional Government but, disappointed by its failure to fully support the National Workshops, he was arrested for joining a violent anti-government demonstration on 15 May. Refusing to defend himself at trial, he served nine years in prison, including four in Belle-Isle, before being freed in 1859.

ALTON-SHÉE, COMTE D' (1810–74). A supporter of Guizot in the Chamber of Peers who in 1847 switched to the Opposition. In 1848, he supported the Republic and became a colonel in the National Guard.

ARCHBISHOP OF PARIS. See AFFRE.

AUMALE, DUC D' (1822–97). Fourth son of Louis-Philippe, governor general of Algeria, September 1847–February 1848. He went into exile in England after the February Revolution.

BARANTE, PROSPER DE (1782–1866). Historian and man of letters noted for his *History of the Dukes of Burgundy* (1824–6). Served in several government posts under Louis-Philippe, including as ambassador to Russia in 1835.

BARBÈS, ARMAND (1809–70). Republican agitator responsible with Blanqui for the uprising of May 1839. Sentenced to prison for life but freed in February 1948. Imprisoned again for revolutionary action in May 1848, he was released in 1854.

BARROT, ODILON (1791–1873). Constitutional monarchist of liberal bent, leader of Centre Left party, and organizer of banquet campaign for electoral reform. Minister of Justice during the beginning of Louis Napoleon's presidency, he went into opposition and was arrested 2 December 1851. He made a brief return to politics in 1872 under Thiers.

BARTHÉLÉMY-SAINT-HILAIRE, JULES (1805–95). Journalist at *Le National* and *Le Constitutionnel*, then professor of ancient philosophy at the Collège de France during the July Monarchy, he was elected as a moderate Republican in 1848 and was briefly Minister of Public Instruction. He was obliged to withdraw from politics after the *coup d'état*.

BÉRANGER, PIERRE-JEAN DE (1780–1857). Poet of the common people, writer of anti-government and anticlerical songs during the Restoration. Although elected as a Republican to the Constituent Assembly, the nostalgia for the Napoleonic era fostered by his songs helped prepare the way for Louis Napoleon.

BLANC, LOUIS (1811–82). The author of the influential *Organization of Labour* (1839), which proposed socialist and cooperative reforms, of a highly critical history of the first ten years of the July Monarchy, and of *The Right to Work* (1848), which inspired the establishment of the National Workshops after Blanc became a member of the Provisional Government. Discredited in the eyes of the workers by the political sabotage of the Workshops and attacked by conservatives, his parliamentary immunity was lifted and he was forced into exile. He would return to politics after 1871.

BLANQUI, LOUIS AUGUSTE (1805–81). A revolutionary socialist imprisoned in 1839 for his role in the May workers' uprising, freed in 1847, and imprisoned again in May 1848 for conspiring against the Second Republic. Released in 1859 after being transported to Algeria for several years, he would be imprisoned several times again for agitating against the State during the Second Empire and the early Third Republic.

BONAPARTE, CHARLES LOUIS NAPOLÉON (1808–73). Nephew of Napoleon I. After Waterloo he lived in exile in Germany, Switzerland, Italy, and England. His attempts in 1836 and 1849 to foment a revolution in his favour ended in failure, the second time with his capture and imprisonment in the fortress of Ham, where he wrote several pamphlets, including one about the solution to pauperism (1844). Other writings combined the idea of a strong central authority with an endorsement of universal suffrage and various populist measures. He escaped from prison in 1846 and went again to England until the 1848 Revolution, when he returned to France. Biding his time, he avoided being associated with either the June uprising or its repression. He became a deputy in September of that year, gaining election in five departments, and won the December presidential election with an overwhelming majority. While his general policies were conservative, he remained the champion of the universal male suffrage the Assembly sought to restrict out of fear of socialism. Prevented by the new constitution from seeking a second term as president in the elections planned for

1852, he seized power on 2 December 1851. Later that month, a national plebiscite endorsed his regime, and in December 1852 another plebiscite approved the transformation of the Republic into the Second Empire. As Emperor Napoleon III (Napoleon's heir, the notional Napoleon II, had died in exile in 1835), his rule, which saw considerable economic expansion and the modernization of Paris, but also an aggressive foreign policy, lasted until France's defeat in its 1870 war with Prussia.

BRÉA, JEAN-BAPTISTE (1790–1848). A distinguished captain in Napoleon's army, he rose through the ranks in subsequent regimes, becoming a field marshal in 1845. In June 1848, he led the troops fighting workers on the Left Bank but was captured and killed.

BUGEAUD, THOMAS-ROBERT (1784–1849). Marshal of France. Although initially opposed to making Algeria a permanent colony, as governor general 1840–7 he became notorious for his brutally effective methods of pacification. In February 1848, Louis-Philippe appointed him army commander but then changed his mind after a hostile response from the National Guard, one reason being his role in the 1834 massacre of innocent bystanders after a riot in the Rue Transnonin. Later that year, Bugeaud threw his support to Louis Napoleon.

CABET, ÉTIENNE (1788–1856). Utopian communist theoretician who also saw his work as recovering the original Christian doctrine of social justice. In 1848 he emigrated to the United States to lead a community named after the one envisioned in his *Voyage to Icaria* (1842).

CAUSSIDIÈRE, MARC (1808–61). Revolutionary journalist who participated in an anti-government uprising in 1834 and then edited the newspaper *La Réforme*. Made prefect of the Paris Police by the Provisional Government, he formed special units of Guardians of the People with names like *Montagnards* (Mountain Men) taken from the French Revolution of 1789. Dismissed from his post in May 1848, he fled the country after the June insurrection and returned to France only in 1859.

CAVAIGNAC, GODEFROY (1801–45). A Republican opponent of Louis-Philippe and active in the Society of the Rights of Man. Held for trial with other conspirators after the uprising of April 1834, he led a mass escape from prison and fled to England. Returning to France in 1840, he wrote for *La Réforme*. His funeral was attended by a large crowd of sympathizers.

CAVAIGNAC, LOUIS-EUGÈNE (1802–57). Brother of Godefroi and army officer. Rose to general in Algeria, of which he became governor general after the February Revolution. In April 1848 he was recalled to Paris as Minister of War and was instrumental in the repression of the June uprising. He served as leader of the Cabinet of ministers until

December 1848, when he was defeated by Louis Napoleon in the election for president. Refusing to take the oath as deputy after the *coup d'état,* he retired from politics.

CHALIER, JOSEPH (1747–93). Jacobin leader in Lyons, executed during a Royalist uprising there and viewed afterwards as a martyr of the Revolution.

CHAMBOLLE, FRANÇOIS-ANDRÉ (1802–83). A journalist and Centre Left deputy in the 1830s and 1840s, he moved to the Right after 1848. He opposed the *coup d'état* and was forced to leave France for a brief period, after which he left politics.

CHAMBORD, COMTE DE (1820–83). Grandson of Charles X, and last descendant of the senior branch of the Bourbon dynasty that was overthrown in 1830. He was considered by the Legitimist party during the reign of Louis Philippe to be the rightful heir to the French throne (as Henri V), but he remained in exile in Austria throughout the Second Republic. He did not press his claim until after the end of the Second Empire, when he gained the support of Louis Philippe's son. He might well have become king had he been willing to accept the tricolour flag of the Revolution.

CHANGARNIER, NICOLAS (1793–1877). Rose to rank of general in Algeria, of which he became governor general April–September 1848, after Cavaignac. Elected to Constituent Assembly in June 1848, he returned to Paris and was appointed commander of the National Guard and of the army troops there. He was responsible for keeping a lid on popular unrest in 1849, notably by expelling demonstrators occupying the Conservatoire des arts et métiers in protest against French intervention in Rome to support the Pope. Hostile to the Republic, he nevertheless became a political opponent of Louis Napoleon in 1851 and was banished for several years after the December *coup d'état.*

CHARLES X. The last king of the senior branch of the Bourbon dynasty, reigned 1824–30. His increasingly reactionary policies led to his overthrow in the July Revolution.

CHATEAUBRIAND, FRANÇOIS RENÉ DE (1767–1848). A leading Romantic writer who also pursued a political career, first under Napoleon (until 1804), and then during the Restoration in the Chamber of Peers, where, though a conservative, he took liberal positions on some issues, notably freedom of the press. Quixotically loyal to the Bourbon dynasty, he refused to take the oath of loyalty to Louis Philippe. He returned to private life and the writing of his memoirs.

COMTE, AUGUSTE (1798–1857). The founder of positivism, a philosophy that rejected introspective knowledge and metaphysical concerns in favour of reliance on science and empirical experience, and that held that social life was as much based on scientific laws and amenable to scientific explanation as the physical world. He is considered to be the inventor of sociology. In later life, he advocated a religion of humanity to fulfil the social function of traditional religion.

CONSIDERANT, VICTOR (1808–93). A utopian thinker, disciple of Fourier, who edited *La Démocratie pacifique* newspaper from 1843 and published several works on the principles of socialism. He also developed the notion of proportional representation in elections. He sat as a left-wing deputy in 1848–9, but his opposition to Louis Napoleon forced him into exile. His attempt to found a utopian community in Texas ended in failure. He later supported the Paris Commune of 1871.

CONSTANT, BENJAMIN (1767–1830). After a somewhat erratic political career during the Revolutionary and Napoleonic eras, he became a leading figure of the liberal opposition during the Restoration, speaking strongly for Greek independence and freedom of the press, and against slavery.

COUSIN, VICTOR (1792–1867). The founder of eclecticism, which sought to draw on the best insights of the various philosophical schools, from the empiricist to the Platonist. For this reason, he considered the history of philosophy to be an important enterprise. Cousin drew on both German Idealism and the Scottish common-sense philosophers. He was suspended from teaching 1821–8 because of his liberal views, but had a distinguished career as a peer and in the July Monarchy. As director of the École Normale supérieure, member of the Académie Française, and Minister of Public Instruction in the 1840s under Thiers, he wielded considerable power over the higher education system.

DANTON, GEORGES (1759–94). One of the chief leaders of the French Revolution and rival of Robespierre. Although considered one of the architects of the Reign of Terror, his relative indulgence for those of diverging views brought him under suspicion, and he was executed after a summary trial.

DESMOULINS, CAMILLE (1760–94). Schoolmate of Robespierre and initially allied with him, his advocacy of clemency to those condemned by Revolutionary tribunals led to his being executed along with Danton.

DUMOURIEZ, CHARLES FRANÇOIS DU PERRIER (1739–1823). Revolutionary general who won the Battle of Valmy in 1792 but who sought to save the life of Louis XVI. His less successful performance in subsequent military engagements brought him under suspicion in France, and so he went over to the side of the European coalition, which nevertheless mistrusted him for his moderate views. He ended his life in English exile.

DUPONT, PIERRE (1821–70). Poet and writer of Republican and socialist political songs, including the militant (but peace-loving) 'Song of the Workers' (1848), which was nicknamed 'the Marseillaise of the people'. Baudelaire wrote an appreciative essay on him. After the *coup d'état*, he was condemned to seven years' transportation to Algeria, but he secured a pardon and later glorified the military campaigns of Napoleon III.

DUPONT DE L'EURE (JACQUES DUPONT, 1767–1853). A noted magistrate under Napoleon, he was a member of the liberal opposition in the Restoration and a minister in the early years of Louis Philippe. In 1848, he was named president of the Provisional Government. He voted for abolition of the death penalty but against the right to work, and he supported Cavaignac against Louis Napoleon. After losing election in 1849 he left politics.

ENFANTIN, BARTHÉLÉMY (1796–1864). A disciple of Saint-Simon, in the 1830s he turned the utopian movement he had joined into a kind of church with himself as 'Father'. His advocacy of socialist ideas and free love led to a brief imprisonment in 1832, following which he went to Egypt in search of his messianic female mate. There he tried unsuccessfully to get the pasha to support his plan for a Suez canal. He returned to France in 1836 and for years sought in vain to serve as a 'royal apostle' to various European rulers. In a second attempt to launch the canal project, he was outmanoeuvred by Ferdinand de Lesseps, who would make the project his own.

FALLOUX, ALFRED DE (1811–86). A Legitimist and Catholic journalist under Louis Philippe, he welcomed the Republic in 1848 but strongly opposed the National Workshops. Named Minister of Public Instruction by Louis Napoleon in December 1848, he authored a law (passed 1850) that now bears his name. It reorganized primary and secondary education, putting the former under clerical control and allowing clergy without university degrees to teach in secondary schools, which were no longer a State monopoly.

FLOCON, FERDINAND (1800–61). Editor in the 1840s of the left-wing *La Réforme* under the patronage of Ledru-Rollin. Minister of Agriculture in the 1848 Provisional Government, he supported Cavaignac in his suppression of the June uprising but opposed Louis Napoleon, who banished him after the *coup d'état*. He was famous for always having his pipe with him.

FOUQUIER-TINVILLE, ANTOINE (1746–95). Prosecutor for the Revolutionary Tribunal and known for his zeal. After the end of the Terror, he was executed with other members of the Tribunal.

FOURIER, CHARLES (1772–1837). Utopian socialist thinker who developed an elaborately detailed vision of communal living spaces he called 'phalansteries', each composed of a 'phalanx' of people representing the range of human characteristics and in which jobs were based on one's interests and desires. His ideal of Harmony included a mixture of advanced and eccentric ideas about gender and sexuality.

FOY, MAXIMILIEN (1775–1825). Napoleonic general who sat as an independent deputy under the Restoration and defended the liberty of the press.

GENOUDE, ANTOINE-EUGÈNE DE (1792–1849). Editor of the Legitimist newspaper *La Gazette de France*. He sought allies among liberals and Republicans in the cause of universal male suffrage, believing that this reform (by enfranchising the rural peasantry) would benefit his party more than the others.

GUIZOT, FRANÇOIS (1787–1874). A leader of the opposition under the Restoration who sought what he believed to be a middle ground between an authoritarian monarchy and popular government. Under Louis Philippe he played a key role, first as Minister of Public Instruction requiring establishment of a primary school in every commune, and then as the conservative-leaning Minister of Foreign Affairs and de facto head of government from 1840. He was attacked for cultivating good relations with Britain and for resisting extension of the electoral franchise. In 1848, he was dismissed by Louis Philippe, too late to prevent the collapse of the July Monarchy. In retirement, he returned to his other vocation of historian.

HENRI V. See CHAMBORD.

HUGO, VICTOR (1802–85). The writer had been made a peer of France by Louis Philippe in 1845. In a June 1848 by-election, he was elected to the Constituent Assembly and also served as mayor of the 8th arrondissement. He supported the Government against the workers' revolt in June and initially sided with Louis Napoleon for president because he hated Cavaignac. In 1849 he moved to the Left with his speeches against poverty and his opposition to the Falloux law. Turning against Louis Napoleon, he was forced into exile after the *coup d'état*. In the novel, however, he is only mentioned as a poet.

JOINVILLE, PRINCE DE (1818–1900). The third son of Louis Philippe. As a naval officer, he served in various campaigns and expeditions in the Mediterranean and as far away as Mexico. Married in 1843 to a daughter of the Portuguese emperor of Brazil, he went into exile in February 1848. He returned to France in 1870.

JOUFFROY, THÉODORE (1760–1842). Eclectic philosopher linked to

Victor Cousin and translator of works by Dugald Stewart and Thomas Reid. He also served as a liberal deputy 1831–42.

LAFARGE, MARIE (1816–52). After a sensational trial, she was sentenced in 1840 for life to hard labour for murdering her husband. The evidence of poisoning was questionable, however, and she continued to proclaim her innocence. She was released by Louis Napoleon in 1852, shortly before her death from tuberculosis.

LAFFITTE, JACQUES (1767–1844). A rich Restoration banker and liberal deputy who spent heavily to support the July Revolution, a move that brought him close to financial ruin in 1831. He was appointed a minister in the new government but was soon dismissed as too progressive; he then sat with the liberal opposition.

LAMARTINE, ALPHONSE DE (1790–1869). After publishing his most famous Romantic poems in the 1820s, he served as a liberal deputy 1833–51. His popular *History of the Girondins* (1847), about the moderate faction in the French Revolution, helped spur demands for political reform. He declared the inauguration of the Second Republic in February 1848 and was a member of its Provisional Government and Minister of Foreign Affairs. His 25 February speech about the military glory associated with the tricolour flag was important in blocking the more militant revolutionaries' demand that the red flag become the national emblem. But his popularity quickly diminished and he won only a few votes in his attempt to become president in December.

LAMENNAIS, FÉLICITÉ DE (1782–1854). In the 1820s a Royalist priest and supporter of papal power, he moved gradually to the Left and founded the liberal Catholic paper *L'Avenir* in 1830. Condemned by Rome, he broke with the Church and embraced broadly humanitarian and socialist views. His book *Words of a Believer* (1834), which recorded his disenchantment and attacked the social order, was extremely popular. He was elected a member of the Constituent Assembly in 1848 and served until the *coup d'état*, but he did not exert much political influence.

LAMORICIÈRE, CHRISTOPHE DE (1806–65). Army general who distinguished himself in various Algerian campaigns including the capture of Constantine in 1837. In politics he would strongly promote colonization efforts. After unsuccessfully trying to install the Duchesse d'Orléans as regent in February 1848, he served in the Constituent Assembly of 1848 as a supporter of Cavaignac and as Minister of War in the second half of that year. He was arrested in the *coup d'état* and lived several years in exile.

LAROMIGUIÈRE, PIERRE DE (1756–1837). Professor of philosophy at the École Normale Supérieure and member of the Academy of Moral and

Political Sciences, interested in distinguishing psychology from physiology. He was an intellectual influence on figures such as Victor Cousin and Armand Marrast.

LEDRU-ROLLIN, ALEXANDRE (1807–74). A left-wing Republican deputy under Louis Philippe and founder of the newspaper *La Réforme*. In 1847, he led the banquet campaign to extend the franchise, and as Minister of the Interior in the 1848 Provisional Government, established universal male suffrage. He replaced the prefects of the former regime with special commissioners with Republican views and defended the right to work. Sidelined by Cavaignac after the June insurrection, he stood unsuccessfully for president in December. Attacked by Changarnier in 1849 for his opposition to the increasing conservatism of the Government, he fled to England and only returned to France in 1871.

LÉOTADE (d. 1850). A Christian Brother whose real name was Louis Bonafous, Léotade was convicted in April 1848 for the murder and attempted rape of 15-year-old Cécile Combettes. The prosecution and trial were suspected of bias, and the real culprit may have been another member of the same religious order who was later sent to the galleys but for another crime. Léotade died in prison.

LEROUX, PIERRE (1797–1871). Of humble background, he excelled in school but was forced to abandon his studies to support his widowed mother. In the 1820s, he wrote for *Le Globe* and became for a time a disciple of Saint-Simon but was put off by what he saw as the oppressiveness of a planned society and coined the word 'socialism' as a name for what he disliked. He later embraced socialism in a more positive sense as an ideal system that would combine freedom and equality, based on mutual aid and free association. He became a close friend of the novelist George Sand. He was elected to the Constituent Assembly in 1848. Although he did not endorse their use of armed force, he defended the workers who rose up in June. He served as a deputy until the *coup d'état*, when he went into exile until 1860.

LOUIS PHILIPPE (1773–1850). As Duc d'Orléans, he belonged to the junior branch of the Bourbon dynasty, but was proclaimed 'King of the French' (rather than 'of France') after the overthrow of his cousin Charles X in July 1830. Initially nicknamed the 'Citizen King' for his lack of pomp and his family-man image (he had five sons and three daughters), his reign favoured the upper financial and manufacturing bourgeoisie. The July Monarchy saw uneven economic (and considerable colonial) expansion, but also increasing unrest, not just among the poor but among all those who were excluded from voting or from other effective political participation. The inflexibility of Louis Philippe and his government on this point was a leading cause for his overthrow in 1848. He died in exile in England.

MABLY, GABRIEL MONNOT DE (1709–85). A significant political thinker of the French Enlightenment, brother of the philosopher Condillac. Defending equality of needs alongside equality before the law, his writings, including the *Rights and Duties of the Citizen* (posthumously published 1789), influenced debates in the early stages of the French Revolution.

MAISTRE, JOSEPH DE (1753–1821). A philosopher and diplomat from Savoy who strongly opposed the ideals of French Revolution, defending instead the absolute authority of kings and popes and a renewed political alliance between Throne and Altar. His reflections on authority and legitimacy, as well as his meditation on evil and the necessity of violence, made a considerable impression even among those who did not share his views, and among those, like the poet Baudelaire, who found in more progressive doctrines a lack of tragic depth.

MALTHUS, THOMAS (1766–1834). Anglican clergyman and political economist, whose most famous work, *An Essay on the Principle of Population* (1798), predicted that population growth must necessarily outstrip increases in food production. The work gave rise to debates about limiting population growth, especially among the lower classes, and whether it should be done by persuasion or force.

MANUEL, JACQUES-ANTOINE (1775–1827). Army officer under Napoleon and lawyer. As a liberal deputy in the Restoration, his eloquent opposition to the French military intervention to re-establish King Ferdinand VII on the Spanish throne led to his expulsion from the Chamber in 1823. His funeral in 1827 was attended by a huge crowd.

MARAT, JEAN-PAUL (1743–93). A radical journalist during the French Revolution. His assassination by Charlotte Corday in July 1793 made him a popular hero whose martyrdom was eulogized by the same Revolutionary leaders who had begun to distance themselves from him before his death.

MARIE (Pierre-Marie de Saint-Georges, known as Marie, 1795–1870). A deputy of the moderate Left from 1842, as a member of the 1848 Provisional Government he organized the National Workshops, but his resistance to workers' demands to make them meaningful enterprises helped spark the June insurrection. He moved to the Right, advocating press censorship, but after Louis Napoleon's election in December opposed the new president. He was not re-elected in 1849 and returned to private life as a lawyer until the 1869s, when he was again elected to the legislature under the Second Empire.

MARRAST, ARMAND (1801–52). A Republican journalist, editor of *Le National* from 1836, in which he attacked France's concessions to Britain in the Pritchard affair. He was one of the organizers of the banned banquet that precipitated the Revolution of February 1848 and served in the Provisional Government and as mayor of Paris later that year. He left politics after being defeated for election in 1849.

MICKIEWICZ, ADAM (1798–1855). Leading Polish Romantic poet who settled in Paris after the failure of the 1830 Polish revolt against Russia. Made professor of Slavic literature at the Collège de France, his lectures were suspended in 1844 because their mystical messianism was seen as politically subversive but especially as an attack on the Church. Under the Second Republic he briefly edited a newspaper favouring democratic and socialist principles, but he supported Louis Napoleon after the *coup d'état*.

MIRABEAU, HONORÉ GABRIEL RIQUETI, COMTE DE (1749–91). After a turbulent youth, he became a leading orator in the first phase of the French Revolution, supporting a constitutional monarchy. After his death, it was discovered that he had accepted money from Royalist sources and his reputation was compromised.

MOLÉ, MATHIEU (1781–1855). A politician who served in various ministerial capacities under Napoleon, the Restoration, and Louis-Philippe, whose government he led as a conservative in the Chamber of Peers 1836–39. As a deputy under the Second Republic, he supported the policies of Cavaignac in 1848, then Louis Napoleon in 1849, but he opposed the *coup d'état* and retired to private life.

MONTALEMBERT, CHARLES DE (1810–70). Liberal Catholic journalist and member of the Chamber of Peers under Louis Philippe. He supported freedom of the press as well as freedom of education, in the sense of allowing the establishment of 'free' (i.e. Catholic) schools outside the State system. As a deputy under the Second Republic, he opposed socialist measures and supported Falloux's law. He accepted the *coup d'état* in the hope of securing legislation favourable to Catholics.

MONTPENSIER, DUC DE (1824–90). Fifth son of Louis Philippe, in 1846 he married the younger sister of the reigning queen of Spain in one of the Spanish marriages that caused friction between France and England because they symbolized closer ties among the various branches of the Bourbon family in southern Europe. After the February Revolution, he moved to Spain, where he later unsuccessfully staked a claim to the throne for himself.

MORELLY, ÉTIENNE-GABRIEL (1717–78). Author of *The Code of Nature* (1755), which set out a utopian vision of an equal and cooperative society without private property.

NAPOLEON, LOUIS. See BONAPARTE.

NÉGRIER, FRANÇOIS DE (1788–1848). A veteran of Napoleon's army who in the 1830s and 1840s served in several campaigns in Algeria, he was killed near the Place de la Bastille fighting the insurgent workers of June 1848.

NEMOURS, DUC DE (1814–96). Second son of Louis Philippe, during the 1830s he served as an army officer in several Algerian campaigns, but in later years lived quietly. After the February Revolution, he went into exile in England. He returned to France in 1871.

ORLÉANS, DUCHESSE D' (1814–58). Protestant German princess who married Louis Philippe's heir in 1837 and was widowed in 1842. In February 1848, she tried unsuccessfully to have herself named as regent for her son, the Comte de Paris, after which she went into exile.

PIDOUX, VICTOR (1807–79). A lawyer and right-wing deputy, 1849–51.

PISCATORY, THÉOBALD (1800–70). A diplomat allied with Guizot, he worked to increase French influence in Greece, whose independence he had strongly supported in the 1820s. He was elected a deputy in 1849 and supported conservative policies, but he opposed the *coup d'état*, after which he returned to private life.

PIUS IX (Pope 1846–78). Initially praised (by Victor Hugo among others) for his progressive views (he freed political prisoners, was sympathetic to Italian nationalism, and reformed the papal government), he reacted to the upheavals of 1848, which included the proclamation of a short-lived Roman Republic that drove him from political power, by moving sharply in a conservative direction. He denounced liberalism, socialism, and the separation of Church and State. In 1854, he would proclaim the dogma of the Immaculate Conception of Mary and in 1870 that of papal infallibility.

PRITCHARD, GEORGE (1796–1883). Missionary and British consul in Tahiti. His opposition to the French annexation of Polynesia in 1843 led to his arrest and his forced return to England. His complaints led the British government to demand an apology and an indemnity from France, which complied, much to the displeasure of nationalist opinion, in what became known as 'the Pritchard affair' of 1844.

PROUDHON, PIERRE-JOSEPH (1809–65). A political writer of working-class background whose *What is Property?* (1840) caused a sensation by its initial (but not at all final) answer: theft. He was active as a journalist under the Second Republic, during which time he also tried to establish a bank of mutual credit to help working people. He became a deputy in a complementary election of April 1848 and expressed views that may be characterized as libertarian socialist or anarchist, but he did not participate in the June uprising, which he thought premature. In 1849 he was convicted for offence against the President and was imprisoned until 1852.

QUINET, EDGAR (1803–75). Historian, poet, and critic; initially a specialist of German thought, he also wrote on the history of religion. He became professor of southern [European] literature at the Collège de France in 1842 but was dismissed in 1846 for using his lectures to attack the Church more than discuss literature. A Republican, he served as a deputy during the Second Republic and opposed Louis Napoleon. He left France at the *coup d'état* and did not return until 1870, after which he resumed his professorship.

RATEAU, JEAN-PIERRE LAMOTTE (1800–87). A right-wing deputy in the Constituent Assembly who in January 1849 proposed its abolition at the behest of Louis Napoleon, so that a new (and, it was anticipated, more conservative) Legislative Assembly could be elected in May of that year.

ROYER-COLLARD, PIERRE-PAUL (1763–1845). As a professor of philosophy under Napoleon, he was influenced by the ideas of Scottish thinkers such as Thomas Reid; in turn, he influenced the thought of Victor Cousin. In the Restoration Chamber of Deputies, he was the leader of the Doctrinaires, a group of constitutional monarchists who rejected absolutism but who were wary of full democracy. He helped shape the ideas of Guizot and Molé.

SAINT-JUST, LOUIS ANTOINE DE (1767–94). A leading orator of the French Revolution and member of the Terrorist Committee of Public Safety. Distinguished for the harshness of his ideology and the eloquence of his speeches, and also for his zeal in conducting military campaigns against the anti-French coalition, he was executed along with Robespierre.

SAINT-SIMON, CLAUDE HENRI DE ROUVROY, COMTE DE (1760–1825). A political and economic theorist who envisioned the rise of an 'industrial' society that glorified all those, workers or business owners, who counted as genuine producers of wealth. He thought political power should be entrusted to economic and technical elites. Combining a practical outlook that came to be associated with modern social science with a messianic Christianity stripped of dogma, he influenced the utopian socialists of the next generation.

STAËL, GERMAINE DE (1760–1817). A political writer who played a key role in the liberal opposition to Napoleon, and the author of the important early Romantic novels *Delphine* (1802) and *Corinne* (1807). She was known for her cosmopolitan spirit and for her forceful personality.

STEUBEN, CHARLES DE (1788–1856). An artist most famous for the series of historical portraits and battle scenes he painted for the Museum of Versailles designed by Louis Philippe to celebrate France's military glories.

TALLEYRAND (Charles Maurice, prince de Talleyrand-Périgord, 1754–1838). A bishop before the French Revolution who became a wily politician, he became a leading diplomat under Napoleon and played a key role in defending French interests for Louis XVIII at the 1814 Congress of Vienna. A member of the Chamber of Peers during the Restoration, he was close to the Doctrinaires and helped Thiers launch his career. In 1830, he helped secure the throne for Louis Philippe.

THIERS, ADOLPHE (1797–1877). Leader of the Orléanist Centre Left and rival of Guizot, he was twice head of government under Louis Philippe. Sidelined in February 1848 but elected to the Constituent Assembly in June, he supported the party of order and the election of Louis Napoleon as President. He opposed the *coup d'état* and was forced to briefly leave France, but he returned to politics in the 1860s as an opposition leader. He played an important diplomatic role after the 1870 Franco-Prussian War and in 1871 organized the siege of Paris to destroy the Commune. He was the first president of the Third Republic, serving until 1873.

WROŃSKI, JÓZEF MARIA HOENE (1776–1853). Of Polish origin, he was an insightful mathematician and an eccentric philosopher, interested in magic and in messianic ideas. He spent most of his life in France and wrote in French.

# EXPLANATORY NOTES

The intention of these notes is to provide information on the full range of the novel's cultural and social references. For items not identified here (usually persons mentioned more than once, or events which require a greater amount of context), please see Appendix 1: Historical Sketch and Appendix 2: Glossary of Historical Figures. On the other hand, no attempt has been made to locate topographical references, except for a few key buildings. Some of the streets named in the book already no longer existed at the moment Flaubert wrote, some have disappeared since then, while others have been renamed at various times, but tracking these changes is not necessary to the comprehension of the story. Readers interested in these details should consult an annotated French edition or a historical guide to Paris.

## PART ONE

5 *L'Art industriel*: in 1839, the year before the one in which Flaubert's story begins, the critic Sainte-Beuve had published an article denouncing what he called 'littérature industrielle', by which he meant explicitly written to make money. Yet, the connotations of the word 'industrial' were not all negative in this period, since it also called to mind the idealistic writings of Saint-Simon (see Appendix 2: Glossary), for whom 'industry' was a positive term for every kind of socially productive activity.

7 *Creole*: in this period, a European person raised in the tropics, especially the West Indian and Indian Ocean French colonies, and whose temperament was therefore considered to be in some degree affected by the climate in ways that many French considered characteristic of local inhabitants of other or mixed race.

*gold coin*: called a louis or a napoleon, this coin was worth 20 francs. Although it is difficult to determine an exact contemporary equivalent, this is a huge tip. In Chapter 2, Frédéric's friend Deslauriers will estimate he could live modestly in Paris for three years on 4,000 francs, or (very roughly) 4 francs a day.

11 *councillor of State*: although its responsibilities have varied in different regimes since the French Revolution, generally speaking the Council of State (Conseil d'État) is the highest judicial body in France dealing with administrative law. It also advises in the drafting of legislation and decrees.

12 *Cygne de la Croix*: the name of this (real) hotel is a pun on the Swan [Sign] of the Cross.

13 *Malebranche, the Scots*: Nicolas Malebranche (1838–1715), Christian rationalist philosopher; the Scots are most likely the 'common sense'

philosophers Dugald Stewart (1753–1828) and Thomas Reid (1710–96), translated by Jouffroy.

13 *Froissart . . . Brantôme*: the Chronicles of Froissart (*c.*1337–*c.*1404) describe the first half of the Hundred Years War; the memoirs of Commines (1447–1511) discuss the kings of the fifteenth century; Pierre de l'Estoile (1564–1611) wrote about France's sixteenth-century wars of religion, while Brantôme (1540–1614) focused on the lives and loves of illustrious men and women.

14 *Monsieur le Censeur*: the school official responsible for student discipline.

15 *Werther . . . Lélia*: iconic Romantic literary characters: Werther in Goethe's *Sorrows of Young Werther* (1774), René from the story of that title by Chateaubriand (1802), Franck in Musset's play *La Coupe et les lèvres* (*The Cup and the Lip*, 1832), Lara from Byron's poem of that title (1813). *Lélia* is the heroine of George Sand's novel of that name (1833).

17 *Rastignac . . . Comédie humaine*: Rastignac, the hero of *Père Goriot* (1835) and a reappearing character in other Balzac novels, is a young man from the impoverished provincial gentry who makes his way to the top of Paris society with the help of various noble ladies. At the time this episode is set, Balzac had not yet given his novels the overall title *The Human Comedy*.

18 *embittered aristocrats in the faubourg*: the Legitimist nobles of the Faubourg Saint-Germain, upset by the overthrow of the Bourbon monarchy of the Restoration and by their loss of influence to capitalists such as Dambreuse, who thrived under the July Monarchy.

20 *Institutes . . . personarum*: Justinian's sixth-century *Institutes* is a compendium of Roman law; the section named here distinguishes between types of legal persons, notably between free men and slaves.

24 *Odéon . . . Revue des deux mondes*: the Odéon was the 'second' national theatre after the Comédie-Française. Located on the Left Bank, it had been occupied by students during the Revolution of 1830. The *Revue des deux mondes* is a leading Paris journal of literature and ideas, founded in 1829.

26 *Reform . . . Humann census*: the reform demanded is the expansion of the franchise to a wider proportion of the middle and professional classes; the National Guard was a volunteer militia, open to all citizens but in practice composed of bourgeois men, since members had to provide their own arms and uniform. In 1841, Minister of Finance Jean Georges Humann had ordered a census designed to calculate tax revenues more accurately but perceived as a way to increase people's tax burden.

*Lemaître . . . Robert Macaire*: Frédéric Lemaître (1800–76) was a leading actor in Romantic melodramas. The dashing fictional bandit Robert Macaire was one of his most famous starring roles.

*Albion . . . Customs Union*: in France, 'Albion'—often preceded by the adjective 'perfidious'—is a derogatory name for Britain. The question 'Are you English?' is in English in the text. Artaxerxes I, king of Persia 471–424 BC, offered gifts to the exiled Athenian politician Themistocles

(524–459 BC), his former wartime enemy. The Prussian-led 1834 customs union (*Zollverein*) of German States, a first step towards the political unification of Germany, worried the French, who began to discuss a similar union with neighbouring countries. The issue was part of a larger debate about free trade.

27 *Zachariaes . . . Ruhrdorffs*: Karl Zachariae and Adolf Rudorff (not Ruhrdorff) were prominent German jurists of the period.

*Marseillaise*: this Revolutionary song, closely identified with the Republican regime, had been replaced during Napoleon's empire with the less bloodthirsty 'Cri du départ' (Parting Cry) and would only become France's national anthem in 1879.

*Voltaire*: famous for his novel *Candide*, and for an enlightened rationalism Flaubert admired, Voltaire (pen name of François-Marie Arouet, 1694–1778) was long dead at the moment Hussonnet makes this joking remark.

*September troubles*: adding to the 1841 unrest caused by the Humann census was an assassination attempt on the Duc d'Aumale that provoked violent police action.

30 *Théâtre Bobino*: not the Montparnasse venue associated with famous singers of the twentieth century, but a vaudeville theatre located near the Luxembourg, also named after an early nineteenth-century Italian performer, and demolished in 1868.

32 *Apollonie*: although the dating is slightly anachronistic, this is usually taken as an allusion to Apollonie Sabatier (1822–90), a former courtesan who hosted a famous literary salon of the later 1840s and 1850s. Baudelaire addressed several poems to her.

*Coreggio, Murillo*: the first is an Italian painter (d. 1534); the second, a Spanish artist (1618–82).

33 *louis*: a gold coin worth 20 francs. See note to p. 7.

*Cherubini . . . Institute*: in 1842, Ingres painted a portrait of the composer Cherubini. That same year saw the inauguration of a large fresco in the assembly room of the École des Beaux-Arts done by Paul Delaroche (1797–1856), known best for historical paintings such as *The Execution of Lady Jane Grey* (1833). The Institute of France includes several prestigious Academies, including the one composed of significant figures in the arts.

34 *Boucher*: François Boucher (1703–70), a painter known for his portraits of women, sometimes in erotic situations.

35 *Callot*: Jacques Callot (1592–1635), printmaker known for his drawings of actors, beggars, Gypsies, and clowns; admired by Baudelaire.

*Phidias and Winckelmann*: the first is a Greek sculptor (490–431 BC), famous for his work on the Parthenon, but also the nickname for James Pradier (see note to p. 50); the second is a German art critic (1717–68) for whom classical Greek art was the summit of perfection.

35 *yataghans*: curved Turkish swords.

36 *National*: newspaper founded in 1830 by a group of liberals including Thiers, and subsidized by Lafitte, to advocate the overthrow of Charles X. Under the July Monarchy, it became the voice of the Republican opposition.

41 *galantine*: a dish of deboned pressed meat, coated with aspic.

43 *chibouks*: long-stemmed Turkish pipes.

*lip-fraoli . . . Tokay*: probably a corrupt pronunciation of Liebfraumilch, a Rhine white wine. Tokay is a sweet Hungarian wine.

47 *Rossini's Stabat*: the Stabat Mater is a medieval hymn to the Virgin Mary which has been set to music by many composers. The version by Gioachino Rossini (1792–1868) was first performed in Paris in January 1842.

48 *National Guard*: see note to p. 26.

50 *Dreux . . . Pradier*: Alfred de Dreux (1808–60), a painter known for equestrian scenes; James Pradier (1792–1852), a prominent sculptor and acquaintance of Flaubert, who had a brief liaison with Pradier's free-spirited wife Louise.

53 *Bastille . . . 'Lord' Guizot*: in 1840, the Government had begun to construct a system of fortifications around the city. Designed to defend the city from foreign enemies, some viewed them as a tool for internal repression. The September laws of 1835 had increased police powers and tightened press censorship in the wake of an assassination attempt against Louis Philippe. Guizot was seen by some as excessively pro-English, especially because of his behaviour in the Pritchard affair (see Appendix 2: Glossary).

*sicut decet*: (Latin) 'as is fitting'.

*lorette*: in the vocabulary of the day, a young woman ready to sell her charms but not quite a mere prostitute. Located somewhere between the working-class grisette (see note to p. 63) and the cocotte of the socialite demi-monde, the *lorette* is named after the parish of Notre-Dame-de-Lorette (Right Bank), in which area of Paris they were supposed to be especially numerous.

54 *yellow gloves of the Jockey Club*: created in 1834, the Jockey Club de Paris was perhaps the most exclusive of social clubs, with a predominantly aristocratic membership. Yellow gloves were a symbol of dandyish dress.

*pointed head*: in phrenology, which linked personality types to formations of the skull, a sign of stubbornness.

*borders of the Rhine*: as an uncompromising nationalist, Regimbart believes France's 'natural' borders include all the territory west of the Rhine that had been annexed by Napoleon.

*Poland*: there was much sympathy in France for Polish nationalism. In the eighteenth century, the country had been partitioned among Prussia, Austria, and Russia. An 1830 rebellion against the Russians had been brutally repressed. The French Government had refused to support the rebels, but many Polish exiles settled in France. In 1846, France's tepid response to the Austrian annexation of the Republic of Cracow, the one remaining partially free Polish city, aggravated many people's discontent with the regime.

55 *'Always him . . . Arnoux'*: a parody of 'Lui', a well-known poem about Napoleon from Victor Hugo's *Les Orientales* (1829).

57 *sealed will*: in France, a confidential will entrusted in a sealed envelope to a notary in the presence of witnesses.

*third-party opposition*: contestation of a legal judgement by someone who is harmed by it but who was not directly a party in the original dispute; normally not permitted under French law.

63 *grisettes*: young working-class women (the name is derived from the colour of their smocks) who entered into relationships and sometimes cohabited with the students they met in the boarding houses of the Quartier Latin. The woman sharing Martinon's flat in Part One would be an example.

65 *Hebes*: Hebe is the Greek goddess of youth.

*tarboosh*: the Arabic name for a fez.

66 *Marquise d'Amaëgui*: a character in Musset's poem 'L'Andalouse' ('The Andalusian Woman'). Hers is a Basque name.

68 *Porte Saint-Martin . . . Dumersan*: a theatre founded in 1781 where many important Romantic dramas were staged; Théophile Dumersan (1780–1849), a prolific author of songs and popular dramas.

73 *Marie*: in addition to their actual birthday, French Catholics celebrated the feast day of the saint after whom they were named. In the case of the Virgin Mary, this would normally be 15 August, Assumption Day (though she had other feast days as well), while Saint Angela (of Foligno) was commemorated in the nineteenth century on 4 January.

76 *Ruysdael*: Jacob van Ruisdael (1629–82), a leading landscape painter of the Dutch golden age.

77 *Odry . . . Oudry . . . animal bump*: Jean-Charles Odry (1781–1853), a comic actor of ungainly appearance for whom Dumersan wrote many parts; Jean-Baptiste Oudry (1686–1755), painter of animal pictures; a joking reference to phrenology (see note to p. 54).

80 *Garde-Meuble*: royal storehouse; the building is now the Navy Ministry.

*slowly*: some editors emend the *lentement* of the 1880 edition to the *lestement* (smartly) of the MS and first edition.

81 *Orsay debating chamber*: a place where young lawyers could practise their oratorical skills.

*Délassements*: the Délassements-Comiques was a theatre on the Boulevard du Temple, nicknamed the 'Boulevard of Crime' after its often lurid melodramas.

*Camarilla . . . Algeria*: a reference to Guizot's clique, and to the Government's decision not to demand war reparations from Morocco after a conflict in 1844 over the demarcation of the Algeria–Morocco border.

82 *féerie*: a theatrical genre adding music, ballet, and spectacular visual effects to a slight fantasy plot.

87 *Keeper of the Seals*: another name for the French Minister of Justice; the title is that of a position in the pre-Revolutionary monarchy.

89 *Atala . . . Feuilles d'automne*: *Atala*, a short novel (1801) by Chateaubriand, set among the Indians of North America; *Cinq-Mars* (1826), Alfred de Vigny's historical novel of early seventeenth-century politics; *Les Feuilles d'automne* (*Autumn Leaves*, 1831), a poetry collection by Victor Hugo. All these works are melancholy in tone.

90 *12 December 1845*: Flaubert was born on 12 December 1821.

## PART TWO

96 *fortifications*: see note to p. 53.

*barrier*: goods entering Paris were subject to a tax levied at customs barriers around the city.

98 *Bourse*: the Stock Exchange.

*Gymnase*: the Gymnase-Dramatique, a comic theatre founded in 1820 on the Boulevard Bonne-Nouvelle.

*Le Siècle . . . Charivari*: the first was a newspaper of the liberal opposition; the second, a satirical journal illustrated by artists such as Daumier and Granville.

101 *a little boy of about three*: there is a problem of chronology here. Since Mme Arnoux had only one child when Frédéric left Paris in what is clearly 1843, it is difficult to see how she can have a son of 'about three' if Frédéric inherits in December 1845, as the text says, and returns to Paris that same month. In his edition, Alan Raitt made a plausible case for correcting 1845 to 1846, since a Seine flood like the one just mentioned occurred in December 1846, while other allusions suggest the first chapters of Part Two all take place in 1847. On the other hand, '1845' is how the text reads in both editions, and there is just enough haziness in the way Frédéric registers facts and recalls events, and enough ambiguity about the degree to which the narrative endorses rather than merely records the character's perceptions, to leave some room for doubt. As we will see, this is not the only chronological problem involving a child.

103 *'the right to make a will' . . . 'Statute of Limitations'*: the right to leave one's money to whomever one liked was controversial in France, which had a tradition of prescribing a certain minimal sharing of assets among family members (who could not be entirely disinherited in favour of mistresses or other children, for example). Deslauriers takes one position here, the opposite one later on. The question of the Statute of Limitations was historically freighted: should there be a time limit on seeking relief from such

questionable legal measures as the French Revolution's seizure of aristocratic property, or other political actions?

*Dunod . . . Troplong*: legal scholars of the eighteenth and nineteenth century.

*debating chamber*: see note to p. 81.

104 *have the vote . . . stand for election to the Chamber*: the property requirement to stand for election to the Chamber of Deputies was even higher than the one to vote, which limited the franchise to perhaps 200,000 men in the whole country.

*Mondor*: a seventeenth-century charlatan who amassed a huge fortune and whose name became proverbial for a very rich man.

105 *Barthélémy*: Auguste Barthélémy (*c.*1796–1867), with his co-author Jules Méry, wrote political songs satirizing the Restoration and early July Monarchy before adopting a more conformist stance. Not to be confused with Barthélémy-Saint-Hilaire (see Appendix 2: Glossary).

108 *Pritchard . . . Bacchante*: for Pritchard, see Appendix 2: Glossary; Antoine Watteau (1684–1721), a painter of delicate pastoral and idyllic scenes; the ancient Greek bacchantes were female devotees of Bacchus (Dionysus), god of wine, and were said to go into such frenzies at their festivals that they tore men to pieces.

110 *Marquise de Pompadour*: mistress of Louis XV (1721–64) and thus associated with a licentious court, but also a woman of intelligence and taste sympathetic to the Enlightenment.

112 *postilion from Longjumeau*: *Le Postillon de Longjumeau* was a popular 1836 comic opera by Adolphe Adam.

*Les Porcherons*: in the eighteenth century, a hamlet outside the Paris walls, popular for its rustic drinking establishments.

113 *Gaspardo le Pêcheur*: 1837 melodrama by Joseph Bouchardy, a playwright known for his complicated plots.

114 *'morbidezza'*: extreme delicacy and softness in the artistic representation of human flesh.

116 *Grassot . . . Celuta*: Paul-Louis-Auguste Grassot (1804–60), a comic actor known for his hoarse voice; Celuta, an American Indian maiden in Chateaubriand's *Les Natchez* (1826).

120 *Ribera*: José de Ribera (1591–1652), Spanish painter with a reputation for dark and gloomy depictions of martyrdoms and other scenes of cruelty.

*Abbé Cœur*: Paul-Louis Cœur (1805–60), a leading Catholic preacher of the 1840s. He will give the funeral oration for Bishop Affre in 1848.

123 *napoleons . . . bag*: 'napoleon' is a more recent name for the 'louis' or 20-franc gold coin. See also note to p. 7. Note that Vatnaz takes the change that should go to Rosanette.

124 *Old Man of the Mountain*: name given by medieval Crusaders to the leader of the 'Assassin' or more properly Haschaschin sect (from which the word

'hashish' is derived). He was a favourite figure in Romantic histories of the Crusades.

126 *Social Contract . . . Revue indépendante*: Jean-Jacques Rousseau's *Social Contract* of 1762, a major influence on subsequent Republican thought; *Revue indépendante*, a journal of democratic and social-humanist views published 1841–8, with which Pierre Leroux and George Sand were associated.

127 *Buzançais . . . food crisis*: bad harvests and floods leading to food shortages had led in the winter of 1846–7 to riots in various parts of France, one of which, in Buzançais, had led to a landowner who had killed a peasant being beaten to death. Despite demands for clemency, three of the rioters were executed in April 1847.

128 *Phalansterians*: the followers of Charles Fourier.

129 *Spanish weddings . . . Saint-Denis*: in October 1846, after a long negotiation, the two daughters of Ferdinand VII of Spain were married, the elder (and reigning queen) to her cousin Francisco, the younger to Louis Philippe's son the Duc de Montpensier. This tightening of ties among branches of the Bourbon family caused a rift between France and England and was a blow to the Anglophile Guizot. Employees of the armoury at Rochefort had been found guilty of malfeasance in January 1847. In the same month, a plan was adopted to reorganize the cathedral chapter of Saint-Denis, a move that caused resentment because of the increased State support for religion it was anticipated to entail.

*La Mode*: a Legitimist weekly focusing on fashion and literature.

*Chambers*: the Chamber of Deputies and the Chamber of Peers.

130 *Royal Crimes . . . Mysteries of the Vatican*: difficult to identify precisely since there were a number of anti-monarchical and anticlerical works with titles such as these circulating at the time.

*Poniatowski . . . Saint Bartholomew's Day*: Prince Josef Poniatowski (1763–1813), a marshal in Napoleon's army, drowned near Leipzig fighting Russia and Prussia, his country's traditional enemies. The 1598 Edict of Nantes granted a limited tolerance to French Protestants. On 24 August 1572, Saint Bartholomew's Day, French Protestants were massacred by Catholic mobs with the presumed complicity of Charles IX.

*the League*: the Catholic League of nobles that fought the Protestants in the sixteenth-century French Wars of Religion.

*Lola Montès*: or Montez, stage name of an Irish actress and dancer (1821–61) famous for her scandalous behaviour, who in 1846 became the mistress of King Ludwig I of Bavaria. The public nature of their relationship and her liberal views were among the factors that led to Ludwig's abdication in 1848. Lola subsequently fled to Britain, then to the United States.

131 *kaolin*: clay mineral used in making porcelain.

*physiologies . . . Toll-keeper*: 'physiologies' were popular, often satirical books of the 1830s, analysing social conditions or depicting the traits and habits of various social types. Balzac's *Physiology of Marriage* of 1829 is the best-known example of the former, and his depiction of the rising bourgeois businessman in the first pages of *The Girl with the Golden Eyes* (1835) is a sociologically acute instance of the latter. Cisy's examples are belated and banal.

138 *Grand Salon*: the room at the annual official art exhibition in which the most remarkable paintings were displayed.

139 *Titian . . . Veronese*: the leading painters of Renaissance Venice, famous for their use of colour.

141 *Turks' heads*: a sign of the Orientalist interests of the artists of the day, but in French *tête de turc* also means scapegoat or target of abuse, and that sense may be present here.

143 *Balzac's "Les Treize"*: Balzac's *The History of the Thirteen* is a collection of three stories (including *The Girl with the Golden Eyes*) that feature the members of a secret society of thirteen men who have vowed mutual assistance in their social and amorous conquests.

145 *Osage*: the name of an American Indian tribe, some of whose members had been exhibited around France during the July Monarchy.

*ribbons*: of the Legion of Honour.

146 *Legitimist . . . Orléanist*: partisans of the overthrown Bourbon dynasty and of Louis Philippe respectively (see Appendix 1: Historical Sketch, p. 396).

*moderate balance*: in French, 'juste milieu', the watchword of Louis-Philippe's monarchy.

147 *Le Siècle*: see note to p. 98.

*on that subject*: notably Lamartine's *Histoire des Girondins*, which appeared in instalments March–June 1847.

*La Reine Margot*: a drama by Alexandre Dumas *père* adapted from his 1845 novel of the same title and premiered in February 1847. Its subject was the civil and religious wars of the sixteenth century, including the events leading up to the St Bartholomew's Day massacre (see note to p. 130).

*Laws of September*: see note to p. 53. Newspaper publishers were obliged to put up a considerable amount of bond money, a burden for all but the rich.

148 *12 May*: perhaps a reference to the plot of 1839 that led to Barbès being sent to prison, but more likely an allusion to a more recent event, Pierre Lecomte's failed attempt to assassinate Louis Philippe at Fontainebleau on 16 April 1846. Thiers had delivered a major speech the month before suggesting, much to the anger of his colleagues, that deputies serving in the Chamber (who were unpaid) be forbidden to accept other Government employment at the same time.

150 *women in their thirties*: in several works, including *The Woman of Thirty* (1842), Balzac had praised the charms of women of this age and

sympathized with those trapped in unhappy marriages and watching their youth slip away.

154 *Lesurques*: famous example of a miscarriage of justice. Executed for murder in 1796, Lesurques's claims of innocence were validated by the discovery of the real culprit.

157 *Henri IV*: the story of this French king (reigned 1589–1610) playing with his children in this manner was the subject of many popular images, including *Henri IV Playing with His Children* by Ingres (1817).

158 *Antony*: the doomed-lover hero of a popular 1831 melodrama by Alexandre Dumas *père*.

159 *filled with gloom*: some editors believe the *sombre* in the printed text should be corrected to *sobre* (sober).

161 *Saint Vincent de Paul*: a French priest (d. 1660), who founded several religious congregations charged with serving the poor and the sick. In 1833, the Saint Vincent de Paul Society was created in Paris by lay Catholics wishing to serve the poor.

164 *red bonnet*: also known as the Phrygian cap, a soft conical Greek cap that in the French Revolution became a widespread emblem of liberty.

*calotte*: the skullcap, commonly called in English by its Italian name of *zucchetto*, worn by Catholic (and some Anglican and other) clergy during formal liturgical rites.

*Concert of Europe . . . Holy Alliance*: Deslauriers imagines a progressive coalition of nations which would replace the conservative alliance of Austria, Prussia, and Russia which had originally been formed to oppose Napoleon and the spread of Revolutionary ideas.

*Lycurgus*: legendary legislator of ancient Sparta.

*"critical repression . . . spontaneity"*: in fact a quotation from *La France mystique* by Alexandre Erdan (1858), a survey of various utopian and religious thinkers and sects.

165 *divine right*: a reference to the early modern theory that kings ruled by divine right and so enjoyed absolute authority over their subjects.

172 *Marcantonio*: the Italian engraver Marcantonio Raimondi (*c*.1475–*c*.1534), known for his prints after paintings by Raphael, Dürer, and others.

176 *General Council*: *Conseil général*, the governing body of each French department.

181 *blungers*: machines for mixing clay and water.

184 *Musset*: Romantic poet and playwright (1810–57) who had a famous affair with George Sand.

*Phèdre . . . Des Grieux*: Phèdre is the tragic heroine of a tragedy by Racine (1677), Dido the abandoned queen of Virgil's *Aeneid*. Shakespeare's Romeo is paired with Des Grieux, the unfortunate hero of *Manon Lescaut* (1731), a novel by the Abbé Prévost.

186 *caro mio, andiamo*: 'let's go, my dear'.

187 *berlin*: a covered travelling carriage with two facing benches.

188 *Bou-Maza*: an Arab chieftain who in 1847 had surrendered to the French army in Algeria. Nominally living as a captive in Paris, he in fact enjoyed a luxurious society life.

189 *Clubstick*: the real winner of the 1847 horse race on which Flaubert based his scene.

*victoria*: a type of two-seated carriage favoured by wealthy women.

*mousquetaire*: Alexandre Dumas *père*'s *The Three Musketeers* was first published as a newspaper serial in 1844, then as a popular illustrated book in 1846.

190 *Louis XI of prostitution*: according to popular legend, Louis XI (reigned 1461–83) was devious and selfish, earning the nickname of 'spider king'. He is a major character in Walter Scott's novel *Quentin Durward* (1823), which was widely read in France.

193 *Garde-Meuble*: see note to p. 80.

194 *Ozaï, a new ballet*: by Casimir Gide (1804–68), premiered 26 April 1847.

*Sainville*: a leading comic actor of the day.

196 *Baucher . . . Comte d'Aure*: riding masters of the day who quarrelled bitterly about the proper principles of dressage (the latter wanted to introduce English methods into France).

197 *Le Flambard*: an approximate translation of this title might be 'The Gay Blade'.

198 *Géricault . . . Parthenon*: Théodore Géricault (1791–1824) painted several works featuring masterful depictions of horses; the Elgin Marbles, taken from the frieze of the Parthenon in Athens, include famous bas-reliefs of the animals.

201 *Drouillard and Benier*: the former was a banker convicted in 1847 of electoral corruption; the latter a Government official responsible for military supply, who was discovered after his death in 1845 to have embezzled large sums of money.

*kris*: a kind of dagger. It is Malay rather than Japanese.

*staunchly*: some editors emend *bravement* to *gravement* (gravely).

203 *Père et Portier*: a vaudeville comedy by Bayard and Varner performed in May 1847.

*Regency . . . Mystères de Paris*: the early eighteenth-century French Regency of Philippe d'Orléans became famous as a period of licence in reaction to the conservatism of Louis XIV; in *Les Mystères de Paris* (1842–3), a wildly popular novel by Eugène Sue, the compassionate prince walks the city streets incognito, helping the poor and the oppressed.

204 *coq de bruyère . . . La Bruyère*: a wood grouse; a famous French moralist (1645–96). The word *bruyère* itself means 'heather'.

205 *Sophie Arnoux*: Cisy, no doubt deliberately, confuses Mme Arnoux with Sophie Arnould (1740–1802), a singer with a reputation for loose morals.

207 *La Fougère*: the author of a *Treatise on Swordfighting* (1825) and of *The Art of Never Being Killed or Wounded in a Duel . . . Even When Facing the World's Best Shot* (1828).

214 *Thiers . . . Les Girondins*: in the 1820s, Thiers had written a history of the French Revolution and in 1845 had started one about the Consulate and the Empire. Jacques-Antoine Dulaure (1755–1835) wrote a history of Paris and Prosper de Barante an innovative account of the dukes of Burgundy. All of these are lengthy works, as is Lamartine's work on the moderate Girondin party of the French Revolution, a bestseller in 1847. One important name missing from this list, and from the novel, is that of Jules Michelet (1798–1874).

215 *Société des Familles*: a secret, revolutionary Republican society (the 'families' were the cells of the group) whose successor, the Société des Saisons, was responsible for the insurrection of May 1839.

*Alibaud*: Louis Alibaud, a soldier of Republican views, had attempted to assassinate Louis Philippe in 1836. He was executed in July of that year.

*Rue Transnonain . . . rifles*: an 1834 anti-government riot in what is now the Rue Beaubourg was violently repressed by soldiers, led by Bugeaud, who killed everyone in a building from which a shot had been fired.

*Mont Saint-Michel . . . suicide*: in this period, the famous abbey was used as a prison, mainly for those convicted of political crimes; Austen and Steuben were co-conspirators of Barbès in the Société des Saisons uprising of May 1839.

216 *Carpentras*: the inhabitants of this southern French town were stereotyped as stupid.

*Funambules . . . Délassements*: like the latter (see note to p. 81), the former was a popular theatre on the Boulevard du Temple.

217 *Don Basilio*: a character in *The Barber of Seville*, a comedy by Beaumarchais (1775), made into an opera by Rossini (1816).

218 *Monsieur Grandin . . . Third Party*: Grandin and Benoist were members of the Chamber of Deputies; the Third Party was formed of deputies who belonged neither to the Right nor to the Left.

*Revue des deux mondes . . . Saint-François lectures*: for the *Revue des deux mondes*, see note to p. 24; the *Imitation of Christ* is a devotional work of the fifteenth century; the *Almanach de Gotha* was the directory of European nobility; the Saint-François lectures were educational talks given at a workmen's association sponsored by the Catholic Church.

219 *Comte d'Artois*: the name by which the future king Charles X was known when he went into exile during the French Revolution.

*pauperism*: in 1844 Louis Napoleon had published *The Extinction of Pauperism*, in which he advanced some progressive ideas, thus enhancing his populist image.

222 *Desolmes . . . Constitution*: Charles Desolmes was a Republican journalist who had translated the *Commentaries on the Laws of England* by the English jurist William Blackstone (1723–80); the English Bill of Rights appeared in 1689. Article 2 is actually a reference to the Declaration of the Rights of Man of 1789 which is placed at the head of the Constitution of 1791. The article affirmed the inalienable right to liberty and the right to resist oppression.

*carbonaro*: (pl. *carbonari*) name given to a Republican conspirator in Italy and France in the early nineteenth century. While some in France had remained Republican, others had rallied to Louis-Philippe's regime.

226 *deed of subrogation*: allows an insurer to assume the rights of the insured and be paid by the debtor.

231 *Directory*: governing executive body of France from 1795 to 1799.

233 *égaud*: local word for a shelter.

239 *tombac*: a kind of unprocessed tobacco smoked in hookahs.

242 *Sainte-Pélagie*: Paris prison (demolished in 1895).

*Lachambeaudie . . . Napoléon*: Lachambeaudie (1807–72) was a writer and composer of songs; for the *Mystères de Paris*, see note to p. 203; the biography of Napoleon published by the Baron de Montbreton de Norvins in 1825–8 was reprinted several times in this period.

243 *reformist banquets*: a series of meetings (tickets were sold by subscription, so they were largely middle-class events) from July 1847 whose purpose was to agitate for electoral reform. They took the form of banquets in order to get around restrictions on political assembly.

*Holland . . . Eastern question*: France had joined Britain in supporting the independence of Belgium from Holland in 1830; for the Spanish marriages, see note to p. 129; Guizot, along with Austrian leader Metternich, supported the cause of the Catholic cantons of Switzerland against the pressures of the Protestant ones, who sought to amend the treaty of 1815 to make the country a more centralized federal state; for the *Zollverein* (customs union) see note to p. 26; in the Mediterranean, the interests of France in Egypt conflicted with Britain's support of the Ottoman Empire.

*Grand Duke Constantine*: second son of Russian Tsar Nicholas I.

*there is nothing, nothing, nothing . . . 'they declare they are satisfied!'*: the first line is from a famous anti-government speech of April 1847, the second cites a widely derided declaration that accusations of corruption against Guizot were unfounded.

244 *Soult . . . Lille*: Marshal Soult, Minister of War, was mocked for having two sentries posted outside his front door; the Jesuits had been expelled from France in 1845 but the ban was not enforced.

*Teste-Cubières*: two Government officials convicted of corruption in July 1847.

*Duchesse de Praslin*: in August 1847 the Duchesse de Praslin-Choiseul was found murdered in her home, probably by her husband, an Orléanist peer. He committed suicide soon afterwards. The Praslin affair was seen as illustrating upper-class immorality.

244 *Chevalier de Maison-Rouge*: a drama adapted in August 1847 from a novel by Alexandre Dumas *père* set in the time of the French Revolution. The patriotic songs it included were enthusiastically applauded by Republicans in the audience.

245 *Démocratie pacifique*: a journal inspired by the ideas of Fourier.

*hymn to Pius IX*: prior to the revolts of 1848, Pius IX (Pope 1846–78), now known for his theological and political conservatism, had given signs of sympathy for liberal political ideas.

246 *Tour de Nesle*: *La Tour de Nesle*, an early Romantic drama by Dumas *père*, includes a famous speech ironically praising 'great ladies' of loose morals.

*white oxen*: a quotation from a well-known song 'Les Bœufs' by the worker-poet Pierre Dupont and the musician Charles Gounod.

253 *New Year*: 1848.

*Palermo*: a revolt in Sicily against King Ferdinand II of Naples.

*12th arrondissement*: the part nearest the Seine of what was the 12th arrondissement of Paris became the 5th when the districts of the expanding city were redefined and their number expanded from twelve to twenty in 1860.

256 *'The pear is ripe'*: the face of Louis-Philippe was often caricatured as that of a pear.

261 *parchment*: Mme Arnoux's son is cured of diphtherial croup by spitting out the membrane blocking his breathing. This could happen, but instances were quite rare.

262 *Girondins*: a popular song from the *Chevalier de Maison-Rouge* (see note to p. 244), it became the national anthem of the Second Republic, 1848–52.

*Frascati's*: café and former gambling hall, at once chic and louche, often mentioned in Balzac's novels.

263 *Boulevard des Capucines*: on 23 February 1848, Government troops killed dozens of demonstrators assembled, shouting against Guizot, in front of the Ministry of Foreign Affairs. What had begun as pressure for a change of minsters became a revolution that overthrew the entire regime.

## PART THREE

265 *He went down*: some editors insert 'towards' here in accordance with the topographical facts that Flaubert is usually careful to respect.

266 *Phrygian cap*: see note to p. 164.

267 *Tuileries*: the palace of the Tuileries, the royal residence inhabited by Louis Philippe and later by Napoleon III, formed the west end of the Louvre and was located beyond the Place du Carrousel. It was set on fire during the 1871 Commune and its ruins demolished in 1883.

272 *Provisional Government*: 24 February 1848, at the Hôtel de Ville.

273 *tricolore*: on 25 February, speaking to a crowd demanding the adoption of the red flag as France's national emblem, Lamartine argued that the tricolour was a symbol of French liberty and military glory, while the socialist red banner signified only bloody violence.

274 *sack of the chateaux . . . forty-five centimes' tax*: the royal chateau of Neuilly and the Rothschild property at Suresnes were pillaged on 25 February; Batignolles was a recently annexed area in north-west Paris; workers in Lyons had destroyed factory machines; on 8 March Ledru-Rollin issued a letter recommending that only staunch Republicans be appointed to Government posts and urging action on the Government's social programme; on 18 March 1848, the Provisional Government, desperately needing money to stabilize its budget, had issued paper currency and imposed a new and unpopular tax of 45 centimes per franc.

276 *Fortelle district*: of Nogent. Earlier in the novel we were told Dambreuse has an estate there.

*Aube*: the French department in which Nogent is located.

*Convention*: the assembly that governed France from 1792 to 1795 is commonly called the National Convention (Convention nationale).

277 *Frenchwoman . . . old person*: Flaubert is distorting a proposal in a feminist Women's Constitution that any woman domiciled in France and who married a Frenchman or took care of an old person should be granted the rights of a citizen.

279 *phalansteries*: the utopian communities envisioned by Fourier.

281 *Prado*: dance hall where Blanqui urged once again that France officially adopt the red flag.

*'La Casquette'*: another song by Pierre Dupont.

*Assemblée nationale*: Royalist newspaper published by former members of Louis-Philippe's regime.

*Thermidor martyrs*: Robespierre, Saint-Just, and the other Revolutionaries executed after being arrested on 10 Thermidor, Year II of the French Revolutionary calendar, or 28 July 1794. The name Thermidor was given to the 'hot' summer period of mid-July to mid-August.

282 *'Azor'*: theatre slang for whistling at a performer (in France, Azor is a dog's name).

284 *The calf's head*: the meaning of this allusion will be revealed to Frédéric and to the reader only in the last chapter.

287 *Ciudadanos . . . nación*: Flaubert found the French text of this speech in a book about the various clubs of the period. He had it translated into Spanish for his novel. Beginning and ending with fraternal greetings, the speaker praises the revolutionary martyrs of his country. He invites his audience to attend a memorial service in their honour in the Paris church of the Madeleine and to listen to a speech about Spanish and worldwide liberty. The original editions omitted the accents and included several

other mistakes in the Spanish text, which modern editions have silently corrected to varying degrees.

289 *Essenes . . . Pingons*: the Essenes were an ascetic Jewish sect that flourished in the century just before and during the time of Christ. The Moravian Church emerged from the Bohemian Reformation; it preached simplicity and communal fellowship; the Jesuits of eighteenth-century Paraguay established 'reductions' or self-sustaining indigenous communities; the Pingons were an extended French family in the Auvergne region that held their possessions in common over several centuries. All of these are mentioned in Étienne Cabet's utopian *Voyage to Icaria* (1842).

291 *La Presse*: a newspaper popular for its publication of serial novels but politically cautious in its late support for the Republic. It would endorse Louis Napoleon for the presidency.

*lectures in the Luxembourg . . . Tyroleans*: the deliberations of the commission charged with labour issues; the Vesuvians were a women's political club, their allegedly loose morals a topic for satirical cartoons; 'Tyroleans' was another name for the 'Mountain Men' police of Caussidière.

292 *National Workshops*: intended to provide gainful employment for Paris workers, the under-budgeted Workshops were soon obliged to repeatedly cut the rate of daily pay. They also failed to set people to work on meaningful projects such as the improvement of the railway network, as had been suggested. Private employers felt threatened by potential competition, while the workers felt cheated of the opportunities promised them and humiliated by being assigned only unskilled work.

296 *that very day*: 22 June 1848.

297 *Christina had Monaldeschi murdered*: living in France after her abdication and conversion to Catholicism, Queen Christina of Sweden (1626–89) had her equerry and lover Monaldeschi assassinated for betraying her schemes for regaining political power somewhere in Europe.

298 *'Diane de Poitiers . . . Henri II'*: for two decades, Diane de Poitiers (1499–1566) exercised considerable personal and political influence as the royal favourite of dauphin, then king Henri II (reigned 1547–59). He was twenty years her junior.

299 *'lovely ladies . . . stage boxes'*: a reference to Rousseau's account in his *Confessions* of the success of his opera, *The Village Soothsayer*, performed before a court audience in 1752.

300 *telegraph tower*: the electric telegraph network was just beginning to be established in the late 1840s. The reference here is most likely to its predecessor, the 'optical' telegraph that used semaphore communication manually relayed from tower to tower.

*A painter*: the Barbizon school of artists is named after a village near Fontainebleau, whose countryside was famously depicted by Corot around 1830 and later by many artists in the following decades.

304 *La Croix-Rousse*: a district of Lyons. Rosanette is thus a native of the same city as Sénécal.

308 *passport*: required since 1792 even for travel within France, though the rule was unevenly enforced. The reference could be more specifically to the *laissez-passer* the Government required of people entering Paris after the June insurrection.

310 *11th arrondissement*: now the 6th (see note to p. 253).

311 *Mobile Guards*: a corps of 24,000 men drawn from the ranks of young unemployed workers and created 25 February 1848 as a kind of parallel to the bourgeois National Guards. It was used by the Government to help crush the June uprising.

313 *grating*: the translation here reflects the emendation of *baquet* (tub) to *barreau*, which makes sense, though a document Flaubert used does speak of a tub of drinking water at the scene.

317 *pineapple purées at the Luxembourg*: the members of the Luxembourg Commission supervising the National Workshops were accused by the Right of treating themselves to sumptuous meals.

318 *Sallesse . . . Péquillet woman*: people of humble station who had distinguished themselves as defenders of the Republic against the workers' insurrection of June 1848.

320 *lion . . . landowner*: an image taken from Thiers's book *On Property* (1848), a conservative reply to Proudhon's claim that property is theft.

'*Light up!*' . . . *Prudhomme on the Barricade*: demonstrators marching in the streets of Paris would demand that residents light up their windows as a show of support. The principles of '89 are those of the French Revolution. Slavery in the French colonies was abolished by a decree of 27 April 1848; 'Joseph Prudhomme', a character invented by Henri Monnier, quickly became an iconic figure of bourgeois stupidity and complacency.

323 *divorce*: legalized by the Revolution in 1792, forbidden by the restored monarchy in 1816, divorce would be legalized again only in 1884.

325 *Gymnase*: see note to p. 98.

329 *zouave cap*: the original Zouaves were a unit of the French infantry raised in Algeria in the 1830s from among a Berber tribe from which their name derives.

*Rateau proposal*: at the behest of President Louis Napoleon, Rateau proposed in January 1849 that the Constituent Assembly dissolve itself and call elections for a new Legislative Assembly that the conservatives were likely to win.

330 *L'Illustration . . . Cham*: the first was one of the first picture weeklies; the second was the pen name of Amédée de Noë (1819–79), a famous caricaturist of the day.

336 *Rue de Poitiers*: Thiers and Falloux met privately with other conservative politicians of the 'Party of Order' at a house in that street.

336 *The President*: Louis Napoleon, elected 10 December 1848 by a land-slide vote.

*the business in the Conservatoire*: on 13 June 1849 demonstrators occupied the Conservatoire des arts et métiers to protest against French intervention in Rome against the Republic that had removed the Pope from political power. Troops commanded by Changarnier expelled them by force. Ledru-Rollin narrowly escaped being killed in the process.

*Phalansterian tail*: Fourier speculated that his system of bodily and social harmony would eventually lead humans to grow a tail with an eye at the end of it, allowing people to see behind them. Fourier's disciple Considerant was caricatured in the press as sporting such a tail.

*Foire aux idées*: a vaudeville revue of 1849 mocking socialist ideas.

340 *prison-ships of Belle-Isle*: a way station for prisoners about to be deported; in fact, they may have been held in a prison on land.

341 *wages book*: a legally required document that served as a disciplinary control on the worker, since employers recorded in it the dates and places of every job held, along with notations about complaints and dismissals.

342 *double election . . . district*: well-known or influential figures might be elected in more than one district and would then choose the one they most wished to represent. By-elections would then be held to fill the vacant seats. While Dambreuse's return to the Legislative Assembly may be dated to May 1849, the by-election is yet to be held over a year later, when Frédéric receives more encouragement, this time from Mme Dambreuse. Like Rosanette's pregnancy, the gestation of Frédéric's candidacy is chronologically fuzzy.

343 *Gobet . . . Chappe*: Nicolas Gobet (1735–81), a mineralogist. If, as has been suggested, the Chappe here is the engineer Claude Chappe (1763–1805), then Delauriers's documentation is not very current.

346 *dismissal of General Changarnier*: in January 1851.

347 *straw . . . under the windows*: it was the custom to dampen the sound of street traffic by this means for the benefit of someone seriously ill in the house.

352 *Chamber's refusal . . . extra funds . . . Dufour*: in February 1851 the Chamber had refused Louis Napoleon's request for a large increase to his personal budget. Chambolle, Pidoux, and Creton were deputies of various conservative stripes who did not join Quantin-Bachard and Dufour in supporting the President and who would return to private life after his seizure of absolute power.

356 *labour*: as has often been remarked (though overlooked by early reviewers), Rosanette gives birth in late February 1851, about two years since she announced her pregnancy in an episode supposed to occur in January 1849 at the time of the Rateau proposal.

360 *red waistcoats*: worn by the Romantic youth of 1830.

365 *crown of rosy pimples*: the *corona veneris*, a sign of advanced syphilis.

367 *Roman Republic . . . priests*: Dussardier lists popular and nationalist uprisings that had been quashed. The liberty trees planted in France in 1848 in imitation of a similar initiative during the French Revolution were cut down in 1850 by order of the Government, which also moved to limit public discussion by closing the political clubs and censoring the press. In that same year, the universal male suffrage proclaimed in 1848 had been substantially restricted by imposing a residency requirement that excluded those who needed to move around to find work, and by the Falloux law the nation's public primary schools were placed under the authority of the local mayor and clergy.

370 *thrush*: a fungal infection.

371 *Lady Gower's lap*: a reference to a painting by Sir Thomas Lawrence (1769–1830).

375 *Le Havre station*: now the Gare Saint-Lazare.

376 *coloured dress*: a sign that Madame Dambreuse is no longer in mourning. Strictly speaking, widows were supposed to wear only black for an entire year, a period here apparently shortened by half.

378 *Petites Affiches*: newspaper in which sales and legal judgements such as seizures were publicized.

383 *next morning*: 2 December, the day of Louis Napoleon's *coup d'état*.

384 *two days later*: to be understood as two days after the *coup d'état*, or 4 December.

385 *prefect's uniform*: Deslauriers has been appointed by the new regime as the chief Government official of the department.

*Tortoni's . . . caryatid*: Tortoni's was famous for its ices; a caryatid is a pillar or other architectural support in the form of a sculpted female figure.

386 *Mostaganem*: a coastal city in Algeria made a French sub-prefecture in 1848.

388 *Werther . . . bread*: in Goethe's novel *The Sorrows of Young Werther* (1774), the hero falls in love with Charlotte, whom he catches in the domestic task of serving bread to her siblings.

*kissed my wrist*: the only such incident in the text involves Rosanette, whose arm is kissed by Frédéric the day of the races.

392 *Froissart*: see note to p. 13.

*The Oxford World's Classics Website*

**www.worldsclassics.co.uk**

- Browse the full range of Oxford World's Classics online

- Sign up for our monthly e-alert to receive information on new titles

- Read extracts from the Introductions

- Listen to our editors and translators talk about the world's greatest literature with our Oxford World's Classics audio guides

- Join the conversation, follow us on Twitter at OWC_Oxford

- Teachers and lecturers can order inspection copies quickly and simply via our website

**www.worldsclassics.co.uk**

**American Literature**

**British and Irish Literature**

**Children's Literature**

**Classics and Ancient Literature**

**Colonial Literature**

**Eastern Literature**

**European Literature**

**Gothic Literature**

**History**

**Medieval Literature**

**Oxford English Drama**

**Philosophy**

**Poetry**

**Politics**

**Religion**

**The Oxford Shakespeare**

A complete list of Oxford World's Classics, including Authors in Context, Oxford English Drama, and the Oxford Shakespeare, is available in the UK from the Marketing Services Department, Oxford University Press, Great Clarendon Street, Oxford OX2 6DP, or visit the website at www.oup.com/uk/worldsclassics.

In the USA, visit www.oup.com/us/owc for a complete title list.

Oxford World's Classics are available from all good bookshops. In case of difficulty, customers in the UK should contact Oxford University Press Bookshop, 116 High Street, Oxford OX1 4BR.

French Decadent Tales
Six French Poets of the Nineteenth
  Century

HONORÉ DE BALZAC    Cousin Bette
Eugénie Grandet
Père Goriot
The Wild Ass's Skin

CHARLES BAUDELAIRE    The Flowers of Evil
The Prose Poems and Fanfarlo

DENIS DIDEROT    Jacques the Fatalist
The Nun

ALEXANDRE DUMAS (PÈRE)    The Black Tulip
The Count of Monte Cristo
Louise de la Vallière
The Man in the Iron Mask
La Reine Margot
The Three Musketeers
Twenty Years After
The Vicomte de Bragelonne

ALEXANDRE DUMAS (FILS)    La Dame aux Camélias

GUSTAVE FLAUBERT    Madame Bovary
A Sentimental Education
Three Tales

VICTOR HUGO    Notre-Dame de Paris

J.-K. HUYSMANS    Against Nature

PIERRE CHODERLOS DE    Les Liaisons dangereuses
LACLOS

MME DE LAFAYETTE    The Princesse de Clèves

GUILLAUME DU LORRIS    The Romance of the Rose
and JEAN DE MEUN

ÉMILE ZOLA

**L'Assommoir**
**The Belly of Paris**
**La Bête humaine**
**The Conquest of Plassans**
**The Fortune of the Rougons**
**Germinal**
**The Kill**
**The Ladies' Paradise**
**The Masterpiece**
**Money**
**Nana**
**Pot Luck**
**Thérèse Raquin**